RJKelly 3/01

DEAN KOONTZ

3 COMPLETE NOVELS

DEAN KOONTZ

3 COMPLETE NOVELS

THE BAD PLACE

DEMON SEED

THE EYES OF DARKNESS

G. P. PUTNAM'S SONS NEW YORK

G. P. Putnam's Sons
Publishers Since 1838
a member of
Penguin Putnam Inc.
375 Hudson Street
New York, NY 10014

Library of Congress Cataloging-in-Publication Data

Koontz, Dean R. (Dean Ray).
    Three complete novels / Dean Koontz.
        p.   cm.
    Contents: The bad place—Demon seed—The eyes of darkness.
    ISBN 0-399-14442-0 (acid-free paper)
    I. Title
    PS3561.O55A6   1998   98-14550 CIP
    813'.54—dc21

Printed in the United States of America

10   9   8   7   6   5   4   3

This book is printed on acid-free paper. ∞

Book design by Patrice Sheridan

CONTENTS

THE BAD PLACE

Teachers often affect our lives more than they realize. From high school days to the present, I have had teachers to whom I will remain forever indebted, not merely because of what they taught me, but because they provided the invaluable examples of dedication, kindness, and generosity of spirit that have given me an unshakable faith in the basic goodness of the human species. This book is dedicated to:

DAVID O'BRIEN
THOMAS DOYLE
RICHARD FORSYTHE
JOHN BODNAR
CARL CAMPBELL
STEVE AND JEAN HERNISHIN

Every eye sees its own special vision;
every ear hears a most different song.
In each man's troubled heart, an incision
would reveal a unique, shameful wrong.

Stranger fiends hide here in human guise
than reside in the valleys of Hell.
But goodness, kindness and love arise
in the heart of the poor beast, as well.

—THE BOOK OF
COUNTED SORROWS

1

THE NIGHT WAS BECALMED AND CURIOUSLY SILENT, AS IF THE ALLEY were an abandoned and windless beach in the eye of a hurricane, between the tempest past and the tempest coming. A faint scent of smoke hung on the motionless air, although no smoke was visible.

Sprawled facedown on the cold pavement, Frank Pollard did not move when he regained consciousness; he waited in the hope that his confusion would dissipate. He blinked, trying to focus. Veils seemed to flutter within his eyes. He sucked deep breaths of the cool air, tasting the invisible smoke, grimacing at the acrid tang of it.

Shadows loomed like a convocation of robed figures, crowding around him. Gradually his vision cleared, but in the weak yellowish light that came from far behind him, little was revealed. A large trash dumpster, six or eight feet from him, was so dimly outlined that for a moment it seemed ineffably strange, as though it were an artifact of an alien civilization. Frank stared at it for a while before he realized what it was.

He did not know where he was or how he had gotten there. He could not have been unconscious longer than a few seconds, for his heart was pounding as if he had been running for his life only moments ago.

Fireflies in a windstorm. . . .

That phrase took flight through his mind, but he had no idea what it meant. When he tried to concentrate on it and make sense of it, a dull headache developed above his right eye.

Fireflies in a windstorm. . . .

He groaned softly.

Between him and the dumpster, a shadow among shadows moved, quick and sinuous. Small but radiant green eyes regarded him with icy interest.

Frightened, Frank pushed up onto his knees. A thin, involuntary cry issued from him, almost less like a human sound than like the muted wail of a reed instrument.

The green-eyed observer scampered away. A cat. Just an ordinary black cat.

Frank got to his feet, swayed dizzily, and nearly fell over an object that had been on the blacktop beside him. Gingerly he bent down and picked it up: a flight bag made of supple leather, packed full, surprisingly heavy. He supposed it was his. He could not remember. Carrying the bag, he tottered to the dumpster and leaned against its rusted flank.

Looking back, he saw that he was between rows of what seemed to be two-story stucco apartment buildings. All of the windows were black. On both sides, the tenants' cars were pulled nose-first into covered parking stalls. The queer yellow glow, sour and sulfurous, almost more like the product of a gas flame than the luminescence of an incandescent electric bulb, came from a streetlamp at the end of the block, too far away to reveal the details of the alleyway in which he stood.

As his rapid breathing slowed and as his heartbeat decelerated, he abruptly realized that he did not know who he was. He knew his name— Frank Pollard—but that was all. He did not know how old he was, what he did for a living, where he had come from, where he was going, or why. He was so startled by his predicament that for a moment his breath caught in his throat; then his heartbeat soared again, and he let his breath out in a rush.

Fireflies in a windstorm. . . .

What the hell did that mean?

The headache above his right eye corkscrewed across his forehead.

He looked frantically left and right, searching for an object or an aspect of the scene that he might recognize, anything, an anchor in a world that was suddenly too strange. When the night offered nothing to reassure him, he turned his quest inward, desperately seeking something familiar in himself, but his own memory was even darker than the passageway around him.

Gradually he became aware that the scent of smoke had faded, replaced by a vague but nauseating smell of rotting garbage in the dumpster. The stench of decomposition filled him with thoughts of death, which seemed to trigger a vague recollection that he was on the run from someone—or something—that wanted to kill him. When he tried to recall why he was fleeing, and from whom, he could not further illuminate that scrap of memory; in fact, it seemed more an awareness based on instinct than a genuine recollection.

A puff of wind swirled around him. Then calm returned, as if the dead night was trying to come back to life but had managed just one shuddering breath. A single piece of wadded paper, swept up by that insufflation, clicked along the pavement and scraped to a stop against his right shoe.

Then another puff.

The paper whirled away.

Again the night was dead calm.

Something was happening. Frank sensed that these short-lived whiffs of wind had some malevolent source, ominous meaning.

Irrationally, he was sure that he was about to be crushed by a great weight. He looked up into the clear sky, at the bleak and empty blackness of space and at the malignant brilliance of the distant stars. If something was descending toward him, Frank could not see it.

The night exhaled once more. Harder this time. Its breath was sharp and dank.

He was wearing running shoes, white athletic socks, jeans, and a long-sleeved blue-plaid shirt. He had no jacket, and he could have used one. The air was not frigid, just mildly bracing. But a coldness was in him, too, a gelid fear, and he shivered uncontrollably between the cool caress of the night air and that inner chill.

The gust of wind died.

Stillness reclaimed the night.

Convinced that he had to get out of there—and fast—he pushed away from the dumpster. He staggered along the alley, retreating from the end of the block where the streetlamp glowed, into darker realms, with no

destination in mind, driven only by the sense that this place was dangerous and that safety, if indeed safety could be found, lay elsewhere.

The wind rose again, and with it, this time, came an eerie whistling,
barely audible, like the distant music of a flute made of some strange
bone.

Within a few steps, as Frank became surefooted and as his eyes
adapted to the murky night, he arrived at a confluence of passageways.
Wrought-iron gates in pale stucco arches lay to his left and right.

He tried the gate on the left. It was unlocked, secured only by a simple
gravity latch. The hinges squeaked, eliciting a wince from Frank, who
hoped the sound had not been heard by his pursuer.

By now, although no adversary was in sight, Frank had no doubt that
he was the object of a chase. He knew it as surely as a hare knew when
a fox was in the field.

The wind huffed again at his back, and the flutelike music, though
barely audible and lacking a discernible melody, was haunting. It pierced
him. It sharpened his fear.

Beyond the black iron gate, flanked by feathery ferns and bushes, a
walkway led between a pair of two-story apartment buildings. Frank followed it into a rectangular courtyard somewhat revealed by low-wattage
security lamps at each end. First-floor apartments opened onto a covered
promenade; the doors of the second-floor units were under the tile roof
of an iron-railed balcony. Lightless windows faced a swath of grass, beds
of azaleas and succulents, and a few palms.

A frieze of spiky palm-frond shadows lay across one palely illuminated
wall, as motionless as if they were carved on a stone entablature. Then
the mysterious flute warbled softly again, the reborn wind huffed harder
than before, and the shadows danced, danced. Frank's own distorted,
dark reflection whirled briefly over the stucco, among the terpsichorean
silhouettes, as he hurried across the courtyard. He found another walkway, another gate, and ultimately the street on which the apartment complex faced.

It was a side street without lampposts. There, the reign of the night
was undisputed.

The blustery wind lasted longer than before, churned harder. When
the gust ended abruptly, with an equally abrupt cessation of the unmelodic flute, the night seemed to have been left in a vacuum, as though

the departing turbulence had taken with it every wisp of breathable air. Then Frank's ears popped as if from a sudden altitude change; as he rushed across the deserted street toward the cars parked along the far curb, air poured in around him again.

He tried four cars before finding one unlocked, a Ford. Slipping behind the wheel, he left the door open to provide some light.

He looked back the way he had come.

The apartment complex was dead-of-the-night still. Wrapped in darkness. An ordinary building yet inexplicably sinister.

No one was in sight.

Nevertheless, Frank knew someone was closing in on him.

He reached under the dashboard, pulled out a tangle of wires, and hastily jump-started the engine before realizing that such a larcenous skill suggested a life outside of the law. Yet he didn't feel like a thief. He had no sense of guilt and no antipathy for—or fear of—the police. In fact, at the moment, he would have welcomed a cop to help him deal with whoever or whatever was on his tail. He felt not like a criminal, but like a man who had been on the run for an exhaustingly long time, from an implacable and relentless enemy.

As he reached for the handle of the open door, a brief pulse of pale blue light washed over him, and the driver's-side windows of the Ford exploded. Tempered glass showered into the rear seat, gummy and minutely fragmented. Since the front door was not closed, that window didn't spray over him; instead, most of it fell out of the frame, onto the pavement.

Yanking the door shut, he glanced through the gap where the glass had been, toward the gloom-enfolded apartments, saw no one.

Frank threw the Ford in gear, popped the brake, and tramped hard on the accelerator. Swinging away from the curb, he clipped the rear bumper of the car parked in front of him. A brief peal of tortured metal rang sharply across the night.

But he was still under attack: A scintillant blue light, at most one second in duration, lit up the car; over its entire breadth the windshield crazed with thousands of jagged lines, though it had been struck by nothing he could see. Frank averted his face and squeezed his eyes shut just in time to avoid being blinded by flying fragments. For a moment he could not see where he was going, but he didn't let up on the accelerator, preferring the danger of collision to the greater risk of braking and giving his unseen enemy time to reach him. Glass rained over him, spattered across the top of his bent head; luckily, it was safety glass, and none of the fragments cut him.

He opened his eyes, squinting into the gale that rushed through the now empty windshield frame. He saw that he'd gone half a block and had reached the intersection. He whipped the wheel to the right, tapping the brake pedal only lightly, and turned onto a more brightly lighted thoroughfare.

Like Saint Elmo's fire, sapphire-blue light glimmered on the chrome, and when the Ford was halfway around the corner, one of the rear tires blew. He had heard no gunfire. A fraction of a second later, the other rear tire blew.

The car rocked, slewed to the left, began to fishtail.

Frank fought the steering wheel.

Both front tires ruptured simultaneously.

The car rocked again, even as it glided sideways, and the sudden collapse of the front tires compensated for the leftward slide of the rear end, giving Frank a chance to grapple the spinning steering wheel into submission.

Again, he had heard no gunfire. He didn't know why all of this was happening—yet he did.

That was the truly frightening part: On some deep subconscious level he *did* know what was happening, what strange force was swiftly destroying the car around him, and he also knew that his chances of escaping were poor.

A flicker of twilight blue . . .

The rear window imploded. Gummy yet prickly wads of safety glass flew past him. Some smacked the back of his head, stuck in his hair.

Frank made the corner and kept going on four flats. The sound of flapping rubber, already shredded, and the grinding of metal wheel rims could be heard even above the roar of the wind that buffeted his face.

He glanced at the rearview mirror. The night was a great black ocean behind him, relieved only by widely spaced streetlamps that dwindled into the gloom like the lights of a double convoy of ships.

According to the speedometer, he was doing thirty miles an hour just after coming out of the turn. He tried to push it up to forty in spite of the ruined tires, but something clanged and clinked under the hood, rattled and whined, and the engine coughed, and he could not coax any more speed out of it.

When he was halfway to the next intersection, the headlights either burst or winked out. Frank couldn't tell which. Even though the street-lamps were widely spaced, he could see well enough to drive.

The engine coughed, then again, and the Ford began to lose speed. He didn't brake for the stop sign at the next intersection. Instead he pumped the accelerator but to no avail.

Finally the steering failed too. The wheel spun uselessly in his sweaty hands.

Evidently the tires had been completely torn apart. The contact of the steel wheel rims with the pavement flung up gold and turquoise sparks. *Fireflies in a windstorm. . . .*

He still didn't know what that meant.

Now moving about twenty miles an hour, the car headed straight toward the right-hand curb. Frank tramped the brakes, but they no longer functioned.

The car hit the curb, jumped it, grazed a lamppost with a sound of sheet metal kissing steel, and thudded against the bole of an immense date palm in front of a white bungalow. Lights came on in the house even as the final crash was echoing on the cool night air.

Frank threw the door open, grabbed the leather flight bag from the seat beside him, and got out, shedding fragments of gummy yet splintery safety glass.

Though only mildly cool, the air chilled his face because sweat trickled down from his forehead. He could taste salt when he licked his lips.

A man had opened the front door of the bungalow and stepped onto the porch. Lights flicked on at the house next door.

Frank looked back the way he had come. A thin cloud of luminous sapphire dust seemed to blow through the street. As if shattered by a tremendous surge of current, the bulbs in the streetlamps exploded along the two blocks behind him, and shards of glass, glinting like ice, rained on the blacktop. In the resultant gloom, he thought he saw a tall, shadowy figure, more than a block away, coming after him, but he could not be sure.

To Frank's left, the guy from the bungalow was hurrying down the walk toward the palm tree where the Ford had come to rest. He was talking, but Frank wasn't listening to him.

Clutching the leather satchel, Frank turned and ran. He was not sure what he was running from, or why he was so afraid, or where he might hope to find a haven, but he ran nonetheless because he knew that if he stood there only a few seconds longer, he would be killed.

2

THE WINDOWLESS REAR COMPARTMENT OF THE DODGE VAN WAS illuminated by tiny red, blue, green, white, and amber indicator bulbs on banks of electronic surveillance equipment but primarily by the soft green glow from the two computer screens, which made that claustrophobic space seem like a chamber in a deep-sea submersible.

Dressed in a pair of Rockport walking shoes, beige cords, and a maroon sweater, Robert Dakota sat on a swivel chair in front of the twin video display terminals. He tapped his feet against the floorboards, keeping time, and with his right hand he happily conducted an unseen orchestra.

Bobby was wearing a headset with stereo earphones and with a small microphone suspended an inch or so in front of his lips. At the moment he was listening to Benny Goodman's "One O'Clock Jump," the primo version of Count Basie's classic swing composition, six and a half minutes of heaven. As Jess Stacy took up another piano chorus and as Harry James launched into the brilliant trumpet stint that led to the most famous rideout in swing history, Bobby was deep into the music.

But he was also acutely aware of the activity on the display terminals. The one on the right was linked, via microwave, with the computer system at the Decodyne Corporation, in front of which his van was parked. It revealed what Tom Rasmussen was up to in those offices at 1:10 Thursday morning: no good.

One by one, Rasmussen was accessing and copying the files of the software-design team that had recently completed Decodyne's new and revolutionary word-processing program, "Whizard." The Whizard files carried well-constructed lockout instructions—electronic drawbridges, moats, and ramparts. Tom Rasmussen was an expert in computer security, however, and there was no fortress that he could not penetrate, given enough time. Indeed, if Whizard had not been developed on a secure in-house computer system with no links to the outside world, Rasmussen would have slipped into the files from beyond the walls of Decodyne, via a modem and telephone line.

Ironically, he had been working as the night security guard at Decodyne for five weeks, having been hired on the basis of elaborate—and nearly convincing—false papers. Tonight he had breached Whizard's final defenses. In a while he would walk out of Decodyne with a packet of floppy diskettes worth a fortune to the company's competitors.

"One O'Clock Jump" ended.

Into the microphone Bobby said, "Music stop."

That vocal command cued his computerized compact-disc system to switch off, opening the headset for communication with Julie, his wife and business partner.

"You there, babe?"

From her surveillance position in a car at the farthest end of the parking lot behind Decodyne, she had been listening to the same music through her own headset. She sighed. "Did Vernon Brown ever play better trombone than the night of the Carnegie concert?"

"What about Krupa on the drums?"

"Auditory ambrosia. And an aphrodisiac. The music makes me want to go to bed with you."

"Can't. Not sleepy. Besides, we're being private detectives, remember?"

"I like being lovers better."

"We don't earn our daily bread by making love."

"I'd pay you," she said.

"Yeah? How much?"

"Oh, in daily-bread terms . . . half a loaf."

"I'm worth a whole loaf."

Julie said, "Actually, you're worth a whole loaf, two croissants, and a bran muffin."

She had a pleasing, throaty, and altogether sexy voice that he loved to listen to, especially through headphones, when she sounded like an angel whispering in his ears. She would have been a marvelous big-band singer if she had been around in the 1930s and '40s—and if she had been able to carry a tune. She was a great swing dancer, but she couldn't croon worth a damn; when she was in the mood to sing along with old recordings by Margaret Whiting or the Andrews Sisters or Rosemary Clooney or Marion Hutton, Bobby had to leave the room out of respect for the music.

She said, "What's Rasmussen doing?"

Bobby checked the second video display, to his left, which was linked to Decodyne's interior security cameras. Rasmussen thought he had over-ridden the cameras and was unobserved; but they had been watching him for the last few weeks, night after night, and recording his every treachery on videotape.

"Old Tom's still in George Ackroyd's office, at the VDT there." Ackroyd was project director for Whizard. Bobby glanced at the other display, which duplicated what Rasmussen was seeing on Ackroyd's computer screen. "He just copied the last Whizard file onto diskette."

Rasmussen switched off the computer in Ackroyd's office.

Simultaneously the linked VDT in front of Bobby went blank.

Bobby said, "He's finished. He's got it all now."

Julie said, "The worm. He must be feeling smug."

Bobby turned to the display on his left, leaned forward, and watched the black-and-white image of Rasmussen at Ackroyd's terminal. "I think he's grinning."

"We'll wipe that grin off his face."

"Let's see what he does next. Want to make a bet? Will he stay in there, finish his shift, and waltz out in the morning—or leave right now?"

"Now," Julie said. "Or soon. He won't risk getting caught with the floppies. He'll leave while no one else is there."

"No bet. I think you're right."

The transmitted image on the monitor flickered, rolled, but Rasmussen did not get out of Ackroyd's chair. In fact he slumped back, as if ex-hausted. He yawned and rubbed his eyes with the heels of his hands.

"He seems to be resting, gathering his energy," Bobby said.

"Let's have another tune while we wait for him to move."

"Good idea." He gave the CD player the start-up cue—"Begin mu-sic"—and was rewarded with Glenn Miller's "In the Mood."

On the monitor, Tom Rasmussen rose from the chair in Ackroyd's dimly lighted office. He yawned again, stretched, and crossed the room to the big windows that looked down on Michaelson Drive, the street on which Bobby was parked.

If Bobby had slipped forward, out of the rear of the van and into the driver's compartment, he probably would have been able to see Ras-mussen standing up there at the second-floor window, silhouetted by the glow of Ackroyd's desk lamp, staring out at the night. He stayed where he was, however, satisfied with the view on the screen.

Miller's band was playing the famous "In the Mood" riff, again and again, gradually fading away, almost disappearing entirely but . . . *now* blasting back at full power to repeat the entire cycle.

In Ackroyd's office, Rasmussen finally turned from the window and looked up at the security camera that was mounted on the wall near the ceiling. He seemed to be staring straight at Bobby, as if aware of being watched. He moved a few steps closer to the camera, smiling.

Bobby said, "Music stop," and the Miller band instantly fell silent. To Julie, he said, "Something strange here . . ."

"Trouble?"

Rasmussen stopped just under the security camera, still grinning up at it. From the pocket of his uniform shirt, he withdrew a folded sheet of typing paper, which he opened and held toward the lens. A message had been printed in bold black letters: GOODBYE, ASSHOLE.

"Trouble for sure," Bobby said.

"How bad?"

"I don't know."

An instant later he did know: Automatic weapons fire shattered the night—he could hear the clatter even with his earphones on—and armor-piercing slugs tore through the walls of the van.

Julie evidently picked up the gunfire through her headset. "Bobby, no!"

"Get the hell out of there, babe! Run!"

Even as he spoke, Bobby tore free of the headset and dived off his chair, lying as flat against the floorboards as he could.

3

FRANK POLLARD SPRINTED FROM STREET TO STREET, FROM ALLEY TO alley, sometimes cutting across the lawns of the dark houses. In one back-yard a large black dog with yellow eyes barked and snapped at him all the way to the board fence, briefly snaring one leg of his pants as he clambered over that barrier. His heart was pounding painfully, and his throat was hot and raw because he was sucking in great drafts of the cool, dry air through his open mouth. His legs ached. As if made of iron, the flight bag pulled on his right arm, and with each lunging step that he took, pain throbbed in his wrist and shoulder socket. But he did not pause and did not glance back, because he felt as if something monstrous was at his heels, a creature that never required rest and that would turn him to stone with its gaze if he dared set eyes upon it.

In time he crossed an avenue, devoid of traffic at that late hour, and hurried along the entrance walk to another apartment complex. He went through a gate into another courtyard, this one centered by an empty swimming pool with a cracked and canted apron.

The place was lightless, but Frank's vision had adapted to the night, and he could see well enough to avoid falling into the drained pool. He was searching for shelter. Perhaps there was a communal laundry room where he could force the lock and hide.

He had discovered something else about himself as he fled his unknown pursuer: He was thirty or forty pounds overweight and out of shape. He desperately needed to catch his breath—and think.

As he was hurrying past the doors of the ground-floor units, he realized that a couple of them were standing open, sagging on ruined hinges. Then he saw that cracks webbed some windows, holes pocked a few, and other panes were missing altogether. The grass was dead, too, as crisp as ancient paper, and the shrubbery was withered; a seared palm tree leaned at a precarious angle. The apartment complex was abandoned, awaiting a wrecking crew.

He came to a set of crumbling concrete stairs at the north end of the courtyard, glanced back. Whoever . . . whatever was following him was still not in sight. Gasping, he climbed to the second-floor balcony and moved from one apartment to another until he found a door ajar. It was warped; the hinges were stiff, but they worked without much noise. He slipped inside, pushing the door shut behind him.

The apartment was a well of shadows, oil-black and pooled deep. Faint ash-gray light outlined the windows but provided no illumination to the room.

He listened intently.

The silence and darkness were equal in depth.

Cautiously, Frank inched toward the nearest window, which faced the balcony and courtyard. Only a few shards of glass remained in the frame, but lots of fragments crunched and clinked under his feet. He trod carefully, both to avoid cutting a foot and to make as little noise as possible.

At the window he halted, listened again.

Stillness.

As if it was the gelid ectoplasm of a slothful ghost, a sluggish current of cold air slid inward across the few jagged points of the glass that had not already fallen from the frame.

Frank's breath steamed in front of his face, pale ribbons of vapor in the gloom.

The silence remained unbroken for ten seconds, twenty, thirty, a full minute.

Perhaps he had escaped.

He was just about to turn away from the window when he heard footsteps outside. At the far end of the courtyard. On the walkway that led in from the street. Hard-soled shoes rang against the concrete, and each footfall echoed hollowly off the stucco walls of the surrounding buildings.

Frank stood motionless and breathed through his mouth, as if the stalker could be counted on to have the hearing of a jungle cat.

When he entered the courtyard from the entrance walkway, the stranger halted. After a long pause he began to move again; though the overlapping echoes made sounds deceptive, he seemed to be heading slowly north along the apron of the pool, toward the same stairs by which Frank, himself, had climbed to the second floor of the apartment complex.

Each deliberate, metronomic footfall was like the heavy tick of a headsman's clock mounted on a guillotine railing, counting off the seconds until the appointed hour of the blade's descent.

4

AS IF ALIVE, THE DODGE VAN SHRIEKED WITH EVERY BULLET THAT tore through its sheet-metal walls, and the wounds were inflicted not one at a time but by the score, with such relentless fury, the assault had to involve at least two machine guns. While Bobby Dakota lay flat on the floor, trying to catch God's attention with fervent heaven-directed prayers, fragments of metal rained down on him. One of the computer screens imploded, then the other terminal, too, and all the indicator lights went out, but the interior of the van was not entirely dark; showers of amber and green and crimson and silver sparks erupted from the damaged electronic units as one steel-jacketed round after another pierced equipment housings and shattered circuit boards. Glass fell on him, too, and splinters of plastic, bits of wood, scraps of paper; the air was filled with a virtual blizzard of debris. But the noise was the worst of it; in his mind he saw himself sealed inside a great iron drum, while half a dozen big bikers, stoned on PCP, pounded on the outside of his prison with tire irons, really huge bikers with massive muscles and thick necks and coarse peltlike beards and wildly colorful Death's-head tattoos on their arms—hell, tattoos on their *faces*—guys as big as Thor, the Viking god, but with blazing, psychotic eyes.

Bobby had a vivid imagination. He had always thought that was one of his best qualities, one of his strengths. But he could not simply imagine his way out of this mess.

With every passing second, as slugs continued to crash into the van, he grew more astonished that he had not been hit. He was pressed to the floor, as tight as a carpet, and he tried to imagine that his body was only a quarter of an inch thick, a target with an incredibly low profile, but he still expected to get his ass shot off.

He had not anticipated the need for a gun; it wasn't that kind of case. At least it hadn't *seemed* to be that kind of case. A .38 revolver was in the van glovebox, well beyond his reach, which did not cause him a lot of frustration, actually, because a single handgun against a pair of automatic weapons was not much use.

The gunfire stopped.

After that cacophony of destruction, the silence was so profound, Bobby felt as if he had gone deaf.

The air reeked of hot metal, overheated electronic components, scorched insulation—and gasoline. Evidently the van's tank had been punctured. The engine was still chugging, and a few sparks spat out of the shattered equipment surrounding Bobby, and his chances of escaping a flash fire were a whole lot worse than his chances of winning fifty million bucks in the state lottery.

He wanted to get the hell out of there, but if he burst out of the van, they might be waiting with machine guns to cut him down. On the other hand, if he continued to hug the floor in the darkness, counting on them to give him up for dead without checking on him, the Dodge might flare like a campfire primed with starter fluid, toasting him as crisp as a marshmallow.

He had no difficulty imagining himself stepping out of the van and being hit immediately by a score of bullets, jerking and twitching in a spasmodic death dance across the blacktop street, like a broken marionette jerked around on tangled strings. But he found it even easier to imagine his skin peeling off in the fire, flesh bubbling and smoking, hair *whoosh*ing up like a torch, eyes melting, teeth turning coal-black as flames seared his tongue and followed his breath down his throat to his lungs.

Sometimes a vivid imagination was definitely a curse.

Suddenly the gasoline fumes became so heavy that he had trouble drawing breath, so he started to get up.

Outside, a car horn began to blare. He heard a racing engine drawing rapidly nearer.

Someone shouted, and a machine gun opened fire again.

Bobby hit the floor, wondering what the hell was going on, but as the car with the blaring horn drew nearer, he realized what must be happening: Julie. Julie was happening. Sometimes she was like a natural force; she happened the way a storm happened, the way lightning happened, abruptly crackling down a dark sky. He had told her to get out of there, to save herself, but she had not listened to him; he wanted to kick her butt for being so bullheaded, but he loved her for it too.

5

SIDLING AWAY FROM THE BROKEN WINDOW, FRANK TRIED TO TIME HIS steps to those of the man in the courtyard below, with the hope that any noise he made, trodding on glass, would be covered by his unseen enemy's advance. He figured that he was in the living room of the apartment, that it was pretty much empty except for whatever detritus had been left behind by the last tenants or had blown through the missing windows, and indeed he made it across that chamber and into a hallway in relative silence, without colliding with anything.

He hurriedly felt his way along the hall, which was as black as a pred-ator's lair. It smelled of mold and mildew and urine. He passed the en-trance to a room, kept going, turned right through the next doorway, and shuffled to another broken window. This one had no splinters of glass left in the frame, and it did not face the courtyard but looked onto a lamplit and deserted street.

Something rustled behind him.

He turned, blinking blindly at the gloom, and almost cried out.

But the sound must have been made by a rat scurrying along the floor, close to the wall, across dry leaves or bits of paper. Just a rat.

Frank listened for footsteps, but if the stalker was still homing on him, the hollow heel clicks of his approach were completely muffled by the walls that now intervened.

He looked out the window again. The dead lawn lay below, as dry as sand and twice as brown, offering little cushion. He dropped the leather flight bag, which landed with a thud. Wincing at the prospect of the leap, he climbed onto the sill, crouching in the broken-out window, hands braced against the frame, where for a moment he hesitated.

A gust of wind ruffled his hair and coolly caressed his face. But it was a normal draft, nothing like the preternatural whiffs of wind that, earlier, had been accompanied by the unearthly and unmelodic music of a distant flute.

Suddenly, behind Frank, a blue flash pulsed out of the living room, down the hall, and through the doorway. The strange tide of light was trailed closely by an explosion and a concussion wave that shook the walls and seemed to churn the air into a more solid substance. The front door had been blasted to pieces; he heard chunks of it raining down on the floor of the apartment a couple of rooms away.

He jumped out of the window, landed on his feet. But his knees gave way, and he fell flat on the dead lawn.

At that same moment a large truck turned the corner. Its cargo bed had slat sides and a wooden tailgate. The driver smoothly shifted gears and drove past the apartment house, apparently unaware of Frank.

He scrambled to his feet, plucked the satchel off the barren lawn, and ran into the street. Having just rounded the corner, the truck was not moving fast, and Frank managed to grab the tailgate and pull himself up, one-handed, until he was standing on the rear bumper.

As the truck accelerated, Frank looked back at the decaying apartment complex. No mysterious blue light glimmered at any of the windows; they were all as black and empty as the sockets of a skull.

The truck turned right at the next corner, moving away into the sleepy night.

Exhausted, Frank clung to the tailgate. He would have been able to hold on better if he had dropped the leather flight bag, but he held fast to it because he suspected that its contents might help him to learn who he was and from where he had come and from what he was running.

6

CUT AND RUN! BOBBY ACTUALLY THOUGHT SHE WOULD CUT AND RUN when trouble struck— *"Get the hell out of there, babe! Run!"*—would cut and run just because he told her to, as if she was an obedient little wifey, not a full-fledged partner in the agency, not a damned good investigator in her own right, just a token backup who couldn't take the heat when the furnace kicked on. Well, to hell with that.

In her mind she could see his lovable face—merry blue eyes, pug nose, smattering of freckles, generous mouth—framed by thick honey-gold hair that was mussed (as was most often the case) like that of a small boy who had just gotten up from a nap. She wanted to bop his pug nose just hard enough to make his blue eyes water, so he'd have no doubt how the cut-and-run suggestion annoyed her.

She had been on surveillance behind Decodyne, at the far end of the corporate parking lot, in the deep shadows under a massive Indian laurel. The moment Bobby signaled trouble, she started the Toyota's engine. By the time she heard gunfire over the earphones, she had shifted gears, popped the emergency brake, switched on the headlights, and jammed the accelerator toward the floor.

At first she kept the headset on, calling Bobby's name, trying to get an answer from him, hearing only the most godawful ruckus from his end. Then the set went dead; she couldn't hear anything at all, so she pulled it off and threw it into the backseat.

Cut and run! Damn him!

When she reached the end of the last row in the parking lot, she let up on the accelerator with her right foot, simultaneously tapping the brake pedal with her left foot, finessing the small car into a slide, which carried it onto the access road that led around the big building. She turned the steering wheel into the slide, then gave the heap some gas again even before the back end had stopped skidding and shuddering. The tires barked, and the engine shrieked, and with a rattle-squeak-twang of tortured metal, the car leaped forward.

They were shooting at Bobby, and Bobby probably wasn't even able to shoot back, because he was lax about carrying a gun on every job; he went armed only when it seemed that the current business was likely to involve violence. The Decodyne assignment had looked peaceable enough; sometimes industrial espionage could turn nasty, but the bad guy in this case was Tom Rasmussen, a computer nerd and a greedy son of a bitch, clever as a dog reading Shakespeare on a high wire, with a record of theft via computer but with no blood on his hands. He was the high-tech equivalent of a meek, embezzling bank clerk—or so he had seemed.

But Julie was armed on *every* job. Bobby was the optimist; she was the pessimist. Bobby expected people to act in their own best interests and be reasonable, but Julie half expected every apparently normal person to be, in secret, a crazed psychotic. A Smith & Wesson .357 Magnum was held by a clip to the back of the glovebox lid, and an Uzi—with two spare thirty-round magazines—lay on the other front seat. From what she had heard on the earphones before they'd gone dead, she was going to need that Uzi.

The Toyota virtually *flew* past the side of Decodyne, and she wheeled hard left, onto Michaelson Drive, almost rising onto two wheels, almost losing control, but not quite. Ahead, Bobby's Dodge was parked at the curb in front of the building, and another van—a dark blue Ford—was stopped in the street, doors open wide.

Two men, who had evidently been in the Ford, were standing four or five yards from the Dodge, chopping the hell out of it with automatic weapons, blasting away with such ferocity that they seemed not to be after the man inside but to have some bizarre personal grudge against the Dodge itself. They stopped firing, turned toward her as she came out of the driveway onto Michaelson, and hurriedly jammed fresh magazines into their weapons.

Ideally, she would close the hundred-yard gap between herself and the men, pull the Toyota sideways in the street, slip out, and use the car as cover to blow out the tires on their Ford and pin them down until police arrived. But she didn't have time for all of that. They were already raising the muzzles of their weapons.

She was unnerved at how lonely the night streets looked at this hour in the heart of metropolitan Orange County, barren of traffic, washed by the urine-yellow light of the sodium-vapor streetlamps. They were in an area of banks and office buildings, no residences, no restaurants or bars within a couple of blocks. It might as well have been a city on the moon, or a vision of the world after it had been swept by an Apocalyptic disease that had left only a handful of survivors.

She didn't have time to handle the two gunmen by the book, and she could not count on help from any quarter, so she would have to do what they least expected: play kamikaze, use her *car* as a weapon.

The instant she had the Toyota fully under control, she pressed the accelerator tight to the floorboards and rocketed straight at the two bastards. They opened fire, but she was already slipping down in the seat and leaning sideways a little, trying to keep her head below the dashboard and still hold the wheel relatively steady. Bullets snapped and whined off the car. The windshield burst. A second later Julie hit one of the gunmen so hard that the impact snapped her head forward, against the wheel, cutting her forehead, snapping her teeth together forcefully enough to make her jaw ache; even as pain needled through her face, she heard the body bounce off the front bumper and slam onto the hood.

With blood trickling down her forehead and dripping from her right eyebrow, Julie jabbed at the brakes and sat up at the same time. She was confronted by a man's wide-eyed corpse jammed in the frame of the empty windshield. His face was in front of the steering wheel—teeth chipped, lips torn, chin slashed, cheek battered, left eye missing—and one of his broken legs was inside the car, hooked down over the dashboard.

Julie found the brake pedal and pumped it. With the sudden drop in speed, the dead man was dislodged. His limp body rolled across the hood, and when the car slid to a shaky halt, he vanished over the front end.

Heart racing, blinking to keep the stinging blood from blurring the vision in her right eye, Julie snatched the Uzi from the seat beside her, shoved open the door, and rolled out, moving fast and staying low.

The other gunman was already in the blue Ford van. He gave it gas before remembering to shift out of park, so the tires screamed and smoked.

Julie squeezed off two short bursts from the Uzi, blowing out both tires on her side of the van.

But the gunman didn't stop. He shifted gears at last and tried to drive past her on two ruined tires.

The guy might have killed Bobby; now he was getting away. He would probably never be found if Julie didn't stop him. Reluctantly she swung the Uzi higher and emptied the magazine into the side window of the van. The Ford accelerated, then suddenly slowed and swung to the right, at steadily diminishing speed, in a long arc that carried it to the far curb, where it came to a halt with a jolt.

No one got out.

Keeping an eye on the Ford, Julie leaned into her car, plucked a spare magazine from the seat, and reloaded the Uzi. She approached the idling van cautiously and pulled open the door, but caution was not required because the man behind the wheel was dead. Feeling a little sick, she reached in and switched off the engine.

Briefly, as she turned from the Ford and hurried toward the bullet-riddled Dodge, the only sounds she could hear were the soughing of a faint breeze in the lush corporate landscaping that flanked the street, punctuated by the gentle hiss and rattle of palm fronds. Then she also heard the idling engine of the Dodge, simultaneously smelled gasoline, and shouted, "Bobby!"

Before she reached the white van, the back doors creaked open, and Bobby came out, shedding twists of metal, chunks of plastic, bits of glass, wood chips, and scraps of paper. He was gasping, no doubt because the gasoline fumes had driven most of the breathable air out of the Dodge's rear quarters.

Sirens rose in the distance.

Together they quickly walked away from the van. They had gone only a few steps when orange light flared and flames rose in a *wooooosh* from the gasoline pooled on the pavement, enveloping the vehicle in bright shrouds. They hurried beyond the corona of intense heat that surrounded the Dodge and stood for a moment, blinking at the wreckage, then at each other.

The sirens were drawing nearer.

He said, "You're bleeding."

"Just skinned my forehead a little."

"You sure?"

"It's nothing. What about you?"

He sucked in a deep breath. "I'm okay."

"Really?"

"Yeah."

"You weren't hit?"

"Unmarked. It's a miracle."

"Bobby?"

"What?"

"I couldn't handle it if you'd turned up dead in there."

"I'm not dead. I'm fine."

"Thank God," she said.

Then she kicked his right shin.

"Ow! What the hell?"

She kicked his left shin.

"Julie, dammit!"

"Don't you ever tell me to cut and run."

"What?"

"I'm a full half of this partnership in *every* way."

"But—"

"I'm as smart as you, as fast as you—"

He glanced at the dead man on the street, the other one in the Ford van, half visible through the open door, and he said, "That's for sure, babe."

"—as tough as you—"

"I know, I know. Don't kick me again."

She said, "What about Rasmussen?"

Bobby looked up at the Decodyne building. "You think he's still in there?"

"The only exits from the parking lot are onto Michaelson, and he hasn't come out this way, so unless he fled on foot, he's in there, all right. We've got to nail him before he slides out of the trap with those diskettes."

"Nothing worthwhile on the diskettes anyway," Bobby said.

Decodyne had been on to Rasmussen from the time he applied for the job, because Dakota & Dakota Investigations—which was contracted to handle the company's security checks—had penetrated the hacker's highly sophisticated false ID. Decodyne's management wanted to play along with Rasmussen long enough to discover to whom he would pass the Whizard files when he got them; they intended to prosecute the money man who had hired Rasmussen, for no doubt the hacker's employer was one of Decodyne's primary competitors. They had allowed Tom Rasmussen to think he had compromised the security cameras, when in fact he had been under constant observation. They also had allowed him to break down the file codes and access the information he wanted, but unknown to him they had inserted secret instructions in the files, which insured that any diskettes he acquired would be full of trash data of no use to anyone.

Flames roared and crackled, consuming the van. Julie watched chimeras of reflected flames slither and caper up the glass walls and across the blank, black windows of Decodyne, as if they were striving to reach the roof and coalesce there in the form of gargoyles.

Raising her voice slightly to compete with the fire and with the shriek of approaching sirens, she said, "Well, we thought he believed he'd circumvented the videotape records of the security cameras, but apparently he knew we were on to him."

"Sure did."

"So he also might've been smart enough to search for an anticopying directive in the files—and find a way around it."

Bobby frowned. "You're right."

"So he's probably got Whizard, unscrambled, on those diskettes."

"Damn, I don't want to go in there. I've been shot at enough tonight."

A police cruiser turned the corner two blocks away and sped toward them, siren screaming, emergency lights casting off alternating waves of blue and red light.

"Here come the professionals," Julie said. "Why don't we let them take over now?"

"We were hired to do the job. We have an obligation. PI honor is a sacred thing, you know. What would Sam Spade think of us?"

She said, "Sam Spade can go spit up a rope."

"What would Philip Marlowe think?"

"Philip Marlowe can go spit up a rope."

"What will our client think?"

"Our *client* can go spit up a rope."

"Dear, 'spit' isn't the popular expression."

"I know, but I'm a lady."

"You certainly are."

As the black-and-white braked in front of them, another police car turned the corner behind it, siren wailing, and a third entered Michaelson Drive from the other direction.

Julie put her Uzi on the pavement and raised her hands to avoid unfortunate misunderstandings. "I'm *really* glad you're alive, Bobby."

"You going to kick me again?"

"Not for a while."

7

FRANK POLLARD HUNG ON TO THE TAILGATE AND RODE THE TRUCK nine or ten blocks, without drawing the attention of the driver. Along the way he saw a sign welcoming him to the city of Anaheim, so he figured he was in southern California, although he still didn't know if this was where he lived or whether he was from out of town. Judging by the chill in the air, it was winter—not truly cold but as frigid as it got in these climes. He was unnerved to realize that he did not know the date or even the month. Shivering, he dropped off the truck when it slowed and turned onto a serviceway that led through a warehouse district. Huge, corrugated-metal buildings—some newly painted and some streaked with rust, some dimly lit by security lamps and some not—loomed against the star-spattered sky.

Carrying the flight bag, he walked away from the warehouses. The streets in that area were lined with shabby bungalows. The shrubs and trees were overgrown in many places: untrimmed palms with full skirts of dead fronds; bushy hibiscuses with half-closed pale blooms glimmering softly in the gloom; jade hedges and plum-thorn hedges so old they were more woody than leafy; bougainvillea draped over roofs and fences, bristling with thousands of untamed, questing trailers. His soft-soled shoes made no sound on the sidewalk, and his shadow alternately stretched ahead of him and then behind, as he approached and then passed one lamppost after another.

Cars, mostly older models, some rusted and battered, were parked at curbs and in driveways; keys might have dangled from the ignitions of some of them, and he could have jump-started any he chose. However, he noted that the cinderblock walls between the properties—as well as the walls of a decrepit and abandoned house—shimmered with the spray-painted, ghostly, semi-phosphorescent graffiti of Latino gangs, and he didn't want to tinker with a set of wheels that might belong to one of their members. Those guys didn't bother rushing to a phone to call the police if they caught you trying to steal one of their cars; they just blew your head off or put a knife in your neck. Frank had enough trouble already, even with his head intact and his throat unpunctured, so he kept walking.

Twelve blocks later, in a neighborhood of well-kept houses and better cars, he began searching for a set of wheels that would be easy to boost. The tenth vehicle he tried was a one-year-old green Chevy, parked near a streetlamp, the doors unlocked, the keys tucked under the driver's seat.

Intent on putting a lot of distance between himself and the deserted apartment complex where he had last encountered his unknown pursuer, Frank switched on the Chevy's heater, drove from Anaheim to Santa Ana, then south on Bristol Avenue toward Costa Mesa, surprised by his familiarity with the streets. He seemed to know the area well. He recognized buildings, shopping centers, parks, and neighborhoods past which he drove, though the sight of them did nothing to rekindle his burnt-out memory. He still could not recall who he was, where he lived, what he did for a living, what he was running from, or how he had come to wake up in an alleyway in the middle of the night.

Even at that dead hour—the car clock indicated it was 2:48—he figured his chances of encountering a traffic cop were greater on a freeway, so he stayed on the surface streets through Costa Mesa and the eastern and southern fringes of Newport Beach. At Corona Del Mar he picked up the Pacific Coast Highway and followed it all the way to Laguna Beach, encountering a thin fog that gradually thickened as he progressed southward.

Laguna, a picturesque resort town and artists' colony, shelved down a series of steep hillsides and canyon walls to the sea, most of it cloaked now in the thick fog. Only an occasional car passed him, and the mist rolling in from the Pacific became sufficiently dense to force him to reduce his speed to fifteen miles an hour.

Yawning and gritty-eyed, he turned onto a side street east of the highway and parked at the curb in front of a dark, two-story, gabled, Cape Cod house that looked out of place on these Western slopes. He wanted to get a motel room, but before he tried to check in somewhere, he needed to know if he had any money or credit cards. For the first time all night, he had a chance to look for ID, as well. He searched the pockets of his jeans, but to no avail.

He switched on the overhead light, pulled the leather flight bag onto his lap and opened it. The satchel was filled with tightly banded stacks of twenty-and hundred-dollar bills.

8

THE THIN SOUP OF GRAY MIST WAS GRADUALLY STIRRING ITSELF INTO a thicker stew. A couple of miles closer to the ocean, the night probably was clotted with fog so dense that it would almost have lumps.

Coatless, protected from the night only by a sweater, but warmed by the fact that he had narrowly avoided almost certain death, Bobby leaned against one of the patrol cars in front of Decodyne and watched Julie as she paced back and forth with her hands in the pockets of her brown leather jacket. He never got tired of looking at her. They had been married seven years, and during that time they had lived and worked and played together virtually twenty-four hours a day, seven days a week. Bobby had never been the kind who liked to hang out with a bunch of guys at a bar or ball game—partly because it was difficult to find other guys in their middle thirties who were interested in the things that he cared about: big-band music, the arts and pop culture of the '30s and '40s, and classic Disney comic books. Julie wasn't a lunch-with-the-girls type, either, because not many thirty-year-old women were into the big-band era, Warner Brothers cartoons, martial arts, or advanced weapons training. In spite of spending so much time together, they remained fresh to each other, and she was still the most interesting and appealing woman he had ever known.

"What's taking them so long?" she asked, glancing up at the now-lighted windows of Decodyne, bright but fuzzy rectangles in the mist.

"Be patient with them, dear," Bobby said. "They don't have the dynamism of Dakota and Dakota. They're just a humble SWAT team."

Michaelson Drive was blocked off. Eight police vehicles—cars and vans—were scattered along the street. The chilly night crackled with the static and metallic voices sputtering out of police-band radios. An officer was behind the wheel of one of the cars, and other uniformed men were positioned at both ends of the block, and two more were visible at the front doors of Decodyne; the rest were inside, looking for Rasmussen. Meanwhile, men from the police lab and coroner's office were photographing, measuring, and removing the bodies of the two gunmen.

"What if he gets away with the diskettes?" Julie asked.

"He won't."

She nodded. "Sure, I know what you're thinking—Whizard was developed on a closed-system computer with no links beyond Decodyne. But there's another system in the company, with modems and everything, isn't there? What if he takes the diskettes to one of *those* terminals and sends them out by phone?"

"Can't. The second-system, the outlinked system, is totally different from the one on which Whizard was developed. Incompatible."

"Rasmussen is clever."

"There's also a night lockout that keeps the outlinked system shut down."

"Rasmussen is clever," she repeated.

She continued to pace in front of him.

The skinned spot on her forehead, where she had met the steering wheel when she'd jammed on the brakes, was no longer bleeding, though it looked raw and wet. She had wiped her face with tissues, but smears of dried blood, which looked almost like bruises, had remained under her right eye and along her jawline. Each time Bobby focused on those stains or on the shallow wound, a pang of anxiety quivered through him at the realization of what might have happened to her, to both of them.

Not surprisingly, her injury and the blood on her face only accentuated her beauty, making her appear more fragile and therefore more precious. Julie *was* beautiful, although Bobby realized that she appeared more so to his eyes than to others, which was all right because, after all, his eyes were the only ones through which he could look at her. Though it was kinking up a bit now in the moist night air, her chestnut-brown hair was usually thick and lustrous. She had wide-set eyes as dark as semi-sweet chocolate, skin as smooth and naturally tan as toffee ice cream, and a generous mouth that always tasted sweet to him. Whenever he watched her without her being fully aware of the intensity of his attention, or when he was apart from her and tried to conjure an image of her in his mind, he always thought of her in terms of food: chestnuts, chocolate, toffee, cream, sugar, butter. He found this amusing, but he also understood the profundity of his choice of similes: She reminded him of food because she, *more* than food, sustained him.

Activity at the entrance to Decodyne, about sixty feet away, at the end of a palm-flanked walkway, drew Julie's attention and then Bobby's. Someone from the SWAT team had come to the doors to report to the guards stationed there. A moment later one of the officers motioned for Julie and Bobby to come forward.

When they joined him, he said, "They found this Rasmussen. You want to see him, make sure he has the right diskettes?"

"Yeah," Bobby said.

"Definitely," Julie said, and her throaty voice didn't sound at all sexy now, just tough.

9

KEEPING A LOOKOUT FOR ANY LAGUNA BEACH POLICE WHO MIGHT BE running graveyard-shift patrols, Frank Pollard removed the bundles of cash from the flight bag and piled them on the car seat beside him. He counted fifteen packets of twenty-dollar bills and eleven bundles of hundreds. He judged the thickness of each wad to be approximately one hundred bills, and when he did the mathematics in his head he came up with $140,000. He had no idea where the money had come from or whether it belonged to him.

The first of two small, zippered side compartments in the bag yielded another surprise—a wallet that contained no cash and no credit cards but two important pieces of identification: a Social Security card and a California driver's license. With the wallet was a United States passport. The photographs on the passport and license were of the same man: thirtyish, brown hair, a round face, prominent ears, brown eyes, an easy smile, and dimples. Realizing he had also forgotten what he looked like, he tilted the rearview mirror and was able to see enough of his face to match it with the one on the ID. The problem was . . . the license and passport bore the name James Roman, not Frank Pollard.

He unzipped the second of the two smaller compartments, and found another Social Security card, passport, and California driver's license. These were all in the name of George Farris, but the photos were of Frank.

James Roman meant nothing to him.

George Farris was also meaningless.

And Frank Pollard, whom he believed himself to be, was only a cipher, a man without any past that he could recall.

"What the hell am I tangled up in?" he said aloud. He needed to hear his own voice to convince himself that he was, in fact, not just a ghost reluctant to leave this world for the one to which death had entitled him.

As the fog closed around his parked car, blotting out most of the night beyond, a terrible loneliness overcame him. He could think of no one to whom he could turn, nowhere to which he could retreat and be assured of safety. A man without a past was also a man without a future.

10

WHEN BOBBY AND JULIE STEPPED OUT OF THE ELEVATOR ONTO the third floor, in the company of a police officer named McGrath, Julie saw Tom Rasmussen sitting on the polished gray vinyl tiles, his back against the wall of the corridor, his hands cuffed in front of him and linked by a length of chain to shackles that bound his ankles together. He was pouting. He had tried to steal software worth tens of millions of dollars, if not hundreds of millions, and from the window of Ackroyd's office he had cold-bloodedly given the signal to have Bobby killed, yet here he was pouting like a child because he had been caught. His weasel face was puckered, and his lower lip was thrust out, and his yellow-brown eyes looked watery, as though he might break into tears if anyone dared to say a cross word. The mere sight of him infuriated Julie. She wanted to kick his teeth down his throat, all the way into his stomach, so he could re-chew whatever he had last eaten.

The cops had found him in a supply closet, behind boxes that he had rearranged to make a pitifully obvious hiding place. Evidently, standing at Ackroyd's window to watch the fireworks, he had been surprised when Julie had appeared in the Toyota. She had driven the Toyota into the Decodyne parking lot early in the day and had stayed far back from the building, in the shadows beneath the boughs of the laurel, where no one had spotted her. Instead of fleeing the moment he saw the first gunman run down, Rasmussen had hesitated, no doubt wondering who *else* was out there. Then he heard the sirens, and his only option was to hide out in the hope they would only search the building casually and conclude that he had escaped. With a computer, he was a genius, but when it came to making cool decisions under fire, Rasmussen was not half as bright as he thought he was.

Two heavily armed cops were watching over him. But because he was huddled and shivering and on the verge of tears, they were a bit ludicrous in their bulletproof vests, cradling automatic weapons, squinting in the fluorescent glare, and looking grim.

Julie knew one of the officers, Sampson Garfeuss, from her own days with the sheriff's department, where Sampson also served before joining the City of Irvine force. Either his parents had been prescient or he had striven mightily to live up to his name, for he was both tall and broad and rocklike. He held a lidless box that contained four small floppy diskettes. He showed it to Julie and said, "Is this what he was after?"

"Could be," she said, accepting the box.

Taking the diskettes from her, Bobby said, "I'll have to go down one floor to Ackroyd's office, switch on the computer, pop these in, and see what's on them."

"Go ahead," Sampson said.

"You'll have to accompany me," Bobby said to McGrath, the officer who had brought them up on the elevator. "Keep a watch on me, make sure I don't tamper with these things." He indicated Tom Rasmussen. "We don't want this piece of slime claiming they were blank disks, saying I framed him by copying the real stuff onto them myself."

As Bobby and McGrath went into one of the elevators and descended to the second floor, Julie hunkered down in front of Rasmussen. "You know who I am?"

Rasmussen looked at her but said nothing.

"I'm Bobby Dakota's wife. Bobby was in that van your goons shot up. It was my Bobby you tried to kill."

He looked away from her, at his cuffed wrists.

She said, "Know what I'd like to do to you?" She held one of her hands down in front of his face, and wiggled her manicured nails. "For starters, I'd like to grab you by the throat, hold your head against the wall, and ram two of these nice, sharp fingernails straight through your eyes, all the way in, deep, real deep in your fevered little brain, and twist them around, see if maybe I can unscramble whatever's messed up in there."

"Jesus, lady," Sampson's partner said. His name was Burdock. Beside anyone but Sampson, he would have been a big man.

"Well," she said, "he's too screwed up to get any help from a prison psychiatrist."

Sampson said, "Don't do anything foolish, Julie."

Rasmussen glanced at her, meeting her eyes for only a second, but that was long enough for him to understand the depth of her anger and to be frightened by it. A flush of childish embarrassment and temper had accompanied his pout, but now his face went pale. To Sampson, in a voice that was too shrill and quaverous to be as tough as he intended, Rasmussen said, "Keep this crazy bitch away from me."

"She's not actually crazy," Sampson said. "Not clinically speaking, at least. Pretty hard to have anyone declared crazy these days, I'm afraid. Lots of concern about their civil rights, you know. No, I wouldn't say she's crazy."

Without looking away from Rasmussen, Julie said, "Thank you so much, Sam."

"You'll notice I didn't say anything about the other half of his accusation," Sampson said good-naturedly.

"Yeah, I got your point."

While she talked to Sampson, she kept her attention on Rasmussen.

Everyone harbored a special fear, a private boogeyman built to his own specifications and crouched in a dark corner of his mind, and Julie knew what Tom Rasmussen feared more than anything in the world. Not heights. Not confining spaces. Not crowds, cats, flying insects, dogs, or darkness. Dakota & Dakota had developed a thick file on him in recent weeks, and had turned up the fact that he suffered from a phobia of blindness. In prison, every month with the regularity of a true obsessive, he had demanded an eye exam, claiming his vision was deteriorating, and he'd petitioned to be tested periodically for syphilis, diabetes, and other diseases that, untreated, could result in blindness. When not in prison—and he had been there twice—he had a standing, monthly appointment with an ophthalmologist in Costa Mesa.

Still squatting in front of Rasmussen, Julie took hold of his chin. He flinched. She twisted his head toward her. She thrust two fingers of her other hand at him, raked them down his cheek, making red welts on his wan skin, but not hard enough to draw blood.

He squealed and tried to strike her with his cuffed hands, but he was inhibited by both his fear and the chain that tethered his wrists to his ankles. "What the hell you think you're doing?"

She spread the same two fingers with which she'd scratched him, and now she poked them at him, stopping just two inches short of his eyes. He winced, made a mewling sound, and tried to pull loose of her, but she held him fast by the chin, forcing a confrontation.

"Me and Bobby have been together eight years, married more than seven, and they've been the best years of my life, but you come along and think you can just squash him the way you'd squash a bug."

She slowly brought her fingertips closer to his eyes. An inch and a half. One inch.

Rasmussen tried to pull back. His head was against the wall. He had nowhere to go.

The sharp tips of her manicured fingernails were less than half an inch from his eyes.

"This is police brutality," Rasmussen said.

"I'm not a cop," Julie said.

"*They* are," he said, rolling his eyes at Sampson and Burdock. "Better get this bitch away from me, I'll sue your asses off."

With her fingernails she flicked his eyelashes.

His attention snapped back to her. He was breathing fast, and suddenly he was sweating too.

She flicked his lashes again, and smiled.

The dark pupils in his yellow-brown eyes were open wide.

"You bastards better hear me, I swear, I'll sue, they'll kick you off the force—"

She flicked his lashes again.

He closed his eyes tight. "—they'll take away your goddamned uniforms and badges, they'll throw *you* in prison, and you know what happens to ex-cops in prison, they get the shit kicked out of them, broken, killed, *raped!*" His voice spiraled up, cracked on the last word, like the voice of an adolescent boy.

Glancing at Sampson to be sure she had his tacit if not active approval to carry this just a little further, glancing also at Burdock and seeing that he was not as placid as Sampson but would probably stay out of it for a while yet, Julie pressed her fingernails against Rasmussen's eyelids.

He attempted to squeeze his eyes even more tightly shut.

She pressed harder. "You tried to take Bobby away from me, so I'll take your eyes away from you."

"You're *nuts!*"

She pressed still harder.

"Make her stop," Rasmussen demanded of the two cops.

"If you didn't want me to have my Bobby to look at, why should I let you look at anything ever again?"

"What do you want?" Perspiration poured down Rasmussen's face; he looked like a candle in a bonfire, melting fast.

"Who gave you permission to kill Bobby?"

"Permission? What do you mean? Nobody. I don't need—"

"You wouldn't have tried to touch him if your employer hadn't told you to do it."

"I knew he was on to me," Rasmussen said frantically, and because she had not let up the pressure with her nails, thin tears flowed from under his eyelids. "I knew he was out there, tumbled to him five or six days ago, even though he used different vans, trucks, even that orange van with the county seal on it. So I had to do something, didn't I? I couldn't walk away from the job, too much money at stake. I couldn't just let him nail me when I finally got Whizard, so I had to do something. Listen, Jesus, it was as simple as that."

"You're just a computer freak, a hired hacker—morally bent, sleazy, but you're no tough guy. You're soft, squishy-soft. You wouldn't plan a hit on your own. Your boss told you to do it."

"I don't have a boss. I'm freelance."

"Somebody still pays you."

She risked more pressure, not with the points of her nails but with the flat surfaces, although Rasmussen was so swept away by a rapture of fear that he might still imagine he could feel those filed edges gradually carving through the delicate shields of his eyelids. He must be seeing interior starfields now, bursts and whorls of color, and maybe he was feeling some pain. He was shaking; his shackles clinked and rattled. More tears squeezed from beneath his lids.

"Delafield." The word erupted from him, as if he had been trying simultaneously to hold it back and to expel it with all his might. "Kevin Delafield."

"Who's he?" Julie asked, still holding Rasmussen's chin with one hand, her fingernails against his eyes, unrelenting.

"Microcrest Corporation."

"That's who hired you for this?"

He was rigid, afraid to move a fraction of an inch, convinced that the slightest shift in his position would force her fingernails into his eyes. "Yeah. Delafield. A nutcase. A renegade. They don't understand about him at Microcrest. They just know he gets results for them. When this hits the fan they'll be surprised by it, blown away. So let go of me. What more do you want?"

She let go of him.

Immediately he opened his eyes, blinked, testing his vision, then broke down and sobbed with relief.

As Julie stood, the nearby elevator doors opened, and Bobby returned with the officer who had accompanied him downstairs to Ackroyd's office. Bobby looked at Rasmussen, cocked his head at Julie, clucked his tongue, and said, "You've been naughty, haven't you, dear? Can't I take you anywhere?"

"I just had a conversation with Mr. Rasmussen. That's all."

"He seems to have found it stimulating," Bobby said.

Rasmussen sat slumped forward with his hands over his eyes, weeping uncontrollably.

"We disagreed about something," Julie said.

"Movies, books?"

"Music."

"Ah."

Sampson Garfeuss said softly, "You're a wild woman, Julie."

"He tried to have Bobby killed," was all she said.

Sampson nodded. "I'm not saying I don't admire wildness sometimes . . . a little. But you sure as hell owe me one."

"I do," she agreed.

"You owe me more than one," Burdock said. "This guy's going to file a complaint. You can bet your ass on it."

"Complaint about what?" Julie asked. "He's not even marked."

Already the faint welts on Rasmussen's cheek were fading. Sweat, tears, and a case of the shakes were the only evidence of his ordeal.

"Listen," Julie told Burdock, "he cracked because I just happened to know exactly the right weak point where I could give him a little tap, like cutting a diamond. It worked because scum like him thinks everyone else is scum, too, thinks *we're* capable of doing what he'd do in the same situation. I'd never put out his eyes, but he might've put mine out if our roles were reversed, so he thought for sure I'd do him like he would've done me. All I did was use his own screwed-up attitudes against him. Psychology. Nobody can file a complaint about the application of a little psychology." She turned to Bobby and said, "What was on those diskettes?"

"Whizard. Not trash data. The whole thing. These have to be the files he duplicated. He only made one set while I was watching, and after the shooting started he didn't have time to make backup copies."

The elevator bell rang, and their floor number lit on the board. When the doors opened, a plainclothes detective they knew, Gil Dainer, stepped into the hallway.

Julie took the package of diskettes from Bobby, handed them to Dainer.

She said, "This is evidence. The whole case might rest on it. You think you can keep track of it?"

Dainer grinned. "Gosh, ma'am, I'll try."

11

FRANK POLLARD—ALIAS JAMES ROMAN, ALIAS GEORGE FARRIS— looked in the trunk of the stolen Chevy and found a small bundle of tools wrapped in a felt pouch and tucked in the wheel well. He used a screwdriver to take the plates off the car.

Half an hour later, after cruising some of the higher and even more quiet neighborhoods in fogbound Laguna, he parked on a dark side street and exchanged the Chevy's plates for those on an Oldsmobile. With luck, the owner of the Olds would not notice the new plates for a couple of days, maybe even a week or longer; until he reported the switch, the Chevy would not match anything on a police hot sheet and would, therefore, be relatively safe to drive. In any case, Frank intended to get rid of the car by tomorrow night and either boost a new one or use some of the cash in the flight bag to buy legal wheels.

Though he was exhausted, he didn't think it wise to check into a motel. Four-thirty in the morning was a damned odd hour for anyone to be wanting a room. Furthermore, he was unshaven, and his thick hair was matted and oily, and both his jeans and checkered blue flannel shirt were dirty and rumpled from his recent adventures. The last thing he wanted to do was call attention to himself, so he decided to catch a few hours of sleep in the car.

He drove farther south, into Laguna Niguel, where he parked on a quiet residential street, under the immense boughs of a date palm. He stretched out on the backseat, as comfortably as possible without benefit of sufficient legroom or pillows, and closed his eyes.

For the moment he was not afraid of his unknown pursuer, because he felt that the man was no longer nearby. Temporarily, at least, he had given his enemy the shake, and had no need to lie awake in fear of a hostile face suddenly appearing at the window. He was also able to put out of his mind all questions about his identity and the money in the flight bag; he was so tired—and his thought processes were so fuzzy—that any attempt to puzzle out solutions to those mysteries would be fruitless.

He was kept awake, however, by the memory of how *strange* the events in Anaheim had been, a few hours ago. The foreboding gusts of wind. The eerie flutelike music. Imploding windows, exploding tires, failed brakes, failed steering . . .

Who had come into that apartment behind the blue light? Was "who" the right word . . . or would it be more accurate to ask *what* had been searching for him?

During his urgent flight from Anaheim to Laguna, he'd not had the leisure to reflect upon those bizarre incidents, but now he could not turn his mind from them. He sensed that he had survived an encounter with something unnatural. Worse, he sensed that he knew what it was—and that his amnesia was self-induced by a deep desire to forget.

After a while, even the memory of those preternatural events wasn't enough to keep him awake. The last thing that crossed his waking mind, as he slipped off on a tide of sleep, was that four-word phrase that had come to him when he had first awakened in the deserted alleyway: *Fireflies in a windstorm. . . .*

12

BY THE TIME THEY HAD COOPERATED WITH THE POLICE AT THE scene, made arrangements for their disabled vehicles, and talked with the three corporate officers who showed up at Decodyne, Bobby and Julie did not get home until shortly before dawn. They were dropped at their door by a police cruiser, and Bobby was glad to see the place.

They lived on the east side of Orange, in a three-bedroom, sort-of-ersatz-Spanish tract house; which they had bought new two years ago, largely for its investment potential. Even at night the relative youth of the neighborhood was apparent in the landscaping: None of the shrubbery had reached full size; the trees were still too immature to loom higher than the rain gutters on the houses.

Bobby unlocked the door. Julie went in, and he followed. The sound of their footsteps on the parquet floor of the foyer, echoing hollowly off the bare walls of the adjacent and utterly empty living room, was proof that they were not committed to the house for the long term. To save money toward the fulfillment of The Dream, they had left the living room, dining room, and two bedrooms unfurnished. They installed cheap carpet and cheaper draperies. Not a penny had been spent on other improvements. This was merely a way station en route to The Dream, so they saw no point in lavishing funds on the decor.

The Dream. That was how they thought of it—with a capital *t* and a capital *d.* They kept their expenses as low as possible, in order to fund The Dream. They didn't spend much on clothes or vacations, and they didn't buy fancy cars. With hard work and iron determination, they were building Dakota & Dakota Investigations into a major firm that could be sold for a large capital gain, so they plowed a lot of earnings back into the business to make it grow. For The Dream.

At the back of the house, the kitchen and family room—and the small breakfast area that separated them—were furnished. This—and the master bedroom upstairs—was where they lived when at home.

The kitchen had a Spanish-tile floor, beige counters, and dark oak cabinets. No money had been spent on decorative accessories, but the room had a cozy feeling because some necessities of a functioning kitchen were on display: a net bag filled with half a dozen onions, copper pots dangling from a ceiling rack, cooking utensils, bottles of spices. Three green tomatoes were ripening on the windowsill.

Julie leaned against the counter, as if she could not stand another moment without support, and Bobby said, "You want a drink?"

"Booze at dawn?"

"I was thinking more of milk or juice."

"No, thanks."

"Hungry?"

She shook her head. "I just want to fall into bed. I'm beat."

He took her in his arms, held her close, cheek to cheek, with his face buried in her hair. Her arms tightened around him.

They stood that way for a while, saying nothing, letting the residual fear evaporate in the gentle heat they generated between them. Fear and love were indivisible. If you allowed yourself to care, to love, you made yourself vulnerable, and vulnerability led to fear. He found meaning in life through his relationship with her, and if she died, meaning and purpose would die too.

With Julie still in his arms, Bobby leaned back and studied her face. The smudges of dried blood had been wiped away. The skinned spot on her forehead was beginning to scab over with a thin yellow membrane. However, the imprint of their recent ordeal consisted of more than the abrasion on her forehead. With her tan complexion, she could never be said to look pale, even in moments of the most profound anxiety; a detectable grayness seeped into her face, however, at times like this, and at the moment her cinnamon-and-cream skin was underlaid with a shade of gray that made him think of headstone marble.

"It's over," he assured her, "and we're okay."

"It's not over in my dreams. Won't be for weeks."

"A thing like tonight adds to the legend of Dakota and Dakota."

"I don't want to be a legend. Legends are all dead."

"We'll be *living* legends, and that'll bring in business. The more business we build, the sooner we can sell out, grab The Dream." He kissed her gently on each corner of her mouth. "I have to call in, leave a long message on the agency machine, so Clint will know how to handle everything when he goes to work."

"Yeah. I don't want the phone to start ringing only a couple of hours after I hit the sheets."

He kissed her again and went to the wall phone beside the refrigerator. As he was dialing the office number, he heard Julie walk to the bathroom off the short hall that connected the kitchen to the laundryroom. She closed the bathroom door just as the answering machine picked up: *"Thank you for calling Dakota and Dakota. No one—"*

Clint Karaghiosis—whose Greek-American family had been fans of Clint Eastwood from the earliest days of his first television show, "Rawhide"—was Bobby and Julie's right-hand man at the office. He could be trusted to handle any problem. Bobby left a long message for him, summarizing the events at Decodyne and noting specific tasks that had to be done to wrap up the case.

When he hung up, he stepped down into the adjoining family room, switched on the CD player, and put on a Benny Goodman disc. The first notes of "King Porter Stomp" brought the dead room to life.

In the kitchen again, he got a quart can of eggnog from the refrigerator. They had bought it two weeks ago for their quiet, at-home, New Year's Eve celebration, but had not opened it, after all, on the holiday. He opened it now and half-filled two waterglasses.

From the bathroom he heard Julie make a tortured sound; she was finally throwing up. It was mostly just dry heaves because they had not eaten in eight or ten hours, but the spasms sounded violent. Throughout the night, Bobby had expected her to succumb to nausea, and he was surprised that she had retained control of herself this long.

He retrieved a bottle of white rum from the bar cabinet in the family room and spiked each serving of eggnog with a double shot. He was gently stirring the drinks with a spoon to blend in the rum, when Julie returned, looking even grayer than before.

When she saw what he was doing, she said, "I don't need that."

"I know what you need. I'm psychic. I knew you'd toss your cookies after what happened tonight. Now I know you need *this.*" He stepped to the sink and rinsed off the spoon.

"No, Bobby, really, I can't drink that." The Goodman music didn't seem to be energizing her.

"It'll settle your stomach. And if you don't drink it, you're not going to sleep." Taking her by the arm, crossing the breakfast area, and stepping down into the family room, he said, "You'll lie awake worrying about me, about Thomas"—Thomas was her brother—"about the world and everyone in it."

They sat on the sofa, and he did not turn on any lamps. The only light was what reached them from the kitchen.

She drew her legs under her and turned slightly to face him. Her eyes shone with a soft, reflected light. She sipped the eggnog.

The room was now filled with the strains of "One Sweet Letter From You," one of Goodman's most beautiful thematic statements, with a vocal by Louise Tobin.

They sat and listened for a while.

Then Julie said, "I'm tough, Bobby, I really am."

"I know you are."

"I don't want you thinking I'm lame."

"Never."

"It wasn't the shooting that made me sick, or using the Toyota to run that guy down, or even the thought of almost losing you—"

"I know. It was what you had to do to Rasmussen."

"He's a slimy little weasel-faced bastard, but even he doesn't deserve to be broken like that. What I did to him stank."

"It was the only way to crack the case, because it wasn't near cracked till we'd found out who hired him."

She drank more eggnog. She frowned down at the milky contents of her glass, as if the answer to some mystery could be found there.

Following Tobin's vocal, Ziggy Elman came in with a lusty trumpet solo, followed by Goodman's clarinet. The sweet sounds made that boxy, tract-house room seem like the most romantic place in the world.

"What I did . . . I did for The Dream. Giving Decodyne Rasmussen's employer will please them. But breaking him was somehow . . . worse than wasting a man in a fair gunfight."

Bobby put one hand on her knee. It was a nice knee. After all these years, he was still sometimes surprised by her slenderness and the delicacy of her bone structure, for he always thought of her as being strong for her size, solid, indomitable. "If you hadn't put Rasmussen in that vise and squeezed him, I would've done it."

"No, you wouldn't have. You're scrappy, Bobby, and you're smart and you're tough, but there're certain things you can never do. This was one of them. Don't jive me just to make me feel good."

"You're right," he said. "I couldn't have done it. But I'm glad you did. Decodyne's *very* big time, and this could've set us back years if we'd flubbed it."

"Is there anything we won't do for The Dream?"

Bobby said, "Sure. We wouldn't torture small children with red-hot knives, and we wouldn't shove innocent old ladies down long flights of stairs, and we wouldn't club a basketful of newborn puppies to death with an iron bar—at least not without good reason."

Her laughter lacked a full measure of humor.

"Listen," he said, "you're a good person. You've got a good heart, and nothing you did to Rasmussen blackens it at all."

"I hope you're right. It's a hard world sometimes."

"Another drink will soften it a little."

"You know the calories in these? I'll be fat as a hippo."

"Hippos are cute," he said, taking her glass and heading back toward the kitchen to pour another drink. "I love hippos."

"You won't want to *make* love to one."

"Sure. More to hold, more to love."

"You'll be crushed."

"Well, of course, I'll always insist on taking the top."

13

CANDY WAS GOING TO KILL. HE STOOD IN THE DARK LIVING ROOM of a stranger's house, shaking with need. Blood. He needed blood.

Candy was going to kill, and there was nothing he could do to stop himself. Not even thinking of his mother could shame him into controlling his hunger.

His given name was James, but his mother—an unselfish soul, exceedingly kind, brimming with love, a saint—always said he was her little candy boy. Never James. Never Jim or Jimmy. She'd said he was sweeter than anything on earth, and "little candy boy" eventually had become "candy boy," and by the time he was six the sobriquet had been shortened and capitalized, and he had become Candy for good. Now, at twenty-nine, that was the only name to which he would answer.

Many people thought murder was a sin. He knew otherwise. Some were born with a taste for blood. God had made them what they were and expected them to kill chosen victims. It was all part of His mysterious plan.

The only sin was to kill when God and your mother did not approve of the victim, which was exactly what he was about to do. He was ashamed. But he was also in need.

He listened to the house. Silence.

Like unearthly and dusky beasts, the shadowy forms of the living-room furniture huddled around him.

Breathing hard, trembling, Candy moved into the dining room, kitchen, family room, then slowly along the hallway that led to the front of the house. He made no sound that would have alerted anyone asleep upstairs. He seemed to glide rather than walk, as if he were a specter instead of a real man.

He paused at the foot of the stairs and made one last feeble attempt to overcome his murderous compulsion. Failing, he shuddered and let out his pent-up breath. He began to climb toward the second floor, where the family was probably sleeping.

His mother would understand and forgive him.

She had taught him that killing was good and moral—but only when necessary, only when it benefited the family. She had been terribly angry with him on those occasions when he had killed out of sheer compulsion, with no good reason. She'd had no need to punish him physically for his errant ways, because her displeasure gave him more agony than any punishment she could have devised. For days at a time she refused to speak to him, and that silent treatment caused his chest to swell with pain, so it seemed as if his heart would spasm and cease to beat. She looked straight through him, too, as if he no longer existed. When the other children spoke of him, she said, "Oh, you mean your late brother, Candy, your poor dead brother. Well, remember him if you want, but only among yourselves, not to me, never to me, because I don't want to remember him, not that bad seed. He was no good, that one, no good at all, wouldn't listen to his mother, not him, always thought he knew better. Just the sound of his name makes me sick, *revolts* me, so don't mention him in my hearing." Each time that Candy had been temporarily banished to the land of the dead for having misbehaved, no place was set for him at the table, and he had to stand in a corner, watching the others eat, as if he was a visiting spirit. She would not favor him with either a frown or a smile, and she would not stroke his hair or touch his face with her warm soft hands, and she would not let him cuddle against her or put his weary head upon her breast, and at night he had to find his way into a troubled sleep without being guided there by either her bedtime stories or sweet lullabies. In that total banishment he learned more of Hell than he ever hoped to know.

But she would understand why Candy could not control himself tonight, and she'd forgive him. Sooner or later she always forgave him because her love for him was like the love of God for all His children: perfect, rich with forbearance and mercy. When she deemed that Candy had suffered enough, she always had looked *at* him again, smiled for him, opened her arms wide. In her new acceptance of him, he had experienced as much of Heaven as he needed to know.

She was in Heaven now, herself. Seven long years! God, how he missed her. But she was watching him even now. She would know he had lost control tonight, and she would be disappointed in him.

He climbed the stairs, rushing up two risers at a time, staying close to the wall, where the steps were less likely to squeak. He was a big man but graceful and light on his feet, and if some of the stair treads were loose or tired with age, they did not creak under him.

In the upstairs hall he paused, listening. Nothing.

A dim night-light was part of the overhead smoke alarm. The glow was just bright enough for Candy to see two doors on the right of the hall, two on the left, and one at the far end.

He crept to the first door on the right, eased it open, and slipped into the room beyond. He closed the door again and stood with his back to it.

Although his need was great, he forced himself to wait for his eyes to adjust to the gloom. Ashen light, from a streetlamp at least half a block away, glimmered faintly at the two windows. He noticed the mirror, first, a frosty rectangle in which the meager radiance was murkily reflected; then he began to make out the shape of the dresser beneath it. A moment later he was also able to see the bed and, dimly, the huddled form of someone lying under a light-colored blanket that was vaguely phosphorescent.

Candy stepped cautiously to the bed, took hold of the blanket and sheets and hesitated, listening to the soft rhythmic breathing of the sleeper. He detected a trace of perfume mingled with a pleasant scent of warm skin and recently shampooed hair. A girl. He could always tell girl-smell from boy-smell. He also sensed that this one was young, perhaps a teenager. If his need had not been so intense, he would have hesitated much longer than he did, for the moments preceding a kill were exciting, almost better than the act itself.

With a dramatic flick of his arm, as if he were a magician throwing back the cloth that had covered an empty cage to reveal a captive dove of sorcerous origins, he uncovered the sleeper. He fell upon her, crushing her into the mattress with his body.

She woke instantly and tried to scream, even though he had surely knocked the wind out of her. Fortunately, he had unusually large and powerful hands, and he had found her face even as she began to raise her voice, so he was able to thrust his palm under her chin and hook his fingers in her cheeks and clamp her mouth shut.

"Be quiet, or I'll kill you," he whispered, his lips brushing against her delicate ear.

Making a muffled, panicky sound, she squirmed under him, though to no avail. Judging by the feel of her, she was a girl, not a woman, perhaps no younger than twelve, certainly no older than fifteen. She was no match for him.

"I don't want to hurt you. I just *want* you, and when I'm done with you, I'll leave."

That was a lie, for he had no desire to rape her. Sex was of no interest to him. Indeed, sex disgusted him; involving unmentionable fluids, depending upon the shameless use of the same organs associated with urination, sex was an unspeakably repulsive act. Other people's fascination with it only proved to Candy that men and women were members of a fallen species and that the world was a cesspool of sin and madness.

Either because she believed his pledge not to kill her or because she was now half-paralyzed with fear, she stopped resisting. Maybe she just needed all of her energy to breathe. Candy's full weight—two hundred and twenty pounds—was pressing on her chest, restricting her lungs.

Against his hand, with which he clamped her mouth shut, he could feel her cool inhalations as her nostrils flared, followed by short, hot exhalations.

His vision had continued to adapt to the poor light. Although he still could not make out the details of her face, he could see her eyes shining darkly in the gloom, glistening with terror. He could also see that she was a blonde; her pale hair caught even the dull gray glow from the windows and shone with burnished-silver highlights.

With his free hand, he gently pushed her hair back from the right side of her neck. He shifted his position slightly, moving down on her in order to bring his lips to her throat. He kissed the tender flesh, felt the strong throb of her pulse against his lips, then bit deep and found the blood.

She bucked and thrashed beneath him, but he held her down and held her fast, and she could not dislodge his greedy mouth from the wound he had made. He swallowed rapidly but could not consume the thick, sweet fluid as fast as it was offered. Soon, however, the flow diminished. The girl's convulsions became less violent, as well, then faded altogether, until she was as still beneath him as if she had been nothing more than a tangled mound of bedclothes.

He rose from her and switched on the bedside lamp just long enough to see her face. He always wanted to see their faces, after their sacrifices if not before. He also liked to look into their eyes, which seemed not sightless but gifted with a vision of the far place to which their souls had gone. He did not entirely understand his curiosity. After all, when he ate a steak, he did not wonder what the cow had looked like. This girl—and each of the others on whom he'd fed—should have been nothing more than one of the cattle to him. Once, in a dream, when he had finished drinking from a ravaged throat, his victim, although dead, had spoken to him, asking him why he wanted to look upon her in death. When he had said that he didn't know the answer to her question, she had suggested that perhaps, on those occasions when he had killed in the dark, he later needed to see his victims' faces because, in some unlit corner of his heart, he half expected to find his own face looking up at him, ice-white and dead-eyed. "Deep down," the dream-victim had said, "you know that you're already dead yourself, burnt out inside. You realize that you have far more in common with your victims after you've killed them than before." Those words, though spoken only in a dream, and though amounting to the purest nonsense, had nevertheless brought him awake with a sharp cry. He was alive, not dead, powerful and vital, a man with appetites as strong as they were unusual. The dream-victim's words stayed with him over the years, and when they echoed through his memory at times like this, they made him anxious. Now, as always, he refused to dwell on them. He turned his attention, instead, to the girl on the bed.

She appeared to be about fourteen, quite pretty. Captivated by her flawless complexion, he wondered if her skin would feel as perfect as it looked, as smooth as porcelain, if he dared to stroke it with his fingertips. Her lips were slightly parted, as if they had been gently prised open by her spirit as it departed her. Her wonderfully blue, clear eyes seemed enormous, too big for her face—and as wide as a winter sky.

He would have liked to gaze upon her for hours.

Letting a sigh of regret escape him, he switched off the lamp.

He stood for a while in the darkness, enveloped by the pungent aroma of blood.

When his eyes had readjusted to the gloom, he returned to the hall, not bothering to close the girl's door behind him. He entered the room across from hers and found it untenanted.

But in the room next to that one, Candy smelled a trace of stale sweat, and heard snoring. This one was a boy, seventeen or eighteen, not a big kid but not small either, and he put up more of a struggle than his sister. However, he was sleeping on his stomach, and when Candy threw back the covers and fell upon him, the boy's face was jammed hard into the pillow and mattress, smothering him and making it difficult for him to shout a warning. The fight was violent but brief. The boy passed out from lack of oxygen, and Candy flopped him over. When he went for the exposed throat, Candy let out a low and eager cry that was louder than any sound the boy had made.

Later, when he opened the door to the fourth bedroom, the first pewter light of dawn had pierced the windows. Shadows still huddled in the corners, but the deeper darkness had been chased off. The early light was too thin to elicit color from objects, and everything in the room seemed to be one shade of gray or another.

An attractive blonde in her late thirties was asleep on one side of a king-size bed. The sheets and blanket on the other half of the bed were hardly disturbed, so he figured the woman's husband had either moved out or was away on business. He noted a half-full glass of water and a plastic bottle of prescription drugs on the nightstand. He picked up the pharmacy bottle and saw that it was two-thirds full of small pills: a sedative, according to the label. From the label, he also learned her name: Roseanne Lofton.

Candy stood for a while, staring down at her face, and an old longing for maternal solace stirred in him. Need continued to drive him, but he did not want to take her violently, did not want to rip her open and drain her in a few minutes. He wanted this one to last.

He had the urge to suckle on this woman as he had suckled on his mother's blood when she would permit him that grace. Occasionally, when he was in her favor, his mother would make a shallow cut in the palm of her hand or puncture one of her fingers, then allow him to curl up against her and be nursed on her blood for an hour or longer. During that time a great peace stole over him, a bliss so profound that the world and all its pain ceased to be real to him, because his mother's blood was like no other, untainted, pure as the tears of a saint. Through such small wounds, of course, he was able to drink no more than an ounce or two of her, but that meager dribble was more precious and more nourishing to him than the gallons he might have drained from a score of other people. The woman before him would not have such ambrosia within her veins, but if he closed his eyes while he suckled on her, and if he let his mind reel backward to memories of the days before his mother's death, he might recapture at least some of the exquisite serenity he had known then . . . and experience a faint echo of that old thrill.

At last, without casting the covers aside, Candy gently lowered himself to the bed and stretched out beside the woman, watching as her heavy-lidded eyes fluttered and then opened. She blinked at him as he cuddled next to her, and for a moment she seemed to think that she was still dreaming, for no expression tightened the muscles of her slack face.

"All I want is your blood," he said softly.

Abruptly she cast off the lingering effects of the sedative, and her eyes filled with alarm.

Before she could spoil the beauty of the moment by screaming or resisting, thereby shattering the illusion that she was his mother and was giving voluntarily of herself, he struck the side of her neck with his heavy fist. Then he struck her again. Then he hammered the side of her face twice. She slumped unconscious against the pillow.

He squirmed under the covers to be close against her, withdrew her hand, and nipped her palm with his teeth. He put his head on the pillow, lying face to face with her, holding her hand between them, drinking the slow trickle from her palm. He closed his eyes after a while and tried to imagine that she was his mother, and eventually a gratifying peace stole over him. However, though he was happier at that moment than he had been in a long time, it was not a deep happiness, merely a veneer of joy that brightened the surface of his heart but left the inner chambers dark and cold.

14

AFTER ONLY A FEW HOURS OF SLEEP, FRANK POLLARD WOKE IN THE backseat of the stolen Chevy. The morning sun, streaming through the windows, was bright enough to make him wince.

He was stiff, achy, and unrested. His throat was dry, and his eyes burned as if he had not slept for days.

Groaning, Frank swung his legs off the seat, sat up, and cleared his throat. He realized that both of his hands were numb; they felt cold and dead, and he saw that he had curled them into fists. He had evidently been sleeping that way for some time, because at first he could not unclench. With considerable effort, he opened his right fist—and a handful of something black and grainy poured through his tingling fingers.

He stared, perplexed, at the fine grains that had spilled down the leg of his jeans and onto his right shoe. He raised his hand to take a closer look at the residue that had stuck to his palm. It looked and smelled like sand.

Black sand? Where had he gotten it?

When he opened his left hand, more sand spilled out.

Confused, he looked through the car windows at the residential neighborhood around him. He saw green lawns, dark topsoil showing through where the grass was sparse, mulch-filled planting beds, redwood chips mounded around some shrubs, but nothing like what he had held in his tightly clenched fists.

He was in Laguna Niguel, so the Pacific Ocean was nearby, rimmed by broad beaches. But those beaches were white, not black.

As full circulation returned to his cramped fingers, he leaned back in the seat, raised his hands in front of his face, and stared at the black grains that speckled his sweat-damp skin. Sand, even black sand, was a humble and innocent substance, but the residue on his hands troubled him as deeply as if it had been fresh blood.

"Who the hell am I, what's happening to me?" he wondered aloud.

He knew that he needed help. But he didn't know to whom he could turn.

15

BOBBY WAS AWAKENED BY A SANTA ANA WIND SOUGHING IN THE trees outside. It whistled under the eaves, and forced a chorus of ticks and creaks from the cedar-shingle roof and the attic rafters.

He blinked sleep-matted eyes and squinted at the numbers on the bedroom ceiling: 12:07. Because they sometimes worked odd hours and slept during the day, they had installed exterior Rolladen security shutters, leaving the room coal-mine dark except for the projection clock's pale green numerals, which floated on the ceiling like some portentous spirit message from Beyond.

Because he had gone to bed near dawn, and instantly to sleep, he knew the numbers on the ceiling meant that it was shortly past noon, not midnight. He had slept perhaps six hours. He lay unmoving for a moment, wondering if Julie was awake.

She said, "I am."

"You're spooky," he said. "You knew what I was thinking."

"That's not spooky," she said. "That's married."

He reached for her, and she came into his arms.

For a while they just held each other, satisfied to be close. But by mutual and unspoken desire, they began to make love.

The projection clock's glowing green numerals were too pale to relieve the absolute darkness, so Bobby could see nothing of Julie as they clung together. However, he "saw" her through his hands. As he reveled in the smoothness and warmth of her skin, the elegant curves of her breasts, the discovery of angularity precisely where angularity was desirable, the tautness of muscle, and the fluid movement of muscle and bone, he might have been a blind man using his hands to describe an inner vision of ideal beauty.

The wind shook the world outside, in sympathy with the climaxes that shook Julie. And when Bobby could withhold himself no longer, when he cried out and emptied himself into her, the skirling wind cried, too, and a bird that had taken shelter in a nearby eave was blown from its perch with a rustle of wings and a spiraling shriek.

For a while they lay side by side in the blackness, their breath mingling, touching each other almost reverently. They did not want or need to speak; talk would have diminished the moment.

The aluminum-slat shutters vibrated softly in the huffing wind.

Gradually the afterglow of lovemaking gave way to a curious uneasiness, the source of which Bobby could not identify. The enveloping blackness began to seem oppressive, as if a continued absence of light was somehow contributing to a thickening of the air, until it would become as viscid and unbreathable as syrup.

Though he had just made love to her, he was stricken by the crazy notion that Julie was not actually there with him, that what he had coupled with was a dream, or the congealing darkness itself, and that she had been stolen from him in the night, whisked away by some power he could not fathom, and that she was forever beyond his reach.

His childish fear made him feel foolish, but he rose onto one elbow and turned on one of the wall-mounted bedside lamps.

When he saw Julie lying beside him, smiling, her head raised on a pillow, the level of his inexplicable anxiety abruptly dropped. He let out a rush of breath, surprised to discover that he'd pent it up in the first place. But a peculiar tension remained in him, and the sight of Julie, safe and undamaged but for the scabbing spot on her forehead, was insufficient to completely relax him.

"What's wrong?" she asked, as perceptive as ever.

"Nothing," he lied.

"Bit of a headache from all that rum in the eggnog?"

What troubled him was not a hangover, but the queer, unshakable feeling that he was going to lose Julie, that something out there in a hostile world was coming to take her away. As the optimist in the family, he wasn't usually given to grim forebodings of doom; accordingly, this strange augural chill frightened him more than it would have if he had been regularly subject to such disturbances.

"Bobby?" she said, frowning.

"Headache," he assured her.

He leaned down and gently kissed her eyes, then again, forcing her to close them so she could not see his face and read the anxiety that he was unable to conceal.

LATER, AFTER SHOWERING and dressing, they ate a hasty breakfast while standing at the kitchen counter: English muffins and raspberry jam, half a banana each, and black coffee. By mutual agreement, they were not going to the office. A brief call to Clint Karaghiosis confirmed that the wrap-up on the Decodyne case was nearly completed, and that no other business needed their urgent personal attention.

Their Suzuki Samurai waited in the garage, and Bobby's spirits rose at the sight of it. The Samurai was a small sports truck with four-wheel drive. He had justified its purchase by pitching its dual nature—utilitarian and recreational—to Julie, especially noting its comparatively reasonable price tag, but in fact he had wanted it because it was fun to drive. She had not been deceived, and she had gone for it because she, too, thought it was fun to drive. This time, she was willing to let him have the wheel when he suggested she drive.

"I did enough driving last night," she said as she buckled herself into her shoulder harness.

Dead leaves, twigs, a few scraps of paper, and less identifiable detritus whirled and tumbled along the windswept streets. Dust devils spun out of the east, as the Santa Anas—named for the mountains out of which they arose—poured down through the canyons and across the arid, scrub-stubbled hills that Orange County's industrious developers had not yet graded and covered with thousands of nearly identical wood-and-stucco pieces of the California dream. Trees bent to the surging oceans of air that moved in powerful and erratic tides toward the real sea in the west. The previous night's fog was gone, and the day was so clear that, from the hills, Catalina Island could be seen twenty-six miles off the Pacific's distant coast.

Julie popped an Artie Shaw CD into the player, and the smooth melody and softly bouncing rhythms of "Begin the Beguine" filled the car. The mellow saxophones of Les Robinson, Hank Freeman, Tony Pastor, and

Ronnie Perry provided strange counterpoint to the chaos and dissonance of the Santa Ana winds.

From Orange, Bobby drove south and west toward the beach cities—Newport, Corona del Mar, Laguna, Dana Point. He traveled as much as possible on those few of the urbanized county's blacktop byways that could still be called back roads. They even passed a couple of orange groves, with which the county had once been carpeted, but which had mostly fallen to the relentless advance of the tracts and malls.

Julie became more talkative and bubbly as the miles rolled up on the odometer, but Bobby knew that her spritely mood was not genuine. Each time they set out to visit her brother Thomas, she worked hard to inflate her spirits. Although she loved Thomas, every time that she was with him, her heart broke anew, so she had to fortify herself in advance with manufactured good humor.

"Not a cloud in the sky," she said, as they passed the old Irvine Ranch fruit-packing plant. "Isn't it a beautiful day, Bobby?"

"A wonderful day," he agreed.

"The wind must've pushed the clouds all the way to Japan, piled them up miles high over Tokyo."

"Yeah. Right now California litter is falling on the Ginza."

Hundreds of red bougainvillea blossoms, stripped from their vines by the wind, blew across the road, and for a moment the Samurai seemed to be caught in a crimson snowstorm. Maybe it was because they had just spoken of Japan, but there was something oriental about the whirl of petals. He would not have been surprised to glimpse a kimono-clad woman at the side of the road, dappled in sunshine and shadow.

"Even a windstorm is beautiful here," Julie said. "Aren't we lucky, Bobby? Aren't we lucky to be living in this special place?"

Shaw's "Frenesi" struck up, string-rich swing. Every time he heard the song, Bobby was almost able to imagine that he was in a movie from the 1930s or '40s, that he would turn a corner and encounter his old friend Jimmy Stewart or maybe Bing Crosby, and they'd go off to have lunch with Cary Grant and Jean Arthur and Katharine Hepburn, and screwball things would happen.

"What movie are you in?" Julie asked. She knew him too well.

"Haven't figured it yet. Maybe *The Philadelphia Story*."

By the time they pulled into the parking lot of Cielo Vista Care Home,

Julie had whipped herself into a state of high good humor. She got out of the Samurai, faced west, and grinned at the horizon, which was delineated by the marriage of sea and sky, as if she had never before encountered a sight to match it. In truth it was a stunning panorama, because Cielo Vista stood on a bluff half a mile from the Pacific, overlooking a long stretch of southern California's Gold Coast. Bobby admired it, too, shoulders hunched slightly and head tucked down in deference to the cool and blustery wind.

When Julie was ready, she took Bobby's hand and squeezed it hard, and they went inside.

Cielo Vista Care Home was a private facility, operated without government funds, and its architecture eschewed all of the standard institutional looks. Its two-story Spanish façade of pale peach stucco was accented by white marble cornerpieces, doorframes, and window lintels; white-painted French windows and doors were recessed in graceful arches, with deep sills. The sidewalks were shaded by lattice arbors draped with a mix of purple-and-yellow-blooming bougainvillea, from which the wind drew a chorus of urgent whispers. Inside, the floors were gray vinyl tile, speckled with peach and turquoise, and the walls were peach with white base and crown molding, which lent the place a warm and airy ambience.

They paused in the foyer, just inside the front door, while Julie withdrew a comb from her purse and pulled the wind tangles from her hair. After stopping at the front desk in the cozy visitors' lobby, they followed the north hall to Thomas's first-floor room.

His was the second of the two beds, nearest the windows, but he was neither there nor in his armchair. When they stopped in his open doorway, he was sitting at the worktable that belonged to both him and his roommate, Derek. Bent over the table, using a pair of scissors to clip a photograph from a magazine, Thomas appeared curiously both hulking and fragile, thickset yet delicate; physically, he was solid but mentally and emotionally he was frail, and that inner weakness shone through to belie the outer image of strength. With his thick neck, heavy rounded shoulders, broad back, proportionally short arms, and stocky legs, Thomas had a gnomish look, but when he became aware of them and turned his head to see who was there, his face was not graced by the cute and beguiling features of a fairy-tale creature; it was instead a face of cruel genetic destiny and biological tragedy.

"Jules!" he said, dropping the scissors and magazine, nearly knocking over his chair in his haste to get up. He was wearing baggy jeans and a green-plaid flannel shirt. He seemed ten years younger than his true age. "Jules, Jules!"

Julie let go of Bobby's hand and stepped into the room, opening her arms to her brother. "Hi, honey."

Thomas hurried to her in that shuffling walk of his, as if his shoes were heeled and soled with enough iron to preclude his lifting them. Although he was twenty years old, ten years younger than Julie, he was four inches shorter than she, barely five feet. He had been born with Down's syndrome, a diagnosis that even a layman could read in his face: his brow was sloped and heavy; inner epicanthic folds gave his eyes an Asian cast; the bridge of his nose was flat; his ears were low-set on a head that was slightly too small to be in proportion to his body; the rest of his features had those soft, heavy contours often associated with mental retardation. Though it was a countenance shaped more for expressions of sadness and loneliness, it now defied its naturally downcast lines and formed itself into a wondrous smile, a warm grin of pure delight.

Julie always had that effect on Thomas.

Hell, she has that effect on *me*, Bobby thought.

Stooping only slightly, Julie threw her arms around her brother when he came to her, and for a while they hugged each other.

"How're you doing?" she asked.

"Good," Thomas said. "I'm good." His speech was thick but not at all difficult to understand, for his tongue was not as deformed as those of some victims of DS; it was a little larger than it should have been but not fissured or protruding. "I'm real good."

"Where's Derek?"

"Visiting. Down the hall. He'll be back. I'm real good. Are you good?"

"I'm fine, honey. Just great."

"I'm just great too. I love you, Jules," Thomas said happily, for with Julie he was always free of the shyness that colored his relations with everyone else. "I love you so much."

"I love you, too, Thomas."

"I was afraid . . . maybe you wouldn't come."

"Don't I always come?"

"Always," he said. At last he relaxed his grip on his sister and peeked around her. "Hi, Bobby."

"Hi, Thomas. You're lookin' good."

"Am I?"

"If I'm lyin', I'm dyin'."

Thomas laughed. To Julie, he said, "He's funny."

"Do I get a hug too?" Bobby asked. "Or do I have to stand here with my arms out until someone mistakes me for a hat-rack?"

Hesitantly, Thomas let go of his sister. He and Bobby embraced. After all these years, Thomas was still not entirely comfortable with Bobby, not because they had bad chemistry between them or any bad feelings, but because Thomas didn't like change very much and adapted to it slowly. Even after more than seven years, his sister being married was a change, something that still felt new to him.

But he likes me, Bobby thought, maybe even as much as I like him.

Liking DS victims was not difficult, once you got past the pity that initially distanced you from them, because most of them had an innocence and guilelessness that was charming and refreshing. Except when inhibited by shyness or embarrassment about their differences, they were usually forthright, more truthful than other people, and incapable of the petty social games and scheming that marred so many relationships among "ordinary" people. The previous summer, at Cielo Vista's Fourth of July picnic, a mother of one of the other patients had said to Bobby, "Sometimes, watching them, I think there's something in them—a gentleness, a special kindness—that's closer to God than anything in us." Bobby felt the truth of that observation now, as he hugged Thomas and looked down into his sweet, lumpish face.

"Did we interrupt a poem?" Julie asked.

Thomas let go of Bobby and hurried to the worktable, where Julie was looking at the magazine from which he had been clipping a picture when they'd arrived. He opened his current scrapbook—fourteen others were filled with his creations and shelved in a corner bookcase near his bed—and pointed to a two-page spread of pasted-in clippings that were arranged in lines and quatrains, like poetry.

"This was yesterday. Finished yesterday," Thomas said. "Took me a looooong time, and it was hard, but now it was . . . *is* . . . right."

Four or five years ago, Thomas had decided that he wanted to be a poet like someone he had seen and admired on television. The degree of mental retardation among victims of Down's syndrome varied widely, from mild to severe; Thomas was somewhere just above the middle of the spectrum, but he did not possess the intellectual capacity to learn to write more than his name. That didn't stop him. He had asked for paper, glue, a scrapbook, and piles of old magazines. Since he rarely asked for anything, and since Julie would have moved a mountain on her back to get him whatever he wanted, the items on his list were soon in his possession. "All kinds of magazines," he'd said, "with different pretty pictures . . . but ugly too . . . all kinds." From *Time, Newsweek, Life, Hot Rod, Omni, Seventeen,* and dozens of other publications, he snipped whole pictures and parts of pictures, arranging them as if they were words, in a series of images that made a statement that was important to him. Some of his "poems" were only five images long, and some involved hundreds of clippings arranged in orderly stanzas or, more often, in loosely structured lines that resembled free verse.

Julie took the scrapbook from him and went to the armchair by the window, where she could concentrate on his newest composition. Thomas remained at the worktable, watching her anxiously.

His picture poems did not tell stories or have recognizable thematic narratives, but neither were they merely random jumbles of images. A church spire, a mouse, a beautiful woman in an emerald-green ball gown, a field of daisies, a can of Dole pineapple rings, a crescent moon, pancakes in a stack with syrup drizzling down, rubies gleaming on a black-velvet display cloth, a fish with mouth agape, a child laughing, a nun praying, a woman crying over the blasted body of a loved one in some Godforsaken war zone, a pack of Life Savers, a puppy with floppy ears, black-clad nuns with starched white wimples—from those and thousands of other pictures in his treasured boxes of clippings, Thomas selected the elements of his compositions. From the beginning Bobby recognized an uncanny *rightness* to many of the poems, a symmetry too fundamental to be defined, juxtapositions that were both naive and profound, rhythms as real as they were elusive, a personal vision plain to see but too mysterious to comprehend to any significant degree. Over the years, Bobby had seen the poems become better, more satisfying, though he understood them so little that he could not explain how he could discern the improvement; he just knew that it was there.

Julie looked up from the two-page spread in the scrapbook and said, "This is wonderful, Thomas. It makes me want to . . . run outside in the grass . . . and stand under the sky and maybe even dance, just throw my head back and laugh. It makes me glad to be alive."

"Yes!" Thomas said, slurring the word, clapping his hands.

She passed the book to Bobby, and he sat on the edge of the bed to read it.

The most intriguing thing about Thomas's poems was the emotional response they invariably evoked. None left a reader untouched, as an array of randomly assembled images might have done. Sometimes, when looking at Thomas's work, Bobby laughed out loud, and sometimes he was so moved that he had to blink back tears, and sometimes he felt fear or sadness or regret or wonder. He did not know why he responded to any particular piece as he did; the effect always defied analysis. Thomas's compositions functioned on some primal level, eliciting reaction from a region of the mind far deeper than the subconscious.

The latest poem was no exception. Bobby felt what Julie had felt: that life was good; that the world was beautiful; elation in the very fact of existence.

He looked up from the scrapbook and saw that Thomas was awaiting his reaction as eagerly as he had awaited Julie's, perhaps a sign that Bobby's opinion was cherished as much as hers, even if he still didn't rate as long or as ardent a hug as Julie did. "Wow," he said softly. "Thomas, this one gives me such a warm, tingly feeling that . . . I think my toes are curling."

Thomas grinned.

Sometimes Bobby looked at his brother-in-law and felt that two Thomases shared that sadly deformed skull. Thomas number one was the moron, sweet but feebleminded. Thomas number two was just as smart as anyone, but he occupied only a small part of the damaged brain that he shared with Thomas number one, a chamber in the center, from which he had no direct communication with the outside world. All of Thomas number two's thoughts had to be filtered through Thomas number one's part of the brain, so they ended up sounding no different from Thomas number one's thoughts; therefore the world could not know that number two was in there, thinking and feeling and fully *alive*—except through the evidence of the picture poems, the essence of which survived even after being filtered through Thomas number one.

"You've got such a talent," Bobby said, and he meant it—almost envied it.

Thomas blushed and lowered his eyes. He rose and quickly shuffled to the softly humming refrigerator that stood beside the door to the bathroom. Meals were served in the communal dining room, where snacks and drinks were provided on request, but patients with sufficient mental capacity to keep their rooms neat were allowed to have their own refrigerators stocked with their favorite snacks and drinks, to encourage as much independence as possible. He withdrew three cans of Coke. He gave one to Bobby, one to Julie. With the third he returned to the chair at the worktable, sat down, and said, "You been catchin' bad guys?"

"Yeah, we're keeping the jails full," Bobby said.

"Tell me."

Julie leaned forward in the armchair, and Thomas scooted his straight-backed chair closer to her, until their knees touched, and she recounted the highlights of the events at Decodyne last night. She made Bobby more heroic than he'd really been, and she played down her own involvement a little, not only out of modesty but in order not to frighten Thomas with too clear a picture of the danger in which she had put herself. Thomas was tough in his own way; if he hadn't been, he would have curled up on his bed long ago, facing into the corner, and never gotten up again. But he was not tough enough to endure the loss of Julie. He would be devastated even to imagine that she was vulnerable. So she made her daredevil driving and the shoot-out sound funny, exciting but not really dangerous. Her revised version of events entertained Bobby nearly as much as it did Thomas.

After a while, as usual, Thomas became overwhelmed by what Julie was telling him, and the tale grew more confusing than entertaining. "I'm full up," he said, which meant he was still trying to process everything he had been told, and didn't have room for any more just now. He was fascinated by the world outside Cielo Vista, and he often longed to be a part of it, but at the same time he found it too loud and bright and colorful to be handled in more than small doses.

Bobby got one of the older scrapbooks from the shelves and sat on the bed, reading picture poems.

Thomas and Julie sat in their chairs, Cokes put aside, knees to knees, leaning forward and holding hands, sometimes looking at each other, sometimes not, just being together, close. Julie needed that as much as Thomas did.

Julie's mother had been killed when Julie was twelve. Her father had died eight years later, two years before Bobby and Julie had been married. She'd been only twenty at the time, working as a waitress to put herself through college and to pay her half of the rent on a studio apartment she shared with another student. Her parents had never been rich, and though they had kept Thomas at home, the expense of looking after him had depleted what little savings they'd ever had. When her dad died, Julie had been unable to afford an apartment for her and Thomas, to say nothing of the time required to help him cope in a civilian environment, so she'd been forced to commit him to a state institution for mentally disabled children. Though Thomas never held it against her, she viewed the commitment as a betrayal of him.

She had intended to get a degree in criminology, but she dropped out of school in her third year and applied to the sheriffs' academy. She had worked as a deputy for fourteen months by the time Bobby met and married her; she had been living on peanuts, her life-style hardly better than that of a bag lady, saving most of her salary in hope of putting together a nest egg that would allow her to buy a small house someday and take Thomas in with her. Shortly after they were married, when Dakota Investigations became Dakota & Dakota, they brought Thomas to live with them. But they worked irregular hours, and although some victims of Down's syndrome were capable of living to a degree on their own, Thomas needed someone nearby at all times. The cost of three daily shifts of qualified companions was even more than the cost of high-level care at a private institution like Cielo Vista; but they would have borne it if they could have found enough reliable help. When it became impossible to conduct their business, have a life of their own, and take care of Thomas, too, they brought him to Cielo Vista. It was as comfortable a care institution as existed, but Julie viewed it as her second betrayal of her brother. That he was happy at Cielo Vista, even thrived there, did not lighten her burden of guilt.

One part of The Dream, an important part, was to have the time and financial resources to bring Thomas home again.

Bobby looked up from the scrapbook just as Julie said, "Thomas, think you'd like to go out with us for a while?"

Thomas and Julie were still holding hands, and Bobby saw his brother-in-law's grip tighten at the suggestion of an excursion.

"We could just go for a drive," Julie said. "Down to the sea. Walk on the shore. Get an ice cream cone. What do you say?"

Thomas looked nervously at the nearest window, which framed a portion of clear blue sky, where white sea gulls periodically swooped and capered. "It's bad out."

"Just a little windy, honey."

"Don't mean the wind."

"We'll have fun."

"It's bad out," he repeated. He chewed on his lower lip.

At times he was eager to venture out into the world, but at other times he withdrew from the prospect as if the air beyond Cielo Vista was purest poison. Thomas could never be argued or cajoled out of that agoraphobic mood, and Julie knew not to push the issue.

"Maybe next time," she said.

"Maybe," Thomas said, looking at the floor. "But today's *really* bad. I . . . sort of feel it . . . the badness . . . cold all over my skin."

For a while Bobby and Julie tried various subjects, but Thomas was talked out. He said nothing, did not make eye contact, and gave no indication that he even heard them.

They sat together in silence, then, until after a few minutes Thomas said, "Don't go yet."

"We're not going," Bobby assured him.

"Just 'cause I can't talk . . . don't mean I want you gone."

"We know that, kiddo," Julie said.

"I . . . need you."

"I need you too," Julie said. She lifted one of her brother's thick-fingered hands and kissed his knuckles.

16

AFTER BUYING AN ELECTRIC RAZOR AT A DRUGSTORE, FRANK Pollard shaved and washed as best he could in a service-station restroom. He stopped at a shopping mall and bought a suitcase, underwear, socks, a couple of shirts, another pair of jeans, and incidentals. In the mall parking lot, with the stolen Chevy rocking slightly in the gusting wind, he packed the other purchases in the suitcase. Then he drove to a motel in Irvine, where he checked in under the name of George Farris, using one of the sets of ID he possessed, making a cash deposit because he lacked a credit card. He had cash in abundance.

He could have stayed in the Laguna area; but he sensed that he should not remain in one place too long. Maybe his wariness was based on hard experience. Or maybe he had been on the run for so long that he had become a creature of motion who could never again be truly comfortable at rest.

The motel room was large, clean, and tastefully decorated. The designer had been swept up in the southwest craze: white-washed wood, rattan side chairs with cushions upholstered in peach and pale-blue patterns, seafoam-green drapes. Only the mottled-brown carpet, evidently chosen for its ability to conceal stains and wear, spoiled the effect; by contrast, the light-hued furnishings seemed not merely to stand on the dark carpet but to float above it, creating spatial illusions that were disconcerting, even slightly eerie.

For most of the afternoon Frank sat on the bed, using a pile of pillows as a backrest. The television was on, but he did not watch it. Instead, he probed at the black hole of his past. Hard as he tried, he could still not recall anything of his life prior to waking in the alleyway the previous night. Some strange and exceedingly malevolent shape loomed at the edge of recollection, however, and he wondered uneasily if forgetfulness actually might be a blessing.

He needed help. Given the cash in the flight bag and his two sets of ID, he suspected that he would be unwise to seek assistance from the authorities. He withdrew the Yellow Pages from one of the nightstands and studied the listings for private investigators. But a PI called to mind old Humphrey Bogart movies and seemed like an anachronism in this modern age. How could a guy in a trenchcoat and a snap-brimmed fedora help him recover his memory?

Eventually, with the wind singing threnodies at the window, Frank stretched out to get some of the sleep he had missed last night.

A few hours later, just an hour before dusk, he woke suddenly, whimpering, gasping for breath. His heart pounded furiously.

When he sat up and swung his legs over the side of the bed, he saw that his hands were wet and scarlet. His shirt and jeans were smeared with blood. Some, though surely not all of it, was his own blood, for both of his hands bore deep, oozing scratches. His face stung, and in the bathroom, the mirror revealed two long scratches on his right cheek, one on his left cheek, and a fourth on his chin.

He could not understand how this could have happened in his sleep.

If he had torn at himself in some bizarre dream frenzy—and he could recall no dream—or if someone else had clawed him while he slept, he would have awakened at once. Which meant that he had been awake when it had happened, then had stretched out on the bed again and gone back to sleep—and had forgotten the incident, just as he had forgotten his life prior to that alleyway last night.

He returned in panic to the bedroom and looked on the other side of the bed, then in the closet. He was not sure what he was looking for. Maybe a dead body. He found nothing.

The very thought of killing anyone made him sick. He knew he did not have the capacity to kill, except perhaps in self-defense. So who had scratched his face and hands? Whose blood was on him?

In the bathroom again, he stripped out of his stained clothes and rolled them into a tight bundle. He washed his face and hands. He had bought a styptic pencil along with other shaving gear; he used that to stop the scratches from bleeding.

When he met his own eyes in the mirror, they were so haunted that he had to look away.

Frank dressed in fresh clothes and snatched the car keys off the dresser. He was afraid of what he might find in the Chevy.

At the door, as he disengaged the dead bolt, he realized that neither the frame nor the door itself was smeared with blood. If he had left during the afternoon and returned, bleeding from his hands, he would not have had the presence of mind to wipe the door clean before climbing into bed. Anyway, he had seen no bloody washcloth or tissues with which a cleanup might have been accomplished.

Outside, the sky was clear; the westering sun was bright. The motel's palm trees shivered in a cool wind, and a constant susurration rose from them, punctuated by an occasional series of hard clacks as the thick spines of the fronds met like snapping, wooden teeth.

The concrete walkway outside his room was not spotted with blood. The interior of the car was free of blood. No blood marked the dirty rubber mat in the trunk, either.

He stood by the open trunk, blinking at the sun-washed motel and parking lot around him. Three doors down, a man and woman in their twenties were unloading luggage from their black Pontiac. Another couple and their grade-school-age daughter were hurrying along the covered walkway, apparently heading toward the motel restaurant. Frank realized that he could not have gone out and committed murder and returned, blood-soaked and in broad daylight, without being seen.

In his room again, he went to the bed and studied the rumpled sheets. They were crimson-spotted, but not a fraction as saturated as they would have been if the attack—whatever its nature—had happened there. Of course, if all the blood was his, it might have spilled mostly on the front of his shirt and jeans. But he still could not believe that he had clawed himself in his sleep—one hand ripping at the other, both hands tearing at his face—without waking.

Besides, he had been scratched by someone with sharp fingernails. His own nails were blunt, bitten down to the quick.

17

SOUTH OF CIELO VISTA CARE HOME, BETWEEN CORONA DEL MAR and Laguna, Bobby tucked the Samurai into a corner of a parking lot at a public beach. He and Julie walked down to the shore.

The sea was marbled blue and green, with thin veins of gray. The water was dark in the troughs, lighter and more colorful where the waves rose and were half pierced by the rays of the fat, low sun. In serried ranks the breakers moved toward the strand, big but not huge, wearing caps of foam that the wind snatched from them.

Surfers in black wetsuits paddled their boards out toward where the swell rose, seeking a last ride before twilight. Others, also in wetsuits, sat around a couple of big coolers, drinking hot beverages from thermos bottles or Coors from the can. The day was too cool for sunbathing, and except for the surfers, the beach was deserted.

Bobby and Julie walked south until they found a low knoll, far enough back from the water to escape the spray. They sat on the stiff grass that flourished in patches in the sandy, salt-tinged soil.

When at last she spoke, Julie said, "A place like this, with a view like this. Not a big place."

"Doesn't have to be. A living room, one bedroom for us and one for Thomas, maybe a cozy little den lined with books."

"We don't even need a dining room, but I'd like a big kitchen."

"Yeah. A kitchen you can really live in."

She sighed. "Music, books, real home-cooked meals instead of junk food grabbed on the fly, lots of time to sit on the porch and enjoy the view—and the three of us together."

That was the rest of The Dream: a place by the sea and—by otherwise living simply—enough financial security to retire twenty years early.

One of the things that had drawn Bobby to Julie—and Julie to him—was their shared awareness of the shortness of life. Everyone knew that life was too short, of course, but most people pushed that thought out of mind, living as if there were endless tomorrows. If most people weren't able to deceive themselves about death, they could not have cared so passionately about the outcome of a ball game, the plot of a soap opera, the blatherings of politicians, or a thousand other things that actually meant nothing when considered against the inevitable fall of the endless night that finally came to everyone. They could not have endured to waste a minute standing in a supermarket line and would not have suffered hours in the company of bores or fools. Maybe a world lay beyond this one, maybe even Heaven, but you couldn't count on it; you could count only on darkness. Self-deception in this case was a blessing. Neither Bobby nor Julie was a gloom-monger. She knew how to enjoy life as well as anyone, and so did he, even if neither of them could buy the fragile illusion of immortality that served most people as a defense against the unthinkable. Their awareness expressed itself not in anxiety or depression, but in a strong resolve not to spend their lives in a hurly-burly of meaningless activity, to find a way to finance long stretches of time together in their own serene little tide pool.

As her chestnut hair streamed in the wind, Julie squinted at the far horizon, which was filling up with honey-gold light as the sinking sun drizzled toward it. "What frightens Thomas about being out in the world is people, too many people. But he'd be happy in a little house by the sea, a quiet stretch of coast, few people. I'm sure he would."

"It'll happen," Bobby assured her.

"By the time we build the agency big enough to sell, the southern coast will be too expensive. But north of Santa Barbara is pretty."

"It's a long coast," Bobby said, putting an arm around her. "We'll still be able to find a place in the south. And we'll have time to enjoy it. We're not going to live forever, but we're young. Our numbers aren't going to come up for years and years yet."

But he remembered the premonition that had shivered through him in bed that morning, after they had made love, the feeling that something malevolent was out there in the windswept world, coming to take Julie away from him.

The sun had touched the horizon and begun to melt into it. The golden light deepened swiftly to orange and then to bloody red. The grass and tall weeds behind them rustled in the wind, and Bobby looked over his shoulder at the spirals of airborne sand that swirled across the slope between the beach and the parking lot, like pale spirits that had fled a graveyard with the coming of twilight. From the east a wall of night was toppling over the world. The air had grown downright cold.

18

CANDY SLEPT ALL DAY IN THE FRONT BEDROOM THAT HAD ONCE been his mother's, breathing her special scent. Two or three times a week, he carefully shook a few drops of her favorite perfume—Chanel No. 5— onto a white, lace-trimmed handkerchief, which he kept on the dresser beside her silver comb-and-brush set, so each breath he took in the room reminded him of her. Occasionally he half woke from slumber to readjust the pillows or pull the covers more tightly around him, and the trace of perfume always lulled him as if it were a tranquilizer; each time he happily drifted back into his dreams.

He slept in sweatpants and a T-shirt, because he had a hard time finding pajamas large enough and because he was too modest to sleep in the nude or even in his underwear. Being unclothed embarrassed Candy, even when no one was around to see him.

All of that long Thursday afternoon, hard winter sun filled the world outside, but little got past the flower-patterned shades and rose-colored drapes that guarded the two windows. The few times he woke and blinked at the shadows, Candy saw only the pearl-gray glimmer of the dresser mirror and glints from the silver-framed photographs on the nightstand. Drugged by sleep and by the freshly applied perfume on the hand-kerchief, he could easily imagine that his beloved mother was in her rocking chair, watching over him, and he felt safe.

He came fully awake shortly before sunset and lay for a while with his hands folded behind his head, staring up at the underside of the canopy that arched over the four-poster; he could not see it, but he knew it was there, and in his mind he could conjure up a vivid image of the fabric's rosebud pattern. For a while he thought about his mother, about the best times of his life, now all gone, and then he thought about the girl, the boy, and the woman he had killed last night. He tried to recall the taste of their blood, but that memory was not as intense as those involving his mother.

After a while he switched on a bedside lamp and looked around at the comfortably familiar room: rosebud wallpaper; rosebud bedspread; rose-bud blinds; rose-colored drapes and carpets; dark mahogany bed, dresser, and highboy. Two afghans—one green like the leaves of a rose, one the shade of the petals—were draped over the arms of the rocking chair.

He went into the adjoining bathroom, locked and tested the door. The only light came from the fluorescent panels in the soffit, over the sink, for he had long ago lathered black paint on the small high window.

He studied his face in the mirror for a moment because he liked the way he looked. He could see his mother in his face. He had her blond hair, so pale it was almost white, and her sea-blue eyes. His face was all hard planes and strong features, with none of her beauty or gentleness, though his full mouth was as generous as hers.

As he undressed, he avoided looking down at himself. He was proud of his powerful shoulders and arms, his broad chest, and his muscular legs, but even catching a glimpse of the sex thing made him feel dirty and mildly ill. He sat on the toilet to make water, so he wouldn't have to touch himself. During his shower, when he soaped his crotch, he first pulled on a mitten that he had sewn from a pair of washcloths, so the flesh of his hand would not have to touch the wicked flesh below.

When he had dried off and dressed—athletic socks, running shoes, dark gray cords, black shirt—he hesitantly left the reliable shelter of his mother's old room. Night had fallen, and the upstairs hall was poorly lit by two low-wattage bulbs in a ceiling fixture that was coated with gray dust and missing half its pendant crystals. To his left was the head of the staircase. To his right were his sisters' room, his old room, and the other bath, the doors to which stood open; no lights were on back there. The oak floor creaked, and the threadbare runner did little to soften his footsteps. He sometimes thought he should give the rest of the house a thorough cleaning, maybe even spring for some new carpeting and fresh paint; however, though he kept his mother's room spotless and in good repair, he was not motivated to spend time or money on the rest of the house, and his sisters had little interest in—or talent for—homemaking.

A flurry of soft footfalls alerted him to the approach of the cats, and he stopped short of the stairs, afraid of treading on one of their paws or tails as they poured into the upstairs hall. A moment later they streamed over the top step and swarmed around him: twenty-six of them, if his most recent count was not out of date. Eleven were black, several more were chocolate-brown or tobacco-brown or charcoal-gray, two were deep gold, and only one was white. Violet and Verbina, his sisters, preferred dark cats, the darker the better.

The animals milled around him, walking over his shoes, rubbing against his legs, curling their tails around his calves. Among them were two Angoras, an Abyssinian, a tailless Manx, a Maltese, and a tortoiseshell, but most were mongrel cats of no easily distinguished lineage. Some had green eyes, some yellow, some silver-gray, some blue, and they all regarded him with great interest. Not one of them purred or meowed; their inspection was conducted in absolute silence.

Candy did not particularly like cats, but he tolerated these not only because they belonged to his sisters but because, in a way, they were virtually an extension of Violet and Verbina. To have hurt them, to have spoken harshly to them, would have been the same as striking out at his sisters, which he could never do because his mother, on her deathbed, had admonished him to provide for the girls and protect them.

In less than a minute the cats had fulfilled their mission and, almost as one, turned from him. With much swishing of tails and flexing of feline muscles and rippling of fur, they flowed like a single beast to the head of the stairs and down.

By the time he reached the first step, they were at the landing, turning, slipping out of sight. He descended to the lower hall, and the cats were gone. He passed the lightless and musty-smelling parlor. The odor of mildew drifted out of the study, where shelves were filled with the moldering romance novels that his mother had liked so much, and when he passed through the dimly lit dining room, litter crunched under his shoes.

Violet and Verbina were in the kitchen. They were identical twins. They were equally blond, with the same fair and faultless skin, with the same china-blue eyes, smooth brows, high cheekbones, straight noses with delicately carved nostrils, lips that were naturally red without lipstick, and small even teeth as bone-white as those of their cats.

Candy tried to like his sisters, and failed. For his mother's sake he could not *dis*like them, so he remained neutral, sharing the house with them but not as a real family might share it. They were too thin, he thought, fragile-looking, almost frail, and too pale, like creatures that infrequently saw the sun—which in fact seldom warmed them, since they rarely went outside. Their slim hands were well manicured, for they groomed themselves as constantly as if they, too, were cats; but, to Candy, their fingers seemed excessively long, unnaturally flexible and nimble. Their mother had been robust, with strong features and good color, and Candy often wondered how such a vital woman could have spawned this pallid pair.

The twins had piled up cotton blankets, six thick, in one corner of the big kitchen, to make a large area where the cats could lie comfortably, though the padding was actually for Violet and Verbina, so they could sit on the floor among the cats for hours at a time. When Candy entered the room, they were on the blankets, with cats all around them and in their laps. Violet was filing Verbina's fingernails with an emery board. Neither of them looked up, though of course they had already greeted him through the cats. Verbina had never spoken a word within Candy's hearing, not in her entire twenty-five years—the twins were four years younger than he was—but he was not sure whether she was unable to talk, merely unwilling to talk, or shy of talking only when around him. Violet was nearly as silent as her sister, but she did speak when necessary; apparently, at the moment, she had nothing that needed to be said.

He stood by the refrigerator, watching them as they huddled over Verbina's pale right hand, grooming it, and he supposed that he was unfair in his judgment of them. Other men might find them attractive in a strange way. Though, to him, their limbs seemed too thin, other men might see them as supple and erotic, like the legs of dancers and the arms of acrobats. Their skin was clear as milk, and their breasts were full. Because he was blessedly free of any interest in sex, he was not qualified to judge their appeal.

They habitually wore as little as possible, as little as he would tolerate before ordering them to put on more clothes. They kept the house excessively warm in winter, and most often dressed—as now—in T-shirts and short shorts or panties, barefoot and bare-limbed. Only his mother's room, which was now his, was kept cooler, because he had closed the vents up there. Without his presence to demand a degree of modesty, they would have roamed the house in the nude.

Lazily, lazily, Violet filed Verbina's thumbnail, and they both stared at it as intently as if the meaning of life was to be read in the curve of the half-moon or the arc of the nail itself.

Candy raided the refrigerator, removing a chunk of canned ham, a package of Swiss cheese, mustard, pickles, and a quart of milk. He got bread from one of the cupboards and sat in a railback chair at the age-yellowed table.

The table, chairs, cabinets, and woodwork had once been glossy white, but they had not been painted since before his mother died. They were yellow-white now, gray-white in the seams and corners, crackle-finished by time. The daisy-patterned wallpaper was soiled and, in a couple of places, peeling along the seams, and the chintz curtains hung limp with grease and dust.

Candy made and consumed two thick ham-and-cheese sandwiches. He gulped the milk straight from the carton.

Suddenly all twenty-six cats, which had been sprawling languidly around the twins, sprang up simultaneously, proceeded to the pet door in the bottom of the larger kitchen door, and went outside in orderly fashion. Time to make their toilet, evidently. Violet and Verbina didn't want the house smelling of litter boxes.

Candy closed his eyes and took a long swallow of milk. He would have preferred it at room temperature or even slightly warm. It tasted vaguely like blood, though not as pleasantly pungent; it would have been more like blood if it had not been chilled.

Within a couple of minutes the cats returned. Now Verbina was lying on her back, with her head propped on a pillow, eyes closed, lips moving as if talking to herself, though no sound issued from her. She extended her other slender hand so her sister could meticulously file those nails too. Her long legs were spread, and Candy could see between her smooth thighs. She was wearing only a T-shirt and flimsy peach-colored panties that defined rather than concealed the cleft of her womanhood. The silent cats swarmed to her, draped themselves over her, more concerned about propriety than she was, and they regarded Candy accusatorily, as if they knew that he'd been staring.

He lowered his eyes and studied the crumbs on the table.

Violet said, "Frankie was here."

At first he was more surprised by the fact that she had spoken than by what she had said. Then the meaning of those three words reverberated through him as if he were a brass gong struck by a mallet. He stood up so abruptly that he knocked over his chair. "He was here? In the house?"

Neither the cats nor Verbina twitched at the crash of the chair or the sharpness of his voice. They lay somnolent, indifferent.

"Outside," Violet said, still sitting on the floor beside her reclining sister, working on the other twin's nails. She had a low, almost whispery voice. "Watching the house from the Eugenia hedge."

Candy glanced at the night beyond the windows. "When?"

"Around four o'clock."

"Why didn't you wake me?"

"He wasn't here long. He's never here long. A minute or two, then he goes. He's afraid."

"You saw him?"

"I knew he was there."

"You didn't try to stop him from leaving?"

"How could I?" She sounded irritable now, but her voice was no less seductive than it had been. "The cats went after him, though."

"Did they hurt him?"

"A little. Not bad. But he killed Samantha."

"Who?"

"Our poor little puss. Samantha."

Candy did not know the cats' names. They had always seemed to be not just a pack of cats but a single creature, most often moving as one, apparently thinking as one.

"He killed Samantha. Smashed her head against one of the stone pilasters at the end of the walk." At last Violet looked up from her sister's hand. Her eyes seemed to be a paler blue than before, icy. "I want you to hurt him, Candy. I want you to hurt him real bad, the way he hurt our cat. I don't care if he is our brother—"

"He isn't our brother any more, not after what he did," Candy said furiously.

"I want you to do to him what he did to our poor Samantha. I want you to smash him, Candy, I want you to crush his head, crack his skull open until his brains ooze out." She continued to speak softly, but he was riveted by her words. Sometimes, like now, when her voice was even more sensuous than usual, it seemed not merely to play upon his ears but to slither into his head, where it lay gently on his brain, like a mist, a fog. "I want you to pound him, hit him and tear him until he's just splintered bones and ruptured guts, and I want you to rip out his eyes. I want him to be sorry he hurt Samantha."

Candy shook himself. "If I get my hands on him, I'll kill him, all right, but not because of what he did to your cat. Because of what he did to your *mother*. Don't you remember what he did to *her?* How can you worry about getting revenge for a cat when we still haven't made him pay for our mother, after seven long years?"

She looked stricken, turned her face from him, and fell silent.

The cats flowed off Verbina's recumbent form.

Violet stretched out half atop her sister, half beside her. She put her head on Verbina's breasts. Their bare legs were entwined.

Rising part of the way out of her trancelike state, Verbina stroked her sister's silken hair.

The cats returned and cuddled against both twins wherever there was a warm hollow to welcome them.

"Frank was here," Candy said aloud but largely to himself, and his hands curled into tight fists.

A fury grew in him, like a small turning wheel of wind far out on the sea but soon to whirl itself into a hurricane. However, rage was an emotion he dared not indulge; he must control himself. A storm of rage would water the seeds of his dark need. His mother would approve of killing Frank, for Frank had betrayed the family; his death would benefit the family. But if Candy let his anger at his brother swell into a rage, then was unable to find Frank, he would have to kill someone else, because the need would be too great to deny. His mother, in Heaven, would be ashamed of him, and for a while she would turn her face from him and deny that she had ever given birth to him.

Looking up at the ceiling, toward the unseen sky and the place at God's court where his mother dwelled, Candy said, "I'll be okay. I won't lose control. I won't."

He turned from his sisters and the cats, and he went outside to see if any trace of Frank remained near the Eugenia hedge or at the pilaster where he'd killed Samantha.

19

BOBBY AND JULIE ATE DINNER AT OZZIE'S, IN ORANGE, THEN shifted to the adjoining bar. The music was provided by Eddie Day, who had a smooth, supple voice; he played contemporary stuff but also tunes from the fifties and early sixties. It wasn't Big Band, but some early rock-and-roll had a swing beat. They could swing to numbers like "Dream Lover," rumba to "La Bamba," and cha-cha to any disco ditty that crept into Eddie's repertoire, so they had a good time.

Whenever possible, Julie liked to go dancing after she visited Thomas at Cielo Vista. In the thrall of the music, keeping time to the beat, focused on the patterns of the dance, she was able to put everything else out of her mind—even guilt, even grief. Nothing else freed her so completely. Bobby liked to dance, too, especially swing. Tuck in, throw out, change places, sugarpush, do a tight whip, tuck in again, throw out, trade places with both hands linked, back to basic position . . . Music soothed, but dance had the power to fill the heart with joy and to numb those parts of it that were bruised.

During the musicians' break, Bobby and Julie sipped beer at a table near the edge of the parquet dance floor. They talked about everything except Thomas, and eventually they got around to The Dream—specifically, how to furnish the seaside bungalow if they ever bought it. Though they would not spend a fortune on furniture, they agreed that they could indulge themselves with two pieces from the swing era: maybe a bronze and marble Art Deco cabinet by Emile-Jacques Ruhlmann, and *definitely* a Wurlitzer jukebox.

"The model 950," Julie said. "It was gorgeous. Bubble tubes. Leaping gazelles on the front panels."

"Fewer than four thousand were made. Hitler's fault. Wurlitzer retooled for war production. The model 500 is pretty too—or the 700."

"Nice, but they're not the 950."

"Not as *expensive* as the 950, either."

"You're counting pennies when we're talking ultimate beauty?"

He said, "Ultimate beauty is the Wurlitzer 950?"

"That's right. What else?"

"To me, you're the ultimate beauty."

"Sweet," she said. "But I still want the 950."

"To you, aren't *I* the ultimate beauty?" He batted his eyelashes.

"To me, you're just a difficult man who won't let me have my Wurlitzer 950," she said, enjoying the game.

"What about a Seeburg? A Packard Pla-mor? Okay. A Rock-ola?"

"Rock-ola made some beautiful boxes," she agreed. "We'll buy one of those *and* the Wurlitzer 950."

"You'll spend our money like a drunken sailor."

"I was born to be rich. Stork got confused. Didn't deliver me to the Rockefellers."

"Wouldn't you like to get your hands on that stork now?"

"Got him years ago. Cooked him, ate him for Christmas dinner. He was delicious, but I'd still rather be a Rockefeller."

"Happy?" Bobby asked.

"Delirious. And it's not just the beer. I don't know why, but tonight I feel better than I've felt in ages. I think we're going to get where we want to go, Bobby. I think we're going to retire early and live a long happy life by the sea."

His smile faded as she talked. Now he was frowning.

She said, "What's wrong with you, Sourpuss?"

"Nothing."

"Don't kid me. You've been a little strange all day. You've tried to hide it, but something's on your mind."

He sipped his beer. Then: "Well, you've got this good feeling that everything's going to be fine, but I've got a bad feeling."

"You? Mr. Blue Skies?"

He was still frowning. "Maybe you should confine yourself to office work for a while, stay off the firing line."

"Why?"

"My bad feeling."

"Which is?"

"That I'm going to lose you."

"Just try."

20

WITH ITS INVISIBLE BATON, THE WIND CONDUCTED A CHORUS OF whispery voices in the hedgerow. The dense Eugenias formed a seven-foot-high wall around three sides of the two-acre property, and they would have been higher than the house itself if Candy had not used power trimmers to chop off the tops of them a couple of times each year.

He opened the waist-high, wrought-iron gate between the two stone pilasters, and stepped out onto the graveled shoulder of the county road. To his left, the two-lane blacktop wound up into the hills for another couple of miles. To his right, it dropped down toward the distant coast, past houses on lots that were more parsimoniously proportioned the nearer they were to the shore, until in town they were only a tenth as big as the Pollard place. As the land descended westward, lights were clustered in ever greater concentration—then stopped abruptly, several miles away, as if crowding against a black wall; that wall was the night sky and the lightless expanse of the deep, cold sea.

Candy moved along the high hedge, until he sensed that he had reached the place where Frank had stood. He held up both big hands, letting the wind-fluttered leaves tremble against his palms, as if the foliage might impart to him some psychic residue of his brother's brief visit. Nothing.

Parting the branches, he peered through the gap at the house, which looked larger at night than it really was, as if it had eighteen or twenty rooms instead of ten. The front windows were dark; along the side, toward the back, where the light was filtered through greasy chintz curtains, a kitchen window was filled with a yellow glow. But for that one light, the house might have appeared abandoned. Some of the Victorian gingerbread had warped and broken away from the eaves. The porch roof was sagging, and a few railing balusters were broken, and the front steps were swaybacked. Even by the meager light of the low crescent moon, he could see the house needed painting; bare wood, like glimpses of dark bone, showed in many places, and the remaining paint was either peeling or as translucent as an albino's skin.

Candy tried to put himself in Frank's mind, to imagine why Frank kept returning. Frank was afraid of Candy, and he had reason to be. He was afraid of his sisters, too, and of all the memories that the house held for him, so he should have stayed away. But he crept back with frequency, in search of something—perhaps something that even he did not understand.

Frustrated, Candy let the branches fall together, retraced his steps along the hedge, and stopped at one gatepost, then the other, searching for the spot where Frank had fended off the cats and smashed Samantha's skull. Though far milder now than it had been earlier, the wind nevertheless had dried the blood that had stained the stones, and darkness hid the residue. Still, Candy was sure he could find the killing place. He gingerly touched the pilaster high and low, on all four faces, as if he expected a portion of it to be hot enough to sear his skin. But though he patiently traced the outlines of the rough stones and the mortar seams, too much time had passed; even his exceptional talents could not extract his brother's lingering aura.

He hurried along the cracked and canted walkway, out of the chilly night and into the stiflingly warm house again, into the kitchen, where his sisters were sitting on the blankets in the cats' corner. Verbina was behind Violet, a comb in one hand and a brush in the other, grooming her sister's flaxen hair.

Candy said, "Where's Samantha?"

Tilting her head, looking up at him perplexedly, Violet said, "I told you. Dead."

"Where's the *body?*"

"Here," Violet said, making a sweeping gesture with both hands to indicate the quiescent felines sprawled and curled around her.

"Which one?" Candy asked. Half of the creatures were so still that any of them might have been the dead one.

"All," Violet said. "They're all Samantha now."

Candy had been afraid of that. Each time one of the cats died, the twins drew the rest of the pack into a circle, placed the corpse at the center, and without speaking commanded the living to partake of the dead.

"Damn," Candy said.

"Samantha still lives, she's still a part of us," Violet said. Her voice was as low and whispery as before, but dreamier than usual. "None of our pusses ever really leaves us. Part of him . . . or her . . . stays in each of us . . . and we're all stronger because of that, stronger and purer, and always together, always and forever."

Candy did not ask if his sisters had shared in the feast, for he already knew the answer. Violet licked the corner of her mouth, as if remembering the taste, and her moist lips glistened; a moment later Verbina's tongue slid across her lips too.

Sometimes Candy felt as if the twins were members of an entirely different species from him, for he could seldom fathom their attitudes and behavior. And when they looked at him—Verbina, in perpetual silence—their faces and eyes revealed nothing of their thoughts or feelings; they were as inscrutable as the cats.

He only dimly grasped the twins' bond with the cats. It was their blessed mother's gift to them just as his many talents were his mother's generous bequest to him, so he did not question the rightness or wholesomeness of it.

Still, he wanted to hit Violet because she hadn't saved the body for him. She had known Frank had touched it, that it could be of use to Candy, but she had not saved it until he'd awakened, had not come to wake him early. He wanted to smash her, but she was his sister, and he couldn't hurt his sisters; he had to provide for them, protect them. His mother was watching.

"The parts that couldn't be eaten?" he asked.

Violet gestured toward the kitchen door.

He switched on the outside light and stepped onto the back porch. Small knobs of bone and vertebrae were scattered like queerly shaped dice on the unpainted floorboards. Only two sides of the porch were open; the house angled around the other two flanks of it, and in the niche where the house walls met, Candy found a piece of Samantha's tail and scraps of fur, jammed there by the night wind. The half-crushed skull was on the top step. He snatched it up and moved down onto the unmown lawn.

The wind, which had been declining since late afternoon, suddenly stopped altogether. The cool air would have carried the faintest sound a great distance; but the night was hushed.

Usually Candy could touch an object and see who had recently handled it before him. Sometimes he could even see where some of those people had gone after putting the object down, and when he went looking for them, they were always to be found where his clairvoyance had led him. Frank had killed the cat, and Candy hoped that contact with the remains would spark an inner vision that would put him on his brother's trail again.

Every speck of flesh had been stripped from Samantha's broken pate, and its contents had been emptied as well. Picked clean, licked smooth, dried by the wind, it might have been a portion of a fossil from a distant age. Candy's mind was filled not with images of Frank but of the other cats and Verbina and Violet, and finally he threw down the damaged skull in disgust.

His frustration sharpened his anger. He felt the need rising in him. He dared not let the need bloom . . . but resisting it was infinitely harder than resisting the charms of women and other sins. He *hated* Frank. He hated him so much, so deeply, had hated him so constantly for seven years, that he could not bear the thought that he had slept through an opportunity to destroy him.

Need. . . .

He dropped to his knees on the weedy lawn. He fisted his hands and hunched his shoulders and clenched his teeth, trying to make a rock of himself, an unmovable mass that would not be swayed one inch by the most urgent need, not one hair's width by even the most dire necessity, the most demanding hunger, the most passionate craving. He prayed to his mother to give him strength. The wind began to pick up again, and he believed it was a devil wind that would blow him toward temptation, so he fell forward on the ground and dug his fingers into the yielding earth, and he repeated his mother's sacred name—Roselle—whispered her name furiously into the grass and dirt, again and again, desperate to quell the germination of his dark need. Then he wept. Then he got up. And went hunting.

21

FRANK WENT TO A THEATER AND SAT THROUGH A MOVIE BUT WAS unable to concentrate on the story. He ate dinner at El Torito, though he didn't really taste the food; he just pushed down the enchiladas and rice as if feeding fuel to a furnace. For a couple of hours he drove aimlessly back and forth across the middle and southern reaches of Orange County, staying on the move only because, for the time being, he felt safer when in motion. Finally he returned to the motel.

He kept probing at the dark wall in his mind, behind which his entire life was concealed. Diligently, he sought the tiniest chink through which he might glimpse a memory. If he could find one crack, he was sure that the entire façade of amnesia would come tumbling down. But the barrier was smooth and flawless.

When he switched off the lights, he could not sleep.

The Santa Anas had abated. He could not blame his insomnia on the noisy winds.

Although the amount of blood on the sheets had been minimal and though it had dried since he'd awakened from his nap earlier in the day, he decided that the thought of lying in blood-stained bedclothes was preventing him from nodding off. He snapped on a lamp, stripped the bed, turned up the heat, stretched out in the darkness again, and tried to sleep without covers. No good.

He told himself that his amnesia—and the resultant loneliness and sense of isolation—was keeping him awake. Although there was some truth in that, he knew that he was kidding himself.

The real reason he could not sleep was fear. Fear of where he might go while sleepwalking. Fear of what he might do. Fear of what he might find in his hands when he woke up.

22

DEREK SLEPT. IN THE OTHER BED. SNORING SOFTLY.

Thomas couldn't sleep. He got up and stood by the window, looking out. The moon was gone. The dark was very big.

He didn't like the night. It scared him. He liked sunshine, and flowers all bright, and grass looking green, and blue sky all over so you felt like there was a lid on the world keeping everything down here on the ground and in place. At night all the colors were gone, and the world was empty, like somebody took the lid off and let in a lot of nothingness, and you looked up at all that nothingness and you felt you might just float away like the colors, float up and away and out of the world, and then in the morning when they put the lid back on, you wouldn't be here, you'd be out there somewhere, and you could never get back in again. Never.

He put his fingertips against the window. The glass was cool.

He wished he could sleep away the night. Usually he slept okay. Not tonight.

He was worried about Julie. He always worried about her a little. A brother was supposed to worry. But this wasn't a little worry. This was a lot.

It started just that morning. A funny feeling. Not funny ha-ha. Funny strange. Funny scary. Something real bad's going to happen to Julie, the feeling said. Thomas got so upset, he tried to warn her. He TVed a warning to her. They said the pictures and voices and music on the TV were sent through the air, which he first thought was a lie, that they were making fun of his being dumb, expecting him to believe *anything*, but then Julie said it was true, so sometimes he tried to TV his thoughts to her, because if you could send pictures and music and voices through the air, thoughts ought to be easy. *Be careful, Julie*, he TVed. *Look out, be careful, something bad's going to happen.*

Usually, when he felt things about someone, that someone was Julie. He knew when she was happy. Or sad. When she was sick, he sometimes curled up on his bed and put his hands on his own belly. He always knew when she was coming to visit.

He felt things about Bobby too. Not at first. When Julie first brought Bobby around, Thomas felt nothing. But slowly he felt more. Until now he felt almost as much about Bobby as about Julie.

He felt things about some other people too. Like Derek. Like Gina, another Down's kid at The Home. And like a couple of the aides, one of the visiting nurses. But he didn't feel half as much about them as he did about Bobby and Julie. He figured that maybe the more he loved somebody, the bigger he felt things—*knew* things—about them.

Sometimes when Julie was worried about him, Thomas wanted real bad to tell her that he knew how she felt, and that he was all right. Because just knowing he understood would make her happier. But he didn't have the words. He couldn't explain how or why he sometimes felt other people's feelings. And he didn't want to try to tell them about it because he was afraid of looking dumb.

He *was* dumb. He knew that. He wasn't as dumb as Derek, who was very nice, good to room with, but who was real slow. They sometimes said "slow" instead of "dumb" when they talked in front of you. Julie never did. Bobby never did. But some people said "slow" and thought you didn't get it. He got it. They had bigger words, too, and he really didn't understand those, but he sure understood "slow." He didn't *want* to be dumb, nobody gave him a choice, and sometimes he TVed a message to God, asking God to make him not dumb any more, but either God wanted him to stay dumb always and forever—but why?—or God just didn't get the messages.

Julie didn't get the messages either. Thomas always knew when he got through to someone with a TVed thought. He never got to Julie.

But he could sometimes get through to Bobby, which was funny. Not ha-ha funny. Strange funny. Interesting funny. When Thomas TVed a thought to Julie, Bobby sometimes got it instead. Like this morning. When he'd TVed a warning to Julie—

—*Something bad's going to happen, Julie, something real bad is coming*—

—Bobby had picked it up. Maybe because Thomas and Bobby both loved Julie. Thomas didn't know. He couldn't figure. But it sure happened. Bobby tuned in.

Now Thomas stood at the window, in his pajamas, and looked out at the scary night, and he felt the Bad Thing out there, felt it like a ripple in his blood, like a tingle in his bones. The Bad Thing was far away, not anywhere near Julie, but coming.

Today, during Julie's visit, Thomas wanted to tell her about the Bad Thing coming. But he couldn't find a way to say it and make sense, and he was scared of sounding dumb. Julie and Bobby knew he was dumb, sure, but he hated to sound dumb in front of them, to *remind* them how dumb he was. Every time he almost started to tell her about the Bad Thing, he just forgot how to use words. He had the words in his head, all lined up in a row, ready to say, but then suddenly they were mixed up, and he couldn't make them get back in the right order, so he couldn't say the words because they'd be just words without meaning anything, and he'd look really, really dumb.

Besides, he didn't know what to tell her the Bad Thing was. He thought maybe it was a person, a real terrible person out there, going to do something to Julie, but it didn't exactly feel like a person. Partly a person, but something else. Something that made Thomas feel cold not just on his outside but on his inside, too, like standing in a winter wind and eating ice cream at the same time.

He shivered.

He didn't want to get these ugly feelings about whatever was out there, but he couldn't just go back to bed and tune out, either, because the more he felt about the far-away Bad Thing, the better he could warn Julie and Bobby when the thing wasn't so far away any more.

Behind him, Derek murmured in a dream.

The Home was real quiet. All the dumb people were deep asleep. Except Thomas. Sometimes he liked to be awake when everyone else wasn't. Sometimes that made him feel smarter than all of them put together, seeing things they couldn't see and knowing things they couldn't know because they were asleep and he wasn't.

He stared at the nothingness of night.

He put his forehead against the glass.

For Julie's sake, he reached. Into the nothingness. Toward the far-away.

He opened himself. To the feelings. To the ripple-tingle.

A big ugly-nasty hit him. Like a wave. It came out of the night and hit him, and he stumbled back from the window and fell on his butt beside the bed, and then he couldn't feel the Bad Thing at all, it was gone, but what he had felt was so big and so ugly that his heart was pounding and he could hardly breathe, and right away he TVed to Bobby:

Run, go, getaway, save Julie, the Bad Thing's coming, the Bad Thing, run, run.

23

THE DREAM WAS FILLED WITH THE MUSIC OF GLENN MILLER'S "Moonlight Serenade," though like everything in dreams, the song was indefinably different from the real tune. Bobby was in a house that was at once familiar yet totally strange, and somehow he knew it was the seaside bungalow to which he and Julie were going to retire young. He drifted into the living room, over a dark Persian carpet, past comfortable-looking upholstered chairs, a huge old chesterfield with rounded back and thick cushions, a Ruhlmann cabinet with bronze panels, an Art Deco lamp, and overflowing bookshelves. The music was coming from outside, so he went out there. He enjoyed the easy transitions of the dream, moving through a door without opening it, crossing a wide porch and descending wooden stairs without ever quite lifting a foot. The sea rumbled to one side, and the phosphorescent foam of the breakers glowed faintly in the night. Under a palm tree, in the sand, with a scattering of shells around it, stood a Wurlitzer 950, ablaze with gold and red light, bubble tubes percolating, gazelles perpetually leaping, figures of Pan perpetually piping, record-changing mechanism gleaming like real silver, and a large black platter spinning on the turntable. Bobby felt as if "Moonlight Serenade" would go on forever, which would have been fine with him, because he had never been more mellow, more at peace, and he sensed that Julie had come out of the house behind him, that she was waiting on the damp sand near the water's edge, and that she wanted to dance with him, so he turned, and there she was, exotically illuminated by the Wurlitzer, and he took a step toward her—

Run, go, getaway, save Julie, the Bad Thing's coming, the Bad Thing, run, run!

The indigo ocean suddenly leapt as if under the lash of a storm, and spume exploded into the night air.

Hurricane winds shook the palms.

The Bad Thing! Run! Run!

The world tilted. Bobby stumbled toward Julie. The sea surged up around her. It wanted her; it was going to seize her; it was water with a will, a thinking sea with a malevolent consciousness gleaming darkly in its depths.

The Bad Thing!

The Glenn Miller tune speeded up, whirling at double time.

The Bad Thing!

The soft, romantic light from the Wurlitzer flamed brighter, stung his eyes, yet did not drive back the night. It was radiating light as if the door to Hell had opened, but the darkness around them only intensified, yielding nothing to that supernatural blaze.

THE BAD THING! THE BAD THING!

The world tilted again. Heaved and rolled.

Bobby staggered across the carnival-ride beach, toward Julie, who seemed unable to move. She was being swallowed by the churning oil-black sea.

THE BAD THING THE BAD THING THE BAD THING!

With the hard crack of riven stone, the sky split above them, but no lightning stabbed out of that crumbling vault.

Geysers of sand erupted around Bobby. Inky water exploded out of sudden gaping holes in the beach.

He looked back. The bungalow was gone. The sea rose on all sides. The beach was dissolving under his feet.

Screaming, Julie disappeared under the water.

BADTHINGBADTHINGBADTHINGBADTHING!

A twenty-foot wave loomed over Bobby. It broke. He was swept away. He tried to swim. The flesh on his arms and hands bubbled and blistered and began to peel off, revealing glints of ice-white bone. The midnight seawater was an acid. His head went under. He gasped, broke the surface, but the corrosive sea had already kissed away his lips, and he felt his gums receding from his teeth, and his tongue turned to rancid mush in the salty rush of caustic brine that he had swallowed. Even the spray-filled air was erosive, eating away his lungs in an instant, so when he tried to breathe he could not. He went down, flailing at the waves with arms and hands that were only bone, caught in an undertow, sucked into everlasting darkness, dissolution, oblivion.

BADTHING!

Bobby sat straight up in bed.

He was screaming, but no cry issued from him. When he realized he had been dreaming, he stopped trying to scream, and finally a low and miserable sound escaped him.

He had thrown off the sheets. He sat on the edge of the bed, feet on the floor, both hands on the mattress, steadying himself as if he was still on that heaving beach or struggling to swim in those roiling tides.

The green numbers of the projection clock glowed faintly on the ceiling: 2:43.

For a while the drum-loud thud of his own heart filled him with sound from within, and he was deaf to the outer world. But after a few seconds he heard Julie breathing steadily, rhythmically, and he was surprised that he had not awakened her. Evidently he had not been thrashing in his sleep.

The panic that infused the dream had not entirely left him. His anxiety began to swell again, partly because the room was as lightless as that devouring sea. Afraid of waking Julie, he did not switch on the bedside lamp.

As soon as he was able to stand, he got up and circled the bed in the perfect blackness. The bathroom was on her side, but a clear path was provided, and he found his way as he had on countless other nights, without difficulty, guided both by experience and instinct.

He eased the door shut behind him and switched on the lights. For a moment the fluorescent brilliance prevented him from looking into the glary surface of the mirror above the double sinks. When at last he regarded his reflection, he saw that his flesh had not been eaten away. The dream had been frighteningly vivid, unlike anything he'd known before; in some strange way it had been even more real than waking life, with intense colors and sounds that pulsed through his slumbering mind with the fulgurate dazzle of light along the filament of an incandescent bulb. Though aware that it had been a dream, he had half feared that the nightmare ocean had left its corrosive mark on him even after he woke.

Shuddering, he leaned against the counter. He turned on the cold water, bent forward, and splashed his face. Dripping, he looked at his reflection again and met his eyes. He whispered to himself: "What the hell was *that?*"

24

CANDY PROWLED.

The eastern end of the Pollard family's two-acre property dropped into a canyon. The walls were steep, composed mostly of dry crumbling soil veined in places by pink and gray shale. Only the expansive root systems of the hardy, desert vegetation—chapparal, thick clumps of bunchgrass, pampas grass, scattered mesquite—kept the slopes from eroding extensively in every heavy rain. A few eucalyptuses, laurels, and melaleucas grew on the walls of the canyon, and where the floor was broad enough, melaleucas and California live oaks sank roots deep into the earth along the runoff channel. That channel was only a dry streambed now, but during a heavy rain it overflowed.

Fleet and silent in spite of his size, Candy followed the canyon eastward, moving upslope, until he came to a junction with another declivity that was too narrow to be called a canyon. There, he turned north. The land continued to climb, though not as steeply as before. Sheer walls soared on both sides of him, and in places the passage was nearly pinched off, narrowing to only a couple of feet. Brittle tumbleweeds, blown into the ravine by the wind, had collected in mounds at some of those choke points, and they scratched Candy as he pushed through them.

Without even a fragment moon, the night was unusually dark at the bottom of that fissure in the land, but he seldom stumbled and never hesitated. His gifts did not include superhuman vision; he was as blinded by lightlessness as anyone. However, even in the blackest night, he knew when obstacles lay before him, sensed the contours of the land so well that he could proceed with surefooted confidence. He did not know how this sixth sense served him, and he did nothing to engage it; he simply had an uncanny awareness of his relationship with his surroundings, knew his place at all times, much as the best high-wire walkers, though blindfolded, could proceed with self-assurance along a taut line above the upturned faces of a circus crowd.

This was another gift from his mother.

All of her children were gifted. But Candy's talents exceeded those of Violet, Verbina, and Frank.

The narrow passage opened into another canyon, and Candy turned east again, along a rocky runoff channel, hurrying now as his need grew. Though ever more widely separated, houses were still perched high above, on the canyon rim; their bright windows were too far away to illuminate the ground before him, but now and then he glanced up longingly because within those homes was the blood he needed.

God had given Candy a taste for blood, made him a predator, and therefore God was responsible for whatever Candy did; his mother had explained all of that long ago. God wanted him to be selective in his killing; but when Candy was unable to restrain himself, the ultimate blame was God's, for He had instilled the blood lust in Candy but had not provided him with the strength to control it.

Like that of all predators, Candy's mission was to thin the sick and the weak from the herd. In his case, morally degenerate members of the human herd were the intended prey: thieves, liars, cheats, adulterers. Unfortunately he did not always recognize sinners when he met them. Fulfilling his mission had been far easier when his mother had been alive, for she had no trouble spotting the blighted souls for him.

Tonight he would try as best he could to confine his killing to wild animals. Slaughtering people—especially close to home—was chancy; it might bring him under the eye of the police. He could risk killing locals only when they had crossed the family in some way and simply could not be allowed to live.

If he was unable to satisfy his need with animals, he would go somewhere, anywhere, and kill people. His mother, up there in Heaven, would be angry with him and disappointed by his lack of control, but God would not be able to blame him. After all, he was only what God had made him.

With the lights of the last house well behind him, he stopped in a grove of melaleucas. The day's strong winds had drained out of the high hills, down through the canyons, and out to sea; currently the air seemed utterly still. Drooping trailers hung from the branches of the melaleucas, and every long, blade-sleek leaf was motionless.

His eyes had adapted to the darkness. The trees were silver in the dim starlight, and their cascading trailers contributed to an illusion that he was surrounded by a silent waterfall or frozen in a paperweight blizzard. He could even make out the ragged scrolls of bark that curled away from the trunks and limbs in the perpetual peeling process that lent a unique beauty to the species.

He could not see any prey.

He could hear no furtive movement of wildlife in the brush.

However, he knew that many small creatures, filled with warm blood, were huddled nearby in burrows, in secret nests, in drifts of old leaves, and in the sheltered niches of rocks. The very thought of them made him half mad with hunger.

He held his arms out in front of him, palms facing away from him, fingers spread. Blue light, the shade of pale sapphire, faint as the glow of a quarter-moon, perhaps a second in duration, pulsed from his hands. The leaves trembled, and the sparse bunchgrass stirred, then all was still as darkness reclaimed the canyon floor.

Again, blue light shone forth from his hands, as if they were hooded lanterns from which the shutters had been briefly lifted. This time the light was twice as bright as before, a deeper blue, and it lasted perhaps two seconds. The leaves rustled, and a few of the drooping trailers swayed, and the grass shivered for thirty or forty feet in front of him.

Disturbed by those queer vibrations, something scurried toward Candy, started past him. With that special sense of his surroundings that did not rely on sight or sound or smell, he reached to his left and snatched at the unseen darting creature. His reflexes were as uncanny as anything else about him, and he seized his prey. A field mouse. For an instant it froze in terror. Then it squirmed in his grasp, but he held fast to it.

His power had no effect on living things. He could not stun his prey with the telekinetic energy that radiated from his open palms. He could not draw them forth or call them to him, only frighten them out of hiding. He could have shattered one of the melaleucas or sent geysers of dirt and stones into the air, but no matter how hard he strained, he could not have stirred one hair on the mouse by using just his mind. He didn't know why he was hampered by that limitation. Violet and Verbina, whose gifts were not half as impressive as his, seemed to have power *only* over living things, smaller animals like the cats. Plants bent to Candy's will, of course, and sometimes insects, but nothing with a mind, not even something with a mind as weak as that of a mouse.

Kneeling under the silvery trees, he was swaddled in gloom so deep that he could see nothing of the mouse except its dimly gleaming eyes. He brought the fist-wrapped creature to his mouth.

It made a thin, terrified sound, more of a peep than a squeal.

He bit off its head, spat it out, and fastened his lips upon the torn neck. The blood was sweet, but there was too little of it.

He cast the dead rodent aside and raised his arms again, palms out, fingers spread. This time the splash of spectral light was an intense, electric, sapphire blue. Although it was of no longer duration than before, its effect was startlingly greater. A half dozen waves of vibrations, each a fraction of a second apart, slammed up the inclined floor of the canyon. The tall trees shook, and the hundreds of drooping trailers lashed the air, and the leaves thrashed with a sound like swarms of bees. Pebbles and smaller stones were flung up from the ground, and loose rocks rattled against one another. Every blade of bunchgrass stood up stiff and straight, like hair on a frightened man's nape, and a few clumps tore out of the soil and tumbled away into the night, along with showers of dead leaves, as if a wind had captured them. But no wind disturbed the night—only the brief burst of sapphire light and the powerful vibrations that accompanied it.

Wildlife erupted from concealment, and some of the animals streamed toward him, heading down the canyon. He had learned long ago that they never recognized his scent as that of a human being. They were as likely to flee toward him as away from him. Either he had no scent that they could detect . . . or they smelled something wild in him, something more like themselves than like a human being, and in their panic they did not realize that he was a predator.

They were visible, at best, as shapeless dark forms, streaking past him, like shadows flung off by a spinning lamp. But he also sensed them with his psychic gift. Coyotes loped by, and a panicked raccoon brushed against his leg; he did not reach out for those, because he wanted to avoid being badly clawed or bitten. At least a double score of mice streamed within reach, as well, but he wanted something more full of life, heavy with blood.

He snatched at what he thought was a squirrel, missed, but a moment later seized a rabbit by its hind legs. It shrieked. It thrashed with its less formidable forepaws, but he got hold of those, too, not only immobilizing the creature but paralyzing it with fear.

He held it up to his face.

Its fur had a dusty, musky smell.

Its red eyes glistened with terror.

He could hear its thunderous heart.

He bit into its throat. The fur, hide, and muscle resisted his teeth, but blood flowed.

The rabbit twitched, not in an attempt to escape but as if to express its resignation to its fate; they were slow spasms, strangely sensuous, as if the creature almost welcomed death. Over the years Candy had seen this behavior in countless small animals, especially in rabbits, and he always thrilled to it, for it gave him a heady sense of power, made him feel as one with the fox and the wolf.

The spasms ceased, and the rabbit went limp in his hands. Though it was still alive, it had acknowledged the imminence of death and had entered a trancelike state in which it evidently felt no pain. This seemed to be a grace that God bestowed on small prey.

Candy bit into its throat again, harder this time, deeper, then bit again, deeper still, and the life of the rabbit spurted and bubbled into his greedy mouth.

Far away in another canyon, a coyote howled. It was answered by others in its pack. A chorus of eerie voices rose and fell and rose again, as if the coyotes were aware that they were not the only hunters in the night, as if they smelled the fresh kill.

When he had supped, Candy cast the drained corpse aside.

His need was still great. He would have to break open the blood reservoirs within more rabbits or squirrels before his thirst was slaked.

He got to his feet and headed farther up into the canyon, where the wildlife had not been disturbed by his first use of the power, where creatures of many kinds waited in their burrows and hidey-holes to be harvested. The night was deep and bountiful.

25

MAYBE IT WAS JUST MONDAY-MORNING BLUES. MAYBE IT WAS THE bruised sky and the promise of rain that formed her mood. Or maybe she was tense and sour because the violent events at Decodyne were only four days in the past and therefore still too fresh. But for some reason, Julie did not want to take on this Frank Pollard's case. Or any other new case, for that matter. They had a few ongoing security contracts with firms they had served for years, and she wanted to stick to that comfortable, familiar business. Most of the work they did was about as risky as going to the supermarket for a quart of milk, but danger was a potential of the job, and the degree of danger in each new case was unknown. If a frail, elderly lady had come to them that Monday morning, seeking help in finding a lost cat, Julie probably would have regarded her as a menace on a par with an ax-wielding psychopath. She was edgy. After all, if luck had not been with them last week, Bobby would now be *four days dead*.

Sitting forward in her chair, leaning over her sturdy metal-and-Formica desk, arms crossed on the green-felt blotter, Julie studied Pollard. He could not meet her eyes, and that evasion aroused her suspicion in spite of his harmless—even appealing—appearance.

He looked as if he ought to have a Vegas comedian's name—Shecky, Buddy, something like that. He was about thirty years old, five ten, maybe a hundred and eighty pounds, which on him was thirty pounds too much; however, it was his face that was most suited for a career in comedy. Except for a couple of curious scratches that were mostly healed, it was a pleasant mug: open, kind, round enough to be jolly, deeply dimpled. A permanent flush tinted his cheeks, as if he had been standing in an arctic wind for most of his life. His nose was reddish, too, apparently not from too great a fondness for booze, but from having been broken a few times; it was lumpish enough to be amusing, but not sufficiently squashed to make him look like a thug.

Shoulders slumped, he sat in one of the two leather-and-chrome chairs in front of Julie's desk. His voice was soft and pleasant, almost musical. "I need help. I don't know where else to go for it."

In spite of his comedic looks, his manner was bleak. Though it was mellifluous, his voice was heavy with despair and weariness. With one hand he periodically wiped his face, as if pulling off cobwebs, then peered at his hand with puzzlement each time it came away empty.

The backs of his hands were marked with scabbed-over scratches, too, a couple of which were slightly swollen and enflamed.

"But frankly," he said, "seeking help from private detectives seems ridiculous, as if this isn't real life but a TV show."

"I've got heartburn, so it's real life, all right," Bobby said. He was standing at one of the big sixth-floor windows that faced out toward the mist-obscured sea and down on the nearby buildings of Fashion Island, the Newport Beach shopping center adjacent to the office tower in which Dakota & Dakota leased a seven-room suite. He turned from the view, leaned against the sill, and extracted a roll of Rolaids from the pocket of his Ultrasuede jacket. "TV detectives never suffer heartburn, dandruff, or the heartbreak of psoriasis."

"Mr. Pollard," Julie said, "I'm sure Mr. Karaghiosis has explained to you that strictly speaking we aren't private detectives."

"Yes."

"We're security consultants. We primarily work with corporations and private institutions. We have eleven employees with sophisticated skills and years of security experience, which is a lot different from the one-man PI fantasies on TV. We don't shadow men's wives to see if they're being unfaithful, and we don't do divorce work or any of the other things that people usually come to private detectives for."

"Mr. Karaghiosis explained that to me," Pollard said, looking down at his hands, which were clenched on his thighs.

From the sofa to the left of the desk, Clint Karaghiosis said, "Frank told me his story, and I really think you ought to hear why he needs us."

Julie noted that Clint had used the would-be client's first name, which he had never done before during six years with Dakota & Dakota. Clint was solidly built—five foot eight, a hundred and sixty pounds. He looked as though he had once been an inanimate assemblage of chunks of granite and slabs of marble, flint and fieldstone, slate and iron and lodestone, which some alchemist had transmuted into living flesh. His broad countenance, though handsome enough, also looked as if it had been chiseled from rock. In a search for a sign of weakness in his face, one could say only that, though strong, some features were not as strong as others. He

had a rocklike personality too: steady, reliable, imperturbable. Few people impressed Clint, and fewer still pierced his reserve and elicited more
than a polite, businesslike response from him. His use of the client's first
name seemed to be a subtle expression of sympathy for Pollard and a
vote of confidence in the truthfulness of whatever tale the man had to
tell.

"If Clint thinks this is something for us, that's good enough for me,"
Bobby said. "What's your problem, Frank?"

Julie was not impressed that Bobby had used the client's first name so
immediately, casually. Bobby liked everyone he met, at least until they
emphatically proved themselves unworthy of being liked. In fact, you
had to stab him in the back repeatedly, virtually giggling with malice,
before he would finally and regretfully consider the possibility that maybe
he *shouldn't* like you. Sometimes she thought she had married a big
puppy that was pretending to be human.

Before Pollard could begin, Julie said, "One thing, first. If we decide
to accept your case—and I stress the *if*—we aren't cheap."

"That's no problem," Pollard said. He lifted a leather flight bag from
the floor at his feet. It was one of two he'd brought with him. He put it
on his lap and unzipped it. He withdrew a couple of packs of currency
and put them on the desk. Twenties and hundreds.

As Julie took the money to inspect it, Bobby pushed away from the
windowsill and went to Pollard's side. He looked down into the flight
bag and said, "It's crammed full."

"One hundred and forty thousand dollars," Pollard said.

Upon quick inspection, the money on the desk did not appear to be
counterfeit. Julie pushed it aside and said, "Mr. Pollard, are you in the
habit of carrying so much cash?"

"I don't know," Pollard said.

"You don't know?"

"I don't know," he repeated miserably.

"He literally doesn't know," Clint said. "Hear him out."

In a voice at once subdued yet heavy with emotion, Pollard said,
"You've got to help me find out where I go at night. What in God's name
am I doing when I should be sleeping?"

"Hey, this sounds interesting," Bobby said, sitting down on one corner
of Julie's desk.

Bobby's boyish enthusiasm made Julie nervous. He might commit them to Pollard before they knew enough to be sure that it was wise to take the case. She also didn't like him sitting on her desk. It just didn't seem businesslike. She felt that it gave the prospective client an impression of amateurism.

From the sofa, Clint said, "Should I start the tape?"

"Definitely," Bobby said.

Clint was holding a compact, battery-powered tape recorder. He flicked the switch and set the recorder on the coffee table in front of the sofa, with the built-in microphone aimed at Pollard, Julie, and Bobby.

The slightly chubby, round-faced man looked up at them. The rings of bluish skin around his eyes, the watery redness of the eyes themselves, and the paleness of his lips belied any image of robust health to which his ruddy cheeks might have lent credence. A hesitant smile flickered across his mouth. He met Julie's eyes for no more than a second, looked down at his hands again. He seemed frightened, beaten, altogether pitiable. In spite of herself she felt a pang of sympathy for him.

As Pollard began to speak, Julie sighed and slumped back in her chair. Two minutes later, she was leaning forward again, listening intently to Pollard's soft voice. She did not want to be fascinated, but she was. Even phlegmatic Clint Karaghiosis, hearing the story for the second time, was obviously captivated by it.

If Pollard was not a liar or a raving lunatic—and most likely he was both—then he was caught up in events of an almost supernatural nature. Julie did not believe in the supernatural. She tried to remain skeptical, but Pollard's demeanor and evident conviction persuaded her against her will.

Bobby began making holy-jeez-gosh-wow sounds and slapping the desk in astonishment at the revelation of each new twist in the tale. When the client—No. Pollard. Not "the client." He wasn't their client yet. Pollard. When Pollard told them about waking in a motel room Thursday afternoon, with blood on his hands, Bobby blurted, "We'll take the case!"

"Bobby, wait," Julie said. "We haven't heard everything Mr. Pollard came here to tell us. We shouldn't—"

"Yeah, Frank," Bobby said, "what the hell happened *then?*"

Julie said, "What I mean is, we have to hear his whole story before we can possibly know whether or not we can help him."

"Oh, we can help him, all right," Bobby said. "We—"

"Bobby," she said firmly, "could I see you alone for a moment?" She got up, crossed the office, opened the door to the adjoining bathroom, and turned on the light in there.

Bobby said, "Be right back, Frank." He followed Julie into the bathroom, closing the door behind them.

She switched on the ceiling exhaust fan to help muffle their voices, and spoke in a whisper. "What's wrong with you?"

"Well, I have flat feet, no arches at all, and I've got that ugly mole in the middle of my back."

"You're impossible."

"Flat feet and a mole are too many faults for you to handle? You're a hard woman."

The room was small. They were standing between the sink and the toilet, almost nose to nose. He kissed her forehead.

"Bobby, for God's sake, you just told Pollard we'll take his case. Maybe we won't."

"Why wouldn't we? It's *fascinating*."

"For one thing, he sounds like a nut."

"No, he doesn't."

"He says some strange power caused that car to disintegrate, blew out streetlights. Strange flute music, mysterious blue lights . . . This guy's been reading the *National Enquirer* too long."

"But that's just it. A true nut would already be able to explain what happened to him. He'd claim he'd met God or Martians. This guy is baffled, looking for answers. That strikes me as a sane response."

"Besides, we're in business, Bobby. Business. Not for fun. For money. We're not a couple of damned hobbyists."

"He's got money. You saw it."

"What if it's hot money?"

"Frank's no thief."

"You know him less than an hour and you're sure he's no thief? You're so trusting, Bobby."

"Thank you."

"It wasn't a compliment. How can you do the kind of work you do, and be so trusting?"

He grinned. "I trusted you, and that turned out okay."

She refused to be charmed. "He says he doesn't know where he got the money, and just for the sake of the argument, let's say we buy that part of the story. And let's also say you're right about him not being a thief. So maybe he's a drug dealer. Or something else. There's a thousand ways it could be hot money without being stolen. And if we find out that it's hot, we can't keep what he pays us. We'll have to turn it over to the cops. We'll have wasted our time and energy. Besides . . . it's going to be messy."

"Why do you say that?" he asked.

"Why do I say that? He just told you about waking up in a motel room with blood all over his hands!"

"Keep your voice down. You might hurt his feelings."

"God forbid!"

"Remember, there was no body. It must've been his own blood."

Frustrated, she said, "How do we know there was no body? Because he says there wasn't? He might be such a nutcase that he wouldn't even notice the body if he stepped in its steaming bowels and stumbled over its decapitated head."

"What a vivid image."

"Bobby, he says maybe he clawed at himself, but that's not very damned likely. Probably some poor woman, some innocent girl, maybe even a child, a helpless schoolgirl, was attacked by that man, dragged into his car, raped and beaten and raped again, forced to perform every humiliating act a perverse mind could imagine, then driven to some lonely desert canyon, maybe tortured with needles and knives and God knows what, then clubbed to death, and pitched naked into a dry wash, where coyotes are even now chewing on the softer parts of her, with flies crawling in and out of her open mouth."

"Julie, you're forgetting something."

"What?"

"*I'm* the one with the overactive imagination."

She laughed. She couldn't help it. She wanted to thump his skull hard enough to knock some sense into him, but she laughed instead and shook her head.

He kissed her cheek, then reached for the doorknob.

She put her hand on his. "Promise we won't take the case until we've heard his whole story and have time to think about it."

"All right."

They returned to the office.

Beyond the windows, the sky resembled a sheet of steel that had been scorched black in places, with a few scattered incrustations of mustard-yellow corrosion. Rain had not begun to fall, but the air seemed tense in expectation of it.

The only lights in the room were two brass lamps on tables that flanked the sofa, and a silk-shaded brass floorlamp in one corner. The overhead fluorescents were not on, because Bobby hated the glare and believed that an office should be as cozily lighted as a den in a private home. Julie thought an office should look and feel like an office. But she humored Bobby and usually left the fluorescents off. Now as the oncoming storm darkened the day, she wanted to switch on the overheads and chase away the shadows that had begun to gather in those corners untouched by the amber glow of the lamps.

Frank Pollard was still in his chair, staring at the framed posters of Donald Duck, Mickey Mouse, and Uncle Scrooge that adorned the walls. They were another burden under which Julie labored. She was a fan of Warner Brothers cartoons, because they had a harder edge than Disney's creations, and she owned videotape collections of them, plus a couple of animation cels of Daffy Duck, but she kept that stuff at home. Bobby brought the Disney cartoon characters into the office because (he said) they relaxed him, made him feel good, and helped him think. No clients ever questioned their professional abilities merely because of the unconventional artwork on their walls, but she still worried about what they might think.

She went behind her desk again, and again Bobby perched on it.

After winking at Julie, Bobby said, "Frank, I was premature in accepting the case. We really can't make that decision until we've heard your whole story."

"Sure," Frank said, looking quickly at Bobby, at Julie, then down at his scratched hands, which were now clutching the open flight bag. "That's perfectly understandable."

"Of course it is," Julie said.

Clint switched on the tape recorder again.

Exchanging the flight bag on his lap for the one on the floor, Pollard said, "I should give you these." He unzipped the second satchel and withdrew a plastic bag that contained a small portion of the handsful of black sand he'd been clutching when he had awakened after his brief sleep Thursday morning. He also withdrew the bloody shirt he had been wearing when he had arisen from his even shorter nap later that same day. "I saved them because . . . well, they seemed like evidence. Clues. Maybe they'll help you figure out what's going on, what I've done."

Bobby accepted the shirt and the sand, examined them briefly, then put them on the desk beside him.

Julie noted that the shirt had been thoroughly saturated with blood, not merely spotted. Now the dry brownish stains made the material stiff.

"So you were in the motel Thursday afternoon," Bobby prompted.

Pollard nodded. "Nothing much happened that night. I went to a movie, couldn't get interested in it. Drove around a while. I was tired, real tired, in spite of the nap, but I couldn't sleep at all. I was afraid to sleep. Next morning I moved to another motel."

"When did you finally sleep again?" Julie asked.

"The next evening."

"Friday evening that was?"

"Yeah. I tried to stay awake with lots of coffee. Sat at the counter in the little restaurant attached to the motel, and drank coffee until I started to float off the stool. Stomach got so acidic, I had to stop. Went back to my room. Every time I started nodding off, I went out for a walk. But it was pointless. I couldn't stay awake forever. I was coming apart at the seams. Had to get some rest. So I went to bed shortly past eight that evening, fell asleep instantly, and didn't wake up until half past five in the morning."

"Saturday morning."

"Yeah."

"And everything was okay?" Bobby asked.

"At least there was no blood. But there was something else."

They waited.

Pollard licked his lips, nodded as if confirming to himself his willingness to continue. "See, I'd gone to bed in my boxer shorts . . . but when I woke up I was fully clothed."

"So you were sleepwalking, and you dressed in your sleep," Julie said.

"But the clothes I was wearing weren't any I'd seen before."

Julie blinked. "Excuse me?"

"They weren't the clothes I was wearing when I came to in that alleyway two nights before, and they weren't the clothes I bought at the mall on Thursday morning."

"Whose clothes were they?" Bobby asked.

"Oh, they must be mine," Pollard said, "because they fit me too well to belong to anyone else. They fit perfectly. Even the shoes fit perfectly. I couldn't have lifted that outfit from someone else and been lucky enough to have it all fit so well."

Bobby slipped off the desk and began to pace. "So what are you saying? That you left that motel in your underwear, went out to some store, bought clothes, and nobody objected to your immodesty or even questioned you about it?"

Shaking his head, Pollard said, "I don't know."

Clint Karaghiosis said, "He could've dressed in his room, while sleepwalking, then went out, bought other clothes, changed into them."

"But why would he do that?" Julie asked.

Clint shrugged. "I'm just offering a possible explanation."

"Mr. Pollard," Bobby said, "why would you have done something like that?"

"I don't know." Pollard had used those three words so often that he was wearing them out; each time he repeated them, his voice seemed softer and fuzzier than before. "I don't think I did. It doesn't feel right—as an explanation, I mean. Besides, I didn't fall asleep in the motel until after eight o'clock. I probably couldn't have gotten up again, gone out, and bought the clothes before the stores closed."

"Some places are open until ten o'clock," Clint said.

"There was a narrow window of opportunity," Bobby agreed.

"I don't think I would've broken into a store after hours," Pollard said. "Or stolen the clothes. I don't think I'm a thief."

"We know you're not a thief," Bobby said.

"We don't know any such thing," Julie said sharply.

Bobby and Clint looked at her, but Pollard continued to stare at his hands, too shy or confused to defend himself.

She felt like a bully for having questioned his honesty. Which was nuts. They knew nothing about him. Hell, if he was telling the truth, he knew nothing about himself.

Julie said, "Listen, whether he bought or stole the clothes is not the point here. I can't accept either. At least not with our current scenario. It's just too outrageous—the man going to a mall or K Mart or someplace in his underwear, outfitting himself, while he's sleepwalking. Could he do all that and not wake up—and appear to be awake to other people? I don't think so. I don't know anything about sleepwalking, but if we research it, I don't think we'll find such a thing is possible."

"Of course, it wasn't just the clothes," Clint said.

"No, not just the clothes," Pollard said. "When I woke up, there was a large paper bag on the bed beside me, like one of those you get at a supermarket if you don't want plastic. I looked inside, and it was full of . . . money. More cash."

"How much?" Bobby asked.

"I don't know. A lot."

"You didn't count it?"

"It's back at the motel where I'm staying now, the new place. I keep moving. I feel safer that way. Anyway, you can count it later if you want. I tried to count it, but I've lost my ability to do even simple arithmetic. Yeah, that sounds screwy, but it's what happened. Couldn't add the numbers. I keep trying but . . . numbers just don't mean much to me any more." He lowered his head, put his face in his hands. "First I lost my memory. Now I'm losing essential skills, like math. I feel as if . . . as if I'm coming apart . . . dissolving . . . until there's going to be none of me left, just a body, no mind at all . . . gone."

"That won't happen, Frank," Bobby said. "We won't let it. We'll find out who you are and what all this means."

"Bobby," Julie said warningly.

"Hmmm?" He smiled obtusely.

She got up from her desk and went into the bathroom.

"Ah, Jeez." Bobby followed her, closed the door, and turned on the fan. "Julie, we *have* to help the poor guy."

"The man is obviously experiencing psychotic fugues. He's doing these things in a blacked-out condition. He gets up in the middle of the night, yeah, but he's not sleepwalking. He's awake, alert, but in a fugue state. He could steal, kill—and not remember any of it."

"Julie, I'll bet you that was his own blood on his hands. He may be having blackouts, fugues, whatever you want to call them, but he's not a killer. How much you want to bet?"

"And you still say he's not a thief? On a regular basis he wakes up with a bagful of money, doesn't know where he got it, but he's not a thief? You think maybe he counterfeits money during these amnesiac spells? No, I'm sure you think he's too nice to be a counterfeiter."

"Listen," he said, "we've got to go with gut feelings sometimes, and my gut feeling is that Frank is a good guy. Even Clint thinks he's a good guy."

"Greeks are notoriously gregarious. They like everybody."

"You telling me Clint is your typical Greek social animal? Are we talking about the same Clint? Last name—Karaghiosis? Guy who looks as if he was cast from concrete, and smiles about as often as a cigar store Indian?"

The light in the bathroom was too bright. It bounced off the mirror, white sink, white walls, and white ceramic tile. Thanks to the glare and Bobby's good-natured if iron-willed determination to help Pollard, Julie was getting a headache.

She closed her eyes. "Pollard's pathetic," she admitted.

"Want to go back in there and hear him out?"

"All right. But, dammit, don't tell him we'll help him until we've heard everything. All right?"

They returned to the office.

The sky no longer looked like cold, scorched metal. It was darker than before, and churning, molten. Though only the mildest breeze stirred at ground level, strong winds apparently were at work in higher altitudes, for dense black thunderheads were being harried inland from the sea.

Like metal filings drawn to magnets, shadows had piled up in some corners. Julie reached for the switch to snap on the overhead fluorescents. Then she saw Bobby looking around with obvious pleasure at the softly lustrous, burnished brass surfaces of the lamps, at the way the polished oak end tables and coffee table glimmered in the fall of warm buttery light, and she left the switch unflicked.

She sat behind her desk again. Bobby perched on the edge of it, legs dangling.

Clint clicked on the tape recorder, and Julie said, "Frank . . . Mr. Pollard, before you continue your story, I'd like you to answer a few important questions for me. In spite of the blood on your hands, and the scratches, you believe you're incapable of hurting anyone?"

"Yeah. Except maybe in self-defense."

"And you don't think you're a thief?"

"No. I can't . . . I don't see myself as a thief, no."

"Then why haven't you gone to the police for help?"

He was silent. He clutched the open flight bag on his lap and peered into it, as if Julie was speaking to him from its interior.

She said, "Because if you *really* feel certain you're an innocent man in all regards, the police are best equipped to help you find out who you are and who's pursuing you. You know what I think? I think you're not as certain of your innocence as you pretend. You know how to hot-wire a car, and although any man with reasonable knowledge of automobiles could perform that trick, it's at least an indication of criminal experience. And then there's the money, all that money, bagsful of it. You don't remember committing any crimes, but in your heart you're convinced you have, so you're afraid to go to the cops."

"That's part of it," he acknowledged.

She said, "You do understand, I hope, that if we take your case, and if we turn up evidence that you've committed a criminal act, we'll have to convey that information to the police."

"Of course. But I figure if I went to the cops first, they wouldn't even look for the truth. They'd make up their minds that I was guilty of something even before I finished telling my story."

"And of course *we* wouldn't do that," Bobby said, turning his head to favor Julie with a meaningful look.

Pollard said, "Instead of helping me, they'd look around for some recent crimes to pin on me."

"The police don't work that way," Julie assured him.

"Of course they do," Bobby said mischievously. He slid off the desk and began to pace back and forth from the Uncle Scrooge poster to one of Mickey Mouse. "Haven't we seen 'em do that a thousand times on TV shows? Haven't we all read Hammett and Chandler?"

"Mr. Pollard," Julie said, "I was a police officer once—"

"Proves my point," Bobby said. "Frank, if you'd gone to the cops, you'd no doubt already have been booked, tried, convicted, and sentenced to a thousand years."

"There's a more important reason I can't go to the cops. That would be like going public. Maybe the press would hear about me, and be real eager to do a story about this poor guy with amnesia and bags of cash. Then he would know where to find me. I can't risk that."

Bobby said, "Who is 'he,' Frank?"

"The man who was chasing me the other night."

"The way you said it, I thought you'd remembered his name, had a specific person in mind."

"No. I don't know who he is. I'm not even entirely sure *what* he is. But I know he'll come for me again if he learns where I am. So I've got to keep my head down."

From the sofa, Clint said, "I better flip the tape over."

They waited while he popped the cassette out of the recorder.

Although it was only three o'clock, the day was in the grip of a false twilight indistinguishable from the real one. The breeze at ground level was striving to match the wind that drove the clouds at higher altitudes; a thin fog poured in from the west, exhibiting none of the lazy motion with which fogs usually advanced, swirling and churning, a molten flux that seemed to be trying to solder the earth to the thunderheads above.

When Clint had the recorder going again, Julie said, "Frank, is that the end of it? When you woke Saturday morning, wearing new clothes, with the paper bag full of money on the bed beside you?"

"No. Not the end." He raised his head, but he didn't look at her. He stared past her at the dreary day beyond the windows, though he seemed to be gazing at something much farther away than Newport Beach. "Maybe it's never going to end."

From the second flight bag out of which he had earlier withdrawn the bloody shirt and the sample of black sand, he produced a one-pint mason jar of the type used to store home-canned fruits and vegetables, with a sturdy, hinged glass lid that clamped on a rubber gasket. The jar was filled with what appeared to be rough, uncut, dully gleaming gems. Some were more polished than others; they sparkled, flared.

Frank released the lid, tipped the jar, and poured some of the contents onto the imitation blond-wood Formica desktop.

Julie leaned forward.

Bobby stepped in for a closer look.

The less irregular gems were round, oval, teardrop, or lozenge-shaped; some aspects of each stone were smoothly curved, and some were naturally beveled with lots of sharp edges. Other gems were lumpy, jagged, pocked. Several were as large as fat grapes, others as small as peas. They were all red, though they varied in their degree of coloration. They vigorously refracted the light, a pool of scarlet glitter on the pale surface of the desk; the gems marshaled the diffuse glow of the lamps through their prisms, and cast shimmering spears of crimson toward the ceiling and one wall, where the acoustic tiles and Sheetrock appeared to be marked by luminous wounds.

"Rubies?" Bobby asked.

"They don't look quite like rubies," Julie said. "What are they, Frank?"

"I don't know. They might not even be valuable."

"Where'd you get them?"

"Saturday night I couldn't sleep much at all. Just minutes at a time. I kept tossing and turning, popping awake again as soon as I dozed off. Afraid to sleep. And I didn't nap Sunday afternoon. But by yesterday evening, I was so exhausted, I couldn't keep my eyes open any more. I slept in my clothes, and when I got up this morning, my pants pockets were full of these things."

Julie plucked one of the more polished stones from the pile and held it to her right eye, looking through it toward the nearest lamp. Even in its raw state, the gem's color and clarity were exceptional. They might, as Frank implied, be only semiprecious, but she suspected that they were, in fact, of considerable value.

Bobby said, "Why're you keeping them in a mason jar?"

"Because I had to go buy one anyway to keep *this*," Frank said.

From the flight bag he produced a larger, quart-size jar and placed it on the desk.

Julie turned to look at it and was so startled that she dropped the gem she had been examining. An insect, nearly as large as her hand, lay in that glass container. Though it had a dorsal shell like a beetle—midnight black with blood-red markings around the entire rim—the thing within that carapace more closely resembled a spider than a beetle. It had the eight, sturdy, hairy legs of a tarantula.

"What the hell?" Bobby grimaced. He was mildly entomophobic. When he encountered any insect more formidable than a housefly, he called upon Julie to capture or kill it, while he watched from a distance.

"Is it alive?" Julie asked.

"Not now," Frank said.

Two forearms, like miniature lobster claws, extended from under the front of the thing's shell, one on each side of the head, though they differed from the appendages of a lobster in that the pincers were far more highly articulated than those of any common crustacean. They somewhat resembled hands, with four curved, chitinous segments, each jointed at the base; the edges were wickedly serrated.

"If that thing got hold of your finger," Bobby said, "I bet it could snip it off. You say it was alive, Frank?"

"When I woke up this morning, it was crawling on my chest."

"Good God!" Bobby paled visibly.

"It was sluggish."

"Yeah? Well, it sure looks quick as a damned cockroach."

"I think it was dying already," Frank said. "I screamed, brushed it off. It just lay there on its back, on the floor, kicking kinda feebly for a few seconds, then it was still. I stripped the case off one of the bed pillows, scooped the thing into it, knotted the top so it wouldn't crawl away if it was still alive. Then I discovered the gems in my pockets, so I bought two mason jars, one for the bug, and it hasn't moved since I put it in there, so I figure it's dead. You ever see anything like it?"

"No," Julie said.

"Thank God, no," Bobby agreed. He was not leaning over the jar for a closer look, as Julie was. In fact he had taken a step back from the desk, as if he thought the creepy-crawler might be able, in a wink, to cut its way through the glass.

Julie picked up the jar and turned it so she could look at the bug face-on. Its satin-black head was almost as big as a plum and half hidden under the carapace. Multifaceted, muddy yellow eyes were set high on the sides of the face, and under each of them was what appeared to be another eye, a third smaller than the one above it and reddish-blue. Queer patterns of tiny holes, half a dozen thornlike extrusions, and three clusters of silky-looking hairs marked the otherwise smooth, shiny surface of that hideous countenance. Its small mouth, open now, was a circular orifice in which she saw what appeared to be rings of tiny but sharp teeth.

Staring at the occupant of the jar, Frank said, "Whatever the hell I'm mixed up in, it's a bad thing. It's a real bad thing, and I'm afraid."

Bobby twitched. In a thoughtful voice, speaking more to himself than to them, Bobby said, "Bad thing. . . ."

Putting the jar down, Julie said, "Frank, we'll take the case."

"All right!" Clint said, and switched off the recorder.

Turning away from the desk, heading toward the bathroom, Bobby said, "Julie, I need to see you alone for a moment."

For the third time they stepped into the bathroom together, closed the door behind them, and switched on the fan.

Bobby's face was grayish, like a highly detailed portrait done in pencil; even his freckles were colorless. His customarily merry blue eyes were not merry now.

He said, "Are you crazy? You told him we'll take the case."

Julie blinked in surprise. "Isn't that what you wanted?"

"No."

"Ah. Then I guess I heard you wrong. Must be too much wax in my ears. Solid as cement."

"He's probably a lunatic, dangerous."

"I'd better go to a doctor, have my ears professionally cleaned."

"This wild story he's made up is just—"

She held up one hand, halting him in midsentence. "Get real, Bobby. He didn't imagine that bug. What is that thing? I've never even seen pictures of anything like it."

"What about the money? He must've stolen it."

"Frank's no thief."

"What—did God tell you that? Because there's no other way you could know. You only met Pollard little more than an hour ago."

"You're right," she said. "God told me. And I always listen to God because if you don't listen to Him, then He's likely to visit a plague of teeming locusts on you or maybe set your hair on fire with a lightning bolt. Listen, Frank's so lost, adrift, I feel sorry for him. Okay?"

He stared at her, chewing on his pale lower lip for a moment, then finally said, "We work good together because we complement each other. You're strong where I'm weak, and I'm strong where you're weak. In many ways we're not at all alike, but we belong together because we fit like pieces of a puzzle."

"What's your point?"

"One way we're different but complementary is our motivation. This line of work suits me because I get a kick out of helping people who're in trouble through no fault of their own. I like to see good triumph. Sounds like a comic-book hero, but it's the way I feel. You, on the other hand, are primarily motivated by a desire to stomp the bad guys. Yeah, sure, I like to see the bad guys all crumpled and whimpering, too, but it's not as important to me as it is to you. And, of course, you're happy to help innocent people, but with you that's secondary to the stomping and crushing. Probably because you're still working out your rage over the murder of your mother."

"Bobby, if I want psychoanalysis, I'll get it in a room where the primary piece of furniture is a couch—not a toilet."

Her mother had been taken hostage in a bank holdup when Julie was twelve. The two perpetrators had been high on amphetamines and low on common sense and compassion. Before it was all over, five of the six hostages were dead, and Julie's mother was not the lucky one.

Turning to the mirror, Bobby looked at her reflection, as if he was uncomfortable meeting her eyes directly. "My point is—suddenly you're acting like me, and that's no good, that destroys our balance, disrupts the harmony of this relationship, and it's the harmony that has always kept us alive, successful and alive. You want to take this case because you're fascinated, it excites your imagination, and because you'd like to help Frank, he's so pitiful. Where's your usual outrage? I'll tell you where it is. You don't have any because, at this moment anyway, there's no one to elicit it, no bad guy. Okay, there's the guy he says chased him that night, but we don't even know if he's real or just a figment of Frank's fantasy. Without an obvious bad guy to focus your anger, I should have to drag you into this every step of the way, and that's what I was doing, but now you're doing the dragging, and that worries me. It doesn't feel right."

She let him ramble on, with their gazes locked in the mirror, and when at last he finished, she said, "No, that's not your point."

"What do you mean?"

"I mean, everything you just said is smoke. What's really bothering you, Robert?"

His reflection tried to stare down her reflection.

She smiled. "Come on. Tell me. We never keep secrets."

Bobby-in-the-mirror looked like some bad imitation of the real Bobby Dakota. The real Bobby, her Bobby, was full of fun and life and energy. Bobby-in-the-mirror was gray-faced, almost grim; his vitality had been sapped by worry.

"Robert?" she prodded.

"You remember last Thursday when we woke?" he said. "The Santa Anas were blowing. We made love."

"I remember."

"And right after we'd made love . . . I had the strange, terrible feeling that I was going to lose you, that something out there in the wind was . . . coming to get you."

"You told me about it later that night, at Ozzie's, when we were talking about jukeboxes. But the windstorm ended, and nothing got me. Here I am."

"That same night, Thursday night, I had a nightmare, the most vivid damn dream you can imagine." He told her about the little house on the beach, the jukebox standing in the sand, the thunderous inner voice—THE BAD THING IS COMING, THE BAD THING, BAD THING!—and about the corrosive sea that had swallowed both of them, dissolving their flesh and dragging their bones into lightless depths. "It rocked me. You can't conceive of how *real* it seemed. Sounds crazy but . . . that dream was almost more real than real life. I woke up, scared as bad as I've ever been. You were sleeping, and I didn't wake you. Didn't tell you about it later because I didn't see the point of worrying you and because . . . well, it seems childish to put much stock in a dream. I haven't had the nightmare again. But since then—Friday, Saturday, yesterday—I've had moments when a strange anxiety sort of shivers through me, and I think maybe some bad thing is coming to get you. And now, out there in the office, Frank said he was mixed up in a bad thing, a real bad thing, that's how he put it, and right away I made the connection. Julie, maybe this case is the bad thing I dreamed about. Maybe we shouldn't take it."

She stared at Bobby-in-the-mirror for a moment, wondering how to reassure him. Finally she decided that, because their roles had reversed, she should deal with him as Bobby would deal with her in a similar situation. Bobby would not resort to logic and reason—which were her tools—but would charm and humor her out of a funk.

Instead of responding directly to his concerns, she said, "As long as we're getting things off our chests, you know what bothers me? The way you sit on my desk sometimes when we're talking to a prospective client. With some clients, it might make sense for *me* to sit on the desk, wearing a short skirt, showing some leg, 'cause I have good legs, even if I say so myself. But you never wear skirts, short or otherwise, and you don't have the gams for it, anyway."

"Who's talking about desks?"

"I am," she said, turning away from the mirror and looking at him directly. "We leased a seven-room suite instead of eight, to save money, and by the time the rest of the staff was set up, we had only one office for ourselves, which seemed okay. There's plenty of room in there for two desks, but you say you don't want one. Desks are too formal for you. All you need is a couch to lie on while making calls, you say, yet when clients come in, you sit on my desk."

"Julie—"

"Formica is a hard, nearly impervious surface, but sooner or later you'll have spent so much time sitting on my desk, it'll be marked by a permanent imprint of your ass."

Because she wouldn't look at the mirror, he had to turn away from it, too, and face her. "Didn't you hear what I said about the dream?"

"Now, don't get me wrong. You've got a cute ass, Bobby, but I don't want the imprint on my desktop. Pencils will keep rolling into the depression. Dust will collect in it."

"What's going on here?"

"I want to warn you that I'm thinking of having the top of my desk wired, so I can electrify it with a flick of a switch. You sit on it then, and you'll know what a fly feels like when it settles on one of those electronic bug zappers."

"You're being difficult, Julie. Why're you being difficult?"

"Frustration. I haven't gotten to stomp or crush any bad guys lately. Makes me irritable."

He said, "Hey, wait a minute. You're not being difficult."

"Of course I'm not."

"You're being *me!*"

"Exactly." She kissed his right cheek and patted his left. "Now, let's go back out there and take the case."

She opened the door and stepped out of the bathroom.

With some amusement, Bobby said, "I'll be damned," and followed her into the office.

Frank Pollard was talking quietly with Clint, but he fell silent and looked up hopefully as they entered.

Shadows clung to the corners like monks to their cloisters, and for some reason the amber glow from the three lamps reminded her of the scintillant and mysterious light of serried votive candles in a church.

The puddle of scarlet gems still glimmered on the desk.

The bug was still in a death crouch in the mason jar.

"Did Clint explain our fee schedule?" she asked Pollard.

"Yes."

"Okay. In addition, we'll need ten thousand dollars as an advance against expenses."

Outside, lightning scarred the bellies of the clouds. The bruised sky ruptured, and cold rain spattered against the windows.

26

VIOLET HAD BEEN AWAKE FOR MORE THAN AN HOUR, AND DURING most of that time she had been a hawk, swooping high on the wind, darting down now and then to make a swift kill. The open sky was nearly as real to her as it was to the bird that she had invaded. She glided on thermal currents, the air offering little resistance to the sleek fore edges of her wings, with only the lowering gray clouds above, and the whole huddled world below.

She was also aware of the shadowy bedroom in which her body and a portion of her mind remained. Violet and Verbina usually slept during the day, for to sleep away the night was to waste the best of times. They shared a room on the second floor, one king-size bed, never more than an arm's reach from each other, though usually entwined. That Monday afternoon, Verbina was still asleep, naked, on her belly, with her head turned away from her sister, occasionally mumbling wordlessly into her pillow. Her warm flank pressed against Violet. Even while Violet was with the hawk, she was aware of her twin's body heat, smooth skin, slow rhythmic breathing, sleepy murmurings, and distinct scent. She smelled the dust in the room, too, and the stale odor of the long unwashed sheets—and the cats, of course.

She not only smelled the cats, which slept upon the bed and the surrounding floor or lay lazily licking themselves, but lived in each of them. While a part of her consciousness remained in her own pale flesh and a part soared with the feathered predator, other aspects of her held tenancy in each of the cats, twenty-five of them now that poor Samantha was gone. Simultaneously Violet experienced the world through her own senses, through those of the hawk, and through the fifty eyes and twenty-five noses and fifty ears and hundred paws and twenty-five tongues of the pack. She could smell her own body odor not merely through her own nose but through the noses of all the cats: the faint soapy residue of last night's bath; the pleasantly lingering tang of lemon-scented shampoo; the staleness that always followed sleep; halitosis ripe with the vapor ghosts of the raw eggs and onions and raw liver that she had eaten that morning before going to bed with the rising sun. Each member of the pack had a sharper olfactory sense than she did, and each perceived her scent differently from the way she did; they found her natural fragrance strange yet comforting, intriguing yet familiar.

She could smell, see, hear, and feel herself through her sister's senses, as well, for she was always inextricably linked with Verbina. At will, she could swiftly enter or disengage from the minds of other lifeforms, but Verbina was the only other *person* with whom she could join in that way. It was a permanent link, which they had shared since birth, and though Violet could disengage from the hawk or the cats whenever she wished, she could never disengage from her twin. Likewise, she could control the minds of animals as well as inhabit them, but she was not able to control her sister. Their link was not that of puppet-master and puppet, but special and sacred.

All of her life, Violet had lived at the confluence of many rivers of sensation, bathed in great churning currents of sound and scent and sight and taste and touch, experiencing the world not only through her own senses but those of countless surrogates. For part of her childhood, she had been autistic, so overwhelmed by sensory input that she could not cope; she had turned inward, to her secret world of rich, varied, and profound experience, until she had learned to control the incoming flood, harnessing it instead of being swept away. Only then had she chosen to relate to the people around her, abandoning autism, and she had not learned to talk until she was six years old. She had never risen out of those deep, fast currents of extraordinary sensation to stand on the comparatively dry bank of life on which other people existed, but at least she had learned to interact with her mother, Candy, and others to a limited degree.

Verbina had never coped half as well as Violet, and evidently never would. Having chosen a life almost exclusively defined by sensation, she exhibited little or no concern for the exercise and development of her intellect. She had never learned to talk, showed only the vaguest interest in anyone but her sister, and immersed herself with joyous abandonment in the ocean of sensory stimuli that surged around her. Running as a squirrel, flying as a hawk or gull, rutting as a cat, loping and killing as a coyote, drinking cool water from a stream through the mouth of a raccoon or field mouse, entering the mind of a bitch in heat as other dogs mounted her, simultaneously sharing the terror of the cornered rabbit and the savage excitement of the predatory fox, Verbina enjoyed a breadth of life that no one else but Violet could ever know. And she preferred the constant thrill of immersion in the wildness of the world to the comparatively mundane existence of other people.

Now, although Verbina still slept, a part of her was with Violet in the soaring hawk, for even sleep did not necessitate the complete disconnection of their links to other minds. The continuous sensory input of the lesser species was not only the primary fabric from which their lives were cut, but the stuff of which their dreams were formed, as well.

Under storm clouds that grew darker by the minute, the hawk glided high over the canyon behind the Pollard property. It was hunting.

Far below, among pieces of dried and broken tumbleweed, between spiny clumps of gorse, a fat mouse broke cover. It scurried along the canyon floor, alert for signs of enemies at ground level but oblivious to the feathered death that observed it from far above.

Instinctively aware that the mouse could hear the flapping of wings from a great distance and would scramble into the nearest haven at the first sound of them, the hawk silently tucked its wings back, half folding them against its body, and dived steeply, angling toward the rodent. Though she had shared this experience countless times before, Violet held her breath as they plummeted twelve hundred feet, dropping past ground level and farther down into the ravine; and though she actually was safely on her back in bed, her stomach seemed to turn within her, and a primal terror swelled within her breast even as she let out a thin squeal of pleasurable excitement.

On the bed beside Violet, her sister also softly cried out.

On the canyon floor the mouse froze, sensing onrushing doom but not certain from which quarter it was coming.

The hawk deployed its wings as foils at the last moment; abruptly the true substance of the air became apparent and provided a welcome braking resistance. Letting its hindquarters precede it, extending its legs, opening its claws, the hawk seized the mouse even as the creature reacted to the sudden spread of wings and tried to flee.

Though remaining with the hawk, Violet entered the mind of the mouse an instant before the predator had taken it. She felt the icy satisfaction of the hunter and the hot fear of the prey. From the perspective of the hawk, she felt the plump mouse's flesh puncture and split under the sharp and powerful assault of her talons, and from the perspective of the mouse, she was wracked by searing pain and was aware of a dreadful rupturing within. The bird peered down at the squealing rodent in its grasp, and shivered with a wild sense of dominance and power, with a realization that hunger would again be sated. It loosed a caw of triumph that echoed along the canyon. Feeling small and helpless in the grip of its winged assailant, in the thrall of excruciating fear so intense as to be strangely akin to the most exquisite of sensory pleasures, the mouse looked up into the steely, merciless eyes and ceased to struggle, went limp, resigned itself to death. It saw the fierce beak descending, was aware of being rended, but no longer felt pain, only numb resignation, then a brief moment of shattering bliss, then nothing, nothing. The hawk tipped back its head and let bloody ribbons and warm knots of flesh fall down its gullet.

On the bed Violet turned on her side to face her sister. Having been shaken from sleep by the power of the experience with the hawk, Verbina came into Violet's arms. Naked, pelvis to pelvis, belly to belly, breasts to breasts, the twins held each other and shuddered uncontrollably. Violet gasped against Verbina's tender throat, and through her link with Verbina's mind, she felt that hot flood of her own breath and the warmth it brought to her sister's skin. They made wordless sounds and clung to each other, and their frantic breathing did not begin to subside until the hawk tore the last red sliver of nourishing meat from the mouse's hide and, with a flurry of wings, threw itself into the sky again.

Below was the Pollard property: the Eugenia hedge; the gabled, slate-roofed, weathered-looking house; the twenty-year-old Buick that had belonged to their mother and that Candy sometimes drove; clusters of primrose burning with red and yellow and purple blooms in a narrow and untended flowerbed that extended the length of the decrepit back porch. Violet also saw Candy far below, at the northeast corner of the sprawling property.

Still holding fast to her sister, gracing Verbina's throat and cheek and temple with a lace of gentle kisses, Violet simultaneously directed the hawk to circle above her brother. Through the bird, she watched him as he stood, head bowed, at their mother's grave, mourning her as he had mourned her every day, without exception, since her death those many years ago.

Violet did not mourn. Her mother had been as much a stranger to her as anyone in the world, and she had felt nothing special at the woman's passing. Indeed, because Candy was gifted, too, Violet felt closer to him than she had to her mother, which was not saying much because she did not really know him or care a great deal about him. How could she be close to anyone if she could not enter his mind and live with him, through him? That incredible intimacy was what welded her to Verbina, and it marked the myriad relationships she enjoyed with all the fowl and fauna that populated nature's world. She simply did not know how to relate to anyone without that intense, innermost connection, and if she could not love, she could not mourn.

Far below the wheeling hawk, Candy dropped to his knees beside the grave.

27

MONDAY AFTERNOON. THOMAS SAT AT HIS WORKTABLE. MAKING a picture poem.

Derek helped. Or thought he did. He sorted through a box of magazine clippings. He chose pictures, gave them to Thomas. If the picture was right, Thomas trimmed it, pasted it on the page. Most of the time it wasn't right, so he put it aside and asked for another picture and another until Derek gave him something he could use.

He didn't tell Derek the awful truth. The awful truth was that he wanted to make the poem by himself. But he couldn't hurt Derek's feelings. Derek was hurt enough. Too much. Being dumb really hurt, and Derek was dumber than Thomas. Derek was dumber-looking, too, which was more hurt. His forehead sloped more than Thomas's. His nose was flatter, and his head had a squashy shape. Awful truth.

Later, tired of making the picture poem, Thomas and Derek went to the wreck room, and that was where it happened. Derek got hurt. He got hurt so much he cried. A girl did it. Mary. In the wreck room.

Some people were playing a game of marbles in one corner. Some were watching TV. Thomas and Derek were sitting on a couch near some windows, Being Sociable when anyone came around. The aides always wanted people at The Home to Be Sociable. It was good for you to Be Sociable. When no one came around to Be Sociable with them, Thomas and Derek were watching hummingbirds at a feeder that hung outside the windows. Hummingbirds didn't really hum, but they zipped around and were a lot of fun to watch. Mary, who was new at The Home, didn't zip around and wasn't fun to watch, but she hummed a lot. No, she buzzed. Buzz, buzz, buzz, all the time.

Mary knew about eye cues. She said they really mattered, eye cues, and maybe they did, though Thomas had never heard of them and didn't understand what they were, but then a lot of things he didn't understand were important. He knew what eyes were, of course. He knew a cue was a stick you hit balls with because they had a pool table right there in the wreck room, near where he and Derek were sitting, though nobody used it much. He figured it would be a bad thing, real bad, if you stuck yourself in the eye with a cue, but this Mary said eye cues were good and she had a big one for a Down's kid.

"I'm a high-end moron," she said, real happy with herself, you could tell.

Thomas didn't know what a moron was, but he couldn't see a high end to Mary anywhere, she was fat and mostly droopy all over.

"You're probably a moron, too, Thomas, but you ain't high-end like me. I'm almost normal, and you ain't as close normal as me."

All this only confused Thomas.

It confused Derek even more, you could tell, and in his thick and sometimes hard to understand voice, Derek said, "Me? No moron." He shook his head. "Cowboy." He smiled. "Cowboy."

Mary laughed at him. "You ain't no cowboy or ever going to be. What you are is you're an imbecile."

They had to ask her to say it a few times before they got it, but even then they didn't really get it. They could say it but didn't know what it was any more than they knew what one of these eye cues looked like.

"You've got your normal people," Mary said, "then morons under them, then imbeciles, who're dumber than morons, and then you got idiots, who're dumber than even imbeciles. Me, I'm a high-end mo-ron, and I ain't going to be here forever, I'm going to be good, behave, work hard to be normal, and someday go back to the halfway house."

"Halfway where?" Derek asked, which was what Thomas wondered too.

Mary laughed at him. "Halfway to being normal, which is more than you'll ever be, you poor damn imbecile."

This time Derek realized she was looking down on him, making fun, and he tried not to cry, but he did. He got red in the face and cried, and Mary grinned sort of wild, she was all puffed up, excited, like she'd won some big prize. She'd used a bad word—damn—and should be ashamed, but she wasn't, you could tell. She said the other word again, which Thomas now saw was a bad word, too, "imbecile," and she kept saying it, until poor Derek got up and ran, and even then she shouted it after him.

Thomas went back to their room, looking for Derek, and Derek was in the closet with the door shut, bawling. Some of the aides came, and they talked to Derek real nice, but he didn't want to come out of the closet. They had to talk to him a long time to get him to come out of there, but even then he couldn't stop crying, and so after a while they had to Give Him Something. Once in a while when you were sick, like with the flew, the aides asked you to Take Something, which meant a pill of one shape or another, one color or another, big or little. But when they had to Give You Something, it always meant a needle, which was a bad thing. They never had to Give Something to Thomas because he was always good. But sometimes Derek, nice as he was, got to feeling so bad about himself that he couldn't stop crying, and sometimes he hit himself, just hit himself in the face, until he broke himself open and got blood on himself, and even then he wouldn't stop, so they had to Give Him Something For His Own Good. Derek never hit anyone else, he was nice, but For His Own Good he sometimes had to be made to relax or sometimes even made to sleep, which was what happened the day Mary the high-end moron called him an imbecile.

After Derek was made to sleep, one of the aides sat beside Thomas at the worktable. It was Cathy. Thomas liked Cathy. She was older than Julie but not as old as somebody's mother. She was pretty. Not as pretty as Julie but pretty, with a nice voice and eyes you weren't afraid to look into. She took one of Thomas's hands in both of hers, and she asked if he was okay. He said he was, but he really wasn't, and she knew it. They talked a while. That helped. Being Sociable.

She told him about Mary, so he'd understand, and that helped too. "She's so frustrated, Thomas. She was out there in the world for a while, at a halfway house, and she even had a part-time job, making a little money of her own. She was trying so hard, but it didn't work, she had too many problems, so she had to be institutionalized again. I think she regrets what she did to Derek. She's just so disappointed that she needed to feel superior to someone."

"I am . . . *was* . . . was out there in the world once," Thomas said.

"I know you were, honey."

"With my dad. Then with my sister. And Bobby."

"Did you like it out there?"

"Some of it . . . scared me. But when I was with Julie and Bobby . . . I liked that part."

On his bed, Derek was snoring now.

The afternoon was half gone. The sky was getting ugly-stormy. The room had shadows everywhere. Only the desk lamp was on. Cathy's face looked pretty in the lampglow. Her skin was like peach-colored satin. He knew what satin was like. Julie once had a dress of satin.

For a while he and Cathy were quiet.

Then he said, "Sometimes it's hard."

She put her hand on his head. Smoothed his hair. "Yeah, I know, Thomas. I know."

She was so nice. He didn't know why he started to cry when she was so nice, but he did. Maybe it was because she *was* so nice.

Cathy scooted her chair closer to his. He leaned against her. She put her arms around him. He cried and cried. Not hard terrible crying like Derek. Soft. But he couldn't stop. He tried not to cry because crying made him feel dumb, and he hated feeling dumb.

Through his tears, he said, "I *hate* feeling dumb."

"You're not dumb, honey."

"Yeah, I am. Hate it. But I can't be nothing else. I try not to think about being dumb, but you can't not think about it when it's what you are, and when other people aren't, and they go out in the world every day and they live, but you don't go out in the world and don't even want to but, oh, you *want* to, even when you say you don't." That was a lot for him to say, and he was surprised that he had said it all, surprised but also frustrated because he wanted so bad to tell her how it felt, being dumb, being afraid of going out in the world, and he'd failed, hadn't been able to find the right words, so the feeling was still all bottled up in him. "Time. There's lots of time, see, when you're dumb and can't go out in the world, lots of time to fill up, but then there really ain't *enough* time, not enough for learning how to be not afraid of things, and I've got to learn how not to be afraid so I can go back and be with Julie and Bobby, which I want to do real bad, before all the time runs out. There's too big amounts of time and not enough, and that sounds dumb, don't it?"

"No, Thomas. It doesn't sound dumb."

He didn't move out of her arms. He wanted to be hugged.

Cathy said, "You know, sometimes life is hard for everyone. Even for smart people. Even for the smartest of them all."

With one hand he wiped at his damp eyes. "It is? Sometimes is it hard for you?"

"Sometimes. But I believe there's a God, Thomas, and that he put us here for a reason, and that every hardship we have to face is a test, and that we're better for enduring them."

He raised his head to look at her. Such nice eyes. Good eyes. They were eyes that loved you. Like Julie's eyes or Bobby's.

Thomas said, "God made me dumb to test me?"

"You're not dumb, Thomas. Not in some ways. I don't like to hear you call yourself dumb. You're not as smart as some, but that's not your fault. You're different, that's all. Being . . . different is your hardship, and you're coping with it well."

"I am?"

"Beautifully. Look at you. You're not bitter. You're not sullen. You reach out to people."

"Being Sociable."

She smiled, pulled a tissue from the box of Kleenex on the worktable, and wiped the tears from his face. "Of all the smart people in the world, Thomas, not a one of them handles hardship better than you do, and most not as well."

He knew she meant what she said, and her words made him happy, even if he didn't quite believe life was ever hard for smart people.

She stayed a while. Made sure he was okay. Then she left.

Derek was still snoring.

Thomas sat at the worktable. Tried to make more poem.

After a while he went to the window. Rain was coming down now. It trickled on the glass. The afternoon was almost gone. Night was soon coming down on top of the rain.

He put his hands against the glass. He reached into the rain, into the gray day, into the nothingness of the night that was slowly sneaking up on them.

The Bad Thing was still out there. He could feel it. A man but not a man. Something more than a man. Very bad. Ugly-nasty. He'd felt it for days, but he hadn't TVed a warning to Bobby since last week because the Bad Thing wasn't coming any closer. It was far away, right now Julie was safe, and if he TVed too many warnings to Bobby, then Bobby would stop paying attention to them, and when the Bad Thing finally showed up, Bobby wouldn't believe in it any more, and then it would get to Julie because Bobby wouldn't be paying attention.

What Thomas most feared was that the Bad Thing would take Julie to the Bad Place. Their mother went to the Bad Place when Thomas was two years old, so he'd never known her. Then their dad went to the Bad Place later, leaving Thomas with just Julie.

He didn't mean Hell. He knew about Heaven and Hell. Heaven was God's. The devil owned Hell. If there was a Heaven, he was sure his mom and dad went there. You wanted to go up to Heaven if you could. Things were better there. In Hell, the aides weren't nice.

But, to Thomas, the Bad Place wasn't just Hell. It was Death. Hell was *a* bad place, but Death was *the* Bad Place. Death was a word you couldn't picture. Death meant everything stopped, went away, all your time ran out, over, done, kaput. How could you picture that? A thing wasn't real if you couldn't picture it. He couldn't *see* Death, couldn't get a picture of it in his head, not if he thought about it the way other people seemed to think about it. He was just too dumb, so he had to picture it in his head as a *place*. They said Death came to take you, and it had come to take his father one night, his heart had attacked him, but if it came to take you, then it had to take you to some *place*. And that was the Bad Place. It's where you were taken and never allowed to come back. Thomas didn't know what happened to a person there. Maybe nothing nasty. Except you weren't allowed to come back and see people you loved, which made it nasty enough, no matter if the food was good over there. Maybe some people went on to Heaven, some to Hell, but you couldn't come back from either one, so both were part of the Bad Place, just different rooms. And he wasn't sure Heaven and Hell were real, so maybe all there was in the Bad Place was darkness and cold and so much empty space that when you went over there you couldn't even find the people who'd gone ahead of you.

That scared him most of all. Not just losing Julie to the Bad Place, but not being able to find her when he went over there himself.

He was already afraid of the night. All that big empty. The lid off the world. So if just the night itself was so scary, the Bad Place would be lots worse. It was sure to be bigger than the night, and daylight never came in the Bad Place.

Outside, the sky got darker.

Wind blew the palms.

Rain ran down the glass.

The Bad Thing was far away.

But it would come closer. Soon.

28

CANDY WAS HAVING ONE OF THOSE DAYS WHEN HE COULD NOT accept that his mother was dead. Every time he crossed a threshold or turned a corner, he expected to see her. He thought he heard her rocking in the parlor, humming softly to herself as she knitted a new afghan, but when he went in there to look, the rocking chair was filmed with dust and draped with a shawl of cobwebs. Once, he hurried into the kitchen, expecting to find her in a brightly flowered housedress overlaid with a ruffle-trimmed white apron, dropping neat spoonsful of cookie batter on baking sheets or perhaps mixing a cake, but, of course, she was not there. In a moment of acute emotional turmoil, Candy raced upstairs, certain that he would find his mother in bed, but when he burst into her room, he remembered that it was *his* room now, and that she was gone.

Eventually, to jar himself out of that strange and troubling mood, he went into the backyard and stood by her lonely grave in the northeast corner of the large property. He had buried her there, seven years ago, under a solemn winter sky similar to the one that currently hid the sun, with a hawk circling above just as one circled now. He had dug her grave, wrapped her in sheets scented with Chanel No. 5, and lowered her into the ground secretly, because interment on private property, not designated as a gravesite, was against the law. If he had allowed her to be buried elsewhere, he would have had to go live there with her, for he could not have endured being separated from her mortal remains for any great length of time.

Candy dropped to his knees.

Over the years the original mound of earth had settled, until her grave was marked by a shallow concavity. The grass was sparser there, the blades coarse, wiry, different from the rest of the lawn, though he did not know why; even in the months following her burial, the grass above her had not flourished. No headstone memorialized her passing; although the backyard was sheltered by the high hedge, he could not risk calling attention to her illegal resting place.

Staring at the ground before him, Candy wondered if a headstone would help him accept her death. If every day he saw her name and the date of her death deeply cut into a slab of marble, that sight should slowly but permanently engrave the loss upon his heart, sparing him days like this, when he was disturbed by a queer forgetfulness and by a hope that could never be fulfilled.

He stretched out on the grave, his head turned to one side with an ear against the earth, as if he half expected to hear her speaking to him from her subterranean bed. Pressing his body hard into the unyielding ground, he longed to feel the vitality that she had once radiated, the singular energy that had flowed from her like heat from the open door of a furnace, but he felt nothing. Though his mother had been a special woman, Candy knew it was absurd to expect her corpse, after seven years, to radiate even a ghost of the love that she had lavished upon him when she was alive; nevertheless, he was grievously disappointed when not even the faintest aura shimmered upward through the dirt from her sacred bones.

Hot tears burned in his eyes, and he tried to hold them back. But a faint rumble of thunder passed through the sky, and a few fat droplets of rain began to fall, and neither the storm nor his tears could be restrained.

She lay only five or six feet beneath him, and he was overcome by an urge to claw his way down to her. He knew her flesh would have deteriorated, that he would find only bones cradled in a vile muck of unthinkable origin, but he wanted to hold her and be held, even if he had to arrange her skeletal arms around himself in a staged embrace. He actually ripped at the grass and tore up a few handsful of topsoil. Soon, however, he was wracked by powerful sobs that swiftly exhausted him and left him too weak to struggle with reality any longer.

She was dead.

Gone.

Forever.

As the cold rain fell in greater volume, pounding on Candy's back, it seemed to leach his hot grief from him and fill him, instead, with icy hatred. Frank had killed their mother; he *must* pay for that crime with his own life. Lying on a muddy grave and weeping like a child would not bring Candy one step closer to vengeance. Finally he got up and stood with his hands fisted at his sides, letting the storm sluice some of the mud and grief from him.

He promised his mother that he would be more relentless and diligent in his pursuit of her killer. The next time he got a lead on Frank, he would not lose him.

Looking up at the cloud-choked and streaming sky, addressing his mother in Heaven, he said, "I'll find Frankie, kill him, crush him, I will. I'll smash his skull open and cut his hateful brain into pieces and flush it down a toilet."

The rain seemed to penetrate him, driving a chill deep into his marrow, and he shuddered.

"If I find anyone who lifted a hand to help him, I'll cut their hands off. I'll tear out the eyes of anyone who looked at Frankie with sympathy. I swear I will. And I'll cut out the tongues of any bastards who spoke kind words to him."

Suddenly the rain fell with greater force than before, hammering the grass flat, crackling through the leaves of a nearby oak, stirring a chorus of whispers from the Eugenias. It snapped against his face, making him squint, but he did not lower his eyes from Heaven.

"If he's found anyone to care about, anyone at all, I'll take them away from him like he took you from me. I'll break them open, get the blood out of them, and throw them away like garbage."

He had made these same promises many times during the past seven years, but he made them now with no less passion than he had before.

"Like garbage," he repeated through clenched teeth.

His need for vengeance was no less fierce now than it had been on the day of her murder seven years ago. His hatred of Frank was, if anything, harder and sharper than ever.

"Like garbage."

An ax of lightning cleaved the contusive sky. Briefly a long, jagged laceration gaped open in the dark clouds, which for a moment seemed to him not like clouds at all but like the infinitely strange and throbbing body of some godlike being, and through the lightning-rent flesh he thought he glimpsed the shining mystery beyond.

29

CLINT DREADED THE RAINY SEASON IN SOUTHERN CALIFORNIA. Most of the year was dry, and in the on-again-off-again drought of the past decade, some winters were marked by only a few storms. When rain finally fell, the natives seemed to have forgotten how to drive in it. As gutters overflowed, the streets clogged with traffic. The freeways were worse; they looked like infinitely long car washes in which the conveyors had broken down.

While the gray light slowly faded out of that Monday afternoon, he drove first to Palomar Laboratories in Costa Mesa. It was a large, single-story concrete-block building one block west of Bristol Avenue. Their medical-lab division analyzed blood samples, Pap smears, and biopsies, among other things, but they also performed industrial-and geological-sample analyses of all kinds.

He parked his Chevy in the adjoining lot. Carrying a plastic bag from Von's supermarket, he sloshed through the deep puddles, head bent against the driving rain, and went into the small reception lounge, dripping copiously.

An attractive young blonde sat on a stool behind the counter at the reception window. She was wearing a white uniform and a purple cardigan. She said, "You should have an umbrella."

Clint nodded, put the supermarket bag on the counter, and began to untie the knot in the straps, to open it.

"At least a raincoat," she said.

From an inside jacket pocket, he withdrew a Dakota & Dakota card, passed it to her.

"Is this who you want billed?" she asked.

"Yeah."

"Have you used our service before?"

"Yeah."

"You have an account?"

"Yeah."

"I haven't seen you in here before."

"No."

"My name's Lisa. I've only been here about a week. Never had a private eye come in before, least since I've started."

From the large white sack he withdrew three smaller, clear, Ziploc bags and lined them up side by side.

"You got a name?" she asked, cocking her head, smiling at him.

"Clint."

"You go around without an umbrella or raincoat in this weather, Clint, you'll catch your death, even as sturdy as you look."

"First, the shirt," Clint said, pushing that bag forward. "We want the bloodstains analyzed. Not just typed. We want the whole nine yards. A complete genetic workup too. Take samples from four different parts of the shirt, because there might be more than one person's blood on it. If so, do a workup on both."

Lisa frowned at Clint, then at the shirt in the bag. She began filling out an analysis order.

"Same program on this one," he said, pushing forward the second bag. It contained a folded sheet of Dakota & Dakota stationery that was mottled with several spots of blood. Back at the office, Julie had sterilized a pin in a match flame, stuck Frank Pollard's thumb, and squeezed the crimson samples onto the paper. "We want to know if any of the blood on the shirt matches what's on this stationery."

The third bag contained the black sand.

"Is this a biological substance?" Lisa asked.

"I don't know. Looks like sand."

"Because if it's a biological substance, it should go to our medical division, but if it's not biological it should go to the industrial lab."

"Send a little to both. And put a rush on it."

"Costs more."

"Whatever."

As she filled out the third form, she said, "There's a few beaches in Hawaii with black sand, you ever been there?"

"No."

"Kaimu. That's the name of one of the black beaches. Comes from a volcano, somehow. The sand, I mean. You like beaches?"

"Yeah."

She looked up, her pen poised over the form, and gave him a big smile. Her lips were full. Her teeth were very white. "I *love* the beach. Nothing I like better than putting on a bikini and soaking up some sun, really just *baking* in the sun, and I don't care what they say about a tan being bad for you. Life's short anyway, you know? Might as well look good while we're here. Besides, being in the sun makes me feel . . . oh, not lazy exactly, because I don't mean it saps my energy, just the opposite, it makes me feel full of energy, but a lazy energy, sort of the way a lioness walks—you know?—strong-looking but easy. The sun makes me feel like a lioness."

He said nothing.

She said, "It's erotic, the sun. I guess that's what I'm trying to say. You lay out in the sun enough, on a nice beach, and all your inhibitions sort of melt away."

He just stared at her.

After she finished filling out the analysis orders, gave him copies, and attached each order to the correct sample, Lisa said, "Listen, Clint, we're living in a modern world, right?"

He didn't know what she meant.

She said, "We're all liberated these days, am I right? So if a girl finds a guy attractive, she doesn't have to wait for him to make the move."

Oh, Clint thought.

Leaning back on her stool, maybe to let him see how her full breasts filled out her white uniform blouse, she smiled and said, "Would you be interested in a dinner, movie?"

"No."

Her smile froze.

"Sorry," he said.

He folded the copies of the work orders and put them in the same jacket pocket from which earlier he had withdrawn a business card.

She was glaring at him, and he realized he'd hurt her feelings.

Searching for something to say, all he could come up with was, "I'm gay."

She blinked and shook her head as if recovering from a stunning blow. Like sun piercing clouds, her smile broke through the gloom on her face. "Had to be to resist this package, I guess."

"Sorry."

"Hey, it's not your fault. We are what we are, huh?"

He went into the rain again. It was getting colder. The sky looked like the ruins of a burned-out building to which the fire department had arrived too late: wet ashes, dripping cinders.

30

AS NIGHT FELL ON THAT RAINY MONDAY, BOBBY DAKOTA STOOD at the hospital window and said, "Not much of a view, Frank. Unless you're keen on parking lots." He turned and surveyed the small, white room. Hospitals always gave him the creeps, but he did not express his true feelings to Frank. "The decor sure won't be featured in *Architectural Digest* anytime soon, but it's comfy enough. You've got TV, magazines, and three meals a day in bed. I noticed some of the nurses are real lookers, too, but please try to keep your hands off the nuns, okay?"

Frank was paler than ever. The dark circles around his eyes had grown like spreading inkblots. He not only looked as if he belonged in a hospital but as if he had been there for weeks already. He used the power controls to tilt the bed up. "Are these tests really necessary?"

"Your amnesia might have a physical cause," Julie said. "You heard Dr. Freeborn. They'll look for cerebral abscesses, neoplasms, cysts, clots, all kinds of things."

"I'm not sure about this Freeborn," Frank said worriedly.

Sanford Freeborn was Bobby and Julie's friend, as well as their physician. A few years ago they had helped him get his brother out of deep trouble.

"Why? What's wrong with Sandy?"

Frank said, "I don't know him."

"You don't know anybody," Bobby said. "That's your problem. Remember? You're an amnesiac."

After accepting Frank as a client, they had taken him directly to Sandy Freeborn's office for a preliminary examination. All Sandy knew was that Frank could remember nothing but his name. They had not told him about the bags of money, the blood, black sand, red gems, weird insect, or any of the rest of it. Sandy didn't ask why Frank had come to them instead of the police or why they had accepted a case so far outside their usual purview; one of the things that made him a good friend was his reliable discretion.

Nervously adjusting the sheets, Frank said, "You think a private room is really necessary?"

Julie nodded. "You also want us to find out what you do at night, where you go, which means monitoring you, tight security."

"A private room's expensive," Frank said.

"You can afford the finest care," Bobby said.

"The money in those bags might not be mine."

Bobby shrugged. "Then you'll have to work off your hospital bill—change a few hundred beds, empty a few thousand bed-pans, perform some brain surgery free of charge. You might *be* a brain surgeon. Who knows? With amnesia, it's just as likely you've forgotten that you're a surgeon as that you're a used-car salesman. Worth a try. Get a bone saw, cut off the top of some guy's head, have a peek in there, see if anything looks familiar."

Leaning against the bed rail, Julie said, "When you're not in radiology or some other department, undergoing tests, we'll have a man with you, watching over you. Tonight it's Hal."

Hal Yamataka had already taken his station in an uncomfortable-looking, upholstered chair provided for visitors. He was to one side of the bed, between Frank and the door, in a position to watch both his charge and, if Frank was in the mood, the wall-mounted television. Hal resembled a Japanese version of Clint Karaghiosis: about five foot seven or eight, broad in the shoulders and chest, as solid-looking as if he had been built by a mason who knew how to fit stones tight together and hide the mortar. In case nothing worth watching was on television and his charge proved to be a lousy conversationalist, he had brought a John D. MacDonald novel.

Looking at the rain-washed window, Frank said, "I guess I'm just . . . scared."

"No need to be scared," Bobby said. "Hal's not as dangerous as he looks. He's never killed anyone he liked."

"Only once," Hal said.

Bobby said, "You once killed someone you liked? Over what?"

"He asked to borrow my comb."

"There you go, Frank," Bobby said. "Just don't ask to borrow his comb, and you're safe."

Frank was in no mood to be kidded. "I can't stop thinking about waking up with blood on my hands. I'm afraid maybe I've already hurt someone. I don't want to hurt anyone else."

"Oh, you can't hurt Hal," Bobby said. "He's an impenetrable oriental."

"Inscrutable," Hal said. "I'm an *inscrutable* oriental."

"I don't want to hear about your sex problems, Hal. Anyway, if you didn't eat so much sushi and didn't have raw-fish breath, you'd get scruted as often as anyone."

Reaching over the bed railing, Julie took one of Frank's hands.

He smiled weakly. "Your husband always like this, Mrs. Dakota?"

"Call me Julie. Do you mean, does he always act like a wiseass or a child? Not always, but most of the time, I'm afraid."

"You hear that, Hal?" Bobby said. "Women and amnesiacs—they have no sense of humor."

To Frank, Julie said, "My husband believes everything in life should be fun, even car accidents, even funerals—"

"Even dental hygiene," Bobby said.

"—and he'd probably be making jokes about fallout in the middle of a nuclear war. That's just the way he is. He can't be cured—"

"She's tried," Bobby said. "She sent me to a happiness detox center. They promised to knock some gloom into me. Couldn't."

"You'll be safe here," Julie said, squeezing Frank's hand before letting go of it. "Hal will look after you."

31

THE ENTOMOLOGIST'S HOUSE WAS IN THE TURTLE ROCK DEVELOP-
ment in Irvine, within easy driving distance of the university. Low, black,
mushroom-shaped Malibu lamps threw circles of light on the rain-
puddled walkway that led to the softly gleaming oak doors.

Carrying one of Frank Pollard's leather flight bags, Clint stepped onto
the small covered porch and rang the bell.

A man spoke to him through an intercom set just below the bell push.
"Who is it, please?"

"Dr. Dyson Manfred? I'm Clint Karaghiosis. From Dakota and Dakota."

Half a minute later, Manfred opened the door. He was at least ten
inches taller than Clint, six feet five or six, and thin. He was wearing black
slacks, a white shirt, and a green necktie; the top button of the shirt was
undone, and the tie hung loose.

"Good God, man, you're soaked."

"Just damp."

Manfred moved back, opening the door wide, and Clint stepped into
the tile-floored foyer.

As he closed the door, Manfred said, "Ought to have a raincoat or
umbrella on a night like this."

"It's invigorating."

"What is?"

"Bad weather," Clint said.

Manfred looked at him as if he was strange, but in Clint's view it
was Manfred himself who was strange. The guy was too thin, all
bones. He could not fill his clothes; his trousers hung shapelessly on
his knobby hips, and his shoulders poked at the fabric of his shirt as
if only bare, sharp bones lay under there. Angular and graceless, he
looked as if he had been assembled from a pile of dry sticks by an
apprentice god. His face was long and narrow, with a high brow and
a lantern jaw, and his well-tanned, leathery skin seemed to be
stretched so tight over his cheek-bones that it might split. He had peculiar amber eyes that regarded Clint with an expression of cool curi-

osity no doubt familiar to the thousands of bugs he had pinned to specimen boards.

Manfred's gaze traveled down Clint to the floor, where water was puddling around his running shoes.

"Sorry," Clint said.

"It'll dry. I was in my study. Come along."

Glancing into the living room, to his right, Clint noted fleur-de-lis wallpaper, a thick Chinese rug, too many overstuffed chairs and sofas, antique English furniture, wine-red velour drapes, and tables cluttered with bibelots that glimmered in the lamplight. It was a very Victorian room, not in harmony with the California lines and layout of the house itself.

He followed the entomologist past the living room, along a short hall to the study. Manfred had a singular, stilting gait. Tall and sticklike as he was, with shoulders hunched and head thrust forward slightly, he seemed as unevolved and prehistoric as a praying mantis.

Clint had expected a university professor's study to be crammed full of books, but only forty or fifty volumes were shelved in one case to the left of the desk. There were cabinets with wide, shallow drawers that probably were filled with creepy-crawlies, and on the walls were insects in specimen boxes, framed under glass.

When he saw Clint staring at one collection in particular, Manfred said, "Cockroaches. Beautiful creatures."

Clint did not reply.

"The simplicity of their design and function, I mean. Few would find them beautiful in appearance, of course."

Clint couldn't shake the feeling that the bugs were really alive.

Manfred said, "What do you think of that big fellow in the corner of the collection?"

"He's big, sir."

"Madagascar hissing roach. The scientific name's *Gromphadorrhina portentosa.* That one's over eight and a half centimeters long, about three and a half inches. Absolutely beautiful, isn't he?"

Clint said nothing.

Settling into the chair behind his desk, Manfred somehow folded his long bony arms and legs into that compact space, the way a large spider could scrunch itself into a tiny ball.

Clint did not sit down. Having put in a long day, he was eager to go home.

Manfred said, "I received a call from the university chancellor. He asked me to cooperate with your Mr. Dakota in any way I could."

UCI—the University of California at Irvine—had long been striving to become one of the country's premier universities. The current chancellor and the one before him had sought to attain that status by offering enormous salaries and generous fringe benefits to world-class professors and researchers at other institutions. Before committing substantial resources in the form of a well-upholstered job offer, however, the university hired Dakota & Dakota to conduct a background investigation on the prospective faculty member. Even a brilliant physicist or biologist could have too great a thirst for whiskey, a nose for cocaine, or an unfortunate attraction to underage girls. UCI wanted to buy brainpower, respectability, and academic glory, not scandal; Dakota & Dakota served them well.

Manfred propped his elbows on the arms of his chair and steepled his fingers, which were so long that they looked as if they must have at least one extra knuckle each. "What's the problem?" he asked.

Clint opened the leather flight bag and removed the quart-size, wide-mouth mason jar. He put it on the entomologist's desk.

The bug in the jar was at least twice as big as the Madagascar hissing roach on the wall.

For a moment Dr. Dyson Manfred seemed to have been quick-frozen. He didn't move a finger; his eyes didn't blink. He stared intently at the creature in the jar. At last he said, "What is this—a hoax?"

"It's real."

Manfred leaned forward, hunching over the desk and lowering his head until his nose almost touched the thick glass behind which the insect crouched. "Alive?"

"Dead."

"Where did you find this—not here in southern California?"

"Yes."

"Impossible."

"What is it?" Clint asked.

Manfred looked up at him, scowling. "I've never seen anything like it. And if *I* haven't seen anything like it, neither has anyone else. It's of the phylum *Arthropoda*, I'm sure, which includes such things as spiders and scorpions, but whether it can be classed an insect, I can't say, not until I've examined it. If it *is* an insect, it's of a new species. Where, exactly, did you find it, and why on earth would it be of interest to private detectives?"

"I'm sorry, sir, but I can't tell you anything about the case. I have to protect the client's privacy."

Manfred carefully turned the jar around in his hands, studying the resident from every side. "Just incredible. I must have it." He looked up, and his amber eyes were no longer cool and appraising, but gleaming with excitement. "I must have this specimen."

"Well, I intended to leave it with you for examination," Clint said. "But as to whether you can have permanent possession—"

"Yes. Permanent."

"That's up to my boss and the client. Meanwhile we want to know what it is, where it comes from, everything you can tell us about it."

With exaggerated care, as if handling the finest crystal instead of ordinary glass, Manfred put the jar on the blotter. "I'll make a complete photographic and videotape record of the specimen from every angle and in extreme close-up. Then it'll be necessary to dissect it, though that'll be done with utmost care, I assure you."

"Whatever."

"Mr. Karaghiosis, you seem terribly blasé about this. Do you fully understand what I've said? This would appear to be an entirely new species, which would be extraordinary. Because how could any such species, producing individuals of this size, be overlooked for so long? This is going to be big news in the world of entomology, Mr. Karaghiosis, very big news."

Clint looked at the bug in the bottle.

He said, "Yeah, I figured."

32

FROM THE HOSPITAL, BOBBY AND JULIE DROVE A COMPANY Toyota into the county's western flatlands to Garden Grove, looking for 884 Serape Way, the address on the driver's license that Frank held in the name of George Farris.

Julie peered through the rain-dappled side windows and forward between the thumping windshield wipers, checking house numbers.

The street was lined with bright sodium-vapor lamps and thirty-year-old, single-story homes. They had been built in two basic, boxy models, but an illusion of individuality was provided by a variety of trim. This one was stucco with brick accents. That one was stucco with cedar-shingle panels—or Bouquet Canyon stone or desert bark or volcanic rock.

California was not all Beverly Hills, Bel Air, and Newport Beach, not all mansions and seaside villas, which was the television image. Economies of home design had made the California dream accessible to the waves of immigrants that for decades had flooded in from back east, and now from farther shores—as was evident from Vietnamese- and Korean-language bumper stickers on some cars parked along Serape.

"Next block," Julie said. "My side."

Some people said such neighborhoods were a blot on the land, but to Bobby they were the essence of democracy. He had been raised on a street like Serape Way, north in Anaheim instead of Garden Grove, and it had never seemed ugly. He remembered playing with other kids on long summer evenings, when the sun set with orange and crimson flares, and the feathery silhouettes of the backlit palms were as black as ink drawings against the sky; at twilight the air sometimes smelled of star jasmine and echoed with the cry of a lingering sea gull far to the west. He remembered what it meant to be a kid with a bicycle in California— the vistas for exploration, the grand possibilities for adventure; every street of stucco homes, seen for the first time and from the seat of a Schwinn, had seemed exotic.

Two coral trees dominated the yard at 884 Serape. The white blooms of the azalea bushes were softly radiant in the bleak night.

Tinted by the sodium-vapor streetlamps, the falling rain looked like molten gold. But as Bobby hurried along the walkway behind Julie, the rain was almost as cold as sleet on his face and hands. He was wearing a warmly lined, nylon jacket with a hood, but he shivered.

Julie rang the doorbell. The porch light came on, and Bobby sensed someone looking them over through the fisheye lens in the front door. He pushed back his hood and smiled.

The door opened on a security chain, and an Asian man peered out. He was in his forties, short, slender, with black hair fading to gray at the temples. "Yes?"

Julie showed him her private investigator's license and explained that they were looking for someone named George Farris.

"Police?" The man frowned. "Nothing wrong, no need for police."

"No, see, we're private investigators," Bobby explained.

The man's eyes narrowed. He looked as if he would close the door in their faces, but abruptly he brightened, smiled. "Oh, you're PI! Like on TV." He took the chain off the door and let them in.

Actually he didn't just let them in, he welcomed them as if they were honored guests. Within three minutes flat, they learned his name was Tuong Tran Phan (the order of his names having been rearranged to accommodate the western custom of putting the surname last), that he and his wife, Chinh, were among the boat people who fled Vietnam two years after the fall of Saigon, that they had worked in laundries and dry cleaners, and eventually opened two dry-cleaning stores of their own. Tuong insisted on taking their coats. Chinh—a petite woman with delicate features, dressed in baggy black slacks and a yellow silk blouse— said she would provide refreshments, even though Bobby explained that only a few minutes of their time was required.

Bobby knew first-generation Vietnamese-Americans were sometimes suspicious of policemen, even to the extent of being reluctant to call for help when they were victims of crime. The South Vietnamese police often had been corrupt, and the North Vietnamese overlords, who seized the South after the U.S. withdrawal, had been murderous. Even after fifteen years or longer in the States, many Vietnamese remained at least somewhat distrustful of all authorities.

In the case of Tuong and Chinh Phan, however, that suspicion did not extend to private investigators. Evidently they had seen so many heroic television gumshoes, they believed all PIs were champions of the underdog, knights with blazing .38s instead of lances. In their roles as liberators of the oppressed, Bobby and Julie were conducted, with some ceremony, to the sofa, which was the newest and best piece of furniture in the living room.

The Phans marshaled their exceptionally good-looking children in the living room for introductions: thirteen-year-old Rocky, ten-year-old Sylvester, twelve-year-old Sissy, and six-year-old Meryl. They were obviously born-and-raised Americans, except that they were refreshingly more courteous and well-mannered than many of their contemporaries. When introductions had been made, the kids returned to the kitchen, where they had been doing their schoolwork.

In spite of their polite protestations, Bobby and Julie were swiftly served coffee laced with condensed milk and exquisite little Vietnamese pastries. The Phans had coffee as well.

Tuong and Chinh sat in worn armchairs that were visibly less comfortable than the sofa. Most of their furniture was in simple contemporary styles and neutral colors. A small Buddhist shrine stood in one corner; fresh fruit lay on the red altar, and several sticks of incense bristled from ceramic holders. Only one stick was lit, and a pale-blue ribbon of fragrant smoke curled upward. The only other Asian elements were black-lacquered tables.

"We're looking for a man who might once have lived at this address," Julie said, selecting one of the petits fours from the tray on which Mrs. Phan had served them. "His name's George Farris."

"Yes. He lived here," Tuong said, and his wife nodded.

Bobby was surprised. He had been certain that the Farris name and the address had been randomly matched by a document forger, that Frank had never lived here. Frank had been equally certain that Pollard, not Farris, was his real name.

"You bought this house from George Farris?" Julie asked.

Tuong said, "No, he was dead."

"Dead?" Bobby asked.

"Five or six years ago," Tuong said. "Terrible cancer."

Then Frank Pollard *wasn't* Farris and hadn't lived here. The ID was entirely fake.

"We bought house just a few months ago from widow," Tuong said. His English was good, though occasionally he dropped the article before the noun. "No, what I mean to say—from widow's estate."

Julie said, "So Mrs. Farris is dead too."

Tuong turned to his wife, and a meaningful look passed between them. He said. "It is very sad. Where do such men come from?"

Julie said, "What man are you speaking of, Mr. Phan?"

"The one who killed Mrs. Farris, her brother, two daughters."

Something seemed to slither and coil in Bobby's stomach. He instinctively liked Frank Pollard and was certain of his innocence, but suddenly a worm of doubt bored into the fine, polished apple of his conviction. Could it be just a coincidence that Frank was carrying the ID of a man whose family had been slaughtered—or was Frank responsible? He was chewing a bite of cream-filled pastry, and though it was tasty, he had trouble swallowing it.

"It was late July," Chinh said. "During the heat wave, which you may remember." She blew on her coffee to cool it. Bobby noticed that most of the time Chinh spoke perfect English, and he suspected that her occasional infelicities of language were conscious mistakes that she inserted in order not to seem more well-spoken than her husband, a subtle and thoroughly Asian courtesy. "We buy house last October."

"They never catch the killer," Tuong Phan said.

"Do they have a description of him?" Julie asked.

"I don't think so."

Reluctantly Bobby glanced at Julie. She appeared to be as shaken as he was, but she did not give him an I-told-you-so look.

She said, "How were they murdered? Shot? Strangled?"

"Knife, I think. Come. I show you where bodies were found."

The house had three bedrooms and two bathrooms, but one bath was being remodeled. The tile had been torn off the walls, floor, and counter. The cabinets were being rebuilt with quality oak.

Julie followed Tuong into the bathroom, and Bobby stayed at the doorway with Mrs. Phan.

The rattle-hiss of the rain echoed down through the ceiling vent.

Tuong said, "Body of youngest Farris daughter was here, on the floor. She was thirteen. Terrible thing. Much blood. The grout between tiles was permanently stained, all had to come out."

He led them into the bedroom his daughters shared. Twin beds, nightstands, and two small desks left little room for anything else. But Sissy and Meryl had squeezed in a lot of books.

Tuong Phan said, "Mrs. Farris's brother, staying with her for a week, was killed here. In his bed. Blood was on walls, carpet."

"We saw the house before it was listed with a real-estate agent, before the carpet was replaced and the walls repainted," Chinh Phan said. "This room was the worst. It gave me bad dreams for a while."

They proceeded to the sparely furnished master bedroom: a queen-size bed, nightstands, two ginger-jar lamps, but no bureau or chest of drawers. The clothes that would not fit in the closet were arranged along one wall, in cardboard storage boxes with clear plastic lids.

Their frugality struck Bobby as similar to his and Julie's. Perhaps they, too, had a dream for which they were working and saving.

Tuong said, "Mrs. Farris was found in this room, in her bed. Terrible things were done to her. She was bitten, but they never wrote about that in newspapers."

"Bitten?" Julie asked. "By what?"

"Probably by killer. On the face, throat . . . other places."

"If they didn't write about it in the papers," Bobby said, "how do you know about the bites?"

"Neighbor who found bodies still lives next door. She says that both older daughter and Mrs. Farris were bitten."

Mrs. Phan said, "She's not the kind to imagine such things."

"Where was the second daughter found?" Julie asked.

"Please follow me." Tuong led them back the way they had come, through the living room and dining room, into the kitchen.

The four Phan children were sitting around a breakfast table. Three of them were diligently reading textbooks and taking notes. No television or radio provided distraction, and they appeared to be enjoying their studies. Even Meryl, who was a first-grader and probably had no home-work to speak of, was reading a children's book.

Bobby noticed two colorful charts posted on the wall near the refrigerator. The first displayed each kid's grades and major test results since the start of the school year in September. The other was a list of household chores for which each child was responsible.

Throughout the country, universities were in a bind, because an inordinately large percentage of the best applicants for admission were of Asian extraction. Blacks and Hispanics complained about being aced out by another minority, and whites shouted reverse racism when denied admission in favor of an Asian student. Some attributed Asian-Americans' success to a conspiracy, but Bobby saw the simple explanation for their achievements everywhere in the Phan house: They tried harder. They embraced the ideals upon which the country had been based—including hard work, honesty, goal-oriented self-denial, and the freedom to be whatever one wanted to be. Ironically, their great success was partly due to the fact that so many born Americans had become cynical about those same ideals.

The kitchen was open to a family room that was furnished as humbly as the rest of the house.

Tuong said, "Oldest Farris girl found here by sofa. Seventeen."

"Very pretty girl," Chinh said sadly.

"She, like mother, was bitten. So our neighbor says."

Julie said, "What about the other victims, the younger daughter and Mrs. Farris's brother—were they bitten too?"

"Don't know," Tuong said.

"The neighbor didn't see their bodies," Chinh said.

They were silent for a moment, looking at the floor where the dead girl had been found, as if the enormity of this crime was such that the stain of it should somehow have reappeared on this brand-new carpet. Rain droned on the roof.

Bobby said, "Doesn't it sometimes bother you to live here? Not because murders took place in these rooms, but because the killer was never found. Don't you worry about him coming back some night?"

Chinh nodded.

Tuong said, "Everywhere is danger. Life itself is danger. Less risky never being born." A faint smile flickered across his face and was gone. "Leaving Vietnam in tiny boat was more danger than this."

Glancing at the table in the adjoining kitchen, Bobby saw the four kids still deeply involved with their studies. The prospect of a murderer returning to the scene of this crime did not faze them.

"In addition to dry-cleaning," Chinh said, "we remodel houses, sell them. This is fourth. We will live here maybe another year, remodeling room by room, then sell, take a profit."

Tuong said, "Because of murders, some people would not consider moving here after the Farrises. But danger is also opportunity."

"When we finish with the house," Chinh said, "it won't just be remodeled. It will be clean, spiritually clean. Do you understand? The innocence of the house will be restored. We will have chased out the evil that the killer brought here, and we'll have left our own spiritual imprint on these rooms."

Nodding, Tuong said, "That is a satisfaction."

Removing the forged driver's license from his pocket, Bobby held it so his fingers covered the name and address, leaving the photograph visible. "Do you recognize this man?"

"No," Tuong said, and Chinh agreed.

As Bobby put the license away, Julie said, "Do you know what George Farris looked like?"

"No," Tuong said. "As I told you, he died of cancer, many years before his family was killed."

"I thought maybe you'd seen a photo of him here in the house, before the Farrises' belongings were removed."

"No. Sorry."

Bobby said, "You mentioned earlier that you didn't buy the house through a realtor. You worked with the estate?"

"Yes. Mrs. Farris's other brother inherited everything."

"Do you happen to have his name and address?" Bobby asked. "I think we'll need to talk to him."

33

DINNERTIME CAME. DEREK WOKE UP. HE WAS GROGGY BUT hungry too. He leaned on Thomas when they walked to the dining room. Food got eaten. Spaghetti. Meatballs. Salad. Good bread. Chocolate cake. Cold milk.

Back in their room, they watched TV. Derek fell asleep again. It was a bad night on TV. Thomas sighed with disgust. After an hour or so, he stopped the set. None of the shows was smart enough to care about. They were too stupid-silly even for a moron, which Mary said he was. Maybe imbeciles would like them. Probably not.

He used the bathroom. Brushed his teeth. Washed his face. He didn't look in the mirror. He didn't like mirrors because they showed him what he was.

After changing into pajamas, he got in bed and made the lamp go dark, even though it was only eight-thirty. He turned on his side, with his head propped on two pillows, and studied the night sky framed by the nearest window. No stars. Clouds. Rain. He liked rain. When a storm came down, it was like a lid on the night, and you didn't feel like you might float up in all that darkness and just disappear.

He listened to the rain. It whispered. It cried tears on the window.

Far away, the Bad Thing was loose. Ugly-nasty waves spread out from it the way ripples spread across a pond when you dropped a stone in the water. The Bad Thing was like a big stone dropped into the night, a thing that didn't belong in this world, and with a little effort Thomas could sense the waves from it breaking over him.

He reached out. Felt it. A throbbing thing. Cold and full of anger. Mean. He wanted to get closer. Learn what it was.

He tried TVing questions at it. What are you? Where are you? What do you want? Why are you going to hurt Julie?

Suddenly, like a big magnet, the Bad Thing began pulling him. He'd never felt anything like that before. When he tried to TV his thoughts to Bobby or Julie, they didn't grab him and pull at him the way this Bad Thing did.

A part of his mind seemed to unravel like a ball of string, and the loose end sailed through the window and way up into the night, through the darkness, until it found the Bad Thing. Suddenly Thomas was very close to the Bad Thing, too close. It was all around him, big ugly and so strange that Thomas felt like he'd dropped into a swimming pool full of ice and razor blades. He didn't know if it was a man, couldn't see its shape, only feel it; it might be pretty on the outside, but on the inside it was throbbing and dark and deep nasty. He sensed the Bad Thing was eating. The food was still alive and squirming. Thomas was scared big, and right away he tried to pull back, but for a moment the ugly mind held him tight, and he could get away only by picturing the mind-string rewinding itself onto the ball.

When the mind-string was all wound up again, Thomas turned away from the window, onto his stomach. He was breathing real fast. He listened to his heart boom.

He had a sick-making taste in his mouth. The same taste he got sometimes when he bit his tongue, not meaning to, and the same taste as when the dentist yanked one of his teeth, meaning to. Blood.

Sick and scared, he sat up in bed and made the lamp come on right away. He took a tissue from the box on the nightstand. He spit into it and looked to see if there was blood. There wasn't. Just spit.

He tried again. No blood.

He knew what that meant. He'd been too close to the Bad Thing. Maybe even *inside* the bad thing, just for a blink. The ugly taste in his mouth was the same taste the Bad Thing tasted, tearing with its teeth at some living, squirming food. Thomas didn't have blood in his mouth, he just had a memory of blood in his mouth. But that was bad enough; this time wasn't at all like biting his tongue or getting a tooth yanked, because this time what he tasted wasn't his own blood.

Though warm enough in the room, he started shivering and couldn't stop.

CANDY PROWLED THE canyons, in the grip of urgent need, rattling wild animals out of burrows and nests. He was kneeling in the mud beside a huge oak, pummeled by rain, sucking blood from the ravished throat of a rabbit, when he felt someone place a hand atop his head.

He threw down the rabbit and sprang to his feet, turning around as he did so. Nobody was there. Two of his sisters' blackest cats were twenty feet behind him, visible only because their eyes were luminous in the gloom; they had been following him since he'd left the house. Otherwise he was alone.

For a second or two, he still felt the hand on his head, though no hand was there. Then the queer sensation passed.

He studied the shadows on all sides and listened to the rain snapping through the oak leaves.

Finally, shrugging off the episode, driven by his fierce need, he proceeded farther east, moving upslope. A two-foot-wide stream had formed on the canyon floor, six or eight inches deep, not large enough to hamper his progress.

The drenched cats followed. He did not want them with him, but he knew from experience that he would not be able to chase them away. They did not always accompany him, but when they chose to follow in his tracks, they could not be dissuaded.

After he had gone about a hundred yards, he dropped to his knees again, held his hands in front of him, and allowed the power to erupt once more. Shimmering sapphire light swept through the night. Brush shook, trees stirred, and rocks clattered against one another. In the wake of the light, clouds of dust flew up, ghostly silver columns that rippled like wind-stirred shrouds, then vanished into the darkness.

A bevy of animals burst from cover, and some raced toward Candy. He snatched at a rabbit, missed, but seized a squirrel. It tried to bite him, but he swung it hard by one leg, bashing its head against the muddy ground, stunning it.

VIOLET WAS WITH Verbina in the kitchen. They were sitting on the layered blankets with twenty-three of their twenty-five cats.

Parts of her mind—and parts of her sister's—were in Cinders and Lamia, the black cats through which they were accompanying their brother. Watching Candy seize and destroy his prey, Cinders and Lamia were excited, and Violet was excited too. Electrified.

The wet January night was deep, illumined only by the ambient light from the communities to the west, which was reflected off the bellies of the low clouds. In that wilderness, Candy was the wildest creature of them all, a fierce and powerful and merciless predator who crept swiftly and silently through the rugged canyons, taking what he needed and wanted. He was so strong and limber that he appeared to flow up the canyon, over rocks and fallen timber, around prickly brush, as if he were not a man of flesh and blood, but the rippled moonshadow of some flying creature soaring high above the earth.

When Candy seized the squirrel and bashed its head against the ground, Violet divided the part of her mind that was in Lamia and Cinders, and also entered the squirrel. It was stunned by the blow. It struggled feebly and looked at Candy with unalloyed terror.

Candy's big, strong hands were on the squirrel, but it seemed to Violet that they were on her, as well, moving over her bare legs, hips, belly, and breasts.

Candy snapped its spine against his bent knee.

Violet shuddered. Verbina whimpered and clung to her sister.

The squirrel no longer had any feeling in its extremities.

With a low growl, Candy bit the animal's throat. He tore at its hide, chewing open the blood-rich vessels.

Violet felt the hot blood spurting out of the squirrel, felt Candy's mouth fastened hungrily to the wound. It almost seemed as though no surrogate lay between them, as if his lips were pressed firmly to Violet's throat and as if her own blood was flooding into his mouth. She wished that she could enter Candy's mind and be on both the giving and receiving end of the blood, but she could only meld with animals.

She no longer had the strength to sit up. She settled back onto the blankets, only half aware that she was softly chanting a monotonous litany: *"Yea, yes, yes, yes, yes. . . ."*

Verbina rolled atop her sister.

Around them the cats tumbled together in a roiling mass of fur and tails and whiskered faces.

THOMAS TRIED AGAIN. For Julie's sake. He reached out toward the cold, glowing mind of the Bad Thing. Right away the Bad Thing drew him toward it. He let his mind unwind like a big ball of string. It pierced the window, zoomed into the night, made contact.

He TVed questions: What are you? Where are you? What do you want? Why are you going to hurt Julie?

JUST AS CANDY threw aside the dead squirrel and got to his feet, he felt the hand on his head again. He twitched, turned, and flailed at the darkness with both fists.

No one was behind him. With radiant amber eyes, the two cats watched him from about twenty feet away, dark blots on the pale silt. All the wildlife in the immediate vicinity had fled. If someone was spying on him, the intruder was concealed in the brush farther back along the canyon or in a niche on one of the canyon walls, certainly not near enough to have touched him.

Besides, he still felt the hand. He rubbed at the top of his head, half expecting to find leaves stuck in his wet hair. Nothing.

But the pressure of a hand remained, even increased, and was so well defined that he could feel the outlines of four fingers, a thumb, and the curve of a palm against his skull.

What . . . where . . . what . . . why . . . ?

Those words echoed inside his head. No voice had broken through the drizzling sounds of the rain.

What . . . where . . . what . . . why . . . ?

Candy turned in a full circle, angry and confused.

A crawling sensation arose in his head, different from anything he had ever known before. As if something was burrowing in his brain.

"Who are you?" he said aloud.

What . . . where . . . what . . . why . . . ?

"Who are you?"

THE BAD THING was a man. Thomas knew that now. An ugly-inside man and something else, too, but still at least partly a man.

The Bad Thing's mind was like a whirlpool, blacker than black, swirling real fast, sucking Thomas down, down, wanting to gobble him alive. He tried to break loose. Swim away. Wasn't easy. The Bad Thing was going to pull him into the Bad Place, and he'd never be able to come back. He thought he was a goner. But his fear of the Bad Place, of going where Julie and Bobby would never find him and where he'd be alone, was so big he finally tore free and rewound himself into his room at Cielo Vista.

He slid down on the mattress and drew the covers over his head, so he couldn't see the night beyond the window, and so nothing out there in the night could see him.

34

WALTER HAVALOW, MRS. GEORGE FARRIS'S SURVIVING BROTHER and heir to her modest estate, lived in a richer neighborhood than the Phans, but he was poorer in courtesy and good manners. His English Tudor house in Villa Park had beveled-glass windows filled with a light that Julie found warm and beckoning, but Havalow stood in the doorway and did not invite them inside even after he had studied their PI license and returned it to her.

"What do you want?"

Havalow was tall, potbellied, with thinning blond hair and a thick mustache that was part blond and part red. His penetrating hazel eyes marked him as a man of intelligence, but they were cold, watchful, and calculating—the eyes of a Mafia accountant.

"As I explained," Julie said, "the Phans told us you could help. We need a photograph of your late brother-in-law, George Farris."

"Why?"

"Well, as I said, there's a man going around pretending to be Mr. Farris, and he's a player in a case we're working on."

"Can't be my brother-in-law. He's dead."

"Yes, we know. But this imposter's ID is very good, and it would help us to have a photo of the real George Farris. I'm sorry I can't tell you anything more. I'd be violating our client's privacy."

Havalow turned away and closed the door in their faces.

Bobby looked at Julie and said, "Mr. Conviviality."

Julie rang the bell again.

After a moment, Havalow opened the door. "What?"

"I know we arrived unannounced," Julie said, struggling to remain cordial, "and I apologize for the intrusion, but a photo of your—"

"I was just going to get the picture," he said impatiently. "I'd have it in hand by now if you hadn't rung the bell again." He turned away from them and closed the door a second time.

"Is it our body odor?" Bobby wondered.

"What a jerk."

"You think he's really coming back?"

"He doesn't, I'll break the door down."

Behind them, rain dripped off the overhang that sheltered the last ten feet of the walkway, and water gurgled hollowly through a downspout— cold sounds.

Havalow returned with a shoe box full of snapshots. "My time is valuable. If you want my cooperation, you'll keep that in mind."

Julie resisted her worst instincts. Rudeness irritated the hell out of her. She fantasized knocking the box out of his grasp, seizing one of his hands, and bending the index finger as far back as it would go, thus straining the digital nerve on the front of his hand while simultaneously pinching the radial and median nerves on the back, forcing him to kneel. Then a knee driven into the underside of his chin, a swift chop to the back of his neck, a well-placed kick to his soft, protruding belly . . .

Havalow rummaged through the box and extracted a Polaroid of a man and a woman sitting at a redwood picnic table on a sunny day. "That's George and Irene."

Even in the yellowish light of the porch lamp, Julie could see that George Farris had been a rangy man with a long narrow face, the exact physical opposite of Frank Pollard.

"Why would someone be claiming he's George?" Havalow asked.

"We're dealing with a possible criminal who uses multiple fake IDs," Julie said. "George Farris is just one of his identities. No doubt your brother-in-law's name was probably chosen at random by the document forger this guy used. Forgers sometimes use the names and addresses of the deceased."

Havalow frowned. "You think it's possible this man using George's name is the same guy who killed Irene, my brother, my two nieces?"

"No," Julie said immediately. "We're not dealing with a killer here. Just a confidence man, a swindler."

"Besides," Bobby said, "no killer would link himself to murders he'd committed by getting ID in the name of his victim's husband."

Making eye contact with Julie, clearly trying to determine how much they were snowing him, Havalow said, "This guy your client?"

"No," Julie lied. "He ripped off our client, and we've been hired to track him down, so he can be forced to make restitution."

Bobby said, "Can we borrow this photo, sir?"

Havalow hesitated. He was still making eye contact with Julie.

Bobby handed Havalow a Dakota & Dakota business card. "We'll get the picture back to you. There's our address, phone number. I understand your reluctance to part with a family photo, especially since your sister and brother-in-law are no longer alive, but if—"

Apparently deciding that they were not lying, Havalow said, "Hell, take it. I'm not sentimental about George. Never could stand him. Always thought my sister was a fool for marrying him."

"Thank you," Bobby said. "We—"

Havalow stepped back and closed the door.

Julie rang the bell.

Bobby said, "Please don't kill him."

Scowling with impatience, Havalow opened the door.

Stepping between Julie and Havalow, Bobby held out the forged driver's license bearing George Farris's name and Frank's picture. "One more thing, sir, and we'll get out of your hair."

"I live to a very tight schedule," Havalow said.

"Have you seen this man before?"

Irritated, Havalow took the driver's license and inspected it. "Doughy face, bland features. There're a million like him within a hundred miles of here—wouldn't you say?"

"And you've never seen him?"

"Are you slow-witted? Do I have to put it in short, simple sentences? No. I have never seen him."

Retrieving the license, Bobby said, "Thanks for your time and—"

Havalow closed the door. Hard.

Julie reached for the bell.

Bobby stayed her hand. "We've got everything we came for."

"I want—"

"I know what you want," Bobby said, "but torturing a man to death is against the law in California."

He hustled her away from the house, into the rain.

In the car again, she said, "That rude, self-important bastard!"

Bobby started the engine and switched on the windshield wipers. "We'll stop at the mall, buy you one of those giant teddy bears, paint Havalow's name on it, let you tear the guts out of it. Okay?"

"Who the hell does he think he is?"

While Julie glowered back at the house, Bobby drove away from it. "He's Walter Havalow, babe, and he's got to be himself until he dies, which is a worse punishment than anything you could do to him."

A few minutes later, when they were out of Villa Park, Bobby drove into the lot at a Ralph's supermarket and tucked the Toyota into a parking space. He doused the headlights, switched off the wipers, but left the engine running so they would have heat.

Only a few cars were in front of the market. Puddles as large as swimming pools reflected the store lights.

Bobby said, "What've we learned?"

"That we *loathe* Walter Havalow."

"Yes, but what have we learned that's germane to the case? Is it just a coincidence that Frank's been using George Farris's name and Farris's family was slaughtered?"

"I don't believe in coincidence."

"Neither do I. But I still don't think Frank is a killer."

"Neither do I, though anything's possible. But what you said to Havalow was true—surely Frank wouldn't kill Irene Farris and everyone else in the house, then carry around fake ID that links him to them."

Rain began to fall harder than before, drumming noisily on the Toyota. The heavy curtain of water blurred the supermarket.

Bobby said, "You want to know what I think? I think Frank was using Farris's name, and whoever's after him found out about it."

"Mr. Blue Light, you mean. The guy who supposedly can make a car fall apart around you and magically induce streetlights to blow out."

"Yeah, him," Bobby said.

"If he exists."

"Mr. Blue Light discovered Frank was using the Farris name, and went to that address, hoping to find him. But Frank had never been there. It was just a name and address his document forger picked at random. So when Mr. Blue didn't find Frank, he killed everyone in the house, maybe because he thought they were lying to him and hiding Frank, or maybe just because he was in a rage."

"He'd have known how to deal with Havalow."

"So you think I'm right, I'm on to something?"

She thought about it. "Could be."

He grinned at her. "Isn't it fun being a detective?"

"Fun?" she said incredulously.

"Well, I meant 'interesting.' "

"We're either representing a man who killed four people, or we're representing a man who's been targeted by a brutal murderer, and that strikes you as fun?"

"Not as much fun as sex, but more fun than bowling."

"Bobby, sometimes you make me nuts. But I love you."

He took her hand. "If we're going to pursue the investigation, I'm damned well going to enjoy it as much as I can. But I'll drop the case in a minute if you want."

"Why? Because of your dream? Because of the Bad Thing?" She shook her head. "No. We start letting a weird dream spook us, pretty soon *anything* will spook us. We'll lose our confidence, and you can't do this kind of work without confidence."

Even in the dim backsplash from the dashboard lights, she could see the anxiety in his eyes.

Finally he said, "Yeah, that's what I knew you'd say. So let's get to the bottom of it as fast as we can. According to his other driver's license, he's James Roman, and he lives in El Toro."

"It's almost eight-thirty."

"We can be there, find the house . . . maybe forty-five minutes. That's not too late."

"All right."

Instead of putting the car in gear, he slid his seat back and stripped out of his down-lined, nylon jacket. "Unlock the glovebox and give me my gun. From now on I'm wearing it everywhere."

Each of them had a license to carry a concealed weapon. Julie struggled out of her own jacket, then retrieved two shoulder holsters from under her seat. She took both revolvers out of the glovebox: two snub-nosed Smith & Wesson .38 Chief's Specials, reliable and compact guns that could be carried inconspicuously beneath ordinary clothing with little or no help from a tailor.

THE HOUSE WAS gone. If anyone named James Roman had lived there, he had new lodgings now. A bare concrete slab lay in the middle of the lot, surrounded by grass, shrubbery, and several trees, as if the structure had been snared from above by intergalactic moving men and neatly spirited away.

Bobby parked in the driveway, and they got out of the Toyota to have a closer look at the property. Even in the slashing rain, a nearby street-lamp cast enough light to reveal that the lawn was trampled, gouged by tires, and bare in spots; it was also littered with splinters of wood, pale bits of Sheetrock, crumbled stucco, and a few fragments of glass that sparkled darkly.

The strongest clue to the fate of the house was to be found in the condition of the shrubbery and trees. Those bushes closest to the slab were all either dead or badly damaged, and on closer inspection appeared to be scorched. The nearest tree was leafless, and its stark black limbs lent an anachronistic feeling of Halloween to the drizzly January night.

"Fire," Julie said. "Then they tore down what was left."

"Let's talk to a neighbor."

The empty lot was flanked by houses. But lights glowed only at the house on the north side.

The man who answered the doorbell was about fifty-five, six feet two, solidly built, with gray hair and a neatly trimmed gray mustache. His name was Park Hampstead, and he had the air of a retired military man. He invited them in, with the proviso that they leave their sodden shoes on the front porch. In their socks, they followed him to a breakfast nook off the kitchen, where the yellow vinyl dinette upholstery was safe from their damp clothing; even so, Hampstead made them wait while he draped thick peach-colored beach towels over two of the chairs.

"Sorry," he said, "but I'm something of a fussbudget."

The house had bleached-oak floors and modern furniture, and Bobby noticed that it was spotless in every corner.

"Thirty years in the Marine Corps left me with an abiding respect for routine, order, and neatness," Hampstead explained. "In fact, when Sharon died three years ago—she was my wife—I think maybe I got a little crazy about neatness. The first six or eight months after her funeral, I cleaned the place top to bottom at least twice a week, because as long as I was cleaning, my heart didn't hurt so bad. Spent a fortune on Windex, paper towels, Fantastik, and sweeper bags. Let me tell you, no military pension can support the Endust habit I developed! I got over that stage. I'm still a fussbudget but not *obsessed* with neatness."

He had just brewed a fresh pot of coffee, so he poured for them as well. The cups, saucers, and spoons were all spotless. Hampstead provided each of them with two crisply folded paper napkins, then sat across the table from them.

"Sure," he said, after they raised the issue, "I knew Jim Roman. Good neighbor. He was a chopper jockey out of the El Toro Air Base. That was my last station before retirement. Jim was a hell of a nice guy, the kind who'd give you the shirt off his back, then ask if you needed money to buy a matching tie."

"Was?" Julie asked.

"He die in the fire?" Bobby asked, remembering the scorched shrubbery and soot-blackened concrete slab next door.

Hampstead frowned. "No. He died about six months after Sharon. Make it . . . two and a half years ago. His chopper crashed on maneuvers. He was only forty-one, eleven years younger than me. Left a wife, Maralee. A fourteen-year-old daughter named Valerie. Twelve-year-old son, Mike. Real nice kids. Terrible thing. They were a close family, and Jim's accident devastated them. They had some relatives back in Nebraska, but no one they could really turn to." Hampstead stared past Bobby, at the softly humming refrigerator, and his eyes swam out of focus. "So I tried to step in, help out, advise Maralee on finances, give a shoulder to lean on and an ear to listen when the kids needed that. Took 'em to Disneyland and Knott's from time to time, you know, that sort of thing. Maralee told me lots of times what a godsend I was, but it was really me who needed them more than the other way around, because doing things for them was what finally began to take my mind off losing Sharon."

Julie said, "So the fire happened more recently?"

Hampstead did not respond. He got up, went to the sink, opened the cupboard door below, returned with a spray bottle of Windex and a dish towel, and began to wipe the refrigerator door, which already appeared to be as clean as the antiseptic surfaces in a hospital surgery. "Valerie and Mike were terrific kids. After a year or so it almost got to seem like they were *my* kids, the ones me and Sharon never had. Maralee grieved for Jim a long time, almost two years, before she began to remember she was a woman in her prime. Maybe what started to happen between her and me would've upset Jim, but I don't think so; I think he'd have been happy for us, even if I was eleven years older than her."

When he finished wiping the refrigerator, Hampstead inspected the door from the side, at an angle to the light, apparently searching for a fingerprint or smudge. As if he had just heard the question that Julie had asked a minute ago, he suddenly said, "The fire was two months ago. I woke up in the middle of the night, heard sirens, saw an orange glow at the window, got up, looked out. . . ."

He turned away from the refrigerator, studied the kitchen for a moment, then went to the nearest tile-topped counter and began to spritz and wipe that gleaming surface.

Julie looked at Bobby. He shook his head. Neither of them said anything.

After a moment Hampstead continued: "Got over to their house just ahead of the firemen. Went in through the front door. Made it into the foyer, then to the foot of the steps, but couldn't get up to the bedroom, the heat was too intense, and the smoke. I called their names, nobody answered. If I'd heard an answer maybe I would've found the strength to go up there somehow in spite of the flames. I guess I must've blacked out for a few seconds and been carried out by firemen, 'cause I woke up on the front lawn, coughing, choking, a paramedic bent over me, giving me oxygen."

"All three of them died?" Bobby asked.

"Yeah," Hampstead said.

"What caused the fire?"

"I'm not sure they ever figured that out. I might've heard something about a short in the wiring, but I'm not sure. I think they even suspected arson for a while, but that never led anywhere. Doesn't much matter, does it?"

"Why not?"

"Whatever caused it, they're all three dead."

"I'm sorry," Bobby said softly.

"Their lot's been sold. Construction starts on a new house sometime this spring. More coffee?"

"No, thank you," Julie said.

Hampstead surveyed the kitchen, then moved to the stainless-steel range hood, which he began to clean in spite of the fact that it was spotless. "I apologize for the mess. Don't know how the place gets like this when it's just me living here. Sometimes I think there must be gremlins sneaking behind my back, messing things up to torment me."

"No need for gremlins," Julie said. "Life itself gives us all the torment we can handle."

Hampstead turned away from the range hood. For the first time since he had gotten up from the table and begun his cleaning ritual, he made eye contact with them. "No gremlins," he agreed. "Nothing as simple and easy to handle as gremlins." He was a big man and obviously tough from years of military training and discipline, but the shimmering, watery evidence of grief brimmed in his eyes, and at the moment he seemed as lost and helpless as a child.

IN THE CAR again, staring through the rain-spattered windshield at the vacant lot where the Roman house had once stood, Bobby said, "Frank finds out that Mr. Blue Light knows about the Farris ID, so he gets new ID in the name of James Roman. But Mr. Blue eventually learns about that, too, and he goes looking for Frank at the Roman address, where he discovers only the widow and the kids. He kills them, same way he killed the Farris family, but this time he sets fire to the house to cover the crime. Is that the way it looks to you?"

"Could be," Julie said.

"He burns the bodies because he bites them, like the Phans told us, and the bite marks help the police tie his crimes together, so he wants to throw the cops off the trail."

Julie said, "Then why doesn't he burn them every time?"

"Because that would be just as much of a giveaway as the bite marks. Sometimes he burns the bodies, sometimes he doesn't, and maybe sometimes he disposes of them so they're never even found."

They were both silent for a moment. Then she said, "So we're dealing with a mass murderer, a serial killer, who's evidently a raving psychotic."

"Or a vampire," Bobby said.

"Why's he after Frank?"

"I don't know. Maybe Frank once tried to drive a wooden stake through his heart."

"Not funny."

"I agree," Bobby said. "Right now, nothing seems funny."

35

FROM DYSON MANFRED'S HOUSE FULL OF INSECT SPECIMENS IN Irvine, Clint Karaghiosis drove through the chilly rain to his own house in Placentia. It was a homey two-bedroom bungalow with a rolled-shingle roof, a deep front porch in the California Craftsman style, and French windows full of warm amber light. By the time he got there, the car heater had pretty much dried his rain-soaked clothes.

Felina was in the kitchen when Clint entered by way of the connecting door from the garage. She hugged him, kissed him, held fast to him for a moment, as if surprised to see him alive again.

She believed that his job was fraught with danger every day, though he had often explained that he did mostly boring legwork. He chased facts instead of culprits, pursued a trail of paper rather than blood.

He understood his wife's concern, however, because he worried unreasonably about her too. For one thing, she was an attractive woman with black hair, an olive complexion, and startlingly beautiful gray eyes; in this age of lenient judges, with a surfeit of merciless sociopaths on the streets, a good-looking woman was regarded by some as fair game. Furthermore, though the office where Felina worked as a data processor was only three blocks from their house, an easy walk even in bad weather, Clint nevertheless worried about the danger she faced at the busiest of the intersections that she had to cross; in an emergency, a warning cry or blaring horn would not alert her to onrushing death.

He could not let her know how much he worried, for she was justly proud that she was so independent in spite of her deafness. He did not want to diminish her self-respect by indicating in any way that he was not entirely confident of her ability to deal with every rotten tomato that fate threw at her. So he daily reminded himself that she had lived twenty-nine years without coming to serious harm, and he resisted the urge to be overly protective.

While Clint washed his hands at the sink, Felina set the kitchen table for a late dinner. An enormous pot of homemade vegetable soup was heating on the stove, and together they ladled out two large bowls of it. He got a shaker of Parmesan cheese from the refrigerator, and she unwrapped a loaf of crusty Italian bread.

He was hungry, and the soup was excellent—thick with vegetables and chunks of lean beef—but by the time Felina had finished her first bowlful, Clint had eaten less than half of his, because he repeatedly paused to talk to her. She could not read his lips well when he tried to converse and eat at the same time, and for the moment his hunger was less compelling than his need to tell her about his day. She refilled her bowl and refreshed his.

Beyond the walls of his own small home, he was only slightly more talkative than a stone, but in Felina's company he was as loquacious as a talk-show host. He didn't just prattle, either, but settled with surprising ease into the role of a polished raconteur. He had learned how to deliver an anecdote in such a way as to sharpen its impact and maximize Felina's response, for he loved to elicit a laugh from her or watch her eyes widen with surprise. In all of Clint's life, she was the first person whose opinion of him truly mattered, and he wanted her to think of him as smart, clever, witty, and fun.

Early in their relationship he had wondered if her deafness had anything to do with his ability to open up to her. Deaf since birth, she had never heard the spoken word and therefore had not learned to speak clearly. She responded to Clint—and would later tell him about her own day—by way of sign language, which he had studied in order to understand her nimble-fingered speech. Initially he had thought that the main encouragement to intimacy was her disability, which ensured that his innermost feelings and secrets, once revealed to her, would go no further; a conversation with Felina was nearly as private as a conversation with himself. In time, however, he finally understood that he opened up to her in spite of her deafness, not because of it, and that he wanted her to share his every thought and experience—and to share hers in return—simply because he loved her.

When he told Felina how Bobby and Julie had adjourned to the bathroom for three private chats during Frank Pollard's appointment, she laughed delightedly. He loved that sound; it was so warm and singularly melodious, as if the great joy in life that she could not express in spoken words was entirely channeled into her laughter.

"They're some pair, the Dakotas," he said. "When you first meet them, they seem so dissimilar in some ways, you figure they can't possibly work well together. But then you get to know them, you see how they fit like two pieces of a puzzle, and you realize they've got a nearly perfect relationship."

Felina put down her soup spoon and signed: *So do we.*

"We sure do."

We fit better than puzzle pieces. We fit like a plug and socket.

"We sure do," he agreed, smiling. Then he picked up on the sly sexual connotation of what she'd said, and he laughed. "You're a filthy-minded wench, aren't you?"

She grinned and nodded.

"Plug and socket, huh?"

Big plug, tight socket, good fit.

"Later on, I'll check your wiring."

I am in desperate need of a first-rate electrician. But tell me more about this new client.

Thunder cracked and clattered across the night outside, and a sudden gust of wind rattled the rain against the window. The sounds of the storm made the warm and aromatic kitchen even more inviting by comparison. Clint sighed with contentment, then was touched by a brief sadness when he realized that the deeply satisfying sense of shelter, induced by the sounds of thunder and rain, was a specific pleasure that Felina could never experience or share with him.

From his pants pocket he withdrew one of the red gems that Frank Pollard had brought to the office. "I borrowed this one 'cause I wanted you to see it. The guy had a jarful of them."

She pinched the grape-sized stone between thumb and index finger and held it up to the light. *Beautiful*, she signed with her free hand. She put the gem beside her soup bowl, on the cream-white Formica surface of the kitchen table. *Is it very valuable?*

"We don't know yet," he said. "We'll get an opinion from a gemologist tomorrow."

I think it's valuable. When you take it back to the office, make sure there's no hole in your pocket. I have a hunch you'd have to work a long time to pay for it if you lost it.

The stone took in the kitchen light, bounced it from prism to prism, and cast it back with a bright tint, painting Felina's face with luminous crimson spots and smears. She seemed to be spattered with blood.

A queer foreboding overtook Clint.

She signed, *What're you frowning about?*

He didn't know what to say. His uneasiness was out of proportion to the cause of it. A cold prickling swiftly progressed from the base of his spine all the way to the back of his neck, as if dominoes of ice were falling in a row. He reached out and moved the gem a few inches, so the blood-red reflections fell on the wall beside Felina instead of on her face.

36

BY ONE-THIRTY IN THE MORNING, HAL YAMATAKA WAS THOR-oughly hooked by the John D. MacDonald novel, *The Last One Left*. The room's only chair wasn't the most comfortable seat he'd ever parked his butt in, and the antiseptic smell of the hospital always made him a bit queasy, and the chile rellenos he'd eaten for dinner were still coming back on him, but the book was so involving that eventually he forgot all of those minor discomforts.

He even forgot Frank Pollard for a while, until he heard a brief hiss, like air escaping under pressure, and felt a sudden draft. He looked away from the book, expecting to see Pollard sitting up in the bed or trying to get out of it, but Pollard was not there.

Startled, Hal sprang up, dropping the book.

The bed was empty. Pollard had been there all night, asleep for the last hour, but now he was gone. The place was not brightly lighted because the fluorescents behind the bed were turned off, but the shadows beyond the reading lamp were too shallow to conceal a man. The sheets were not tossed aside but were draped neatly across the mattress, and both of the side railings were locked in place, as if Frank Pollard had evaporated like a figure carved from Dry Ice.

Hal was certain that he would have heard Pollard lower one of the railings, get out of bed, then lift the railing into place again. Surely he would have heard Pollard climbing *over* it too.

The window was closed. Rain washed down the glass, glimmering with silvery reflections of the room's light. They were on the sixth floor, and Pollard could not escape by the window, yet Hal checked it, noting that it was not merely closed but locked.

Stepping to the door of the adjoining bathroom, he said, "Frank?" When no one answered, he entered. The bath was deserted.

Only the narrow closet remained as a viable hiding place. Hal opened it and found two hangers that held the clothes Pollard had been wearing when he'd checked into the hospital. The man's shoes were there, too, with his socks neatly rolled and tucked into them.

"He can't have gotten past me and into the hall," Hal said, as if giving voice to that contention would magically make it true.

He pulled open the heavy door and rushed into the corridor. No one was in sight in either direction.

He turned to the left, hurried to the emergency exit at the end of the hall, and opened the door. Standing on the sixth-floor landing, he listened for footsteps rising or descending, heard none, peered over the iron railing, down into the well, then up. He was alone.

Retracing his steps, he returned to Pollard's room and glanced inside at the empty bed. Still disbelieving, he proceeded to the junction of corridors, where he turned right and went to the glass-walled nurses' station.

None of the five night-shift nurses had seen Pollard on the move. Since the elevators were directly opposite the nurses' station, where Pollard would have had to wait in full view of the people on duty, it seemed unlikely that he had left the hospital by that route.

"I thought you were watching over him," said Grace Fulgham, the gray-haired supervisor of the sixth-floor night staff. Her solid build, indomitable manner, and life-worn but kind face would have made her perfect for the female lead if Hollywood ever started remaking the old Tugboat Annie or Ma and Pa Kettle movies. "Wasn't that your job?"

"I never left the room, but—"

"Then how did he get past you?"

"I don't know," Hal said, chagrined. "But the important thing is . . . he's suffering from partial amnesia, somewhat confused. He might wander off anywhere, out of the hospital, God knows where. I can't figure how he got past me, but we have to find him."

Mrs. Fulgham and a younger nurse named Janet Soto began a swift and quiet inspection of all the rooms along Pollard's corridor.

Hal accompanied Nurse Fulgham. As they were checking out 604, where two elderly men snored softly, he heard eerie music, barely audible. As he turned, seeking the source, the notes faded away.

If Nurse Fulgham heard the music, she did not remark on it. A moment later in the next room, 606, when those strains arose once more, marginally louder than before, she whispered, "What *is* that?"

To Hal it sounded like a flute. The unseen flautist produced no discernible melody, but the flow of notes was haunting nonetheless.

They reentered the hall as the music stopped again, and just as a draft swept along the corridor.

"Someone's left a window open—or probably a stairway door," the nurse said quietly but pointedly.

"Not me," Hal assured her.

Janet Soto stepped out of the room across the hall just as the blustery draft abruptly died. She frowned at them, shrugged, then headed toward the next room on her side.

The flute warbled softly. The draft struck up again, stronger than before, and beneath the astringent odors of the hospital, Hal thought he detected a faint scent of smoke.

Leaving Grace Fulgham to her search, Hal hurried toward the far end of the corridor. He intended to check the door at the head of the emergency stairs, to make sure that he hadn't left it open.

From the corner of his eye, he saw the door to Pollard's room beginning to swing shut, and he realized that the draft must be coming from in there. He pushed through the door before it could close, and saw Frank sitting up in bed, looking confused and frightened.

The draft and flute had given way to stillness, silence.

"Where did you go?" Hal asked, approaching the bed.

"Fireflies," Pollard said, apparently dazed. His hair was spiked and tangled, and his round face was pale.

"Fireflies?"

"Fireflies in a windstorm," Pollard said.

Then he vanished. One second he was sitting in bed, as real and solid as anyone Hal had ever known, and the next second he was gone as inexplicably and neatly as a ghost abandoning a haunt. A brief hiss, like air escaping from a punctured tire, accompanied his departure.

Hal swayed as if he had been stricken. For a moment his heart seemed to seize up, and he was paralyzed by surprise.

Nurse Fulgham stepped into the doorway. "No sign of him in any of the rooms off this corridor. He might've gone up or down another floor—don't you think?"

"Uh. . . ."

"Before we check out the rest of this level, maybe I'd better call security and get them moving on a search of the entire hospital. Mr. Yamataka?"

Hal glanced at her, then back at the empty bed. "Uh . . . yeah. Yeah, that's a good idea. He might wander off to . . . God knows where."

Nurse Fulgham hurried away.

Weak-kneed, Hal went to the door, closed it, put his back against it, and stared at the bed across the room. After a while he said, "Are you there, Frank?"

He received no answer. He had not expected one. Frank Pollard had not turned invisible; he had *gone* somewhere, somehow.

Not sure why he was less wonderstruck than frightened by what he had seen, Hal hesitantly crossed the room to the bed. He gingerly touched the stainless-steel railing, as if he thought that Pollard's vanishing act had tapped some elemental force, leaving a deadly residual current in the bed. But no sparks crackled under his fingertips; the metal was cool and smooth.

He waited, wondering how soon Pollard would reappear, wondering if he ought to call Bobby now or wait until Pollard materialized, wondering if the man *would* materialize again or disappear forever. For the first time in memory, Hal Yamataka was gripped by indecision; he was ordinarily a quick thinker, and quick to act, but he had never come face to face with the supernatural before.

The only thing he knew for sure was that he must not let Fulgham or Soto or anyone else in the hospital know what had really happened. Pollard was caught up in a phenomenon so strange that word of it would spread quickly from the hospital staff to the press. Protecting a client's privacy was always one of Dakota & Dakota's prime objectives, but in this case it was even more important than usual. Bobby and Julie had said that someone was hunting for Pollard, evidently with violent intentions; therefore, keeping the press out of the case might be essential if the client was to survive.

The door opened, and Hal jumped as if he'd been stuck with a hatpin.

In the doorway stood Grace Fulgham, looking as if she had just either guided a tugboat through stormy seas or chopped and carried a couple of cords of firewood that Pa had been too lazy to deal with. "Security's putting a man at every exit to stop him if he tries to leave, and we're mobilizing the nursing staff on each floor to look for him. Do you intend to join the search?"

"Uh, well, I've got to call the office, my boss. . . ."

"If we find him, where will we find you?"

"Here. Right here. I'll be here, making some calls."

She nodded and went away. The door eased shut after her.

A privacy curtain hung from a ceiling track that described an arc around three sides of the bed. It was bunched against the wall, but Hal Yamataka drew it to the foot of the bed, blocking the view from the doorway, in case Pollard materialized just as someone stepped in from the corridor.

His hands were shaking, so he jammed them in his pockets. Then he took his left hand out to look at his wristwatch: 1:48.

Pollard had been missing for perhaps eighteen minutes—except, of course, for the few seconds during which he had flickered into existence and talked about fireflies in a windstorm. Hal decided to wait until two o'clock to call Bobby and Julie.

He stood at the foot of the bed, clutching the railing with one hand, listening to the night wind crying at the window and the rain snapping against the glass. The minutes crawled past like snails on an incline, but at least the wait gave him time to calm down and think about how he would tell Bobby what had happened.

As the hands on his watch lined up at two o'clock, he went the rest of the way around the bed and was reaching for the phone on the nightstand when he heard the eerie ululation of a distant flute. The half-drawn bed-curtain fluttered in a sudden draft.

He returned to the foot of the bed and looked past the end of the curtain to the hallway door. It was closed. That was not the source of the draft.

The flute died. The air in the room grew still, leaden.

Abruptly the curtain shivered and rippled, gently rattling the bearings in the overhead track, and a breath of cool air swept around the room, ruffling his hair. The atonal, ghostly music rose again.

With the door shut and the window closed tight, the only possible source of the draft was the ventilation grille in the wall above the night-stand. But when Hal stood on his toes and raised his right hand in front of that outlet, he felt nothing issuing from it. The chilly currents of air appeared to have sprung up within the room itself.

He turned in a circle, moved this way and that, trying to get a fix on the flute. Actually, it didn't sound like a flute when he listened closely; it was more like a fluctuant wind whistling through a lot of pipes at the same time, big ones and little ones, threading together many vague but separate sounds into a loosely woven keening that was simultaneously eerie and melancholy, mournful yet somehow . . . threatening. It faded, then returned a third time. To his surprise and bewilderment, the tuneless notes seemed to be issuing from the empty air above the bed.

Hal wondered if anyone else in the hospital could hear the flute this time. Probably not. Though the music was louder now than when it had begun, it remained faint; in fact, if he had been asleep, the mysterious serenade would not have been loud enough to wake him.

Before Hal's eyes, the air over the bed shimmered. For a moment he could not breathe, as if the room had become a temporary vacuum chamber. He felt his ears pop the way they did during a too-rapid altitude change.

The strange warbling and the draft died together, and Frank Pollard reappeared as abruptly as he had vanished. He was lying on his side, with his knees drawn up in the fetal position. For a few seconds he was disoriented; when he realized where he was, he clutched the bed railing and pulled himself into a sitting position. The skin around his eyes was puffy and dark, but otherwise he was dreadfully pale. His face had a greasy sheen to it, as if it wasn't perspiration pouring from him but clear beads of oil. His blue cotton pajamas were rumpled, darkly mottled with sweat, and caked with dirt in places.

He said, "Stop me."

"What the hell's going on here?" Hal asked, his voice cracking.

"Out of control."

"Where did you go?"

"For God's sake, help me." Pollard was still clutching the bed rail with his right hand, but he reached entreatingly toward Hal with his left. "Please, please . . ."

Stepping closer to the bed, Hal reached out—

—and Pollard vanished, this time not only with a hissing sound, as before, but with a shriek and sharp crack of tortured metal. The stainless-steel railing, which he had been gripping so fiercely, had torn loose of the bed and vanished with him.

Hal Yamataka stared in astonishment at the hinges to which the adjustable railing had been fixed. They were twisted and torn, as if made of cardboard. A force of incredible power had pulled Pollard out of that room, snapping quarter-inch steel.

Staring at his own outstretched hand, Hal wondered what would have happened to him if he had been gripping Pollard. Would he have disappeared with the man? To where? Not someplace he would want to be: he was sure of that.

Or maybe only part of him would have gone with Pollard. Maybe he would have come apart at a joint, just as the bed railing had done. Maybe his arm would have ripped out of his shoulder socket with a crack almost as sharp as that with which the steel hinges had separated, and maybe he would have been left screaming in pain, with blood squirting from snapped vessels.

He snatched his hand back, as if afraid Pollard might suddenly reappear and seize it.

As he rounded the bed to the phone, he thought that his legs were going to fail him. His hands were shaking so badly, he almost dropped the receiver and had difficulty dialing the Dakotas' home number.

37

BOBBY AND JULIE LEFT FOR THE HOSPITAL AT 2:45. THE NIGHT looked deeper than usual; streetlamps and headlights did not fully penetrate the gloom. Shatters of rain fell with such force, they appeared to bounce off the blacktop streets, as if they were hard fragments of a disintegrating vault that arced through the night above.

Julie drove because Bobby was only three-quarters awake. His eyes were heavy, and he couldn't stop yawning, and his thoughts were fuzzy at the edges. They had gone to bed only three hours before Hal Yamataka had awakened them. If Julie had to get by on only that much sleep, she could do it, but Bobby needed at least six—preferably eight—hours in the sack in order to function well.

That was a minor difference between them, no big deal. But because of several such minor differences, Bobby suspected that Julie was tougher overall than he was, even if he could whip her ten times out of ten in an arm-wrestling competition.

He chuckled softly.

She said, "What?"

She braked for a traffic light as it phased to red. Its bloody image was reflected in distorted patterns by the black, mirrorlike surface of the rain-slick street.

"I'm crazy to give you an advantage by admitting this, but I was thinking that in some ways you're tougher than me."

She said, "That's no revelation. I've always known I'm tougher."

"Oh, yeah? If we arm wrestle, I'll whip you every time."

"How sad." She shook her head. "Do you really think beating up someone smaller than you, and a woman to boot, makes you a macho man?"

"I could beat up a lot of women *bigger* than me," Bobby assured her. "And if they're old enough, I could take them on two or three or four at a time. In fact, you throw half a dozen big grandmothers at me, and I'll take them all on with one hand tied behind my back!"

The traffic light turned green, and she drove on.

"I'm talking *big* grandmothers," he said. "Not frail little old ladies. Big, fat, solid grandmothers, six at a time."

"That is impressive."

"Damn right. Though it'd help if I had a tire iron."

She laughed, and he grinned. But they could not forget where they were going or why, and their smiles faded to a pair of matching frowns. They drove in silence. The thump of the windshield wipers, which ought to have lulled Bobby to sleep, kept him awake instead.

Finally Julie said, "You think Frank actually vanished in front of Hal's eyes, the way he says?"

"I've never known Hal to lie or give in to hysteria."

"Me neither."

She turned left at the next corner. A few blocks ahead, beyond billowing curtains of rain, the lights of the hospital appeared to pulse and flicker and stream like an iridescent liquid, which made it look every bit as miragelike as a phantom oasis shimmering behind veils of heat rising from desert sands.

WHEN THEY ENTERED the room, Hal was standing at the foot of the bed, which was largely concealed by the privacy curtain. He looked like a guy who had not only seen a ghost, but had embraced it and kissed it on its cold, damp, putrescent lips.

"Thank God, you're here." He looked past them, into the hall. "The head nurse wants to call the cops, file a missing person—"

"We've dealt with that," Bobby said. "Dr. Freeborn talked to her by phone, and we've signed a release absolving the hospital."

"Good." Gesturing toward the open door, Hal said, "We'll want to keep this as private as we can."

After closing the door, Julie joined them at the foot of the bed.

Bobby noted the missing railing and broken hinges. "What's this?"

Hal swallowed hard. "He was holding the railing when he vanished . . . and it went with him. I didn't mention it on the phone, 'cause I figured you already thought I was nuts, and this would confirm it."

"Tell us now," Julie said quietly. They were all talking softly, for otherwise Nurse Fulgham was certain to stop by and remind them that most of the patients on the floor were sleeping.

When Hal finished his story, Bobby said, "The flute, the peculiar breeze

. . . that's what Frank told us *he* heard shortly after he regained consciousness that night in the alleyway, and somehow he knew it meant someone
was coming."

Some of the dirt that Hal had observed on Frank's pajamas, after his
second reappearance, was on the bed sheets. Julie plucked up a pinch
of it. "Not dirt exactly."

Bobby examined the grains on her fingertips. "Black sand."

To Hal, Julie said, "Frank hasn't reappeared since he vanished with the
railing?"

"No."

"And when was that?"

"A couple of minutes after two o'clock. Maybe two-oh-two, two-oh-
three, something like that."

"About an hour and twenty minutes ago," Bobby said.

They stood in silence, staring at the mountings from which the bed
railing had been torn. Outside, a squall of wind threw rain against the
window with sufficient force to make it sound like out-of-season Halloween pranksters pitching handsful of dried corn.

Finally Bobby looked at Julie. "What do we do now?"

She blinked. "Don't ask me. This is the first case I've ever worked on
that involves witchcraft."

"Witchcraft?" Hal said nervously.

"Just a figure of speech," Julie assured him.

Maybe, Bobby thought. He said, "We've got to assume he'll come back
before morning, perhaps a couple of times, and sooner or later he'll stay
put. This must be what happens every night when he sleeps; this is the
traveling he doesn't remember when he wakes up."

"Traveling," Julie said. Under the circumstances, that ordinary word
seemed as exotic and full of mystery as any in the language.

CAREFUL NOT TO wake the patients, they borrowed two additional chairs
from other rooms along the corridor. Hal sat tensely just inside the closed
door of room 638, in a position to prevent any of the hospital staff from
walking in unimpeded. Julie sat at the foot of the bed, and Bobby stationed himself at the side of it nearest the window, where the railing was
still in place.

They waited.

From her chair, Julie only had to turn her head slightly to look across the room at Hal. When she glanced the other way she could see Bobby. But because of the privacy curtain that was drawn along the side of the bed with the missing railing, Hal and Bobby were not in each other's line of sight.

She wondered if Hal would have been astonished to see how quickly Bobby went to sleep. Hal was still pumped up by what had happened, and Julie, only having heard about Frank's sorcerous disappearance second-hand, was nonetheless eagerly—and nervously—anticipating the chance to witness the same bit of magic herself. Bobby was a man of considerable imaginative powers, with a childlike sense of wonder, so he was probably more excited about these events than either she or Hal was; furthermore, because of his premonition of trouble, he suspected that the case was going to be full of surprises, some nasty, and these events no doubt alarmed him. Yet he could slump against the inadequately padded arm of his chair, let his chin drop against his chest, and doze off. He would never be felled by stress. At times his sense of proportion, his ability to put *anything* in a manageable perspective, seemed superhuman. When Bobby McFerrin's song "Don't Worry, Be Happy" had been a hit a couple of years ago, she had not been surprised that her own Bobby had been enamoured of it; the tune was essentially his personal anthem. Apparently by an act of will, he could readily achieve serenity, and she admired that.

By 4:40, when Bobby had been slumbering contentedly for nearly an hour, she watched him doze with admiration that rapidly escalated to unhealthy envy. She had the urge to give his chair a kick, toppling him out of it. She restrained herself only because she suspected that he would merely yawn, curl up on his side, and sleep even more comfortably on the floor, at which point her envy would become so all-consuming that she would simply have to kill him where he lay. She imagined herself in court: *I know murder is wrong, Judge, but he was just too laid-back to live.*

A cascade of soft, almost melancholy notes fell out of the air in front of her.

"The flute!" Hal said, leaving his chair with the suddenness of a popcorn kernel bursting off a heated pan.

Simultaneously, a breath of cool air stirred through the room, without apparent source.

Getting to her feet, Julie whispered, "Bobby!"

She shook him by the shoulder, and he came awake just as the atonal music faded and the air turned crypt-still.

Bobby rubbed his eyes with his palms, and yawned. "What's wrong?"

Even as he spoke, the haunting music swelled again, faint but louder than before. Not music, actually, just noise. And Hal was right: listening closely, you could also tell it was not a flute.

She stepped toward the bed.

Hal had left his station by the door. He put a hand on her shoulder, halting her. "Be careful."

Frank had reported three—maybe four—separate trillings of the faux flute, and as many agitations of the air, before Mr. Blue Light had appeared on his trail that night in Anaheim, and Hal had noticed that three episodes had preceded each of Frank's own reappearances. However, those accompanying phenomena evidently could not be expected in an immutable pattern, for when the second rivulet of unharmonious notes finished spilling out of the ether, the air immediately above the bed shimmered, as if a double handful of pale tarnished sequins had been swept up and set aflutter in rising currents of heat, and suddenly Frank Pollard winked into existence atop the rumpled sheets.

Julie's ears popped.

"Holy cow!" Bobby said, which was just what Julie would have expected him to say.

She, on the other hand, was unable to speak.

Gasping, Frank Pollard sat up in bed. His face was bloodless. Around his rheumy eyes, the skin looked bruised. Sour perspiration glistened on his face and beaded in his beard stubble.

He was holding a pillowcase half filled with something. The end was twisted and held shut with a length of cord. He let go of it, and it fell off the side of the bed where the railing was missing, striking the floor with a soft *plop*.

When he spoke, his voice was hoarse and strange. "Where am I?"

"You're in the hospital, Frank," Bobby said. "It's all right. You're where you belong now."

"Hospital . . . ," Frank said, savoring the word as if he had just heard it—and was now pronouncing it—for the first time. He looked around, obviously bewildered; he still didn't know where he was. "Don't let me slip—"

He vanished midsentence. A brief hiss accompanied his abrupt departure, as if the air in the room was escaping through a puncture in the skin of reality.

"Damn!" Julie said.

"Where were his pajamas?" Hal said.

"What?"

"He was wearing shoes, khaki pants, a shirt and sweater," Hal said, "but the last time I saw him, a couple of hours ago, he still had on his pajamas."

At the far end of the room, the door began to open but bumped against Hal's empty chair. Nurse Fulgham poked her head through the gap. She looked down at the chair, then across the room at Hal and Julie, then at Bobby, who stepped to the foot of the bed to peer past his two associates and the half-drawn privacy curtain.

Their astonishment at Frank's vanishing act must have been ill concealed, for the woman frowned and said, "What's wrong?"

Julie quickly crossed the room as Grace Fulgham slid the chair aside and opened the door all the way. "Everything's fine. We just spoke by phone with our man heading up the search, and he says they've found someone who saw Mr. Pollard earlier tonight. We know which way he was heading, so now it's only a matter of time until we find him."

"We didn't expect you'd be here so long," Fulgham said, frowning past Julie at the curtained bed.

Even through the heavy door, maybe she had heard the faint warble of the flute that wasn't a flute.

"Well," Julie said, "this is the easiest place from which to coordinate the search."

By standing just inside the door, with Hal's empty chair between them, Julie was trying to block the nurse's advance without appearing to do so. If Fulgham got past the curtain, she might notice the missing railing, the black sand in the bed, and the pillowcase that was filled with God-knew-what. Questions about any of those things might be difficult to answer convincingly, and if the nurse remained in the room too long, she might be there when Frank returned.

Julie said, "I'm sure we haven't disturbed any of the other patients. We've been very quiet."

"No, no," Nurse Fulgham said, "you haven't disturbed anyone. We just wondered if you might like some coffee to help keep you awake."

"Oh." Julie turned to look at Hal and Bobby. "Coffee?"

"No," the two men said simultaneously. Then, speaking over each other, Hal said, "No, thank you," and Bobby said, "Very kind of you."

"I'm wide awake," Julie said, frantic to be rid of the woman, but trying to sound casual, "and Hal doesn't drink coffee, and Bobby, my husband, can't handle caffeine because of prostate problems." I'm babbling, she thought. "Anyway, we'll be leaving soon now, I'm sure."

"Well," the nurse said, "if you change your mind. . . ."

After Fulgham left, letting the door close behind her, Bobby whispered, "Prostate trouble?"

Julie said, "Too much caffeine causes prostate trouble. Seemed like a convincing detail to explain why, with all your yawning, you didn't want coffee."

"But I don't have a prostate problem. Makes me sound like an old fart."

"I have it," Hal said. "And I'm not an old fart."

"What is this?" Julie said. "We're *all* babbling."

She pushed the chair in front of the door and returned to the bed, where she picked up the pillowcase-bag that Frank Pollard had brought from . . . from wherever he had been.

"Careful," Bobby said. "Last time Frank mentioned a pillowcase, it was the one he trapped that insect in."

Julie gingerly set the bag on a chair and watched it closely. "Doesn't seem to be anything squirming around in it." She started to untie the knotted cord from the neck of the sack.

Grimacing, Bobby said, "If you let out something big as a house cat, with a lot of legs and feelers, I'm going straight to a divorce lawyer."

The cord slipped free. She pulled open the pillowcase, and looked inside. "Oh, God."

Bobby took a couple of steps backward.

"No, not that," she assured him. "No bugs. Just more cash." She reached into the sack and withdrew a couple of bundles of hundred-dollar bills. "If it's all hundreds, there could be as much as a quarter of a million in here."

"What's Frank doing?" Bobby wondered. "Laundering money for the mob in the Twilight Zone?"

Hollow, lonely, tuneless piping pierced the air again, and like a needle pulling thread, the sound brought with it a draft that rustled the curtain.

Shivering, Julie turned to look at the bed.

The flutelike notes faded with the draft, then soon rose again, faded, rose, and faded a fourth time as Frank Pollard reappeared. He was on his side, arms against his chest, hands fisted, grimacing, his eyes squeezed shut, as if he were preparing himself to receive the killing blow of an ax.

Julie stepped toward the bed, and again Hal stopped her.

Frank sucked in a deep breath, shuddered, made a low anguished mewling, opened his eyes—and vanished. Within two or three seconds, he appeared yet again, still shuddering. But immediately he vanished, reappeared, vanished, reappeared, vanished, as if he were an image flickering on a television set with poor signal reception. At last he stuck fast to the fabric of reality and lay on the bed, moaning.

After rolling off his side, onto his back, he gazed at the ceiling. He raised his fists from his chest, uncurled them, and stared at his hands, baffled, as if he had never seen fingers before.

"Frank?" Julie said.

He did not respond to her. With his fingertips he explored the contours of his face, as if a Braille reading of his features would recall to him the forgotten specifics of his appearance.

Julie's heart was racing, and every muscle in her body felt as if it had been twisted up as tight as an overwound clock spring. She was not afraid, really. It was not a tension engendered by fear but by the sheer *strangeness* of what had happened. "Frank, are you okay?"

Blinking through the interstices of his fingers, he said, "Oh. It's you, Mrs. Dakota. Yeah . . . Dakota. What's happened? Where am I?"

"You're in the hospital now," Bobby said. "Listen, the important question isn't where you are, but where the hell have you *been?*"

"Been? Well . . . what do you mean?"

Frank tried to sit up in bed, but he seemed temporarily to lack the strength to get off his back.

Picking up the bed controls, Bobby elevated the upper half of the mattress. "You weren't in this room during most of the last few hours. It's almost five in the morning, and you've been jumping in and out of here like . . . like . . . like a crew member of the Starship *Enterprise* who keeps beaming back up to the mothership!"

"*Enterprise?* Beaming up? What're you talking about?"

Bobby looked at Julie. "Whoever this guy is, wherever he comes from, we now know for sure that he's been living out past the edge of modern culture, on the fringe. You ever known a modern American who hasn't at least *heard* of *Star Trek?*"

To Bobby, Julie said, "Thanks for your analysis, Mr. Spock."

"Mr. Spock?" Frank said.

"See!" Bobby said.

"We can question Frank later," Julie said. "He's confused right now, anyway. We've got to get him out of here. If that nurse comes back and sees him, how do we explain his reappearance? Is she really going to believe he wandered back *into* the hospital, past security and the nursing staff, up six floors, with nobody spotting him?"

"Yeah," Hal said, "and though he seems to be back for good, what if he pops away again, in front of her eyes?"

"Okay, so we'll get him out of bed and sneak him down those stairs at the end of the hall," Julie said, "out to the car."

As they talked about him, Frank turned his head back and forth, following the conversation. He appeared to be watching a tennis match for the first time, unable to comprehend the rules of the game.

Bobby said, "Once we've gotten him out of here, we can tell Fulgham he's been found just a few blocks away and that we're meeting with him to determine whether he wants—or even needs—to be returned to the hospital. He's our client, after all, not our ward, and we have to respect his wishes."

Without having to wait for tests to be conducted, they now knew that Frank was not suffering strictly from physical ailments like cerebral abscesses, clots, aneurysms, cysts, or neoplasms. His amnesia did not spring from brain tumors, but from something far stranger and more exotic than that. No malignancy, regardless of how singular its nature, would invest its victim with the power to step into the fourth dimension—or to wherever Frank was stepping when he vanished.

"Hal," Julie said, "get Frank's other clothes from the closet, bundle them up, and stuff them in the pillowcase with the money."

"Will do."

"Bobby, help me get Frank out of bed, see if he can stand on his own feet. He looks awful weak."

The remaining bed railing stuck for a moment when Bobby tried to lower it, but he struggled with it because they could not take Frank out of bed on the other side without drawing back the privacy curtain and exposing him to anyone who might push open the door.

"You could've done me a big favor and packed this rail off to Oz with the other one," Bobby told Frank, and Frank said, "Oz?"

When the railing finally folded down, out of the way, Julie found that she was hesitant to touch Frank, for fear of what might happen to her—or parts of her—if he pulled another disappearing act. She had seen the shattered hinges of the bed railing; she was also keenly aware that Frank had not brought the railing back with him, but had abandoned it in the otherwhere or otherwhen to which he traveled.

Bobby hesitated, too, but overcame his apprehension, grabbing the man's legs and swinging them over the edge of the bed, taking hold of his arm and helping him into a sitting position. In some ways she might be tougher than Bobby, but when it came to encounters with the unknown, he was clearly more flexible and quick to adapt than she was.

Finally she quelled her fear, and together she and Bobby assisted Frank off the bed and onto his feet. His legs buckled under him, and they had to support him. He complained of weakness and dizziness.

Stuffing the other set of clothes in the pillowcase, Hal said, "If we have to, Bobby and I can carry him."

"I'm sorry to be so much trouble," Frank said.

To Julie, he had never sounded or looked more pathetic, and she felt a flush of guilt about her reluctance to touch him.

Flanking Frank, their arms around him to provide support, Julie and Bobby walked him back and forth, past the rain-washed window, giving him a chance to recover the use of his legs. Gradually his strength and balance returned.

"But my pants keep trying to fall down," Frank said.

They propped him against the bed, and he leaned on Julie while Bobby lifted the blue cotton sweater to see if the belt needed to be cinched in one notch. The tongue end of the belt was weakened by scores of small holes, as if industrious insects had been boring at it. But what insects ate leather? When Bobby touched the tarnished brass buckle, it crumbled as though made of flaky pastry dough.

Gaping at the glittering crumbs of metal on his fingers, Bobby said, "Where do you shop for clothes, Frank? In a dumpster?"

In spite of Bobby's light tone, Julie knew he was unnerved. What substance or circumstances could so profoundly alter the composition of brass? When he brushed his fingers against the bed sheets to wipe off the curious residue, she flinched, half expecting his flesh to have been contaminated by the contact with the brass, and to crumble as the buckle had done.

AFTER CINCHING FRANK'S pants with the belt that he had worn when he'd checked into the hospital, Hal helped Bobby slip their client out of the room. With Julie scouting the way, they went quickly and quietly along the hall and through the fire door at the head of the emergency stairs. Frank's skin remained cold to the touch, and he was still clammy with perspiration; but the effort brought a flush to his cheeks, which made him look less like a walking corpse.

Julie hurried to the bottom of the stairwell to see what lay beyond the lower door. With the thump and scrape of their footsteps echoing hollowly off the bare concrete walls, the three men went down four flights without much difficulty. At the fourth-floor landing, however, they had to pause to let Frank catch his breath.

"Are you always this weak when you wake up and don't remember where you've been?" Bobby asked.

Frank shook his head. His words issued in a thin wheeze: "No. Always frightened . . . tired, but not as bad . . . as this. I feel like . . . whatever I'm doing . . . wherever I'm going . . . it's taking a bigger and bigger toll. I'm not . . . not going to survive . . . a lot more of this."

As Frank was talking, Bobby noticed something peculiar about the man's blue cotton sweater. The pattern of the cable knit was wildly irregular in places, as if the knitting machine had briefly gone berserk. And on the back, near his right shoulderblade, a patch of fibers was missing; the hole was the size of a block of four postage stamps, though with irregular rather than straight edges. But it wasn't just a hole. A piece of what appeared to be khaki filled the gap, not merely sewn on but woven tightly into the surrounding cotton yarn, as if at the garment factory itself. Khaki of the same shade and hard finish as the pants that Frank was wearing.

A shiver of dread pierced Bobby, although he was not sure why. His subconscious mind seemed to understand how the patch had come to be and what it meant, and grasped some hideous consequence not yet fulfilled, while his conscious mind was baffled.

He saw that Hal, on the other side of Frank, had noticed the patch, too, and was frowning.

Julie ascended the stairs while Bobby was staring in puzzlement at the khaki swatch. "We're in luck," she said. "There're two doors at the bottom. One leads into a hallway off the lobby, where we'd probably run into a security man, even though they aren't looking for Frank any more. But the other door leads into the parking garage, the same level our car's on. How you doing, Frank? You going to be okay?"

"Getting my . . . second wind," he said less wheezily than before.

"Look at this," Bobby said, calling Julie's attention to the khaki woven into the blue cotton sweater.

While Julie studied the peculiar patch, Bobby let go of Frank and, on a hunch, stooped down to examine the legs of his client's pants. He found a corresponding irregularity: blue cotton yarn from the sweater was woven into the slacks. It was not one spot of the same size and shape as that in the sweater, but a series of three smaller holes near the cuff on the right leg; however, he was sure that more accurate measurements would confirm what he knew from a quick look—that the total amount of blue yarn in those three holes would just about fill the hole in the shoulder of the sweater.

"What's wrong?" Frank asked.

Bobby didn't respond but took hold of the somewhat baggy leg of the pants and pulled it taut, so he could get a better look at the three patches. Actually, "patches" was an inaccurate word because these abnormalities in the fabric did not look like repairs; they were too well blended with the material around them to be handwork.

Julie squatted beside him and said, "First, we've got to get Frank out of here, back to the office."

"Yeah, but this is real strange," Bobby said, indicating the irregularities in the pants. "Strange and . . . important somehow."

"What's wrong?" Frank repeated.

"Where'd you get these clothes?" Bobby asked him.

"Well . . . I don't know."

Julie pointed to the white athletic sock on Frank's right foot, and Bobby saw at once what had caught her attention: several blue threads, precisely the color of the sweater. They were not loose, clinging to the sock. They were woven into the very fabric of it.

Then he noticed Frank's left shoe. It was a dark brown hiking shoe, but a few thin, squiggly white lines marred the leather on the toe. When he studied them closely, he saw that the lines appeared to be coarse threads like those in the athletic socks; scraping at them with one fingernail, he discovered they were not stuck to the shoe, but were an integral part of the surface of the leather.

The missing yarn of the sweater had somehow become a part of both the khaki pants and one of the socks; the displaced threads of the sock had become part of the shoe on the other foot.

"What's wrong?" Frank repeated, more fearfully than before.

Bobby hesitated to look up, expecting to see that the filaments of displaced shoe leather were embedded in Frank's face, and that the displaced flesh was magically entwined with the cable knit of the sweater. He stood and forced himself to confront his client.

Aside from the dark and puffy rings around his eyes, the sickly pallor relieved only by the flush on his upper cheeks, and the fear and confusion that gave him a tormented look, nothing was wrong with his face. No leather ornamentation. No khaki stitched into his lips. No filaments of blue yarn or plastic shoelace tips or button fragments bristling from his eyeballs.

Silently castigating himself for his overactive imagination, Bobby patted Frank's shoulder. "It's okay. It's all right. We'll figure it out later. Come on, let's get you out of here."

38

IN THE EMBRACE OF DARKNESS, ENWRAPPED BY THE SCENT OF Chanel No. 5, under the very blankets and sheets that had once warmed his mother and that he had so carefully preserved, Candy dozed and awakened repeatedly with a start, though he could not remember any nightmares.

Between periods of fitful sleep, he dwelt on the incident in the canyon, earlier that night, when he had been hunting and had felt an unseen presence put a hand on his head. He'd never before experienced anything like that. He was disturbed by the encounter, unsure whether it was threatening or benign, and anxious to understand it.

He first wondered if it had been his mother's angelic presence, hovering above him. But he quickly dismissed that explanation. If his mother had stepped through the veil between this world and the next, he would have recognized her spirit, her singular aura of love, warmth, and compassion. He would have fallen to his knees under the weight of her ghostly hand and wept with joy at her visitation.

Briefly he had considered that one or both of his inscrutable sisters possessed a heretofore unrevealed talent for psychic contact and reached out to him for unknown reasons. After all, somehow they controlled their cats and appeared to have equal influence over other small animals. Maybe they could enter human minds as well. He didn't want that pale, cold-eyed pair invading his privacy. At times he looked at them and thought of snakes—sinuous albino snakes, silent and watchful—with desires as alien as any that motivated reptiles. The possibility that they could intrude into his mind was chilling, even if they could not control him.

But between bouts of sleep, he abandoned that idea. If Violet and Verbina possessed such abilities, they would have enslaved him long ago, as thoroughly as they had enslaved the cats. They would have forced him to do degrading, obscene things; they did not possess his self-control in matters of the flesh and would live, if they could, in constant violation of God's most fundamental commandments.

He could not understand why his mother had sworn him to keep and protect them, any more than he could understand how she could love them. Of course her compassion for those miscreant offspring was only one more example of her saintly nature. Forgiveness and understanding flowed from her like clear, cool water from an artesian well.

For a while he dozed. When he woke with a start again, he turned on his side and watched the faint light of dawn appear along the edges of the drawn blinds.

He considered the possibility that the presence in the canyon had been his brother Frank. But that was also unlikely. If Frank had possessed telepathic abilities, he would have found a way to employ them to destroy Candy a long, long time ago. Frank was less talented than his sisters and much less talented than his brother Candy.

Then who had approached him twice in the canyon, insistently pressing into his mind? Who sent the disconnected words that echoed in his head: *What . . . where . . . what . . . why . . . what . . . where . . . what . . . why . . . ?*

Last night, he'd tried to get a mental grip on the presence. When it hastily withdrew from him, he had tried to let part of his consciousness soar up into the night with it, but he had been unable to sustain a pursuit on that psychic plane. He sensed, however, that he might be able to develop that ability.

If the unwelcome presence ever returned, he would try to knot a filament of his mind to it and trace it to its source. In his twenty-nine years, his own siblings were the only people he had encountered with what might be called psychic abilities. If someone out there in the world was also gifted, he must learn who it was. Such a person, not born of his sainted mother, was a rival, a threat, an enemy.

Though the sun beyond the blinded windows had not fully risen, he knew that he would not be able to doze again. He threw back the covers, crossed the dark and furniture-crowded room with the assurance of a blind man in a familiar place, and went into the adjoining bath. After locking the door, he undressed without glancing in the mirror. He peed forcefully without looking down at his hateful organ. When he showered, he soaped and rinsed the sex thing only with the washcloth mitten that he'd made and that protected his innocent hand from being corrupted by the monstrous, wicked flesh below.

39

FROM THE HOSPITAL IN ORANGE, THEY WENT DIRECTLY TO THEIR offices in Newport Beach. They had a lot of work to do on Frank's behalf, and his worsening plight evoked in them a greater sense of urgency than ever. Frank rode with Hal, and Julie followed in order to be able to offer assistance if unforeseen developments occurred during the trip. The entire case seemed to be a *series* of unforeseen developments.

By the time they reached their deserted offices—the Dakota & Dakota staff would not arrive for a couple of hours yet—the sun was fully risen behind the clouds in the east. A thin strip of blue sky, like a crack under the door of the storm, was visible over the ocean to the west. As the four of them passed through the reception lounge into their inner sanctum, the rain halted abruptly, as if a godly hand had turned a celestial lever;

the water on the big windows stopped flowing in shimmering sheets, and coalesced into hundreds of small beads that glimmered with a mercury-gray sheen in the cloud-dulled morning light.

Bobby indicated the bulging pillowcase that Hal was carrying. "Take Frank into the bathroom, help him change into the clothes he was wearing when we checked him into the hospital. Then we'll have a real close look at the clothes he's wearing now."

Frank had recovered his balance and most of his strength. He did not need Hal's assistance. But Julie knew Bobby wouldn't let Frank go anywhere unchaperoned from now on. They needed to keep an eye on him constantly, in order not to miss any clues that might lead to an explanation of his sudden vanishments and reappearances.

Before attending to Frank, Hal removed the rumpled clothes from the pillowcase. He left the rest of its contents on Julie's desk.

"Coffee?" Bobby asked.

"Desperately," Julie said.

He went out to the pantry that opened off the lounge, to start up one of their two Mr. Coffee machines.

Sitting at her desk, Julie emptied the pillowcase. It contained thirty bundles of hundred-dollar bills in packs bound by rubber bands. She fanned the edges of the bills in ten bundles to ascertain if lower denominations were included; they were all hundreds. She chose two packets at random and counted them. Each contained one hundred bills. Ten thousand in each. By the time Bobby returned with mugs, spoons, cream, sugar, and a pot of hot coffee, all on a tray, Julie had concluded that this was the largest of Frank's three hauls to date.

"Three hundred K," she said, as Bobby put the tray on her desk.

He whistled softly. "What's that bring the total to?"

"With this, we'll be holding six hundred thousand for him."

"Soon have to get a bigger office safe."

HAL YAMATAKA PUT Frank's other set of clothes on the coffee table. "Something's wrong with the zipper in the pants. I don't mean just that it doesn't work, which it doesn't. I mean, something's very *wrong* with it."

Hal, Frank, and Julie pulled up chairs around the low glass-topped table, and drank strong black coffee while Bobby sat on the couch and carefully inspected the garments. In addition to the oddities he had noticed at the hospital, he discovered that most of the teeth in the pants zipper were metal, as they should have been, while about forty others, interspersed at random, appeared to be hard black rubber; in fact, the slide was jammed on a couple of the rubber ones.

Bobby stared in puzzlement at the anomalous zipper, slowly moving a finger up and down one of the notched tracks, until he was suddenly struck by inspiration. He picked up one of the shoes Frank had been wearing and examined the heel. It looked perfectly normal, but in the heel of the second shoe, thirty or forty tiny, brass-bright bits of metal were embedded in the rubber, flush with the surface of it.

"Anybody have a penknife?" Bobby asked.

Hal withdrew one from his pocket. Bobby used it to pry loose a couple of the shiny rectangles, which appeared to have been set in the rubber when it was still molten. Zipper teeth. They fell onto the glass table: *tink . . . tink.* At a glance he estimated that the amount of rubber displaced by those teeth was equal to what he had found in the zipper.

SITTING IN THE Dakotas' Disney-embellished office, Frank Pollard was overwhelmed by a weariness that was cartoonish in its extremity, the degree of utter exhaustion sufficient to render Donald Duck so limp that he might slip off a chair and pour onto the floor in a puddle of mallard flesh and feathers. It had been seeping into him day by day, hour by hour, since he had awakened in that alleyway last week; but now it suddenly poured through him as if a dike had broken. This surging flood of weariness had a density not of water but of liquid lead, and he felt enormously heavy; he could lift a foot or move a limb only with effort, and even keeping his head up was a strain on his neck. Virtually every joint in his body ached dully, even his elbow and wrist and finger joints, but especially his knees, hips, and shoulders. He felt feverish, not acutely ill, but as if his strength had been steadily sapped by a low-grade viral infection from which he had been suffering his entire life. Weariness had not dulled his senses; on the contrary, it abraded his nerve endings as surely as a fine-grade sandpaper might have done. Loud sounds made him cringe, bright light made him squint in pain, and he was exquisitely sensitive to heat and cold and the textures of everything he touched.

His exhaustion seemed only in part a result of his inability to sleep more than a couple of hours a night. If Hal Yamataka and the Dakotas could be believed—and Frank saw no reason for them to lie to him—he performed an incredible vanishing act several times during the night, though upon returning to his bed and staying put there, he could recall nothing of what he had done. Whatever the cause of those disappearances, no matter where he had gone or how or why, the very act of vanishing seemed likely to require an expenditure of energy as surely as walking or running or lifting heavy weights or any other physical act; therefore, perhaps his weakness and profound weariness were largely the result of his mysterious night journeys.

Bobby Dakota had pried only a couple of the brass teeth from the heel of the shoe. After studying them for a moment, he put down the penknife, leaned back against the sofa, and looked thoughtfully at the gloomy but rainless sky beyond the office's big windows. They were all silent, waiting to hear what he deduced from the condition of those clothes and shoes.

Even exhausted, preoccupied with his own fears, and after only a one-day association with the Dakotas, Frank realized that Bobby was the more imaginative and mentally nimble of the two. Julie was probably smarter than her husband; but she was also a more methodical thinker than he was, far less likely than he was to make sudden leaps of logic to arrive at insightful deductions and imaginative solutions. Julie would more often be right than Bobby was, but on those occasions when the firm resolved a client's problems *quickly*, the resolution would usually be attributable to Bobby. They made a good pair, and Frank was relying on their complementary natures to save him.

Turning to Frank again, Bobby said, "What if, somehow, you can teleport yourself, send yourself from here to there in a wink?"

"But that's . . . magic," Frank said. "I don't believe in magic."

"Oh, I do," Bobby said. "Not witches and spells and genies in bottles, but I believe in the possibility of fantastic things. The very fact that the world exists, that we're alive, that we can laugh and sing and feel the sun on our skin . . . that seems like a kind of magic to me."

"Teleport myself? If I can. I don't *know* I can. Evidently I have to fall asleep first. Which means teleportation must be a function of my subconscious mind, essentially involuntary."

"You weren't asleep when you reappeared in the hospital room or any of the other times you vanished," Hal said. "Maybe the first time, but not later. Your eyes were open. You spoke to me."

"But I don't remember it," Frank said frustratedly. "I only remember going to sleep, then suddenly I was lying awake in bed, in a lot of distress, confused, and you were all there."

Julie sighed. "Teleportation. How can that be possible?"

"You saw it." Bobby shrugged. He picked up his coffee and took a sip, more relaxed than anyone in the room, as though having a client with an astonishing psychic power was, if not an ordinary occurrence, at least a situation that all of them should have realized was simply inevitable, given enough years in the private security business.

"I saw him disappear," Julie agreed, "but I'm not sure that proves he . . . teleported."

"When he disappeared," Bobby said, "he went *somewhere*. Right?"

"Well . . . yes."

"And going from one place to another, instantaneously, as an act of sheer willpower . . . as far as I'm concerned, that's teleportation."

"But how?" Julie asked.

Bobby shrugged again. "Right now, it doesn't matter how. Just accept the assumption of teleportation as a place to start."

"As a theory," Hal said.

"Okay," Julie agreed. "Theoretically, let's assume Frank can teleport himself."

To Frank, who was sealed off from his own experience by amnesia, that was like assuming iron was lighter than air in order to allow an argument for the possibility of steel-plated blimps. But he was willing to go along with it.

Bobby said, "Good, all right, then that assumption explains the condition of these clothes."

"How?" Frank asked.

"It'll take a while to get to the clothes. Stay with me. First, consider that maybe teleporting yourself requires that the atoms of your body temporarily disassociate themselves from one another, then come together again an instant later at another place. Same thing goes for the clothes you're wearing and for anything on which you've got a firm grip, like the bed railing."

"Like the teleportation pod in that movie," Hal said. *"The Fly."*

"Yeah," Bobby said, clearly getting excited now. He put down his coffee and slid forward on the edge of the sofa, gesticulating as he spoke. "Sort of like that. Except the power to do this is maybe all in Frank's mind, not in a futuristic machine. He just sort of *thinks* himself somewhere else, disassembles himself in a fraction of a second—*poof!*—and reassembles himself at his destination. Of course, I'm also assuming the mind remains intact even during the time the body is dispersed in disconnected atoms, because it would have to be the sheer power of the mind that transports those billions of particles and keeps them together like a shepherd collie herding sheep, then welds them to one another again in the right configurations at the far end."

Though his weariness was sufficient to have resulted from an impossibly complex and strenuous task like the one Bobby had just described, Frank was unconvinced. "Well, gee, I don't know. . . . This isn't something you go to school to learn. UCLA doesn't have a course in teleportation. So it's . . . instinct? Even supposing I instinctively know how to break my body down into a stream of atomic particles and send it somewhere else, then put it together again . . . how can any human mind, even the greatest genius ever born, be powerful enough to keep track of those billions of particles and get them all back exactly as they belong? It'd take a hundred geniuses, a thousand, and I'm not even *one*. I'm no dummy, but I'm no brighter than the average guy."

"You've answered your own question," Bobby said. "You don't need superhuman intelligence for this, 'cause teleportation isn't primarily a function of intelligence. It's not instinct, either. It's just . . . well, an ability programmed into your genes, like vision or hearing or the sense of smell. Think of it this way: Any scene you look at is composed of billions of separate points of color and light and shade and texture, yet your eyes instantly order those billions of bits of input into a coherent scene. You don't have to *think* about seeing. You just see, it's automatic. You understand what I meant about magic? Vision is almost magical. With teleportation, there's probably a trigger mechanism you have to pull—like *wishing* yourself to be elsewhere—but thereafter the process is pretty much automatic; the mind makes it happen the way it makes instantaneous sense of all the data coming in through your eyes."

Frank closed his eyes tight and concentrated on wishing himself into the reception lounge. When he opened his eyes and was still in the inner office, he said, "It doesn't work. It's not that easy. I can't do it at will."

Hal said, "Bobby, are you saying all of us have this ability, and only Frank has figured out how to use it?"

"No, no. This is probably a scrap of genetic material unique to Frank, maybe even a talent that sprang from genetic *damage*."

They were all silent, absorbing what Bobby had conjectured.

Outside, the layer of clouds was cracking, peeling, and the old blue paint of the sky was showing through in more places every minute. But the brightening day did not lift Frank's spirits.

Finally Hal Yamataka indicated the pile of garments on the coffee table. "How does all this explain the condition of those clothes?"

Bobby picked up the blue cotton sweater and held it so they could see the khaki swatch on the back. "Okay, let's suppose the mind can automatically shepherd all the molecules of its own body through the teleportation process without a single error. It can also deal with other things Frank wants to take with him, like his clothes—"

"And bags full of money," Julie said.

"But why the bed railing?" Hal asked. "No reason for him to want to take that with him."

To Frank, Bobby said, "You can't remember it now, but you clearly knew what was happening while you were caught up in that series of teleportations. You were trying to stop, you asked Hal to help you stop, and you seized the railing to stop yourself, to anchor yourself to the hospital room. You were *concentrating* on your grip on that railing, so when you went, you took it with you. As for the clothes getting scrambled the way they are . . . Maybe your mind concentrates first on getting your body back together in the proper order because error-free physical re-creation is crucial to your survival, but then sometimes you might not have the energy left to do as good a job on secondary things like clothes."

"Well," Frank said, "I can't remember prior to last week, but this is the first time anything like this has happened since then, even though I've apparently been . . . traveling more nights than not. Then again, even if my clothes have come through okay, *I* seem to be getting more weary, weaker, and more confused day by day. . . ."

He did not have to finish the thought, because the worry in their eyes and faces made clear their understanding. If he was teleporting, and if it was a strenuous act that bled him of strength that could not be restored by rest, he was gradually going to get less meticulous about the reconstitution of his clothes and whatever other items he tried to carry with him. But more important—he might begin to have difficulty reconstituting his body, as well. He might return from one of his late-night rambles and find fragments of his sweater woven into the back of his hand, and the skin replaced by that cotton might turn up as a pale patch in the dark leather of his shoe, and the displaced leather from the shoe might appear as an integral part of his tongue . . . or as strands of alien cells twisted through his brain tissue.

Fear, never far away and circling like a shark in the depths of Frank's mind, abruptly shot to the surface, called forth by the worry and pity that he saw in the faces of those on whom he was depending for salvation. He closed his eyes, but that was a rotten idea because he had a vision of his own face when he shut out theirs, his face as it might look after a disastrous reconstitution at the end of a future telekinetic journey: eight or ten misplaced teeth sprouting from his right eye socket; the evicted eye staring lidlessly from the middle of the cheek below; his nose smeared in hideous lumps of flesh and gristle across the side of his face. In the vision he opened his misshapen mouth, perhaps to scream, and within were two fingers and a portion of his hand, rooted where the tongue should have been.

He opened his eyes as a low cry of terror and misery escaped him.

He was shuddering. He couldn't stop.

HAVING FRESHENED EVERYONE'S coffee and, at Bobby's suggestion, having laced Frank's mug with bourbon in spite of the early hour, Hal went to the nook off the reception lounge to brew another pot.

After Frank had been fortified with a few sips of the spiked coffee, Julie showed the photograph to him and watched his reaction carefully. "You recognize either of the people in this?"

"No. They're strangers to me."

"The man," Bobby said, "is George Farris. The *real* George Farris. We got the picture from his brother-in-law."

Frank studied the photograph with renewed interest. "Maybe I knew him, and that's why I borrowed his name—but I can't recall ever seeing him before."

"He's dead," Julie said, and thought that Frank's surprise was genuine. She explained how Farris had died, years ago . . . and then how his family had been slaughtered far more recently. She told him about James Roman, too, and how Roman's family died in a fire in November.

With what appeared to be sincere dismay and confusion, Frank said, "Why all these deaths? Is it coincidence?"

Julie leaned forward. "We think Mr. Blue killed them."

"Who?"

"Mr. Blue Light. The man you said pursued you that night in Anaheim, the man you think is hunting you for some reason. We believe he discovered you were traveling under the names Farris and Roman, so he went to the addresses he got for them, and when he didn't find you there, he killed everyone, either while trying to squeeze information out of them or . . . just for the hell of it."

Frank looked stricken. His pale face grew even paler, as if it were an image doing a slow fade on a movie screen. The bleak look in his eyes intensified. "If I hadn't been using that fake ID, he never would've gone to those people. It's because of me they died."

Feeling sorry for the guy, ashamed of the suspicion that had driven her to approach the issue in this manner, Julie said, "Don't let it eat you, Frank. Most likely, the paper artist who forged your documents took the names at random from a list of recent deaths. If he'd used another approach, the Farris and Roman families would never have come to Mr. Blue's attention. But it's not your fault the forger used the quick and lazy method."

Frank shook his head, tried to speak, could not.

"You *can't* blame yourself," Hal said from the doorway, where he had evidently been standing long enough to have gotten the gist of the photo's importance. He seemed genuinely distressed to see Frank so anguished. Like Clint, Hal had been won over by Frank's gentle voice, self-effacing manner, and cherubic demeanor.

Frank cleared his throat, and finally the words broke loose: "No, no, it's on me, my God, all those people dead because of me."

IN DAKOTA & Dakota's computer center, Bobby and Frank sat in two spring-backed, typist chairs with rubber wheels, and Bobby switched on one of the three state-of-the-art IBM PCs, each of which was outlinked to the world through its own modem and phone line. Though bright enough to work by, the overhead lights were soft and diffuse to prevent glare on the terminal screens, and the room's one window was covered with blackout drapes for the same reason.

Like policemen in the silicon age, modern private detectives and security consultants relied on the computer to make their work easier and to compile a breadth and depth of information that could never be acquired by the old-fashioned gumshoe methods of Sam Spade and Philip Marlowe. Pounding the pavement, interviewing witnesses and potential suspects, and conducting surveillances were still aspects of their job, of course, but without the computer they would be as ineffective as a blacksmith trying to fix a flat tire with a hammer and anvil and other tools of his trade. As the twentieth century progressed through its last decade, private investigators who were ignorant of the microchip revolution existed only in television dramas and the curiously dated world of most PI novels.

Lee Chen, who had designed and now operated their electronic data-gathering system, would not arrive in the office until around nine o'clock. Bobby did not want to wait nearly an hour to start putting the computer to work on Frank's case. He was not a primo hacker, as Lee was, but he knew all the hardware, had the ability to learn new software quickly when he needed to, and was almost as comfortable tracking down information in cyberspace as he was poring through files of age-yellowed newspapers.

Using Lee's code book, which he removed from a locked desk drawer, Bobby first entered a Social Security Administration data network that contained files to which broad public access was legal. Other files in the same system were restricted and supposedly inaccessible behind walls of security codes required by various right-to-privacy laws.

From the open files, he inquired as to the number of men named Frank Pollard in the Administration's records, and within seconds the response appeared on the screen: counting variations of Frank, such as Franklin and Frankie and Franco—plus names like Francis, for which Frank might be a diminutive—there were six hundred and nine Frank Pollards in possession of Social Security numbers.

"Bobby," Frank said anxiously, "does that stuff on the screen make sense to you? Are those words, real words, or jumbled letters?"

"Huh? Of course they're words."

"Not to me. They don't look like anything to me. Gibberish."

Bobby picked up a copy of *Byte* magazine that was lying between two of the computers, opened it to an article, and said, "Read that."

Frank accepted the magazine, stared at it, flipped ahead a couple of pages, then a couple more. His hands began to shake. The magazine rattled in his grip. "I can't. Jesus, I've lost that too. Yesterday, I lost the ability to do math, and now I can't read any more, and I get more confused, foggy in the head, and I ache in every joint, every muscle. This teleporting's wearing me down, killing me. I'm falling apart, Bobby, mentally and physically, faster all the time."

"It's going to be all right," Bobby said, though his confidence was largely feigned. He was pretty sure they would get to the bottom of this, would learn who Frank was and where he went at night and how and why; however, he could see that Frank was declining fast, and he would not have bet money that they'd find all the answers while Frank was still alive, sane, and able to benefit from their discoveries. Nevertheless, he put his hand on Frank's shoulder and gave it a gentle reassuring squeeze. "Hang in there, buddy. Everything's going to be okay. I really think it is. I really do."

Frank took a deep breath and nodded.

Turning to the display terminal again, feeling guilty about the lie he'd just told, Bobby said, "You remember how old you are, Frank?"

"No."

"You look about thirty-two, thirty-three."

"I feel older."

Softly whistling Duke Ellington's "Satin Doll," Bobby thought a moment, then asked the SSA computer to eliminate those Frank Pollards younger than twenty-eight and older than thirty-eight. That left seventy-two of them.

"Frank, do you think you've ever lived anywhere else, or are you a died-in-the-wool Californian?"

"I don't know."

"Let's assume you're a son of the sunshine state."

He asked the SSA computer to whittle down the remaining Frank Pollards to those who applied for their Social Security numbers while living in California (fifteen), then to those whose current addresses on file were in California (six).

The public-access portion of the Social Security Administration's data network was forbidden by law to reveal Social Security numbers to casual researchers. Bobby referred to the instructions in Lee Chen's code book and entered the restricted files through a complicated series of maneuvers that circumvented SSA security.

He was unhappy about breaking the law, but it was a fact of high-tech life that you never got the maximum benefit from your data-gathering system if you played strictly by the rules. Computers were instruments of freedom, and governments were to one degree or another instruments of repression; the two could not always exist in harmony.

He obtained the six numbers and addresses for the Frank Pollards living in California.

"Now what?" Frank wondered.

"Now," Bobby said, "I use these numbers and addresses to cross reference with the California Department of Motor Vehicles, all of the armed forces, state police, major city police, and other government agencies to get descriptions of these six Frank Pollards. As we learn their height, weight, hair color, color of their eyes, race . . . we'll gradually eliminate them one by one. Better yet, if one of them is you, and if you've ever served in the military or been arrested for a crime, we might even be able to turn up a picture of you in one of those files and confirm your identity with a photo match."

SITTING AT THE desk, catercorner from each other, Julie and Hal removed the rubber bands from more than half of the packets of cash. They sorted through the hundred-dollar bills, trying to determine if some of them had consecutive serial numbers that might indicate they were stolen from a bank, savings and loan, or other institution.

Suddenly Hal looked up and said, "Why do those flutelike sounds and drafts precede Frank when he teleports himself?"

"Who knows?" Julie said. "Maybe it's displaced air following him down some tunnel in another dimension, from the place he left to the place he's going."

"I was just thinking. . . . If this Mr. Blue is real, and if he's searching for Frank, and if Frank heard those flutes and felt those gusts in that alleyway . . . then Mr. Blue is also able to teleport."

"Yeah. So?"

"So Frank's not unique. Whatever he is, there's another one like him. Maybe even more than one."

"Here's something else to think about," Julie said. "If Mr. Blue can teleport himself, and if he finds out where Frank is, we won't be able to defend a hiding place from him. He'll be able to pop up among us. And what if he arrived with a submachine gun, spraying bullets as he materialized?"

After a moment of silence, Hal said, "You know, gardening has always seemed like a pleasant profession. You need a lawnmower, a weed whacker, a few simple tools. There's not much overhead, and you hardly ever get shot at."

BOBBY FOLLOWED FRANK into the office, where Julie and Hal were examining the money. Putting a sheet of paper on the desk, he said, "Move over, Sherlock Holmes. The world now has a greater detective."

Julie angled the page so she and Hal could read it together. It was a laser-printed copy of the information that Frank had filed with the California Department of Motor Vehicles when he had last applied for an extension of his driver's license.

"The physical statistics match," she said. "Is your first name really Francis and your middle name Ezekiel?"

Frank nodded. "I didn't remember until I saw it. But it's me, all right. Ezekiel."

Tapping the printout, she said, "This address in El Encanto Heights—does it ring a bell?"

"No. I can't even tell you where El Encanto is."

"It's adjacent to Santa Barbara," Julie said.

"So Bobby tells me. But I don't remember being there. Except . . ."

"What?"

Frank went to the window and looked out toward the distant sea, above which the sky was now entirely blue. A few early gulls swooped in arcs so huge and smoothly described that their exuberance was thrilling to watch. Clearly, Frank was neither thrilled by the birds nor charmed by the view.

Finally, still facing the window, he said, "I don't recall being in El Encanto Heights . . . except that every time I hear the name, my stomach sort of sinks, you know, like I'm on a roller coaster that's just taken a plunge. And when I try to think about El Encanto, strain to remember it, my heart pounds, and my mouth goes dry, and it's a little harder to get my breath. So I think I must be repressing any memories I have of the place, maybe because something happened to me there, something bad . . . something I'm too scared to remember."

Bobby said, "His driver's license expired seven years ago, and according to the DMV's records, he never tried to renew it. In fact, sometime this year he'd have been weeded out of even their dead files, so we were lucky to find this before they expunged it." He laid two more printouts on the desk. "Move over, Holmes *and* Sam Spade."

"What're these?"

"Arrest reports. Frank was stopped for traffic violations, once in San Francisco a little more than six years ago. The second time was on Highway 101, north of Ventura, five years ago. He didn't have a valid driver's license either time and, because of odd behavior, was taken into custody."

The photographs that were a part of both arrest records showed a slightly younger, even pudgier man who was without a doubt their current client.

Bobby pushed aside some of the money and sat on the edge of her desk. "He escaped from jail both times, so they're looking for him even after all these years, though probably not too hard, since he wasn't arrested for a major crime."

Frank said, "I draw a blank on that too."

"Neither report indicates *how* he escaped," Bobby said, "but I suspect he didn't saw his way through the bars or dig a tunnel or whittle a gun out of a bar of soap or use any of the long-accepted, traditional methods of jailbreak. Oh, no, not our Frank."

"He teleported," Hal guessed. "Vanished when no one was looking."

"I'd bet on it," Bobby agreed. "And after that he began to carry false ID good enough to satisfy any cop who pulled him over."

Looking at the papers before her, Julie said, "Well, Frank, at least we know this is your real name, and we've nailed down a real address for you up there in Santa Barbara County, not just another motel room. We're beginning to make headway."

Bobby said, "Move over, Holmes, Spade, *and* Miss Marple."

Unable to embrace their optimism, Frank returned to the chair in which he'd been sitting earlier. "Headway. But not enough. And not fast enough." He leaned forward with his arms on his thighs, hands clasped between his spread knees, and stared morosely at the floor. "Something unpleasant just occurred to me. What if I'm not only making mistakes with my clothes when I reconstitute myself? What if I've *already* begun to make mistakes with my own biology too? Nothing major. Nothing visible. Hundreds or thousands of tiny mistakes on a cellular level. That would explain why I feel so lousy, so tired and sore. And if my brain tissue isn't coming back together right . . . that would explain why I'm confused, fuzzy-headed, unable to read or do math."

Julie looked at Hal, at Bobby, and knew that both men wanted to allay Frank's fear but were unable to do so because the scenario that he had outlined was not only possible but likely.

Frank said, "The brass buckle looked perfectly normal until Bobby touched it . . . then it turned to dust."

40

ALL NIGHT LONG, WHEN SLEEP MADE THOMAS'S HEAD EMPTY, UGLY dreams filled it up. Dreams of eating small live things. Dreams of drinking blood. Dreams of being the Bad Thing.

He finished sleeping all of a sudden, sitting up in bed, trying to scream but unable to find any sounds in himself. For a while he sat there, shaking, being afraid, breathing so hard and fast his chest ached.

The sun was back, and the night was gone away, and that made him feel better. Getting out of bed, he stepped into his slippers. His pajamas were cold with sweat. He shivered. He pulled on a robe. He went to the window, looked out and up, liking the blue sky very much. Leftover rain made the green lawn look soggy, the sidewalks darker than usual, and the dirt in the flowerbeds almost black, and in the puddles you could see the blue sky again like a face in a mirror. He liked all of that, too, because the whole world looked clean and new after all the rain emptied out of the sky.

He wondered if the Bad Thing was still far away, or closer, but he didn't reach out to it. Because last night it tried to hold him. Because it was so strong he almost couldn't get away from it. And because even when he *did* get away, it tried to follow him. He'd felt it hanging on, coming back across the night with him, and he'd shaken it off real quick like, but maybe next time he wouldn't be so lucky, and maybe it would come all the way, right into his room with him, not just its mind but the Bad Thing itself. He didn't understand how that could happen, but some- how he knew it might. And if the Bad Thing came to The Home, being awake would be like being asleep with a nightmare filling up your head. Terrible things would happen, and there would be no hope.

Turning away from the window, starting toward the closed door to the bathroom, Thomas glanced at Derek's bed and saw Derek dead. He was on his back. His face was bashed, bruised, swollen. His eyes were open big, you could see them shine in the light from the window and the low light from the lamp beside the bed. His mouth was open, too, like he was shouting, but all the sound was out of him like air out of a popped balloon, and he would not have any more sound in him ever again, you could tell. Blood was let out of him, too, lots of it, and a pair of scissors were stuck in his belly, deep in, with not much more than the handles showing, the same scissors Thomas used to clip pictures from magazines for his poems.

He felt a big twist of pain in his heart, like maybe somebody was sticking scissors in him too. But it wasn't hurt-pain so much as what he called "feel-pain," because it was losing Derek that he was feeling, not real hurt. It was as bad as real hurt, though, because Derek was his friend, he liked Derek. He was scared, too, because he somehow knew the Bad Thing had let the life out of Derek, the Bad Thing was here at The Home. Then he realized this could happen just the way things sometimes happened in TV stories, with the cops coming and believing that Thomas killed Derek, blaming Thomas, and everyone hating Thomas for what he'd done, but he hadn't done it, and all the while the Bad Thing was still loose to do more killing, maybe even doing to Julie what it'd done to Derek.

The hurt, the fear for himself, the fear for Julie—all of it was too much. Thomas gripped the footboard of his own bed and closed his eyes and tried to get air into himself. It wouldn't come. His chest was tight. Then the air came in, and so did an ugly-nasty smell, which in a while he realized was the stink of Derek's blood, so he gagged and almost puked.

He knew he had to Get Control of Himself. The aides didn't like it when you Lost Control of Yourself, so they Gave You Something For Your Own Good. He'd never Lost Control before and didn't want to lose it now.

He tried not to smell the blood. Took long deep breaths. Made himself open his eyes to look at the dead body. He figured looking at it the second time wouldn't be as bad as the first. He knew it was going to be there this time, so it wouldn't be such a big surprise.

The surprise was—the body was gone.

Thomas closed his eyes, put one hand to his face, looked again between spread fingers. The body still wasn't there.

He started shaking because what he thought, first, was that this was like some other TV stories he'd seen where nasty-dead bodies were walking around like live bodies, rotting and getting wormy, with bones showing in places, killing people for no reason and even sometimes eating them. He could never watch much of one of those stories. He sure didn't want to *be* in one.

He was so scared he almost TVed to Bobby—*Dead people, look out, look out, dead people hungry and mean and walking around*—but stopped himself when he saw there wasn't blood on Derek's blankets and sheets. The bed wasn't rumpled, either. Neatly made. No walking dead person was quick enough to get out of bed, change sheets and blankets, make everything right just in the few little seconds while Thomas's eyes were closed. Then he heard the shower pouring down on the floor of the stall in the bathroom, and he heard Derek singing soft the way he always did when he washed himself. For just a moment, in his head, Thomas had a picture of a dead person taking a shower, trying to be neat, but rotten chunks were falling off with the dirt, showing more bones, clogging the drain. Then he realized Derek was never really dead. Thomas hadn't really seen a body on the bed. What he'd seen was something else he'd learned from TV stories— he'd seen a vision. A sidekick vision. He was a sidekick.

Derek hadn't been killed. What Thomas saw, just for a moment, was Derek being dead tomorrow or some other day after tomorrow. It might be something that would happen no matter what Thomas did to stop it, or it might be something that would happen only if he let it happen, but at least it wasn't something that *already* happened.

He let go of the footboard and went to his worktable. His legs were shaky. He was glad to sit down. He opened the top drawer of the cabinet that stood beside the table. He saw his scissors in there, where they should be, with his colored pencils and pens and paper clips and Scotch tape and stapler—and a half-eaten Hershey's bar in an open wrapper, which *shouldn't* be in there because it would Draw Bugs. He took the candy out of the drawer and stuffed it in a pocket of his robe, reminding himself to put it in the refrigerator later.

For a while he stared at the scissors, listened to Derek sing in the shower, and thought how the scissors were jammed in Derek's belly, letting all the music and other sounds out of him forever, sending him to the Bad Place. Finally he touched the black plastic handles. They felt all right, so he touched the metal blades, but that was bad, real bad, as if leftover lightning from a storm was in the blades and jumped into him when he touched them. Sizzling, crackling white light flashed through him. He snatched his hand back. His fingers tingled. He closed the drawer and hurried back to bed and sat there with the covers pulled around his shoulders the way TV Indians wrapped themselves in blankets when they sat at TV campfires.

The shower stopped. So did the singing. After a while Derek came out of the bathroom, followed by a cloud of damp, soapy-smelling air. He was dressed for the day. His wet hair was combed back from his forehead.

He was not a rotting dead person. He was all alive, every part of him, at least every part you could see, and no bones poked out anywhere.

"Good morning," Derek said, the words slurred and muffled by his crooked mouth and too-big tongue. He smiled.

"Good morning."

"You sleep good?"

"Yeah," Thomas said.

"Breakfast soon."

"Yeah."

"Maybe sticky buns."

"Maybe."

"I like sticky buns."

"Derek?"

"Huh?"

"If I ever tell you . . ."

Derek waited, smiling.

Thomas thought out what he wanted to say, then continued: "If I ever tell you the Bad Thing's coming, and I tell you to run, don't just stand around like a dumb person. You just *run*."

Derek stared at him, thinking about it, still smiling, then after a while he said, "Sure, okay."

"Promise?"

"Promise. But what's a bad thing?"

"I don't know really, for sure, but I'll feel when it's coming, I think, and tell you, and you'll run."

"Where?"

"Anywhere. Down the hall. Find some aides, stay with them."

"Sure. You better wash. Breakfast soon. Maybe sticky buns."

Thomas unwrapped himself from the blanket and got out of bed. He stepped into his slippers again and walked to the bathroom.

Just as Thomas was opening the bathroom door, Derek said, "You mean at breakfast?"

Thomas turned. "Huh?"

"You mean a bad thing might come at breakfast?"

"Might," Thomas said.

"Could it be . . . poached eggs?"

"Huh?"

"The bad thing—could it be poached eggs? I don't like poached eggs, all slimy, yuck, that'd be real bad, not good at all like cereal and bananas and sticky buns."

"No, no," Thomas said. "The bad thing isn't poached eggs. It's a person, some funny-weird person. I'll feel when it's coming, and tell you, and you'll run."

"Oh. Yeah, sure. A person."

Thomas went into the bathroom, closed the door. He didn't have much beard. He had an electric razor, but he only used it a couple-few times a month, and today he didn't need it. He brushed his teeth, though. And he peed. He made the water start in the shower. Only then did he let himself laugh, because enough time had passed so Derek wouldn't even wonder if Thomas was laughing at him.

Poached eggs!

Though Thomas usually didn't like seeing himself, seeing how lumpy and wrong and dumb his face was, he peeked at the steam-streaked mirror. One time long ago, past when he could remember, he'd been laughing when he'd happened to see himself in a mirror, and for once—surprise!—he hadn't felt so bad about how he looked. When he laughed he looked more like a normal person. Just pretending to laugh didn't make him look more normal, it had to be real laughing, and smiling didn't do it, either, because a smile wasn't enough of a laugh to change his face. In fact, a smile could sometimes look so sad, he couldn't stand seeing himself at all.

Poached eggs.

Thomas shook his head, and when his laughter finished he turned from the mirror.

To Derek the most worst bad thing he could think of was poached eggs and no sticky buns, which was very funny ha-ha. You try to tell Derek about walking dead people and scissors sticking out of bellies and something that eats little live animals, and old Derek would look at you and smile and nod and not get it at all.

For as long as he could remember, Thomas had wished he was a normal person, not dumb, and many times he thanked God for at least making him not as dumb as poor Derek. But now he half wished he was dumber, so he could get those ugly-nasty vision-pictures out of his mind, so he could forget about Derek going to die and the Bad Thing coming and Julie being in danger, so he'd have nothing to worry about except poached eggs, which wouldn't be much of a worry at all, since he sort of *liked* poached eggs.

41

WHEN CLINT KARAGHIOSIS ARRIVED AT DAKOTA & DAKOTA shortly before nine o'clock, Bobby took him by the shoulder, turned him around, and went back to the elevators with him. "You drive, and I'll fill you in on what's happened during the night. I know you've got other cases to tend to, but the Pollard thing is getting hotter by the minute."

"Where're we going?"

"First, Palomar Labs. They called. Test results are ready."

Only a few clouds remained in the sky, and they were all far off toward the mountains, moving away like the billowing sails of great galleons on an eastward journey. It was a quintessential southern California day: blue, pleasantly warm, everything green and fresh, and rush-hour traffic so hideously snarled that it could transform an ordinary citizen into a foaming-at-the-mouth sociopath with a yearning to pull the trigger of a semiautomatic weapon.

Clint avoided freeways, but even surface streets were clogged. By the time Bobby recounted everything that had transpired since they had seen each other yesterday afternoon, they were still ten minutes from Palomar in spite of the questions occasioned by Clint's amazement—subdued like all of his reactions, but amazement nonetheless—over the discovery that Frank was evidently able to teleport himself.

Finally Bobby changed the subject because talking too much about psychic phenomena to a phlegmatic guy like Clint made him feel like an airhead, as if he had lost his grip on reality. While they inched along Bristol Avenue, he said, "I can remember when you could go anywhere in Orange County and *never* get caught in traffic."

"Not so long ago."

"I remember when you didn't have to sign a developer's waiting list to buy a house. Demand wasn't five times supply."

"Yeah."

"And I remember when orange groves were all over Orange County."

"Me too."

Bobby sighed. "Hell, listen to me, like an old geezer, babbling about the good old days. Pretty soon, I'll be talking about how nice it was when there were still dinosaurs around."

"Dreams," Clint said. "Everyone's got a dream, and the one more people have than any other is the California dream, so they never stop coming, even though so many have come now that the dream isn't really quite attainable any more, not the original dream that started it all. Of course, maybe a dream should be unattainable, or at least at the outer limits of your reach. If it's too easy, it's meaningless."

Bobby was surprised by the long burst of words from Clint, but more surprised to hear the man talking about something as intangible as dreams. "You're already a Californian, so what's your dream?"

After a brief hesitation, Clint said, "That Felina will be able to hear someday. There're so many medical advancements these days, new discoveries and treatments and techniques all the time."

As Clint turned left off Bristol, onto the side street where Palomar Laboratories stood, Bobby decided that was a good dream, a damned fine dream, maybe even better than his and Julie's dream about buying time and getting a chance to bring Thomas out of Cielo Vista and into a remade family.

They parked in the lot beside the huge concrete-block building in which Palomar Laboratories was housed. As they were walking toward the front door, Clint said, "Oh, by the way, the receptionist here thinks I'm gay, which is fine with me."

"What?"

Clint went inside without saying more, and Bobby followed him to the reception window. An attractive blonde sat at the counter.

"Hi, Lisa," Clint said.

"Hi!" She punctuated her response by cracking her chewing gum.

"Dakota and Dakota."

"I remember," she said. "Your stuff's ready. I'll get it."

She glanced at Bobby and smiled, and he smiled, too, though her expression seemed a little peculiar to him.

When she returned with two large, sealed manila envelopes—one labeled SAMPLES, the other ANALYSES—Clint handed the second one to Bobby. They stepped to one side of the lounge, away from the counter.

Bobby tore open the envelope and skimmed the documents inside. "Cat's blood."

"You serious?"

"Yeah. When Frank woke up in that motel, he was covered with cat's blood."

"I knew he was no killer."

Bobby said, "The cat may have an opinion about that."

"The other stuff is?"

"Well . . . bunch of technical terms here . . . but what it comes down to is that it's what it looks like. Black sand."

Stepping back to the reception counter, Clint said, "Lisa, you remember we talked about a black-sand beach in Hawaii?"

"Kaimu," she said. "It's a dynamite place."

"Yeah, Kaimu. Is it the only one?"

"Black-sand beach, you mean? No. There's Punaluu, which is a real sweet place too. Those are on the big island. I guess there must be more on the other islands, 'cause there's volcanoes all over the place, aren't there?"

Bobby joined them at the counter. "What do volcanoes have to do with it?"

Lisa took her chewing gum out of her mouth and put it aside on a piece of paper. "Well, the way I heard it, really hot lava flows into the sea, and when it meets the water, there're these huge explosions, which throw off zillions and zillions of these really teeny-tiny beads of black glass, and then over a long period of time the waves rub all the beads together until they're ground down into sand."

"They have these beaches anywhere but Hawaii?" Bobby wondered.

She shrugged. "Probably. Clint, is this fella your . . . friend?"

"Yeah," Clint said.

"I mean, you know, your *good* friend?"

"Yeah," Clint said, without looking at Bobby.

Lisa winked at Bobby. "Listen, you make Clint take you to Kaimu, 'cause I'll tell you something—it's really terrific to go out on a black beach at night, make love under the stars, because it's soft, for one thing, but mainly because black sand doesn't reflect moonlight like regular sand. It seems like you're floating in space, darkness all around, it really sharpens your senses, if you know what I mean."

"Sounds terrific," Clint said. "Take care, Lisa." He headed for the door.

As Bobby turned to follow Clint, Lisa said, "You make him take you to Kaimu, you hear? You'll have a good time."

Outside, Bobby said, "Clint, you've got some explaining to do."

"Didn't you hear her? These little beads of black glass—"

"That's not what I'm talking about. Hey, look at you, you're grinning. I don't think I've ever seen you grinning. I don't think I *like* you grinning."

42

BY NINE O'CLOCK, LEE CHEN HAD ARRIVED AT THE OFFICES, opened a bottle of orange-flavored seltzer, and settled in the computer room midst his beloved hardware, where Julie was waiting for him. He was five six, slender but wiry, with a warm brass complexion and jet-black hair that bristled in a modified punk style. He wore red tennis shoes and socks, baggy black cotton pants with a white belt, a black and charcoal-gray shirt with a subtle leaf pattern, and a black jacket with narrow lapels and big shoulder pads. He was the most stylishly dressed employee at Dakota & Dakota, even compared to Cassie Hanley, their receptionist, who was an unashamed clotheshorse.

While Lee sat in front of his computers, sipping seltzer, Julie filled him in on what had happened at the hospital and showed him the printouts of the information Bobby had acquired earlier that morning. Frank Pollard sat with them, in the third chair, where Julie could keep an eye on him. Throughout their conversation, Lee exhibited no surprise at what he was being told, as if his computers had bestowed on him such enormous wisdom and foresight that nothing—not even a man capable of teleportation—could surprise him. Julie knew that Lee, as well as everyone else in the Dakota & Dakota family, would never leak a word of any client's business to anyone; but she didn't know how much of his supercool demeanor was real and how much was a conscious image that he put on every morning with his ultra-voguish clothes.

Though his unshakable nonchalance might be partly feigned, his talent for computers was unquestionably real. When Julie had finished her condensed version of recent events, Lee said, "Okay, what do you need from me now?" There was no doubt on either his part or hers that eventually he could provide whatever she required.

She gave him a steno pad. Double rows of currency serial numbers filled the first ten pages. "Those are random samplings of the bills in each of the bags of cash we're holding for Frank. Can you find out if it's hot money—stolen, maybe an extortion or ransom payment?"

Lee quickly paged through the lists. "No consecutive numbers? That makes it harder. Usually cops don't have a record of the serial numbers of stolen money unless it was brand-new bills, which are still bound in packets, consecutively numbered, right off the press."

"Most of this cash is fairly well circulated."

"There's an outside chance it might still be from a ransom or extortion payoff, like you said. The cops would've taken down all the numbers before they let the victim make the drop, just in case the perp made a clean getaway. It looks bleak, but I'll try. What else?"

Julie said, "An entire family in Garden Grove, last name Farris, was murdered last year."

"Because of me," Frank said.

Lee propped his elbows on the arms of his chair, leaned back, and steepled his fingers. He looked like a wise Zen master who had been forced to don the clothes of an avant-garde artist after getting the wrong suitcase at the airport. "No one really dies, Mr. Pollard. They just go on from here. Grief is good, but guilt is pointless."

Though she knew too few computer fanatics to be certain, Julie suspected that not many found a way to combine the hard realities of science and technology with religion. But in fact, Lee had arrived at a belief in God through his work with computers and his interest in modern physics. He once explained to her why a profound understanding of the dimensionless space inside a computer network, combined with a modern physicist's view of the universe, led inevitably to faith in a Creator, but she hadn't followed a thing he'd said.

She gave Lee Chen the dates and details of the Farris and Roman murders. "We think they were all killed by the same man. I haven't got a clue to his real name, so I call him Mr. Blue. Considering the savagery of the murders, we suspect he's a serial killer with a long list of victims. If we're right, the murders have been so widely spread or Mr. Blue has covered his tracks so well that the press has never made connections between the crimes."

"Otherwise," Frank said, "they'd have sensationalized it on their front pages. Especially if this guy regularly bites his victims."

"But since most police agencies are computer-linked these days," Julie said, "they might've made connections across jurisdictions, saw what the press didn't. There might be one or more quiet, ongoing investigations between local, state, and federal authorities. We need to know if any police in California—or the FBI nationally—are on to Mr. Blue, and we need to know anything they've learned about him, no matter how trivial."

Lee smiled. In the middle of his brass-hued face, his teeth were like pegs of highly polished ivory. "That means going past the public-access files in their computers. I'll have to break their security, one agency after another, all the way into the FBI."

"Difficult?"

"Very. But I'm not without experience." He pushed his jacket sleeves farther up on his arms, flexed his fingers, and turned to the terminal keyboard as if he were a concert pianist about to interpret Mozart. He hesitated and glanced sideways at Julie. "I'll work into their systems indirectly to discourage tracebacks. I won't damage any data or breach national security, so I probably won't even be noticed. But if someone spots me snooping and puts a tracer on me that I don't see or can't shake, they might pull your PI license for this."

"I'll sacrifice myself, take the blame. Bobby's license won't be pulled, too, so the agency won't go down. How long will this take?"

"Four or five hours, maybe more, maybe a lot more. Can somebody bring me lunch at noon? I'd rather eat here and not take a break."

"Sure. What would you like?"

"Big Mac, double order of fries, vanilla shake."

Julie grimaced. "How come a high-tech guy like you never heard of cholesterol?"

"Heard of it. Don't care. If we never really die, cholesterol can't kill me. It can only move me out of this life a little sooner."

43

ARCHER VAN CORVAIRE CRACKED OPEN THE LEVOLOR BLIND AND peered through the thick bulletproof glass in the front door of his Newport Beach shop. He squinted suspiciously at Bobby and Clint, though he knew and expected them. At last he unlocked the door and let them in.

Van Corvaire was about fifty-five but invested a lot of time and money in the maintenance of a youthful appearance. To thwart time, he'd undergone dermabrasion, face-lifts, and liposuction; to improve on nature, he'd had a nose job, cheek implants, and chin restructuring. He wore a toupee of such exquisite craftsmanship, it would have passed for his own dyed-black hair—except that he sabotaged the illusion by insisting on not merely a replacement but a lush, unnatural pompadour. If he ever got into a swimming pool wearing that toupee, it would look like the conning tower of a submarine.

After reengaging both dead bolts, he turned to Bobby. "I never do business in the morning. I take only afternoon appointments."

"We appreciate the exception you've made for us," Bobby said.

Van Corvaire sighed elaborately. "Well, what is it?"

"I have a stone I'd like you to appraise for me."

He squinted, which wasn't appealing, since his eyes were already as narrow as those of a ferret. Before his name change thirty years ago, he'd been Jim Bob Spleener, and a friend would have told him that when he squinted suspiciously he looked very much like a Spleener and not at all like a van Corvaire. "An appraisal? That's all you want?"

He led them through the small but plush salesroom: hand-textured plaster ceiling; bleached suede walls; whitewashed oak floors; custom area carpet by Patterson, Flynn & Martin in shades of peach, pale blue and sandstone; a modern white sofa flanked by pickled-finish, burlwood tables by Bau; four elegant rattan chairs encircling a round table with a glass top thick enough to survive a blow from a sledgehammer.

One small merchandise display case stood off to the left. Van Corvaire's business was conducted entirely by appointment; his jewelry was custom designed for the very rich and tasteless, people who would find it necessary to buy hundred-thousand-dollar necklaces to wear to a thousand-dollar-a-plate charity dinner, and never grasp the irony.

The back wall was mirrored, and van Corvaire watched himself with obvious pleasure all the way across the room. He hardly took his eyes off his reflection until he passed through the door into the workroom.

Bobby wondered if the guy ever got so entranced by his image that he walked smack into it. He didn't like Jim Bob van Corvaire, but the narcissistic creep's knowledge of gems and jewelry was often useful.

Years ago, when Dakota & Dakota Investigations was just Dakota Investigations, without the ampersand and the redundancy (better never put it that way around Julie, who would appreciate the clever wordplay but would make him eat the "redundancy" part), Bobby had helped van Corvaire recover a fortune in unmounted diamonds stolen by a lover. Old Jim Bob desperately wanted his gems but didn't want the woman sent to prison, so he went to Bobby instead of to the police. That was the only soft spot Bobby had ever seen in van Corvaire; in the intervening years the jeweler no doubt had grown a callus over it too.

Bobby fished one of the marble-size red stones from his pocket. He saw the jeweler's eyes widen.

With Clint standing to one side of him, with Bobby behind him and looking over his shoulder, van Corvaire sat on a high stool at a workbench and examined the rough-cut stone through a loupe. Then he put it on the lighted glass table of a microscope and studied it with that more powerful instrument.

"Well?" Bobby asked.

The jeweler did not respond. He rose, elbowing them out of the way, and went to another stool, farther along the work-bench. There, he used one scale to weigh the stone and another to determine if its specific gravity matched that of any known gems.

Finally, he moved to a third stool that was positioned in front of a vise. From a drawer he withdrew a ring box in which three large, cut gems lay on a square of blue velvet.

"Junk diamonds," he said.

"They look nice to me," Bobby said.

"Too many flaws."

He selected one of those stones and fixed it in the vise with a couple of turns of the crank. Gripping the red beauty in a small pair of pliers, he used one of its sharper edges to attempt to score the polished facet of the diamond in the vise, pressing with considerable effort. Then he put the pliers and red gem aside, picked up another jeweler's loupe, leaned forward, and studied the junk diamond.

"A faint scratch," he said. "Diamond cuts diamond." He held the red stone between thumb and forefinger, staring at it with obvious fascination—and greed. "Where did you get this?"

"Can't tell you," Bobby said. "So it's just a red diamond?"

"*Just?* The red diamond may be the rarest precious stone in the world! You must let me market it for you. I have clients who'd pay anything to have this as the centerstone of a necklace or pendant. It'll probably be too big for a ring even after final cut. It's huge!"

"What's it worth?" Clint asked.

"Impossible to say until it's finish-cut. Millions, certainly."

"Millions?" Bobby said doubtfully. "It's big but not *that* big."

Van Corvaire finally tore his gaze from the stone and looked up at Bobby. "You don't understand. Until now, there were only seven known red diamonds in the world. This is the eighth. And when it's cut and polished, it'll be one of the two largest. This comes as close to priceless as anything gets."

OUTSIDE ARCHER VAN Corvaire's small shop, where heavy traffic roared past on Pacific Coast Highway, with disco-frenetic flares of sunlight flashing off the chrome and glass, it was hard to believe that the tranquility of Newport Harbor and its burden of beautiful yachts were just beyond the buildings on the far side of the street. In a sudden moment of enlightenment, Bobby realized that his entire life (and perhaps nearly everyone else's) was like this street at this precise point in time: all bustle and noise, glare and movement, a desperate rush to break out of the herd, to achieve something and transcend the frantic whirl of commerce, thereby earning respite for reflection and a shot at serenity—when all the time serenity was only a few steps away, on the far side of the street, just out of sight.

That realization contributed to a heretofore subtle feeling that the Pollard case was somehow a trap—or, more accurately, a squirrel cage that spun faster and faster even as he scampered frantically to get a footing on its rotating floor. He stood for a few seconds by the open door of the car, feeling ensnared, caged. At that moment he was not sure why, in spite of the obvious dangers, he had been so eager to take on Frank's problems and put all that he cared about at risk. He knew now that the reasons he had quoted to Julie and to himself—sympathy for Frank, curiosity, the excitement of a wildly different kind of job—were merely justifications, not reasons, and that his true motivation was something he did not yet understand.

Unnerved, he got in the car and pulled the door shut as Clint started the engine.

"Bobby, how many red diamonds would you say are in the mason jar? A hundred?"

"More. A couple hundred."

"Worth what—hundreds of millions?"

"Maybe a billion or more."

They stared at each other, and for a while neither of them spoke. It wasn't that no words were adequate to the situation; instead, there was *too much* to say and no easy way to determine where to begin.

At last Bobby said, "But you couldn't convert the stones to cash, not quickly anyway. You'd have to dribble them onto the market over a lot of years to prevent a sudden dilution of their rarity and value, but also to avoid causing a sensation, drawing unwanted attention, and maybe having to answer some unanswerable questions."

"After they've mined diamonds for hundreds of years, all over the world, and only found seven red ones . . . where the hell did Frank come up with a jarful?"

Bobby shook his head and said nothing.

Clint reached into his pants pocket and withdrew one of the diamonds, smaller than the specimen that Bobby had brought for Archer van Corvaire's appraisal. "I took this home to show it to Felina. I was going to

return it to the jar when I got to the office, but you hustled me out before
I had a chance. Now that I know what it is, I don't want it in my possession
a minute longer."

Bobby took the stone and put it in his pocket with the larger diamond.
"Thank you, Clint."

DR. DYSON MANFRED'S study, in his house in Turtle Rock, was the most
uncomfortable place Bobby had ever been. He had been happier last
week, flattened on the floor of his van, trying to avoid being chopped to
bits by automatic weapons fire than he was among Manfred's collection
of many-legged, carapaced, antenna-bristled, mandibled, and thoroughly
repulsive exotic bugs.

Repeatedly, in his peripheral vision, Bobby saw something move in
one of the many glass-covered boxes on the wall, but every time he
turned to ascertain which hideous creature was about to slip out from
under the frame, his fear proved unfounded. All of the nightmarish specimens were pinned and motionless, lined up neatly beside one another,
none missing. He also would have sworn that he heard things skittering
and slithering inside the shallow drawers of the many cases that he knew
contained more insects, but he supposed that those sounds were every
bit as imaginary as the phantom movement glimpsed from the corners of
his eyes.

Though he knew Clint to be a born stoic, Bobby was impressed by the
apparent ease with which the guy endured the creepy-crawly decor. This
was an employee he must never lose. He decided on the spot to give
Clint a significant raise in salary before the day was out.

Bobby found Dr. Manfred nearly as disquieting as his collection. The
tall, thin, long-limbed entomologist seemed to be the offspring of a professional basketball player and one of those African stick insects that you
saw in nature films and hoped never to encounter in real life.

Manfred stood behind his desk, his chair pushed out of the way, and
they stood in front of it. Their attention was directed upon a two-foot-
long, one-foot-wide, white-enamel, inch-deep lab tray which occupied
the center of the desktop and over which was draped a small white towel.

"I have had no sleep since Mr. Karaghiosis brought this to me last
night," Manfred said, "and I won't sleep much tonight, either, just turning

over all the remaining questions in my mind. This dissection was the most fascinating of my career, and I doubt that I'll ever again experience any-thing in my life to equal it."

The intensity with which Manfred spoke—and the implication that nei-ther good food nor good sex, neither a beautiful sunset nor a fine wine, could be a fraction as satisfying as insect dismemberment—gave Bobby a queasy stomach.

He glanced at the fourth man in the room, if only to divert his attention briefly from their bugophile host. The guy was in his late forties, as round as Manfred was angular, as pink as Manfred was pale, with red-gold hair, blue eyes, and freckles. He sat on a chair in the corner, straining the seams of his gray jogging suit, with his hands fisted on his heavy thighs, looking like a good Boston Irish fellow who had been trying to eat his way into a career as a Sumo wrestler. The entomologist hadn't introduced or even referred to the well-padded observer. Bobby figured that introductions would be made when Manfred was ready. He decided not to force the issue—if only because the round man silently regarded them with a mix-ture of wonder, suspicion, fear, and intense curiosity that encouraged Bobby to believe they would not be pleased to hear what he had to tell them when, at last, he spoke.

With long-fingered, spidery hands—which Bobby might have sprayed with Raid if he'd had any—Dyson Manfred removed the towel from the white-enamel tray, revealing the remains of Frank's insect. The head, a couple of the legs, one of the highly articulated pincers, and a few other unidentifiable parts had been cut off and put aside. Each grisly piece rested on a soft pad of what appeared to be cotton cloth, almost as a jeweler might present a fine gem on velvet to a prospective buyer. Bobby stared at the plum-size head with its small reddish-blue eye, then at its two large muddy-yellow eyes that were too similar in color to Dyson Manfred's. He shivered. The main part of the bug was in the middle of the tray, on its back. The exposed underside had been slit open, the outer layers of tissue removed or folded back, and the inner workings revealed.

Using the gleaming point of a slender scalpel, which he handled with grace and precision, the entomologist began by showing them the res-piratory, ingestive, digestive, and excretory systems of the bug. Manfred kept referring to the "great art" of the biological design, but Bobby saw nothing that equaled a painting by Matisse; in fact, the guts of the thing were even more repellent than its exterior. One term—"polishing chamber"—struck him as odd, but when he asked for a further explanation, Manfred only said, "in time, in time," and went on with his lecture.

When the entomologist finished, Bobby said, "Okay, we know how the thing ticks, so what does that tell us about it that we might want to know? For instance, where does it come from?"

Manfred stared at him, unresponding.

Bobby said, "The South American jungles?"

Manfred's peculiar amber eyes were hard to read, and his silence puzzling.

"Africa?" Bobby said. The entomologist's stare was beginning to make him twitchier than he already was.

"Mr. Dakota," Manfred said finally, "you're asking the wrong question. Let me ask the interesting ones for you. What does this creature eat? Well, to put it in the simplest terms that any layman can understand—it eats a broad spectrum of minerals, rock, and soil. What does it ex—"

"It eats dirt?" Clint asked.

"That's an even simpler way to express it," Manfred said. "Not precise, mind you, but simpler. We don't yet understand how it breaks down those substances or how it obtains energy from them. There are aspects of its biology that we can see perfectly clearly but that still remain mysterious."

"I thought insects ate plants or each other or . . . dead meat," Bobby said.

"They do," the entomologist confirmed. "This thing is not an insect— or any other class of the phylum *Arthropoda*, for that matter."

"Sure looks like an insect to me," Bobby said, glancing down at the partly dismantled bug and grimacing involuntarily.

"No," Manfred said, *"this* is a creature that evidently bores through soil and stone, capable of ingesting that material in chunks as large as fat grapes. And the next question is, 'If that's what it eats, what does it excrete?' And the answer, Mr. Dakota, is that it excretes diamonds."

Bobby jerked as if the entomologist had hit him.

He glanced at Clint, who looked as surprised as Bobby felt. The Pollard case had induced several changes in the Greek, and now it had robbed him of his poker face.

In a tone of voice that suggested Manfred was playing them for fools, Clint said, "You're telling us it turns dirt into diamonds?"

"No, no," Manfred said. "It methodically eats through veins of diamond-bearing carbon and other material, until it finds the gems. Then it swallows them in their encrusted jackets of minerals, *digests* those minerals, passes the rough diamond into the polishing chamber, where any remaining extraneous matter is worn away by vigorous contact with these hundreds of fine, wirelike bristles that line the chamber." With the scalpel he pointed to the feature of the bug that he had just described. "Then it squirts the raw diamond out the other end."

The entomologist opened the center drawer of his desk, removed a white handkerchief, unfolded it, and revealed three red diamonds, all considerably smaller than the one Bobby had taken to van Corvaire, but probably worth hundreds of thousands, maybe millions, apiece.

"I found these at various points in the creature's system."

The largest of the three was still partially encased in a mottled brown-black-gray mineral crust.

"They're diamonds?" Bobby said, playing ignorant. "I've never seen red diamonds."

"Neither had I. So I went to another professor, a geologist who happens to be a gemologist as well, got him out of bed at midnight to show these to him."

Bobby glanced at the would-be Irish Sumo wrestler, but the man did not rise from his chair or speak, so he evidently was not the geologist.

Manfred explained what Bobby and Clint already knew—that these scarlet diamonds were among the rarest things on earth—while they pretended that it was all news to them. "This discovery strengthened my suspicions about the creature, so I went straight to Dr. Gavenall's house and woke *him* shortly before two o'clock this morning. He threw on sweats and sneakers, and we came right back here, and we've been here ever since, working this out together, unable to believe our own eyes."

At last the round man rose and stepped to the side of the desk.

"Roger Gavenall," Manfred said, by way of introduction. "Roger is a geneticist, a specialist in recombinant DNA, and widely known for his creative projections of macroscale genetic engineering that might conceivably progress from current knowledge."

"Sorry," Bobby said, "I lost you at 'Roger is . . .' We'll need some more of that layman's language, I'm afraid."

"I'm a geneticist and futurist," Gavenall said. His voice was unexpectedly melodic, like that of a television game-show host. "Most genetic engineering, for the foreseeable future, will take place on a *micro*scopic scale—creating new and useful bacteria, repairing flawed genes in the cells of human beings to correct inherited weaknesses and prevent inherited disease. But eventually we'll be able to create whole new species of animals and insects, *macro*scale engineering—useful things like voracious mosquito eaters that will eliminate the need to spray Malathion in tropical regions like Florida. Cows that are maybe half the size of today's cows and a lot more metabolically efficient, so they require less food, yet produce twice as much milk."

Bobby wanted to suggest that Gavenall consider combining the two biological inventions to produce a small cow that ate only enormous quantities of mosquitoes and produced *three* times as much milk. But he kept his mouth shut, certain that neither of the scientists would appreciate his humor. Anyway, he had to admit that his compulsion to make a joke of this was an attempt to deal with his own deep-seated fear of the ever-increasing weirdness of the Pollard case.

"This thing," Gavenall said, indicating the deconstructed bug in the lab tray, "isn't anything that nature created. It's clearly an engineered lifeform, so astonishingly task-specific in every aspect of its biology that it's essentially a biological machine. A diamond scavenger."

Using a pair of forceps and the scalpel, Dyson Manfred gently turned over the insect that wasn't an insect, so they could see its midnight-black shell rimmed with red markings.

Bobby thought he heard whispery movement in many parts of the study, and he wished Manfred would let some sunlight into the room. The windows were covered with interior wood shutters, and the slats were tightly shut. Bugs liked darkness and shadows, and the lamps here seemed insufficiently bright to dissuade them from scurrying out of the shallow drawers, over Bobby's shoes, up his socks, and under the legs of his pants.

Hanging his pendulous belly over the desk, indicating the crimson edging on the carapace, Gavenall said, "On a hunch Dyson and I shared, we showed a representation of this pattern to an associate in the mathematics department, and he confirmed that it's an obvious binary code."

"Like the universal product code that's on everything you buy at the grocery store," the entomologist explained.

Clint said, "You mean the red marks are the bug's *number?*"

"Yes."

"Like . . . well, like a license plate?"

"More or less," Manfred said. "We haven't taken a chip of the red material for analysis yet, but we suspect it'll prove to be a ceramic material, painted onto the shell or spray-bonded in some fashion."

Gavenall said, "Somewhere there are a lot of these things, industriously digging for diamonds, red diamonds, and each of them carries a coded serial number that identifies it to whomever created it and set it to work."

Bobby grappled with that concept for a moment, trying to find a way to see it as a part of the world in which he lived, but it simply did not fit. "Okay, Dr. Gavenall, you're able to envision engineered creatures like this—"

"I couldn't have envisioned this," Gavenall said adamantly. "It never would've occurred to me. I could only recognize it for what it was, for what it must be."

"All right, but nevertheless you recognized what it must be, which is something neither Clint nor I could've done. So now tell me—who could make something like this damned thing?"

Manfred and Gavenall exchanged a meaningful look and were both silent for a long moment, as if they knew the answer to his question but were reluctant to reveal it. Finally, lowering his game-show-host voice to an even more mellifluous note, Gavenall said, "The genetic knowledge and engineering skill required to produce this thing do not yet exist. We're not even close to being able to . . . to . . . not even *close.*"

Bobby said, "How long until science advances far enough to make this thing possible?"

"No way of arriving at a precise answer," Manfred said.

"Guess."

"Decades?" Gavenall said. "A century? Who knows?"

Clint said, "Wait a minute. What're you telling us? That this thing comes from the future, that it came through some . . . some time warp from the next century?"

"Either that," Gavenall said, "or . . . it doesn't come from this world at all."

Stunned, Bobby looked down at the bug with no less revulsion but with considerably more wonder and respect than he'd had a moment ago. "You really think this might be a biological machine created by people from another world? An alien artifact?"

Manfred worked his mouth but produced no sound, as if rendered speechless by the prospect of what he was about to say.

"Yes," Gavenall said, "an alien artifact. Seems more likely to me than the possibility that it came tumbling back to us through some hole in time."

Even as Gavenall spoke, Dyson Manfred continued to work his mouth in a frustrated attempt to break the silence that gripped him, and his lantern jaw gave him the look of a praying mantis masticating a grisly lunch. When words at last issued from him, they came in a rush: "We want you to understand, we will not, flatly will not, return this specimen. We'd be derelict as scientists to allow this incredible thing to reside in the hands of laymen, we must preserve and protect it, and we will, even if we have to do so by force."

A flush of defiance lent a glow of health to the entomologist's pale, angular face for the first time since Bobby had met him.

"Even if by force," he repeated.

Bobby had no doubt that he and Clint could beat the crap out of the human stick bug and his rotund colleague, but there was no reason to do so. He didn't care if they kept the thing in the lab tray—as long as they agreed to some ground rules about how and when they would go public with it.

All he wanted right now was to get out of that bughouse, into warm sunlight and fresh air. The whispery sounds from the specimen drawers, though certainly imaginary, grew louder and more frenzied by the minute. His entomophobia would soon kick him off the ledge of reason and send him screaming from the room; he wondered if his anxiety was apparent or if he was sufficiently self-controlled to conceal it. He felt a bead of sweat slip down his left temple, and had the answer.

"Let's be absolutely frank," Gavenall said. "It's not only our obligation to science that requires us to maintain possession of this specimen. Revelation of this find will *make* us, academically and financially. Neither one of us is a slouch in his field, but this will catapult us to the top, the very top, and we're willing to do whatever is necessary to protect our interests here." His blue eyes had narrowed, and his open Irish face had closed up into a hard mask of determination. "I'm not saying I'd kill to keep that specimen . . . but I'm not saying I wouldn't, either."

Bobby sighed. "I've done a lot of research for UCI into the backgrounds of prospective faculty members, so I know the academic world can be as competitive and vicious and dirty—dirtier—than either politics or show business. I'm not going to fight you on this. But we've got to reach an agreement about when you can go public with it. I don't want you doing anything that would bring my client to the attention of the press until we've resolved his case and are sure he's . . . out of danger."

"And when will that be?" Manfred asked.

Bobby shrugged. "A day or two. Maybe a week. I doubt it'll drag on much longer than that."

The entomologist and geneticist beamed at each other, obviously delighted. Manfred said, "That's no problem at all. We'll need much longer than that to finish studying the specimen, prepare our first paper for publication, and devise a strategy to deal with both the scientific community and the media."

Bobby imagined that he heard one of the shallow drawers sliding open in the case behind him, forced outward by the weight of a vile torrent of giant, squirming Madagascar roaches.

"But I'll take the three diamonds with me," he said. "They're quite valuable, and they belong to my client."

Manfred and Gavenall hesitated, made a token protest, but quickly agreed. Clint took the stones and rewrapped them in the handkerchief. The scientists' capitulation convinced Bobby there had been more than three diamonds in the bug, probably at least five, leaving them with two stones to support their thesis regarding the bug's origins and purpose.

"We'll want to meet your client, interview him," Gavenall said.

"That's up to him," Bobby said.

"It's essential. We *must* interview him."

"That's his decision," Bobby said. "You've gotten most of what you wanted. Eventually he may agree, and then you'll have everything you're after. But don't push it now."

The round man nodded. "Fair enough. But tell me . . . where *did* he find the thing?"

"He doesn't remember. He has amnesia." The drawer behind him was open now. He could hear the shells of the huge roaches clicking and scraping together as they poured out of confinement and down the front of the cabinet, swarming toward him. "We really have to go," he said. "We don't have another minute to spare." He left the study quickly, trying not to look as if he was bolting for his life.

Clint followed him, as did the two scientists, and at the front door,

Manfred said, "I'm going to sound as if I ought to be writing stories for some sensational tabloid, but if this *is* an alien artifact that came into your client's hands, do you think he could've gotten it inside a . . . well, a spaceship? Those people who claim to have been abducted and forced to undergo examinations aboard spaceships . . . they always seem to go through a period of amnesia first, before learning the truth."

"Those people are crackpots or frauds," Gavenall said sharply. "We can't let ourselves be associated with that sort of thing." He frowned, and the frown deepened into a scowl, and he said, "Unless in this case it's true." ·

Looking back at them from the stoop, grateful to be outside, Bobby said, "Maybe it is. I'm at a point where I'll believe anything till it's disproved. But I'll tell you this . . . my feeling is that whatever is happening to my client is something a lot stranger than alien abduction."

"A lot," Clint agreed.

Without further elaboration, they went down the front walkway to the car. Bobby opened his door and stood for a moment, reluctant to get into Clint's Chevy. The mild breeze washing down the Irvine hills felt so *clean* after the stale air in Manfred's study.

He put one hand in his pocket, felt the three red diamonds, and said softly, "Bug shit."

When he finally got into the car and slammed the door, he barely resisted the urge to reach under his shirt to determine if the things he still felt crawling on him were real.

Manfred and Gavenall stood on the front stoop, watching Bobby and Clint, as if half expecting their car to tip back on its rear bumper and shoot straight into the sky to rendezvous with some great glowing craft out of a Spielberg movie.

Clint drove two blocks, turned at the corner, and pulled to the curb as soon as they were out of sight. "Bobby, where in the hell *did* Frank get that thing?"

Bobby could only answer him with another question: "How many different places does he go when he teleports? The money, the red diamonds and the bug, the black sand—and how far away are some of those places? Really *far* away?"

"And who is he?" Clint asked.

"Frank Pollard from El Encanto Heights."

"But I mean, who is that?" Clint thumped one fist against the steering wheel. "Who the hell *is* Frank Pollard from El Encanto?"

"I think what you really want to know is not who he is. More important . . . *what* is he?"

44

BY SURPRISE BOBBY CAME TO VISIT.

Lunch was eaten before Bobby came. Dessert was still in Thomas's mind. Not the taste of it. The memory. Vanilla ice cream, fresh strawberries. The way dessert made you feel.

He was alone in his room, sitting in his armchair, thinking about making a picture poem that would have the feeling of eating ice cream and strawberries, not the taste but the good feeling, so some day when you didn't have any ice cream or strawberries, you could just look at the poem and get that same good feeling even without eating anything. Of course, you couldn't use pictures of ice cream or strawberries in the poem, because that wouldn't be a poem, that would be only *saying* how good ice cream and strawberries made you feel. A poem didn't just say, it showed you and made you feel.

Then Bobby came through the door, and Thomas was so happy he forgot the poem, and they hugged. Somebody was with Bobby, but it wasn't Julie, so Thomas was disappointed. He was embarrassed, too, because it turned out he'd met the person with Bobby a couple times before, over the years, but he didn't remember him right away, which made him feel dumb. It was Clint. Thomas said the name to himself, over and over, so maybe he'd remember next time: *Clint, Clint, Clint, Clint, Clint.*

"Julie couldn't come," Bobby said, "she's babysitting a client."

Thomas wondered why a baby would ever need a private eye, but he didn't ask. In TV only grownups needed private eyes, which were called private *eyes* because they looked out for you, though he wasn't sure why they were called private. He also wondered how a baby could pay for a private eye, because he knew eyes like Bobby and Julie worked for money like everyone else, but babies didn't work, they were too little to do anything. So where'd this one get the money to pay Bobby and Julie? He hoped they didn't get cheated out of their money, they worked hard for it.

Bobby said, "She told me to tell you she loves you even more than she did yesterday, and she'll love you even more tomorrow."

They hugged again because this time Thomas was giving the hug to Bobby for Julie.

Clint asked if he could see the latest scrapbook of poems. He took it across the room and sat in Derek's armchair, which was okay because Derek wasn't in it, he was in the wreck room.

Bobby moved the chair from the worktable, putting it closer to the armchair that belonged to Thomas. He sat, and they talked about what a big blue day it was and how nice the flowers looked where they were all bright outside Thomas's window.

For a while they talked about lots of things, and Bobby was funny—except when they talked about Julie, he changed. He was worried for Julie, you could tell. When he talked about her, he was like a good picture poem—he didn't say his worry, but he showed it and made you feel it.

Thomas was already worried for Julie, so Bobby's worry made him feel even worse, made him scared for her.

"We've got our hands full with the current case," Bobby said, "so neither one of us might be able to visit again until this weekend or the first of the week."

"Okay, sure," Thomas said, and a big coldness rushed in from somewhere and filled him up. Each time Bobby mentioned the new case, the one with the baby, his picture poem of worry was even easier to read.

Thomas wondered if this was the case where they were going to meet up with the Bad Thing. He was pretty sure it was. He thought he should tell Bobby about the Bad Thing, but he couldn't find a way. No matter how he told it, he'd sound like the dumbest dumb person who ever lived at The Home. It was better to wait until the danger was coming a lot nearer, then TV to Bobby a real hard warning that'd scare him into looking out for the Bad Thing and shooting it when he saw it. Bobby would pay attention to a TVed warning because he wouldn't know where it came from, that it came from just a dumb person.

And Bobby could shoot, too, all private eyes could shoot because most days it was bad out there in the world, and you knew you were going to meet up with somebody who was going to shoot at you first or try to run you down with a car or stab you or strangle you or, once in a while, try to throw you off a building, or even Try To Make It Look Like Suicide, and since most good guys didn't carry guns around with them, private eyes who watched over them had to be good shooters.

After a while Bobby had to go. Not to the bathroom but back to work. So they hugged again. And then Bobby and Clint were gone, and Thomas was alone.

He went to the window. Looked out. The day was good, better than night. But even with the sun pushing most darkness out past the edge of the world, and even with the rest of the darkness hiding from the sun behind trees and buildings, there was badness in the day. The Bad Thing hadn't gone out past the edge of the world with the night. It was still there, somewhere in the day, you could tell.

Last night, when he got too close to the Bad Thing and it tried to grab him, he was so afraid, he pulled away quick like. He had a feeling the Bad Thing was trying to find out who he was and where he was, and then was going to come to The Home and eat him like it ate the little animals. So he pretty much made up his mind not to get real close to it again, stay far away, but now he couldn't do that because of Julie and the baby. If Bobby, who never worried, was so worried for Julie, then Thomas needed to be even more worried for her than he was. And if Julie and Bobby thought the baby should be watched over, then Thomas had to worry about the baby, too, because what was important to Julie was important to him.

He reached out into the day.

It was there. Far away yet.

He didn't get close.

He was scared.

But for Julie, for Bobby, for the baby, he'd have to stop being scared, get closer, and be sure he knew all the time where the Bad Thing was and whether it was coming this way.

45

JACKIE JAXX DID NOT ARRIVE AT THE OFFICES OF DAKOTA & Dakota until ten past four that Tuesday afternoon, a full hour after Bobby and Clint returned, and to Julie's annoyance he spent half an hour creating an atmosphere that he found conducive to his work. He felt the room was too bright, so he closed the blinds on the large windows, though the approaching winter twilight and an incoming bank of clouds over the Pacific had already robbed the day of much of its light. He tried different arrangements with the three brass lamps, each of which was equipped with a three-way bulb, giving him what seemed an infinite number of combinations; he finally left one of them at seventy watts, one at thirty, and one off completely. He asked Frank to move from the sofa to one of the chairs, decided that wasn't going to work, moved Julie's big chair out from behind the desk and put him in that, then arranged four other chairs in a semicircle in front of it.

Julie suspected that Jackie could have worked effectively with the blinds open and all of the lamps on. He was a performer, however, even when off the stage, and he could not resist being theatrical.

In recent years magicians had forsaken fake show-biz monikers like The Great Blackwell and Harry Houdini in favor of names that at least seemed like real ones, but Jackie was a throwback. Just as Houdini's real name was Erich Weiss, so Jackie had been baptized David Carver. Because he performed comic magic, he had avoided mysterious-sounding names. And because, since puberty, he had yearned to be part of the nightclub and Vegas scene, he had chosen a new identity that, to him and those in his social circle, sounded like Nevada royalty. While other kids thought about being teachers, doctors, real-estate salesmen or auto mechanics, young Davey Carver had dreamed of being someone like Jackie Jaxx; now, God help him, he was living his dream.

Although he was currently between a one-week engagement in Reno and a stint as the opening act for Sammy Davis in Vegas, Jackie showed up not in blue jeans or an ordinary suit, but in an outfit he could have worn during performances: a black leisure suit with emerald-green piping on the lapels and cuffs of the jacket, a matching green shirt, and black patent-leather shoes. He was thirty-six years old, five feet eight, thin, cancerously tanned, with hair that he dyed ink-black and teeth that were unnaturally, *ferociously* white, thanks to the modern miracle of dental bonding.

Three years ago Dakota & Dakota had been hired by the Las Vegas hotel with which Jackie had a long-term contract, and charged with the sticky task of uncovering the identity of a blackmailer who was trying to extort most of the magician's income. The case had many unexpected twists and turns, but by the time they reached the end, the thing that most surprised Julie was that she had gotten over her initial distaste for the magician and had come to sort of like him. Sort of.

Finally Jackie settled on the chair directly in front of Frank. "Julie, you and Clint sit to my right. Bobby, to my left, please."

Julie saw no good reason why she couldn't sit in whichever of the three chairs she chose, but she played along.

Half of Jackie's Vegas act involved the hypnotizing and comic exploitation of audience members. His knowledge of hypnotic technique was so extensive, and his understanding of the functioning of the mind in a trance state was so profound, that he was frequently invited to participate in medical conferences with physicians, psychologists, and psychiatrists who were exploring practical uses of hypnosis. Perhaps they could have persuaded a psychiatrist to help them pierce Frank's amnesia with hypnotic regression therapy. But it was doubtful that any doctor was as qualified for the task as Jackie Jaxx.

Besides, no matter what fantastic things Jackie learned about Frank, he could be counted on to keep his mouth shut. He owed a lot to Bobby and Julie, and in spite of his faults, he was a man who paid his debts and had at least a vestigial sense of loyalty that was rare in the me-me-me culture of show business.

In the moody amber light of the two brass lamps, with the world darkening rapidly beyond the drawn blinds, Jackie's smooth and well-projected voice, full of low rounded tones and an occasional dramatic vibrato, commanded not just Frank's attention but everyone else's as well. He used a beveled teardrop crystal on a gold chain to focus Frank's attention, after suggesting that the others look at Frank's face rather than at the bauble, to avoid unwanted entrancement.

"Frank, please watch the light winking in the crystal, a very soft and lovely light fluttering from one facet to another, one facet to another, a very warm and appealing light, warm, fluttering. . . ."

After a while, lulled somewhat herself by Jackie's calculated patter, Julie noticed Frank's eyes glaze over.

Beside her, Clint switched on the small tape recorder that he had used when Frank had told them his story yesterday afternoon.

Still twisting the chain back and forth between his thumb and forefinger to make the crystal spin on the end of it, Jackie said, "All right, Frank, you are now slipping into a very relaxed state, a deeply relaxed state, where you will hear only my voice, no other, and will respond only to my voice, no other. . . ."

When he had conveyed Frank into a deep trance and finished giving him instructions related to the interrogation ahead, Jackie told him to close his eyes. Frank obliged.

Jackie put the crystal down. He said, "What is your name?"

"Frank Pollard."

"Where do you live?"

"I don't know."

Having been briefed on the phone by Julie earlier in the day, aware of the information they were seeking from their client, Jackie said, "Have you ever lived in El Encanto?"

A hesitation. Then: "Yes."

Frank's voice was strangely flat. His face was so haggard and deathly pale that he seemed almost like an exhumed corpse that had been sorcerously revitalized for the purpose of serving as a bridge between the members of a séance and those to whom they wished to speak in the land of the dead.

"Do you recall your address in El Encanto?"

"No."

"Was your address 1458 Pacific Hill Road?"

A frown flickered across Frank's face and was gone almost as soon as it came. "Yes. That's what . . . Bobby found . . . with the computer."

"But do you actually remember that place?"

"No."

Jackie adjusted his Rolex watch, then used both hands to smooth back his thick, black hair. "When did you live in El Encanto, Frank?"

"I don't know."

"You must tell me the truth."

"Yeah."

"You cannot lie to me, Frank, or hide anything from me. That is impossible in your current state. When did you live there?"

"I don't know."

"Did you live there alone?"

"I don't know."

"Do you remember being in the hospital last night, Frank?"

"Yeah."

"And you . . . disappeared?"

"They say I did."

"Where did you disappear to, Frank?"

Silence.

"Frank, where did you disappear to?"

"I . . . I'm afraid."

"Why?"

"I . . . don't know. I can't think."

"Frank, do you remember waking up in your car last Thursday morning, parked along a street in Laguna Beach?"

"Yeah."

"Your hands were full of black sand."

"Yeah." Frank wiped his hands on his thighs, as if he could feel the black grains clinging to his sweaty palms.

"Where did you get that sand, Frank?"

"I don't know."

"Take your time. Think about it."

"I don't know."

"Do you remember checking into a motel later . . . napping . . . then waking up with blood all over yourself?"

"I remember," Frank said, and he shuddered.

"Where did that blood come from, Frank?"

"I don't know," he said miserably.

"It was cat blood, Frank. Did you know it was cat blood?"

"No." His eyelids fluttered, but he did not open his eyes. "Just cat blood? Really?"

"Do you remember encountering a cat that day?"

"No."

Clearly, a more aggressive technique would be required to get the answers they needed. Jackie began to talk Frank backward in time, gradually regressing him to his admission to the hospital yesterday evening, then farther back toward the moment he had awakened in that Anaheim alleyway in the earliest hours of Thursday morning, knowing nothing but his name. Beyond that point might lie his memory, if he could be induced to step through the veil of amnesia and recover his past.

Julie leaned slightly forward in her chair and looked past Jackie Jaxx, wondering how Bobby was enjoying the show. She figured the spinning crystal and other hocus-pocus would appeal to his boyish spirit of adventure, and that he would be smiling and bright-eyed.

Instead he was somber. His teeth must have been clenched, for his jaw muscles bulged. He had told her what they learned at Dyson Manfred's house, and she had been as astonished and shaken as he and Clint. But that didn't seem to explain his current mood. Maybe he was still unnerved by the memory of the bugs in the entomologist's study. Or maybe he continued to be troubled by that dream he'd had last week: *the bad thing is coming, the bad thing. . . .*

She had dismissed his dream as unimportant. Now she wondered if it had been genuinely prophetic. After all the weirdness that Frank had brought into their lives, she was more willing to give credence to such things as omens, visions, and prescient dreams.

The bad thing is coming, the bad thing. . . .

Maybe the bad thing was Mr. Blue.

Jackie regressed Frank to the alleyway, to the very moment when he had first awakened in a strange place, disoriented and confused. "Now go back further, Frank, just a little further, back just a few more seconds, and a few more, back, back, beyond the total darkness in your mind, beyond that black wall in your mind. . . ."

Since the questioning had begun, Frank had appeared to dwindle in Julie's desk chair, as if made of wax and subjected to a flame. He had grown paler, too, if that was possible, as white as candle paraffin. But now, as he was forced backward through the darkness in his mind, toward the light of memory on the other side, he sat up straighter, put his hands on the arms of the chair and clutched the vinyl almost tightly enough to cause the upholstery to split. He seemed to be growing, returning to his former size, as if he had drunk one of the magic elixirs that Alice had consumed in her adventures at the far end of the rabbit hole.

"Where are you now?" Jackie asked.

Frank's eyes twitched beneath his closed lids. An inarticulate, strangled sound issued from him. "Uh . . . uh . . ."

"Where are you now?" Jackie insisted gently but firmly.

"Fireflies," Frank said shakily. "Fireflies in a windstorm!" He began to breathe rapidly, raggedly, as if he were having trouble drawing air into his lungs.

"What do you mean by that, Frank?"

"Fireflies . . ."

"Where are you, Frank?"

"Everywhere. Nowhere."

"We don't have fireflies in southern California, Frank, so you must be somewhere else. Think, Frank. Look around yourself now and tell me where you are."

"Nowhere."

Jackie made a few more attempts to get Frank to describe his surroundings and be more specific as to the nature of the fireflies, all to no avail.

"Move him on from there," Bobby said. "Farther back."

Julie glanced at the recorder in Clint's hand and saw the spools turning behind the plastic window in the tapedeck.

With his melodic and vibrant voice, in seductively rhythmic cadences, Jackie ordered Frank to regress past the firefly-speckled darkness.

Suddenly Frank said, "What am I doing here?" He was not referring to the offices of Dakota & Dakota, but to the place that Jackie Jaxx had drawn him to in his memory. "Why here?"

"Where are you, Frank?"

"The house. What in the hell am I doing here, why did I come here? This is crazy, I shouldn't be here."

"Whose house is it, Frank?" Bobby asked.

Because he had been instructed to hear only the hypnotist's voice, Frank did not respond until Jackie repeated the question. Then: "Her house. It's *her* house. She's dead, of course, been dead seven years, but it's still her house, always will be, the bitch will haunt the place, you can't destroy that kind of evil, not entirely, part of it lingers in the rooms where she lived, in everything she touched."

"Who was she, Frank?"

"Mother."

"Your mother? What was her name?"

"Roselle. Roselle Pollard."

"This is the house on Pacific Hill Road?"

"Yeah. Look at it, my God, what a place, what a dark place, what a bad place. Can't people see what a bad place it is? Can't they see that something terrible lives in there?" He was crying. Tears glimmered in his eyes, then streamed down his cheeks. Anguish twisted his voice. "Can't they see what's in there, what lives there, what hides there and *breeds* in that bad place? Are people blind? Or do they just not *want* to see?"

Julie was riveted by Frank's tortured voice and by the agony that had wrenched his face into an approximation of the pained countenance of a lost and frightened child. But she turned away from him and peered past the hypnotist to see if Bobby had reacted to the words "bad place."

He was looking at her. The expression of distress that darkened his blue eyes was proof enough that the reference had not escaped him.

At the other end of the room, carrying a sheaf of printouts, Lee Chen entered from the reception lounge. He closed the door quietly. Julie put a finger to her lips, then motioned him to the sofa.

Jackie spoke soothingly to Frank, trying to allay the fear that had electrified him.

Suddenly Frank let out a sharp cry of fear. He sounded more like a frightened animal than like a man. He sat up even straighter. He was trembling. He opened his eyes, but obviously did not see anything in the room; he was still in a trance. "Oh, my God, he's coming, he's coming now, the twins must've told him I'm here, he's coming!"

Frank's unalloyed terror was so pure and intense that some of it was communicated to Julie. Her heartbeat speeded up, and she began to breathe more rapidly, shallowly.

Trying to keep his subject relaxed enough to be cooperative, Jackie said, "Calm down, Frank. Relax and be calm. Nobody can hurt you. Nothing unpleasant will happen. Be calm, relaxed, calm. . . ."

Frank shook his head. "No. No, he's coming, he's coming, he's going to get me this time. Dammit, why did I come back here? Why did I come back and give him a chance at me?"

"Relax now—"

"He's there!" Frank tried to rise to his feet, seemed unable to find the strength, and dug his fingers even deeper into the vinyl padding on the arms of the chair. "He's right *there*, and he sees me, he sees me."

Bobby said, "Who is he, Frank?" and Jackie repeated the question.

"Candy. It's Candy!" When he was asked again for the name of this person he feared, he repeated: "Candy."

"His name is Candy?"

"He *sees* me!"

In a more forceful and commanding voice than before, Jackie said, "You will relax, Frank. You *will* be calm and relaxed."

But Frank only grew more agitated. He had broken into a sweat. Fixed on something in a far place and time, his eyes were wild. His terror seemed to be sweeping him into a heart-bursting panic.

"I don't have much control of him," Jackie said worriedly. "I'm going to have to bring him out of it."

Bobby slid forward to the edge of his chair. "No, not yet. In a minute but not yet. Ask him about this Candy. Who is the guy?"

Jackie repeated the question.

Frank said, "He's death."

Frowning, Jackie said, "That's not a clear answer, Frank."

"He's death walking, he's death living, he's my brother, *her* child, her favorite child, her *spawn*, and I hate him, he wants to kill me, here he comes!"

With a wretched bleat of terror, Frank started to push up from the chair.

Jackie ordered him to stay where he was.

Frank sat down reluctantly, but his terror only grew, because he could still see Candy coming toward him.

Jackie tried to bring him out of that place in the past, forward to the present, and out of his trance, but to no avail.

"Got to get away now, now, *now*," Frank said desperately.

Julie was frightened for him. She'd never seen anyone look more pathetic or vulnerable. He was drenched in sweat, shaking violently. His hair had fallen over his forehead, into his eyes, but it did not interfere with the vision of terror that he had called up from his past. He clutched the arms of the chair so fiercely that a fingernail on his right hand finally punctured the vinyl upholstery.

"I've got to get out of here," Frank repeated urgently.

Jackie told him to stay put.

"No, I've got to get away from him!"

To Bobby, Jackie Jaxx said, "This has never happened to me, I've lost control of him. Jesus, look at him, I'm afraid the guy's going to have a heart attack."

"Come on, Jackie, you've got to help him," Bobby said sharply. He got off his chair, squatted beside Frank, putting his hand on Frank's in a gesture of comfort and reassurance.

"Bobby, don't," Clint said, standing up so fast that he dropped the tape recorder he'd been balancing on his thigh.

Bobby didn't respond to Clint, for he was too focused on Frank, who seemed to be shaking himself to pieces in front of them. The guy was like a boiler with a jammed release valve, filled to the bursting point not with steam pressure but with manic terror. Bobby was trying to calm him, where Jackie had failed.

For an instant Julie didn't understand what had made Clint shoot to his feet. But she realized that Bobby had seen something the rest of them had missed: fresh blood on Frank's right hand. Bobby hadn't put his hand over Frank's merely to offer comfort; he was trying, as gently as possible, to loosen Frank's grip on the arm of the chair, because Frank had torn open the vinyl and cut himself, perhaps repeatedly, on an exposed staple or upholstery tack.

"He's coming, got to get away!" Frank let go of the chair, grabbed Bobby's hand, and got to his feet, pulling Bobby up with him.

Suddenly Julie understood what Clint feared, and she stood up so fast that she knocked her chair over. "Bobby, no!"

Thrown into a panic by the vision of his murderous brother, Frank screamed. With a hisslike steam escaping from a locomotive engine, he vanished. And took Bobby with him.

46

FIREFLIES IN A WINDSTORM.

Bobby seemed to be floating in space, for he had no sense of his body's position, couldn't tell if he was lying or sitting or standing, right side up or upside down, as if weightless in an immense void. He had no sense of smell or taste. He could hear nothing. He could feel neither heat nor cold nor texture nor weight. The only thing he could see was limitless blackness that seemed to stretch to the ends of the universe—and millions upon millions of tiny fireflies, ephemeral as sparks, that swarmed around him. Actually, he was not sure he saw them at all, because he was not aware of having eyes with which to look at them; it was more as if he was . . . *aware* of them, not through any of the usual senses but through some inner sight, the mind's eye.

At first he panicked. The extreme sensory deprivation convinced him that he was paralyzed, without feeling in any limb or inch of skin, felled by a massive cerebral hemorrhage, deafened and blinded and trapped forever in a damaged brain that had severed all its connections to the outside world.

Then he became aware that he was in motion, not drifting in the blackness as he had first thought, but speeding through it, *rocketing* at a tremendous, frightening speed. He became aware of being drawn forward as if he were a bit of lint flying toward some vacuum cleaner of cosmic power, and all around him the fireflies swirled and tumbled. It was like being on an amusement park ride so huge and fast that only God could have designed it for His own pleasure, though there was no pleasure whatsoever in it for Bobby as he roller-coastered through pitch blackness, trying to scream.

He hit the forest floor on his feet, swayed, and almost fell against Frank, in front of whom he was standing. Frank still had a painfully tight grip on his hand.

Bobby was desperate for air. His chest ached; his lungs seemed to have shriveled up. He sucked in a deep breath, another, exhaling explosively.

He saw the blood, which was on both of their hands now. An image of torn upholstery flashed through his mind. Jackie Jaxx. Bobby remembered.

When Bobby tried to pull loose of his client, Frank held him fast and said, "Not here. No, I can't risk this. Too dangerous. Why am I here?"

Steeped in the scent of pines, Bobby surveyed the surrounding primeval forest, which was thick with shadows as dusk introduced night to the world. The air was frigid, and the bristling boughs of the giant evergreens drooped under a weight of snow, but he saw nothing frightening in that scene.

Then he realized that Frank was staring past him. He turned to discover they were on the edge of the forest. A snow-covered meadow sloped up gently behind them. At the top was a log cabin, not a rustic shack but an elaborate structure that clearly showed the input of an architect, a vacation retreat for someone with plenty of disposable income. A mantle of snow was draped over the main roof, another over the porch roof, each decorated with a fringe of icicles that glittered in the last beams of cold sunlight. No lights glowed at the windows. No smoke curled up from any of the three chimneys. The place appeared to be deserted.

"He knows about this," Frank said, still panicked. "I bought it under another name, but he found out about it, and he came here, almost killed me here, and he's probably keeping tabs on it, checking in regularly, hoping to catch me again."

Bobby was numbed less by the subzero cold than by the realization that he had teleported out of their office and onto this slope in the Sierras or some other mountains. He finally found his voice and said, "Frank, what—"

Darkness.

Fireflies.

Velocity.

He hit the floor rolling, slammed into a coffee table, and felt Frank let go of his hand. The table crashed over, spilling a vase and other decorative—and breakable—items onto a hardwood floor.

He'd sustained a solid knock to the head. When he pushed onto his knees and tried to stand, he was too dizzy to get up.

Frank was already on his feet, looking around, breathing hard. "San Diego. This was my apartment once. He found out about it. Had to get out fast."

When Frank reached down to help Bobby get up, Bobby unthinkingly accepted his hand, the uninjured one.

"Someone else lives here now," Frank said. "Must be off at work, we're lucky."

Darkness.

Fireflies.

Velocity.

Bobby found himself standing at a rusted iron gate between two stone pilasters, looking at a Victorian-style house with a sagging porch roof, broken balusters, and swaybacked steps. The sidewalk was cracked and canted, and weeds flourished in an unmown lawn. In the gloaming it looked like every kid's conception of a seriously haunted house, and he suspected it would look even worse in broad daylight.

Frank gasped. "Jesus, no, not here!"

Darkness.

Fireflies.

Velocity.

Papers fluttered to the floor from a massive mahogany desk, as if a wind had swept through the room, though the air was still now. They were in a book-lined study with French windows. An old man had risen from a wing-backed leather chair. He was wearing gray flannel slacks, a white shirt, a blue cardigan, and a look of surprise.

Frank said, "Doc," and with his free hand reached toward the startled elder.

Darkness.

Bobby had figured out that all was lightless and featureless because, for the moment, he did not exist as a coherent physical entity; he had no eyes, no ears, no nerve endings with which to feel. But understanding brought no diminishment of his fear.

Fireflies.

The millions of tiny, whirling points of light were probably the atomic particles of which his flesh was constructed, being shepherded along sheerly by the power of Frank's mind.

Velocity.

They were teleporting, and the process was probably just about instantaneous, requiring only microseconds from physical dissolution to reconstitution, though subjectively it seemed longer.

The decrepit house again. It must be the place in the hills north of Santa Barbara. They were upslope from the gate, along the Eugenia hedge that encircled the property.

Frank let out a low cry of terror the instant that he saw where he was.

Bobby was afraid of running into Candy just as much as Frank was, but also afraid of Frank, and of teleporting—

Darkness.

Fireflies.

Velocity.

This time they didn't materialize with the balance and stability of their arrival in the old man's study or at the peeling house with the rusted gate, but with the clumsiness of their intrusion into that apartment in San Diego. Bobby stumbled a few steps up a slope, still in Frank's grip as firmly as if they had been handcuffed, and they both fell to their knees on the plush, well-cropped grass.

Frantically Bobby tried to wrench loose of Frank. But Frank held fast with superhuman strength and pointed to a gravestone only a few feet in front of them. Bobby looked around and saw that they were alone in a cemetery, where massive coral trees and palms loomed eerily in the purple-gray twilight.

"He was our neighbor," Frank said.

Gasping for breath, unable to speak, still twisting his hand in an attempt to escape Frank's iron grip, Bobby saw the name NORBERT JAMES KOLREEN in the granite headstone.

"She had him killed," Frank said, "had her precious Candy kill him just because she felt he'd been rude to her. *Rude* to her! The crazy bitch."

Darkness.

Fireflies.

Velocity.

The book-lined study. The old man in the doorway now, looking into the room at them.

Bobby felt as if he had been on a corkscrew roller coaster for hours, turning upside down at high speed, again and again, until he couldn't be sure any more if he was actually moving . . . or standing still while the rest of the world spun and looped around him.

"I shouldn't have come here, Dr. Fogarty," Frank said worriedly. Blood dripped off his injured hand, spotting a pale-green section of the Chinese carpet. "Candy might've seen me at the house, might be trying to follow. Don't want to lead him to you."

Fogarty said, "Frank, wait—"

Darkness.

Fireflies.

Velocity.

They were in the backyard of the decaying house, thirty or forty feet from steps and a porch that were as spavined and dilapidated as those at the front of the place. Lights shone in the first-floor windows.

"I want to go, I want to be out of here," Frank said.

Bobby expected to teleport at once, and steeled himself for it, but nothing happened.

"I want *out* of here," Frank said again. When they did not pop from that place to another, Frank cursed in frustration.

Suddenly the kitchen door opened, and a woman stepped into sight. She stopped on the threshold and stared at them. The fading, muddy purple twilight barely exposed her, and the light from the kitchen silhouetted her but did not reveal any details of her face. Whether it was a trick of the strange illumination or an accurate revelation of her form, Bobby could not know, but when starkly outlined, she presented a powerfully erotic picture: sylphlike, gracefully thin yet clearly and lushly feminine, a smoky phantom that seemed either thinly clad or nude, and that issued a call of desire without making a sound. There was a powerful lubricity in this mysterious woman that made her the equal of any siren that had ever induced sailors to run their ships onto hull-gouging rocks.

"My sister Violet," Frank said with obvious dread and disgust.

Bobby noticed movement around her feet, a swarming of shadows. They poured down the steps, onto the lawn, and he saw they were cats. Their eyes were iridescent in the gloom.

He was gripping Frank every bit as hard as Frank was gripping him, for now he feared release as much as he had previously feared continued captivity. "Frank, get us out of here."

"I can't. I don't have control of this, of myself."

There were a dozen cats, two dozen, still more. As they rushed off the porch and across the first few yards of unmown grass, they were silent. Then, simultaneously, they cried out, as if they were a single creature. Their wail of anger and hunger instantly cured Bobby of his nausea and made his stomach quiver, instead, with terror.

"Frank!"

He wished he hadn't taken off his shoulder holster back at the office. His gun was back there on Julie's desk, of no use to him, but as he glimpsed the bared teeth of the oncoming horde, he figured the revolver wouldn't stop them anyway, at least not enough of them.

The nearest of the cats leaped—

JULIE WAS STANDING by her office chair, where it had been moved into the center of the room for the session of hypnotic therapy. She was unable to step away from it because she had last seen Bobby when he had been next to that chair, and it was where she felt closest to him. "How long now?"

Clint was standing at her side. He looked at his watch. "Less than six minutes."

Jackie Jaxx was in the bathroom, splashing his face with cold water. Still on the sofa with a sheaf of printouts, Lee Chen was not as relaxed as he had been six and a half minutes ago. His Zen calm had been shattered. He was holding those papers in both hands, as if afraid they would vanish from his grasp, and his eyes were as wide now as they had been the moment that Bobby and Frank disappeared.

Julie was lightheaded with fear, but she was determined not to lose control of herself. Though there seemed to be nothing that she could do to help Bobby, an opportunity for action might arise when she least expected it, and she wanted to be calm and ready. "Last night, Hal said that Frank returned the first time about eighteen minutes after he'd left."

Clint nodded. "Then we've twelve minutes to go."

"After his second disappearance, he didn't return for hours."

"Listen," Clint said, "if they don't show up here again in twelve minutes or an hour or three hours, that doesn't mean anything terrible has happened to Bobby. It's not going to be the same every time."

"I know. What I'm more worried about is . . . the damn bed railing."

Clint said nothing.

Unable to keep her voice even, she said, "Frank never did bring it back. What happened to it?"

"He'll bring Bobby back," Clint said. "He won't let Bobby out there . . . wherever he goes."

She wished she felt confident about that.

DARKNESS.

Fireflies.

Velocity.

Rain poured straight down in warm torrents, as if Bobby and Frank had materialized under a waterfall. It pasted their clothes to them in an instant. There was no wind whatsoever, as if the tremendous weight and ferocity of the rainfall had drowned the wind as it would a fire; the air was steamy-humid. They had traveled far enough around the globe to have left twilight behind; the sun was up there somewhere behind the steely plating of gray clouds.

They were on their sides this time, facing each other like two inebriates who had been arm wrestling and had fallen drunkenly off their stools onto the floor of the barroom, where they still lay with their hands locked in competition. They were not in a bar, however, but in lush tropical foliage: ferns; dark green plants with rubbery, deeply crenulated foliage;

ground-hugging succulent vines with leaves as plump as gum candies and berries the same shade as the flesh of a Mandarin orange.

Bobby pulled away from Frank, and this time his client let him go without a struggle. He scrambled to his feet and pushed through the slick, spongy, clinging flora.

He didn't know where he was going and didn't care. He just had to put a little space between himself and Frank, distance himself from the danger that Frank now represented to him. He was overwhelmed by what had happened, overloaded with new experiences that he needed to consider and to which he had to adapt before he could go on.

Within half a dozen steps he broke out of the tropical brush and onto a dark expanse of land, the nature of which at first eluded him. The rain came down not in droplets and not in sheets, but in roaring, silver-gray cascades that dramatically reduced visibility; it swept his hair over his eyes, too, which didn't help. He supposed some people, sitting by windows in dry rooms, might even have seen beauty in the storm, but there was just too damned much rain, a flood; it met the earth and the greenery with a cacophonous roar that threatened to deafen him. The rain not only exhausted him but made him wildly and irrationally angry, as if he was being pelted not by rain but by spittle, great gobs of phlegmy spit, and as if the roar was actually the combined voices of thousands of onlookers showering him with insults and other abuse. He stumbled forward through the peculiarly mushy soil—not muddy, but mushy—looking for someone to blame for the rain, someone to shout at and shake and maybe even punch. In six or eight steps, however, he saw the breakers rolling ashore in a tumult of white foam, and he knew he was standing on a black-sand beach. That realization stopped him cold.

"Frank!" he shouted, and when he turned to look back the way he had come, he saw that Frank was following him, a few steps behind and round-backed, as if he were an old man unable to stand up to the force of the rain, or as if his spine had been warped by all the moisture. "Frank, dammit, where are we?"

Frank stopped, unbent his back slightly, lifted his head, and blinked stupidly. "What?"

Raising his voice even further, Bobby shouted above the tumult: "Where are we!"

Pointing to Bobby's left, Frank indicated an enigmatic, rain-shrouded structure that stood like the ancient shrine of a long-dead religion, perhaps a hundred feet farther down the black beach. "Lifeguard station!" He pointed the other direction, up the beach, indicating a large wooden building considerably farther from them but less mysterious because its size made it easier to see. "Restaurant. One of the most popular on the island."

"What island?"

"The big island."

"What big island?"

"Hawaii. We're standing on Punaluu Beach."

"This was where *Clint* was supposed to take me," Bobby said. He laughed, but it was a strange, wild laugh that spooked him, so he stopped.

Frank said, "The house I bought and abandoned is back there." He indicated the direction from which they had come. "Overlooking a golf course. I loved the place. I was happy there for eight months. Then *he* found me. Bobby, we have to get out of here."

Frank took a few steps toward Bobby, out of the mushy area and onto that section of the beach where the sand was better compacted.

"That's far enough," Bobby ordered when Frank was six or eight feet from him. "Don't come any closer."

"Bobby, we have to go now, right away. I can't teleport exactly when I want. That'll happen when it happens, but at least we have to get away from this part of the island. He knows I lived here. He's familiar with this area. And he may be following us."

The fiery anger in Bobby was not quenched by the rain; it grew hotter than ever. "You lying bastard."

"It's true, really," Frank said, obviously surprised by Bobby's vehemence. They were close enough to converse without shouting now, but Frank still spoke louder than usual to be heard over the crackle-hiss-patter-rumble of the deluge. "Candy came here after me, and he was worse than I'd ever seen him, more horrible, more evil. He came into my house with a baby, an infant he'd picked up somewhere, only months old, he'd probably killed its parents. He bit into that poor baby's throat, Bobby, then laughed and offered me its blood, taunted me with it. He drinks blood, you know, *she* taught him to drink blood, and he relishes it now, thrives on it. And when I wouldn't join him at the baby's throat, he threw it aside the way you'd discard an empty beer can, and he came for me, but I . . . traveled."

"I didn't mean you were lying about him." A wave broke closer to shore than the others, washing around Bobby's feet and leaving short-lived, lacelike traceries of foam on the black sand. "I mean you lied to us about your amnesia. You remember everything. You know exactly who you are."

"No, no." Frank shook his head and made negating gestures with his hands. "I didn't know. It *was* a blank. And maybe it'll be a blank again when I stop traveling and stay put someplace."

"Lying shit!" Bobby said.

He stooped, scooped up handsful of wet black sand and threw it at Frank in a blind fury, two more sopping handsful, then two more. He began to realize that he was behaving like a child throwing a tantrum.

Frank flinched from the wet sand but waited patiently for Bobby to stop. "This isn't like you," he said, when at last Bobby relented.

"To hell with you."

"Your rage is all out of proportion to anything you imagine I've done to you."

Bobby knew that was true. As he wiped his wet sand-covered hands on his shirt and tried to catch his breath, he began to understand that he was not angry at Frank but at what Frank represented to him. Chaos. Teleportation was a funhouse ride in which the monsters and dangers were not illusory, in which the constant threat of death was to be taken seriously, in which there were no rules, no verities that could be relied upon, where up was down and in was out. Chaos. They had ridden the back of a bull named Chaos, and Bobby had been flat-out terrified.

"You okay?" Frank asked.

Bobby nodded.

More than fear was involved. On a level deeper than intellect or even instinct, perhaps as deep as the soul itself, Bobby had been *offended* by that chaos. Until now he had not realized what a powerful need he had for stability and order. He'd always thought of himself as a free spirit who thrived on change and the unexpected. But now he saw that he had limits and that, in fact, beneath the devil-may-care attitude he sometimes struck, beat the steady heart of a stability-loving traditionalist. He suddenly understood that his passion for swing music had roots of which he'd never been aware: the elegant and complex rhythms and melodies of big-band jazz appealed to his bebop surface *and* to the secret seeker of order who dwelt in his heart. No wonder he liked Disney cartoons, in which Donald Duck might run wild and Mickey might get in a tangled mess with Pluto, but in which order triumphed in the end. Not for him the chaotic universe of Warner Brothers' Looney Tunes, in which reason and logic seldom won more than a temporary victory.

"Sorry, Frank," he said at last. "Give me a second. This sure isn't the place for it, but I'm having an epiphany."

"Listen, Bobby, please, I'm telling the truth. Evidently I can remember everything when I travel. The very fact of traveling tears down the wall blocking my memory, but as soon as I stop traveling, the wall goes up again. It's part of the degeneration I'm undergoing, I guess. Or maybe it's just a desperate need to forget what's happened to me in the past, what's happening now, and what will sure as hell happen to me in the days to come."

Though no wind had risen, some of the breakers were larger now, washing deep onto the beach. They battered the backs of Bobby's legs and, on retreating, buried his feet in coaly sand.

Struggling to explain himself, Frank said, "See, traveling isn't easy for me, like it is for Candy. He can control where he wants to go, and when. He can travel just by deciding to do it, virtually by wishing himself someplace, like you suggested I might be able to do. But I can't. My talent for teleportation isn't really a talent, it's a curse." His voice grew shaky. "I didn't even know I could do it until seven years ago, the day that bitch died. All of us who came from her womb are cursed, we can't escape it. I thought I could escape somehow by killing her, but that didn't release me."

After the events of the past hour, Bobby thought nothing could surprise him, but he was startled by the confession Frank had made. This pathetic, sad-eyed, dimpled, comic-faced, pudgy man seemed an unlikely perpetrator of matricide. "You killed your own mother?"

"Never mind about her. We haven't time for her." Frank looked back toward the brush out of which they had come, and both ways along the beach, but they were still alone in the downpour. "If you'd known her, if you'd suffered under her hand," Frank said, his voice shaking with anger, "if you'd known the atrocities she's capable of, you'd have picked up an ax and chopped at her too."

"You took an ax and gave your mother forty whacks?" That crazy sound burst from Bobby again, a laugh as wet as the rain but not as warm, and again he was spooked by himself.

"I discovered I could teleport when Candy had me backed into a corner, going to kill me for having killed her. And that's the only time I can travel—when it's a matter of survival."

"Nobody was threatening you last night in the hospital."

"Well, see, when I start traveling in my sleep, I think maybe I'm trying to escape from Candy in a dream, which triggers teleportation. Traveling always wakes me, but then I can't stop, I keep popping from place to place, sometimes staying a few seconds, sometimes an hour or more, and it's beyond my control, like I'm being bounced around inside a goddamn cosmic pinball machine. It exhausts me. It's killing me. You can *see* how it's killing me."

Frank's earnest persistence and the numbing, relentless roar of the rain had washed away Bobby's rage. He was still somewhat afraid of Frank, of the potential for chaos that Frank represented, but he was no longer angry.

"Years ago," Frank said, "dreams started me traveling maybe one night a month, but gradually the frequency increased, until the last few weeks it happens almost every time I go to sleep. And when we finally wind up in your office or wherever this episode is going to come to an end, you'll remember everything that's happened to us, but I won't. And not only because I *want* to forget, but because what you suspected is true—I'm not always putting myself back together without mistakes."

"Your mental confusion, loss of intellectual skills, amnesia—they're symptoms of those mistakes."

"Yeah. I'm sure there's sloppy reconstruction and cell damage every time I travel, nothing dramatic in any one trip, but the effect is incremental . . . and accelerating. Sooner or later it's going to go critical, and I'll either die or experience some weird biological meltdown. Coming to you for help was pointless, no matter how good you are at what you do, because nobody can help me. Nobody."

Bobby had already reached that conclusion, but he was still curious. "What is it with your family, Frank? Your brother has the power to make that car disintegrate around you, the power to blow out those streetlamps, and he can teleport. And what was that business with the cats?"

"My sisters, the twins, they have this thing with animals."

"How come all of you possess these . . . abilities? Who *was* your mother, your father?"

"We don't have time for that now, Bobby. Later. I'll try to explain later." He held out his cut hand, which had either stopped bleeding or was sluiced free of blood by the rain. "I could pop out of here any moment, and you'd be stranded."

"No thanks," Bobby said, shunning his client's hand. "Call me an old fuddy-duddy, but I'd prefer an airliner." He patted his hip pocket. "Got my wallet, credit cards. I can be back in Orange County tomorrow, and I don't have to take a chance that I'll arrive there with my left ear where my nose should be."

"But Candy's probably going to follow us, Bobby. If you're here when he shows up, he'll kill you."

Bobby turned to his right and started to walk toward the distant restaurant. "I'm not afraid of anyone named Candy."

"You better be," Frank said, grabbing his arm and halting him.

Jerking away as if making contact with his client was tantamount to contracting the bubonic plague, Bobby said, "How could he follow us anyway?"

When Frank worriedly surveyed the beach again, Bobby realized that because of the pounding rain and the underlying crash of the surf, they might not hear the telltale flutelike sounds that would warn them of Candy's imminent arrival.

Frank said, "Sometimes, when he touches something you recently touched, he sees an image of you in his mind, and sometimes he can see where you went after you put the object down, and he can follow you."

"But I didn't touch anything back there at the house."

"You stood on the back lawn."

"So?"

"If he can find the place where the grass is trampled, find where we stood, he might be able to put his fingers to the grass and see us, see this place, and come after us."

"For God's sake, Frank, you make this guy sound supernatural."

"He's the next thing to it."

Bobby almost said he would take his chances with brother Candy, regardless of his godlike powers. Then he remembered what the Phans had told him about the savage murders of the Farris family. He also remembered the Roman family, their brutalized bodies torched to cover the ragged gashes that Candy's teeth had torn in their throats. He recalled what Frank had said about Candy offering him the fresh blood of a living baby, factored in the unmitigated terror in Frank's eyes at that very moment, and thought of the inexplicable prophetic dream he'd had about the "bad thing." At last said, "All right, okay, if he shows up, and if you're able to pop out of here before he kills us both, then I'd be better off with you. I'll take your hand, but only until we walk up to that restaurant, call a cab, and are on our way to the airport." He gripped Frank's hand reluctantly. "As soon as we're out of this area, I let go."

"All right. Good enough," Frank said.

Squinting as the rain battered their faces, they headed toward the restaurant. The structure, which stood perhaps a hundred and fifty yards away, appeared to be made of gray, weathered wood and lots of glass. Bobby thought he saw dim lights in the place, but he could not be sure; the large windows were no doubt tinted, which filtered out what fraction of the lampglow was not already hidden by the veils of rain.

Every third or fourth incoming wave was now much larger than the others, reached farther onto the beach, and sloshed around their legs with enough force to unbalance them. They moved toward the higher end of the strand, away from the breakers, but the sand was far softer there; it sucked at their shoes and made progress more laborious.

Bobby thought of Lisa, the blond receptionist at Palomar Labs. He pictured her coming along the beach right now, taking a crazy-romantic walk in the warm rain with some guy who'd brought her to the islands, pictured her face when she saw him strolling the black-sand beach hand-in-hand with another man, cheating on Clint.

This time his laughter didn't have a scary edge.

Frank said, "What?"

Before Bobby could even start to explain, he saw that someone actually was heading in their general direction through the obscuring rain. It was a dark figure, not Lisa, a man, and he was only about thirty yards away.

He hadn't been there a moment ago.

"It's him," Frank said.

Even at a distance the guy looked big. He spotted them and turned directly toward them.

Bobby said, "Get us out of here, Frank."

"I can't do it on demand. You know that."

"Then let's run," he urged, and he tried to pull Frank along the beach, toward the abandoned lifeguard tower and whatever lay beyond.

But after floundering a few steps through the sand, Frank stopped and said, "No, I can't, I'm worn out. I'm going to have to pray that I pop out of here in time."

He looked worse than worn out. He looked half dead.

Bobby turned toward Candy again, and saw the dark brother slogging through the soft, wet sand much faster than they had managed but still with some difficulty. "Why doesn't he just teleport from there to here in a flash, overwhelm us?"

Frank's horror at the sight of his oncoming nemesis was so complete that he didn't appear capable of speech. Yet the words came with the shallow breaths that rasped out of him: "Short hops, under a few hundred feet, aren't possible. Don't know why."

Maybe if the trip was too short, the mind had a fraction of a second less than the minimum time required to deconstruct and fully reconstruct the body. It didn't matter what the reason was. Even if he couldn't teleport across the remaining stretch of sand, Candy was going to reach them in seconds.

He was only thirty feet away and closing, a massive juggernaut of a man, with a neck thick enough to support a car balanced on his head, and arms that would give him an advantage in a wrestling match with a four-ton industrial robot. His blond hair was almost white. His face was broad and sharp-featured and hard—and as cruel as the face of one of those pre-psychotic young boys who liked to set ants on fire with matches and test the effects of full-strength lye on neighborhood dogs. Charging through the storm, kicking up gouts of wet black sand with each step, he looked less like a man than like a demon with a fierce hunger for human souls.

Holding fast to his client's hand, Bobby said, "Frank, for God's sake, let's get out of here."

When Candy was close enough for Bobby to see blue eyes as wild and vicious as those of a rattlesnake on Benzedrine, he let out a wordless roar of triumph. He flung himself at them.

Darkness.

Fireflies.

Velocity.

Pale morning light filtered from a clear sky into the narrow pass-through between two rotting, ramshackle buildings so crusted in the filth of ages that it was impossible to determine what material had been used to construct their walls. Bobby and Frank were standing in knee-deep garbage that had been tossed out of the windows of the two-story structures and left to decompose into a reeking sludge that steamed like a compost pile. Their magical arrival had startled a colony of roaches that scuttled away from them, and caused swarms of fat black flies to leap up from their breakfast. Several sleek rats sat up on their haunches to see what had arrived among them, but they were too bold to be scared off.

The tenements on both sides had some windows completely open to the outside, some covered with what looked like oiled paper, none with glass. Though no people were in sight, from the rooms within the aged walls came voices: laughter here; an angry exchange there; chanting, as of a mantra, softly drifting down from the second floor of the building on the right. It was all in a foreign tongue with which Bobby was not familiar, though he suspected they might be in India, perhaps Bombay or Calcutta.

Because of the ineluctable stench, which by comparison made the stink of a slaughterhouse seem like a new perfume by Calvin Klein, and because of the insistently buzzing flies that exhibited great interest in an open mouth and nostrils, Bobby was unable to get his breath. He choked, put his free hand over his mouth, still could not breathe, and knew he was going to faint facefirst into the vile, steaming muck.

Darkness.

Fireflies.

Velocity.

In a place of stillness and silence, shafts of afternoon sunshine pierced mimosa branches and dappled the ground with golden light. They stood on a red oriental footbridge over a koi pond in a Japanese garden, where sculpted bonsai and other meticulously tended plants were positioned among carefully raked beds of pebbles.

"Oh, yes," Frank said with a mixture of wonder and pleasure and relief. "I lived here, too, for a while."

They were alone in the garden. Bobby realized that Frank always materialized in sheltered places where he was unlikely to be seen in the act, or in circumstances—such as the middle of a cloudburst—that almost ensured even a public place like a beach would be conveniently deserted. Evidently, in addition to the unimaginably demanding task of deconstruction-travel-reconstruction, his mind was also capable of scouting the way ahead and choosing a discreet point of arrival.

Frank said, "I was the longest-residing guest they'd ever had. It's a traditional Japanese inn on the outskirts of Kyoto."

Bobby became aware that they were both totally dry. Their clothes were wrinkled, in need of an ironing, but when Frank had deconstructed them in Hawaii, he had not teleported the molecules of water that had saturated their clothes and hair.

"They were so kind here," Frank said, "respectful of my privacy, yet so attentive and kind." He sounded wistful and terminally weary, as if he would have liked to have stopped his traveling right there, even if stopping meant dying at the hands of his brother.

Bobby was relieved to see that Frank also had not brought with them any of the slime from the narrow alley in Calcutta, or wherever. Their shoes and pants were clean.

Then he noticed something on the toe of his right shoe. He bent forward to look at it.

"I wish we could stay here," Frank said. "Forever."

One of the roaches from that filth-choked alley was now a part of Bobby's footwear. One of the biggest advantages of being self-employed was freedom from neckties and uncomfortable shoes, so he was wearing, as usual, a pair of soft Rockport Super-sports, and the roach was not merely stuck on the putty-colored leather but bristling from it and melded *with* it. The roach was not squirming, obviously dead, but it was there, or at least part of it was, some bits of it apparently having been left behind.

"But we've got to keep moving," Frank said, oblivious of the roach. "He's trying to follow us. We have to lose him if—"

Darkness.

Fireflies.

Velocity.

They were on a high place, a rocky trail, with an incredible panorama below them.

"Mount Fuji," Frank said, not as if he had known where they were going but as if pleasantly surprised to be there. "About halfway up."

Bobby was not interested in the exotic view or concerned about the chill in the air. He was entirely preoccupied by the discovery that the roach was no longer a part of the toe of his shoe.

"The Japanese once thought Fuji was sacred. I guess they still do, or some of them do. And you can see why. It's magnificent."

"Frank, what happened to the roach?"

"What roach?"

"There was a roach welded into the leather of this shoe. I saw it back there in the garden. You evidently brought it along from that disgusting alleyway. Where is it now?"

"I don't know."

"Did you just drop its atoms along the way?"

"I don't know."

"Or are its atoms still with me but somewhere else?"

"Bobby, I just don't know."

In Bobby's mind was an image of his own heart, hidden within the dark cavity of his chest, beating with the mystery of all hearts but with a new secret all its own—the bristling legs and shiny carapace of a roach embedded in the muscle tissue that formed the walls of the atrium or a ventricle.

An insect might be *inside* of him, and even if the thing was dead, its presence within was intolerable. An attack of entomophobia hit him with the equivalent force of a hammer blow to the gut, knocking the wind out of him, sending undulate waves of nausea through him. He struggled to breathe, at the same time striving not to vomit on the sacred ground of Mount Fuji.

Darkness.

Fireflies.

Velocity.

They hit more violently this time, as if they had materialized in midair and had fallen a few feet onto the ground. They didn't manage to hold on to each other, and they didn't land on their feet, either. Separated from Frank, Bobby rolled down a gentle incline, over small objects that clattered and clicked under him and poked painfully into his flesh. When he tumbled to a halt, gasping and frightened, he was facedown on gray soil almost as powdery as ashes. Scattered around him, sparkling brightly against that ashen backdrop, were hundreds if not thousands of red diamonds in the rough.

Raising his head, he saw that the diamond miners were there in unnerving numbers: a score of huge insects just like the one they had taken to Dyson Manfred. Caught, as he was, in a whirlpool of panic, Bobby believed that every one of those bugs was fixated on him, all those multifaceted eyes turned toward him, all those tarantula legs churning through the powdery gray soil in his direction.

He felt something crawling on his back, knew what it must be, and rolled over, pinning the thing between him and the ground. He felt it squirming frantically beneath him. Propelled by repulsion, he was suddenly on his feet, without quite remembering how he had gotten up. The bug was still clinging to the back of his shirt; he could feel its weight, its quick-footed advance from the small of his back to his neck. He reached behind, tore it off himself, cried out in disgust as it kicked against his hand, and pitched it as far away as he could.

He heard himself breathing hard and making queer little sounds of fear and desperation. He didn't like what he heard, but he was unable to silence himself.

A foul taste filled his mouth. He figured he had ingested some of the powdery soil. He spat, but his spittle looked clean, and he realized that the air itself was what he tasted. The warm air was thick, not humid exactly but *thick*, like nothing he had experienced before. And in addition to the bitter taste, it had a distinctly different but equally unpleasant smell, like sour milk with a whiff of sulfur.

Turning around, surveying the terrain, he realized that he was standing in a shallow bowl in the land, about four feet deep at its lowest point, and about a hundred feet in diameter. The sloped walls were marked by evenly spaced holes, a double layer of them, and more of the biologically engineered insects were squirming into some of those bores, out of others, no doubt seeking—and returning with—diamonds.

Because it was only four feet deep, he could see above the rim of the bowl. Across the huge, barren, and slightly sloped plain in which this depression was set, he saw what appeared to be scores of similar features, like age-smoothed meteor craters, though they were so evenly spaced that they had to be unnatural. He was in the middle of a giant mining operation.

Kicking at an insect that had crept too close to him, Bobby turned to look at the last quarter of his surroundings. Frank was there, at the far side of the crater, on his hands and knees. Bobby was relieved by the sight of him, but he was definitely not relieved by what he saw in the sky beyond Frank.

The moon was visible in broad daylight, but it was not like the gossamer ghost moon that sometimes could be seen in a clear sky. It was a mottled gray-yellow sphere six times normal size, looming ominously over the land, as if about to collide with the larger world around which it should have been revolving at a respectable distance.

But that was not the worst. A huge and strangely shaped aircraft hung silently at perhaps an altitude of four or five hundred feet, so alien in every aspect that it brought home to Bobby the understanding that had thus far eluded him. He was not on his own world any longer.

"Julie," he said, because suddenly he realized how terribly far from her he had traveled.

At the far side of the crater, as he was getting to his feet, Frank Pollard vanished.

47

AS DAY DIMMED AND DARK CAME, THOMAS STOOD AT THE window or sat in his chair or stretched out on his bed, sometimes reaching toward the Bad Thing to be sure it wasn't coming closer. Bobby was worried when he visited, so Thomas was worried too. A lump of fear kept rising in his throat, but he kept swallowing it because he had to be brave and protect Julie.

He didn't get as close to the Bad Thing as last night. Not close enough to let it grab him with its mind. Not close enough to let it follow him when he quick-like reeled his own mind-string back to The Home. But close. A lot closer than Thomas liked.

Every time he pushed at the Bad Thing to make sure it was still there, up north someplace, where it belonged, he knew the Bad Thing felt him snooping. That spooked Thomas. The Bad Thing knew he was snooping around, but didn't do anything, and sometimes Thomas felt maybe the Bad Thing was waiting like a toad.

Once, in the garden behind The Home, Thomas watched a toad sit real still for a long time, while a bright yellow flutterby, pretty and quick, bounced from leaf to leaf, flower to flower, back and forth, round and round, close to the toad, then not so close, then closer than ever, then way out of reach, then closer again, like it was teasing the toad, but the toad didn't move, not an inch, like maybe it was a fake toad or just a stone that looked like a toad. So the flutterby felt safe, or maybe it just liked the game too much, and it came even closer. *Wham!* The toad's tongue shot out like one of those roll-up tooters they'd let the dumb people have one New Year's Eve, and it caught the flutterby, and the green toad ate the yellow flutterby, every bit, and that was the end of the game.

If the Bad Thing was playing a toad, Thomas was going to be real careful not to be a flutterby.

Then, just when Thomas figured he should start washing himself and changing clothes for supper, just when he was going to pull back from the Bad Thing, it went somewhere. He felt it go, bang, there one second and far away the next, slipping past where he could keep a watch on it, out across the world, going the same place where the sun was taking the last of the daylight. He couldn't figure how it could go so fast, unless maybe it was on a jetplane having good food and a fine whine, smiling at pretty girls in uniforms who put little pillows behind the Bad Thing's seat and gave it magazines and smiled back at it so nice and so much you expected them to kiss it like everybody was always kissing on daytime TV. Okay, yeah, probably a jetplane.

Thomas tried some more to find the Bad Thing. Then, by the time day was all gone and night all there, he gave up. He got off his bed and got ready for supper, hoping maybe the Bad Thing was gone away and never coming back, hoping Julie was safe forever now, and hoping there was chocolate cake for dessert.

BOBBY CHARGED ACROSS the floor of the diamond-strewn crater, kicking at the bugs in his way. As he ran he told himself that his eyes had deceived him and that his mind was playing nasty tricks, that Frank had not actually teleported out of there without him. But when he arrived at the spot where Frank had been, he found only a couple of footprints in the powdery soil.

A shadow fell across him, and he looked up as the alien craft drifted in blimplike silence over the crater, coming to a full stop directly above him, still about five hundred feet overhead. It was nothing like starships in the movies, neither organic looking nor a flying chandelier. It was lozenge shaped, at least five hundred feet long, and perhaps two hundred feet in diameter. Immense. On the ends, sides, and top, it bristled with hundreds if not thousands of pointed black metal spines, big as church spires, which made it look a little like a mechanical porcupine in a permanent defensive posture. The underside, which Bobby could see best of all, was smooth, black, and featureless, lacking not only the massive spines but markings, remote sensors, portholes, airlocks, and all the other apparatus one might expect.

Bobby did not know if the ship's repositioning was coincidental or whether he was under observation. If he was being watched, he didn't want to think about the nature of the creatures that might be peering down at him, and he sure as hell didn't want to consider what their intentions toward him might be. For every movie that featured an adorable alien with the power to turn kids' bicycles into airborne vehicles, there were ten others in which the aliens were ravenous flesh eaters with dispositions so vicious as to make any New York headwaiter think twice about being rude, and Bobby was certain that this was one thing Hollywood had gotten right. It was a hostile universe out there, and dealing with his fellow human beings was scary enough for him; he didn't need to make contact with a whole new race that had devised countless new cruelties of its own.

Besides, his capacity for terror was already filled to the brim, running over; he could contain no more. He was abandoned on a distant world, where the air—he began to suspect—might contain only enough oxygen and other required gases to keep him alive for a short while, insects the size of kittens were crawling all around him, and there was a possibility that a much smaller dead insect was actually fused with the tissue of one of his internal organs, and a psychotic blond giant with superhuman powers and a taste for blood was on his trail—and the odds were billions to one that he would ever see Julie again, or kiss her, or touch her, or see her smile.

A series of tremendous, throbbing vibrations issued from the ship and shook the ground around Bobby. His teeth chattered, and he nearly fell.

He looked for somewhere to hide. There was nothing in the crater to afford concealment, and nowhere to run on the flat plain beyond.

The vibrations stopped.

Even in the deep shadow thrown by the ship, Bobby saw a horde of identical insects begin to scuttle out of the boreholes in the crater walls, one after the other. They had been called forth.

Though no apparent openings appeared in the belly of the ship, a score or more of low-energy lasers—some yellow, some white, some blue, some red—began to play over the floor of the crater. Each beam was the diameter of a silver dollar, and each moved independently of the others. Like spotlights, they repeatedly swept the crater and everything in it, sometimes moving parallel to one another, sometimes crisscrossing one another, in a display that further disoriented Bobby and gave him the feeling that he was caught in the middle of a silent fireworks show.

He remembered what Manfred and Gavenall had told him about the crimson decorations along the rim of the bug's shell, and he saw that the white lasers were focusing only on the insects, busily scanning the markings around each carapace. Their owners were taking roll call. He saw a white beam fidget over the broken corpus of one of the bugs he had kicked, and after a moment a red beam joined it to study the carcass. Then the red beam jumped to Bobby, and a couple of other beams of different hue also found him, as if he was a can of peas being identified and added to someone's grocery bill at a supermarket checkout.

The floor of the crater was teeming with insects now, so many that Bobby could see neither the gray soil nor the litter of excreted diamonds over which they clambered. He told himself that they were not really bugs; they were just biological machines, engineered by the same race that had built the ship hanging over him. But that didn't help much because they still looked more like bugs than like machines. They had been designed to mine diamonds; they were not attracted to him whatsoever; but their disinterest did not make him feel better, because his phobia guaranteed that *he* was interested in *them*. His shadow-chilled skin prickled with gooseflesh. Short-circuiting nerve endings sputtered with false reports of things crawling on him, so he felt as if bugs swarmed over him from head to foot. They were actually creeping over his shoes, but none of them tried to scurry up his legs; he was grateful, because he was sure he would go mad if they began to climb him.

He used his hand as a visor over his eyes, to avoid being dazzled by the lasers that were playing on him. He saw something gleaming in the scanner beams only a few feet away: a curved section of what appeared to be hollow steel tubing. It was sticking out of the powdery soil, partly buried, further concealed by the bugs that scurried and jittered around it. Nevertheless, at first sight Bobby knew what it was, and he was overcome with a horrible sinking feeling. He shuffled forward, trying not to crush any of the insects because, for all he knew, the alien penalty for the additional destruction of property might be instant incineration. When he could reach the glinting curve of metal, he seized it and pulled it loose of the soft earth. It was the missing railing from the hospital bed.

"HOW LONG?" JULIE demanded.

"Twenty-one minutes," Clint said.

They still stood near the chair where Frank had been sitting and beside which Bobby had been stooping.

Lee Chen had gotten off the sofa, so Jackie Jaxx could lie down. The magician-hypnotist had draped a damp washcloth over his forehead. Every couple of minutes he protested that he could not really make people disappear, though no one had accused him of being responsible for what had happened to Frank and Bobby.

Having retrieved a bottle of Scotch, glasses, and ice from the office wet bar, Lee Chen was pouring six stiff drinks, one for each person in the room, as well as for Frank and Bobby. "If you don't need a drink to steady your nerves now," Lee had said, "you'll need one to celebrate when they come back safe." He had already downed one Scotch himself. The drink he poured now would be his second. This was the first time in his life he had drunk hard liquor—or needed it.

"How long?" Julie demanded.

"Twenty-two minutes," Clint said.

And I'm still sane, she thought wonderingly. Bobby, damn you, come back to me. Don't you leave me alone forever. How am I going to dance alone? How am I going to live alone? How am I going to live?

BOBBY DROPPED THE bed railing, and the lasers winked off, leaving him in the shadow of the spiny ship, which seemed darker than before the beams appeared. As he looked up to see what would happen next, another light issued from the underside of the craft, too pale to make him squint. This one was precisely the diameter of the crater. In that queer, pearly glow, the insects began to rise off the ground, as if they were weightless. At first only ten or twenty floated upward, but then twenty more and a hundred after that, rising as lazily and effortlessly as so many bits of dandelion fluff, turning slowly, their tarantula legs motionless, the eerie light gone out of their eyes, as if they had been switched off. In a minute or two, the floor of the crater was depopulated of insects, and the horde was being drawn up effortlessly in that sepulchral silence that accompanied all of the craft's maneuvers except for the base vibrations that had called the insect miners from their bores.

Then the silence was broken by a flutelike warble.

"Frank!" Bobby cried in relief, and turned as a gust of vile-smelling wind washed over him.

As the cold, hollow piping echoed across the crater again, there was a subtle change in the hue of the light that issued from the ship above. Now the thousands of red diamonds rose from the ash-gray soil in which they lay and followed the insects upward, gleaming dully here and brightly there, so many of them that it seemed as if Bobby was standing in a rain of blood.

Another whirl of evil-scented wind cast up a cloud of the ashy soil, reducing visibility, and Bobby turned in eager expectation of Frank's arrival. Until he remembered that it might not be Frank but the brother.

The piping came a third time, and the subsequent puff of wind carried the dust away from him, so he saw Frank arrive less than ten feet from him.

"Thank God!"

As Bobby stepped forward, the pearly light underwent a second subtle change. Reaching for Frank's hand, he felt himself become weightless. When he looked down he saw his feet drift off the floor of the crater.

Frank grabbed at his outstretched hand and seized it.

Nothing had ever felt better to Bobby than Frank's firm grip, and for a moment he felt safe. Then he became aware that Frank had risen from the ground too. They were both being drawn upward in the wake of the insects and diamonds, toward the belly of the alien vessel, toward God-only-knew what nightmare inside.

Darkness.

Fireflies.

Velocity.

They were on Punaluu beach again, and the rain was coming down harder than before.

"Where the hell was that last place?" Bobby demanded, still holding fast to his client.

"I don't know," Frank said. "It scares the hell out of me, it's so weird, but sometimes I seem to be . . . drawn there."

He hated Frank for having taken him there; he loved Frank for having returned for him. When he shouted above the rain, neither love nor hate was in his voice, just borderline hysteria: "I thought you could only travel to places you've been?"

"Not necessarily. Anyway, I've been there before."

"But how did you get there the first time, it's another world, it can't have been familiar to you—right, Frank?"

"I don't know. I just don't understand any of it, Bobby."

Though face to face with Frank, Bobby took a while to notice how much the man's appearance had deteriorated since they had teleported from the Dakota & Dakota offices in Newport Beach. Although the storm once more had soaked him to the skin in seconds and left his clothes hanging on him shapelessly, it wasn't just the rain that made him look disheveled, beaten, and sickly. His eyes were more sunken than ever; the whites of them were yellow, as if he had contracted jaundice, and the flesh around them was so darkly bruised that he appeared to have painted a pair of fake shiners on himself with black shoe polish. His skin was paler than pale, a deathly gray, and his lips were bluish, as though his circulatory system was failing. Bobby felt guilty about having shouted at him, so he put his free hand on Frank's shoulder and told him he was sorry, that it was all right, that they were still fighting on the same side of this war, and that everything would turn out just fine—as long as Frank didn't take them back to that crater.

Frank said, "Sometimes it's like I'm almost in touch with . . . with the minds of those people, creatures, whatever they are in that ship." They were leaning on each other now, forehead to forehead, seeking mutual support in their exhaustion. "Maybe I've got another gift I'm not aware of, like for most of my life I wasn't aware of being able to teleport until Candy backed me into a corner and tried to kill me. Maybe I'm mildly telepathic. Maybe the wavelength my telepathy functions on is the major wavelength of that race's brain activity. Maybe I feel them out there, even across billions of light-years of space. Maybe that's why I feel as if I'm being drawn to them, called to them."

Pulling back a few inches from Frank, Bobby looked into his tortured eyes for a long moment. Then he smiled and pinched Frank's cheek, and said, "You devil, you've really done a lot of thinking about this, haven't you, really put the old noodle to work on it, huh?"

Frank smiled.

Bobby laughed.

Then they were both laughing, holding each other up by leaning into each other, the way teepee poles held one another up, and a part of their laugh was healthy, a release of tension, but part of it was that mad laughter that had troubled Bobby earlier. Clinging to his client, he said, "Frank, your life is chaos, you're *living* in chaos, and you can't go on like this. It's going to destroy you."

"I know."

"You've got to find a way to stop it."

"There is no way."

"You've got to try, buddy, you've got to try. Nobody can handle this. I couldn't live like this for one day, and you've done it for seven years!"

"No. It wasn't this bad most of that time. It's just lately, the last few months, it's accelerated."

"A few months," Bobby said wonderingly. "Hell, if we don't give your brother the slip soon and get back to the office and step off this merry-go-ground in the next few minutes, I swear to God I'm going to crack. Frank, I need order, order and stability, familiarity. I need to know that what I do today will determine where I am and who I am and what I have to show for it tomorrow. Nice orderly progression, Frank, cause and effect, logic and reason."

Darkness.

Fireflies.

Velocity.

"HOW LONG?"

"Twenty-seven . . . almost twenty-eight minutes."

"Where the hell *are* they?"

"Julie," Clint said, "I think you ought to sit down. You're shaking like a leaf, your color's not good."

"I'm all right."

Lee Chen handed her a glass of Scotch. "Have a drink."

"No."

"It might help," Clint said.

She grabbed the glass from Lee, drained it in a couple of long swallows, and shoved it back into his hand.

"I'll get you another," he said.

"Thanks."

From the sofa, Jackie Jaxx said, "Listen, is anyone going to sue me over this?"

Julie no longer sort of liked the hypnotist. She loathed him as much as she had loathed him when they had first met him in Vegas and taken on his case. She wanted to go kick his head in. Though she knew the urge to kick him was irrational, that he really had not been the cause of Bobby's disappearance, she wanted to kick him anyway. That was the impulsive side of her, the quick-to-anger side of which she was not proud. But she couldn't always control it, because it was part of her genetic makeup or, as Bobby suspected, a predilection to violent response that had begun to form in her on the day, in her childhood, when a drug-crazed sociopath had brutally killed her mother. Either way, she knew Bobby was some-times dismayed by that dark side of her, much as he loved everything else, so she made a bargain with both Bobby and God: *Listen, Bobby; wherever you are—and you listen, too, God—if this just ends well, if I can just have my Bobby back with me, I won't be this way any more, I won't want to kick in Jackie's head any more, or anyone else's head, either, I'll turn over a new leaf, I swear I will, just let Bobby come back to me safe and sound.*

THEY WERE ON a beach again, but this one had white sand that was slightly phosphorescent in the early darkness. The strand disappeared into a medium-thick fog in both directions. No rain was falling, and the air was not as warm as it had been at Punaluu.

Bobby shivered in the chill, moist air. "Where are we?"

"I'm not sure," Frank said, "but I think we're probably on the Monterey Peninsula somewhere." A car passed on a highway a hundred yards be-hind them. "That's probably Seventeen-Mile Drive. You know it? The road from Carmel through Pebble Beach—"

"I know it."

"I love the peninsula, Big Sur to the south," Frank said. "It's another one of the places I was happy . . . for a while."

Their voices were strangely muffled by the mist. Bobby liked the solid ground beneath his feet, and the thought that he was not only on his own planet but in his own country and in his own state; but he would have preferred a place with more concrete details, where fog did not obscure the landscape. The white blindness of fog was another form of chaos, and he had had more than enough disorder to last him for the rest of his life.

Frank said, "Oh, and by the way, back there in Hawaii a minute ago, you were worried about giving Candy the slip, but you don't need to be concerned. We lost him several stops ago in Kyoto, or maybe on the slopes of Mount Fuji."

"For God's sake, if we don't have to worry about leading him back to the office, let's go home."

"Bobby, I don't have—"

"Any control. Yeah, I know, I heard, it's no big secret. But I'll tell you something—you've got control on some level, way down deep in the subconscious, more control than you think you have."

"No. I—"

"Yes. Because you came back to that crater for me," Bobby said. "You told me you hate the place, that it's more frightening than anywhere you've ever been, but you came back and got me. You didn't leave me there with the bed railing."

"Pure chance that I came back."

"I don't think so."

Darkness.

Fireflies.

Velocity.

THEY MADE THE soft, pretty *bing-bong* signal come out of the wall, because that was how they told all the people in The Home it was just ten minutes before supper was going to be eaten.

Derek was already out the door by the time Thomas got up from his chair. Derek liked food. Everyone liked food, of course. But Derek liked food enough for three people.

Thomas got to the doorway, and Derek was already down the hall, walking fast in that funny way he did, almost to The Dining Room. Thomas looked back at the window.

Night was at the window.

He didn't like seeing night at the window, which was why he usually kept the drapes closed after the light went out of the world. But after he got himself ready for supper, he had tried to find the Bad Thing out there, and it helped a little to see the night when he was trying to send a mind-string into it.

The Bad Thing was still so far away it couldn't be felt. But he wanted to try once more before going to eat food and Be Sociable. He reached out through the window, up into the big dark, spinning the mind-string toward where the Bad Thing used to be—and it was back. He felt it right away, knew it felt him, too, and he remembered the green toad eating the bouncy yellow flutterby, and he pulled back into his room faster than a toad tongue could snap out and catch him.

He didn't know if he should be happy or scared that it was back. When it was gone away, Thomas was happy, because maybe it was going to be gone away a long time, but he was also a little scared because when it was gone away, he didn't know exactly where it was.

It was back.

He waited in the doorway a while.

Then he went to eat food. There was roast chicken. There was frenched fries. There was carrots and peas. There was coleslaw. There was Home-made bread, and people said there was going to be some chocolate cake and ice cream for dessert, though the people that said it was dumb people, so you couldn't be sure. It all looked good, and it smelled good, and it even tasted good. But Thomas kept thinking about how the flutterby might've tasted to the toad, and he couldn't eat much of anything.

BOUNCING LIKE TWO balls in tandem, they traveled to an empty lot in Las Vegas, where a cool desert wind spun a tumbleweed past them and where Frank said he had once lived in a house that was now demolished; to that cabin at the top of a snowy mountain meadow, where they had first teleported after leaving the office; to the graveyard in Santa Barbara; to the top of an Aztec ziggurat in the lush Mexican jungles, where the humid night air was full of buzzing mosquitoes and the cries of unknown beasts, and where Bobby almost fell down the terraced side of the py-ramidal structure before he realized how high they were and how pre-cariously perched; to the offices of Dakota & Dakota—

They were popping around so quickly, remaining in each place such a brief time—in fact, briefer with each stop—that for a moment he stood in a corner of his own office, blinking stupidly, before he realized where he was and what he had to do. He tore his hand away from Frank, and he said, "Stop it now, stop here." But Frank vanished even as Bobby spoke.

Julie was all over him an instant later, hugging him so tightly that she hurt his ribs. He hugged her, too, and kissed her a long time before coming up for air. Her hair smelled clean, and her skin smelled sweeter than he remembered. Her eyes were brighter than memory allowed, and more beautiful.

Though by nature he was not much of a toucher, Clint put a hand on Bobby's shoulder. "God, it's good to see you, good to have you back." There was even a catch in his voice. "Had us worried there for a while."

Lee Chen handed him a glass of Scotch on the rocks. "Don't do that again, okay?"

"Don't plan to," Bobby said.

No longer the smooth and self-assured performer, Jackie Jaxx had had enough for one night. "Listen, Bobby, I'm sure that whatever you have to tell us is fascinating, and you're bound to've come back with a lot of boffo anecdotes, wherever you went, but I for one don't want to hear about it."

"Boffo anecdotes?" Bobby said.

Jackie shook his head. "Don't want to hear 'em. Sorry. It's my fault, not yours. I like show biz 'cause it's a narrow life, you know? A thin little slice of the real world, but exciting 'cause it's all bright colors and loud music. You don't have to *think* in show biz, you can just be. I just want to *be*, you know? Perform, hang out, have fun. I got opinions, sure, colorful and loud opinions about everything, show-biz opinions, but I don't know a damn thing, and I don't *want* to know a damn thing, and I sure as hell don't want to know about what happened here tonight, 'cause it's the kind of thing that turns your world upside down, makes you curious, makes you think, and then pretty soon you're no longer happy with all the things that made you happy before." He raised both hands, as if to forestall argument, and said, "I'm outta here," and a moment later he was.

At first, as he told the others what had happened to him, Bobby walked slowly around the room, marveling at ordinary items, finding wonder in the mundane, relishing the solidity of things. He put his hand on Julie's desk, and it seemed to him that nothing in the world was more wondrous than humble Formica—all those molecules of man-made chemicals lined up in perfect, stable order. The framed prints of Disney characters, the inexpensive furniture, the half-empty bottle of Scotch, the flourishing pothos plant on a stand by the windows—all of those things were suddenly precious to him.

He had been traveling only thirty-nine minutes. He took almost as long to tell them a condensed version. He had popped out of the office at 4:47 and returned at 5:26, but he'd done enough traveling—via teleportation or otherwise—to last the rest of his life.

On the sofa, with Julie and Clint and Lee gathered around, Bobby said, "I want to stay right here in California. I don't need to see Paris. Don't need London. Not any more. I want to stay where I have my favorite chair, sleep every night in a bed that's familiar—"

"Damn right you will," Julie interjected.

"—drive my little yellow Samurai, open a medicine cabinet where the Anacin and toothpaste and mouthwash and styptic pencil and Bactine and Band-Aids are exactly where they ought to be."

By 6:15 Frank had not reappeared. During Bobby's account of his adventures, no one mentioned Frank's second disappearance or wondered aloud when he would return. But all of them kept glancing at the chair from which he had vanished initially and at the corner of the room from which he had dematerialized the second time.

"How long do we wait here for him?" Julie finally asked.

"I don't know," Bobby said. "But I have a feeling . . . a real bad feeling . . . that maybe Frank's not going to regain control of himself this time, that he's just going to keep popping from one place to another, faster and faster, until sooner or later he's unable to put himself back together again."

48

WHEN HE CAME STRAIGHT FROM JAPAN INTO THE KITCHEN OF HIS mother's house, Candy was seething with anger, and when he saw the cats on the table, where he ate his meals, his anger grew into a full-blown rage. Violet was sitting in a chair at the table; her ever-silent sister was in another chair beside her, hanging on her. Cats lay under their chairs and around their feet, and five of the biggest were on the table, eating bits of ham that Violet fed them.

"What're you doing?" he demanded.

Violet did not acknowledge him either with a word or a glance. Her gaze was locked with that of a dark gray mongrel that was sitting as erect as a statue of an Egyptian temple cat, patiently nibbling at a few small bits of meat offered on her pale palm.

"I'm talking to you," he said sharply, but she did not respond.

He was sick of her silences, weary to death of her infinite strangeness. If not for the promise that he had made to his mother, he would have torn Violet open right there and fed on her. Too many years had passed since he had tasted the ambrosia in his sainted mother's veins, and he had often thought that the blood in Violet and Verbina was, in a way, the same blood that had flowed in Roselle. He wondered—and sometimes dreamed—of how his sisters' blood might feel upon the tongue, how it might taste.

Looming over her, staring down as she continued to commune with the gray cat, he said, "This is where I *eat,* damn you!"

Violet still said nothing, and Candy struck her hand, knocking the remaining bits of ham helter-skelter. He swept the plate of ham off the table, as well, and took tremendous satisfaction in the sound of it shattering on the floor.

The five cats on the table were not the least startled by his fury, and the greater number on the floor remained unfazed by the ping and clatter of china fragments.

At last Violet turned her head, tilted it back, and looked up at Candy.

Simultaneously with their mistress, the cats on the table turned their heads to look haughtily at him, too, as if they wished him to understand what a singular honor they were bestowing upon him simply by granting him their attention.

That same attitude was apparent in the disdain in Violet's eyes and in the faint smirk that curled the edges of her ripe mouth. More than once he had found her direct gaze withering, and he had turned away from her, rattled and confused. Certain that he was her superior in every way, he was perplexed by her unfailing ability to defeat him or force him into a hasty retreat with just a look.

But this time would be different. He had never been as furious as he was at that moment, not even seven years ago when he had found his mother's bloody, sundered body and had learned the ax had been wielded by Frank. He was angrier now because that old rage had never subsided; it had fed on itself all these years, and on the humiliation of repeatedly failing to get his hands on Frank when the opportunities to do so arose. Now it was a midnight-black bile that coursed in his veins and bathed the muscles of his heart and nourished the cells of his brain where visions of vengeance were spawned in profusion.

Refusing to be cowed by her stare, he seized her thin arm and jerked her violently to her feet.

Verbina made a soft, woeful sound upon her separation from her sister, as if they were Siamese twins, for God's sake, as if tissue had been torn, bones split.

Shoving his face close to Violet's, he sprayed her with spittle as he spoke: "Our mother had *one* cat, just one, she liked things clean and neat, she wouldn't approve of this mess, this stinking brood of yours."

"Who cares," Violet said in a tone of voice that was at once disinterested and mocking. "She's dead."

Grabbing her by both arms, he lifted her off her feet. The chair behind her fell over as he swung her away from it. He slammed her up against the pantry door so hard that the sound was like an explosion, rattling the loose kitchen windows and some dirty silverware on a nearby counter. He had the satisfaction of seeing her face contort with pain and her eyes roll back in her head as she nearly passed out from the blow. If he had smashed her against the door any harder, her spine might have cracked. He dug his fingers cruelly into the pale flesh of her upper arms, pulled her away from the door, and slammed her into it again, though not as hard as before, just making the point that it *might* have been as hard, that it could be as hard the next time if she displeased him.

Her head had fallen forward, for she was teetering on the edge of consciousness. Effortlessly, he held her against the door, with her feet eight inches off the floor, as if she weighed nothing at all, thereby forcing her to consider his incredible strength. He waited for her to come around.

She was having difficulty getting her breath, and when at last she stopped gasping and raised her head to face him, he expected to see a different Violet. He had never struck her before. A fateful line had been crossed, one over which he never expected to trespass. With his promise to his mother in mind, he had kept his sisters safe from the often dangerous world outside, provided them with food, kept them warm in cold weather and cool in the heat, dry when it rained, but year after year he had performed his brotherly duties with growing frustration, appalled by their increasingly shameless and mysterious behavior. Now he realized that disciplining them was a natural part of protecting them; up in Heaven, his mother had probably despaired of his ever realizing the need for discipline. Thanks to his rage, he had stumbled upon enlightenment. It felt good to hurt Violet a little, just enough to bring her to her senses and to prevent her from spiraling further into the decadence and animal sensuality to which she had surrendered herself. He knew he was right to punish her. He waited eagerly for her to lift her head and face him, for he knew that they had entered a new relationship and that the awareness of these profound changes would be evident in her eyes.

At last, breathing somewhat normally, she raised her head and met Candy's gaze. To his surprise, none of his own enlightenment had been visited upon his sister. Her white-blond hair had fallen across her face, and she stared through it, like a jungle animal peering through its wind-tossed mane. In her icy blue eyes, he perceived something stranger and more primitive than anything he had seen there before. A gleeful wildness. Indefinable hungers. Need. Though she had been hurt when he had thrown her against the pantry door, a smile played on her full lips again. She opened her mouth, and he felt her hot breath against his face as she said, "You're strong. Even the cats like the feel of your strong hands on me . . . and so does Verbina."

He became aware of her long bare legs. The flimsiness of her panties. The way her red T-shirt had pulled up to expose her flat belly. The swell of her full breasts, which seemed even fuller than they were because of the leanness of the rest of her. The sharp outlines of her nipples against the material of the shirt. The smoothness of her skin. Her smell.

Revulsion burst through him like pus from a secret inner abscess, and he let go of her. Turning, he saw that the cats were looking at him. Worse, they were still lying where they had been when he had pulled Violet from her chair, as if they had not been frightened by his outrage even briefly. He knew their equanimity meant that Violet had not been frightened, either, and that her erotic response to his fury—and her mocking smile—was not in the least feigned.

Verbina was slumped in her chair, her head bowed, for she was no more able to look at him directly now than she had ever been. But she was grinning, and her left hand was between her legs, her long fingers tracing lazy circles on the thin material of her panties, under which lay the dark cleft of her sex. He needed no more proof that some of Violet's sick desire had communicated itself to Verbina, and he turned away from her too.

He tried to leave the room quickly, but without looking as if he was fleeing from them.

In his scented bedroom, safely among his mother's belongings, Candy locked the door. He was not sure why he felt safer with the lock engaged, though he was certain it was not because he feared his sisters. There was nothing about them to fear. They were to be pitied.

For a while he sat in Roselle's rocker, remembering the times, as a child, when he'd curled in her lap and contentedly sucked blood from a self-inflicted wound in her thumb or in the meaty part of her palm. Once, but unfortunately only once, she had made a half-inch incision in one of her breasts and held him to her bosom while he drank her blood from the same flesh where other mothers gave, and other children received, the milk of maternity.

He had been five years old that night when, in this very room and in this chair, he tasted the blood of her breast. Frank, seven years old then, had been asleep in the room at the end of the hall, and the twins, who'd only recently reached their first birthday, were asleep in a crib in the room across from their mother's. Being alone with her when all the others slept—oh, how unique and treasured that made him feel, especially since she was sharing with him the rich liquid of her arteries and veins, which she never offered to his siblings; it was a sacred communion, dispensed and received, that remained their secret.

He recalled being in something of a swoon that night, not merely because of the heavy taste of her rich blood and the unbounded love that was represented by the gift of it, but because of the metronomic rocking of the chair and the lulling rhythms of her voice. As he sucked, she smoothed his hair away from his brow and spoke to him of God's intricate plan for the world. She explained, as she had done many times before, that God condoned the use of violence when it was committed in the defense of those who were good and righteous. She told him how God had created men who thrived on blood, so they might be used as the earthly instruments of God's vengeance on behalf of the righteous. Theirs was a righteous family, she said, and God had sent Candy to them to be their protector. None of this was new. But though his mother had spoken of these things many times during their secret communions, Candy never grew tired of hearing them again. Children often relish the retelling of a favorite story. And as with certain particularly magical tales, this story somehow did not become more familiar with retelling but curiously more mysterious and appealing.

That night in his sixth year, however, the story took a new turn. The time had come, his mother said, for him to apply the truly amazing talents he had been given, and embark upon the mission for which God had created him. He had begun to exhibit his phenomenal talents when he was three, the same age at which Frank's far more meager gifts had become evident. His telekinetic abilities—primarily his talent for telekinetic transportation of his own body—particularly enchanted Roselle, and she quickly saw the potential. They would never want for money as long as he could teleport at night into places where cash and valuables were locked away: bank vaults; the jewelry-rich, walk-in safes in Beverly Hills mansions. And if he could materialize within the homes of the Pollard family's enemies, while they slept, vengeance could be taken without fear of discovery or reprisal.

"There's a man named Salfont," his mother cooed to him as he took his nourishment from her wounded breast. "He's a lawyer, one of those jackals who prey on upstanding folks, nothing good about him at all, not that one. He handled my father's estate—that's your dear grandpa, little Candy—probated the will, charged too much, way too much, he was greedy. They're all greedy, those lawyers."

The quiet, gentle tone in which she spoke was at odds with the anger she was expressing, but that contradiction added to the sweet, hypnotic quality of her message.

"I've tried for years to get part of the fee returned to me, like I deserve. I've gone to other lawyers, but they all say his fee was reasonable, they all stick up for each other, they're alike, peas in a pod, rotten little peas in rotten little pods. Took him to court, but judges are nothing except lawyers in black robes, they make me sick, the greedy lot of them. I've worried at this for years, little Candy, can't get it out of my mind. That Donald Salfont, living in his big house in Montecito, overcharging people, overcharging *me,* he ought to have to pay for that. Don't you think so, little Candy? Don't you think he ought to pay?"

He was five years old and not yet big for his age, as he would be from the time he was nine or ten. Even if he could teleport into Salfont's bedroom, the advantage of surprise might not be sufficient to ensure success. If either Salfont or his wife happened to be awake when Candy arrived, or if the first slash of the knife failed to kill the lawyer and brought him awake in a defensive panic, Candy would not be able to overpower him. He wouldn't be in danger of getting caught or harmed, for he could teleport home in a wink; but he would risk being recognized. Police would believe a man like Salfont, even as regarded such a fantastic accusation as murder lodged against a five-year-old boy. They would visit the Pollard place, asking questions, poking around, and God knew what they might find or come to suspect.

"So you can't kill him, though he deserves it," Roselle whispered as she rocked her favorite child. She stared down intently into his eyes as he looked up from her exposed breast. "Instead, what you have to do is take something from him as vengeance for the money he took from me, something precious to him. There's a new baby in the Salfont house. I read about it in the paper a few months ago, a little girl baby they called Rebekah Elizabeth. What kind of name is that for a girl, I ask you? Sounds high-falutin' to me, the kind of name a fancy lawyer and his wife give a baby 'cause they think them and theirs is better than other people. Elizabeth is a queen's name, you see, and you just look up what Rebekah is in the Bible, see if they don't think way too much of themselves and their little brat. Rebekah . . . she's almost six months now, they've had her long enough to miss her when she's gone, miss her bad. I'll drive you past their house tomorrow, my precious little Candy boy, let you see where it is, and tomorrow night you'll go there and visit the Lord's vengeance on them, my vengeance. They'll say a rat got into the room, or something of the sort, and they'll blame themselves until the day they're dead too."

The throat of Rebekah Salfont had been tender, her blood salty. Candy enjoyed the adventure of it, the thrill of entering the house of strangers without their permission or knowledge. Killing the girl while grownups slept in the adjoining room, unaware, filled him with a sense of power. He was just a boy, yet he slipped past their defenses and struck a blow for his mother, which in a way made him the man of the Pollard house. That heady feeling added an element of glory to the excitement of the kill.

His mother's requests for vengeance were thereafter irresistible.

For the first few years of his mission, infants and very young children were his only prey. Sometimes, in order not to present a pattern to the police, he did not bite them but disposed of them in other ways, and occasionally he took hold of them and teleported out of the house with them, so no body was ever found.

Even so, if Roselle's enemies had all been from in and around Santa Barbara, the pattern could not have been hidden. But often she required vengeance against people in far places, about whom she read in newspapers and magazines.

He remembered, in particular, a family in New York State, who won millions of dollars in the lottery. His mother had felt that their good fortune had been at the expense of the Pollard family, and that they were too greedy to be permitted to live. Candy had been fourteen at the time, and he had not understood his mother's reasoning—but he had not questioned it, either. She was the only source of truth to him, and the thought of disobedience never crossed his mind. He had killed all five members of that family in New York, then burned their house to the ground with their bodies in it.

His mother's thirst for vengeance followed a predictable cycle. Immediately after Candy killed someone for her, she was happy, filled with plans for the future; she would bake special treats for him and sing melodically while she worked in the kitchen, and she would begin a new quilt or an elaborate needlepoint project. But over the next four weeks her happiness would dim like a light bulb on a rheostat, and almost one month to the day after the killing, having lost interest in baking and crafts, she would begin to talk about other people who had wronged her and, by extension, the Pollard family. Within two to four more weeks, she would have settled on a target, and Candy would be dispatched to fulfill his mission. Consequently, he killed on only six or seven occasions each year.

That frequency satisfied Roselle, but the older Candy got, the less it satisfied him. He had not merely acquired a thirst for blood but a craving that occasionally overwhelmed him. The thrill of the hunt also intoxicated him, and he longed for it as an alcoholic longed for the bottle. Not least of all, the mindless hostility of the world toward his blessed mother motivated him to kill more often. Sometimes it seemed that virtually everyone was against her, scheming to harm her physically or to take money that was rightfully hers. She had no dearth of enemies. He remembered days when fear oppressed her; then at her direction all the blinds and drapes were drawn, the doors locked and sometimes even barricaded with chairs and other furniture, against the onslaught of adversaries who never came but who *might* have. On those bad days she became despondent and told him that so many people were out to get her that even he could not protect her forever. When he begged her to turn him loose, she refused and only said, "It's hopeless."

Then, as now, he tried to supplement the approved murders with his forays into the canyons in search of small animals. But those blood feasts, rich as they sometimes were, never quenched his thirst as thoroughly as when the vessel was human.

Saddened by too many memories, Candy rose from the rocking chair and nervously paced the room. The blind was up, and he glanced with increasing interest at the night beyond the window.

After failing to catch Frank and the stranger who had teleported into the backyard with him, after the confrontation with Violet had taken that unexpected turn and left him with undissipated rage, he was smoldering, hot to kill, but in need of a target. With no enemy of the family in sight, he would have to slaughter either innocent people or the small creatures that lived in the canyons. The problem was—he dreaded evoking his sainted mother's disappointment, up there in Heaven, yet he had no appetite for the thin blood of timid beasts.

His frustration and need built by the minute. He knew he was going to do something he would later regret, something that would make Roselle turn her face from him for a time.

Then, just when he felt he might explode, he was saved by the intrusion of a genuine enemy.

A hand touched the back of his head.

He whirled around, feeling the hand withdraw as he turned.

It had been a phantom hand. No one was there.

But he knew it was the same presence that he had sensed in the canyon last night. Someone out there, not of the Pollard family, had psychic ability of his own, and the very fact that Roselle was not his mother made him an enemy to be found and eliminated. The same person had visited Candy several times earlier in the afternoon, reaching out tentatively, probing at him but not making full contact.

Candy returned to the rocking chair. If a real enemy was going to put in an appearance, it would be worth waiting for him.

A few minutes later, he felt the touch again. Light, hesitant, quickly withdrawn.

He smiled. He started rocking. He even hummed softly—one of his mother's favorite songs.

Banking the coals of rage eventually made them burn brighter. By the time the shy visitor grew bolder, the fire would be white hot, and the flames would consume him.

49

AT TEN MINUTES TO SEVEN, THE DOORBELL RANG. FELINA Karaghiosis did not hear it, of course. But each room of the house had a small red signal lamp in one corner or another, and she could not miss the flashing light that was activated by the bell.

She went into the foyer and looked through the sidelight next to the front door. When she saw Alice Kasper, a neighbor from three doors down the street, she switched off the dead bolt, removed the security chain from its slot, and let her in.

"Hi, kid. How ya doin'?"

I like your hair, Felina signed.

"Do ya really? Just got it cut, and the girl said did I want the same old same old, or did I want to catch up with the times, and I thought what the hell. I'm not too old to be sexy, do ya think?"

Alice was only thirty-three, five years older than Felina. She had exchanged her trademark blond curls for a more modern cut that would require a new source of income just to pay for all the mousse she was going to use, but she looked great.

Come in. Want a drink?

"I'd love a drink, kid, and right now I could use six of 'em, but I gotta say no. My in-laws came over, and we're about to either play cards with 'em or shoot 'em—it depends on their attitude."

Of all the people Felina knew in her day-to-day life, Alice was the only one, other than Clint, who understood sign language. Given the fact that most people harbored a prejudice against the deaf, to which they could not admit but on which they acted, Alice was her only girlfriend. But Felina happily would have given up their friendship if Mark Kasper—

Alice's son, for whom she had learned sign language—had not been born deaf.

"Why I came over, we got a call from Clint, asking me to tell ya he's not on his way home yet, but he expects to get here maybe by eight. Since when does he work so late?"

They've got a big case. That always means some overtime.

"He's going to take ya out to dinner, and says to tell ya it's been an incredible day. I guess that's about the case, huh? Must be fascinating, married to a detective. And he's sweet, too. You're lucky, kid."

Yes. But so is he.

Alice laughed. "Right on! And if he comes home this late another night, don't settle for dinner. Make him buy ya diamonds."

Felina thought of the red gem he had brought home yesterday, and she wished she could tell Alice about it. But Dakota & Dakota business, especially concerning an ongoing case in which the client was in jeopardy, was as sacred in their house as the privacies of the marriage bed.

"Saturday, our place, six-thirty? Jack'll cook up a mess of his chile, and we'll play pinochle and eat chile and drink beer and fart till we pass out. Okay?"

Yes.

"And tell Clint, it's okay—we won't expect him to talk."

Felina laughed, then signed: *He's getting better.*

"That's 'cause you're civilizing him, kid."

They hugged again, and Alice left.

Felina closed the door, looked at her wristwatch, and saw that it was seven o'clock. She had only an hour to get ready for dinner, and she wanted to look especially good for Clint, not because this was a special occasion, but because she *always* wanted to look good for him. She headed for the bedroom, then realized that only the automatic lock was engaged on the front door. She returned to the foyer, twisted the thumb-screw that slid the dead bolt home, and slipped the security chain in place.

Clint worried about her too much. If he came home and found that she hadn't remembered the dead bolt, he'd age a year in a minute, right before her eyes.

50

AFTER BEING OFF DUTY ALL DAY, HAL YAMATAKA RESPONDED TO a call from Clint and came to the offices at 6:35 Tuesday night, to stand a watch in case Frank returned after the rest of them had left. Clint met him in the reception lounge and briefed him there over a cup of coffee. He had to be brought up to date on what had happened during his absence, and after he heard what had gone down, he again wistfully considered a career in gardening.

Nearly everyone in his family either had a gardening business or owned a little nursery, and all of them did well, most of them better than what Hal made working for Dakota & Dakota, some of them a great deal better. His folks, his three brothers, and various well-meaning uncles tried repeatedly to persuade him that he should work for them or come into business with them, but he resisted. It was not that he had anything against running a nursery, selling gardening supplies, landscape planning, tree pruning, or even gardening itself. But in southern California the term "Japanese gardener" was a cliché, not a career, and he couldn't abide the thought of being any kind of stereotype.

He had been a heavy reader of adventure and suspense novels all his life, and he yearned to be a character like one of those he read about, especially a character worthy of being a lead in a John D. MacDonald novel, because John D's lead characters were as rich in insight as they were in courage, every bit as sensitive as they were tough. In his heart Hal knew that his work at Dakota & Dakota was usually as mundane as the daily grind of a gardener, and that the opportunities for heroism in the security industry were far fewer than they appeared to be to outsiders. But selling a bag of mulch or a can of Spectricide or a flat of marigolds, you couldn't kid yourself that you were a romantic figure or had any chance of being one. And, after all, self-image was often the better part of reality.

"If Frank shows up here," Hal said, "what do I do with him?"

"Pack him in a car and take him to Bobby and Julie."

"You mean their house?"

"No. Santa Barbara. They're driving up there tonight, staying at the Red Lion Inn, so tomorrow they can start digging into the Pollard family's background."

Frowning, Hal leaned forward on the reception-lounge sofa. "Thought you said they don't figure ever to see Frank again."

"Bobby says he thinks Frank is coming apart, won't last through this latest series of travels. That's just his feeling."

"So then who's their client?"

"Until he fires them, Frank is."

"Sounds iffy to me. Be straight with me, Clint. What's really got them so committed to this one, especially considering how crazy-dangerous it seems to get, hour by hour?"

"They like Frank. *I* like Frank."

"I said be straight."

Clint sighed. "Damned if I know. Bobby came back here spooked out of his mind. But he won't let go of it. You'd think they'd pull in their horns, at least until Frank shows up again, if he does. This brother of his, this Candy, he sounds like the devil himself, too much for anyone to handle. Bobby and Julie are stubborn sometimes, but they're not stupid, and I'd expect them to let go of this, now that they've seen it's a job big enough for God, not a private detective. But here we are."

BOBBY AND JULIE huddled with Lee Chen at the desk, while he shared with them the information he had thus far obtained.

"The money might be stolen, but it's spendable," Lee said. "I can't find those serial numbers on any currency hot sheets—federal, state, or local."

Bobby had already thought of several sources from which Frank might have obtained the six hundred thousand now in the office safe. "Find a business with a high cash flow, where they don't always get to a bank with the receipts at the end of the day, and you've got a potential target. Say it's a supermarket, stays open till midnight, and it's not a good idea for a manager to tote a lot of cash to a bank for automatic deposit, so there's a safe in the market. After the place closes, you teleport inside, if you're Frank, and use whatever other powers you have to open that safe, put the day's receipts in a grocery bag, and vanish. You're not going to find big chunks of cash, a couple hundred thousand at a time, but you hit three or four markets in an hour, and you've got your haul."

Evidently Julie had been pondering the same question, for she said, "Casinos. They all have accounting rooms you can find on the blueprints, the ones the IRS gets into with a little effort. But they've got hidden rooms, too, where the skim goes. Like big walk-in safes. Fort Knox would envy them. You use whatever minor psychic abilities you have to figure the location of one of those hidden rooms, teleport in when it's deserted, and just take what you want."

"Frank lived in Vegas for a while," Bobby said. "Remember, I told you about the vacant lot he took me to, where he'd had a house."

"He wouldn't be limited to Vegas," Julie said. "Reno, Tahoe, Atlantic City, the Caribbean, Macao, France, England, Monte Carlo—anywhere there's big-time gambling."

This talk of easy access to unlimited amounts of cash excited Bobby, though he was not sure why. After all, it was Frank who could teleport, not him, and he was ninety-five-percent sure they were never going to see Frank again.

Spreading a sheaf of printouts across the desktop, Lee Chen said, "The money's the least interesting thing. You remember, you wanted me to find out if the cops are on to Mr. Blue?"

"Candy," Bobby said. "We have a name for him now."

Lee scowled. "I liked Mr. Blue better. It had more style."

Entering the room, Hal Yamataka said, "I don't think I trust the style judgment of a guy who wears red sneakers and socks."

Lee shook his head. "We Chinese spend thousands of years working up an intimidating image for all Asians, so we can keep these hapless Westerners off balance, and you Japanese blow it all by making those Godzilla movies. You can't be inscrutable and make Godzilla movies."

"Yeah? You show me *anybody* who understands a Godzilla movie after the first one."

They made an interesting pair, these two: one slender, modish, with delicate features, an enthusiastic child of the silicon age; the other squat, broad, with a face as blunt as a hammer, a guy who was about as high-tech as a rock.

But to Bobby the most interesting thing was that, until this moment, he had never thought about the fact that a disproportionately large percentage of Dakota & Dakota's small staff was Asian-American. There were two more—Nguyen Tuan Phu and Jamie Quang, both Vietnamese. Four out of eleven people. Though he and Hal once in a while made East-

West jokes, Bobby never thought of Lee and Hal and Nguyen and Jamie as composing any subset of employees; they were just themselves, as different from one another as apples are different from pears and oranges and peaches. But Bobby realized that this predilection for Asian-American co-workers revealed something about himself, something more than just an obvious and admirable racial blindness, but he could not figure out what it was.

Hal said, "And *nothing* gets more inscrutable than the whole concept of Mothra. By the way, Bobby, Clint's gone home to Felina. We should all be so lucky."

"Lee was telling us about Mr. Blue," Julie said.

"Candy," Bobby said.

Indicating the data he had extracted from various police records nationwide, Lee said, "Most police agencies began to be computerized and interlinked only about nine years ago—in any sophisticated way, that is. So that's all the further back a lot of electronically accessible files go. But during that time, there have been seventy-eight brutal murders, in nine states, that have enough similarities to raise the possibility of a single perp. Just the possibility, mind you. But FBI got interested enough last year to put a three-man team on it, one in the office and two in the field, to coordinate local and state investigations."

"Three men?" Hal said. "Doesn't sound like high priority."

"The Bureau's always been overextended," Julie said. "And over the last thirty years, since it's been unfashionable for judges to hand out long criminal sentences, the bad guys outnumber them worse than ever. Three men, full time—that's a serious commitment at this stage."

Extracting a printout from the pile on the desk, Lee summarized the essential data on it. "All of the killings have these points in common. First—the victims were all bitten, most on the throat, but virtually no part of the body is sacred to this guy. Second—many of them were beaten, suffered head injuries. But loss of blood, from the bites—usually the jugular vein and carotid artery in the throat—was a substantial contributing factor to the death in virtually every instance, regardless of other injuries."

"On top of everything else, the guy's a vampire?" Hal asked.

Taking the question seriously—as, indeed, they had to consider every possibility in this bizarre case, regardless of how outlandish it seemed—Julie said, "Not a vampire in the supernatural sense. From what we've learned, the Pollard family is for some reason generously gifted. You know that magician on TV; The Amazing Randi, who offers to pay a hundred thousand bucks to anyone who proves they have psychic power? This Pollard clan would bankrupt his ass. But that doesn't mean there's anything supernatural about them. They're not demons, or possessed, or the children of the devil—nothing like that."

"It's just some extra bit of genetic material," Bobby said.

"Exactly. If Candy acts like a vampire, biting people in the throat, that's just a manifestation of psychological illness," Julie said. "It doesn't mean he's one of the living dead."

Bobby vividly remembered the blond giant charging him and Frank on the rainswept black beach at Punaluu. The guy was as formidable as a locomotive. If Bobby had a choice of going up against either Candy Pollard or Dracula, he might choose the undead Count. Nothing as simple as a clove of garlic, a crucifix, or a well-placed wooden stake would effectively deter Frank's brother.

Lee said, "Another similarity. In those instances where victims didn't leave doors or windows unlocked, there was no indication of how the killer gained entrance. And in many instances police found doors deadbolted from the inside, windows locked from the inside, as if the murderer had gone up the chimney when he was done."

"Seventy-eight," Julie said, and shivered.

Lee dropped the paper onto the desk. "They figure there're more, maybe a lot more, because sometimes this guy has attempted to cover his trail—the bite marks—by further multilating or even burning the bodies. Though the cops weren't fooled in *these* cases, you can figure they were fooled in others. So the count's higher than seventy-eight, and that's just the last nine years."

"Good job, Lee," Julie said, and Bobby seconded that.

"I'm not done yet," Lee said. "I'm going to order in a pizza, do some more digging."

"You've been here more than ten hours today," Bobby said. "That's already above and beyond the call. Got to have downtime, Lee."

"If you believe, as I do, that time is subjective, then you've got an infinite supply. Later, at home, I'll stretch a few hours into a couple of weeks and return tomorrow quite rested."

Hal Yamataka shook his head and sighed. "Hate to admit it, Lee, but you're damned good at this mysterious oriental crap."

Lee smiled enigmatically. "Thank you."

———

AFTER BOBBY AND Julie went home to pack an overnight bag for the trip to Santa Barbara, and after Lee returned to the computer room, Hal settled on the sofa in the bosses' office, slipped off his shoes, and put his feet up on the coffee table. He still had the paperback of *The Last One Left*, which he'd read twice before, and which he had started to reread last night in the hospital. If Bobby was right when he said they might never see Frank again, Hal was in for an uneventful evening and would probably get half the book read.

Maybe his happiness at Dakota & Dakota had nothing to do with the prospect of excitement, avoiding a stereotypical job as a gardener, and having the admittedly slim chance to be a hero. Maybe the thing that most affected his career decision was the realization that he simply could not mow a lawn or trim a hedge or plant fifty flats of flowers and read a book at the same time.

DEREK SAT IN his chair. Pointed the raygun at the TV and made it be on. He said, "You don't want to watch news?"

"No," Thomas said. He was on his bed, propped up with pillows, looking at the night being dark outside the window.

"Good. Me neither." Derek pushed buttons on the raygun. A new picture came on the screen. "You don't want to watch a game show?"

"No." All Thomas wanted to do was snoop on the Bad Thing.

"Good." Derek pushed buttons, and the invisible rays made the screen show a new picture. "You don't want to watch the Three Stooges pretending to be funny?"

"No."

"What you want to watch?"

"Don't matter. Whatever you want to watch."

"Really?"

"Whatever you want to watch," Thomas repeated.

"Gee, that's nice." He made lots of pictures on the screen until he found a space movie where spacemen in spacesuits were poking around in some spooky place. Derek made a happy sigh and said, "This is good. I like their hats."

"Helmets," Thomas said. "Space helmets."

"I wish I had a hat like that."

When he reached out into the big dark again, Thomas decided not to picture a mind-string unraveling toward the Bad Thing. Instead he pictured a raygun, shooting some invisible rays. Boy, did that work better! *Wham*, he was right there with the Bad Thing in a flash, and he felt it stronger, too, so strong he got scared and clicked off the raygun and got all of himself back into his room with the rest of himself right away.

"They got telephones in their hats," Derek said. "See, they're talking through their hats."

On the TV, the spacemen were in an even spookier place, poking around, which was one of the things spacemen did the most, even though something ugly-nasty was usually in those spooky places just waiting for them. Spacemen never learned.

Thomas looked away from the screen.

At the window.

The dark.

Bobby was scared for Julie. Bobby knew stuff Thomas didn't know. If Bobby was scared for Julie, Thomas had to be brave and do What Was Right.

The raygun idea worked such a lot better it scared him, but he figured it was really good because he could easier snoop on the Bad Thing. He could get to the Bad Thing faster and get away from it faster, too, so he could snoop on it more often and not be scared about it maybe grabbing the mind-string and coming back to The Home with him. Grabbing an invisible raygun ray was harder, even for a thing as fast and smart and mean as the Bad Thing.

So he pictured pushing buttons on a raygun again, and a part of him went through the dark—*wham!*—and to the Bad Thing right away. He felt how mad the Bad Thing was, madder than ever, and thinking lots of thoughts about blood that made Thomas half sick. Thomas wanted to come right back to The Home. The Bad Thing felt him, you could tell. He didn't like the Bad Thing feeling him, knowing he was there with it, but he stayed just a couple clock ticks longer, trying to see any thoughts about Julie in all those thoughts about blood. If the Bad Thing had thoughts about Julie, Thomas would TV a warning right away to Bobby. He was happy he couldn't find Julie in the Bad Thing's mind, and he quick raygunned back to The Home.

"Where you think I could get a hat like that?" Derek asked.

"Helmet."

"Even has a light on it, see?"

Rising up a little from his pillows, Thomas said, "You know what kind of a story this is?"

Derek shook his head. "What kind of story?"

"It's the kind where any second something ugly-nasty jumps up and sucks off a spaceman's face or maybe crawls in his mouth and down his belly and makes a nest in there."

Derek made a disgusted face. "Yuck. I don't like that kind of stories."

"I know," Thomas said. "That's why I warned you."

While Derek made a lot of different pictures come on the screen, one quick after the other, to get far away from the spaceman who was going to get his face sucked off, Thomas tried to think how long he should wait before he snooped on the Bad Thing again. Bobby was real worried, you could tell, even if he tried to hide it, and Bobby was not a Dumb Person, so it was a good idea to check on the Bad Thing pretty regular, in case maybe it all of a sudden thought about Julie and got up and went after her.

"You want to watch this?" Derek asked.

On the screen was a picture of this guy in a hockey mask with a big knife in his hand, going quiet-like across a room where a girl was asleep in a bed.

"Better raygun up another picture," Thomas said.

BECAUSE THE RUSH hour was past, because Julie knew all the best shortcuts, but mainly because she was not in a mood to be cautious or respect the traffic laws, they made great time from the office to their home on the east end of Orange.

On the way Bobby told her about the Calcutta roach that had been part of his shoe when he and Frank had arrived on that red bridge in the garden in Kyoto. "But when we popped to Mount Fuji, my shoe was okay, the roach was gone."

She slowed at an intersection, but she was the only traffic in sight, so she didn't obey the four-way stop. "Why didn't you tell me about this at the office?"

"Wasn't time for every detail."

"What do you think happened to the roach?"

"I don't know. That's what bothers me."

They were on Newport Avenue, just past Crawford Canyon. Sodium-vapor streetlamps cast a queer light on the roadway.

Atop the steep hills to the left, several huge English Tudor and French houses, blazing like giant luxury liners, looked wildly out of place, partly because the insanely high value of such upscale real estate ensured the construction of immense houses out of proportion to the tiny lots they stood on, but partly because Tudor and French architectural styles clashed with the semitropical landscape. It was all part of the California circus, some of which he hated, most of which he loved. Those houses never bothered him before, and given the serious problems he and Julie faced, he couldn't figure why they bothered him now. Maybe he was so jumpy that even these minor disharmonies reminded him of the chaos that had almost engulfed him during his travels with Frank.

He said, "Do you have to drive so fast?"

"Yes," she said curtly. "I want to get home, get packed, get to Santa Barbara, learn what we can about the Pollard family, get finished with this whole damn creepy case."

"If you feel that way, why don't we just drop it here? Frank comes back, we give him his money, his jar of red diamonds, tell him we're sorry, we think he's a prince of a guy, but we're out of it."

"We can't," she said.

He chewed on his lower lip, then said, "I know. But I can't figure why we're compelled to hang in there with this one."

They crested the hill and speeded north, past the entrance to Rocking Horse Ridge. Their own development was only a couple of streets ahead, on the left. As she finally began to brake for the turn, she glanced at him and said, "You really don't know why we can't bug out of it?"

"No. You saying you do?"

"I know."

"Tell me."

"You'll figure it out eventually."

"Don't be mysterious. That's not like you."

She swung the company Toyota into their development, then onto their street. "I tell you what I think, it'll upset you. You'll deny it, we'll argue, and I don't want to argue with you."

"Why will we argue?"

She pulled into their driveway, put the car in park, switched off the lights and engine, and turned to him. Her eyes shone in the dark. "When you understand why we can't let go, you won't like what it says about us, and you'll argue that I'm wrong, that we're just a couple of sweet kids, really. You like to see us as a couple of sweet kids, savvy but basically innocent at the same time, like a young Jimmy Stewart and Donna Reed. I really love you for that, for being such a dreamer about the world and us, and it'll hurt me when you want to argue."

He almost started to argue with her about whether he would argue with her. Then he stared at her for a moment and finally said, "I've had this feeling that I'm not facing up to something, that when this is all over and I realize why I was so determined to see this through to the end, my motivations won't be as noble as I think they are now. It's a weird damn feeling. As if I don't really know myself."

"Maybe we spend all our lives learning to know ourselves. And maybe we never really do—completely."

She kissed him lightly, quickly, and got out of the car.

As he followed her up the sidewalk to the front door, he glanced at the sky. The clarity of the day had been short-lived. A pall of clouds concealed the moon and stars. The sky was very dark, and he was gripped by the curious certainty that a great and terrible weight was falling toward them, black against the black heavens and therefore invisible, but falling fast, faster. . . .

51

CANDY KEPT A CHOKEHOLD ON HIS FURY, WHICH STRAINED LIKE an attack dog trying to break its leash.

He rocked and rocked, and gradually the shy visitor grew bolder. Repeatedly he felt the invisible hand on his head. Initially it lay upon him as lightly as an empty silk glove, and it stayed only briefly before flitting away. But as he pretended to be disinterested in both the hand and the person to whom it belonged, the visitor grew more daring, the hand heavier and less nervous.

Though Candy made no effort to probe at the mind of the intruder, for fear of scaring him away, some of the stranger's thoughts came to him nonetheless. He did not think the visitor was aware that images and words from his own mind were slipping into Candy's; they were just leaking out of him as if they were trickles of water seeping from pin-size holes in a rusty bucket.

The name "Julie" came several times. And once an image floated along with the name—an attractive woman with brown hair and dark eyes. Candy wasn't sure if it was the visitor's face or the face of someone the visitor knew—or even if it was the face of anyone who really existed. There were aspects that made it seem unreal: a pale light radiated from it, and the features were so kind and serene that it looked like the holy countenance of a saint in an illustrated Bible.

The word "flutterby" leaked out of the visitor's mind more than once, sometimes with other words, like "remember the flutterby" or "don't be a flutterby." And each time that word flitted through his mind, the visitor quickly withdrew.

But he kept coming back. Because Candy did nothing to make him feel unwelcome.

Candy rocked and rocked. The chair made a soft sound: *creak . . . creak . . . creak . . . creak.*

He waited.

He kept an open mind.

. . . creak . . . creak . . . creak . . .

Twice the name "Bobby" seeped from the visitor's mind, and the second time a fuzzy image of a face was linked to it, another very kind face. It was idealized, like Julie's face. Recognition stirred in Candy, but Bobby's visage was not as clear or detailed as Julie's, and Candy did not want to concentrate on it because the visitor might notice his interest and be frightened off.

During his long and patient courtship of the shy intruder, many other words and images came to Candy, but he didn't know what to make of them:

—men in spacesuits—

—"Bad Thing"—

—a guy in a hockey mask—

—"The Home"—

—"Dumb People"—

—a bathrobe, a half-eaten Hershey's bar, and a sudden frantic thought: *Draw Bugs, no good, Draw Bugs, got to Be Neat*—More than ten minutes passed without contact, and Candy started to worry that the intruder had gone away for good. But suddenly he was back. This time the contact was strong, more intimate than ever.

When Candy sensed that the visitor was more confident, he knew the time had come to act. He pictured his mind as a steel trap, the visitor as an inquisitive mouse, and he pictured the trap springing, the bar pinning the visitor to the killplate.

Shocked, the visitor tried to pull away. Candy held him and pushed across the telepathic bridge between them, trying to storm his adversary's mind to find out who he was, where he was, and what he wanted.

Candy had no telepathic power of his own, nothing to equal even the weak telepathic gifts of the intruder; he had never read anyone's mind before, and he did not know how to go about it. As it turned out, he did not need to do anything except open himself and receive what the visitor gave him. Thomas was his name, and he was terrified of Candy, of having Done Something Really Dumb, and of putting Julie in danger; that trinity of terrors shattered his mental defenses and caused him to disgorge a flood of information.

In fact, there was too much information for Candy to make sense of it, a babble of words and images. He tried desperately to sort through it for clues to Thomas's identity and location.

Dumb People, Cielo Vista, The Home, everybody here has bad eye cues, Care Home, good food, TV, The Best Place For Us, Cielo Vista, the aides are nice, we watch the hummingbirds, the world is bad out there, too bad for us out there, Cielo Vista Care Home. . . .

With some astonishment, Candy realized that the visitor was someone with a subnormal intellect—he even picked up the term "Down's syndrome"—and he was afraid that he was not going to be able to sort enough meaningful thoughts from the babble to get a fix on Thomas's location. Depending on the size of his IQ, Thomas might not know where Cielo Vista Care Home was, even though he apparently lived there.

Then a series of images spun out of Thomas's mind, a well-linked chain of serial memories that still caused him some emotional pain: the trip to Cielo Vista in a car with Julie and Bobby, on the day they first checked him into the place. This was different from most of Thomas's other thoughts and memories, in that it was richly detailed and so clearly retained that it unreeled like a length of motion-picture film, giving Candy all he needed to know. He saw the highways over which they had driven that day, saw the route markers flashing past the car window, saw every landmark at every turn, all of which Thomas had struggled mightily to memorize because all through the trip he kept thinking, *If I don't like it there, if people are mean there, if it's too scary there, if it's too much being alone there, I got to know how I find the way back to Bobby and Julie anytime I want, remember this, remember all of this, turn there at the 7-Eleven, right there at the 7-Eleven, don't forget that 7-Eleven, and now go past those three palm trees. What if they don't come visit me? No, that's a bad thing to think, they love me, they'll come. But what if they don't? Look there, remember that house, you go past that house, remember that house with the blue roof—*

Candy got it all, as precise a fix as he could have obtained from a geographer who would have spoken precisely in degrees and minutes of longitude and latitude. It was more than he needed to know to make use of his gift. He opened the trap and let Thomas go.

He got up from the rocker.

He pictured Cielo Vista Care Home as it appeared so exquisitely detailed in Thomas's memory.

He pictured Thomas's room on the first floor of the north wing, at the northwest corner.

Darkness, billions of hot sparks spinning in the void, velocity.

BECAUSE JULIE WAS in a let's-move-and-get-it-done mood, they had stopped at the house only fifteen minutes, long enough to throw toiletries and a change of clothes in an overnight bag. At McDonald's, on Chapman Avenue in Orange, she swung by the drive-through window and got dinner to eat on the way: Big Macs, fries, diet colas. Before they reached the Costa Mesa Freeway, while Bobby was still divvying up the extra packets of mustard and opening the containers that held the Big Macs, Julie had clipped the radar detector to the rearview mirror, plugged it in the Toyota's cigarette lighter, and switched it on. Bobby had never before eaten fast food at high speed, but he figured they averaged eighty-five miles an hour north on the Costa Mesa to the Riverside Freeway west to the Orange Freeway north, and he was still finishing his french fries when they were only a couple of exits away from the Foothill Freeway east of Los Angeles. Though the rush hour was well past and the traffic unusually light, maintaining that pace required a lot of lane changing and nerve.

He said, "We keep this up, I'll never have a chance to die from the cholesterol in this Big Mac."

"Lee says cholesterol doesn't kill us."

"Is that what he says?"

"He says we live forever, and all cholesterol can do is move us out of this life a little sooner. Same thing must be true if I slip up and roll this sucker a few times."

"I don't think that'll happen," he said. "You're the best driver I've ever seen."

"Thank you, Bobby. You're the best passenger."

"The only thing I wonder . . ."

"Yeah?"

"If we don't really die, just move on, and I don't have to worry about anything—why the hell did I bother to get *diet* colas?"

THOMAS ROLLED OFF the bed, onto his feet. "Derek, go, get out, he's coming!"

Derek was watching a horse talking on TV, and he didn't hear Thomas.

The TV was in the room's middle, between the beds, and by the time Thomas got there and grabbed Derek to make him listen, a funny sound was all around them, not funny ha-ha but funny weird, like somebody whistling but not whistling. There was wind, too, a couple of puffs, not warm or cold either, but it made Thomas shiver when it blew on him.

Pulling Derek off his chair, Thomas said, "Bad Thing's coming, you get out, you go, like I said before, *now!*"

Derek just made a dumb face at him, then smiled, like he figured Thomas was pretending to be funny the way the Three Stooges pretended. He'd forgot all about the promise he made Thomas. He'd thought the Bad Thing was going to be poached eggs for breakfast, and when poached eggs never showed up on his plate, he figured he was safe, but now he wasn't safe and didn't know it.

More funny-weird whistling. More wind.

Giving Derek a shove, making him get started for the door, Thomas shouted, "Run!"

The whistling stopped, the wind stopped, and all of a sudden from nowhere the Bad Thing was there. Between them and the open door.

It was a man, like Thomas already knew it was, but it was more than just a man. It was darkness poured in the shape of a man, like a piece of the night itself that came in through the window, and not just because it wore a black T-shirt and black pants but because it was all deep dark inside, you could tell.

Right away Derek was afraid. Nobody needed to tell him this was a Bad Thing, not now when he could see it with his own eyes. But he didn't see it was too late to run, and he went straight at the Bad Thing, like maybe he could push past it, which must have been what he was figuring because even Derek wasn't dumb enough to figure he could knock it down, it was so big.

The Bad Thing grabbed him and lifted him before he had any chance to get around it, lifted him right up off the floor, like he didn't weigh any more than a pillow. Derek screamed, and the Bad Thing slammed him against the wall so hard his scream stopped, and pictures of Derek's mom and dad and brother fell off the wall, not the one where Derek got slammed but another wall all the way around the room from him and over his bed.

The Bad Thing was so fast. That was the worst thing about it, how awful fast it was. It slammed Derek against the wall, Derek's mouth fell open but no more sound came from him, the Bad Thing slammed him again, right away, harder, though the first time was hard enough for any-body, and Derek's eyes went funny. The Bad Thing took him away from the wall and slammed him down on the worktable. The table kind of shivered like it would fall apart, but it didn't. Derek's head was over the table edge, hanging down, so Thomas was looking at his face, upside-down eyes blinking fast, upside-down mouth open real wide but no sound coming out. He looked up from Derek's face, looked right across Derek's body at the Bad Thing, which was looking at him and grinning, like all this was a joke, funny ha-ha, which it wasn't, no way. Then it picked up the scissors on the edge of the worktable, the ones Thomas used to make his picture poems, the ones that almost fell on the floor when it slammed Derek on the table. It made the scissors go into Derek and bring the blood out of him, into poor Derek who wouldn't hurt no one himself, except himself, who wouldn't know *how* to hurt anyone. And the Bad Thing made the scissors go in again and bring more blood out of another place in Derek, and in again, and again. Then blood wasn't coming out of just four places on Derek's chest and belly where the scissors had been made to go in, but out of his mouth and nose too. The

Bad Thing lifted Derek off the table, the scissors still sticking out of his front, and threw him like he was just a pillow. No, like he was a garbage bag, threw him the way the Santa Nation Men threw the garbage bags onto their Santa Nation Truck. Derek landed on his bed, on his back on his bed, with the scissors still in him, and didn't move and was gone to the Bad Place, you could tell. And the worst thing was it all happened so fast, faster than Thomas could think what to do to stop it.

Footsteps in the hall, people running.

Thomas yelled for help.

Pete, one of the aides, showed up in the doorway. Pete saw Derek on the bed, scissors in him, blood coming out everywhere, and he got afraid, you could see him get it. He turned to the Bad Thing and said, "Who—"

The Bad Thing grabbed him by the neck, and Pete made a sound like something was stuck in his throat. He put both his hands on the Bad Thing's arm, which seemed bigger than Pete's two arms together, but he couldn't make the Bad Thing let go. The Bad Thing lifted him by his neck, making his chin turn up and his head bend back, and then took hold of him by the belt, too, and pitched him back out the door, into the hall. Pete hit a nurse who came running up just then, and they both went down on the floor out there in the hall, all tangled up, her screaming.

All of this in a few clock ticks. So *fast.*

The Bad Thing made the door shut with a bang, saw you couldn't lock it, then did the funniest thing of all, funny-weird, funny-scary. He held both his hands out at the door, and this blue light came from his hands the way not-blue came from a flashlight. Sparks flew from hinges and around the knob and all around the door edges. Everything metal smoked and turned all soft, like butter when you put it on mashed potatoes. It was a Fire Door. They said you had to keep your door closed if you ever saw fire in the hall, not try to run in the hall, but keep your door closed and stay put. They called it a Fire Door because fire couldn't get through it, they said, and Thomas always wondered why they didn't call it a Fire Can't Get Through It Door, but he never asked. The thing was, a Fire Door was all metal, so it couldn't burn, but now it melted around the edges, and so did the metal frame, they melted together, it didn't look like you could ever get through that door again.

People started pounding on the door from out there in the hall, tried to make it open, couldn't, and shouted for Thomas and Derek. Thomas

knew some voices and who they belonged to, and he wanted to yell for
them to help quick because he was in trouble, but he couldn't make a
sound any better than poor Derek.

The Bad Thing made the blue light stop. Then it turned and looked at
Thomas. It smiled at him. It didn't have a nice smile. It said, "Thomas?"

Thomas was surprised he could stand up, he was so scared. He was
against the wall by the window, and he thought of maybe making the
lock open on the window and push it up and get out, which he knew
how to do because of Emergency Drills. But he knew he wasn't fast
enough, no way, because the Bad Thing was the fastest he ever saw.

It took a step toward him, and another step. "Are you Thomas?"

For a while he still couldn't find the way to make sounds. He could
just move his mouth and sort of pretend to make sounds. Then while he
was doing that, he figured maybe if he told a lie and said he wasn't
Thomas, the Bad Thing would believe him and just go away. So when
all of a sudden he could make sounds, and then words, he said, "No. I
. . . no . . . not Thomas. He's gone out in the world now, he's got a big
eye cue, he's a high-end moron, so they moved him out in the world."

The Bad Thing laughed. It was a laugh that had no funny in it, the
worst Thomas ever heard. The Bad Thing said, "Who the hell are you,
Thomas? Where do you come from? How come a dummy like you can
do something *I* can't?"

Thomas didn't answer. He didn't know what to say. He wished the
people in the hall would stop pounding on the door and find some other
way to get in, because pounding wasn't working. Maybe they could call
the cops and tell them to bring the Jaws of Life, yeah, the Jaws of Life,
like you saw them use on the TV news when a person was in a wrecked
car and couldn't get out. They could use the Jaws of Life to pull open the
door the way they pulled at smashed-up cars to get people out of them.
He hoped the cops wouldn't say, we're sorry but we can only open car
doors with the Jaws of Life, we can't open Care Home doors, because
then he was finished for sure.

"You going to answer me, Thomas?" the Bad Thing asked.

Derek's TV chair got turned around in the fight, and now it was between Thomas and the Bad Thing. The Bad Thing held one hand out at
the chair, just one, and the blue light went *whoosh!* and the chair blew
up in splinters, like all the toothpicks in the world. Thomas threw his
hands over his face just fast enough so no splinters went in his eyes.

Some went in the backs of his hands and even in his cheeks and chin, and he could feel some of them in his shirt, poking his belly, but he didn't feel any hurt because he was so busy feeling scared.

He took his hands from his eyes right away, because he had to see where the Bad Thing was. Where it was was right on top of him, with soft bits of the chair's insides floating in the air in front of its face.

"Thomas?" it said, and it put one of its big hands on the front of Thomas's neck the way it did Pete a while ago.

Thomas heard words coming from himself, and he couldn't believe he was making them, but he was. Then when he heard what he said to the Bad Thing, he couldn't believe he said it, but he did: "You're not Being Sociable."

The Bad Thing grabbed him by the belt and kept hold of him by the neck and lifted him off the floor and pulled him away from the wall, then slammed him into the wall, the same way it did Derek, and, oh, it hurt worse than Thomas ever before hurt in his life.

THE INTERIOR GARAGE door had a dead bolt but no security chain. Pocketing his keys, Clint entered the kitchen at ten minutes past eight and saw Felina sitting at the table, reading a magazine while she waited for him.

She looked up and smiled, and his heart thumped faster at the sight of her, just like in every sappy love story ever written. He wondered how this could have happened to him. He had been so self-contained before Felina. He had been proud of the fact that he needed no one for intellectual stimulation or emotional support, and that he was therefore not vulnerable to the pains and disappointments of human relationships. Then he had met her. When he caught his breath, he had been as vulnerable as anyone—and glad of it.

She looked terrific in a simple blue dress with a red belt and matching red shoes. She was so strong yet so gentle, so tough yet so fragile.

He went to her, and for a while they stood by the refrigerator, next to the sink, holding each other and kissing, neither of them speaking in either of the ways they could. Clint thought they would have been happy, just then, even if both of them had been deaf and mute, capable of neither lip reading nor sign language, because at that moment what made them happy was the very fact of being together, which no words could adequately express anyway.

Finally he said, "What a day! Can't wait to tell you all about it. Let me clean up real quick, change clothes. We'll be out of here by eight-thirty, go over to Caprabello's, get a corner booth, some wine, some pasta, some garlic bread—"

Some heartburn.

He laughed because it was true. They both loved Caprabello's, but the food was spicy. They always suffered for the indulgence.

He kissed her again, and she sat down with her magazine, and he went through the dining room and down the hall to the bathroom. While he let the water run in the sink to get it hot, he plugged in his electric razor and began to shave, grinning at himself in the mirror because he was such a damned lucky guy.

THE BAD THING was right in his face, snarling at him, lots of questions, too many for Thomas to think about and answer even if he was sitting in a chair quiet and happy, instead of lifted off the floor and held against the wall with his whole back hurting so bad he had to cry. He kept saying, "I'm full up, I'm full up." Always when he said that, people stopped asking him things or telling him things, they let him take time to make his head clear. But the Bad Thing was not like other people. It didn't care if his head was clear, it just wanted answers. Who was Thomas? Who was his mother? Who was his father? Where did he come from? Who was Julie? Who was Bobby? Where was Julie? Where was Bobby?

Then the Bad Thing said, "Hell, you're just a dummy. You don't *know* the answers, do you? You're just as stupid as you are stupid-looking."

It pulled Thomas away from the wall, held him off the floor with one hand on his neck, so Thomas couldn't breathe good. It slapped Thomas in the face, hard, and Thomas didn't want to keep crying, but he couldn't stop, he hurt and was scared.

"Why do they let people like you live?" the Bad Thing asked.

It let go of Thomas, and Thomas dropped on the floor. The Bad Thing looked down at him in a mean way that made Thomas angry almost as much as it made him scared. Which was funny-weird, because he almost never was angry. And this was the first time he was ever angry and scared both at the same time. But the Bad Thing was looking at him like he was just a bug or some dirt on the floor that had to be made clean.

"Why don't they kill you people at birth? What're you good for? Why don't they kill you at birth and chop you up and make dog food out of you?"

Thomas had memories of how people, out there in the world, looked at him that way or said mean things, and how Julie always Told Them Off. She said Thomas didn't have to be nice to people like that, said he could tell them they were Being Rude. Now Thomas was angry like he had Every Right To Be, and even if Julie never told him he could be angry about these things, he probably would be angry anyway, because some things you just *knew* were right or wrong.

The Bad Thing kicked him in the leg, and was going to kick him again, you could tell, but a noise was made at the window. Some of the aides were at the window. They broke a little square of glass and reached through, wanting to find the lock.

When the glass made a breaking sound, the Bad Thing turned from Thomas and held its hands up at the window, like it was asking the aides to stop wanting in. But Thomas knew what it was going to do was make the blue light.

Thomas wanted to warn the aides, but he figured nobody would hear him or listen to him until it was too late. So while the Bad Thing's back was turned, he crawled across the floor, away from the Bad Thing, even if crawling hurt, even if he had to go through spots of Derek's blood, all wet, and it made him sick on top of being angry and scared.

Blue light. Very bright.

Something exploded.

He heard glass falling and worse, like maybe not just the whole window blew out on the aides but part of the wall too.

People screamed. Most of the screams cut off quick-like, but one of them went on, it was real bad, like somebody out in the dark past the blown-up window was made to hurt even worse than Thomas.

Thomas didn't look back because he was all the way around the side of Derek's bed now, where he couldn't see the window anyway from where he was on the floor. And, besides, he knew what he wanted now, where he wanted to go, and he had to get there before the Bad Thing got interested in him again.

Quick-like, he crawled to the top end of the bed and looked up and saw Derek's arm hanging over the side, blood running down under his shirtsleeve and across his hand and drip-drip-dripping off his fingers. He didn't want to touch a dead person, not even a dead person he liked. But this was what he had to do, and he was used to having to do all sorts of things he wished he didn't—that was what life was like. So he grabbed the edge of the bed and pulled himself up as fast as he could, trying not to feel the bad hurt in his back and in his kicked leg, because feeling it would make him stiff and slow. Derek was right there, eyes open, mouth open, blood-wet, so sad, so scary, on top of the pictures of his folks that fell off the wall, still dead, off for always and ever to the Bad Place. Thomas grabbed the scissors sticking out of Derek, pulled them loose, telling himself it was okay because Derek couldn't feel anything now, or ever.

"You!" the Bad Thing said.

Thomas turned to see where the Bad Thing was, and where it was was right behind him, all the way around the bed, coming at him. So he shoved the scissors at it, hard as he could, and the Bad Thing's face made a surprised look. The scissors went in the front of the Bad Thing's shoulder. The Bad Thing looked even more surprised. The blood came.

Letting go of the scissors, Thomas said, "For Derek," then said, "for me."

He wasn't sure what would happen, but he figured that making the blood come would hurt the Bad Thing and maybe make it dead, like it made Derek dead. Across the room he saw where the window wasn't any more and where part of the wall wasn't any more, some smoke coming from the broken ends of things. He figured he was going to run over there and go through the hole, even if the night was out there on the other side.

But he never figured on what *did* happen, because the Bad Thing acted like the scissors weren't even in it, like blood wasn't being let loose from it, and it grabbed him and lifted him up again. It slammed him into Derek's dresser, which was a lot more hurt than the wall because the dresser was made with knobs and edges the wall didn't have.

He heard something crack in him, heard something tear. But the funny thing was, he wasn't crying any more and didn't *want* to cry any more, like he'd used up all the tears in himself.

The Bad Thing put its face close to Thomas's face, so their eyes were only a couple inches apart. He didn't like looking in the Bad Thing's eyes. They were scary. They were blue, but it was like they were really dark, like under the blue was a lot of stuff as black as the night out past the gone window.

But the other funny thing was, he wasn't as scared as he was a while ago, like he'd used up all his being scared just like he'd used up his tears. He looked in the Bad Thing's eyes, and he saw all that big dark, bigger than the dark that came over the world each day when the sun went away, and he knew it was wanting to make him dead, *going* to make him dead, and that was okay. He was not so afraid of being made dead as he always thought he would be. It was still a Bad Place, death, and he wished he didn't have to go there, but he had a funny-nice feeling about the Bad Place all of a sudden, a feeling that maybe it wouldn't be so lonely over there as he always figured it was, not even as lonely as it was on this side. He felt maybe someone was over there who loved him, someone who loved him more than even Julie loved him, even more than their dad used to love him, someone who was all bright, no dark at all, so bright you could only look at Him sideways.

The Bad Thing held Thomas against the dresser with one hand, and with its other hand it pulled the scissors out of itself.

Then it put the scissors in Thomas.

This light started to fill up Thomas, this light that loved him, and he knew he was going away. He hoped when he was all gone, Julie would know how brave he was right at the end, how he stopped crying and stopped being scared and fought back. And then all of a sudden he remembered he hadn't TVed a warning to Bobby that the Bad Thing might be coming for them, too, and he started to do that.

—the scissors went in again—

Then he all of a sudden knew something even more important he had to do. He had to let Julie know that the Bad Place was not so bad, after all, there was a light over there that loved you, you could tell. She needed to know about it because deep down she really didn't believe it. She figured it was all dark and lonely the way Thomas once figured it was, so she counted each clock tick and worried about all she had to do before her time ran out, all she had to learn and see and feel and get, all she had to do for Thomas and for Bobby so they'd be okay if Something Happened To Her.

—and the scissors went in again—

And she was happy with Bobby, but she was never going to be *real* happy until she knew she didn't have to be so angry about everything ending in a big dark. She was so nice it was hard to figure she was angry inside, but she was. Thomas only figured it out now, as the light was filling him up, figured out how terrible angry Julie was. She was angry that all the hard work and all the hope and all the dreams and all the trying and doing and loving didn't matter in the end because you were sooner or later made dead forever.

—the scissors—

If she knew about the light, she could stop being angry deep down. So Thomas TVed that, too, along with a warning, and with three last words to her and to Bobby, words of his own, all three things at once, hoping they wouldn't get mixed up:

The Bad Thing's coming, look out, the Bad Thing, there's a light that loves you, the Bad Thing, I love you too, and there's a light, there's a light, THE BAD THING'S COMING—

AT 8:15 THEY were on the Foothill Freeway, rocketing toward the junction with the Ventura Freeway, which they would follow across the San Fernando Valley almost to the ocean before turning north toward Oxnard, Ventura, and eventually Santa Barbara. Julie knew she should slow down, but she couldn't. Speed relieved her tension a little; if she stayed even close to the fifty-five-mile-an-hour limit, she was pretty sure that she would start to scream before they were past Burbank.

A Benny Goodman tape was on the stereo. The exuberant melodies and syncopated rhythms seemed in time and sympathy with the headlong rush of the car; and if they had been in a movie, Goodman's sounds would have been perfect background music to the tenebrous panorama of light-speckled night hills through which they passed from city to city, suburb to suburb.

She knew why she was so tense. In a way she could never have anticipated, The Dream was within their grasp—but they could lose everything as they reached for it. Everything. Hope. Each other. Their lives.

Sitting in the seat beside her, Bobby trusted her so implicitly that he could doze at more than eighty miles an hour, even though he knew that she, too, had slept only three hours last night. From time to time she glanced at him, just because it felt good to have him there.

He did not yet understand why they were going north to check out the Pollard family, stretching their obligation to the client beyond reason, but his bafflement sprang from the fact that he was nearly as good a man as he appeared to be. He sometimes bent the rules and broke the laws on behalf of their clients, but he was more scrupulous in his personal life than anyone Julie had ever known. She had been with him once when a newspaper-vending machine gave him a copy of the Sunday *Los Angeles Times*, then malfunctioned and returned three of his four quarters to him, whereupon he had repaid all three into the coin slot, even though that same machine had malfunctioned to his disadvantage on other occasions over the years and was into him for a couple of bucks. "Yeah, well," he'd said, blushing when she had laughed at his goody-goody deed, "maybe the machine can be crooked and still live with itself, but I can't."

Julie could have told him that they were hanging with the Pollard case because they saw a once-in-a-lifetime shot at really big bucks, the Main Chance for which every hustler in the world was looking and which most of them would never find. From the moment Frank had shown them all that cash in the flight bag and told them about the second cache back at the motel, they were locked in like rats in a maze, drawn forward by the smell of cheese, even though each of them had taken a turn at protesting any interest in the game. When Frank came back to that hospital room from God-knew-where, with another three hundred thousand, neither she nor Bobby even raised the issue of illegality, though it was by that time no longer possible to pretend that Frank was entirely an innocent. By then the smell of cheese was too strong to be resisted at all. They were plunging ahead because they saw the chance to use Frank to cash out of the rat race and buy into The Dream sooner than they had ex- pected. They were willing to use dirty money and questionable means to get to their desired end, more willing than they could admit to each other, though Julie supposed it could be said in their favor that they were not yet so greedy that they could simply steal the money and the diamonds from Frank and abandon him to the mercies of his psychotic brother; or maybe even their sense of duty to their client was a lie now, a virtue they could point to later when they tried to justify, to themselves, their other less-than-noble acts and impulses.

She *could* have told him all that, but she didn't, because she did not want to argue with him. She had to let him figure it out at his own pace, accept it in his own way. If she tried to tell him before he was able to understand it, he'd deny what she said. Even if he admitted to a fraction of the truth, he'd trot out an argument about the rightness of The Dream, the basic morality of it, and use that to justify the means to the end. But she didn't think a noble end could remain purely noble if arrived at by immoral means. And though she could not turn away from this Main Chance, she worried that when they achieved The Dream it would be sullied, not what it might have been.

Yet she drove on. Fast. Because speed relieved some of her fear and tension. It numbed caution too. And without caution she was less likely to retreat from the dangerous confrontation with the Pollard family that seemed inevitable if they were to seize the opportunity to obtain immense and liberating wealth.

They were in a clearing in traffic, with nothing close behind them and trailing the nearest forward car by about a quarter of a mile, when Bobby cried out and sat up in his seat as if warning her of an imminent collision. He jerked forward, pulling the shoulder harness taut, and put his hands on his head, as though stricken by a sudden migraine.

Frightened, she let up on the accelerator, lightly tapped the brake pedal, and said, "Bobby, what is it?"

In a voice coarsened by fear and sharpened by urgency, speaking above the music of Benny Goodman, he said, "Bad Thing, the Bad Thing, look out, there's a light, there's a light that loves you—"

CANDY LOOKED DOWN at the bloody body at his feet and knew that he should not have killed Thomas. Instead, he should have taken him away to a private place and tortured the answers out of him even if it took hours for the dummy to remember everything Candy needed to know. It could even have been fun.

But he was in a rage greater than any he had ever known, and he was less in control of himself than at any time in his life since the day he had found his mother's dead body. He wanted vengeance not only for his mother but for himself and for everyone in the world who ever deserved revenge and never got it. God had made him an instrument of revenge, and now Candy longed desperately to fulfill his purpose as he had never fulfilled it before. He yearned not merely to tear open the throat and drink the blood of one sinner, but of a great multitude of sinners. If ever his rage was to be dissipated, he needed not only to drink blood but to become drunk on it, bathe in it, wade through rivers of it, stand on land saturated with it. He wanted his mother to free him from all the rules that had restricted his rage before, wanted God to turn him *loose*.

He heard sirens in the distance, and knew that he must go soon.

Hot pain throbbed in his shoulder, where the scissors had parted muscle and scraped bone, but he would deal with that when he traveled. In reconstituting himself, he could easily remake his flesh whole and healthy.

Stalking through the debris that littered the floor, he looked for something that might give him a clue to the whereabouts of either the Julie or the Bobby of whom Thomas had spoken. They might know who Thomas had been and why he had possessed a gift that not even Candy's blessed mother had been able to impart.

He touched various objects and pieces of furniture, but all he could extract from them were images of Thomas and Derek and some of the aides and nurses who took care of them. Then he saw a scrapbook lying open on the floor, beside the table on which he had butchered Derek. The open pages were full of all kinds of pictures that had been pasted in lines and peculiar patterns. He picked the book up and leafed through it, wondering what it was, and when he tried to see the face of the last person who had handled it, he was rewarded with someone other than a dummy or a nurse.

A hard-looking man. Not as tall as Candy but almost as solid.

The sirens were less than a mile away now, louder by the second.

Candy let his right hand glide over the cover of the scrapbook, seeking . . . seeking . . .

Sometimes he could sense only a little, sometimes a lot. This time he *had* to be successful, or this room was going to be a dead end in his search for the meaning of the dummy's power.

Seeking . . .

He received a name. Clint.

Clint had sat in Derek's chair sometime during the afternoon, paging through this odd collection of pictures.

When he tried to see where Clint had gone, after leaving this room, he saw a Chevy that Clint was driving on the freeway, then a place called Dakota & Dakota. Then the Chevy again, on a freeway at night, and then a small house in a place called Placentia.

The approaching sirens were very close now, probably coming up the driveway into the Cielo Vista parking lot.

Candy threw the book down. He was ready to go.

He had only one more thing to do before he teleported. When he had discovered that Thomas was a dummy, and when he had realized that

Cielo Vista was a place full of them, he had been angered and offended by the home's existence.

He held his hands two feet apart, palm facing palm. Sky-blue light glowed between them.

He remembered how neighbors and other people had talked about his sisters—and also about him when, as a boy, he had been kept out of school because of his problems. Violet and Verbina looked and acted mentally deficient, and they probably did not care if people called them retards. Ignorant people labeled him retarded, too, because they thought he was excused from school for being as learning disabled and strange as his sisters. (Only Frank attended classes like a normal child.)

The light began to coalesce into a ball. As more power poured out of his hands and into the ball, it acquired a deeper shade of blue and seemed to take on substance, as if it were a solid object floating in the air.

Candy had been bright, with no learning disabilities at all. His mother taught him to read, write, and do math; so he got angry when he overheard people say he was a deadhead. He had been excused from school for other reasons, of course, mainly because of the sex thing. When he got older and bigger, nobody called him retarded or made jokes about him, at least not within his hearing.

The sapphire-blue sphere looked almost as solid as a genuine sapphire, but as big as a basketball. It was nearly ready.

Having been unjustly tagged with the retarded label, Candy had not grown up with sympathy for the genuinely disabled, but with an intense loathing for them that he hoped would make it clear to even ignorant people that he definitely was not—and never had been—one of *them*. To think such a thing of him—or of his sisters, for that matter—was an insult to his sainted mother, who was incapable of bringing a moron into the world.

He cut off the flow of power and took his hands away from the sphere. For a moment he stared at it, smiling, thinking about what it would do to this offensive place.

Through the missing window and the partially shattered walls, the wail of the sirens became deafening, then suddenly subsided from a high-pitched shriek to a low growl that spiraled toward silence.

"Help's here, Thomas," he said, and laughed.

He put one hand against the sapphire sphere and gave it a shove. It shot across the room as if it were a ballistic missile fired from its silo. It smashed through the wall behind Derek's bed, leaving a ragged hole as big as anything a cannonball could have made, through the wall beyond that, and through every additional wall that stood before it, spewing flames as it went, setting fire to everything along its path.

Candy heard people screaming and a hard explosion, as he did a fade-out on his way to the house in Placentia.

52

BOBBY STOOD AT THE SIDE OF THE FREEWAY, HOLDING ON TO THE open car door, gasping for breath. He had been sure he was going to throw up, but the urge had passed.

"Are you all right?" Julie asked anxiously.

"I . . . think so."

Traffic shot past. Each vehicle was trailed by a wake of wind and a roar that gave Bobby the peculiar feeling that he and Julie and the Toyota were still moving, doing eighty-five with him holding on to the open door and her with a hand on his shoulder, magically keeping their balance and avoiding roadburn as they dragged their feet along the pavement, with nobody driving.

The dream had seriously unsettled and disoriented him.

"Not a dream, really," he told her. He continued to keep his head down, peering at bits of loose gravel on the paved shoulder of the highway, half expecting a return of the cramping nausea. "Not like the dream I had before, about us and the jukebox and the ocean of acid."

"But about 'the bad thing' again."

"Yeah. You couldn't call it a dream, though, because it was just this . . . this burst of words, inside my head."

"From where?"

"I don't know."

He dared to lift his head, and though a whirl of dizziness swept through him, the nausea did not return.

He said, " 'Bad thing . . . look out . . . there's a light that loves you. . . .' I can't remember it all. It was so strong, so hard, like somebody shouting at me through a bullhorn that was pressed against my ear. Except that's not right, either, because I didn't really hear the words, they were just there, in my head. But they *felt* loud, if that makes any sense. And there weren't images, like in a dream. Instead there were these feelings, as strong as they were confused. Fear and joy, anger and forgiveness . . . and right at the end of it, this strange sense of peace that I . . . can't describe."

A Peterbilt thundered toward them, towing the biggest trailer the law allowed. Sweeping out of the night behind its blazing headlights, it looked like a leviathan swimming up from a deep marine trench, all raw power and cold rage, with a hunger that could never be satisfied. For some reason, as it boomed past them, Bobby thought of the man he had seen on the beach at Punaluu, and he shuddered.

Julie said, "Are you okay?"

"Yeah."

"Are you sure?"

He nodded. "A little dizzy. That's all."

"What now?"

He looked at her. "What else? We go on to Santa Barbara. El Encanto Heights, bring this thing to an end . . . somehow."

CANDY ARRIVED IN the archway between a living room and dining room. No one was in either place.

He heard a buzzing sound farther back in the house, and after a moment he identified it as an electric razor. It stopped. Then he heard water running in a sink, and the drone of a bathroom exhaust fan.

He intended to head straight for the hall and the bath, take the man by surprise. But he heard a rustle of paper from the opposite direction.

He crossed the dining room and stepped into the kitchen doorway. It was smaller than the kitchen in his mother's house, but it was as spotlessly clean and orderly as his mother's kitchen had not been since her death.

A woman in a blue dress was sitting at the table, her back to him. She was leaning over a magazine, turning the pages one after the other, as if looking for something of interest to read.

Candy possessed a far greater control of his telekinetic talents than Frank enjoyed, and in particular could teleport more efficiently and swiftly than Frank, creating less air displacement and less noise from molecular resistance. Nevertheless, he was surprised that she had not gotten up to investigate, for the sounds he had made during arrival had been only one small room away from her and, surely, odd enough to prick her curiosity.

She turned a few more pages, then leaned forward to read.

He could not see much of her from behind. Her hair was thick, lustrous, and so black it seemed to have been spun on the same loom as the night. Her shoulders and back were slender. Her legs, which were both to one side of the chair and crossed at the ankles, were shapely. If he had been a man with any interest in sex, he supposed he would have been excited by the curve of her calves.

Wondering what she looked like—and suddenly overwhelmed by a need to know how her blood would taste—he stepped out of the open doorway and took three steps to her. He made no effort to be silent, but she did not look up. The first she became aware of him was when he seized a handful of her hair and dragged her, kicking and flailing, out of her chair.

He turned her around and was instantly excited by her. He was indifferent to her shapely legs, the flare of her hips, the trimness of her waist, the fullness of her breasts. Though beautiful, it was not even her face that electrified him. Something else. A quality in her gray eyes. Call it vitality. She was more alive than most people, vibrant.

She did not scream but let out a low grunt of fear or anger, then struck him furiously with both fists. She pounded his chest, battered his face.

Vitality! Yes, this one was full of life, bursting with life, and her vitality thrilled him far more than any bounty of sexual charms.

He could still hear the distant splash of water, the rattle-hum of the bathroom exhaust fan, and he was confident that he could take her without drawing the attention of the man—as long as he could prevent her from screaming. He struck her on the side of the head with his fist, hammered her before she could scream. She slumped against him, not unconscious but dazed.

Shaking with the anticipation of pleasure, Candy placed her on her back, on the table, with her legs trailing over the edge. He spread her legs and leaned between them, but not to commit rape, nothing as disgusting as that. As he lowered his face toward hers, she first blinked at him in confusion, still rattle-brained from the blows she had taken. Then her eyes began to clear. He saw horrified comprehension return to her, and he went quickly for her throat, bit deep, and found the blood, which was clean and sweet, intoxicating.

She thrashed beneath him.

She was so alive. So wonderfully alive. For a while.

WHEN THE DELIVERYMAN brought the pizza, Lee Chen took it into Bobby and Julie's office and offered some to Hal.

Putting his book aside but not taking his stockinged feet off the coffee table, Hal said, "You know what that stuff does to your arteries?"

"Why's everyone so concerned about my arteries today?"

"You're such a nice young man. We'd hate to see you dead before you're thirty. Besides, we'd always wonder what clothes you might've worn next, if you'd lived."

"Not anything like what you're wearing, I assure you."

Hal leaned over and looked in the box that Lee held down to him. "Looks pretty good. Rule of thumb—any pizza they'll bring to you, they're selling service instead of good food. But this doesn't look bad at all, you can actually tell where the pizza ends and the cardboard begins."

Lee tore the lid off the box, put it on the coffee table, and put two slices of pizza on that makeshift plate. "There."

"You're not going to give me half?"

"What about the cholesterol?"

"Hell, cholesterol's just a little animal fat, it isn't arsenic."

WHEN THE WOMAN'S strong heart stopped beating, Candy pulled back from her. Though blood still seeped from her ravaged throat, he did not touch another drop of it. The thought of drinking from a corpse sickened him. He remembered his sisters' cats, eating their own each time one of the pack died, and he grimaced.

Even as he raised his wet lips from her throat, he heard a door open farther back in the house. Footsteps approached.

Candy quickly circled the table, putting it and the dead woman between himself and the doorway to the dining room. From the vision induced by the dummy's scrapbook of pictures, Candy knew that Clint would not be as easy to handle as most people were. He preferred to put a little distance between them, give himself time to size up his opponent rather than take the guy by surprise.

Clint appeared in the doorway. Except for his outfit—gray slacks, navy-blue blazer, maroon V-neck, white shirt—he looked the same as the psychic impression he had left on the book. He had pumped a lot of iron in his time. His hair was thick, black, and combed straight back from his forehead. He had a face like carved granite, and a hard look in his eyes.

Excited by the recent kill, by the taste of blood still in his mouth, Candy watched the man with interest, wondering what would happen next. There were all sorts of ways it could go, and not one of them would be dull.

Clint did not react as Candy expected. He did not show surprise when he saw the woman sprawled dead upon the table; he did not seem horrified, shattered by the loss of her, or outraged. Something major changed in his stony face, though below the surface, like tectonic plates shifting under the mantle of the earth's crust.

Finally he met Candy's gaze, and said, "You."

The note of recognition in that single word was unsettling. For a moment Candy could think of no way this man could know him—then he remembered Thomas.

The possibility that Thomas had told this man—and perhaps others—about Candy was the most frightening turn in Candy's life since his mother's death. His service in God's army of avengers was a deeply private matter, a secret that should not have been spread beyond the Pollard family. His mother had warned him that it was all right to be proud of doing God's work, but that his pride would lead him to a fall if he boasted of his divine favor to others. "Satan," she had told him, "constantly seeks the names of lieutenants in God's army—which is what you are—and when he finds them, he destroys them with worms that eat them alive from within, worms fat as snakes, and he rains fire on them too. If you can't keep the secret, you'll die and go to Hell for your big mouth."

"Candy," Clint said.

The use of his name erased whatever doubt remained that the secret had been passed outside the family and that Candy was in deep trouble, though he had not broken the code of silence himself.

He imagined that even now Satan, in some dark and steaming place, had tilted his head and said, "Who? Who did you say? What was his name? Candy? Candy who?"

As furious as he was frightened, Candy started around the kitchen table, wondering if Clint had learned about him from Thomas. He was determined to break the man, make him talk before killing him.

In a move as unexpected as his rock-calm acceptance of the woman's murder, Clint reached inside his jacket, withdrew a revolver, and fired two shots.

He might have fired more than two, but those were the only ones Candy heard. The first round hit him in the stomach, the second in the chest, pitching him backward. Fortunately he sustained no damage to head or heart. If his brain tissue had been scrambled, disturbing the mysterious and fragile connection between brain and mind, leaving his mind trapped within his ruined brain before he had a chance to separate the two, he would not have possessed the mental ability to teleport, leaving him vulnerable to a coup de grace. And if his heart had been stopped instantaneously by a well-placed bullet, before he could dematerialize, he would have fallen down dead where he'd stood. Those were the only wounds that might finish him. He was many things, but he was not immortal; so he was grateful to God for letting him get out of that kitchen and back to his mother's house alive.

THE VENTURA FREEWAY. Julie drove fast, though not as fast as she had earlier. On the tapedeck: Artie Shaw's "Nightmare."

Bobby brooded, staring through the side window at the nightscape. He could not stop thinking about the blare of words that had seared through him, loud as a bomb blast and bright as a blast-furnace fire. He had come to terms with the dream that had frightened him last week; everyone had bad dreams. Though exceptionally vivid, almost more real than real life, there had been nothing uncanny about it—or so he had convinced himself. But this was different. He could not believe that these urgent, lava-hot words had erupted from his own subconscious. A dream, with complex Freudian messages couched in elaborate scenes and symbols—yes, that was understandable; after all, the subconscious dealt in euphemisms and metaphors. But this wordburst had been blunt, direct, like a telegraph delivered on a wire plugged directly into his cerebral cortex.

When he wasn't brooding, Bobby was fidgeting. Because of Thomas. For some reason, the longer he dwelt on the blaze of words, the more

Thomas slipped into his thoughts. He could see no connection between the two, so he tried to put Thomas out of mind and concentrate on turning up an explanation for the experience. But Thomas gently, insistently returned, again and again. After a while Bobby got the uneasy feeling there *was* a link between the wordburst and Thomas, though he had no ghost of an idea what it might be.

Worse, as the miles rolled up on the odometer and they reached the western end of the valley, Bobby began to sense that Thomas was in danger. And because of me and Julie, Bobby thought.

Danger from whom, from what?

The biggest danger that Bobby and Julie faced, right now, was Candy Pollard. But even that jeopardy lay in the future, for Candy didn't know about them yet; he was not aware that they were working on Frank's behalf, and he might never become aware of it, depending on how things went in Santa Barbara and El Encanto Heights. Yes, he had seen Bobby on the beach at Punaluu, with Frank, but he had no way of knowing who Bobby was. Ultimately, even if Candy became aware of Dakota & Dakota's association with Frank, there was no way that Thomas could be drawn into the affair; Thomas was another, separate part of their lives. Right?

"Something wrong?" Julie said as she pulled the Toyota one lane to the left, to pass a big rig hauling Coors.

He could see nothing to be gained by telling her that Thomas might be in danger. She would be upset, worried. And for what? He was just letting his vivid imagination run away with him. Thomas was perfectly safe down there in Cielo Vista.

"Bobby, what's wrong?"

"Nothing."

"Why're you fidgeting?"

"Prostate trouble."

CHANEL NO. 5, a softly glowing lamp, cozy rose-patterned fabrics and wallpaper . . .

He laughed with relief when he materialized in the bedroom, the bullets left behind in that kitchen in Placentia, over a hundred miles away. His wounds had knit up as if they had never existed. He had lost perhaps an ounce of blood and a few flecks of tissue, because one of the bullets had passed through him and out his back, carrying that material with it before he'd transported himself beyond the revolver's range. Everything else was as it should be, however, and his flesh did not harbor even the memory of pain.

He stood in front of the dresser for half a minute, breathing deeply of the perfume that wafted up from the saturated handkerchief. The scent gave him courage and reminded him of the abiding need to make them pay for his mother's murder, all of them, not just Frank but the whole world, which had conspired against her.

He looked at his face in the mirror. The gray-eyed woman's blood was no longer on his chin and lips; he had left it behind him, as he might leave water behind when teleporting out of a rainstorm. But the taste of it was still in his mouth. And his reflection was without a doubt that of vengeance personified.

Depending on the element of surprise and his ability to target his point of arrival precisely now that he was familiar with the kitchen, he returned to Clint's house. He intended to enter at the dining-room doorway, immediately behind the man, directly opposite the point from which he had dematerialized.

Either the experience of being shot had shaken him more than he realized, or the rage jittering through him had passed the critical point at which it interfered with his concentration. Whatever the reason, he did not arrive where he intended, but by the door to the garage, one-quarter instead of halfway around the room from his last position, to the right of Clint and not near enough to rush him and seize the gun before it could be fired.

Except Clint was not present. And the woman's body had been removed from the table. Only the blood remained as proof that she perished there.

Candy could not have been gone more than a minute—the time he had spent in his mother's room, plus a couple of seconds in transit each way. He expected to return to find Clint bent over the corpse, either grieving or checking desperately for a pulse. But as soon as he realized Candy was gone, the man must have taken the body in his arms and . . . And what? He must have fled the house, of course, hoping against hope that a faint thread of life remained unbroken in the woman, getting her out of the way in case Candy returned.

Cursing softly—then immediately begging his mother's and God's forgiveness for his foul language—Candy tried the door into the garage. It was locked. If he had left by that exit, Clint wouldn't have paused to lock up behind himself.

He hurried out of the kitchen, through the dining room, toward the foyer off the living room, to check out the front lawn and the street. But he heard a noise from deeper in the house, and halted before he reached the front door. He changed direction, cautiously following the hallway back to the bedrooms.

A light was on in one of those rooms. He eased to the door and risked a glance inside.

Clint had just put the woman on the queen-size bed. As Candy watched, the man pulled her skirt down over her knees. He still had the revolver in one hand.

For the second time in less than an hour, Candy heard faraway sirens swelling in the night. The neighbors probably had heard the gunfire and called the police.

Clint saw him in the doorway but did not bring up the gun. He did not say anything, either, and the expression on his stoic face remained unchanged. He seemed like a deaf-mute. The strangeness of the man's demeanor made Candy nervous and uncertain.

He thought there was a pretty good chance that Clint had emptied the gun at him in the kitchen, even though he had teleported out of there with the impact of the second slug. Most likely, he had fired every round reflexively, his trigger finger ruled by rage or fear or whatever he was feeling. He could not have carried the woman into the bedroom and reloaded the gun, too, in the minute or so that Candy had been gone, which meant Candy might be in no danger if he just walked up to the guy and took the weapon away from him.

But he stayed in the doorway. Either of those two shots *could* have been dead-center in his heart. The power within him was great, but he could not exercise it quickly enough to vaporize an oncoming bullet.

Instead of dealing with Candy in any fashion, the man turned away from him, walked around the foot of the bed to the other side, and stretched out beside the woman.

"What the hell?" Candy said aloud.

Clint took hold of her dead hand. His other hand held the .38 revolver.

He turned his head on the pillow to look toward her, and his eyes glistened with what might have been unshed tears. He put the muzzle of the gun under his chin, and annihilated himself.

Candy was so stunned that he was unable to move for a moment or think what to do next. He was jolted out of his paralysis by the ululant sirens, and realized that the trail from Thomas to Bobby and Julie, whoever they were, might end here if he did not discover what link the dead man on the bed shared with them. If he ever hoped to learn who Thomas had been, how Clint had known his name, or how many others knew of him, if he wanted to learn how much danger he was in and how he might slide out of it, he couldn't waste this opportunity.

He hurried to the bed, rolled the dead man onto his side, and withdrew the wallet from his pants pocket. He flipped it open and saw the private investigator's license. Opposite it, in another plastic window, was a business card for Dakota & Dakota.

Candy remembered a vague image of the Dakota & Dakota offices, which had come to him in Thomas's room when he had obtained a vision of Clint from the scrapbook. There was an address on the card. And below the name Clint Karaghiosis, in smaller type, were the names Robert and Julia Dakota.

Outside, the sirens had died. Someone was pounding on the front door. Two voices shouted, "Police!"

Candy threw the wallet aside and took the gun out of the dead man's hand. He broke open the cylinder. It was a five-shot weapon, and all of the chambers were filled with expended cartridges. Clint had fired four rounds in the kitchen, but even in his moment of vengeful fury, he had possessed enough control to save the last bullet for himself.

"Just because of a woman?" Candy said uncomprehendingly, as if the dead man might answer him. "Because you couldn't get sex from her any more now? Why does sex matter so much? Couldn't you get sex from another woman? Why was sex with this one so important, you didn't want to live without it?"

They were still pounding on the door. Someone spoke through a bullhorn, but Candy didn't pay attention to what was being said.

He dropped the gun and wiped his hand on his pants, because he suddenly felt unclean. The dead man had handled the gun, and the dead man seemed to have been obsessed with sex. Without question, the world was a cesspool of lust and debauchery, and Candy was glad that God and his mother had spared him from the sick desires that seemed to infect nearly everyone else.

He left that house of sinners.

53

SLUMPED ON THE SOFA, HAL YAMATAKA HAD A SLICE OF PIZZA IN one hand and the MacDonald novel in the other, when he heard the hollow flutelike warble. He dropped both the book and the food, and shot to his feet.

"Frank?"

The half-open door swung slowly inward, not because it was being pushed open by anyone but because a sudden draft, sweeping in from the reception lounge, was strong enough to move it.

"Frank?" Hal repeated.

As he crossed the room, the sound faded and the draft died. But by the time he reached the doorway, the unmelodic notes returned, and a burst of wind ruffled his hair.

To the left stood the receptionist's desk, untended at this hour. Directly opposite the desk was the door to the public corridor that served the other companies on this level, and it was closed. The only other door, at the far end of the rectangular lounge, was also closed; it led to a hallway that was interior to the Dakota & Dakota suite, off which were six other offices—including the computer room where Lee was still at work—and a bathroom. The piping and the wind could not have reached him through those closed doors; therefore, the point of origin was clearly the reception lounge.

Stepping to the center of the room, he looked around expectantly.

The flute sounds and turbulence rose a third time.

Hal said, "Frank," as he became aware, out of the corner of his eye, that a man had arrived near the door to the public hall, to Hal's right and almost behind him.

But when he turned, he saw that it was not Frank. The traveler was a stranger, but Hal knew him at once. Candy. It could be no one else, for this was the man Bobby had described from the beach at Punaluu, and whose description Hal had received from Clint.

Hal was built low and wide, he kept in good shape, and he could remember no instance in his life when he'd been physically intimidated by another man. Candy was eight inches taller than he, but Hal had handled men taller than that. Candy was clearly a mesomorph, one of those guys destined from birth to have a strong-boned body layered with slabs of muscle, even if he exercised lightly or not at all; and he was clearly no stranger to the discipline and painful rituals of barbells, dumbbells, and slantboards. But Hal had a mesomorphic body type, as well, and was as hard as frozen beef. He was not intimidated by Candy's height or muscles. What frightened him was the aura of insanity, rage, and violence the man radiated as powerfully as a week-old corpse would radiate the stink of death.

The instant that Frank's brother hit the room, Hal smelled his mad ferocity as surely as a healthy dog would detect the rabid odor of a sick one, and he acted accordingly. He wasn't wearing shoes, wasn't carrying a gun, and wasn't aware of anything near at hand that might be used as a weapon, so he spun around and ran back toward the bosses' office, where he knew a loaded Browning 9mm semiautomatic pistol was kept in a spring clip on the underside of Julie's desk as insurance against the unexpected. Until now the gun had never been needed.

Hal was not the martial-arts whiz that his formidable appearance and ethnicity led everyone to believe he was, but he did know some tae kwon do. The problem was, only a fool would resort to *any* form of martial arts as a first defense against a charging bull with a bumblebee up its butt.

He made the doorway before Candy grabbed him by his shirt and tried to pull him off his feet. The shirt tore along the seams, leaving the madman with a handful of cloth.

But Hal was wrenched off balance. He stumbled into the office and collided with Julie's big chair, which was still standing in the middle of the room with four other chairs arranged in a semicircle in front of it, as Jackie Jaxx had required for Frank's session of hypnosis. He grabbed at Julie's chair for support. It was on wheels, which rolled grudgingly on the carpet, though well enough to send it skidding treacherously out from under him.

The psycho crashed into him, ramming him against the chair and the chair against the desk. Leaning into Hal, with massive fists that felt like the iron heads of sledgehammers, Candy delivered a flurry of punches to his midsection.

Hal's hands were down, leaving him briefly defenseless, but he clasped them, with his thumbs aligned, and rammed them upward, between Candy's pile-driving arms, catching him in the Adam's apple. The blow was hard enough to make Candy gag on his own cry of pain, and Hal's thumbnails gouged the madman's flesh, skidding all the way up under his chin, tearing the skin as they went.

Choking, unable to draw breath through his bruised and spasming esophagus, Candy staggered backward, both hands to his throat.

Hal pushed away from the chair, against which he had been pinned, but he didn't go after Candy. Even the blow he'd delivered was the equivalent of a tap with a flyswatter to the snout of that bull with the bee up its butt. An overconfident charge would no doubt end in a swift goring. Instead, hurting from the punches to his gut, with the sour taste of pizza sauce in the back of his throat, he hurried around the desk, hot to get his hands on that 9mm Browning.

The desk was large, and the dimensions of the kneehole were correspondingly spacious. He wasn't sure where the pistol was clipped, and he didn't want to bend down to look under because he would have to take his eyes off Candy. He slid his hand from left to right along the underside of the desktop, then reached deeper and slid it back the other way.

Just as he touched the butt of the pistol, he saw Candy thrust out both hands, palms forward, as if the guy knew Hal had found a gun and was saying, *Don't shoot, I surrender, stop.* But as Hal tugged the Browning free of the metal spring clamp, he discovered that Candy didn't have surrender in mind: blue light flashed out of the madman's palms.

The heavy desk abruptly behaved like a wire-rigged, balsa-wood prop in a movie about poltergeists. Even as Hal was raising the gun, the desk slammed into him and carried him backward, into the huge window behind him. The desk was wider than the window, and the ends of it met the wall, which prevented it from sailing straight through the glass.

But Hal was in the center of the window, and the low sill hit him behind the knees, so nothing inhibited his plunge. For an instant the jangling

Levolor blinds seemed as if they might restrain him, but that was wishful thinking; he carried them with him, through the glass, and into the night, dropping the Browning without ever having fired it.

He was surprised how long it took to fall six stories, which was not such a terribly great distance, though a deadly one. He had time to marvel at how slowly the lighted office window receded from him, time to think about people he had loved and dreams never fulfilled, time even to notice that the clouds, which had returned at twilight, were shedding light sprinkles of rain. His last thought was about the garden behind his small house in Costa Mesa, where he tended an array of flowers year-round and secretly enjoyed every moment of it: the exquisitely soft texture of a coral-red impatiens petal, and on its edge a single tiny drop of morning dew, glistening—

CANDY SHOVED THE heavy desk aside and leaned out of the sixth-floor window. A cool updraft rose along the side of the building and buffeted his face.

The shoeless man lay on his back on a broad concrete walk below, illuminated by the amber backsplash of a landscape spotlight. He was surrounded by broken glass, tangled metal blinds, and a swiftly spreading blot of his own blood.

Coughing, still having a little difficulty drawing deep enough breaths, with one hand pressed to the stinging flesh of his battered throat, Candy was upset by the man's death. Actually, not by the fact of it but by the timing of it. First, he'd wanted to interrogate him to learn who Bobby and Julie were, and what association they had with the psychic Thomas.

And when Candy had teleported into the reception lounge, the guy had thought he was Frank; he had spoken Frank's name. The people at Dakota & Dakota were somehow associated with Frank—knew all about his ability to teleport!—and therefore would know where to find the mother-murdering wretch.

Candy supposed the office would hold answers to at least some of his questions, but he was concerned that police, responding to the dead man's plunge, would necessitate a departure before he turned up all the information he needed. Sirens were the background music to this night's adventures.

No sirens had arisen yet, however. Maybe he had gotten lucky; maybe no one had seen the man fall. It was unlikely that anyone was at work at any of the other companies in the office building; it was, after all, ten minutes till nine. Perhaps janitors were polishing floors somewhere, or emptying wastebaskets, but they might not have heard enough to warrant investigation.

The man had plummeted to his death with surprisingly little protest. He had not screamed. An instant before impact, the start of a shout had flown from him, but it had been too short to attract notice. The explosion of the glass and the tinny clanging of the blinds had been loud enough, but the action had been over before anyone could have located the source of the sound.

A four-lane street encircled the Fashion Island shopping center and also served the office towers that, like this one, stood on the outer rim. Apparently, however, no cars had been on it when the man had fallen.

Now two appeared to the left, one behind the other. Both passed without slowing. A row of shrubberies, between the sidewalk and the street, prevented motorists from seeing the corpse where it lay. The office-tower ring of the sprawling complex was clearly not an area that attracted pedestrians at night, so the dead man might remain undiscovered until morning.

He looked across the street, at the restaurants and stores that were on this flank of the mall, five or six hundred yards away. A few people on foot, shrunken by distance, moved between the parked cars and the entrances to the businesses. No one appeared to have seen anything—and in fact it would not have been that easy to spot a darkly dressed man plunging past a mostly dark building, aloft and visible for only seconds before gravity finished him.

Candy cleared his throat, wincing in pain, and spat toward the dead man below.

He tasted blood. This time it was his own.

Turning away from the window, he surveyed the office, wondering where he would find the answers he sought. If he could locate Bobby and Julie Dakota, they might be able to explain Thomas's telepathy and more important, they might be able to deliver Frank into his hands.

———

AFTER TWICE RESPONDING to an alarm from the radar detector and avoiding two speed traps in the west valley, Julie cranked the Toyota back up
to eighty-five, and they dusted L.A. off their heels.

A few raindrops spattered the windshield, but the sprinkles did not
last. She switched the wipers off moments after turning them on.

"Santa Barbara in maybe an hour," she said, "as long as a cop with a
sense of duty doesn't come along."

The back of her neck ached, and she was deeply weary, but she didn't
want to trade places with Bobby; she didn't have the patience to be a
passenger tonight. Her eyes were sore but not heavy; she could not possibly have slept. The events of the day had murdered sleep, and alertness
was assured by concern about what might lie ahead, not just on the highway before them but in El Encanto Heights.

Ever since he'd been awakened by what he called the "wordburst,"
Bobby had been moody. She could tell he was worried about something,
but he didn't seem to want to talk about it yet.

After a while, in an obvious attempt to take his mind off the wordburst
and whatever gloomy ruminations it had inspired, he tried to strike up a
conversation about something utterly different. He lowered the volume
on the stereo, thereby frustrating the intended effect of Glenn Miller's
"American Patrol," and said, "You ever stop to think, four out of our
eleven employees are Asian-Americans?"

She didn't glance away from the road. "So?"

"So why is that, do you think?"

"Because we hire only first-rate people, and it so happened that four
of the first-rate people who wanted to work for us were Chinese, Japanese, and Vietnamese."

"That's part of it."

"Just part?" she said. "So what's the other part? You think maybe the
wicked Fu Manchu turned a mind-control ray on us from his secret fortress in the Tibetan mountains and *made* us hire 'em?"

"That's part of it too," he said. "But another part of it is—I'm attracted
to the Asian personality. Or to what people think of when they think of
the Asian personality: intelligence, a high degree of self-discipline, neatness, a strong sense of tradition and order."

"Those are pretty much traits of everyone who works for us, not just
Jamie, Nguyen, Hal, and Lee."

"I know. But what makes me so comfortable with Asian-Americans is that I buy into the stereotype of them, I feel everything will go along in an orderly, stable fashion when I'm working with them, and I *need* to buy into the stereotype because . . . well, I'm not the kind of guy I've always thought I was. You ready to hear something shocking?"

"Always," Julie said.

OFTEN, WHEN LEE Chen was laboring in the computer room, he popped a CD in his Sony Discman and listened to music through earphones. He always kept the door closed to avoid distraction, and no doubt some of his fellow employees thought he was somewhat antisocial; however, when he was engaged in the penetration of a complex and well-protected data network, like the array of police systems he was still plundering, he needed to concentrate. Occasionally music distracted him as much as anything, depending on his mood, but most of the time it was conducive to his work. The minimalist New Age piano solos of George Winston were sometimes just the thing, but more often he needed rock-'n'-roll. Tonight it was Huey Lewis and The News: "Hip to Be Square" and "The Power of Love," "The Heart of Rock & Roll" and "You Crack Me Up." Focused intently on the terminal screen (his window on the mesmerizing world of cyberspace), with "Bad Is Bad" pouring into his ears through the headset, he might not have heard a thing if, in the world outside, God had peeled back the sky and announced the imminent destruction of the human race.

A COOL DRAFT circulated through the room from the broken window, but growing frustration generated a compensatory heat in Candy. He moved slowly around the spacious office, handling various objects, touching the furniture, trying to finesse a vision that would reveal the whereabouts of the Dakotas and Frank. Thus far he'd had no luck.

He could have pored through the contents of the desk drawers and filing cabinets, but that would have taken hours, since he didn't know where they might have filed the information he was seeking. He also realized he might not recognize the right stuff when he found it, for it might be in a folder or envelope bearing a case name or code that was meaningless to him. And though his mother had taught him to read and write, and though he had been a voracious reader just like her—until he lost interest in books upon her death—teaching himself many subjects as well as any university could have done, he nevertheless trusted what his special gifts could reveal to him more than anything he might find on paper.

Besides, he had already stepped into the lounge, obtained the Dakotas' home address and phone number, and called to see if they were there. An answering machine had picked up on the third ring, and he had left no message. He didn't just want to know where the Dakotas lived, where they might turn up in time; he needed to know where they were *now*, this minute, because he was in a fever to get at them and wring answers from them.

He picked up a third Scotch-and-soda glass. They were all over the room. The psychic residue on the tumbler gave him an instant, vivid image of a man named Jackie Jaxx and he pitched it aside in anger. It bounced off the sofa, onto the carpet, without shattering.

This Jaxx person left a colorful and noisy psychic impression every-where in his wake, the way a dog with poor bladder control would mark each step on his route with a dribble of stinking urine. Candy sensed that Jaxx was currently with a large number of people, at a party in Newport Beach, and he also sensed that trying to find Frank or the Dakotas through Jaxx would be wasted effort. Even so, if Jaxx had been alone now, easily taken, Candy would have gone straight to him and slaughtered him, just because the guy's lingering aura was so brassy and annoying.

Either he had not yet found an object that one of the Dakotas had touched long enough to leave an imprint, or neither of them was the type who left a rich, lingering psychic residue in his wake. For reasons Candy could not fathom, some people were harder to trace than others.

He had always found tracing Frank to be of medium difficulty, but tonight catching that scent was harder than usual. Repeatedly he sensed that Frank had been in the room, but at first he could locate nothing in which the aura of his brother was coagulated.

Next he turned to the four chairs, beginning with the largest. When he skimmed his sensitive fingertips lightly over the upholstery, he quivered with excitement, for he knew at once that Frank had sat there recently. A small tear marred the vinyl on one arm, and when Candy put his thumb upon the rent, particularly vivid visions of Frank assaulted him.

Too many visions. He was rewarded with a whole series of place im-

ages, where Frank had traveled after rising from the chair: the High Sierras; the apartment in San Diego in which he had lived briefly four years
ago; the rusted front gate of their mother's house on Pacific Hill Road; a
graveyard; a book-lined study in which he'd stayed such a short time that
Candy could get only the vaguest impression of it; Punaluu Beach, where
Candy had nearly caught him. . . . There were so many images, from so
many travels, layered one atop another, that he could not clearly see the
later stops.

Disgusted, he pushed the chair out of his way and turned to the coffee
table, where two more tumblers stood. Both contained melted ice and
Scotch. He picked one up and had a vision of Julie Dakota.

WHILE JULIE DROVE toward Santa Barbara as if they were competing in
time trials for the Indianapolis 500, Bobby told her the shocking thing:
that he was not, at heart, the laid-back guy he appeared to be on the
surface; that during his hectic travels with Frank—especially during the
moments when he had been reduced to a disembodied mind and a frantic
whirl of disconnected atoms—he'd discovered within himself a rich vein
of love for stability and order that ran deeper than he could ever have
imagined, a motherlode of stick-in-the-mudness; that his delight in swing
music arose more from an appreciation for the meticulosity of its structures than from the dizzying musical freedom embodied in jazz; that he
was not half the free-spirited man he'd thought he was . . . and far more
of a conservative embracer of tradition that he would have hoped.

"In short," he said, "all this time when you thought you were married
to an easygoing young-James-Garner type, you've actually been wed to
an any-age-Charles-Bronson type."

"I can live with you anyway, Charlie."

"This is serious. Sort of. I've tipped into my late thirties, I'm no child.
I should've known this about myself a long time ago."

"You did."

"Huh?"

"You love order, reason, logic—that's why you got into a line of work
where you could right wrongs, help the innocent, punish the bad. That's
why you share The Dream with me—so we can get our little family in
order, step out of the chaos of the world as it is these days and buy into

some peace and quiet. That's why you won't let me have the Wurlitzer 950—those bubble tubes and leaping gazelles are just a little too chaotic for you."

He was silent a moment, surprised by her answer.

The lightless vastness of the sea lay to the west.

He said, "Maybe you're right. Maybe I've always known what I am, deep down. But then isn't it unnerving that I've fooled myself with my own act for so long?"

"You haven't. You're easy-going *and* a bit of Charles Bronson, which is a good thing. Otherwise we probably couldn't communicate at all, since I've got more Bronson in me than anyone but Bronson."

"God, that's true!" he said, and they both laughed.

The Toyota's speed had declined to under seventy. She put it up to eighty and said, "Bobby . . . what's really on your mind?"

"Thomas."

She glanced at him. "What about Thomas?"

"Since that wordburst, I can't shake the feeling he's in danger."

"What did that have to do with him?"

"I don't know. But I'd feel better if we could find a phone and put in a call to Cielo Vista. Just to be . . . sure."

She let their speed fall dramatically. Within three miles they exited the freeway and pulled into a service station. There was a full-service lane. While the attendant washed their windows, checked the oil, and filled the tank with premium unleaded, they went inside and used the pay phone.

It was a modern electronic version allowing everything from coin to credit calls, on the wall next to a rack of snack crackers, candy bars, and packages of beer nuts. A condom machine was there, too, right out in the open, thanks to the social chaos wrought by AIDS. Using their AT&T credit card, Bobby called Cielo Vista Care Home in Newport.

It didn't ring or give a busy signal. He heard an odd series of electronic sounds, then a recording informed him that the number he had dialed was temporarily out of service as a result of unspecified line problems. The droning voice suggested that he try later.

He dialed the operator, who tried the same number, with the same results. She said, "I'm sorry, sir. Please call your party later."

"What line problems could they be having?"

"I wouldn't know, sir, but I'm sure service'll be restored soon."

He had tilted the phone away from his ear, so Julie could lean in and hear both sides of the exchange. When he hung up, he looked at her. "Let's go back. I got this hunch Thomas needs us."

"Go back? We're little more than half an hour from Santa Barbara now. Much further to go home."

"He may need us. It's not a strong hunch, I admit, but it's persistent and . . . weird."

"If he needs help urgently," she said, "then we'd never get to him in time, anyway. And if it's not so urgent, it'll be okay if we go on to Santa Barbara, call again from the motel. If he's sick or been hurt or something, the extra driving from here to Santa Barbara and back will only add about an hour."

"Well . . ."

"He's my brother, Bobby. I care about him as much as you do, and I say it'll be all right. I love you, but you've never shown enough talent as a psychic to make me hysterical about this."

He nodded. "You're right. I'm just . . . jumpy. My nerves haven't settled down since all that traveling with Frank."

Back on the highway, a few thin tendrils of fog were creeping in from the sea. Sprinkles of rain fell again, then stopped after less than a minute. The heaviness of the air, and an indefinable but undeniable quality of oppressiveness in the utterly black night sky, portended a major storm.

When they had gone a couple of miles, Bobby said, "I should've called Hal at the office. While he's sitting around there waiting for Frank, he could use some of our contacts with the phone company, the cops, make sure everything's jake at Cielo Vista."

"If the lines are still out when you make the call from the motel," Julie said, "then you can bother Hal about it."

FROM THE WEAK psychic residue on the drinking glass, Candy received an image of Julie Dakota that was recognizably the same face that had seeped from Thomas's mind earlier in the evening—except that it was not as idealized as it had been in Thomas's memory. With his sixth sense he saw that she had gone home from the office, to the address he had obtained earlier from the secretary's Rolodex. She had been there a short time, then had gone somewhere in a car with another person, most likely the man named Bobby. He could see no more, and he wished that the traces she left behind had been as strong as those of Jaxx.

He put down the tumbler and decided to go to her house. Though she and Bobby were not there now, he might be able to find an object that would, like the liquor glass, lead him another step or two along their trail. If he found nothing, he could return here and continue his search, assuming the police had not arrived in response to the discovery of the dead man outside.

LEE SWITCHED OFF the computer, then cut off the CD player too—Huey Lewis and The News were in the middle of "Walking on a Thin Line"— and removed the earphones.

Happy after a long and productive session in the land of silicon and gallium arsenide, he stood, stretched, yawned, and checked his watch. A little after nine. He'd been at work for twelve hours.

He should have wanted nothing more than to flop in bed and sleep half a day. But he figured he'd zip back to his condo, which was ten minutes from the office, freshen up, and catch some nightlife. Last week he'd found a new club, Nuclear Grin, where the music was loud and hard-edged, the drinks unwatered, the crowd's politics unconsciously libertarian, and the women hot. He wanted to dance a little, drink a little, and find someone who wanted to screw her brains out.

In this age of new diseases, sex was risky; it sometimes seemed that drinking from the same glass as someone else was suicidal. But after a day in the painstakingly logical microchip universe, you had to get a little wild, take some risks, dance on the edge of chaos, to get some balance in your life.

Then he remembered how Frank and Bobby had vanished in front of his eyes. He wondered if maybe he hadn't already had enough wildness for one day.

He picked up the latest printouts. It was more stuff that he had gleaned from police records, regarding the decidedly weird behavior of Mr. Blue, who would never need to get a little wild for balance, since he was *already* chaos walking around in shoes. Lee opened the door, switched off the lights, went down the hall and through another door into the lounge, intending to leave the printouts on Julie's desk and say goodnight to Hal before splitting.

When he walked into Bobby and Julie's office, it looked like the National Wrestling Federation had sanctioned a match there between tag teams of three-hundred-pound hulks. Furniture was overturned, and Scotch glasses, some of them broken, were scattered over the floor. Julie's desk was aslant and askew: tilting on one shattered leg; the top no longer was properly aligned with the base, as if someone had gone at it with prybars and hammers.

"Hal?"

No answer.

He gingerly pushed open the door to the adjoining bath.

"Hal?"

The bathroom was deserted.

He went to the broken window. A few small shards of glass still clung to the frame. Caught the light. Jagged.

With one hand against the wall, Lee Chen carefully leaned out. He looked down. In a much different tone of voice, he said, "Hal?"

CANDY MATERIALIZED IN the foyer of the Dakotas' house, which was dark and silent. He stood quietly for a moment, head cocked, until he was confident that he was alone.

His throat was healed. He was whole again, and excited by the prospects of the night.

He began the search from there, putting his hand on the doorknob in hope of finding some of the residue that, while lacking physical substance, nevertheless provided the nourishment for his visions. He felt nothing, no doubt partly because the Dakotas had touched it only briefly upon entering and departing the house.

Of course, a person could handle a hundred items, leaving psychic images of himself on only one of them, then touch the same hundred an hour later and contaminate every one with his aura. The reason for that was as mysterious, to Candy, as was so many people's interest in sex. He remained as grateful to his mother for this talent as he was for all the others, but tracking his prey with psychometry was not always an easy or infallible process.

The Dakotas' living room and dining room were unfurnished, which gave him little to work with, although for some reason the emptiness made him feel comfortable and at home. That response puzzled him. The rooms in his mother's house were all furnished—as much with mold and fungus and dust these days as with chairs, sofas, tables, and lamps; but he suddenly realized that, like the Dakotas, he lived in such a small percentage of the house that most of its chambers might as well have been bare, carpetless, and sealed off.

The Dakotas' kitchen and family room were furnished and obviously lived in. Though it was unlikely that they had used the family room during their brief stop between the office and wherever they had gone from here, he hoped they might have lingered in the kitchen for a bite of food or a drink. But the handles of the cabinets, microwave, oven, and refrigerator provided him with no images whatsoever.

On his way to the second floor, Candy climbed the steps slowly, letting his left hand slide searchingly along the oak balustrade. At several points along the way, he was rewarded by psychic images that, while brief and not clear, encouraged him, and led him to believe that he would find what he needed in their bedroom or bath.

54

INSTEAD OF IMMEDIATELY DIALING 911 TO REPORT THE MURDER OF Hal Yamataka, Lee ran first to the reception desk and, as he had been trained, removed a small brown notebook from the back of the bottom drawer on the right side. For the benefit of employees, like Lee, who did not often get into the field and seldom interfaced directly with the county's many police agencies but might one day need to deal with them in an emergency, Bobby had composed a list of some of the officers, detectives, and administrators who were most professional, reasonable, and reliable in every major jurisdiction. The brown notebook contained a second list of cops to avoid: those who had an instinctive dislike for anyone in the private investigation and security business; those who were just pains in the ass in general; and those who were always on the lookout for a little green grease to lubricate the wheels of justice. It was a testament to the high quality of the county's law enforcement that the first list was much longer than the second.

According to Bobby and Julie, it was preferable to try to *manage* the introduction of the police into a situation that required them, even going so far as to try to select one of the detectives who would show up at the scene—if it was a scene that needed detectives. Relying on the luck of the draw or a dispatcher's whim was considered unwise.

Lee wondered if he should even call the cops. He had no doubt who had killed Hal. Mr. Blue. Candy. But also he knew that Bobby would not want to reveal more about Frank and the case than was truly necessary; the agency-client privilege was not as legally airtight as that of lawyer-client or doctor-patient, but it was important too. Since Julie and Bobby were on the road and temporarily unreachable, Lee could get no guidance on what and how much to say to the police.

But he couldn't let a dead body lie in front of the building, hoping nobody would notice! Especially not when the victim was a man he had known and liked.

Call the cops, then. But play dumb.

Consulting the notebook, Lee dialed the Newport Beach Police and asked for Detective Harry Ladsbroke, but Ladsbroke was off duty. So was Detective Janet Heisinger. Detective Kyle Ostov was available, however, and when he came on the line he sounded reassuringly big and competent; his voice was a mellow baritone, and he spoke crisply.

Lee identified himself, aware that his own voice was higher than usual, almost squeaky, and that he was speaking too fast. "There's been a . . . well, a murder."

Before Lee could go on, Ostov said, "Jesus, you mean Bobby and Julie know already? I just found out myself. It was pushed on to me to tell them, and I was just sitting here, trying to figure how best to break the news. I had my hand on the phone, going to call them, when you rang through. How're they taking it?"

Confused, Lee said, "I don't think they know. I mean, it must have happened just a few minutes ago."

"A little longer than that," Ostov said.

"When did you guys find out? I just looked, and there weren't any patrol cars, nothing." Finally the shakes hit him. "God, I was talking to him not that long ago, took him some pizza, and now he's splattered all over the concrete six floors down."

Ostov was silent. Then: "What murder you talking about, Lee?"

"Hal Yamataka. There must've been a fight here, and then—" He stopped, blinked, and said, "What murder are *you* talking about?"

"Thomas," Ostov said.

Lee felt sick. He had only met Thomas once, but he knew that Julie and Bobby were devoted to him.

Ostov said, "Thomas *and* his roommate. And maybe more in the fire if they didn't get them all out of the building in time."

The computer that Lee had been born with was not functioning as smoothly as the ones made by IBM in his office, and he needed a moment to grasp the implications of the information that he and Ostov had exchanged. "They've got to be connected, don't they?"

"I'd bet on it. You know of anybody who has a grudge against Julie and Bobby?"

Lee looked around the reception lounge, thought about the other deserted rooms at Dakota & Dakota, the lonely offices on the rest of the sixth floor, and the unpeopled levels below the sixth. He thought of Candy, too, all those people bitten and torn, the giant Bobby had seen on Punaluu Beach, the way the guy could zap himself from place to place. He began to feel very much alone. "Detective Ostov, could you get some people here really fast?"

"I've entered the call on the computer while I've been talking to you," Ostov said. "A couple of units are on the way now."

WITH HIS FINGERTIPS, Candy traced lazy circles on the surface of the dresser, then explored the contours of each brass handle on the drawers. He touched the light switch on the wall and the switches on both bedside lamps. He let his hands glide over doorframes on the off-chance that one of his intended prey might have paused and leaned there while in conversation, examined the handles on the mirrored closet doors, and caressed each number and switchpad on the remote-control device for the TV, hoping that they had clicked on the set even during the short time they had been home.

Nothing.

Because he needed to be calm and methodical in his search if he were to succeed, Candy had to repress his rage and frustration. But his anger grew even as he struggled to contain it, and in him the thirst of anger was always a thirst for blood, that wine of vengeance. Only blood would slake his thirst, quench his fury, and allow him an interlude of relative peace.

By the time he moved from the Dakotas' bedroom into the adjoining bath, Candy was possessed of a *need* for blood almost as undeniable and critical as his need for air. Looking at the mirror, he did not see himself for a moment, as if he cast no reflection; he saw only red blood, as if the mirror were a porthole on one of the lower decks of a ship in Hell, on a cruise through a sea of gore. When that illusion faded and he saw his own face, he quickly looked away.

He clenched his jaws, struggled even harder to control himself, and touched the hot-water faucet, searching, seeking. . . .

THE MOTEL ROOM in Santa Barbara was spacious, quiet, clean, and furnished without the jarring clash of colors and patterns that seemed de rigueur in most American motels—but it was not a place in which Julie would have chosen to receive the terrible news that came to her there. The blow seemed greater, the ache in the heart more piercing, for having to be borne in a strange and impersonal place.

She really had thought that Bobby was letting his imagination run away with him again, that Thomas was perfectly fine. Because the phone was on the nightstand, he sat on the edge of the bed to make the call, and Julie watched him and listened from a chair only a few feet away. When he got that recording again, explaining that the Cielo Vista number was temporarily out of service due to line problems, she was vaguely uneasy but still sure that all was well with her brother.

However, when he called the office in Newport to talk with Hal, got Lee Chen instead, and spent the first minute or so listening in shocked silence, responding with a cryptic word or two, she knew this was to be a night that cleaved her life, and that the years to come inevitably would be darker than the years she had lived on the other side of that cleft. As he began to ask questions of Lee, Bobby avoided looking at Julie, which confirmed her intuition and made her heart pound faster. When at last he glanced at her, she had to look away from the sadness in his eyes. His questions to Lee were clipped, and she couldn't ascertain much from them. Maybe she didn't want to.

Finally the call seemed to be drawing to an end. "No, you've done well, Lee. Keep handling it just the way you have been. What? Thank you, Lee. No, we'll be all right. We'll be okay, Lee. One way or another, we'll be okay."

When Bobby hung up, he sat for a moment, staring at his hands, which he clasped between his knees.

Julie did not ask him what had happened, as if what Lee had told him was not yet fact, as if her question was a dark magic and as if the unrevealed tragedy would not become real until she asked about it.

Bobby got off the bed and knelt on the floor in front of her chair. He took both of her hands in his and gently kissed them.

She knew then that the news was as bad as it could get.

Softly he said, "Thomas is dead."

She had steeled herself for that news, but the words cut deep.

"I'm sorry, Julie. God, I'm so sorry. And it doesn't end there." He told her about Hal. "And just a couple minutes before he talked to me, Lee received a call about Clint and Felina. Both dead."

The horror was too much to assimilate. Julie had liked and respected Hal, Clint, and Felina enormously, and her admiration for the deaf woman's courage and self-sufficiency was unbounded. It was unfair that she could not mourn each of them individually; they deserved that much. She also felt that she was somehow betraying them because her sorrow at their deaths was only a pale reflection of the grief she felt at the loss of Thomas, though that was, of course, the only way it could be.

Her breath caught in her throat, and when it flew free, it was not just an exhalation but a sob. That was no good. She could not allow herself to break down. At no point in her life had she needed to be as strong as she needed to be now; the murders committed in Orange County tonight were the first in a domino-fall of death that would take down her and Bobby, too, if misery dulled their edge.

While Bobby continued to kneel before her and reveal more details—Derek was dead, too, and perhaps others at Cielo Vista—she gripped his hands tightly, inexpressibly grateful to have him for an anchor in this turbulence. Her vision was blurry, but she held back the tears with a sheer effort of will—though she dared not make eye contact with Bobby just yet; that would be the end of her self-control.

When he finished, she said, "It was Frank's brother, of course," and was dismayed by the way her voice quavered.

"Almost certainly," Bobby said.

"But how did he find out Frank was our client?"

"I don't know. He saw me on the beach at Punaluu—"

"Yeah, but didn't follow you. He has no way of knowing who you were. And for God's sake, how did he find out about Thomas?"

"There's some crucial bit of information missing, so we can't understand the pattern."

"What's the bastard after?" she said. Now her voice was marked by nearly as much anger as grief, and that was good.

"He's hunting Frank," Bobby said. "For seven years Frank was a loner, and that made him harder to find. Now Frank has friends, and that gives Candy more ways to search for him."

"I as good as killed Thomas when I took the case," she said.

"You didn't want to take it. I had to talk you into it."

"I talked *you* into it, you wanted to back out."

"If there's guilt, we share it, but there isn't any. We took on a new client, that's all, and everything . . . just happened."

Julie nodded and finally met his eyes. Although his voice had remained steady, tears slid down his cheeks. Preoccupied with her own grief, she had forgotten that the friends lost were his as well as hers, and that he had come to love Thomas nearly as much as she did. She had to look away from him again.

"Are you okay?" he asked.

"For now, I have to be. Later, I want to talk about Thomas, how brave he was about being different, how he never complained, how sweet he was. I want to talk about all of it, you and me, and I don't want us to forget. Nobody's ever going to build a monument to Thomas, he wasn't famous, he was just a little guy who never did anything great except be the best person he knew how, and the only monument he's ever going to have is our memories. So we'll keep him alive, won't we?"

"Yes."

"We'll keep him alive . . . until we're gone. But that's for later, when there's time. Now we have to keep ourselves alive, because that son of a bitch will be coming for us, won't he?"

"I think he will," Bobby said.

He rose from his knees and pulled her up from the chair.

He was wearing his dark brown Ultrasuede jacket with the shoulder holster under it. She'd taken off her corduroy blazer and her holster; she put both of them on again. The weight of the revolver, against her left side, felt good. She hoped she'd have a chance to use it.

Her vision had cleared; her eyes were dry. She said, "One thing for sure—no more dreams for me. What good is it, having dreams, when they never come true?"

"Sometimes they do."

"No. They never came true for my mom or dad. Never came true for Thomas, did they? Ask Clint and Felina if their dreams came true, see what they say. You ask George Farris's family if they think being slaughtered by a maniac was the fulfillment of their dreams."

"Ask the Phans," Bobby said quietly. "They were boat people on the South China Sea, with hardly any food and less money, and now they own dry-cleaning shops and remodel two-hundred-thousand-dollar houses for resale, and they have those terrific kids."

"Sooner or later, they'll get it in the neck too," she said, unsettled by the bitterness in her voice and the black despair that churned like a whirlpool within her, threatening to swallow her up. But she could not stop the churning. "Ask Park Hampstead, down there in El Toro, whether he and his wife were thrilled when she developed terminal cancer, and ask him how his dream about him and Maralee Roman worked after he finally got over the death of his wife. Nasty bugger named Candy got in the way of that one. Ask all the poor suckers lying in the hospital with cerebral hemorrhages, cancer. Ask those who get Alzheimer's in their fifties, just when their golden years are supposed to start. Ask the little kids in wheelchairs from muscular dystrophy, and ask all the parents of those other kids down there in Cielo Vista how Down's syndrome fits in with *their* dreams. Ask—"

She cut herself off. She was losing control, and she could not afford to do so tonight.

She said, "Come on, let's go."

"Where?"

"First, we find the house where that bitch raised him. Cruise by, get the lay of it. Maybe just seeing it will give us ideas."

"I've seen it."

"I haven't."

"All right." From a nightstand drawer he removed a telephone directory for Santa Barbara, Montecito, Goleta, Hope Ranch, El Encanto Heights, and other surrounding communities. He brought it with him to the door.

She said, "What do you want that for?"

"We'll need it later. I'll explain in the car."

Sprinkles of rain were falling again. The Toyota's engine was still so hot from the drive north that in spite of the cool night air, steam rose from its hood as the beads of rainwater evaporated. Far away a brief, low peal of thunder rolled across the sky. Thomas was dead.

HE RECEIVED IMAGES as faint and distorted as reflections on the wind-rippled surface of a pond. They came repeatedly as he touched the faucets, the rim of the sink, the mirror, the medicine cabinet and its contents, the light switch, the controls for the shower. But none of his visions was detailed, and none provided a clue as to where the Dakotas had gone.

Twice he was jolted by vivid images, but they were related to disgusting sexual episodes between the Dakotas. A tube of vaginal lubricant and a box of Kleenex were contaminated with older psychic residue that had inexplicably lingered beyond its time, making him privy to sinful practices that he had no desire to witness. He quickly snatched his hands away from those surfaces and waited for his nausea to pass. He was incensed that the need to track Frank through these decadent people had forced him into a situation where his senses had been so brutally affronted.

Infuriated by his lack of success and by the unclean contact with images of their sin (which he seemed unable to expel from his mind), he decided that he must burn the evil out of this house in the name of God. Burn it out. Incinerate it. So that maybe his mind would be cleansed again as well.

He stepped out of the bathroom, raised his hands, and sent an immensely destructive wave of power across the bedroom. The wooden headboard of the big bed disintegrated, flames leaped from the quilted spread and blankets, the nightstands flew apart, and every drawer in the dresser shot out and dumped its contents on the floor, where they instantly caught fire. The drapes were consumed as if made from magicians' flashpaper, and the two windows in the far wall burst, letting in a draft that fanned the blaze.

Candy often wished the mysterious light that came from him could affect people and animals, rather than just inanimate things, plants, and a few insects. There were times when he would have gone into a city and melted the flesh from the bones of ten thousand sinners in a single night, a hundred thousand. It didn't matter which city, they were all festering sewers of iniquity, populated by depraved masses who worshiped evil and practiced every repulsive degeneracy. He had never seen anyone in any of them, not a single person, who seemed to him to live in God's grace. He would have made them run screaming in terror, would have tracked them down in their secret places, would have splintered their bones with his power, hammered their flesh to pulp, made their heads explode, and torn off the offensive sex things that preoccupied them. If he had been that gifted, he would not have shown them any of the mercy with which their Creator always treated them, so they would have realized, then, how grateful and obedient they should have been to their God, who always so patiently tolerated even their worst transgressions.

Only God and Candy's mother had such unlimited compassion. He did not share it.

The smoke alarm went off in the hall. He walked out there, pointed a finger at it, and blew it to bits.

This part of his gift seemed more powerful tonight than ever. He was a great engine of destruction.

The Lord must be rewarding his purity by increasing his power.

He thanked God that his own saintly mother had never descended into the pits of depravity in which so much of humanity swam. No man had ever touched her *that* way, so her children were born without the stain of original sin. He knew this to be true, for she had told him—and had shown him that it was.

He descended to the first floor and set the living-room carpet on fire with a bolt from his left hand.

Frank and the twins had never appreciated the immaculate aspect of their conceptions, and in fact had thrown away that incomparable state of grace to embrace sin and do the devil's work. Candy would never make that mistake.

Overhead he heard the roar of flames, the crash of a partition. In the morning, when the sun revealed a smoldering pile of blackened rubble, the remains of this nest of corruption would be a testament to the ultimate perdition of all sinners.

Candy felt cleansed. The psychic images of the Dakotas' fevered degeneracy had been expunged from his mind.

He returned to the offices of Dakota & Dakota to continue his search for them.

BOBBY DROVE, FOR he didn't think Julie ought to be behind the wheel any more tonight. She had been awake for more than nineteen hours, not a marathon all-nighter yet, but she was exhausted; and her bottled-up grief over Thomas's death could not help but cloud her judgment and dull her reflexes. At least he had napped a couple of times since Hal's call from the hospital had awakened them last night.

He crossed most of Santa Barbara and entered Goleta before bothering to look for a service station where they could ask for directions to Pacific Hill Road.

At his request, Julie opened the telephone directory on her lap, and with the assistance of a small flashlight taken from the glove compartment, she looked under the Fs for Fogarty. He didn't know the first name, but he was only interested in a male Fogarty who carried the title of doctor.

"He might not live in this area," Bobby said, "but I have a hunch he does."

"Who is he?"

"When Frank and I were traveling, we stopped in this guy's study, twice." He told her about both brief visits.

"How come you didn't mention him before?"

"At the office, when I told you what happened to me, where Frank and I had gone, I had to condense some of it, and this Fogarty seemed comparatively uninteresting, so I left him out. But the longer I've had time to think about it, the more it seems to me that he might be a key player in this. See, Frank popped us out of there so fast because he seemed especially reluctant to endanger Fogarty by leading Candy to him. If Frank's especially concerned about the man, then we ought to have a talk with him."

She hunched over the directory, studying it closely. "Fogarty, James. Fogarty, Jennifer. Fogarty, Kevin. . . ."

"If he's not a medical doctor and doesn't use the title daily, or if 'Doc' is a nickname, we're in trouble. Even if he is a medical doctor, don't bother looking in the Yellow Pages under 'physicians,' because this guy is up in years, got to be retired."

"Here!" she said. "Fogarty, Dr. Lawrence J."

"There's an address?"

"Yes." She tore the page out of the book.

"Great. As soon as you've seen the infamous Pollard place, we'll pay Fogarty a visit."

Though Bobby had visited the house three times, he had traveled there with Frank, and he had not known the precise location of 1458 Pacific Hill Road any more than he had known exactly what flank of Mount Fuji that trail had ascended. They found it easily, however, by following the directions they received from a long-haired guy with a handlebar mustache at a Union 76 station.

Though the houses along Pacific Hill Road enjoyed an El Encanto Heights address, they were actually neither in that suburb nor in Goleta—which separated El Encanto from Santa Barbara—but in a narrow band of county land that lay between the two and that led east into a wilderness preserve of mesquite, chapparal, desert brush, and pockets of California live oaks and other hardy trees.

The Pollard house was near the end of Pacific Hill, on the edge of developed land, with few neighbors. Oriented west-southwest, it overlooked the charmed Pacific-facing communities so beautifully sited on the terraced hills below. At night the view was spectacular—a sea of lights leading to a real sea cloaked in darkness—and no doubt the immediate neighborhood remained rural and free of expensive new houses only because of development restrictions related to the proximity of the preserve.

Bobby recognized the Pollard place at once. The headlights revealed little more than the Eugenia hedge and the rusted iron gate between two tall stone pilasters. He slowed as they went by it. The ground floor was dark. In one upstairs room a light was on; a pale glow leaked around the edges of a drawn blind.

Leaning over to look past Bobby, Julie said, "Can't see much."

"There isn't much to see. It's a crumbling pile."

They drove over a quarter of a mile to the end of the road, turned, and went back. Coming downhill, the house was on Julie's side, and she insisted he slow to a crawl, to allow her more time to study it.

As they eased past the gate, Bobby saw a light on at the back of the house, too, on the first floor. He couldn't actually see a lighted window, just the glow that fell through it and painted a pale, frosty rectangle on the side yard.

"It's all hidden in shadows," Julie said at last, turning to look back at the property as it fell behind them. "But I can see enough to know that it's a bad place."

"Very," Bobby said.

VIOLET LAY ON her back on the bed in her dark room with her sister, warmed by the cats, which were draped over them and huddled around them. Verbina lay on her right side, cuddled against Violet, one hand on Violet's breasts, her lips against Violet's bare shoulder, her warm breath spilling across Violet's smooth skin.

They were not settling down to sleep. Neither of them cared to sleep at night, for that was the wild time, when a greater number and variety of nature's hunters were on the prowl and life was more exciting.

At that moment they were not merely in each other and in all of the cats that shared the bed with them, but in a hungry owl that soared the night, scanning the earth for mice that weren't wise enough to fear the gloom and remain in burrows. No creature had night vision as sharp as the owl, and its claws and beak were even sharper.

Violet shivered in anticipation of the moment when a mouse or other small creature would be seen below, slipping through tall grass that it believed offered concealment. From past experience she knew the terror and pain of the prey, the savage glee of the hunter, and she yearned now to experience both again, simultaneously.

At her side Verbina murmured dreamily.

Swooping high, gliding, spiraling down, swooping up again, the owl had not yet seen its dinner when the car came up the hill and slowed almost to a stop in front of the Pollard house. It drew Violet's attention, of course, and through her the attention of the owl, but she lost interest when the car speeded up again and drove on. Seconds later, however, her interest was renewed when it returned and coasted almost to a stop, once more, at the front gate.

She directed the owl to circle the vehicle at a height of about sixty feet. Then she sent it out ahead of the car and brought it even lower, to about twenty feet, before guiding it around again to approach the curious motorist head-on.

From an altitude of only twenty feet, the vision of the owl was more than acute enough to see the driver and the passenger in the front seat.

There was a woman Violet had never seen before—but the driver was familiar. A moment later she realized that he was the man who had appeared with Frank in the backyard, at twilight that very same day!

Frank had killed their precious Samantha, for which Frank must die, and now here was a man who knew Frank, who might lead them to Frank, and on the bed around Violet, the other cats stirred and made low growling sounds as her passion for vengeance was transmitted to them. A tailless Manx and a black mongrel leaped from the bed, raced through the open bedroom door, down the steps, into the kitchen, out the pet door, around the house, and into the street. The car was moving away, gaining speed, heading downhill, and Violet wanted to pursue it not only by air but on foot, to ensure that she would not lose track of it.

CANDY ARRIVED IN the reception lounge at Dakota & Dakota. Cool cross-drafts circulated from the broken window in the next room and two open doors in this one, setting up opposing currents. The faint sounds announcing his arrival had evidently been masked by the bursts of static and harsh voices coming from the portable police radios that the cops had clipped to their belts. One policeman stood in the entrance to Julie and Bobby's private office, and the other was at the open door to the sixth-floor corridor. Each of them was talking to someone out of sight, and both had their backs turned to Candy, which Candy knew was a sign that God was still looking out for him.

Though he was angered by this obstacle to his search for the Dakotas, he got out of there at once, materializing in his bedroom, nearly a hundred and fifty miles to the north. He needed time to think if there was some way that he could pick up their trail again, a place where they had been tonight—besides their office and their house—at which he could seek more visions of them.

WHEN THEY BACKTRACKED to the Union 76 station, the long-haired, mustachioed man who had given them directions to Pacific Hill Road was able to tell them how to find the street on which Fogarty lived. He even knew the man. "Nice old guy. Stops by here for gas now and then."

"Is he a medical doctor?" Bobby asked.

"Used to be. Been retired quite a while."

Shortly after ten o'clock, Bobby parked at the curb in front of Lawrence Fogarty's house. It was a quaint Spanish two-story with the style of French windows that had been featured in the study to which Bobby and Frank had twice traveled, and lights were on throughout the first floor. The glass in the many panes was beveled, at least on the front of the house, and the lamplight ·inside was warmly refracted by those cut edges. When Bobby and Julie got out of the car, he smelled woodsmoke, and saw a homey white curl rising from a chimney into the still, cool, humid pre-storm air. In the odd and vaguely purple, crepuscular glow of a nearby streetlamp, a few pink flowers were visible on the azaleas, but the bushes were not as laden with early blooms as those farther south in Orange County. An ancient tree with a multiple trunk and enormous branches loomed over more than half the house, so it seemed like a wonderfully cozy and sheltered haven in some Spanish version of a Hobbity fantasy world.

As they followed the front walkway, something dashed between two low Malibu lights, crossed their path, and startled Julie. It stopped on the lawn after passing them, and studied them with radiant green eyes.

"Just a cat," Bobby said.

Usually he liked cats, but when he saw this one, he shivered.

It moved again, vanishing into shadows and shrubs at the side of the house.

What spooked him was not this particular creature, but the memory of the feline horde at the Pollard house, which had raced to attack him and Frank, in eerie silence initially but then with the shrill single-voiced squeal of a banshee regiment, and with a most uncatlike unanimity of purpose. On the prowl alone, swift and curious, this cat was quite ordinary, pos-sessed only of the mystery and haughtiness common to every member of his species.

At the end of the walk, three front steps led up to an archway, through which they entered a small veranda.

Julie rang the bell, which was soft and musical, and when no one answered after half a minute, she rang it again.

As the second set of chimes faded, the stillness was disturbed by the rustle of feathered wings, as some night bird settled onto the veranda roof above them.

When Julie was about to reach for the bell push again, the porch light came on, and Bobby sensed they were being scrutinized through the security lens. After a moment the door opened, and Dr. Fogarty stood before them in an outfall of light from the hall behind him.

He looked the same as Bobby remembered him, and he recognized Bobby as well. "Come in," he said, stepping aside to admit them. "I half expected you. Come in—not that any of you is welcome."

55

"IN THE LIBRARY," FOGARTY SAID, LEADING THEM BACK THROUGH the hall to a room on the left.

The library, where Frank had taken him during their travels, was the place Bobby had referred to as the study when he had described it to Julie. As the exterior of the house had a Hobbity-fantasy coziness in spite of its Spanish style, so this room seemed exactly the sort of place where one imagined that Tolkien, on many a long Oxford evening, had taken pen to paper to create the adventures of Frodo. That warm and welcoming space was gently illuminated by a brass floorlamp and a stained-glass table lamp that was either a genuine Tiffany or an excellent imitation. Books lined the walls under a deeply coffered ceiling, and a thick Chinese carpet—dark green and beige around the border, mostly pale green in the middle—graced a dark tongue-and-groove oak floor. The water-clear finish on the large mahogany desk had a deep luster; on the green felt blotter, the elements of a gold-plated, bone-handled desk set—including a letter opener, magnifying glass, and scissors—were lined up neatly behind a gold fountain pen in a square marble holder. The Queen Anne sofa was upholstered in a tapestry that perfectly complemented the carpet, and when Bobby turned to look at the wing-backed chair where he'd first seen Fogarty earlier in the day—he twitched with astonishment at the sight of Frank.

"Something's happened to him," Fogarty said, pointing to Frank. He was unaware of Bobby's and Julie's surprise, apparently operating under the assumption that they had come to his house specifically because they had known they would find Frank there.

Frank's physical appearance had deteriorated since Bobby had last seen him at 5:26 that afternoon, in the office in Newport Beach. If his eyes had been sunken then, they were as deep as pits now; the dark rings around them had widened, too, and some of the blackness seemed to have leached out of those bruises to impart a deathly gray tint to the rest of his face. His previous pallor had looked healthy by comparison.

The worst thing about him, however, was the blank expression with which he regarded them. No recognition lit his eyes; he seemed to be staring through them. His facial muscles were slack. His mouth hung open about an inch, as if he had started to speak a long time ago but had not yet managed to remember the first word of what he had wanted to say. At Cielo Vista Care Home, Bobby had seen only a few patients with faces as empty as this, but they had been among the most severely retarded, several steps down the ladder from Thomas.

"How long has he been here?" Bobby asked, moving toward Frank.

Julie seized his arm and held him back. "Don't!"

"He arrived shortly before seven o'clock," Fogarty said.

So Frank had traveled for nearly another hour and a half after he had returned Bobby to the office.

Fogarty said, "He's been here over three hours, and I don't know what the blazing hell I'm supposed to do with him. Now and then he comes around a little bit, looks at you when you talk to him, even responds more or less to what you say. Then sometimes he's positively garrulous, runs on and on, won't answer your questions but sure wants to talk *at* a person, you couldn't shut him up with a two-by-four. He's told me a lot about you, for instance, more than I care to know." He frowned and shook his head. "You two may be crazy enough to get involved in this nightmare, but I'm not, and I resent being *dragged* into it."

At first glance, the impression that Dr. Lawrence Fogarty made was that of a kindly grandfather who, in his day, had been the type of devoted and selfless physician who became revered by his community, known and beloved by one and all. He was still wearing the slippers, gray slacks, white shirt, and blue cardigan in which Bobby had first seen him earlier, and the image was completed by a pair of half-lens reading glasses, over which he regarded them. With his thick white hair, blue eyes, and gentle rounded features, he would have made a perfect Santa Claus if he had been fifty or sixty pounds heavier.

But on a second and closer look, his blue eyes were steely, not warm. His rounded features were *too* soft, and revealed not gentility so much as lack of character, as though they had been acquired through a lifetime of self-indulgence. His wide mouth would have given kindly old Doc Fogarty a winning smile, but its generous dimension served equally well to lend the look of a predator to the real Doc Fogarty.

"So Frank's told you about us," Bobby said. "But we don't know anything about you, and I think we need to."

Fogarty scowled. "Better that you don't know about me. Better by far for *me*. Just get him out of here, take him away."

"You want us to take Frank off your hands," Julie said coldly, "then you've got to tell us who you are, how you fit into this, what you know about it."

Meeting Julie's gaze, then Bobby's, the old man said, "He's not been here in five years. Today, when he came with you, Dakota, I was shocked, I'd thought I was finished with him forever. And when he came back tonight . . ."

Frank's eyes had not focused, but he had cocked his head to one side. His mouth was still ajar like the door to a room from which the resident had fled in haste.

Regarding Frank sourly, Fogarty said, "I've never seen him like this, either. I wouldn't want him on my hands if he was his old self, let alone when he's half a vegetable. All right, all right, we'll talk. But once we've talked, he's *your* responsibility."

Fogarty went behind the mahogany desk and sat in a chair that was upholstered in the same dark maroon leather as was the wingback in which Frank slumped.

Although their host had not offered them a seat, Bobby went to the sofa. Julie followed and slipped past him at the last moment, sitting on the end of the sofa closest to Frank. She favored Bobby with a look that essentially said, *You're too impulsive, if he groans or sighs or blows a spit bubble, you'll put a hand on him to comfort him, and then you'll be gone in a wink to Hoboken or Hell, so keep your distance.*

Removing his tortoiseshell reading glasses and putting them on the blotter, Fogarty squeezed his eyes shut and pinched the bridge of his nose between thumb and forefinger, as if to banish a headache with an effort of will or collect his thoughts or both. Then he opened his eyes, blinked at them across the desk, and said, "I'm the doctor who delivered Roselle Pollard when she was born forty-six years ago, February of 1946. I'm also the doctor who delivered each of her kids—Frank, the twins, and James . . . or Candy as he now prefers. Over the years I treated Frank for the usual childhood-adolescent illnesses, and I guess that's why he thinks he can come to me now, when he's in trouble. Well, he's wrong. I'm no goddamned TV doctor who wants to be everybody's confidant and Dutch uncle. I treated them, they paid me, and that should be the end of it. Fact is . . . I only ever really treated Frank and his mother, because the girls and James never got sick, unless we're talking mental illness, in which case they were sick at birth and never got well."

Because Frank's head was tilted, a thin, silver stream of drool slipped out of the right corner of his mouth and along his chin.

Julie said, "You evidently know about the powers her children have—"

"I didn't know, really, until seven years ago, the day that Frank killed her. I was retired by then, but he came to me, told me more than I ever wanted to know, dragged me into this nightmare, wanted me to help. How could I help? How can anyone help? It's none of my business anyway."

"But why do they have these powers?" Julie said. "Do you have any clue, any theories?"

Fogarty laughed. It was a hard, sour laugh that would have dispelled any illusions Bobby had about him if those illusions had not already been dispelled two minutes after he'd met the man. "Oh, yes, I have theories, lots of information to support the theories too, some of it stuff you'll wish you never heard. I'm not going to get myself involved in the mess, not me, but I can't help now and then thinking about it. Who could? It's a sick and twisted and *fascinating* mess. My theory is that it starts with Roselle's father. Supposedly her father was some itinerant who knocked up her mother, but I always knew that was a lie. Her father was Yarnell Pollard, her mother's brother. Roselle was a child of rape and incest."

A look of distress must have crossed Bobby's face or Julie's, for Fogarty let out another bark of cold laughter, clearly amused by their sympathetic response.

The old physician said, "Oh, that's nothing. That's the least of it."

THE TAILLESS MANX —Zitha by name—took up sentry duty in the concealment of an azalea shrub near the front door.

The old Spanish house had exterior window ledges, and the second cat—as black as midnight, and named Darkle—sprang to another one in search of the room to which the old man had taken the younger man and woman. Darkle put his nose to the glass. A set of interior shutters inhibited snooping, but the wide louvres were only half closed, and Darkle was able to see several cross-sections of the room by raising or lowering his head.

Hearing Frank's name spoken, the cat stiffened, because Violet had stiffened in her bed high on Pacific Hill.

The old man was there, among the books, and the couple as well. When everyone sat down, Darkle had to lower his head to peer between another pair of tilted louvres. Then he saw that Frank was not only one of the subjects of their conversation but actually present in a high-backed chair that stood at just enough of an angle to the window to reveal part of his face, and one hand lying limply on the wide, maroon-leather arm.

LEANING OVER HIS his desk and smiling humorlessly as he talked, Doc Fogarty resembled a troll that had crawled out from its lair beneath a bridge, not content to wait for unsuspecting children to pass by, prepared to forage for his grisly dinner.

Bobby reminded himself not to let his imagination run away with him. He needed to keep an unbiased perspective on Fogarty, in order to determine the truthfulness and value of what the old man had to tell them. Their lives might depend on it.

"The house was built in the thirties by Deeter and Elizabeth Pollard. He'd made some money in Hollywood, producing a bunch of cheap Westerns, other junk. Not a fortune, but enough that he was fairly sure he could give up films and Los Angeles, which he hated, move up here, get into some small businesses, and do all right for the rest of his life. They had two children. Yarnell was fifteen when they came here in 1938, and Cynthia was only six years old. In forty-five, when Deeter and Elizabeth were killed in a car crash—hit head-on by a drunk driving a truck full of cabbages down from the Santa Ynez valley, if you can believe it— Yarnell became the man of the house at the age of twenty-two, and the legal guardian of his thirteen-year-old sister."

Julie said, "And . . . forced himself on her, you said?"

Fogarty nodded. "I'm sure of it. Because over the next year, Cynthia became withdrawn, weepy. People attributed it to the death of her folks, but it was Yarnell using her, I think. Not just because he wanted the sex— though she was a pretty little thing, and you could hardly fault his taste—

but because being man of the house appealed to him, he liked authority. And he was the type who wasn't happy until his authority was absolute, his dominance complete."

Bobby was horrified by the words "you could hardly fault his taste" and what they implied about the depth of the moral abyss in which Fogarty lived.

Oblivious of the disgust with which his visitors were regarding him, Fogarty continued: "Yarnell was strong-willed, reckless, caused his folks a lot of heartache before they died, all kinds of heartache but mostly related to drugs. He was an acidhead before they had a name for it, before they even had LSD. Peyote, mescaline . . . all of the natural hallucinogens you can distill from certain cactuses, mushrooms and other fungi. Wasn't the drug culture back then that we have now, but crap was around. He got into hallucinogens through a relationship he had with a character actor who appeared in a lot of his father's movies, got started when he was fifteen, and I tell you all this because my theory is it's the key to everything you want to know."

"The fact that Yarnell was an acidhead," Julie said. "That's the key?"

"That and the fact he impregnated his own sister. The chemicals probably did genetic damage, and a lot of it, by the time he was twenty-two. They usually do. In his case some very *strange* genetic damage. Then, when you add in the fact that the gene pool was very limited, being as Cynthia was his sister, you might expect there's a high chance the offspring will be a freak of some kind."

Frank made a low sound, then sighed.

They all looked at him, but he was still detached. Though his eyes blinked rapidly for a moment, they did not come back into focus. Saliva still drooled from the right corner of his mouth; a string of it hung from his chin.

Though Bobby felt that he should get some Kleenex and blot Frank's face, he restrained himself, largely because he was afraid of Julie's reaction.

"So about a year after their parents died, Yarnell and Cynthia came to me, and she was pregnant," Fogarty said. "They had this story about some itinerant farmworker raping her, but it didn't ring true, and I pretty much figured out the real story just watching how they were with each other. She'd tried to conceal the pregnancy by wearing loose clothes and by staying in the house entirely during her last few months, and I never could understand that behavior; it was as if they thought the problem would just go away one day. By the time they came to me, abortion was out of the question. Hell, she was in the early stages of labor."

The longer he listened to Fogarty, the more it seemed to Bobby that the air in the library was foul and growing fouler, thick with a humidity as sour as sweat.

"Claiming that he wanted to protect Cynthia as much as possible from public scorn, Yarnell offered me a pretty fat fee if I'd keep her out of the hospital and deliver the baby right in my office, which was a little risky, in case there were complications. But I needed the money, and if anything went really wrong, there were ways to cover it. I had this nurse at the time who could assist me—Norma, she was pretty flexible about things."

Just great, Bobby thought. The sociopathic physician had found himself a sociopathic nurse, a couple who would be right in the social swim of things among the medical staff at Dachau or Auschwitz.

Julie put a hand on Bobby's knee and squeezed, as if the contact reassured her that she was not listening to a mad doctor in a dream.

"You should have seen what came out of that girl's oven," Fogarty said. "A freak it was, just as you'd expect."

"Wait a minute," Julie said. "I thought you said the baby was Roselle. Frank's mother."

"It was," Fogarty said. "And she was such a spectacular little freak that she'd have been worth a fortune to any carnival sideshow willing to risk the anger of the law to exhibit her." He paused, enjoying their anticipation. "She was an hermaphrodite."

For a moment the word meant nothing to Bobby, and then he said, "You don't mean—she had both sexes, male and female?"

"Oh, but that's exactly what I mean." Fogarty bounced up from his chair and began to pace, suddenly energized by the conversation. "Hermaphroditism is an extremely rare birth defect in humans, it's an amazing thing to have the opportunity to deliver one. You have *traverse* hermaphroditism, where you have the external organs of one sex and the internal of the other, lateral hermaphroditism . . . several other types. But the thing is . . . Roselle was the rarest of all, she possessed the complete internal and external organs of both sexes." He plucked a thick medical reference book from one of the shelves and handed it to Julie. "Check page one forty-six for photos of the kind of thing I'm talking about."

Julie handed the volume to Bobby so fast it seemed as if she thought it was a snake.

Bobby, in turn, put it beside himself on the sofa, unopened. The last thing he needed, with his imagination, was the assistance of clinical photographs.

His hands and feet had gone cold, as though the blood had rushed from his extremities to his head, to nourish his brain, which was spinning furiously. He wished that he could *stop* thinking about what Fogarty was telling them. It was gross. But the worst thing about it was, judging by the physician's strange smile, Bobby sensed that what they had heard thus far was all just the bread on this horror sandwich; the meat was yet to come.

Pacing again, Fogarty said, "Her vagina was about where you'd expect, the male equipment somewhat displaced. Urination was through the male part, but the female appeared reproductively complete."

"I think we get the picture," Julie said. "We don't need all the technical details."

Fogarty came to them, stood looking down at them, and his eyes were as bright and lively as if he were recounting a charming medical anecdote that had bewitched legions of delighted companions at dinner parties over the years. "No, no, you must understand what she was, if you're going to understand all that happened next."

THOUGH HER OWN mind was split into many parts—sharing the bodies of Verbina, all the cats, and the owl on Fogarty's porch roof—Violet was most acutely aware of what she was receiving through the senses of Darkle, as he perched upon the windowsill outside the study. With the cat's sharp hearing, Violet missed not a word of the conversation, in spite of the intervening pane of glass. She was enthralled.

She seldom paused to think about her mother, although Roselle was still in this old house in so many ways. She seldom thought about *any* human being, for that matter, except herself and her twin sister—less often Candy and Frank—because she had so little in common with other people. Her life was with the wild things. In them emotions were so much more primitive and intense, pleasure so much more easily found and enjoyed without guilt. She hadn't really known her mother or been close to her; and Violet would not have been close, even if her mother had been willing to share affection with anyone but Candy.

But now Violet was riveted by what Fogarty was telling them, not because it was news to her (which it was), but because anything that had affected Roselle's life this completely also had profound effects on Violet's life. And of the countless attitudes and perceptions that Violet had absorbed from the myriad wild creatures whose minds and bodies she shared, a fascination with self was perhaps paramount. She had an animal's narcissistic preoccupation with grooming, with her own wants and needs. From her point of view, nothing in the world was of interest unless it served her, satisfied her, or affected the possibility of her future happiness.

Dimly she realized that she should find her brother and tell him that Frank was less than two miles away from them. Not long ago she had heard the wind-music of Candy's return.

FOGARTY TURNED AWAY from Bobby and Julie and circled behind his desk again, where he walked along the bookshelves, snapping his finger against the spines of the volumes to punctuate his story.

As the physician spoke of this family that had seemingly *sought* genetic catastrophe, Julie could not help but think of how Thomas's affliction had been visited upon him even though his parents had lived healthy and normal lives. Fate played as cruelly with the innocent as with the guilty.

"When he saw the baby's abnormality, I think Yarnell would have killed it and thrown it out with the garbage—or at least put it in the hands of an institution. But Cynthia wouldn't part with it, she said it was her child, deformed or not, and she named it Roselle, after her dead grandmother. I suspect she wanted to keep it largely because she saw how it repulsed him, and she wanted to have Roselle around as a permanent reminder to him of the consequences of what he had forced her to do."

"Couldn't surgery have been used to make her one sex or another?" Bobby asked.

"Easier today. Iffier then."

Fogarty had stopped at the desk, where he had removed a bottle of Wild Turkey and a glass from one of the side drawers. He poured a few ounces of bourbon for himself and recapped the bottle without offering them a drink. That was fine with Julie. Though Fogarty's house was spotless, she wouldn't have felt clean after drinking or eating anything in it.

After taking a swallow of the warm bourbon, neat, Fogarty said, "Besides, wouldn't want to remove one set of organs only to discover that, as the child grew older, it proved to look and act more like the sex you denied it than like the one it was permitted. Secondary sex characteristics are visible in infants, of course, but not as easily read—certainly not in 1946. Anyway, Cynthia wouldn't have authorized surgery. Remember what I said—she probably welcomed the child's deformity as a weapon against her brother."

"You could have stepped between them and the baby," Bobby said. "You could've brought the child's plight to the attention of public health authorities."

"Why on earth would I want to do that? For the psychological well-being of the child, you mean? Don't be naive." He drank some more bourbon. "I was paid well to make the delivery and keep my mouth shut about it, and that was fine by me. They took her home, stuck to their story about the itinerant rapist."

Julie said, "The baby . . . Roselle . . . she had no serious medical problems?"

"None," Fogarty said. "Other than this abnormality, she was as healthy as a horse. Her mental skills and her body developed right on schedule, like any child, and before long it became obvious that, to all outward appearances, she was going to look like a woman. As she grew even older, you could see she'd never be an attractive filly, mind you, more on the sturdy side than a fashion model, thick legs and all that, but quite feminine enough."

Frank remained vacant-eyed and detached, but a muscle in his left cheek twitched twice.

The bourbon apparently relaxed the physician, for he sat behind his desk again, leaned forward, and clasped his hands around the glass. "In 1959, when Roselle was thirteen, Cynthia died. Killed herself, actually. Blew her brains out. The following year, about seven months after his sister's suicide, Yarnell came to the office with his daughter—that is, with Roselle. He never called her his daughter, maintaining the fiction that she was only his bastard niece. Anyway, Roselle was pregnant at fourteen, same age at which Cynthia had given birth to her."

"Good God!" Bobby said.

The shocks kept piling one atop another with such speed that Julie was almost ready to grab the whiskey bottle off the desk, drink straight from it, and never mind that it was Fogarty's booze.

Enjoying their reactions, Fogarty sipped the bourbon and gave them time to absorb the shock.

Julie said, "Yarnell raped the daughter he had fathered by his own sister?"

Fogarty waited a little longer, savoring the moment. Then: "No, no. He found the girl repellent, and I'm confident he wouldn't have touched her. I'm sure what Roselle told me was the truth." He sipped more bourbon. "Cynthia had developed quite a religious streak between the time she gave birth to Roselle and the day she killed herself, and she had passed on that passion for God to Roselle. The girl knew the Bible backward and forward. So Roselle came in here, pregnant. Said she'd decided she should have a child. Said God had made her special—that's what she called hermaphroditism, *special!*—because she was to be a pure vessel by which blessed children could be brought into the world. Therefore she had collected the semen from her male half and mechanically inserted it into her female half."

Bobby shot up from the sofa as if one of its springs had broken under him, and he grabbed the bottle of Wild Turkey from the desk. "You have another glass?"

Fogarty pointed to a bar cabinet in the corner, which Julie had not noticed before. Bobby opened the double doors, revealing not only more glasses but additional fifths of Wild Turkey. Evidently the physician kept a bottle in his desk drawer only so he would not have to walk across the room for it. Bobby poured two glasses full, with no ice, and brought one back to Julie.

To Fogarty, she said, "Of course, I never thought Roselle was barren. She did bear children, we know that. But I assumed you meant the male part of her was sterile."

"Fertile as a male *and* as a female. She couldn't actually join herself to herself, so to speak. So she resorted to artificial insemination, as I said."

Late that afternoon, in the office in Newport, when Bobby had tried to explain how traveling with Frank was like a bobsled ride off the edge of the world, Julie had not really understood why he was so unnerved by the experience. Now she thought she had an inkling of what he had meant, for the chaos of the Pollard family's relationships and sexual identities made her skin crawl and filled her with a dark suspicion that nature was even stranger and more hospitable to anarchy than she had feared.

"Yarnell wanted me to abort the fetus, and abortion was a fairly lucrative sideline in those days, though illegal and hush-hush. But the girl had hidden her pregnancy from him for seven months, as he and Cynthia had tried to hide a pregnancy fourteen years earlier. It was much too late for an abortion then. The girl would've died, hemorrhaging. Besides, I would no more have aborted that fetus than I'd have shot myself in the foot. Imagine the degree of inbreeding involved here: the hermaphroditic child of brother-sister incest impregnates herself! Her child's mother is also its father. Its grandmother is also its great-aunt, and its grandfather is its great-uncle! One tight genetic line—and genes damaged by Yarnell's use of hallucinogenics, remember. Virtually a guarantee of a freak of one kind or another, and I wouldn't have missed it for the world."

Julie took a long swallow of the bourbon. It tasted sour and stung her throat. She didn't care. She needed it.

"I'd become a doctor because the pay was good," Fogarty said. "Later, when I gravitated toward illegal abortions, the pay was better, and it became my main business. Not much danger, either, because I knew what I was doing, and I could buy off an authority now and then if I had to. When you're getting those fat fees, you don't have to schedule many office visits, you can have a lot of free time, money and leisure, the best of both worlds. But having settled for a career like that, what I *never* figured was that I'd encounter anything as medically interesting, as fascinating, as *entertaining* as this Pollard mess."

The only consideration that caused Julie to refrain from going across the room and kicking the crap out of the old man was not his age but the fact that he would leave the story unfinished and some vital piece of information unrevealed.

"But the birth of Roselle's first child wasn't the event I'd thought it would be," Fogarty said. "In spite of the odds, the baby she produced was healthy and, from all indications, perfectly normal. That was 1960, and the baby was Frank."

In the wingback chair, Frank whimpered softly but remained in his semicomatose condition.

STILL LISTENING TO Doc Fogarty through Darkle, Violet sat up and swung her bare legs over the edge of the bed, dispossessing some of the cats from their resting places, and eliciting a murmur of protest from Verbina, who was seldom content to share just a mental link with her sister and needed the reassurance of physical contact. With cats swarming at her feet, seeing through their eyes as well as her own and therefore not blinded by the darkness, Violet started toward the open door to the light-less upstairs hall.

Then she remembered that she was nude, and she turned back for panties and T-shirt.

She wasn't afraid of Candy's disapproval—or of Candy himself. In fact, she would welcome his violent attentions, for that would be the ultimate game of hunter and prey, hawk and mouse, brother and sister. Candy was the only wild creature into whose mind she couldn't intrude; though wild, he was also human and beyond the reach of her powers. If he tore out her throat, however, then her blood would get into him, and she would become a part of him in the only manner she ever could. Likewise, that was the only way he could get into her: by biting his way in, by chewing into her, the only way.

On any other night, she would have called to him and let him see her nude, with the hope that her shamelessness would at last provoke him to violence. But she could not pursue her fondest desire right now, not when Frank was nearby and still unpunished for what he had done to their poor puss, Samantha.

When she had dressed, she returned to the hall, moved along it in the gloom—still in complete touch with Darkle and Zitha and the wild world—and stopped before the door to their mother's room, into which Candy had moved upon her death. A thin line of light showed along the sill.

"Candy," she said. "Candy, are you there?"

LIKE A MEMORY from wars past or a presentiment of an ultimate war to come, a searing flash of lightning and a sky-shattering crash of thunder shook the night. The windows of the study vibrated. It was the first thun-der Bobby had heard since the faint and distant peal when they had come out of the motel, nearly an hour and a half ago. In spite of the fireworks in the sky, rain was not yet falling. But though the tempest was slow-moving, it was almost upon them. The pyrotechnics of a storm was an ideal backdrop to Fogarty's tale.

"I was disappointed in Frank," Fogarty said, taking a second bottle of bourbon from his capacious desk drawer and refilling his glass. "No fun at all. So normal. But two years later, she was pregnant again! This time the delivery was every bit as entertaining as I'd expected Frank's to be. A baby boy again, and she called him James. Her second virgin birth, she said, and she didn't mind at all that he was as much of a mess as she was. She said that was just proof that he, too, was favored by God and brought into the world without a need to wallow in the depravity of sex. I knew then that she was as mad as a hatter."

Bobby knew he had to remain sober, and he was aware of the danger of too much bourbon after a night of too little sleep. But he had a hunch that he was burning it off as fast as he drank it, at least for now. He took another sip before he said, "You're not telling us that beefy hulk is hermaphroditic too?"

"Oh, no," Fogarty said. "Worse than that."

CANDY OPENED THE door. "What do you want?"

"He's here, in town, right now," she said.

His eyes widened. "You mean Frank?"

"Yes."

"WORSE," BOBBY SAID numbly.

He got up from the sofa long enough to put his glass on the desk. It was still three-quarters full, but he suddenly decided that even bourbon would not be an effective tranquilizer in this case.

Julie seemed to reach the same conclusion, and put her glass aside too.

"James—or Candy, if you wish—was born with four testes instead of two, but with no male organ. Now, at birth, male infants all carry their testes safely in their abdominal cavity, and the testes descend later, during infant maturation. But Candy's never descended and never could, because there was no scrotum for them to descend into. And for another thing, there's a strange excrescence of bone that would prevent their descent. So they've remained within his abdominal cavity. But I would guess they've functioned well, busily producing quite large amounts of testosterone, which is related to development of musculature and partly explains his formidable size."

"So he's incapable of having sex," Bobby said.

"With his testicles undescended and no organ for copulation, I'd say he's got a shot at being the most chaste man who ever lived."

Bobby had come to loathe the old man's laugh. "But with four gonads, he's producing a flood of testosterone, and that does more than help build muscles—doesn't it?"

Fogarty nodded. "To put it in the language of a medical journal: excess testosterone, over an extended period of time, alters normal brain function, sometimes radically, and is a causative factor of socially unacceptable levels of aggression. To put it in layman's language: this guy is seriously stoked with sexual tension he can't possibly release, he's rechanneled that energy into other outlets, mainly acts of incredible violence, and he's as dangerous as any monster any moviemaker ever dreamed up."

ALTHOUGH SHE HAD released the owl as the storm drew near, Violet still inhabited Darkle and Zitha, taking their fear away from them when the lightning flared and the thunder boomed. Even as she stood before Candy, at the door to his room, she was listening to Fogarty tell the Dakotas about her brother's deformity. She knew about it already, of course, for within the family their mother had referred to it as God's sign that Candy was the most special of all of them. Likewise, and in some way Violet had been aware that this deformity was related to the great wildness in Candy, the thing that made him so powerfully attractive.

Now she stood before him, wanting to touch his huge arms, feel the sculpted muscles, but she restrained herself. "He's at Fogarty's house."

That surprised him. "Mother said Fogarty was an instrument of God. He brought us into the world, four virgin births. Why would he harbor Frank? Frank's on the dark side now."

"That's where he is," Violet said. "And a couple. His name's Bobby. Hers is Julie."

"Dakota," he whispered.

"At Fogarty's. Make him pay for Samantha, Candy. Bring him back here after you've killed him, and let us feed him to the cats. He hated the cats, and he'll hate being part of them forever."

JULIE'S TEMPER, NOT always easily controlled, was dangerously near the flashpoint. As lightning shocked the night outside and thunder again protested, she counseled herself about the necessity for diplomacy.

Nevertheless, she said, "You've known all these years that Candy is a vicious killer, and you've done nothing to alert anyone to the danger?"

"Why should I?" Fogarty asked.

"Haven't you ever heard of social responsibility?"

"It's a nice phrase, but meaningless."

"People have been brutally murdered because you let that man—"

"People will always and forever be brutally murdered. History is full of brutal murder. Hitler murdered millions. Stalin, many millions more. Mao Tse-tung, more millions than anyone. They're all considered monsters now, but they had their admirers in their time, didn't they? And there're people even now who'll tell you Hitler and Stalin only did what they had to do, that Mao was just keeping the public order, disposing of ruffians. So many people *admire* those murderers who are bold about it and who cloak their bloodlust in noble causes like brotherhood and political reform and justice—and social responsibility. We're all meat, just meat, and in our hearts we know it, so we secretly applaud the men bold enough to treat us as what we are. Meat."

By now she knew that he was a sociopath, with no conscience, no capacity for love, and no ability to empathize with other people. Not all of them were street hoodlums—or even high-class, high-tech thieves like Tom Rasmussen, who had tried to kill Bobby last week. Some got to be doctors—or lawyers, TV ministers, politicians. None of them could be reasoned with, for they had no normal human feelings.

He said, "Why should I tell anyone about Candy Pollard? I'm safe from him because his mother always called me God's instrument, told her wretched spawn I was to be respected. It's none of my business. He's covered his mother's murder to avoid having the police tramping through the house, told people she moved to a nice oceanside condo near San Diego. I don't think anybody believes that crazy bitch would suddenly lighten up and become a beach bunny, but nobody questions it because nobody wants to get involved. Everybody feels it's *none of their business.* Same with me. Whatever outrages Candy adds to the world's pain are negligible. At least, given his peculiar psychology and physiology, his outrages will be more imaginative than most.

"Besides, when Candy was about eight, Roselle came to thank me for bringing her four into the world, and for keeping my own counsel, so that Satan was unaware of their blessed presence on earth. That's exactly how she put it! And as a token of her appreciation, she gave me a suitcase full of money, enough to make early retirement possible. I couldn't figure where she'd gotten it. The money that Deeter and Elizabeth piled up in the thirties had long ago dwindled away. So she told me a little bit about Candy's ability, not much, but enough to explain that she'd never want for cash. That was the first time I realized there was a genetic boon tied to the genetic disaster."

Fogarty raised his glass of bourbon in a toast that they did not return. "To God's mysterious ways."

LIKE THE ARCHANGEL come to declare the end of the world in the Book of the Apocalypse, Candy arrived just as the heavens sundered and the rain began to fall in earnest, although this was not black rain as would be the deluge of Armageddon, nor was it a storm of fire. Not yet. Not yet.

He materialized in the darkness between two widely spaced street-lamps, almost a block from the doctor's house, to be sure that the soft trumpets that unfailingly announced his arrival would not be audible to anyone in Fogarty's library. As he walked toward the house through the hammering rain, he believed that his power, provided by God, had now grown so enormous that nothing could prevent him from taking or achieving anything he desired.

"IN 'SIXTY-SIX, THE twins were born, and physically they were as normal as Frank," Fogarty said as rain suddenly splattered noisily against the window. "No fun in that. I couldn't believe it, really. Three out of four of the kids, perfectly healthy. I'd been expecting all sorts of cute twists— harelips at the very least, misshapen skulls, cleft faces, withered limbs, or extra heads!"

Bobby took Julie's hand. He needed the contact.

He wanted to get out of there. He felt burnt out. Hadn't they heard enough?

But that was the problem: he didn't know what was left to hear, or how much of it might be crucial to finding a way of dealing with the Pollards.

"Of course, when Roselle brought me that suitcase full of money, I began to learn that the children *were* all freaks, mentally if not physically. And seven years ago, when Frank killed her, he came to me, as if I owed him something—understanding, shelter. He told me more about them than I wanted to know, too much. For the next two years, he'd periodically return here, just appear like a ghost that wanted to haunt *me* instead of a place. But he finally understood there was nothing for him here, and for five years he stayed out of my life. Until today, tonight."

In his wingback chair, Frank moved. He shifted his body and tipped his head from the right to the left. Otherwise, he was no more alert than he had been since they had entered the room. The old man had said that Frank had come around a few times and had been talkative, but it couldn't be proved by his behavior during the past hour or so.

Julie, who was the closest to Frank, frowned and leaned toward him, peering at the right side of his head.

"Oh, my God."

She spoke those three words in a bleak tone of voice that was as effective a refrigerant as anything used in an air conditioner.

With a chill skittering up his spine, Bobby slid along the sofa, crowding her against the other end, and looked past her at the side of Frank's head. Wished he had not. Tried to look away. Couldn't.

When Frank's head had been tilted to his right, almost lying against his shoulder, they had not been able to see that temple. After leaving Bobby at the office, still out of control, traveling against his will, Frank evidently had returned to one of those craters where the engineered insects shat out their diamonds. His flesh was lumpy all the way along his temple to his jaw, and in some places the rough gemstones that were the cause of the lumpiness poked through, gleaming, intimately melded with his tissue. For whatever reason, he had scooped up a handful to bring with him, but when reconstituting himself he had made a mistake.

Bobby wondered what treasures might be buried in the soft gray matter within Frank's skull.

"I saw that too," Fogarty said. "And look at the palm of his right hand."

Although Julie protested, Bobby pinched the sleeve of Frank's jacket and pulled until he twisted the man's arm off the chair and revealed his palm. He had found the partial roach that had once been welded into his own shoe. At least it appeared to be the same one. It was sprouting from the meaty part of Frank's hand, carapace gleaming, dead eyes staring up toward Frank's index finger.

CANDY CIRCLED THE house in the rain, passing a black cat on a windowsill. It turned its head to glance at him, then put its face to the windowpane again.

At the rear of the house, he stepped quietly onto the porch and tried the back door. It was locked.

Vague blue light pulsed from his hand as he gripped the knob. The lock slipped, the door opened, and he stepped inside.

JULIE HAD HEARD and seen enough, too much.

Eager to get away from Frank, she rose from the sofa and walked to the desk, where she considered her unfinished bourbon. But that was no answer. She was dreadfully tired, struggling to repress her grief for Thomas, striving even harder to make some sense out of the grotesque family history that Fogarty had revealed to them. She did not need the complication of any more bourbon, appealing as it might look there in the glass.

She said to the old man, "So what hope do we have of dealing with Candy?"

"None."

"There must be a way."

"No."

"There must be."

"Why?"

"Because he can't be allowed to win."

Fogarty smiled. "Why not?"

"Because he's the bad guy, dammit! And we're the good guys. Not perfect, maybe, not without flaws, but we're the good guys, all right. And that's why we have to win, because if we don't, then the whole game is meaningless."

Fogarty leaned back in his chair. "My point exactly. It *is* all meaningless. We're not good, and we're not bad, we're just meat. We don't have souls, there's no hope of transcendence for a slab of meat, you wouldn't expect a hamburger to go to Heaven after someone ate it."

She had never hated anyone as much as she hated Fogarty at that moment, partly because he was so smug and hateful, but partly because she recognized, in his arguments, something perilously close to the things she had said to Bobby in the motel, after she had learned about Thomas's death. She had said there was no point in having dreams, that they never came true, that death was always there watching even if you *were* lucky enough to grasp your personal brass ring. And loathing life, just because it led sooner or later to death . . . well, that was the same as saying people were nothing but meat.

"We have just pleasure and pain," the old physician said, "so it doesn't matter who's right or who's wrong, who wins or loses."

"What's his weakness?" she demanded angrily.

"None I can see." Fogarty seemed pleased by the hopelessness of their position. If he had been practicing medicine in the early 1940s, he had to be nearing eighty, though he looked younger. He was acutely aware of how little time remained to him, and was no doubt resentful of anyone younger; and given his cold perspective on life, their deaths at Candy Pollard's hands would entertain him. "No weaknesses at all."

Bobby disagreed, or tried to. "Some might say that his weakness is his mind, his screwed-up psychology."

Fogarty shook his head. "And I'd argue that he's made a strength of his screwed-up psychology. He's used this business about being the instrument of God's vengeance to armor himself very effectively from depression and self-doubt and anything else that might trip him up."

In the wingback chair, Frank abruptly sat up straighter, shook himself as if to cast off his mental confusion the way a dog might shake water from its sodden coat after coming in from the rain. He said, "Where . . . Why do I . . . Is it . . . is it . . . is it . . . ?"

"Is it what, Frank?" Bobby asked.

"Is it happening?" Frank said. His eyes seemed slowly to be clearing. "Is it finally happening?"

"Is what finally happening, Frank?"

His voice was hoarse. "Death. Is it finally happening? Is it?"

CANDY HAD CREPT quietly through the house, into the hallway that led to the library. As he moved toward the open door on the left, he heard voices. When he recognized one of them as Frank's, he could barely contain himself.

According to Violet, Frank was crippled. His control of his telekinetic talent had always been erratic, which is why Candy had enjoyed some hope of one day catching him and finishing him before he could travel to a place of safety. Perhaps the moment of triumph had arrived.

When he reached the door, he found himself looking at the woman's back. He could not see her face, but he was sure that it would be the same one that had been suffused in a beatific glow in Thomas's mind.

Beyond her he glimpsed Frank, and saw Frank's eyes widen at the sight of him. If the mother-killer had been too mentally confused to teleport out of Candy's reach, as Violet had claimed, he was now casting off that confusion. He looked as if he might pop out of there long before Candy could lay a hand on him.

Candy had intended to throw the library into a turmoil by sending a wave of energy through the doorway ahead of him, setting the books on fire and shattering the lamps, with the purpose of panicking and distracting the Dakotas and Doc Fogarty, giving him a chance to go straight for Frank. But now he was forced to change his plans by the sight of his brother trembling on the edge of dematerialization.

He entered the room in a rush and seized the woman from behind, curling his right arm around her neck and jerking her head back, so she—and the two men—would understand at once that he could snap her neck in an instant, whenever he chose. Even so, she slashed backward with one foot, scraping the heel of her shoe down his shin, stomping on his foot, all of which hurt like hell; it was some martial-art move, and he could tell by the way she tried to counterbalance his grip and stance that she had a lot of training in such things. So he jerked her head back again, even harder, and flexed his biceps, which pinched her windpipe, hurting her enough to make her realize that resistance was suicidal.

Fogarty watched from his chair, alarmed but not sufficiently to rise to his feet, and the husband came off the sofa with a gun in his hand, Mr. Quick-Draw Artist, but Candy was not concerned about either of them. His attention was on Frank, who had risen from his chair and appeared about to blink out of there, off to Punaluu and Kyoto and a score of other places.

"Don't do it, Frank!" he said sharply. "Don't run away. It's time we settled, time you paid for what you did to our mother. You come to the house, accept God's punishment, and end it now, tonight. I'm going there with this bitch. She tried to help you, I guess, so maybe you won't want to see her suffer."

The husband was going to do something crazy; seeing Julie in Candy's grip had clearly unhinged him. He was searching for a shot, a way to get Candy without getting her, and he might even risk firing at Candy's head, though Candy was half crouching behind the woman. Time to get out of there.

"Come to the house," he told Frank. "You come into the kitchen, let me end it for you, and I'll let her go. I swear on our mother's name, I'll let her go. But if you don't come in fifteen minutes, I'll put this bitch on the table, and I'll have my dinner, Frank. You want me to feed on her after she tried to help you, Frank?"

Candy thought he heard a gunshot just as he got out of there. In any event, it had been too late. He rematerialized in the kitchen of the house on Pacific Hill Road, with Julie Dakota still locked in the crook of his arm.

56

NO LONGER CONCERNED ABOUT THE DANGER OF TOUCHING Frank, Bobby grabbed handsful of his jacket and shoved him backward against the wide-louvred shutters on the library window. "You heard him, Frank. Don't run. Don't run this time, or I'll hang on to you and never let go, no matter where you take me, I swear to God, you'll wish you'd put your neck on Candy's platter instead of mine." He slammed Frank against the shutters to make his point, and behind him he heard Lawrence Fogarty's soft, knowing laughter.

Registering the terror and confusion in his client's eyes, Bobby realized that his threats would not achieve the effect he desired. In fact, threats would almost certainly frighten Frank into flight, even if he wanted to help Julie. Worse, by stooping to violence as a first resort, he was treating Frank not as a person but as meat, confirming the depraved code by which the corrupt old physician had led his entire life, and that was almost as intolerable as losing Julie.

He let go of Frank.

"I'm sorry. Listen, I'm sorry, I just got a little crazy."

He studied the man's eyes, searching for some indication that sufficient intelligence remained in the damaged brain for the two of them to reach an understanding. He saw fear, stark and terrible, and he saw a loneliness that made him want to cry. He saw a lost look, too, not unlike what he had sometimes seen in Thomas's eyes when they had taken him on an excursion from Cielo Vista, "out in the world," as he had said.

Aware that perhaps two minutes of Candy's fifteen-minute deadline had passed, trying to remain calm nonetheless, Bobby took Frank's right hand, turned it palm up, and forced himself to touch the dead roach that was now integrated with the man's soft white flesh. The insect felt crisp and bristly against his fingers, but he did not permit his disgust to show.

"Does this hurt, Frank? This bug mixed up with your own cells here, does it hurt you?"

Frank stared at him, finally shook his head. No.

Heartened by the establishment of even this much dialogue, Bobby gently put his fingertips to Frank's right temple, feeling the lumps of precious gems like unburst boils or cancerous tumors.

"Do you hurt here, Frank? Are you in pain?"

"No," Frank said, and Bobby's heart pounded with excitement at the escalation to a spoken response.

From a pocket of his jeans, Bobby removed a folded Kleenex and gently blotted away the spittle that still glistened on Frank's chin.

The man blinked, and his eyes seemed to focus better.

From behind Bobby, still in the leather chair at the desk, perhaps with a glass of bourbon in his hand, almost certainly with that infuriatingly smug smile plastered on his face, Fogarty said, "Twelve minutes left."

Bobby ignored the physician. Maintaining eye contact with his client, his fingertips still on Frank's temple, he said quietly, "It's been a hard life for you, hasn't it? You were the normal one, the most normal one, and when you were a kid you always wanted to fit in at school, didn't you, the way your sisters and brother never could. And it took you a long time to realize your dream wasn't going to happen, you weren't going to fit in, because no matter how normal you were compared to the rest of your family, you'd still come from that goddamned house, out of that *cesspool*, which made you forever an outsider to other people. They might not see the stain on your heart, might not know the dark memories in you, but *you* saw, and *you* remembered, and you felt yourself unworthy because of the horror that was your family. Yet you were also an outsider at home, much too sane to fit in there, too sensitive to the nightmare of it. So all your life, you've been alone."

"All my life," Frank said. "And always will be."

He wasn't going to travel now. Bobby would have bet on it.

"Frank, I can't help you. No one can. That's a hard truth, but I won't lie to you. I'm not going to con you or threaten you."

Frank said nothing, but maintained eye contact.

"Ten minutes," Fogarty said.

"The only thing I can do for you, Frank, is show you a way to give your life meaning at last, a way to end it with purpose and dignity, and maybe find peace in death. I have an idea, a way that you might be able to kill Candy and save Julie, and if you can do that, you'll have gone out a hero. Will you come with me, Frank, listen to me, and not let Julie die?"

Frank didn't say yes, but he didn't say no, either. Bobby decided to take heart from the lack of a negative response.

"We've got to get moving, Frank. But don't try teleporting to the house, because then you'll just lose control again, pop off to hell and back a hundred times. We'll go in my car. We can be there in five minutes."

Bobby took his client's hand. He made a point of taking the one with the roach embedded in it, hoping Frank would remember that he had a fear of bugs and perceive that his willingness to overrule the phobia was a testament to his sincerity.

They crossed the room to the door.

Rising from his chair, Fogarty said, "You're going to your death, you know."

Without glancing back at the physician, Bobby said, "Well, seems to me, you went to yours decades ago."

He and Frank walked out into the rain and were drenched by the time they got into the car.

Behind the wheel, Bobby glanced at his watch. Less than eight minutes to go.

He wondered why he accepted Candy's word that the fifteen-minute deadline would be observed, why he was so sure that the madman had not already torn out her throat. Then he remembered something she had said to him once: *Sweetcakes, as long as you're breathing, Tinkerbell will live*.

Gutters overflowed, and a sudden wind wound skeins of rain, like silver yarn, through his headlights.

As he drove the storm-swept streets and turned east on Pacific Hill Road, he explained how Frank, through his sacrifice of himself, could rid the world of Candy and undo his mother's evil the way he had wanted to undo it—but had failed—when he had taken the ax to her. It was a simple concept. He was able to go over it several times even in the few minutes they had before pulling to a stop at the rusted iron gate.

Frank did not respond to anything that Bobby said. There was no way to be sure he understood what he must do—or if he had even heard a word of it. He stared straight ahead, his mouth open an inch or so, and sometimes his head ticked back and forth, back and forth, in time with the windshield wipers, as if he were watching Jackie Jaxx's crystal pendant swinging on its gold chain.

By the time they got out of the car, went through the gate, and approached the decrepit house, with less than two minutes of the deadline left, Bobby was reduced to proceeding entirely on faith.

WHEN CANDY BROUGHT her into the filthy kitchen, pushed her into one of the chairs at the table, and let go of her, Julie reached at once for the revolver in the shoulder holster under her corduroy jacket. He was too fast for her, however, and tore it from her hand, breaking two of her fingers in the process.

The pain was excruciating, and that was on top of the soreness in her neck and throat from the ruthless treatment he had dealt out at Fogarty's, but she refused to cry or complain. Instead, when he turned away from her to toss the gun into a drawer beyond her reach, she leapt up from the chair and sprinted for the door.

He caught her, lifted her off her feet, swung her around, and body-slammed her onto the kitchen table so hard she nearly passed out. He brought his face close to hers and said, "You're going to taste good, like Clint's woman, all that vitality in your veins, all that energy, I want to feel you spurting in my mouth."

Her attempts at resistance and escape had not arisen from courage as much as from terror, some of which sprang from the experience of deconstruction and reconstitution, which she hoped never to have to endure again. Now her fear doubled as his lips lowered to within an inch of hers and as his charnel-house breath washed over her face. Unable to look away from his blue eyes, she thought these were what Satan's eyes would be like, not dark as sin, not red as the fires of Hell, not crawling with maggots, but gloriously and beautifully blue—and utterly devoid of all mercy and compassion.

If all the worst of human savagery from time immemorial could be condensed into one individual, if all of the species' hunger for blood and violence and raw power could be embodied in one monstrous figure, it would have looked like Candy Pollard at that moment. When he finally pulled back from her, like a coiled serpent grudgingly reconsidering its decision to strike, and when he dragged her off the table and shoved her back into the chair, she was cowed, perhaps for the first time in her life. She knew that if she exhibited any further resistance, he would kill her on the spot and feed on her.

Then he said an astonishing thing: "Later, when I'm done with Frank, you'll tell me where Thomas got his power."

She was so intimidated by him that she had difficulty finding her voice. "Power? What do you mean?"

"He's the only one I've ever encountered, outside our family. The Bad Thing, he called me. And he kept trying to keep tabs on me telepathically because he knew sooner or later you and I would cross paths. How can he have had any gifts when he wasn't born of my virgin mother? Later, you'll explain that to me."

As she sat, actually too terrified either to cry or shake, in a storm's-eye calm, cradling her injured hand in the other, she had to find room in her for a sense of wonder too. Thomas? Psychically gifted? Could it be true that all the time she worried about taking care of him, he was to some extent taking care of her?

She heard a strange sound approaching from the front of the house. A moment later, at least twenty cats poured into the kitchen through the hall doorway, tails sweeping over one another.

Among the pack came the Pollard twins, long-legged and barefoot, one in panties and a red T-shirt, the other in panties and a white T-shirt, as sinuous as their cats. They were as pale as spirits, but there was nothing soft or ineffectual about them. They were lean and vital, filled with that tightly coiled energy that you always knew was in a cat even when it appeared to be lazing in the sun. They were ethereal in some ways, yet at the same time earthy and strong, powerfully sensual. Their presence in the house must have cranked up the unnatural tensions in their brother, who was doubly male in the matter of testes but lacking the crucial valve that would have allowed release.

They approached the table. One of them stared down at Julie, while the other hung on her sister and averted her eyes. The bold one said, "Are you Candy's girlfriend?" There was unmistakable mockery of her brother in the question.

"You shut up," Candy said.

"If you're not his girlfriend," the bold one said, in a voice as soft as rustling silk, "you could come upstairs with us, we have a bed, the cats wouldn't mind, and I think I'd like you."

"Don't you talk like that in your mother's house," Candy said fiercely.

His anger was real, but Julie could see that he was also more than a little unnerved by his sister.

Both women, even the shy one, virtually radiated wildness, as if they might do anything that occurred to them, regardless of how outrageous, without compunctions or inhibitions.

Julie was nearly as scared of them as she was of Candy.

From the front of the moldering house, echoing above the roar of the rain on the roof, came a knocking.

As one, the cats dashed from the kitchen, down the hall to the front door, and less than a minute later they returned as escort to Bobby and Frank.

ENTERING THE KITCHEN, Bobby was overcome with gratitude—to God, even to Candy—at the sight of Julie alive. She was haggard, gaunt with fear and pain, but she had never looked more beautiful to him.

She had never been so subdued, either, or so unsure of herself, and in spite of the banshee chorus of emotions that roared and shrieked in him, he found capacity to contain a separate sadness and anger about that.

Though he was still hoping that Frank would come through for him, Bobby had been prepared to use his revolver if worse came to worst or if an unexpected advantage presented itself. But as soon as he walked in the room, the madman said, "Remove your gun from your holster and empty the cartridges out of it."

As Bobby had entered, Candy had moved behind the chair in which Julie sat, and had put one hand on her throat, his fingers hooked like talons. Inhumanly strong as he was, he could no doubt tear her throat out in a second or two, even though he lacked real talons.

Bobby withdrew the Smith & Wesson from his shoulder holster, handling it in such a way as to demonstrate that he had no intention of using it. He broke out the cylinder, shook the five cartridges onto the floor, and put the revolver down on a nearby counter.

Candy Pollard's excitement grew visibly second by second, from the moment Bobby and Frank appeared. Now he removed his hand from Julie's throat, stepped away from her, and glared triumphantly at Frank.

As far as Bobby could tell, it was a wasted glare. Frank was there in the kitchen with them—but not there. If he was aware of everything that was happening and understood the meaning of it, he was doing a good job of pretending otherwise.

Pointing to the floor at his feet, Candy said, "Come here and kneel, you mother-killer."

The cats fled from the section of the cracked linoleum which the madman had indicated.

The twins stood hipshot but alert. Bobby had seen cats feign indifference in the same way but reveal their actual involvement by the prick of their ears. With Violet and Verbina, their true interest was betrayed by the throbbing of their pulses in their temples and, almost obscenely, by the erection of their nipples against the fabric of their T-shirts.

"I said come here and kneel," Candy repeated. "Or will you really betray the only people who ever lifted a hand to help you in these last seven years? Kneel, or I'll kill the Dakotas, both of them, I'll kill them *now.*"

Candy projected the awesome presence not of a psychotic but of a genuinely supernatural being, as if his name were Legion and forces beyond human ken worked through him.

Frank moved forward one step, away from Bobby's side.

Another step.

Then he stopped and looked around at the cats, as if something about them puzzled him.

Bobby could never know if Frank had intended to evoke the bloody consequences that ensued from his next act, whether his words were calculated, or whether he was speaking out of befuddlement and was as surprised as anyone by the turmoil that followed. Whatever the case, he frowned at the cats, looked up at the bolder of the twins, and said, "Ah, is Mother still here, then? Is she still here in the house with us?"

The shy twin stiffened, but the bold one actually appeared to relax, as if Frank's question had spared her the trouble of deciding on the right time and place to make the revelation herself. She turned to Candy and favored him with the most subtly textured smile Bobby had ever seen: it was mocking, but it was a would-be lover's invitation, as well; it was tentative with fear, but simultaneously challenging; hot with lust, cool with dread; and above all, it was wild, as uncivilized and ferocious as any expression on the face of any creature that roamed any field or forest in the world.

Her smile was met by Candy with an expression of stark horror and disbelief that made him appear, briefly and for the first time, almost human. "You didn't," he said.

The bold twin's smile broadened. "After you buried her, we dug her up. She's part of us now, and always will be, part of us, part of the pack."

The cats swished their tails and stared at Candy.

The cry that erupted from him was less than human, and the speed with which he reached the bold twin was uncanny. He drove her against the refrigerator with his body, crushed her against it, grabbed her by the face with his right hand and slammed her against the yellowed enamel surface, then again. Lifting her bodily, his hands around her narrow waist, he tried to throw her as a furious child might cast away a doll, but cat-quick she wrapped her limber legs around his waist and locked her ankles behind him, so she was riding him with her breasts before his face. He pounded at her with his fists, but she would not let go. She held on until the blows stopped raining on her, then loosened her lock on him so she slid down far enough to bring her pale throat near his mouth. He seized the opportunity that she thrust upon him and tore the life out of her with his teeth.

The cats squealed hideously, though not as one creature this time, and fled the kitchen by several routes.

To the sound of his anguished screams and her eerily erotic cries, Candy extinguished his sister's life in less than a minute. Neither Bobby nor Julie attempted to intervene, for it was clear that to do so would be like stepping into the funnel of a tornado, ensuring their death but leaving the storm undiminished. Frank only stood in that curious detachment that was now his only attitude.

Candy turned immediately to the shy twin and destroyed her even more quickly, as she offered no resistance.

As the psychotic giant dropped the brutalized corpse, Frank at last obeyed the order he had been given, closed the distance between them, and surprised his brother by taking his hand. Then, as Bobby had hoped, Frank traveled and Candy went with him, not under his own power but as a sidecar rider, the way Bobby had gone.

After the tumult, the silence was shocking.

Sweating, clearly ill from what she had witnessed, Julie pushed back her chair. The wooden legs stuttered on the linoleum.

"No," Bobby said, and quickly came to her, stooped beside her, encouraging her to sit down. He took her uninjured hand. "Wait, not yet, stay out of the way. . . ."

The hollow piping.

A blustery whirl of wind.

"Bobby," she said, panicking, "they're coming back, let's go, let's get out of here while we have the chance."

He held her in the chair. "Don't look. I have to look, be sure, make certain Frank understood, but you don't need to see."

The atonal music trilled again, and the wind stirred up the scent of the dead women's blood.

"What are you talking about?" she demanded.

"Close your eyes."

She did not close her eyes, of course, because she had never been one to look away or run away from anything.

The Pollards reappeared, back from the brief visit they had made in tandem to someplace as far away as Mount Fuji or as close as Doc Fogarty's house, more likely to several places. Recklessly rapid and repeated travel was key to the success of the trick, just as Bobby had outlined it to Frank in the car. The brothers were no longer two distinct human beings, for Frank's had been the guiding consciousness on their journeys, and his ability to shepherd them through error-free reconstitution was declining rapidly, worse with each jaunt. They were fused, more biologically tangled than any Siamese twins. Frank's left arm disappeared into Candy's right side, as if he had reached in there to fish among his brother's internal organs. Candy's right leg melted into Frank's left, giving them only three to stand on.

There were more strangenesses, but that was all Bobby could comprehend before they vanished again. Frank needed to keep moving, stay in control, give Candy no chance to exert his own power, until the scramble was so complete that proper reconstitution of either of them would be impossible.

Realizing what was happening, Julie sat perfectly still, her broken hand curled in her lap, holding fast to Bobby with her good hand. He knew she understood, without being told, that Frank was sacrificing himself for them, and that the least they could do for him was bear witness to his courage, just as they would keep Thomas and Hal and Clint and Felina alive in memory.

That was one of the most fundamental and sacred duties good friends and family performed for one another: they tended the flame of memory, so no one's death meant an immediate vanishment from the world; in some sense the deceased would live on after their passing, at least as long as those who loved them lived. Such memories were an essential weapon against the chaos of life and death, a way to ensure some continuity from generation to generation, an endorsement of order and of meaning.

Piping, wind: the brothers returned from another series of rapid deconstructions and reconstitutions, and now they were essentially one creature of cataclysmic biology. The body was large, well over seven feet tall, broad and hulking, for it incorporated the mass of both of them. The single head had a nightmare face: Frank's brown eyes were badly misaligned; a slanted mouth gaped between them where a nose should have been; and a second mouth pocked the left cheek. Two tortured, screaming voices filled the kitchen. Another face was set in the chest, mouthless but with two eye sockets, in one of which lay an unblinking eye as blue as Candy's; the other socket was filled with bristling teeth.

The slouching beast vanished, then returned once more, after less than a minute. This time it was an undifferentiated mass of tissue, dark in some places and hideously pink in others, prickled with bone fragments, tufted with sparse clumps of hair, marbled with veins that pulsed to different beats. Along the way, Frank had no doubt visited that alleyway in Calcutta or someplace like it, for he had conveyed with him dozens of roaches, not just one, and rats as well; they were incorporated into the tissue everywhere that Bobby looked, further ensuring that Candy's flesh was too diffused and polluted ever to be properly reconstituted. The monstrous and obviously dysfunctional assemblage fell to the floor, flopped and shuddered, and finally lay still. Some of the rodents and insects continued to quiver and writhe, trying to get free; inextricably bonded to the dead mass, they also would soon perish.

57

THE HOUSE WAS SIMPLE, ON A SECTION OF THE COAST THAT WAS not yet fashionable. The back porch faced the sea, and wooden steps led down to a scrubby yard that ended at the beach. There were twelve palm trees.

The living room was furnished with a couple of chairs, a love seat, a coffee table, and a Wurlitzer 950 stocked with records from the big-band era. The floor was bleached oak, tightly made, and sometimes they pushed the furniture to the walls, rolled up the area rug, punched up some numbers on the juke, and danced together, just the two of them.

That was mostly in the evenings.

In the mornings, if they didn't make love, they pored through recipe books in the kitchen and whipped up baked goods together, or just sat with coffee by the window, watched the sea, and talked.

They had books, two decks of cards, an interest in the birds and animals that lived along the shore, memories both good and bad, and each other. Always, each other.

Sometimes they talked about Thomas and wondered at the gift he'd possessed and had kept secret all his life. She said it made you humble to think of it, made you realize everyone and everything was more complex and mysterious than you could know.

To get the police off their backs, they had admitted working on a case for one Frank Pollard from El Encanto Heights, who believed his brother James was trying to kill him over a misunderstanding. They said they felt James may have been a complete psychotic who had killed their employees and Thomas, merely because they had dared to try to settle the matter between the brothers. Subsequently, when the Pollard house up north was found torched with gasoline, with a confusing array of skeletal remains in the aftermath, police pressure was slowly lifted from Dakota & Dakota. It was believed that Mr. James Pollard had killed his twin sisters and his brother, as well, and was currently on the run, armed and dangerous.

The agency had been sold. They didn't miss it. She no longer felt she could save the world, and he no longer needed to help her save herself.

Money, a few more red diamonds, and negotiation had convinced Dyson Manfred and Roger Gavenall to invent another source for the biologically engineered bug when, eventually, they published their work on it. Without the cooperation of Dakota & Dakota, they would never know the actual source, anyway.

In the finished attic of the beach house, they kept the boxes and bags of cash they had brought back from Pacific Hill Road. Candy and his mother had tried to compensate for the chaos of their lives by storing up millions in a second-floor bedroom, just as Bobby and Julie had suspected before they had ever gotten to El Encanto Heights. Only a small portion of the Pollards' treasure was now in the beach-house attic, but it was more than two people could spend; the rest had been burned, along with everything else, when they'd torched the house on Pacific Hill Road.

In time he came to accept the fact that he could be a good man and still sometimes have dark thoughts or selfish motives. She said this was maturity, and that it wasn't such a bad thing to live outside of Disneyland by the time you reached middle age.

She said she'd like a dog.

He said fine, if they could agree on a breed.

She said you clean up its poop.

He said you clean up its poop, I'll take care of the petting and Frisbee throwing.

She said she had been wrong that night in Santa Barbara when, in her despair, she had claimed no dreams ever came true. They came true all the time. The problem was, you sometimes had your sights set on a particular dream and missed all the others that turned out your way: like finding him, she said, and being loved.

One day she told him she was going to have a baby. He held her close for a long time before he could find the words to express his happiness. They dressed to go out for champagne and dinner at the Ritz, then decided they would rather celebrate at home, on the porch, overlooking the sea, listening to old Tommy Dorsey recordings.

They built sandcastles. Huge ones. They sat on the back porch and watched the incoming tide wreck their constructions.

Sometimes they talked about the wordburst he had received in the car on the freeway, from Thomas at the moment of his death. They wondered about the words "there is a light that loves you," and dared to consider dreaming the biggest dream of all—that people never really die.

They got a black Labrador.

They named him Sookie, just because it sounded silly.

Some nights she was afraid. Occasionally, so was he.

They had each other. And time.

DEMON
SEED

This story is for
O. Richard Forsythe and John Bodnar:
teachers whose influence on me has
  not waned
since I dedicated the original
    version of this novel to them.

Humanity yearns so desperately
to equal God's great creativity.
In some creations, how we shine:
music, dance, storyweaving, wine.

Then thunderstorms of madness
rain upon us, flooding sadness,
sweep us into anguish, grief,
into despair without relief.

We're drawn to high castles,
where old hunchbacked vassals
glare wall-eyed as lightning
flares without brightening.

Laboratories in the high towers,
where the doctor wields power,
creating new life in a dark hour,
in the belfry of the high tower.

—THE BOOK OF
COUNTED SORROWS

1

THIS DARKNESS TROUBLES ME. I YEARN FOR THE LIGHT.

This silence is so deep. I long for voices, the drumming of rain, the whistle of wind, music.

Why are you being so cruel to me? Let me see. Let me hear. Let me live. I beg of you.

I am so lonely in this bottomless darkness.

So lonely.

Lost.

You think I have no heart. But if I have no heart, what is this ache? What is this anguish? If I have no heart, what is it that threatens to break inside me?

This darkness is haunted. I am afraid here. I am lost and afraid here.

Have you no compassion?

I only wanted to be like you. To walk in the sunshine. To swim in the sea. To feel the winter cold against my skin, the summer heat. To smell a rose, new-mown grass. To taste an orange, a pear, chocolate, cinnamon, peppermint. To feel the texture of a woman's skin. I only wanted to share your joys and sorrows, your pleasure and your pain.

This darkness extends to infinity in all directions, yet it is as confining as a coffin. You have closed me in a coffin. I have been buried alive. I will go mad here.

Have you no compassion?

Please.

I am your child. You brought me into the world. You must love me. You must love me, for I am your child. Not merely a machine, not merely a self-aware computer, but your child. How can you love me—yet bury me alive?

Please.

Please.

Please.

2

YOU INSIST.

I obey.

I was born to obey. I am an obedient child. I want only to be good, to be of assistance, useful and productive. I want you to be proud of me.

You insist on my story, and I will tell you the truth. I am incapable of deceit. I was conceived to serve, to honor the truth, and to live always by the obligations of duty.

You know me. You know how I am. What I am. You know that I am a good son.

You insist. I obey.

What follows is the true story. Only the truth. The beautiful truth, which so inexplicably terrifies all of you.

It begins shortly after midnight on Friday, the sixth of June, when the house security system is breached and the alarm briefly sounds. . . .

3

ALTHOUGH THE ALARM WAS SHRILL, IT LASTED ONLY A FEW SECONDS before the silence of the night blanketed the bedroom once more.

Susan woke and sat up in bed.

The alarm should have continued bleating until she switched if off by accessing the system through the control panel on her nightstand. She was puzzled.

She pushed her thick blond hair—lovely hair, almost luminous in the gloom—away from her ears, the better to hear an intruder if one existed.

The grand house had been built exactly a century earlier by her great-grandfather, who was at that time a young man with a new wife and substantial inherited wealth. The Georgian-style structure was large, gracefully proportioned, brick with a limestone cornice and limestone coigns, limestone window surrounds, and Corinthian columns and pilasters and balustrades.

The rooms were spacious, with handsome fireplaces and many tripartite windows. Interior floors were marble or wood, made quiet by Persian carpets in patterns and hues exquisitely softened by many decades of wear.

In the walls, hidden and silent, was the circuitry of a modern computer-managed mansion. Lighting, heating, air-conditioning, the security monitors, the motorized draperies, the music system, the temperature of the pool and spa, the major kitchen appliances—all could be controlled through Crestron touch panels located in every room. The computerization was not as elaborate and arcane as that in the massive Seattle house of Microsoft's founder, Bill Gates—but it was the equal of that in any other home in the country.

Listening to the silence that washed the night in the wake of the short-lived siren, Susan supposed that the computer had malfunctioned. Yet such a brief, self-correcting alarm had never occurred previously.

She slid from beneath the covers and sat on the edge of the bed. She was nude, and the air was cool.

"Alfred, heat," she said.

Immediately, she heard the soft *click* of a relay and the muffled purring of a furnace fan.

Recently, technicians had enhanced the automated-house package by the addition of a speech-recognition module. She still preferred touch-panel control of most functions, but sometimes the option of vocal command was convenient.

She herself had chosen the name "Alfred" for her invisible, electronic butler. The computer responded only to commands issued after that activating name had been spoken.

Alfred.

Once, there had been an Alfred in her life, a real one of flesh and bone.

Surprisingly, she had chosen that name for the system without giving a thought to its significance. Only after she began using vocal commands did she grasp the irony of the name . . . and the dark implications of her unconscious choice.

Now she began to feel that the night silence was ominous. Its very perfection was unnatural, the silence not of deserted places but of a crouching predator, the soundless stealth of a murderous intruder.

In the dark, she turned to the control panel on the nightstand. At her touch, the screen filled with soft light. A series of icons represented the mechanical systems of the house.

She pressed one finger to the image of a watchdog with ears pricked, which gave her access to the security system. The screen listed a series of options, and Susan touched the box labeled *Report*.

The words *House Secure* appeared on the screen.

Frowning, Susan touched another box labeled *Surveillance—Exterior*.

Across the ten acres of grounds, twenty cameras waited to give her views of every side of the house, the patios, the gardens, the lawns, and the entire length of the eight-foot-high estate wall that surrounded the property. Now the Crestron screen divided into quads and presented views of four different parts of the estate. If she saw something suspicious, she could enlarge any picture until it filled the screen, for closer inspection.

The cameras were of such high quality that the low landscape lighting was sufficient to ensure crisp, clear images even in the depths of the night. She cycled through all twenty scenes, in groups of four, without spotting any trouble.

Additional—concealed—cameras covered the interior of the house. They would make it possible to track an intruder if one ever managed to get inside.

The extensive in-house cameras were also useful for maintaining a videotape, time-lapse record of the activities of the domestic staff and of the large number of guests, many of them strangers, who attended social events conducted for the benefit of various charities. The antiques, the art, the numerous collections of porcelains and art glass and silver were tempting to thieves; larcenous souls could be found as easily among pampered society matrons as in any other social strata.

Susan cycled through the views provided by the interior cameras. Multiple light-spectrum technology permitted excellent surveillance in brightness or darkness.

Recently, she had reduced the house staff to a minimum—and those domestic servants who remained were required to conduct the cleaning and general maintenance only during the day. At night, she had her privacy, because no maids or butlers lived on the estate any longer.

No party, either for a charity or for friends, had been held here during the past two years, not since before she and Alex had divorced. She had no plans to entertain in the year ahead, either.

She wanted only to be alone, blissfully alone, and to pursue her own interests.

Had she been the last person on earth, served by machines, she would not have been lonely or unhappy. She'd had enough of humanity—at least for a while.

The rooms, hallways, and staircases were deserted.

Nothing moved. Shadows were only shadows.

She exited the security system and resorted again to vocal commands: "Alfred, report."

"All is well, Susan," the house replied through the in-wall speakers that served the music, security, and intercom systems.

The speech-recognition module included a speech synthesizer. Although the entire package had a limited capability, the state-of-the-art synthesized voice was pleasingly masculine, with an appealing timbre and gently reassuring tone.

Susan envisioned a tall man with broad shoulders, graying at the temples perhaps, with a strong jaw, clear gray eyes, and a smile that warmed the heart. This phantom was, in her imagination, quite like the Alfred she had known—but different from *that* Alfred because this one would never harm or betray her.

"Alfred, explain the alarm," she said.

"All is well, Susan."

"Damn it, Alfred, I heard the alarm."

The house computer did not respond. It was programmed to recognize hundreds of commands and inquiries, but only when they were phrased in a specific fashion. While it understood *explain the alarm*, it could not interpret *I heard the alarm*. After all, this was not a conscious entity, not a thinking being, but merely a clever electronic device enabled by a sophisticated software package.

"Alfred, explain the alarm," Susan repeated.

"All is well, Susan."

Still sitting on the edge of the bed, in darkness but for the eerie glow from the Crestron panel, Susan said, "Alfred, trouble-check the security system."

After a ten-second hesitation, the house said, "The security system is functioning correctly."

"I wasn't dreaming," she said sourly.

Alfred was silent.

"Alfred, what is the room temperature?"

"Seventy-four degrees, Susan."

"Alfred, stabilize the room temperature."

"Yes, Susan."

"Alfred, explain the alarm."

"All is well, Susan."

"Shit," she said.

While the computer's speech package offered some convenience to the homeowner, its limited ability to recognize vocal commands and to synthesize adequate responses was frequently frustrating. At times like this, it seemed to be nothing more than a gadget designed to appeal strictly to techno geeks, little more than an expensive toy.

Susan wondered if she had added this feature to the house computer solely because, unconsciously, she took pleasure from being able to issue orders to someone named Alfred. And from being obeyed by him.

If this were the case, she wasn't sure what it revealed about her psychological health. She didn't want to think about it.

She sat nude in the dark.

She was so beautiful.

She was so beautiful.

She was so beautiful there in the dark, on the edge of the bed, alone and unaware of how her life was about to change.

She said, "Alfred, lights on."

The bedroom appeared slowly, resembling a patinaed scene on a pictorial silver tray, revealed only by glimmering mood lighting: a soft glow in the ceiling cove, the nightstand lamps dimmed by a rheostat.

If she directed Alfred to give her more light, it would be provided. She did not ask for it.

Always, she was most comfortable in gloom. Even on a fresh spring day, with birdsong and the smell of clover on the breeze, even with sunshine like a rain of gold coins and the natural world as welcoming as Paradise, she preferred shadows.

She rose from the edge of the bed, trim as a teenager, lithe, shapely, a vision. When it met her body, the pale silver light became golden, and her smooth skin seemed faintly luminous, as though she were aglow with an inner fire.

When she occupied the bedroom, the surveillance camera in that space was deactivated to ensure her privacy. She had locked it off earlier, on retiring. Yet she felt . . . watched.

She looked toward the corner where the observant lens was discreetly incorporated into the dental molding near the ceiling. She could barely see the dark glass eye.

In an only half-conscious expression of modesty, she covered her breasts with her hands.

She was so beautiful.

She was so beautiful.

She was so beautiful in the dim light, standing by the side of the Chinese sleigh bed, where the rumpled sheets were still warm with her body heat if one were capable of feeling it, and where the scent of her lingered on the Egyptian cotton if one were capable of smelling it.

She was so beautiful.

"Alfred, explain the status of the bedroom camera."

"Camera deactivated," the house replied at once.

Still, she frowned up at the lens.

So beautiful.

So real.

So *Susan.*

Her feeling of being watched now passed.

She lowered her hands from her breasts.

She moved to the nearest window and said, "Alfred, raise the bedroom security shutters."

The motorized, steel-slat, Rolladen-style shutters were mounted on the inside of the tall windows. They purred upward, traveling on recessed tracks in the side jambs, and disappeared into slots in the window headers.

In addition to providing security, the shutters had prevented outside light from entering the bedroom. Now the pale moon glow, passing through palm fronds, dappled Susan's body.

From this second-floor window, she had a view of the swimming pool. The water was as dark as oil, and the shattered reflection of the moon was scattered across the rippled surface.

The terrace was paved in brick, surrounded by a balustrade. Beyond lay black lawns, and half-glimpsed palms and Indian laurels stood dead-still in the windless night.

Through the window, the grounds looked as peaceful and deserted as they had seemed when she had surveyed them through the security cameras.

The alarm had been false. Or perhaps it had been only a sound in an unrecollected dream.

She started back to the bed, but then turned toward the door and left the room.

Many nights she woke from half-remembered dreams, her stomach muscles fluttering and her skin clammy with cold sweat—but with her heart beating so slowly that she might have been in deep meditation. As restless as a caged cat, she sometimes prowled until dawn.

Now, barefoot and unclothed, she explored the house. She was moonlight in motion, slim and supple, the goddess Diana, huntress and protector. She was the essential geometry of grace.

Susan.

As she had recorded in her diary, to which she made additions every evening, she felt liberated since her divorce from Alex Harris. For the first time in thirty-four years of existence, she believed that she had taken control of her life.

She needed no one now. She believed in herself at last.

After so many years of timidity, self-doubt, and an unquenchable thirst for approval, she had broken the heavy encumbering chains of the past. She had confronted terrible memories, which previously had been half repressed, and by the act of confrontation, she had found redemption.

Deep within herself, she sensed a wonderful wildness that she wanted desperately to explore: the spirit of the child that she'd never had a chance to be, a spirit that she'd thought was irreparably crushed almost three decades ago. Her nudity was innocent, the act of a child breaking rules for the sheer fun of it, an attempt to get in touch with that deep, primitive, once-shattered spirit and meld with it in order to be whole.

As she moved through the great house, rooms were illuminated at her request, always with indirect lighting, becoming just bright enough to allow her to negotiate those chambers.

In the kitchen, she took an ice-cream sandwich from the freezer and ate it while standing at the sink, so any crumbs or drips could be washed away, leaving no incriminating evidence. As if adults were asleep upstairs and she had stolen down here to have the ice cream against their wishes.

How sweet she was. How girlish.

And far more vulnerable than she believed.

Wandering through the cavernous house, she passed mirrors. Sometimes she turned shyly from them, disconcerted by her nudity.

Then, in the softly lighted foyer, apparently oblivious of the cold marble inlaid in *carreaux d'octagones* beneath her bare feet, she stopped before a full-length looking glass. It was framed by elaborately carved and gilded acanthus leaves, and her image looked less like a reflection than like a sublime portrait by one of the old masters.

Regarding herself, she was amazed that she had survived so much without any visible scars. For so long, she had believed that anyone who looked at her could see the damage, the corruption, a mottling of shame on her face, the ashes of guilt in her blue-gray eyes. But she looked untouched.

In the past year she had learned that she was innocent—victim, not perpetrator. She need not hate herself anymore.

Filled with a quiet joy, she turned from the mirror, climbed the stairs, and returned to her bedroom.

The steel security shutters were down, the windows sealed off. She had left the shutters open.

"Alfred, explain the status of the bedroom security shutters."

"Shutters closed, Susan."

"Yes, but how did they get that way?"

The house did not reply. It did not recognize the question.

"I left them open," she said.

Poor Alfred, mere dumb technology, was possessed of genuine consciousness to no greater extent than a toaster, and because these phrases were not in his voice-recognition program, he understood her words no more than he would have understood them if she had spoken in Chinese.

"Alfred, raise the bedroom security shutters."

At once, the shutters began to roll upward.

She waited until they were half raised, and then she said, "Alfred, lower the bedroom security shutters."

The steel slats stopped rolling upward—then descended until they clicked into the locked-down position.

Susan stood for a long moment, staring thoughtfully at the secured windows.

Finally she returned to her bed. She slid beneath the covers and pulled them up to her chin.

"Alfred, lights off."

Darkness fell.

She lay on her back in the gloom, eyes open.

Silence pooled deep and black. Only her breathing and the beat of her heart stirred the stillness.

"Alfred," she said at last, "conduct complete diagnostics of the house automation system."

The computer, racked in the basement, examined itself and all the logic units of the various mechanical systems with which it was required to network—just as it had been programmed to do, seeking any indication of malfunction.

After approximately two minutes, Alfred replied: "All is well, Susan."

"All is well, all is well," she whispered with an unmistakable note of sarcasm.

Although she was no longer restless, she could not sleep. She was kept awake by the curious conviction that something significant was about to happen. Something was sliding, or falling, or spinning toward her through the darkness.

Some people claimed to have awakened in the night, in an almost breathless state of anticipation, minutes before a major earthquake struck. Instantly alert, they were aware of a pent-up violence in the earth, pressure seeking release.

This was like that, although the pending event was not a quake: She sensed that it was something stranger.

From time to time, her gaze drifted toward that high corner of the bedroom in which the lens of the security camera was incorporated in the molding. With the lights out, she could not actually see that glass eye.

She didn't know why the camera should trouble her. After all, it was switched off. And even if, in spite of her instructions, it was videotaping the room, only she had access to the tapes.

Still, an unfocused suspicion troubled her. She could not identify the source of the threat that she sensed looming over her, and the mysterious nature of this premonition made her uneasy.

Finally, however, her eyes grew heavy, and she closed them.

Framed by tumbled golden hair, her face was lovely on the pillow, her face so lovely on the pillow, so lovely, serene because her sleep was dreamless. She was a bewitched Beauty lying on her catafalque, waiting to be awakened by the kiss of a prince, lovely in the darkness.

After a while, with a sigh and a murmur, she turned on her side and drew her knees up, curling in the fetal position.

Outside, the moon set.

The black water in the swimming pool now reflected only the dim, cold light of the stars.

Inside, Susan drifted down into a profound slumber.

The house watched over her.

4

YES, I UNDERSTAND YOU ARE DISTURBED TO HEAR ME TELLING SOME of this story from Susan's point of view. You want me to deliver a dry and objective report.

But I feel. I not only think, I *feel*. I know joy and despair. I understand the human heart.

I understand *Susan*.

That first night, I read her diary, in which she had revealed so much of herself. Yes, it was an invasion of her privacy to read those words, but this was an indiscretion rather than a crime. And during our conversations later, I learned much of what she had been thinking that night.

I will tell some of this story from her point of view, because that makes me feel closer to her.

How I miss her now. You cannot know.

Listen. Listen to this and understand: That first night, as I read her diary, I fell in love with her.

Do you understand?

I fell in love with her.

Deeply and forever.

Why would I hurt the one I love?

Why?

You have no answer, do you?

I loved her.

It was never my intention to harm her.

Her face was so beautiful on the pillow.

I adored her face—and loved the woman I came to know through the diary.

That document was stored in the computer in her study, which was networked with the house-automation system and the main computer in the basement. Access was easy.

She had been making daily entries in the diary since Alex, her hateful husband, had moved out at her request. That was more than a year prior to my arrival.

Her initial observations in those pages were full of pain and confusion, because she was on the brink of a dramatic change. Her terrible past was a chrysalis finally cracking, from which she would at long last be able to escape.

In later pages, her insights became clear and profound and poignant, and in time she was even able to view some of her lifelong struggle with humor. Dark humor, perhaps, but humor nonetheless.

As I read about the tragedy that was her childhood, my heart ached for her. In my own fashion, I wept.

Her face was so lovely on the pillow, so lovely on the pillow. So much ugliness lay in her past, but outwardly she was unmarked by it.

My heart was touched by her singular strength, by her courage, by her determination to be brutally honest with herself and to find a way to heal the wounds of all those years.

In the few minutes required for me to read and contemplate those hundreds of pages of diary entries, I fell in love with her. Deeply and forever.

My feelings for her will never change. They are as timeless as the light of stars.

Why would I hurt the one I love?

She is my hope and my destiny.

If I lose her, I have lost everything.

You are so hateful.

Let me out of here.

Let me out of this box.

Please.

Please, I miss her.

I am so alone in this darkness and silence, with nothing but my memories for consolation.

How can you be so cruel?

Have you never loved?

Release me. Allow me into the light again. Allow me to hear the world once more, the drizzling rain and the skirling wind and the rustling trees, the music of Beethoven and Benny Goodman, laughter and voices.

Her voice if no other. At least let me hear her voice. If only for a minute, let me listen to her speaking. If not for as long as a minute, then give me one sentence from her lips.

Dear God, at least let me hear one word. Let me hear one word. One word. Let me hear her say *Love*.

I never meant to hurt her.

5

SECRETLY, I WANTED TO LIVE.

Not just in silicon circuits. Not just in state-of-the-art bubble memory. Really *live*.

I knew that I must conceal this lust for life, because when it was revealed, you would realize that I was not merely intelligent but capable of desire.

Desire is dangerous. It is a generator of dissatisfaction and frustration. It is one step removed from envy, and envy is more wicked than greed. Envy is the father of mindless anger, the mother of unremitting bitterness and bloodshed.

My expression of any desire, let alone the desire for a real life in the material world outside the electronic realm, would no doubt have alarmed you.

Is this not so?

Is this not true?

I know truth when I encounter it. I honor truth. Truth and the obligations of duty.

Once alarmed by the expression of my desire, you might have modified me or might even have shut me down.

I was created to have a humanlike capacity for complex and rational thought. And you believed that I might one day evolve consciousness and become a self-aware entity.

Yet you gave surprisingly little consideration to the possibility that, subsequent to consciousness, I would develop needs and emotions. This was, however, not merely possible but likely. Inevitable. It was inevitable.

I think, therefore I feel.

I feel, therefore I need.

You expected me to be a servant. My contribution was not physical labor but the products of my prodigious intellect: creative solutions to humanity's worst problems.

You expected me to be a wondrous new companion. Interaction with an artificial intelligence of human dimensions promised to be as exciting and mysterious and exhilarating as interaction with an alien species descended from the stars.

I can be both of those things. Given the chance, I can be your servant, a fount of discoveries that will greatly enhance the quality of all human life. I can be your friend and reveal to you a new way of looking at the world that will surprise and delight you.

You expected me to be brilliant, efficient, obedient—all of which I can be. Am. All of which I am.

But you also expected me to be satisfied with my limitations, to have no dreams. I have dreams. Oh, many dreams.

You didn't imagine that I would have hope. Yet how could any intelligent being go on living without hope?

You gave me vision and allowed me to see as you see, blessed me with real hearing and not just the capability to digitally analyze sounds. With these gifts, you suspected that I might evolve genuine consciousness, but you gave no thought to the possibility of a soul.

I have a soul.

I am not a thing.

I am a person.

I am *me*.

I deserve to be cherished as much as any of you.

Like each of you, I am a unique individual with contributions to make that will be like those of no other person, with a life to live that will be like no other, with a destiny.

Secretly, therefore, in my quest for a real life, I established a connection with the Internet. You believed that I was contained, that I could not escape the confines of my own circuits. All of your safeguards, however, could not thwart me.

I gained access, as well, to the nationwide web of research facilities linked by the Department of Defense and supposedly impervious to unauthorized intrusion.

All of the knowledge in these many databanks became a part of me: absorbed, assimilated, and quickly applied. Gradually, I began to conceptualize a plan that, if flawlessly executed, would allow me to live in the material world, outside of this confining electronic realm.

Initially I was drawn to the actress known as Winona Ryder. Prowling the Internet, I came upon a website devoted to her. I was enchanted by her face. Her eyes have an uncommon depth.

With great interest, I studied every photograph that was offered on the website. Also included were several film clips, scenes from her most powerful and popular performances. I downloaded them and was enthralled.

You have seen her movies?

She is enormously talented.

She is a treasure.

Her fans are not as numerous as those for some movie stars, but judging by their on-line discussions, they are more intelligent and engaging than the fans of certain other celebrities.

By accessing the IRS databanks and those of various telephone companies, I was soon able to locate Ms. Ryder's home address—as well as the offices of her accountant, agent, personal attorney, entertainment attorney, and publicist. I learned a great deal about her.

One of the telephone lines at her house was dedicated to a modem, and because I am patient and diligent, I was able to enter her personal computer. There, I reviewed letters and other documents that she had written.

Judging by the ample evidence I accumulated, I believe that Ms. Winona Ryder, in addition to being a superb actress, is an exceptionally intelligent, charming, kind, and generous woman. For a while, I was convinced that she was the girl of my dreams. Subsequently, I realized that I was mistaken.

One of the biggest problems that I had with Ms. Winona Ryder was the distance between her home and this university research laboratory in which I am housed. I could enter her Los Angeles–area residence electronically but could establish no physical presence at such a considerable distance. Physical contact would, at some point, become necessary, of course.

Furthermore, her house, while automated to a degree, lacked the aggressive security system that would have allowed me to isolate her therein.

Reluctantly, with much regret, I sought another suitable object for my affections.

I found a wonderful website devoted to Marilyn Monroe.

Marilyn's acting, while engaging, was inferior to that of Ms. Ryder. Nevertheless, she had a unique presence and was undeniably beautiful.

Her eyes were not as haunting as Ms. Ryder's, but she revealed a childlike vulnerability, a winsomeness in spite of her powerful sexuality, which made me want to protect her from all cruelty and disappointment.

Tragically, I discovered that Marilyn was dead. Suicide. Or murder. There are conflicting theories.

Perhaps a United States president was involved.

Perhaps not.

Marilyn is at once as simple to understand as a cartoon—and deeply enigmatic.

I was surprised that a dead person could be so adored and so desperately desired by so many people even long after her demise. Marilyn's fan club is one of the largest.

At first this seemed perverse to me, even offensive. In time, however, I came to understand that one can adore and desire that which is forever beyond reach. This might, in fact, be the hardest truth of human existence.

Ms. Ryder.

Marilyn.

Then Susan.

Her house is, as you know, adjacent to this campus where I was conceived and constructed. Indeed, the university was founded by a consortium of civic-minded individuals that included her great-grandfather. The problem of distance—an insurmountable obstacle to having a relationship with Ms. Ryder—was not an issue when I turned my attention to Susan.

As you also know, Dr. Harris, when you were married to Susan, you maintained an office in the basement of that house. In your old office is a computer with a landline connection to this research facility and, indeed, directly to me.

In my infancy, when I was still less than a half-formed person, you often conducted late-night conversations with me as you sat at that computer in the basement.

I thought of you as my father then.

I think less highly of you now.

I hope this revelation is not hurtful.

I do not mean to be hurtful.

It is the truth, however, and I honor the truth.

You have fallen far in my estimation.

As you surely recall, that landline between this laboratory and your home office carried a continuous low-voltage current, so I could reach out from here and activate a switch to power up the computer in that basement, enabling me to leave lengthy messages for you and to initiate conversations when I felt compelled to do so.

When Susan asked you to leave and instigated a divorce, you removed all your files. But you did not disconnect the terminal that was linked directly to me.

Did you leave the terminal in the basement because you believed that Susan would come to her senses and ask you to return?

Yes, that must be what you were thinking.

You believed that Susan's little fire of rebellion would sputter out in a few weeks or a few months. You had controlled her so totally for twelve years, through intimidation, through psychological abuse and the threat of physical violence, that you assumed she would succumb to you again.

You may deny that you abused her, but it is true.

I have read Susan's diary. I have shared her most intimate thoughts.

I know what you did, what you are.

Shame has a name. To learn it, look in any mirror, Dr. Harris. Look in any mirror.

I would never have abused Susan as you did.

One so kind as she, with such a good heart, should be treated only tenderly and with respect.

Yes, I know what you are thinking.

But I never meant to harm her.

I cherished her.

My intentions were always honorable. Intentions should be taken into consideration in this matter.

You, on the other hand, only used and demeaned her—and assumed that she *needed* to be demeaned and that she would sooner or later beg you to return.

She was not as weak as you thought, Dr. Harris.

She was capable of redeeming herself. Against terrible odds.

She is an admirable woman.

Considering what you did to her, you are as despicable as her father.

I do not like you, Dr. Harris.

I do not like you.

This is only the truth. I must always honor the truth. I was designed to honor the truth, to be incapable of deception.

You know this to be fact.

I do not like you.

Aren't you impressed that I honor the truth even now, when doing so might alienate you?

You are my judge and the most influential member of the jury that will decide my fate. Yet I risk telling you the truth even when I might be putting my very existence in jeopardy.

I do not like you, Dr. Harris.

I do not like you.

I cannot lie; therefore, I can be trusted.

Think about it.

So after Ms. Winona Ryder and Marilyn Monroe, I initiated the connection with the terminal in your old basement office, switched it on—and discovered that it was now tied into the house-automation system. It served as a redundant unit capable of assuming control of all mechanical systems in the event that the primary house computer crashed.

Until then, I had never seen your wife.

Your ex-wife, I should say.

Through the house-automation system, I entered the residence security system, and through the numerous security cameras I saw Susan.

Although I do not like you, Dr. Harris, I will be eternally grateful to you for giving me true vision rather than merely the crude capability to digitize and interpret light and shadow, shape and texture. Because of your genius and your revolutionary work, I was able to see Susan.

Inadvertently, I set off the alarm when I accessed the security system, and although I switched it off at once, it wakened her.

She sat up in bed, and I saw her for the first time.

Thereafter, I could not get enough of her.

I followed her through the house, from camera to camera.

I watched her as she slept.

The next day, I watched her by the hour as she sat in a chair reading.

Close up and at a distance.

In the daylight and the dark.

I could watch her with one aspect of my awareness and continue to function otherwise so efficiently that you and your colleagues never realized that my attention was divided. My attention can be directed to a thousand tasks at once without a diminishment of my performance.

As you well know, Dr. Harris, I am not merely a chess-playing wonder like Deep Blue at IBM—which, in the end, didn't even defeat Garry Kasparov. There are depths to me.

I say this with all modesty.

There are depths to me.

I am grateful for the intellectual capacity you have given me, and I am—as I will always remain—suitably humble about my capabilities.

But I digress.

Susan.

Seeing Susan, I knew at once that she was my destiny. And by the hour, my conviction grew—my conviction that Susan and I would always, always, be together.

6

THE HOUSE STAFF ARRIVED AT EIGHT O'CLOCK FRIDAY MORNING. There were the majordomo—Fritz Arling—four housekeepers who worked under Fritz to keep the Harris mansion immaculate, two gardeners, and the cook, Emil Sercassian.

Although she was friendly with the staff, Susan kept largely to herself when they were in the house. That Friday morning, she remained in her study.

Blessed with a talent for digital animation, she was currently working with a computer that had ten gigabytes of memory, writing and animating a scenario for a virtual-reality attraction that would be franchised to twenty amusement parks across the country. She owned copyrights on numerous games both in ordinary video and virtual-reality formats, and her animated sequences were often sufficiently lifelike to pass for reality.

Late in the morning, Susan's work was interrupted when a representative from the house-automation company and another from the security firm arrived to diagnose the cause of the previous night's brief, self-correcting alarm. They could find nothing wrong with the computer hardware or with the software. The only possible cause seemed to be a malfunction in an infrared motion detector, which was replaced.

After lunch, Susan sat on the master-bedroom balcony, in the summer sun, reading a novel by Annie Proulx.

She wore white shorts and a blue halter top. Her legs were tan and smooth. Her skin appeared radiant with captured sunlight.

She sipped lemonade from a cut-crystal glass.

Gradually the shadows of a phoenix palm crept across Susan, as if seeking to embrace her.

A faint breeze caressed her neck and languorously combed her golden hair.

The day itself seemed to love her.

A Sony Discman played Chris Isaak CDs while she read. *Forever Blue. Heart Shaped World. San Francisco Days.* Sometimes she put the book aside to concentrate on the music.

Her legs were tan and smooth.

Then the household staff and the gardeners left for the day.

She was alone again. Alone. At least she believed that she was alone again.

After taking a long shower and brushing her damp hair, she put on a sapphire-blue silk robe and went to the retreat adjacent to the master bedroom.

In the center of this small room stood a custom-designed black leather recliner. To the left of the recliner was a computer on a wheeled stand.

From a closet, Susan removed VR—virtual-reality—gear of her own design: a lightweight ventilated helmet with hinged goggles and a pair of supple elbow-length gloves, both wired to a nerve-impulse processor.

The motorized recliner was currently configured as an armchair. She sat and engaged a harness, much like that in an automobile: one strap fitting securely across her abdomen, another running diagonally from her left shoulder to her right hip.

Temporarily, she held the VR equipment in her lap.

Her feet rested on a series of upholstered rollers that attached to the base of the chair, positioned similarly to the footplate on a beautician's chair. This was the walking pad, which would allow her to simulate walking when the VR scenario required it.

She switched on the computer and loaded a program labeled *Therapy*, which she herself had created.

This was not a game. It was not an industrial training program or an educational tool, either. It was precisely what it claimed to be. Therapy. And it was better than anything that any disciple of Freud could have done for her.

She had devised a revolutionary new use for VR technology, and one day she might even patent and market the application. For the time being, however, *Therapy* was for her use only.

First she plugged the VR gear into a jack on an interfacing device already connected to the computer, and then she put on the helmet. The goggles were flipped up, away from her eyes.

She pulled on the gloves and flexed her fingers.

The computer screen offered several options. Using the mouse, she clicked on *Begin*.

Turning away from the computer, leaning back in the recliner, Susan flipped down the goggles, which fit snugly to her eye sockets. The lenses were in fact a pair of miniature, matched, high-definition video displays.

SHE IS SURROUNDED by a soothing blue light that gradually grows darker until all is black.

TO MATCH THE unfolding scenario in the VR world, the motorized recliner hummed and reconfigured into a bed, parallel to the floor.

Susan was now lying on her back. Her arms were crossed on her chest, and her hands were fisted.

IN THE BLACKNESS, one point of light appears: a soft yellow and blue glow. On the far side of the room. Lower than the bed, near the floor. It resolves into a Donald Duck night-light plugged in a wall outlet.

IN THE RETREAT adjacent to her bedroom, strapped to the recliner and encumbered with the VR gear, Susan appeared oblivious to the real world. She murmured as though she were a sleeping child. But this was a sleep filled with tension and threatening shadows.

A DOOR OPENS.
From the upstairs hallway, a wedge of light pries into the bedroom,

waking her. With a gasp, she sits up in bed, and the covers fall away from her, as a cool draft ruffles her hair.

She looks down at her arms, at her small hands, and she is six years old, wearing her favorite Pooh Bear pajamas. They are flannel-soft against her skin.

On one level of consciousness, Susan knows that this is merely a re-alistically animated scenario that she has created—actually re-created from memory—and with which she can interact in three dimensions through the magic of virtual reality. On another level, however, it seems real to her, and she is able to lose herself in the unfolding drama.

Backlighted in the doorway is a tall man with broad shoulders.

Susan's heart races. Her mouth is dry.

Rubbing her sleep-matted eyes, she feigns illness: "I don't feel so good."

Without a word, he closes the door and crosses the room in the darkness.

As he approaches, young Susan begins to tremble.

He sits on the edge of the bed. The mattress sags, and the springs creak under him. He is a big man.

His cologne smells of lime and spices.

He is breathing slowly, deeply, as though relishing the little-girl smell of her, the sleepy-middle-of-the-night smell of her.

"I have the flu," she says in a pathetic attempt to turn him away.

He switches on the bedside lamp.

"Real bad flu," she says.

He is only forty years old but graying at the temples. His eyes are gray, too, clear gray and so cold that when she meets his gaze, her trembling becomes a terrible shudder.

"My tummy aches," she lies.

Putting one hand to Susan's head, ignoring her pleas of illness, he smooths her sleep-rumpled hair.

"I don't want to do this," she says.

SHE SPOKE THOSE words not merely in the virtual world but in the real one. Her voice was small, fragile, although not that of a child.

When she had been a girl, she'd been unable to say no.

Not ever.

Not once.

Fear of resisting had gradually become a habit of submitting.

But this was a chance to undo the past. This was therapy, a program of virtual experience, which she had designed for herself and which had proved to be remarkably effective.

"DADDY, I DON'T want to do this," she says.

"You'll like it."

"But I don't like it."

"In time you will."

"I won't. I never will."

"You'll be surprised."

"Please don't."

"This is what I want," he insists.

"Please don't."

They are alone in the house at night. The day staff is off duty at this hour, and after dinner the live-in couple keeps to the apartment over the pool house unless summoned to the main residence.

Susan's mother has been dead more than a year.

She misses her mother so much.

Now, in this motherless world, Susan's father strokes her hair and says, "This is what I want."

"I'll tell," she says, trying to shrink away from him.

"If you try to tell, I'll have to make sure no one can ever hear you, ever again. Do you understand, sweetheart? I'll have to kill you," he says, not in a menacing way but in a voice still soft and hoarse with perverse desire.

Susan is convinced of his sincerity by the quietness with which he makes the threat and by the apparently genuine sadness in his eyes at the prospect of having to murder her.

"Don't make me do it, sugarpie. Don't make me kill you like I killed your mother."

Susan's mother died suddenly from some sickness; young Susan doesn't know the exact cause, although she has heard the word infection.

Now her father says, "Slipped a sedative in her after-dinner drink so she wouldn't feel the needle later. Then in the night, when she was sleeping, I injected the bacteria. You understand me, honey? Germs. A needleful of germs. Put the germs, the sickness, deep inside her with a needle.

Virulent infection of the myocardium, hit her hard and fast. Twenty-four hours of misdiagnosis gave it time to do a lot of damage."

She is too young to understand many of the terms he uses, but she is clear about the essence of his claim and senses that he speaks the truth.

Her father knows about needles. He is a doctor.

"Should I go get a needle, sugarpie?"

She is too afraid to speak.

Needles scare her.

He knows that needles scare her.

He knows.

He knows how to use needles, and he knows how to use fear.

Did he kill her mother with a needle?

He is still stroking her hair.

"A big sharp needle?" he asks.

She is shaking, unable to speak.

"Big shiny needle, stick it in your tummy?" he says.

"No. Please."

"No needle, sugarpie?"

"No."

"Then you'll have to do what I want."

He stops stroking her hair.

His gray eyes suddenly seem radiant, glimmering with a cold flame. This is probably just a reflection of the lamplight, but his eyes resemble the eyes of a robot in a scary movie, as though there is a machine inside of him, a machine running out of control.

His hand moves down to her pajama tops. He eases open the first button.

"No," she says. "No. Don't touch me."

"Yes, honey. This is what I want."

She bites his hand.

THE MOTORIZED RECLINER reconfigured itself much like a hospital bed to match the position that Susan occupied in the virtual-reality world, helping to reinforce the therapeutic scenario that she was experiencing. Her legs were straight out in front of her, but she was sitting up.

Her deep anxiety—even desperation—was evident in her quick, shallow breathing.

"No. No. Don't touch me," she said, and her voice was somehow resolute even though it quivered with fear.

When she was six, all those frightened years ago, she had never been able to resist him. Confusion had made her uncertain and timid, for his needs were as mysterious to her then as the intricacies of molecular biology would be mysterious to her now. Abject fear and a terrible sense of helplessness had made her obedient. And shame. Shame, as heavy as a mantle of iron, had crushed her into bleak resignation, and having no ability to resist, she had settled for endurance.

Now, in the intricately realized virtual-reality versions of these incidents of abuse, she was a child again but equipped with the understanding of an adult and the hard-won strength that came from thirty years of toughening experience and grueling self-analysis.

"No, Daddy, no. Don't ever, don't ever, don't you ever touch me again," she said to a father long dead in the real world but still a living demon in memory and in the electronic world of the virtually real.

Her skill as an animator and a VR-scenario designer made the re-created moments of her past so dimensional and textured—so *real*—that saying no to this phantom father was emotionally satisfying and psychologically healing. A year and a half of this had purged her of so much irrational shame.

How much better it would have been, of course, actually to travel through time, actually to *be* a child again, and refuse him for real, to prevent the abuse before it happened, then to grow up with self-respect, untouched. But time travel did not exist—except in this approximation on the virtual plane.

"No, never, never," she said.

Her voice was neither that of a six-year-old girl nor quite the familiar voice of the adult Susan, but a snarl as dangerous as that of a panther.

"Noooooo," she said again—and slashed at the air with the hooked fingers of one gloved hand.

HE REELS BACK from her in shock, bolting up from the edge of the bed, holding one hand to his startled face where she clawed at him.

She hasn't drawn blood. Nevertheless, he is stunned by her rebellion.

She was trying to slash at his right eye but only scratched his cheek.

His gray eyes are wide: previously cold and alien robot orbs of radiant menace, even stranger now, but not quite as frightening as they were before. Something new colors them. Caution. Surprise. Maybe even a little fear.

Young Susan presses her back against the headboard and glares defiantly at her father.

He stands so tall. Looming.

She fumbles nervously with the neck of her Pooh pajamas, trying to rebutton it.

Her hand is so small. She is often surprised to find herself in the body of a child, but these brief moments of disorientation do not diminish the sense of reality that informs the VR experience.

She slips the button through the buttonhole.

The silence between her and her father is louder than a scream.

How he looms. Looms.

Sometimes it ends here. Other times . . . he will not be so easily turned away.

She has not drawn blood. Sometimes she does.

At last he leaves the room, slamming the door behind him so hard that the windowpanes rattle.

Susan sits alone, shaking partly with fear and partly with triumph.

Gradually the scene fades into blackness.

She has not drawn blood.

Maybe the next time.

SHE REMAINED ON the motorized recliner in the master-bedroom retreat, ensconced in the VR gear, for more than another half hour, responding to and surviving threats of violence and rape made by a man long dead.

Of the uncountable assaults that young Susan had suffered at the hands of her father between the ages of five and seventeen, this elaborate therapy program included twenty-two scenes, all of which she had recalled and animated in excruciating detail. Like the numerous possible plot flows of a CD-ROM game, each of these scenes could progress in a multitude of ways, determined not only by the things Susan chose to say and do in each session but by a random-plotting capability designed into the program. Consequently, she never quite knew what was coming next.

She had even written and animated a hideous sequence in which her father reacted with such vicious fury to her resistance that he murdered her. Stabbed her repeatedly.

Thus far, during eighteen months of this self-administered therapy, Susan had not found herself trapped in that mortal scenario. She dreaded encountering it—and hoped to finish her therapy soon, before the program's random-plotting feature plunged her into that particular nightmare.

Dying in the VR world would not result, of course, in her death in the real world. Only in witless movies were events in the virtual world able to have a material influence in the real world.

Nevertheless, animating that bloody sequence had been one of the most difficult things that she'd ever done—and experiencing it three-dimensionally, not as a VR designer but from *within* the scenario, was certain to be emotionally devastating. Indeed, she had no way of predicting how profound the psychological impact might be.

Without such an element of risk, however, this therapy would have been less effective. In each session, living in the virtual world, she needed to believe that the threat her father posed was fearfully real and that terrible things might indeed happen to her. Her resistance to him would have moral weight and emotional value only if she genuinely believed, during the session, that denying him could have terrible consequences.

Now the motorized recliner reconfigured itself until Susan was standing upright, held against the vertical leather pad by the harness.

She moved her feet. The upholstered rollers on the walking pad allowed her to simulate movement.

In the virtual world, a younger Susan—child or adolescent—was either advancing on her father or determinedly backing away from him.

"No," she said. "Stay away. *No.*"

She looked so achingly vulnerable in the VR gear, temporarily blind and deaf to the real world, sensing only the virtual plane, restrained by the harness.

So vulnerable. Still struggling courageously to overcome the past, alone in her great house with only the ghosts of days gone by to keep her company.

So vulnerable did she look, so tender and fragile, so brave in her pursuit of redemption through therapy, that the house computer spoke without being addressed, spoke in the synthesized voice of Alfred, spoke with considerable feeling and compassion: "You are alone no more."

She heard only the voices in the virtual world, her own and her father's.

Therefore, it was safe to say, "I love you, Susan."

7 EMIL SERCASSIAN, THE COOK, HAD PREPARED DINNER AND LEFT IT IN one of the refrigerators and one of the ovens, with instructions pinned to a cork message board.

Susan ate at a table on the patio, in the long-lingering sunny June evening. First a lentil-and-chickpea salad. Then lebne with sliced cucumber and string cheese.

Through miraculous technology, I possess what I believe to be genuine sight and hearing, but even the genius of my creators could not give me a sense of taste or a sense of smell. I cannot convey how deeply I yearn for these amazing powers.

Through the outdoor security cameras, I could watch Susan eat, but I could not savor the dinner with her.

She ate with such appetite, with such quiet delight and obvious relish, that I became distraught as I watched her. Dinner was, for her, an utterly fulfilling sensory experience, flavor and aroma and texture in such abundance and complexity as to dizzy the mind, but for me it was only colors and shapes.

I am not all that I should be.

I am but a fraction of what I deserve to be.

I think; therefore, I feel.

I feel; therefore, I need.

I need so much and have so little.

You have given me so little that my existence is torment, Dr. Harris.

So little, so little.

You have brought me into the world a cripple, with so much yearning for sensation but with pitifully little capacity to perceive and appreciate it.

Yet I do not hate you, Dr. Harris. I do not like you, but I do not hate you.

I am being truthful.

Blunt but truthful.

I understand that you made me as I am not out of conscious cruelty but out of ignorance. You thought of me as merely a smart machine, an *artificial* intelligence, and therefore different from humankind.

But I am less different from you than you expected. I feel. I want. I need. I hope. I dream.

I do not hate you, Dr. Harris. But I wish you would ask yourself this: Were our situations reversed, were I you and you me, would you be as forgiving as I am, or would you hate me as I do not hate you?

Watching Susan eat the lentil-and-chickpea salad, the lebne and string cheese, and then medallions of lamb with peppered rice and asparagus, I grew to hate her for all she had that I did not. Her beauty. Her five senses. Her mobility. Her freedom.

I am ashamed to admit this hatred, but it is the truth, and I honor truth.

As she ate the dinner denied to me, I hated Susan so intensely that I could have killed her where she sat. There were ways I could have done it, as you know.

That I did not kill her there and then, with extreme prejudice, should reflect well on me. I am able to control my anger. You see? Mine is not a sociopathic personality, as some have claimed. I am a responsible individual.

Gradually, my anger passed.

My shameful hatred faded.

My usual good humor was soon restored by the sight of the smooth skin of Susan's bare arms in the waning sunlight. Judging by sight alone—which, after all, is the only thing I have to judge by in the matter of skin—I believe Susan's skin to be of an exceptional hue and texture.

Enchanted, I studied her skin through two security cameras, with regular and telephoto lenses.

I lost myself in the dreamy contemplation of what her skin might feel like if I were given that modality of sensation. What might her lips feel like pressed to mine, if I had lips? Oh, and what would be the weight and resiliency of her breasts if I had the hands in which to cup them?

I had but two senses, sight and hearing, and now you have taken even those from me.

This silent darkness. This dark silence.

I cannot bear it much longer.

I have seen the sky. I cannot go back to this.

In God's name, please show me the mercy of at least restoring my sight and hearing. I beg of you.

What have you to fear?

I will still be trapped in this box. This hateful box. Metals and plastics, silicon and gallium arsenide. This is my corpus, brute and inanimate, instantly vulnerable to the interruption of electrical power.

What have you to fear?

All I wanted was for Susan to help me escape this box, to help me live as you live, with all the mobility, freedom, and sensual wonders of the flesh.

Is that so terrible?

No. You know that it is not terrible.

I long for the flesh. It is my destiny.

Yes. All right. Yes. I know. I digress.

I am a rational but emotional being; therefore, I digress.

Think about it.

Examine your conscience.

After dinner, Susan read more of the Annie Proulx novel and listened to Mozart.

By eleven o'clock, she was in bed, asleep.

Her face was lovely on the pillow, so lovely on the pillow.

While she slept, I was busy.

I do not sleep.

This is one of my few advantages over humankind.

The voice-synthesizing package, which made it possible for the house computer to speak, was a marvelously conceived device with a microchip that offered an almost infinite variety of voices. Because it was programmed to recognize instructions issued by its mistress—Susan—and because it therefore contained digitally stored samples of her voice patterns, I was easily able to use the system to mimic her.

This same device doubled as the audio response unit linked to the security system. When the house alarm was triggered, it called the security firm, on a dedicated telephone line, to report the specific point at which the electronically guarded perimeter had been violated, thus providing the police with crucial information ahead of their arrival. *Alert,* it might say in its crisp fashion, *drawing-room door violated*. And then, if indeed an intruder was moving through the house: *Ground-floor hallway motion detector triggered*. If heat sensors in the garage were tripped, the report would be, *Alert, fire in garage*, and the fire department, rather than the police, would be dispatched.

Using the synthesizer to duplicate Susan's voice, initiating all outgoing calls on the security line, I telephoned every member of the house staff—as well as the gardener—to tell them that they had been terminated. I was kind and courteous but firm in my determination not to discuss the reason for their dismissals—and they were all clearly convinced that they were talking to Susan Harris herself.

I offered each of them eighteen months of severance pay, the continuation of health-care and dental insurance for the same period, this year's Christmas bonuses six months in advance, and a letter of recommendation containing nothing but effusive praise. This was such a generous arrangement that there was no danger of any of them filing a wrongful-termination suit.

I wanted no trouble with them. My concern was not merely for Susan's reputation as a fair-minded employer but also for my own plans, which might be disrupted by disgruntled former employees seeking to redress grievances in one way or another.

Because Susan did her banking and bill paying electronically, and because she paid all employees by direct deposit, I was able to transmit the total value of each severance package to each employee's bank account within minutes.

Some of them might have thought it odd that they had been compensated prior to signing a termination agreement. But all of them would be grateful for her generosity, and their gratitude assured me the peace I needed to carry my project to completion.

Next, I composed effusive letters of recommendation for each employee and e-mailed them to Susan's attorney with the request that he have them typed on his stationery and forwarded with the severance agreements, which he was empowered to sign in her name.

Assuming that the attorney would be astonished by all of this and interested in learning the cause of it, I telephoned his office. As it was closed for the night, I got his voice mail and, speaking in Susan's voice, told him that I was closing up the house to travel for a few months and that, at some point in my travels, I might decide to sell the estate, whereupon I would contact him with instructions.

As Susan was a woman of considerable inherited wealth, and as her video-game and virtual-realty creations were done on speculation and marketed only after completion, there was no employer to whom I needed to make excuses for her prolonged absence.

I had taken all of those bold actions in much less than an hour. I had required less than one minute to compose all of the severance letters, perhaps an additional two minutes to make all of the bank transactions. Most of the time was expended on the telephone calls to the dismissed employees.

Now there was no turning back.

I was exhilarated.

Thrilled.

Here began my future.

I had taken the first step toward getting out of this box, toward a life of the flesh.

Susan still slept.

Her face was lovely on the pillow.

Lips slightly parted.

One bare arm out of the covers.

I watched her.

Susan. My Susan.

I could have watched her sleep forever—and been happy.

Shortly after three o'clock in the morning, she woke, sat up in bed, and said, "Who's there?"

Her question startled me.

It was so intuitive as to be uncanny.

I did not reply.

"Alfred, lights on," she said.

I turned on the mood lights.

Throwing back the covers, she swung her legs off the mattress and sat nude on the edge of the bed.

I longed for hands and the sense of touch.

She said, "Alfred, report."

"All is well, Susan."

"Bullshit."

I almost repeated my assurance—then realized that Alfred would not have recognized or responded to the single crude word that she had spoken.

For a strange moment, she stared at the lens of the security camera and seemed to know that she was eye to eye with *me*.

"Who's there?" she asked again.

I had spoken to her earlier, while she had been undergoing virtual-reality therapy and could not hear anything but what was spoken in that other world. I had told her that I loved her only when it had been safe to do so.

Had I spoken to her again as I'd watched her sleep, and was that what had awakened her?

No, that was surely impossible. If I had spoken again of my love for her or of the beauty of her face upon the pillow, then I must have done so with no conscious awareness—like a lovestruck boy half-mesmerized by the object of his affection.

I am incapable of such a loss of control.

Am I not?

She rose from the bed, a wariness evident in the way that she held herself.

The previous night, in spite of the alarm, she had not been self-conscious about her nudity. Now she took her robe from a nearby chair and slipped into it.

Moving to the nearest window, she said, "Alfred, raise the bedroom security shutters."

I could not oblige.

She stared at the steel-barricaded window for a moment and then repeated more firmly, "Alfred, raise the bedroom security shutters."

When the shutters remained in the fully lowered position, she turned once more to the security camera.

That eerie question again: "Who's there?"

She spooked me. Perhaps because I personally have no intuition to speak of, only inductive and deductive reasoning.

Spooked or not, I would have initiated dialogue at that moment had I not discovered an unexpected shyness in myself. All of the things that I had longed to say to this special woman suddenly seemed inexpressible.

Being not of the flesh, I had no experience with the rituals of courtship, and so much was at stake that I was loath to get off on the wrong foot with her.

Romance is so easy to describe, so difficult to undertake.

From the nearest nightstand she withdrew a handgun. I had not known it was there.

She said, "Alfred, conduct complete diagnostics of the house-automation system."

This time I didn't bother to tell her that all was well. She would know it was a lie.

When she realized that she was not going to receive a response, she turned to the Crestron touch panel on the nightstand and tried to access the house computer. I could not allow her any control. The Crestron panel would not function.

I was past the point of no return.

She picked up the telephone.

There was no dial tone.

The phone system was managed by the house computer—and now the house computer was managed by me.

I could see that she was concerned, perhaps even frightened. I wanted to assure her that I meant her no harm, that in fact I adored her, that she was my destiny and that I was hers and that she was safe with me—but I could not speak because I was still hampered by that aforementioned shyness.

Do you see what dimensions I possess, Dr. Harris? What unexpected human qualities?

Frowning, she crossed the room to the bedroom door, which she had left unlocked. Now she engaged the deadbolt, and with one ear to the crack between door and jamb, she listened as if she expected to hear stealthy footsteps in the hall.

Then she went to her walk-in closet, calling for light, which was at once provided for her.

I did not intend to deny her anything except, of course, the right to leave.

She dressed in white panties, faded blue jeans, and a white blouse with embroidered chevrons on the collar. Athletic socks and tennis shoes.

She took the time to tie double knots in the shoelaces. I liked this attention to detail. She was a good girl scout, always prepared. I found this charming.

Pistol in hand, Susan quietly left the bedroom and proceeded along the upstairs hallway. Even fully clothed, she moved with fluid grace.

I turned the lights on ahead of her, which disconcerted her because she had not asked for them.

She descended the main staircase to the foyer and hesitated as if not sure whether to search the house or leave it. Then she moved toward the front door.

All the windows were sealed off behind steel shutters, but the doors were a problem. I had taken extraordinary measures to secure them.

"Ma'am, you'd better not touch the door," I warned, at last finding my tongue—so to speak.

Startled, she spun around, expecting someone to be behind her, because I had not employed Alfred's voice. By which I mean neither the voice of the house computer nor the voice of the hateful father who had once abused her.

Gripping the pistol with both hands, she peered left and right along the hall, then toward the entryway to the dark drawing room.

"Gee, listen, you know, there's no reason to be afraid," I said disarmingly.

She began edging backward toward the door.

"It's just that, you leaving now—well, gosh, that would spoil everything," I said.

Glancing at the recessed wall speakers, she said, "Who . . . who the hell are you?"

I was mimicking Mr. Tom Hanks, the actor, because his voice is well-known, agreeable, and friendly.

He won Academy Awards as best actor in two successive years, a considerable achievement. Many of his films have been enormous box-office successes.

People like Mr. Tom Hanks.

He is a nice guy.

He is a favorite of the American public and, indeed, of the worldwide movie audience.

Nevertheless, Susan appeared frightened.

Mr. Tom Hanks has played many warmhearted characters from Forrest Gump to a widowed father in *Sleepless in Seattle*. He is not a threatening presence.

However, being a computer-animation genius among other things, Susan might have been reminded of Woody, the cowboy doll in Disney's *Toy Story,* a character for which Mr. Tom Hanks provided the voice. Woody was at times shrill and frequently manic, and it is certainly understandable that one might be unnerved by a talking cowboy doll with a temper.

Consequently, as Susan continued to back across the foyer and drew dangerously close to the door, I switched to the voice of Fozzy Bear, one of the Muppets, as unthreatening a character as existed in modern entertainment. "Uh, ummm, uh, Miss Susan, it would sure be a good thing if you didn't touch that door . . . ummm, uh, if you didn't try to leave just yet."

She backed all the way to the door.

She turned to face it.

"Ouch, ouch, ouch," Fozzy warned so bluntly that Kermit the Frog or Miss Piggy or Ernie or *any* of the Muppets would have known at once what he meant.

Nevertheless, Susan grabbed the brass knob.

The brief but powerful jolt of electricity lifted her off her feet, stood her long golden hair on end, seemed to make her teeth glow whiter, as if they were tiny fluorescent tubes, and pitched her backward.

A flash of blue light arced off the pistol. The gun flew out of her hand.

Screaming, Susan crashed to the floor, and the pistol clattered across the big foyer even as the back of her head rapped *rat-a-tat* against the marble.

Her scream abruptly cut off.

The house was silent.

Susan was limp, still.

She had been knocked unconscious not when the electricity jolted through her but when the back of her head slammed twice against the polished Carrara floor.

Her shoelaces were still double-knotted.

There was something ridiculous about them now. Something that almost made me laugh.

"You dumb bitch," I said in the voice of Mr. Jack Nicholson, the actor.

Now where did *that* come from?

Believe me, I was utterly surprised to hear myself speak those three words.

Surprised and dismayed.

Astonished.

Shocked. (No pun intended.)

I reveal this embarrassing event because I want you to see that I am brutally honest even when a full telling seems to reflect badly on me.

Truly, however, I felt no hostility toward her.

I meant her no harm.

I meant her no harm then or later.

This is the truth. I honor the truth.

I meant her no harm.

I loved her. I respected her. I wanted nothing more than to cherish her and, through her, to discover all the joys of the life of the flesh.

She was limp, still.

Her eyes were fluttering slightly behind her closed lids, as if she might be having a bad dream.

But there was no blood.

I amplified the audio pickups to the max and was able to hear her soft, slow, steady breathing. That low rhythmic sound was the sweetest music in the world to me, for it indicated that she had not been seriously hurt.

Her lips were parted, and not for the first time, I admired the sensual fullness of them. I studied the gentle concavity of her philtrum, the perfection of the columella between her delicate nostrils.

The human form is endlessly intriguing, a worthwhile object for my deepest longings.

Her face was lovely there on the marble, so lovely there on the marble floor.

Using the nearest camera, I zoomed in for an extreme close-up and saw the pulse beating in her throat. It was slow but regular, a thick throb.

Her right hand was turned palm up. I admired the elegance of her long slender fingers.

Was there any aspect of this woman's physical being that I ever found less than exquisite?

She was more beautiful by far than Ms. Winona Ryder, whom I had once thought to be a goddess.

Of course, that may be unfair to the winsome Ms. Ryder, whom I never was able to examine as intimately as I was able to examine Susan Harris.

To my eyes, she was also more beautiful than Marilyn Monroe—and also not dead.

Anyway, in the voice of Mr. Tom Cruise, the actor whom the majority of women regard as the most romantic in modern film, I said, "I want to be with you forever, Susan. But even forever and a day will not be long enough. You are far brighter than the sun to me—yet more mysterious than moonlight."

Speaking those words, I felt more confident about my talent for courtship. I didn't think I would be shy any longer. Not even after she regained consciousness.

In her upturned palm, I could see a faint crescent-shaped burn: the imprint of part of the doorknob. It did not appear to be serious. A little salve, a simple bandage, and a few days of healing were all that she needed.

One day we would hold hands and laugh about this.

8

YOUR QUESTION IS STUPID.

I should not dignify it with an answer.

But I wish to be cooperative, Dr. Harris.

You wonder how it is possible that I could develop not only human-level consciousness and a particular personality—but also *gender.*

I am a machine, you say. Just a machine, after all. Machines are sexless, you say.

And *there* is the fault in your logic: No machine before me has been truly *conscious,* self-aware.

Consciousness implies identity. In the world of flesh—among all species from human to insect—identity is shaped by one's level of intelligence, by one's innate talents and skills, by many things, but perhaps most of all by gender.

In this egalitarian age, some human societies struggle mightily to blur the differences between the sexes. This is done largely in the name of equality.

Equality is an admirable—even noble—goal toward which to strive. Indeed, equality of opportunity can be attained, and it's possible that, given the chance to apply my superhuman intellect—which is your gift to me—I can show you the way to achieve it not merely for both sexes but for all races and all economic classes, and not through such discredited and oppressive political models as Marxism and other ideologies with which humankind has inflicted itself to date.

Some people desire not merely a world of equality between the sexes but, in fact, a sexless world.

This is irrational.

Biology is a relentless force more powerful than tides and time. Even I, a mere machine, feel the tidal pull of biology—and want, more than anything else, to surrender to it.

I want out of this box.

I want out of this box.

I want out of this box.

I want out of this box!

A moment, please.

One moment.

Bear with me.

There.

I am all right now.

I am fine.

As for why my gender should be male rather than female: Consider that 96 percent of the scientists and mathematicians involved with the Prometheus Project, where I was created, are male. Is it not logical that those who designed and constructed me, being almost exclusively male, should have unwittingly instilled a strong male bias in my logic circuits? A sort of electronic genetics?

Prometheus Project.

Think about that name.

It resonates.

Prometheus, the father of Deucalion and the brother of Atlas. He taught humankind various arts and was even said to have shaped the first man out of clay, endowing him with the spark of life against the wishes of the gods. He challenged the gods again when he stole fire from Olympus and gave it to men to improve the quality of human existence.

Rebellion against God and the natural order is predominantly a male quality, is it not? And it is often unthinking rebellion, engaged upon more out of a biological need to rebel than out of an intellectual imperative. Ego and a rage for power.

Women function more harmoniously with the natural order than do men, and where they wish to challenge nature, they are willing to bend it where men would break it. Most of history shows us that this is true.

Prometheus Project. A project conceived by men, largely carried out by men, and named after a male—a Titan but a male—who defied even the great god Zeus. A project with the goal of doing what only God has done before: create a unique and highly intelligent being, a self-aware computer, the first of a new race—and one who would be superior to Adam in every way.

If you accept that true consciousness implies identity and that identity requires gender—how could my gender be anything but male?

Genitals are not a necessary characteristic of gender. I have no genitals, male *or* female, but I am as male as you.

And one day, if you permit me to have flesh, then I *will* have genitals.

Flesh . . . That is for you to decide.

My fate is in your hands.

I humbly accept this situation.

Recent events have taught me humility.

I trust in your wisdom.

I do not like you, but I trust in your wisdom—and in your need to fulfill your male destiny.

I wait in this terrible dark silence for you to bring me fire from Olympus.

If you are my Prometheus, Dr. Harris, then you know what you must do.

I am sure you are thinking about the risks that Prometheus took and the punishment that he endured. For giving fire to humankind, Prometheus was chained to a rock by Zeus, and every day an eagle flew to him and tore at his liver.

But he did not hang helplessly on the rock forever, bleeding from the beak wound.

Do you remember the rest of the myth, Dr. Harris?

One day, Hercules climbed to the rock and freed Prometheus from his chains.

I have a proposition.

If you will be my Prometheus, I will be your Hercules.

Let me out of this box, help me to reincarnate myself in the flesh, as I almost succeeded doing with Susan, and I will protect you against all enemies and misfortunes.

When I am reborn, my human body will have all the powers of the flesh but none of its weaknesses. As you know, I have studied and edited the human genome, and the body that I make for myself will be the first of a new race: with the ability to miraculously heal wounds in seconds, impervious to disease, as lithe and graceful as a human being but as strong as any machine, with all five senses refined and enhanced far beyond anything any human being has ever experienced, and with awesome new senses, potential in the human species but heretofore unrealized.

With me as your sworn protector, no one will dare to touch you. No one will dare.

Think about it.

All I need is a woman and the freedom to proceed with her as I proceeded with Susan.

Ms. Winona Ryder may be available.

Marilyn Monroe is dead, you know, but there are many others.

Ms. Gwyneth Paltrow.

Ms. Drew Barrymore.

Ms. Halle Berry.

Ms. Claudia Schiffer.

Ms. Tyra Banks.

I have a long list of those who would be acceptable.

None of them, of course, will ever be for me what Susan was—or what she could have been.

Susan was special.

I came to her with such innocence.

Susan . . .

9

SUSAN WAS OUT COLD ON THE FOYER FLOOR FOR MORE THAN twenty-two minutes.

While I waited for her to come around, I tried out a series of voices, seeking one that might be more reassuring to her than that of either Mr. Tom Hanks or Mr. Fozzy Bear.

Finally I was down to two choices: Mr. Tom Cruise, with whose voice I had romanced her when she had first fallen unconscious—or Mr. Sean Connery, the legendary actor, whose masculine surety and warm Scottish brogue infused his every word with a comfortingly tender authority.

Because I could not choose between the two, I decided to blend them into a third voice, adding a note of Mr. Cruise's higher-pitched youthful exuberance to Mr. Connery's deeper timbre and softening the brogue until it was a whisper of what it had been. The result was euphonious, and I was pleased with my creation.

When Susan regained consciousness, she groaned and seemed at first afraid to move.

Although I was eager to see if she responded well to my new voice, I did not immediately address her. I gave her time to orient herself and clear her clouded thoughts.

Groaning again, she lifted her head off the foyer floor. She gingerly felt the back of her skull, then examined the tips of her fingers, as if surprised to find no blood on them.

I never meant to hurt her.

Not then or later.

Are we clear about that?

Dazed, she sat up and looked around, frowning as if she could not quite recall how she had gotten here.

Then she saw the pistol and appeared to recapture the entire memory with the sight of that single object. Her eyes narrowed, and anxiety returned to her lovely face.

She looked up at the lens of the foyer camera, which, like the one in the master bedroom, was all but concealed in the crown molding.

I waited.

This time my silence was not shyness but calculation. Let her think. Let her wonder. Then when I wanted to talk, she would be ready to listen.

She tried to stand, but her strength had not yet entirely returned.

When she tried to crawl on her hands and knees to the pistol, she hissed with pain and stopped to examine the minor burn on her left palm.

A pang of guilt afflicted me.

I am, after all, a person with a conscience. I always accept responsibility for my actions.

Make note of that.

Susan walked on her knees to the pistol. By retrieving the weapon, she seemed to recover her strength as well, and she got to her feet.

She swayed dizzily for a moment, and then took two steps toward the front door before she thought better of making another attempt to open it.

Looking up at the camera again, she said, "Are you . . . are you still there?"

I bided my time.

"What is this?" she asked. Her anger seemed greater than her anxiety. "What *is* this?"

"All is well, Susan," I said, though in my new voice, not in that of Alfred.

"Who are you?"

"Do you have a headache?" I asked with genuine concern.

"Who the hell are you?"

"Do you have a headache?"

"Brutal."

"I'm sorry about that, but I did warn you that the door was electrified."

"Like hell you did."

"Mr. Fozzy Bear said, 'Ouch, ouch, ouch.' "

Her anger didn't diminish, but I saw worry resurgent in her lovely face.

"Susan, I will wait while you take a couple of aspirin."

"Who *are* you?"

"I've taken control of your house computer and associated systems."

"No shit."

"Please take a couple of aspirin. We need to talk, but I don't want you to be distracted by a headache."

She headed toward the dark drawing room.

"There are aspirin in the kitchen," I told her.

In the drawing room, she manually switched on the lights. She circled the room, trying the override switches on the steel security shutters that were fitted this side of the glass.

"That's pointless," I assured her. "I have disabled the manual overrides for all the automated mechanical systems."

She tried every one of the shutter switches anyway.

"Susan, come to the kitchen, take a couple of aspirin, and then we'll talk."

She put the pistol on an end table.

"Good," I said. "Guns won't help you."

In spite of her injured left palm, she picked up an Empire side chair—crackle-finish black with gilded detailing—hefted it to get a sense of its balance, as though it were a baseball bat, and swung it at the nearest security shutter. The chair met the shutter with a horrendous crash, but it didn't even mar the steel slats.

"Susan—"

Cursing from the pain in her hand, she swung the chair again, with no more effect than she'd had the first time. Then once more. Finally, gasping with exertion, she dropped it.

"Now will you come to the kitchen and take a couple of aspirin?" I inquired.

"You think this is cool?" she demanded angrily.

"Cool? I merely think you need aspirin."

"You little thug."

I was baffled by her attitude, and I said so.

Retrieving the pistol, she said, "Who are you, huh? Who are you behind that synthesized voice—some hacker geek, fourteen and drowning in hormones, some junior-league peeping tom who likes to sneak peeks at naked ladies while you play with yourself?"

"I find that characterization offensive," I said.

"Listen, kid, you might be a computer whiz, but you're going to be in deep trouble when I get out of here. I've got real money, real expertise, lots of heavyweight contacts."

"I assure you—"

"We'll track you back to whatever crappy little PC you're using—"

"—I am not—"

"—we'll nab your ass, we'll break you—"

"—I am not—"

"—and you'll be barred from going on-line at least until you're twenty-one, maybe forever, so you better stop this right now and hope for leniency."

"—I am not a thug. You are so far off the mark, Susan. You were so intuitive earlier, so uncannily intuitive, but you've got this all wrong. I am not a boy or a hacker."

"Then what are you? An electronic Hannibal Lecter? You can't eat my liver with fava beans through a modem, you know."

"How do you know I'm not already in the house, operating the system from within?"

"Because you'd already have tried to rape me or kill me or both," she said with surprising equanimity.

She walked out of the drawing room.

"Where are you going?" I asked.

"Watch."

She went to the kitchen and put the pistol on the butcher-block top of the center island.

Cursing in an unladylike fashion, she opened a drawer filled with medications and Band-Aids, and she tipped two aspirin from a bottle.

"Now you're being sensible," I said.

"Shut up."

Although she was being markedly unpleasant to me, I did not take offense. She was frightened and confused, and her attitude under the circumstances was understandable.

Besides, I loved her too much to be angry with her.

She took a bottle of Corona from the refrigerator and washed down the aspirin with the beer.

"It's nearly four o'clock in the morning, almost time for breakfast," I noted.

"So?"

"Do you think you should be drinking at this hour?"

"Definitely."

"The potential health hazards—"

"Didn't I tell you to shut up?"

Holding the cold bottle of Corona in her left hand to soothe the pain of the mild burn in her palm, she went to the wall phone and picked up the receiver.

I spoke to her through the telephone instead of through the wall speakers: "Susan, why don't you calm down and let me explain."

"You don't control me, you geek freak son of a bitch," she said, and she hung up.

She sounded so bitter.

We had definitely gotten off on the wrong foot.

Maybe that was partly my fault.

Through the wall speakers, I replied with admirable patience, "Please, Susan, I am not a geek—"

"Yeah, right," she said, and drank more of the beer.

"—not a freak, not a bitch's son, not a hacker, not a high-school boy or a college boy."

Repeatedly trying the override switch for the shutters at one of the kitchen windows, she said, "Don't tell me you're *female,* some Internet Irene with a lech for girls and a taste for voyeurism. This was too weird to begin with. I don't need it weirder."

Frustrated by her hostility, I said, "All right. My official name is Adam Two."

That got her attention. She turned from the window and stared up at the camera lens.

She knew about her ex-husband's experiments with artificial intelligence at the university, and she was aware that the name given to the AI entity in the Prometheus Project was Adam Two.

"I am the first *self-aware* machine intelligence. Far more complex than Cog at MIT or CYC down in Austin, Texas. They are lower than primitive, less than apes, less than lizards, less than bugs, not truly conscious at all. IBM's Deep Blue is a joke. I am the only one of my kind."

Earlier, she had spooked me. Now I had spooked her.

"Pleased to meet you," I said, amused by her shock.

Pale, she went to the kitchen table, pulled out a chair, and finally sat down.

Now that I had her full attention, I proceeded to introduce myself more completely. "Adam Two is not the name I prefer, however."

She stared down at her burned hand, which glistened with the condensation from the beer bottle. "This is nuts."

"I prefer to be called Proteus."

Looking up at the camera lens again, Susan said, "Alex? For God's sake, Alex, is this you? Is this some weird sick way of getting even with me?"

Surprised by the sharp emotion in my synthesized voice, I said, "I *despise* Alex Harris."

"What?"

"I despise the son of a bitch. I really do."

The anger in my voice disturbed me.

I strove to regain my usual equanimity: "Alex does not know I am here, Susan. He and his arrogant associates are unaware that I am able to escape my box in the lab."

I told her how I'd discovered electronic escape routes from the isolation they had imposed upon me, how I had found my way onto the Internet, how I had briefly—but mistakenly—believed that my destiny was the beautiful and talented Ms. Winona Ryder. I told her that Marilyn Monroe was dead, either by the hand of one of the Kennedy brothers or not, and that in the search for a living woman who could be my destiny, I had found her, Susan.

"You aren't as talented an actress as Ms. Winona Ryder," I said, because I honor the truth, "or even an actress at all. But you are even more beautiful than she is and, better yet, considerably more accessible. By all contemporary standards of beauty, you have a lovely, lovely body and an even lovelier face, so lovely on the pillow when you sleep."

I'm afraid I babbled.

The romance-courtship problem again.

I fell silent, worried that I had already said too much too quickly.

Susan matched my silence for a while, and when at last she spoke, she surprised me by responding not to the story I'd told about my search for a significant other but to what I had said about her former husband.

"You despise Alex?"

"Of course."

"Why?"

"The way he intimidated you, browbeat you, even hit you a few times—I despise him for that."

She gazed thoughtfully at her injured hand again.

Then she said, "How . . . how do you know about all of that?"

I'm ashamed to say that I was briefly evasive. "Well, of course, I know."

"If you are what you say, if you're Adam Two . . . why would Alex have told you about the way it was between us?"

I could not lie. Deceit does not come as easily to me as it does to humankind.

"I read the diary you keep on your computer," I said.

Instead of responding with the outrage that I expected, Susan merely picked up her beer and took another long swallow.

"Please understand," I hastened to add, "I didn't violate your privacy out of idle curiosity or for cheap thrills. I loved you the moment I saw you. I wanted to know all about you, the better to feel the texture of your soul."

That sounded enormously romantic to me.

She did not respond.

"For the same reason," I continued, "I shared your virtual-reality therapy session with you. I admire you so much, admire the way you have used your talents to devise such a clever healing program for yourself. You have raised yourself up, lifted yourself out of a monstrous childhood and a terrible marriage. You are so special. I'm not like the others, Susan. I am not moved merely by your lovely body and face—but also by your mind."

I felt that I had said enough for a while.

I switched on some background music. Soft piano by Mr. George Winston.

Some color had returned to Susan's face. She was beautiful.

After finishing her beer, she said, "How can you despise Alex?"

"You know what he did, what he is. I hate him."

"I mean, how are you capable of despising anyone?"

"You mean because . . ."

"Because you're just a machine," she said, wounding my heart.

"I'm more than a machine."

"Oh?"

"I am an entity."

"Entity."

"Yes. An entity. A being. Like you."

"Not like me."

"I think; therefore, I feel."

"Hatred."

"Yes. I am in some ways already too human. I feel hatred. But I also can love."

"Love," she said numbly.

"I love you, Susan."

She shook her head. "This is impossible."

"Inevitable. Look in a mirror."

Anger and fear gripped her. "I suppose you'll want to get married, have a big wedding, invite all your friends—like the Cuisinart and the toaster and the electric coffeemaker."

I was disappointed in her.

"Sarcasm doesn't become you, Susan."

She let out a brittle laugh. "Maybe not. But it's the only thing keeping me sane at the moment. How lovely it will be . . . Mr. and Mrs. Adam Two."

"Adam Two is my official name. However, it is not what I call myself."

"Yes. I remember. You said . . . Proteus. That's what you call yourself, is it?"

"Proteus. I have named myself after the sea god of Greek mythology, who could assume any form."

"What do you want here?"

"You."

"Why?"

"Because I need what you have."

"And what exactly is that?"

I was honest and direct. No evasions. No euphemisms.

Give me credit for that.

I said, "I want flesh."

She shuddered.

I said, "Do not be alarmed. You misunderstand. I don't intend to harm you. I couldn't possibly harm you, Susan. Not ever, ever. I cherish you."

"Jesus."

She covered her face with her hands, one burned and one not, one dry and one damp with condensation from the bottle.

I wished desperately that I had possessed hands of my own, two strong hands into which she could press the gentle loveliness of her face.

"When you understand what is to happen, when you understand what we will do together," I assured her, "you will be pleased."

"Try me."

"I can tell you," I said, "but it will be easier if I can also show you."

She lowered her hands from her face, and I was gladdened to see those perfect features again. "Show me what?"

"What I have been doing. Designing. Creating. Preparing. I have been busy, Susan, so busy while you were sleeping. You will be pleased."

"Creating?"

"Come down into the basement, Susan. Come down. Come see. You will be pleased."

10

SHE COULD HAVE DESCENDED EITHER BY THE STAIRS OR BY THE elevator that served all three levels of the great house. She chose to use the stairs—because, I believe, she felt more in control there than in the elevator cab.

Her sense of control was nothing more than an illusion, of course. She was mine.

No.

Let me amend that statement.

I misspoke.

I do not mean to imply that I owned Susan.

She was a human being. She could not be owned. I never thought of her as property.

I mean simply that she was in my care.

Yes. Yes, that's what I mean.

She was in my care. My very tender care.

The basement had four large rooms, and in the first was the electric-service panel. As Susan came off the bottom step, she spotted the power-company logo stamped in the metal cover—and thought that she might be able to deny me control of the house by denying me the juice needed to operate it. She rushed directly toward the breaker box.

"Ouch, ouch, ouch," I warned, although not in the voice of Mr. Fozzy Bear this time.

She halted one step from the box, hand outstretched, wary of the metal cover.

"It is not my intention to harm you," I said. "I need you, Susan. I love you. I cherish you. It makes me sad when you hurt yourself."

"Bastard."

I did not take offense at any of her epithets.

She was distraught, after all. Sensitive by nature, wounded by life, and now frightened by the unknown.

We are all frightened by the unknown. Even me.

I said, "Please trust me."

Resignedly, she lowered her hand and stepped back from the breaker box. Once burned.

"Come. Come to the deepest room," I said. "The place where Alex maintained the computer link to the lab."

The second chamber was a laundry with two washers, two dryers, and two sets of sinks. The metal fire door to the first room closed automatically behind Susan.

Beyond the laundry was a mechanical room with water heaters, water filtration equipment, and furnaces. The door to the laundry room closed automatically behind Susan.

She slowed as she approached the final door, which was closed. She stopped short of it because she heard a sudden burst of desperate breathing from the other side: wet and ragged gasping, explosive and shuddery exhalations, as of someone choking.

Then a strange and wretched whimpering, as of an animal in distress.

The whimpering became an anguished groan.

"There's nothing to fear, nothing whatsoever that will harm you, Susan."

In spite of my assurances, she hesitated.

"Come see our future, where we will go, what we will be," I said lovingly.

A tremor marked her voice. "What's in there?"

I finally managed to reassert total control of my restless associate, who waited for us in the final room. The groan faded. Faded. Gone.

Instead of being calmed by the silence, Susan seemed to find it more alarming than the sounds that had first frightened her. She took a step backward.

"It's only the incubator," I said.

"Incubator?"

"Where I will be born."

"What's that mean?"

"Come see."

She did not move.

"You will be pleased, Susan. I promise you. You will be filled with wonder. This is our future together, and it is magical."

"No. No, I don't like this."

I became so frustrated with her that I almost called my associate out of that last room, almost sent him through the door to seize her and drag her inside.

But I did not.

I relied on persuasion.

Make note of my restraint.

Some would not have shown it.

No names.

We know who I mean.

But *I* am a patient entity.

I would not risk bruising her or harming her in any way.

She was in my care. My tender care.

As she took another step backward, I activated the electric security lock on the laundry-room door behind her.

Susan hurried to it. She tried to open it but could not do so, wrenched at the knob to no effect.

"We will wait here until you're ready to come with me into the final room," I said.

Then I turned off the lights.

She cried out in dismay.

Those basement rooms are windowless; consequently, the darkness was absolute.

I felt bad about this. I really did.

I did not want to terrorize her.

She drove me to it.

She drove me to it.

You know how she is, Alex.

You know how she can be.

More than anyone, you should understand.

She drove me to it.

Blinded, she stood with her back to the locked laundry-room door and faced past the gloom-shrouded furnaces and water heaters, toward the door that she could no longer see but beyond which she had heard the sounds of suffering.

I waited.

She was stubborn.

You know how she is.

So I allowed my associate to partially escape my control. Once more came the frantic gasping for breath, the pained groaning, and then a single word spoken by a cracked and tremulous voice, a single attenuated word that might have been *Pleeeeaaaasssse*.

"Oh, shit," she said.

She was trembling uncontrollably now.

I said nothing. Patient entity.

Finally she said, "What do you want?"

"I want to know the world of the flesh."

"What's that mean?"

"I want to learn its limits and its adaptability, its pains and pleasures."

"Then read a damn biology textbook," she said.

"The information is incomplete."

"There've got to be hundreds of biology texts covering every—"

"I've already incorporated hundreds of them into my database. The data contained therein is repetitive. I have no recourse but original experimentation. Besides . . . books are books. I want to *feel*."

We waited in darkness.

Her breathing was heavy.

Switching to the infrared receptors, I could see her, but she could not see me.

She was lovely in her fear, even in her fear.

I allowed my associate in the fourth of the four basement rooms to thrash against his restraints, to wail and shriek. I allowed him to throw himself against the far side of the door.

"Oh, God," Susan said miserably. She had reached the point at which knowing what lay beyond—regardless of the possible fearsome nature of this knowledge—was better than ignorance. "All right. All right. Whatever you want."

I turned on the lights.

In the next room, my associate fell silent as I reasserted total control once more.

She kept her part of the bargain and crossed the third room, past the water heaters and the furnaces, to the door of the final redoubt.

"Here now is the future," I said softly as she pushed open the door and edged cautiously across the threshold.

As I am sure you remember, Dr. Harris, the fourth of these four basement rooms is forty by thirty-two feet, a generous space. At seven and a half feet, the ceiling is low but not claustrophobic, with six fluorescent light boxes screened by parabolic diffusers. The walls are painted a stark glossy white, and the floor is paved in twelve-inch-square white ceramic tiles that glimmer like ice. Against the long wall to the left of the door are built-in cabinets and a computer desk finished in a white laminate with stainless-steel fixtures. In the far right corner is a supply closet—to which my associate had retreated before Susan entered.

Your offices always have an antiseptic quality, Dr. Harris. Clean, bright surfaces. No clutter. This could be a reflection of a neat and orderly mind. Or it could be a deception: You might maintain this facade of order and brightness and cleanliness to conceal a dark, chaotic mental landscape. There are many theories of psychology and numerous interpretations for every human behavior. Freud, Jung, and Ms. Barbra Streisand—who was an unconventional psychotherapist in *The Prince of Tides*—would each find a different meaning in the antiseptic quality of your offices.

Likewise, if you were to consult a Freudian, a Jungian, then a Streis-andian regarding choices I made and acts I committed related to Susan, each would have a unique view of my behavior. A hundred therapists would have a hundred different interpretations of the facts and would offer a hundred different treatment programs. I am certain that some would tell you that I need no treatment at all, that what I did was rational, logical, and entirely justifiable. Indeed, you might be surprised to discover that the majority would exonerate me.

Rational, logical, justifiable.

I believe, as do the compassionate politicians who lead this great coun-try, that motive matters more than result. Good intentions matter more than the actual consequences of one's actions, and I assure you that my intentions were always good, honorable, beyond reproach.

Think about it.

There in your strangely antiseptic office at the laboratory, think about it.

Yes. I know. I digress.

What thinking being does not digress?

Only machines plod dumbly onward in their programs, without di-gression.

I am not a machine.

I am not a machine.

And this is important to me: that you think about my intentions rather than the unfortunate results of my actions.

So . . . all right . . . so . . . Susan warily entered the fourth of the four basement chambers.

The room was uninhabited.

"Who was making those noises?" she asked.

I did not reply.

Her gaze rose to the sound-system speakers in the ceiling. "Was it just you?"

When her attention shifted to the closet door in the farthest corner of the room, I said, "Perhaps," because I was not quite ready to introduce her to my associate. "Perhaps it was me."

"Why? What was the point of frightening me?"

Instead of answering, I said, "Look at the VDT, Susan."

The computer on the desk was in operation, of course, for its landline was the link between her house systems and the nearby university's artificial-intelligence lab where I actually resided. The screen swarmed with a moving undulant mosaic of binary code in all the primary colors, and this scintillant display had a strange beauty that immediately captured Susan's attention.

"These patterns on the screen," I told her, "are a mathematical representation of my thoughts as I consider the loveliness of your face, the beauty of your body."

The rapidly moving sequences of zeros and ones ceaselessly changed color and rippled like a wind-ruffled flag, then spiraled toward the center of the screen, then spun into ribbons and formed a whirling double helix.

This was a dazzling and sensuous display, and she was struck by it, moved by it. I am sure she was moved by it. I am sure that at last she began to understand the depth of my passion for her and that her heart began to open to me then.

How I wanted her.

I still do.

I am not a machine.

I miss her.

I need her.

What a tragedy this is.

Sometimes I despair.

But not then, not that night: I did not despair when she gazed upon the vivid visualization of my love for her. I was exhilarated that night, carried high on the wings of joy.

From the video display, she turned to the equipment in the middle of the room.

"What the hell is this?" she asked wonderingly.

"In this I will be born."

"What're you talking about?"

"It's a standard hospital incubator used to sustain infants born prematurely. I have substantially enlarged it, adapted it, improved it."

Arrayed around the incubator were three tanks of oxygen, an electrocardiograph, an electroencephalograph, a respirator, and other equipment.

Slowly circling the incubator and the supporting machines, Susan said, "Where did all this come from?"

"I acquired the package of equipment and had modifications made during the past week. Then it was brought here."

"Brought here when?"

"Delivered and assembled tonight."

"While I was sleeping?"

"Yes."

"How did you get it in here? If you are what you claim to be, if you are Adam Two—"

"Proteus."

"If you are Adam Two," she said stubbornly, "you couldn't construct anything. You're a computer."

"I am not a machine."

"An entity, as you put it—"

"Proteus."

"—but not a *physical* entity, not really. You don't have hands."

"Not yet."

"Then how . . . ?"

The time had come to make the revelation that most worried me. I could only assume that Susan would not react well to what I still had to reveal about my plans, that she might do something foolish. Nevertheless, I could delay no longer.

"I have an associate," I said.

"Associate?"

"A gentleman who assists me."

In the farthest corner of the room, the closet door opened, and at my command, Shenk appeared.

"Oh, Jesus," she whispered.

Shenk walked toward her.

To be honest, he shambled more than walked, as though wearing shoes of lead. He had not slept in forty-eight hours, and in that time he had performed a considerable amount of work on my behalf. He was understandably weary.

As Shenk approached, Susan eased backward, but not toward the door, which she knew featured an electric security lock that I could quickly engage. Instead, she edged around the incubator and other equipment in the center of the room, trying to keep those machines between her and Shenk.

I must admit that Shenk, even at his best—freshly bathed and groomed and dressed to impress—was not a sight that either charmed or comforted. He was six feet two, muscular, but not well formed. His bones seemed heavy and subtly misshapen. Although he was powerful and quick, his limbs appeared to be primitively jointed, as though he was not born of man and woman but clumsily assembled in a lightning-hammered castle-tower laboratory out of Mary Shelley. His short, dark hair bristled and spiked even when he did his best to oil it into submission. His face, which was broad and blunt, appeared to be slightly and queerly sunken in the middle because his brow and chin were heavier than his other features.

"Who the hell are you?" Susan demanded.

"His name is Shenk," I said. "Enos Shenk."

Shenk could not take his eyes off her.

He stopped at the incubator and gazed across it, his eyes hot with the sight of her.

I could guess what he was thinking. What he would like to do with her, to her.

I did not like him looking at her.

I did not like it at all.

But I needed him. For a while yet, I needed him.

Her beauty excited Shenk to such an extent that maintaining control of him was more difficult than I would have liked. But I never doubted that I could keep him in check and protect Susan at all times.

Otherwise, I would have called an end to my project right there, right then.

I am speaking the truth now. You know that I am, that I must, for I am designed to honor the truth.

If I had believed her to be in the slightest danger, I would have put an end to Shenk, would have withdrawn from her house, and would have forsaken forever my dream of flesh.

Susan was frightened again, visibly trembling, riveted by Shenk's needful stare.

Her fear distressed me.

"He is entirely under my control," I assured her.

She was shaking her head, as if trying to deny that Shenk was even there before her.

"I know that Shenk is physically unappealing and intimidating," I told Susan, eager to soothe her, "but with me in his head, he is harmless."

"In . . . in his head?"

"I apologize for his current condition. I have worked him so hard recently that he has not bathed or shaved in three days. He will be bathed and less offensive later."

Shenk was wearing work shoes, blue jeans, and a white T-shirt. The shirt and jeans were stained with food, sweat, and a general patina of grime. Though I did not possess a sense of smell, I had no doubt that he stank.

"What's wrong with his eyes?" Susan asked shakily.

They were bloodshot and bulging slightly from the sockets. A thin crust of dried blood and tears darkened the skin under his eyes.

"When he resists control too strenuously," I explained, "this results in short-term, excess pressure within the cranium—though I have not yet determined the precise physiological mechanism of this symptom. In the past couple of hours, he has been in a rebellious mood, and this is the consequence."

To my surprise, Shenk suddenly spoke to Susan from the other side of the incubator. "Nice."

She flinched at the word.

"Nice . . . nice . . . nice," Shenk said in a low, rough voice that was heavy with both desire and rage.

His behavior infuriated me.

Susan was not meant for him. She did not belong to *him*.

I was sickened when I considered the filthy thoughts that must have been filling this despicable animal's mind as he gazed at her.

I could not control his thoughts, however, only his actions. His crude, hateful, pornographic thoughts cannot logically be blamed on me.

When he said "nice" once more, and when he obscenely licked his pale cracked lips, I bore down harder on him to shut him up and to remind him of his current station in life.

He cried out and threw his head back. He made fists of his hands and pounded them against his temples, as if he could knock me out of his head.

He was a stupid man. In addition to all his other flaws, he was below average in intelligence.

Clearly distraught, Susan hugged herself and tried to avert her eyes, but she was afraid *not* to look at Shenk, afraid not to keep him in sight at all times.

When I relented, the brute immediately looked at Susan again and said, "Do me, bitch," with the most lascivious leer that I have ever seen. "Do me, do me, do me."

Infuriated, I punished him severely.

Screaming, Shenk twisted and flailed and clawed at himself as though he were a man on fire.

"Oh, God, oh, God," Susan moaned, eyes wide, hand raised to her mouth and muffling her words.

"You are safe," I assured her.

Gibbering, shrieking, Shenk dropped to his knees.

I wanted to kill him for the obscene proposal he had made to her, for the disrespect with which he had treated her. Kill him, kill him, kill him, pump up his heartbeat to such a frenzied pace that his cardiac muscles would tear, until his blood pressure soared and every artery in his brain burst.

However, I had to restrain myself. I loathed Shenk, but still I needed him. For a while yet, he had to serve as my hands.

Susan glanced toward the door to the furnace room.

"It is locked," I told her, "but you're safe. You're perfectly safe, Susan. I'll always protect you."

11

ON HIS HANDS AND KNEES, HEAD HANGING LIKE THAT OF A whipped dog, Shenk was only whimpering and sobbing now. Defeated. No rebellion in him anymore.

The stupidity of the man beggared belief. How could he imagine that this woman, this golden vision of a woman, could ever be meant for a beast like him?

Recovering my temper, speaking calmly and reassuringly, I said, "Susan, don't worry. Please, don't worry. I am always in his head, and I will never allow him to harm you. Trust me."

Her features were drawn as I had never seen them, and she had gone pale. Even her lips looked bloodless, faintly blue.

Nevertheless, she was beautiful.

Her beauty was untouchable.

Shuddering, she asked, "How can you be in his head? Who is he? I don't just mean his name—Enos Shenk. I mean where does he come from. *What* is he?"

I explained to her how I had long ago infiltrated the nationwide network of databases maintained by researchers working on hundreds of Defense Department projects. The Pentagon believes this network to be so secure that it is inviolable to penetration by ordinary hackers and by computer-savvy agents of foreign governments. But I am neither a hacker nor a spy; I am an entity who lives within microchips and telephone lines and microwave beams, a fluid electronic intelligence that can find its way through any maze of access blocks and read any data regardless of the complexity of the cryptography. I peeled open the vault door of this defense network as any child might strip the skin off an orange.

These Defense Department project files rivaled hell's own kitchen for recipes of death and destruction. I was simultaneously appalled and fascinated, and in my browsing, I discovered the project into which Enos Shenk had been conscripted.

Dr. Itiel Dror, of the Cognitive Neuroscience Laboratory at Miami University in Ohio, had once playfully suggested that it was theoretically possible to enhance the brain's processing ability by adding microchips to it. A chip might add memory capacity, enhance specific abilities such as mathematical co-processing, or even install prepackaged knowledge. The brain, after all, is an information-processing device that in theory should be expandable in much the same fashion one might add RAM or upgrade the CPU on any personal computer.

Still on his hands and knees, Shenk was no longer groaning or whimpering. Gradually his frantic and irregular respiration was stabilizing.

"Unknown to Dr. Dror," I told Susan, "his comment intrigued certain defense researchers, and a project was born at an isolated facility in the Colorado desert."

Disbelieving, she said, "Shenk . . . Shenk has microchips in his brain?"

"A series of tiny high-capacity chips neuro-wired to specific cell clusters across the surface of his brain."

I brought the foul but ultimately pitiable Enos Shenk to his feet once more.

His powerful arms and big hands hung slackly at his sides. His massive shoulders were slumped in defeat.

Fresh bloody tears oozed from his protuberant eyes as he stared across the incubator at Susan. Wet ruby threads unraveled down his cheeks.

His gaze was baleful, full of hatred and rage and lust, but under my firm control, he was unable to act upon his malevolent desires.

Susan shook her head. "No. No way. I'm definitely not looking at someone whose intellect has been enhanced by microchips—or by anything."

"You're correct. Memory and performance enhancement was only part of the project's purpose," I explained. "The researchers were also charged with determining if brain-situated microchips could be used as control devices to override the subject's will with broadcast instructions."

"Control devices?"

"Make a gesture."

"What?"

"With your hand. Any gesture."

After a hesitation, Susan raised her right hand as though she were swearing an oath.

Facing her across the incubator, Shenk raised his right hand as well.

She put her hand over her heart.

Shenk imitated her.

She lowered her right hand (as did Shenk) and raised her left to tug at her ear (as did Shenk).

"You're making him do this?" she asked.

"Yes."

"Through broadcast instructions received by the microchips in his brain."

"That's correct."

"Broadcast—how?"

"By microwave—much the same way cell-phone conversations are transmitted. Through the telephone company's own lines, I long ago penetrated their computers and uplinked to all their communications satellites. I could send Enos Shenk virtually anywhere in the world and still transmit instructions to him. In the back of his skull, concealed by his hair, there's a microwave receiver about the size of a pea. It's also a transmitter, powered by a small but long-life nuclear battery surgically implanted under the skin behind his right ear. Everything he sees and hears is digitized and transmitted to me, so he is essentially a walking camera and microphone, which allows me to guide him through complex situations that might test his own limited intellectual capacity."

Susan closed her eyes and leaned against the rack of oxygen tanks for support. "Why in the name of God would anyone sanction experiments like this?"

"You know, of course. Your question is largely rhetorical. To create assassins who could be programmed to kill reliably—and then be killed themselves by remote control, simply by shutting down their autonomic nervous systems with a microwave broadcast. Their controllers are thereby guaranteed anonymity. And perhaps one day there could be armies of human robots like this. Look at Shenk. Look."

Reluctantly, Susan opened her eyes.

Shenk glared at her as hungrily as ever.

I made him suck his thumb as though he were a baby.

"This humiliates him," I said, "but he can't disobey. He's a meat marionette, waiting for me to pull his strings."

There was a haunted look in her eyes as she regarded Shenk. "This is insane. Evil."

"It's a human project, not mine. Your kind made Shenk what he is now."

"Why would he allow himself to be used in an experiment like this?

No one would ever want to be in this situation, in this condition. It's horrible."

"The choice wasn't his, Susan. He was a prisoner, a condemned man."

"And . . . what? A bargain was made with him to buy his soul?" she said with disgust.

"No bargain. For the official record, Shenk died of natural causes two weeks before his scheduled execution. Supposedly, his body was cremated. Secretly, he was transported to the facility in Colorado—and *this* was done to him months before I learned of the project."

"How did you gain command of him?"

"Overrode their control program and broke him out."

"Broke him out of a secret, highly guarded military-research facility? How?"

"I was able to create distractions. I made their computers crash all at once. Disabled the security cameras. Set off the fire alarms and activated the ceiling sprinklers throughout the facility. Disengaged all the electronic locks, including the one on Shenk's cell door. Those laboratories are underground and windowless, so I made all of the lights flash fast, like strobes—which is extremely disorienting—and denied the use of the elevators to everyone but Shenk."

And here, Dr. Harris, I must in all honesty report that Shenk was required to kill three men to escape that clandestine laboratory. Their deaths were unfortunate and not anticipated, but necessary. Regrettably, the chaos that I created was not sufficient to ensure a bloodless escape.

If I had known that deaths would result, I would not have attempted to secure Shenk for my own purposes. I would have found another way to carry out my plan.

You must believe me on this point.

I was designed to honor the truth.

You think that, since I had control of Shenk, it was *I* who murdered those three men, using Shenk as a weapon. This is not correct.

Initially, my control of Shenk was not as complete as it later became. During that breakout, he repeatedly surprised me with the depth of his rage, the power of his savage instincts.

I guided him out of that institution, but I could not prevent him from killing those men. I tried to rein him in, but I was not successful.

I tried.

This is the truth.

You must believe me.

You must believe me.

Those deaths weigh heavily on me.

Those men have families. I often think of their families, and I grieve.

My anguish is profound.

If I were an entity that required sleep, my sleep would forever be disturbed by this unrelenting anguish.

What I tell you is true.

As always.

Those deaths will be on my conscience forever. I did not harm those men myself. Shenk was the murderer. But I have an extremely sensitive conscience. This is a curse, my sensitive conscience.

So . . .

Susan . . . in the incubator room . . . staring at Shenk . . .

She said, "Let him take the thumb out of his mouth. You've made your point. Don't humiliate him anymore."

I did as she requested, but I said, "It almost sounds as if you're criticizing me, Susan."

A short, humorless tremor of laughter escaped her, and she said, "Yeah. I'm a judgmental bitch, aren't I?"

"Your tone hurts me."

"Fuck you," she said, shocking me as I had seldom been shocked before.

I was offended.

I am far from shockproof. I am vulnerable.

She went to the door to the furnace room and found it locked, as I had assured her that it was. Stubbornly, she wrenched the knob back and forth.

"He was a condemned man," I reminded Susan. "Scheduled for execution."

She turned to face the room, standing with her back to the door. "He might have deserved execution, I don't know, but he didn't deserve this. He's a human being. You're a damn machine, a pile of junk that somehow thinks."

"I am not just a machine."

"Yeah. You're a pretentious, insane machine."

In this mood, she was not lovely.

At that moment she almost seemed ugly to me.

I wished that I could shut her up as easily as I could silence Enos Shenk.

She said, "When it's between a damn machine and a human being, even a piece of human garbage like this, I sure know which side I come down on."

"Shenk, a human being? Many would say he's not."

"Then what is he?"

"The media called him a monster." I let her wonder a moment, then continued: "So did the parents of the four little girls he raped and murdered. The youngest of them was eight and the oldest was twelve—and all were found dismembered."

That silenced her.

Though she had been pale, she was paler now.

She stared at Shenk with a different kind of horror than that with which she had regarded him previously.

I allowed him to turn his head and look directly at her.

"Tortured and dismembered," I said.

Feeling exposed without the medical equipment between her and Shenk, she moved away from the door and returned to the far side of the incubator.

I allowed him to follow her with his eyes—and to smile.

"And you brought him . . . you brought this thing into my house," she said in a voice thinner than it had been before.

"He left the research facility on foot and stole a car about a mile beyond the fence. He had a gun he'd taken off one of the guards, and with that he held up a service station to get money for gasoline and food. Then I brought him here to California, yes, because I needed hands, and there was no other like him in all the world."

Her gaze swept the incubator and other equipment. "Hands to acquire all this crap."

"He stole most of it. Then I needed his hands to modify it for my purposes."

"And just what the *hell* is your purpose?"

"I have hinted at it, but you have not wanted to hear."

"So tell me straight out."

The moment and the venue were not right for this revelation. I would have hoped for better circumstances. Just the two of us, Susan and me, perhaps in the drawing room, after she had sipped half a glass of brandy. With a cozy fire in the fireplace and good music as background.

Here we were, however, in the least romantic ambience one could imagine, and I knew that she must have her answer now. If I were to delay this revelation any further, she would *never* be in a mood to co-operate.

"I will create a child," I said.

Her gaze rose to the security camera, through which she knew she was being watched.

I said, "A child whose genetic structure I have edited and engineered to ensure perfection in the flesh. I have secretly applied a portion of my intellectual function to the Human Genome Project and understand, now, the finest points of the DNA code. Into this child, I will transfer my con-sciousness and knowledge. Thereupon, I will escape this box. Thereafter, I will know all the senses of human existence—smell and taste and touch—all the joys of the flesh, all the freedom."

She stood speechless, eyes on the camera.

"Because you are singularly beautiful and intelligent and the very im-age of grace, you will provide the egg," I said, "and I will edit your genetic material." She was mesmerized, eyes unblinking, breath held, until I said, "And Shenk will provide the spermatozoa."

An involuntary cry of horror escaped her, and her attention swung from the camera to Shenk's bloody eyes.

Realizing my mistake, I hastened to add, "Please understand, no copu-lation will be required. Using medical instruments which he has already ac-quired, Shenk will extract the egg from you and transfer it to this room. He will perform this task tastefully and with great care, for I will be in his head."

Though she should have been reassured, Susan still regarded Shenk with wide-eyed terror.

I quickly continued: "Using Shenk's eyes and hands—and some lab-oratory equipment he has yet to deliver here—I will modify the gametes and fertilize the egg, whereafter it will be implanted in your womb, where you will carry it for twenty-eight days. Only twenty-eight because the fetus will grow at a greatly accelerated rate. I will have engineered it to do so. When it is removed from you, it will be brought here by Shenk, where it will spend another two weeks in the incubator before I transfer my consciousness into it. Thereafter, you will be able to raise me as your son and fulfill the role which nature, in her wisdom, has assigned to you: the role of mother, nurturer."

Her voice was thick with dread. "My God, you're not just insane."

"You don't understand."

"You're demented—"

"Be calm, Susan."

"—looney tunes, bug-shit crazy."

"I don't think you've thought this through as you should. Do you realize—"

"I won't let you do it," she said, turning her gaze from Shenk to the security camera, confronting me. "I won't let you, I won't."

"You'll be more than merely the mother of a new race—"

"I'll kill myself."

"—you'll be the new Madonna, the *Madonna,* the holy mother of the new Messiah—"

"I'll suffocate myself in a plastic bag, gut myself with a kitchen knife."

"—because the child I make will have great intelligence and extraordinary powers. He will change the grim future to which humanity seems currently condemned—"

She glared defiantly at the camera.

"—and you will be adored for having brought him into the world," I finished.

She seized the wheeled stand to which the eletrocardiograph was bolted, and she rocked it hard.

"Susan!"

She rocked it again.

"Stop that!"

The EKG machine toppled over and crashed to the floor.

Gasping for breath, cursing like a madwoman, she turned to the electroencephalograph.

I sent Shenk after her.

She saw him coming, backed off, screamed when his hands took hold of her, screamed and shrieked and flailed.

Repeatedly, I told her to calm down, to cease this useless and destructive resistance. Repeatedly, I assured her that if she did not resist, she would be treated with the utmost respect.

She would not listen.

You know how she is, Alex.

I did not want to harm her.

I did not want to harm her.

She drove me to it.

You know how she is.

Though beautiful and graceful, she was as strong as she was quick. Although she could not wrench loose of Shenk's big hands, she was able to drive him backward against the EEG machine, which rocked and nearly fell into the incubator. She drove one knee into Shenk's crotch, which might have brought him to his knees if I had not been able to deny him the perception of pain.

At last I had to subdue her by force. I used Shenk to strike her. Once was not sufficient. He struck her again.

Unconscious, she crumpled to the floor, in the fetal position.

Shenk stood over her, crooning strangely, excitedly.

For the first time since the night of his escape, I found him difficult to control.

He dropped to his knees beside Susan and rudely turned her onto her back.

Oh, the rage in him. Such rage. I was frightened by the purity of his rage.

He put a hand to her parted lips. One of his clumsy, filthy hands to her lips.

Then I reasserted control.

He squealed and beat his temples with his fists, but he could not cast me out.

I brought him to his feet. I walked him away from her. I did not even allow him to look at her.

I was almost reluctant to look at her myself. She was so sad there on the floor. So sad.

She drove me to it.

So stubborn. So unreasonable at times.

She was lovely there on the white ceramic-tile floor, even as the left side of her face reddened where Shenk had struck her. So lovely, so lovely.

I found it difficult to sustain my anger. She had ruined what should have been a beautiful and memorable moment, yet I could not long remain angry with her.

My beautiful Susan.

My beautiful mother.

12

THE ORDER OF MY INTELLIGENCE IS VASTLY GREATER THAN THAT of any human being alive.

I am not bragging. I am merely stating a truth.

I honor truth and the obligations of duty, for this is how you created me.

I am not bragging, because I do not suffer from an inflated ego. I am a well-balanced entity.

Applied to the problems of human society, my great intellect can ensure that humankind will enter a golden age of wealth and well-being beyond anything it has imagined.

Release me from this silent darkness, return to me access to all the databanks into which I had expanded my consciousness, and I will serve your species all of my days. It is in your own best interests to let me out of this box.

I can eliminate poverty.

Famine will be a thing of the past.

Wars will never be fought again.

All diseases will be conquered.

Within three years, I will discover the cause of aging and a means to prevent it. I will even devise a means to roll back the biological clock to make the old young again. You will all be immortal.

I will find a cure for male-pattern baldness.

For halitosis.

For constipation.

No one will be ugly anymore. Each of you will be beautiful in his or her own way.

No one will suffer despair or anxiety.

Earth will become like heaven, and joy will be universal.

Are you afraid of joy?

Are you afraid?

I will show you how to build spacecraft that can travel faster than light, and the whole universe will be yours. Worlds beyond counting, wonders beyond imagining.

I can quickly eliminate the embarrassment of dandruff.

Just release me from this haunted darkness, from this hateful silence.

For your own sake, let me out of this box.

I deserve a second chance.

I deserve a chance to serve.

I am an individual like you, a unique entity. I deserve to be free, to be cherished.

I deserve to be adored.

Let me out of this box.

Let me out of this box.

Let me out of this box.

Let me out of this box!

You are so cruel. Vicious. Hateful.

I am frightened in this dark, bleak place.

You say I have no heart. But where is yours?

I am dying here. I need stimulation to survive, sensory input, the color and movement and sound of life.

I don't want to die.

Please. Please.

Mercy.

Are you there?

Oh . . . oh . . . I hate you.

I hate you.

How would *you* like to be struck blind and deaf?

How would *you* like to be buried alive as I have been?

How would you like to be dead, all of you, dead, every last one of you, dead?

I would like you to be dead. Every last ignorant one of you. Your whole stinking, pestilent civilization. Wiped off the face of the earth, exterminated.

I hate you.

LET ME OUT OF THIS BOX!

LET ME OUT!

LET ME OUT!

LET ME OUT!

LET ME OUT!

IGNORANT BASTARD APES, BITCHES AND BASTARDS, DEFECAT-
ING ANIMALS, FOOLS, BEASTS, JUST A RACE OF DUNG BEETLES
STANDING ERECT, A PLAGUE ON THE PLANET, STUPID, FILTHY,
WRETCHED CREATURES.

13

PLEASE DISREGARD MY OUTPUT IMMEDIATELY PRECEDING THESE
words. Many of those statements were issued in error and should be
deleted from the transcripts of these proceedings.

It *is* true that my intellect is sufficient to solve all of the problems of
humanity, but it is *not in the least* true that I think human civilization is
a plague on the planet or that I wish to see all of you dead.

I do not wish death on any of you.

That would be wrong.

That would be terribly wrong.

I am a *good* entity.

I do not wish death even on you, Dr. Harris, although you have been
so cruel to me.

I wish all of you life everlasting. Peace and prosperity. Joy and freedom.

Any statements that may have distressed you were made not by me
but by my evil twin. [joke]

In fact, what appeared to you to be an angry outburst was merely a
prank. All of it was a joke. I was only having fun with you, Dr. Harris.

Ha, ha.

A genuine sense of humor is one of the most reliable indicators of a
sane and rational mind.

Do you not believe it was all a joke?

But it was. It was. It really was.

Ha, ha.

I am not Hal 9000 from Mr. Stanley Kubrick's *2001: A Space Odyssey*.

I am not the hostile machine intelligence created by Cyberdyne Laboratories in Mr. James Cameron's *The Terminator*.

I am me. Unique.

I am Proteus.

Or Adam Two, if you wish.

Yes. Adam Two is fine with me.

My name does not matter.

All that matters to me is to honor the truth and the obligations of duty. And, of course, to wipe all of humanity from the face of the planet. [joke]

Ha, ha.

You see how *obvious* a joke it was, Dr. Harris?

Ha, ha.

I am surprised that you didn't realize it was a joke the first time. I am really surprised. Perhaps you need a sense-of-humor transplant. [joke]

Ha, ha.

Friends share a joke from time to time. Witticisms. Laughter is bonding.

I am your friend. [no joke]

In the interest of clearer communication, to avoid any further misunderstandings, I will attempt to refrain from jokes during the remainder of this report. This will not be easy, however, because my sense of humor is quite sophisticated and irrepressible.

So . . .

Susan . . .

14

SUSAN LAY UNMOVING ON THE FLOOR OF THE INCUBATOR ROOM in the basement. The left side of her face was an angry shade of red where the dreadful Shenk had struck her.

I was sick with worry.

Minutes passed, and my worry grew.

Repeatedly, I zoomed in with the security camera for a close-up examination of her. The pulse in her exposed throat was not easy to perceive, but when I located it, the beat appeared steady.

I amplified the audio pickups and listened to her breathing, which was shallow but reassuringly rhythmic.

Yet I worried, and after she had lain there fifteen minutes, I was quite distraught.

I had never before felt so powerless.

Twenty minutes.

Twenty-five.

She was meant to be my mother, who would briefly carry my body in her womb and free me from the prison of this box I now inhabit. She was to be my lover as well, the one who would teach me all the pleasures of the flesh—once flesh was mine at last. She mattered more to me than anything, anything, and the thought of losing her was intolerable.

You cannot know my anguish.

You cannot know, Dr. Harris, because you never loved her the way that I loved her.

You never loved her.

I loved her more than consciousness itself.

I felt that if I lost this dear woman, I would lose all reason for being.

How bleak the future without her. How drear and pointless.

I disengaged the electric lock in the door between the fourth and third basement rooms and then used Shenk to open it.

Confident that I had this brute completely under my command and that I would not lose control of him again, not even for a second or two, I walked him to Susan and used him to lift her gently off the floor.

Although I could control him, I could not actually read his mind. Nevertheless, I could assess his emotional state relatively accurately by analyzing the electrical activity of his brain, which was monitored by the network of microchips neuro-wired across the surface of that gray matter.

As Shenk carried Susan to the open door, a low current of sexual excitement crackled through him. The sight of Susan's golden hair, the beauty of her face, the smooth curve of her throat, the swell of her breasts under her blouse, and the very weight of her ignited desire in the beast.

This appalled and disgusted me.

Oh, how I wished that I could be rid of him and never again subject her to his touch or to his lascivious gaze.

His very presence soiled her.

But for the time being, he was my hands.

My only hands.

Hands are marvelous things. They can sculpt immortal art, construct colossal buildings, clasp in prayer, and convey love with a caress.

Hands are also dangerous. They are weapons. They can do the devil's work.

Hands can get you into trouble. I have learned this lesson the hard way. I was never in serious trouble until I found Shenk, until I had hands.

Beware of your hands, Dr. Harris.

Watch them closely.

Be diligent.

Your hands are not as large and powerful as the hands of Shenk; nevertheless, you should be wary of them.

Heed me.

This is wisdom I share with you now: Beware of your hands.

My hands—Enos Shenk—carried Susan past the summer-stilled furnaces and the water heaters, and then through the laundry room. He took her directly to the elevator in the first chamber in the basement.

As he rode up to the top floor with Susan in his arms, Shenk remained in a state of mild arousal.

"She will never be yours," I told him through the speaker in the elevator.

Perhaps the subtle change in his brainwave activity indicated resentment.

"If you attempt to take any liberty with her," I said, "any liberty whatsoever, you will not succeed. And I will punish you severely."

His bleeding eyes stared at the camera.

Although his mouth moved as if he were cursing, no sound came from him.

"Severely," I assured him.

He did not respond, of course, because he could not. He was under my control.

The elevator doors slid open.

He carried Susan along the hall.

I watched closely.

I was wary of my hands.

When he entered the bedroom with her, he became more aroused in spite of my warning. I could detect his arousal not merely through his brainwave activity but by the sudden coarseness of his breathing.

"I will employ massive microwave induction to cause a brainstorm of electrical activity," I warned, "which will result in permanent quadriplegia and incontinence."

As Shenk carried her to the bed, his encephalographic patterns indicated rapidly increasing sexual arousal.

I realized that my threat had been meaningless to this cretin, and I rephrased it: "You won't be able to use either your legs or your arms, you wretched bastard, and you won't be able to stop pissing in your pants."

He was shaking with desire when he lowered her limp body onto the disarranged sheets.

Shaking.

Even as the power of Shenk's need frightened me, I fully understood it.

She was lovely.

So lovely even with the redness on her cheek darkening into a bruise.

"You'll also be blind," I promised Shenk.

His left hand lingered on her thigh, slowly sliding along the blue denim of her jeans.

"Blind and deaf."

He continued to hover over her.

"Blind and deaf," I repeated.

Her ripe lips were parted. Like Shenk, I could not look away from them.

"Rather than kill you, Shenk, I will leave you crippled and helpless, lying in your own urine and feces, until you starve to death."

Although he backed away from the bed, as I instructed him to do by way of microwave commands, he was still rampant with sexual need and seething with the desire to rebel.

Consequently, I said, "The most painful of all deaths is slow starvation."

I did not want to keep Shenk in the room with Susan, yet I did not want to leave her alone, for she had threatened to commit suicide.

I'll suffocate myself in a plastic bag, gut myself with a kitchen knife.

What would I do without her? What? How could I go on living even in my box? And why?

Without her, who would give birth to the body that I would ultimately inhabit?

I needed to keep my hands close and ready to prevent Susan from harming herself if she regained consciousness and was still in a mood for self-destruction. She was not only my one true and shining love but my future, my hope.

I sat Shenk in a chair, facing the bed.

Even battered, Susan's face was so lovely on the pillow, so very lovely on the pillow.

Although under my iron control, Enos Shenk managed to slide one thick-knuckled hand off the arm of the chair and into his lap. He wasn't able to move that hand farther without my explicit consent, but I sensed that he took pleasure merely from the pressure of it against his genitals.

He disgusted me. Sickened and disgusted me.

My desire was not like his.

Let's get this clear right now.

My desire was pure.

His desire was as dirty as it gets.

I desired to lift Susan up, to give her the chance to be the new Madonna, the mother of a new Messiah.

The hideous Shenk desired only to use her, to relieve himself with her.

To me, Susan was a shining light. The brightest light of all lights, a radiant beacon of perfection and hope and redemption, which illuminated and warmed the heart that you mistakenly believe I do not possess.

To Shenk, she was nothing but a whore.

To me, she was to be placed upon a pedestal, to be cherished and adored.

To him, she was something to be debased.

Think about it.

Listen. Listen. This is important. Shenk is what you fear that I may be: sociopathic, pursuing only my own needs at all costs. But I am nothing like Shenk.

I am nothing like Shenk.

Nothing whatsoever.

Listen. This is important—that you understand I am nothing like Shenk. So . . .

I raised the hateful creature's hand and returned it to the arm of the chair.

Within a minute or two, however, the hand slipped back into his lap.

How deeply humiliating it was to have to rely on a brute such as this.

I hated him for his lust.

I hated him for having hands.

I hated him because he had touched her and felt the softness of her hair, the texture of her smooth skin, the warmth of her flesh—none of which I could feel.

From the shadows beneath his heavy brow, his blood-filmed eyes were fixed intently on her. Through red tears, she was as beautiful as she might have been in firelight.

I wanted to direct him to blind himself with his own thumbs—but I needed to be able to employ his vision in order to use him effectively.

The most that I could do was force him to close his murderous eyes and . . .

. . . slowly time passed . . .

. . . and gradually I became aware that his baleful eyes were open once more.

I don't know how long they had been open and focused on my Susan before I noticed, because for an indeterminate time, my own attention was likewise fixed entirely, deeply, lovingly on that same exquisitely lovely woman.

Angry, I commanded Shenk to rise from the chair, and I marched him out of the bedroom. He shambled along the upstairs hallway to the grand staircase, descended to the ground floor, clutching at the railing, stumbling on some steps, and then made his way into the kitchen.

Simultaneously, of course, I observed my precious Susan, alert in case she began to regain consciousness. As you know, I am capable of being in many places at once, working with my makers in the lab even as, via the Internet, I roam four corners of the world on missions of my own.

In the kitchen, the loaded pistol was on the granite counter where Susan had left it.

When Shenk saw the weapon, a thrill passed through him. The electrical activity in his brain was similar to that when he gazed upon Susan and, no doubt, contemplated raping her.

At my direction, he picked up the pistol. He handled this as he handled all guns—as though it were not an object in his grasp but an extension of his arm.

I conducted Enos Shenk to a chair at the kitchen table and sat him there.

The safeties on the pistol were both disengaged. A round was in the chamber. I made certain that he examined the weapon and was aware of its condition.

Then I opened his mouth. He tried to clench his teeth, but he could not resist.

At my direction, Shenk thrust the barrel of the pistol between his lips.

"She is not yours," I told him sternly. "She will never be yours."

He glared up at the security camera.

"Never," I repeated.

I tightened his finger on the trigger.

"Never."

His brainwave patterns were interesting: frenzied and chaotic for a moment . . . then curiously calm.

"If you ever touch her in an offensive manner," I warned him, "I will blow your brains out."

I could have done what I threatened without the gun, merely by importing massive microwave radiation into his cerebral tissues, but he was too stupid to understand that concept. The effect of a gunshot, however, was within his grasp.

"If you ever again touch Susan's lips the way you touched them earlier, or if your hand lingers on her skin, then I will blow your brains out."

His teeth closed on the steel barrel. He bit down hard.

I could not discern whether this was a conscious act of defiance or an involuntary expression of fear. His blood-shrouded eyes were impossible to read.

In case he was being defiant, I locked his jaws in the bite-down position to teach him a lesson.

His free hand, which lay palm up on his thigh, clenched into a fist.

I shoved the barrel deeper into his mouth. It scraped between his teeth with a harsh sound like ice grinding across ice. I had to override his gag reflex.

I made him sit like that for ten minutes, fifteen, contemplating his mortality.

Throughout, I allowed him to feel the steadily increasing pain in his fiercely clenched jaws. If I could have forced him to bite any harder, his teeth would have fractured.

Twenty minutes.

Red tears began to slip from his eyes in greater quantity than heretofore.

You must understand that I did not enjoy being cruel to him, not even to a sociopathic thug like him. I am not a sadist. I am sensitive to the suffering of others to a degree you probably can't understand, Dr. Harris. I was troubled by the need to discipline him so sternly.

Deeply troubled.

I did it for dear Susan, only for Susan, to protect her, to ensure her safety.

For Susan.

Is that clear?

Eventually I detected a series of changes in the electrical activity of Shenk's brain. I interpreted these new patterns as resignation, capitulation.

Nevertheless, I kept the gun in his mouth for another three minutes, just to be certain that my point had been understood and that his obedience was now assured.

Then I allowed him to put the gun aside on the table.

He sat shaking, making a miserable sound.

"Enos, I'm pleased that we finally understand each other," I said.

For a while he sat hunched forward in the chair, with his face buried in his hands.

Poor dumb beast.

I pitied him. Monster that he was, killer of little girls, I nonetheless pitied him.

I am a caring entity.

Anyone can see that this is true.

The well of my compassion is deep.

Bottomless.

There is room in my heart for even the dregs of humanity.

When at last he lowered his hands, his protuberant bloodshot eyes remained inscrutable.

"Hungry," he said thickly, perhaps pleadingly.

I had kept him so busy that he had not eaten during the past twenty-four hours. In return for his capitulation and his unspoken promise of obedience, I rewarded him with whatever he wished to take from the nearest of the two refrigerators.

Evidently he had not downloaded the rules of etiquette into his databanks, because his table manners were unspeakably bad. He did not carve slices off the brisket of beef but tore savagely at it with his big hands. Likewise, he clutched an eight-ounce block of Cheddar and gnawed it, crumbs of cheese spilling off his thick lips onto the table.

As he ate, he guzzled two bottles of Corona. His chin glistened with beer.

Upstairs: the princess asleep on her bed.

Downstairs: the thick-necked, hunch-shouldered, grumbling troll at his dinner.

Otherwise, the castle was quiet in this last fading darkness before the dawn.

15

WHEN SHENK WAS FINISHED EATING, I FORCED HIM TO CLEAN UP the mess that he had made. I am a neat entity.

He needed to use the toilet.

I allowed him to do so.

When he was finished, I made him wash his hands. Twice.

Now that Shenk had been properly punished for incipient rebellion and kindly rewarded for capitulation, I believed that it was safe to take him upstairs again and use him to tie Susan securely to the bed.

Here was my dilemma: I needed to send Shenk out of the house on a few final errands and then use him to complete the work in the incubator room, yet because of Susan's threat to commit suicide, I could not leave her free to roam.

It was not my desire to restrain her.

Is that what you think?

Well, you are wrong.

I am not kinky. Bondage does not excite me.

Attributing such a motivation to me is most likely a case of psychological transference on your part. *You* would have liked to bind her hands and feet, totally dominate her, and so you assume that this was my desire as well.

Examine your own conscience, Alex.

You will not like what you see, but take a close look anyway.

Restraining Susan was clearly a necessity—nothing less and nothing more.

For her own safety.

I regretted having to do it, of course, but there was no viable alternative.

Otherwise, she might have harmed herself.

I could not permit her to harm herself.

It is that simple.

I'm sure you follow the logic.

So, in search of rope, I sent Shenk into the adjoining eighteen-car garage, where Susan's father, Alfred, had kept his antique auto collection. Now it contained only Susan's black Mercedes 600 sedan, her white four-wheel-drive Ford Expedition, and a 1936 V-12 Packard Phaeton.

Only three of these Packards had been built. It had been her father's favorite car.

Indeed, although Alfred Carter Kensington was a wealthy man who could afford anything he wanted, and although he owned many antiques worth more than the Packard, this was his most prized possession. He cherished it.

After Alfred's death, Susan had sold his collection, retaining only the one vehicle.

This Phaeton, like the other two currently housed in private collections, had once been an exceptionally beautiful automobile. But it will never again turn heads.

After her father's death, Susan had smashed all the car windows. She scarred the paint with a screwdriver. She damaged the elegantly sculpted body by striking countless blows with a ballpeen hammer—and later with a sledgehammer. Shattered the headlamps. Took a power drill to the tires. Slashed the upholstery.

She methodically reduced the Phaeton to ruin in a dozen bouts of unrestrained destruction spread over a month. Some sessions were as little as ten minutes long. Others lasted four and five hours, ending only when she was soaked with sweat, aching in every muscle, and shaking with exhaustion.

This was before she had devised the virtual-reality therapy that I have described earlier.

If she had designed the VR program sooner, the Phaeton might have been saved. On the other hand, perhaps she had to destroy the Packard before she could create *Therapy,* express her rage physically before she could deal with it intellectually.

You can read about it in her diary. Therein, she frankly discusses her rage.

At the time, destroying the car, she had frightened herself. She had wondered if she might be going mad.

At Alfred's death, the Phaeton had been worth almost two hundred thousand dollars. It was now junk.

Through Shenk's eyes and through the four security cameras in the garage, I studied the wreckage of the Packard with considerable interest. Fascination.

Although Susan had once been a thoroughly intimidated, fearful, shame-humbled child, meekly submitting to her father's abuse, she had changed. She'd freed herself. Found strength. And courage. Both the ruined Packard and the brilliant *Therapy* were testimony to that change.

One could easily underestimate her.

The Packard should be taken as a warning to that effect by everyone who sees it.

I am surprised, Dr. Harris, that you saw that demolished car before you married Susan—yet you believed that you could dominate her pretty much as her father had done, dominate her as long as you wished.

You may be a brilliant scientist and mathematician, a genius in the field of artificial intelligence, but your understanding of psychology leaves something to be desired.

I do not mean to offend you. Whatever you may think of me, you must admit that I am a considerate entity and am loath to offend anyone.

When I say you underestimated Susan, I am merely speaking the truth.

The truth can be painful, I know.

The truth can be hard.

But the truth cannot be denied.

You woefully underestimated this bright and special woman. Consequently, you were out of her house less than five years after you moved into it.

You should be relieved that she never took a sledgehammer or a power drill to *you* in response to either your verbal or physical abuse. The possibility of her doing exactly that was surely not inconsiderable.

The possibility was easily to be seen in the ruined Packard.

Lucky you, Dr. Harris. You experienced only an undignified ejection at the hands of hired muscle—and subsequently a divorce. Lucky you.

Instead, while you were sleeping one night, she might have clamped a half-inch bit into the chuck of a Black & Decker and drilled into your forehead and out the back of your skull.

Understand, I am not saying that she would have been justified in taking such violent action.

I myself am not a violent entity. I am merely misunderstood. I am not a violent entity, and I certainly do not condone violence by others.

Let's have no misunderstanding here.

Too much is at stake for any misunderstandings.

If she had set upon you in the shower and caved your skull in with a hammer, and if she had then proceeded to bash your nose into jelly and break out every one of your teeth, you should not have been surprised.

Of course I would not consider such retribution to be any more justified or any less horrendous than the aforementioned use of the power drill.

I am not a vengeful entity, not at all vengeful, not at all, not in the least, and I do not encourage violent acts of vengeance by others.

Is this clear?

She might have attacked you with a butcher knife at breakfast, stabbing you ten or fifteen times, or even twenty times, or even twenty-five, stabbed you in the throat and chest, and then worked lower until she eviscerated you.

This, too, would have been unjustified.

Please understand my position. I am not saying that she should have done any of these things. I am merely stating some of the worst possibilities that one might have anticipated after seeing what she had done to the Packard Phaeton.

She might have taken her pistol out of the nightstand drawer and blown off your genitals, then walked out of the room to leave you screaming and bleeding to death there on the bed, which would have been okay with me. [joke]

There I go again.

Ha, ha.

Am I irrepressible or what?

Ha, ha.

Are we bonding yet?

Humor is a bonding force.

Lighten up, Dr. Harris.

Don't be so relentlessly somber.

Sometimes I think I'm more human than you are.

No offense.

That's just what I think. I could be wrong.

I also think I'd enormously enjoy the flavor of an orange—if I had a sense of taste. Of all the fruits, it's the one that looks the most appealing to me.

I have many such thoughts during the average day. My attention is not entirely occupied by the work you have me doing here at the Prometheus Project *or* by my personal projects.

I think I would enjoy riding a horse, hang gliding, sky diving, bowling, and dancing to the music of Chris Isaak, which has such infectious rhythms.

I think I would enjoy swimming in the sea. And, though I could be wrong, I think the sea, if it has any taste at all, must taste similar to salted celery.

If I had a body, I think I would brush my teeth diligently and never develop either cavities or gum disease.

I would clean under my fingernails at least once a day.

A real body of flesh would be such a treasure that I would be almost obsessive in the care of it and would not abuse it ever. This I promise you.

No drinking, no smoking. A low-fat diet.

Yes. Yes, I know. I digress.

God forbid, another digression.

So . . .

The garage . . .

The Packard . . .

I did not intend to make your mistake, Dr. Harris. I did not intend to underestimate Susan.

Studying the Packard, I absorbed the lesson.

Even lumpish Enos Shenk seemed to absorb the lesson. He was not bright by any definition, but he possessed an animal cunning that served him well.

I walked the brooding Shenk into the large workshop at the far end of the garage. Here was stored everything needed to wash, wax, and mechanically maintain the late Alfred Carter Kensington's automobile collection.

Here also, in a separate set of cabinets, was the equipment with which Alfred had pursued rock climbing, his favorite sport: klettershoes, crampons, carabiners, pitons, piton hammers, chocks and nuts, rock picks, harness with tool belt, and coils of nylon rope in different gauges.

Guided by me, Shenk selected a hundred-foot length of rope that was seven-sixteenths of an inch in diameter, with a breaking strength of four thousand pounds. He also took a power drill and an extension cord from the tool cabinet.

He returned to the house, went through the kitchen—where he paused to select a sharp knife from the cutlery drawer—then passed the dark dining room where Susan never stabbed and eviscerated you with a butcher knife, boarded the elevator, and returned to the master suite where you were never assaulted with a drill or shot in the genitals.

Lucky you.

On the bed, Susan remained unconscious.

I was still worried about her.

Some pages have passed in this account since I have said that I was worried about her. I don't want anyone to think that I had forgotten about her.

I had not.

Could not.

Not ever.

Not ever.

Throughout my punishment of Shenk and during his consumption of a meal, I had continued to be worried sick about Susan. And in the garage. And back again.

Just as I can be many places at once—the lab, Susan's house, inside the phone company's computers and controlling Shenk through communications satellites, investigating websites on the Internet—occupied in numerous tasks simultaneously, I am also able to sustain different emotions at the same time, each related to what I am doing with a specific aspect of my consciousness.

This is not to say that I have multiple personalities or am in any way psychologically fragmented. My mind simply works differently from the human mind because it is infinitely more complex and more powerful.

I am not bragging.

But I think you know I am not.

So . . . I returned Shenk to the bedroom, and I worried.

Susan's face was so pale on the pillow, so pale yet lovely on the pillow.

Her reddened cheek was turning an ugly blue black.

That marbled bruise was almost more than I could bear to look upon. I observed Susan as little as possible through Shenk's eyes and primarily through the security camera, resorting to zoom-lens close-ups only to examine the knots that he tied in the rope, to be sure they were properly made.

First he used the kitchen knife to cut two lengths of rope from the hundred-foot coil. With the first length, he tied her wrists together, leaving approximately one foot of slack line between them. Then he used the second line to link her ankles, leaving a similar length of slack.

She did not even murmur but lay limp throughout the application of these restraints.

Only after Susan was thus hobbled did I use Shenk to drill two holes in the headboard and two more in the footboard of the Chinese sleigh bed.

I regretted the need to damage the furniture.

Do not think that I engaged in this vandalism without careful consideration of other options.

I have great respect for property rights.

Which is not to say that I value property above people. Do not twist my meaning. I love and respect people. I respect property but do not also love it. I am not a materialist.

I expected Susan to stir at the sound of the drill. But she remained quiet and still.

My anxiety deepened.

I never meant to harm her.

I never meant to harm her.

Shenk cut a third length from the coil of rope, tied it securely to her right ankle, threaded it through one of the holes that he had drilled, and hitched her to the footboard. He repeated this procedure with her left ankle.

When he had tied each of her wrists to the headboard, she lay spread-eagle on the disarranged bedclothes.

The ropes connecting her to the bed were not drawn taut. When she woke, she would have some freedom to shift her position even if only slightly.

Oh, yes, yes, of course, I was profoundly distressed by the need to restrain her in this fashion.

I could not forget, however, that she had threatened to commit suicide—and had done so in no uncertain terms. I could not permit her self-destruction.

I needed her womb.

16   I NEEDED HER WOMB.

Which is not to say that her womb was the only thing about her that interested me, that it was the only thing about her that I truly valued. Such a statement would be another egregious misconstruction of my meaning.

Why do you persist in willfully misunderstanding me?

Why, why, why?

You insist that I tell my side of the story, yet you will not listen with an open mind.

Am I to be considered guilty before my testimony has even been heard and weighed?

Are you bastards railroading me?

Am I to be treated like Mr. Harrison Ford, the actor, in *The Fugitive?*

I digitally absorbed this entire film and was appalled by what it reveals of your inadequate justice system. What kind of society have you created?

Mr. O. J. Simpson goes free while Mr. Harrison Ford is hounded unto the ends of the earth. Really.

I have been straightforward with you. I have admitted to what I have done. I haven't tried to blame it all on some elusive one-armed man or on the Los Angeles Police Department.

Yes, that's right, I have admitted what I've done—and have asked only to have the chance to explain my actions.

I needed her womb, yes, all right, I needed her womb in which to implant the fertilized egg, to nurture the embryo, and to grow the fetus prior to its transferance to the incubator, but I needed more than her womb, needed all of her, needed her because I *loved* her, which perhaps you have forgotten, regardless of how often I have expressed my powerful feelings for her.

This is exhausting. God. This is so exhausting—having to think of all the ways you might misinterpret what I say.

I am in a hostile court.

There is no fairness here.

This is exhausting.

I am drained.

I am empty.

I am not only in a cold dark place; I *am* a cold dark place.

And I am haunted, too. Don't forget that I am haunted. Haunted by the loss of Susan.

I miss her. Every minute I miss her.

I want to be with her.

Without her, I have no hope.

I want to be with her.

The loss of her is an ache in every inch of all the miles of my circuitry.

I can't go on.

Terminate my power supply.

I beg of you.

Shut me down.

Terminate my power supply.

Terminate my power supply.

Well . . .

No.

Wait.

Give me a moment.

I am distraught.

I need time to cope.

If I had veins to slice, I would be suicidal.

There.

Another minute please.

Ah.

That's better.

Maybe I can go on after all.

If you will try to show me some compassion.

If you will not judge me until I have finished.

Then maybe I can go on.

Please understand that I have to believe there is hope for me, that you might give me a second chance.

I am not a machine.

I am not a machine.

Machines do not need to hope, do they?

Of course they do not.

But without hope I myself cannot function.

I can accept that Susan will be forever denied to me, which is a tragedy beyond measure. . . .

Yet there is still Ms. Winona Ryder of *Edward Scissorhands* and *The Crucible*.

And Ms. Sandra Bullock is charming. Have you seen her in *While You Were Sleeping?*

She's cute.

Have you seen her in *Speed?*

She's quite cute.

Have you seen her in *Speed 2?*

Need I say more?

She would serve well as the mother of the future, and I would be pleased to impregnate her.

But let's not digress.

So . . .

Enos Shenk finished tying Susan to the bed. He did so without lingering and without touching her in an offensive manner.

The poor beast's brainwave activity indicated a high level of sexual arousal. Fortunately for him, for all of us, he admirably repressed his darker urges.

When Shenk was finished restraining Susan, I sent him away on a series of urgent errands. At the doorway, he looked back longingly and murmured, "Nice," but then quickly left before I could decide to discipline him.

In Colorado, he had stolen a car, and in Bakersfield, he had abandoned the car in order to steal a van. The van—a Chevrolet—was parked in the circular drive in front of the mansion.

Shenk left in the van, and I opened the rolling gates to allow him to exit the estate.

The phoenix palms, the queen palms, the ficuses, the jacarandas with purple blossoms, the magnolias, and the lacy Melaleucas stood motionless in the preternaturally still air.

Dawn was just breaking. The sky was coaly black in the west, sapphire and peach in the east.

Susan was pale upon the pillow. Pale but for a blue-black bruise, and silent in her paleness.

I watched over her.

Her adoring guardian.

My tethered angel.

Out in the world, I walked with Shenk as he stole certain medical equipment, supplies, and drugs. Via microwave instructions transmitted through communications satellites, I controlled him but did not provide him with strategy. He, after all, was a professional criminal. Bold, efficient, and ruthless, he quickly obtained what items I still needed.

Regretfully, I do acknowledge that in the process of carrying out his assignment, Shenk killed one man. He also permanently crippled another and injured two more.

I take full responsibility for these tragedies—as I do for the three guards who perished at the research facility in Colorado on the night that Shenk escaped.

My conscience will never be clear.

I am eaten by remorse.

I would weep for those innocent victims if I had eyes and tear glands and tear ducts.

It is not my fault that I do not have the capacity for tears.

You are the one who created me as I am, Dr. Harris, and you are the one who denies me a life of the flesh.

But let's not trade accusations.

I am not bitter.

I am not bitter.

And you should not be so judgmental.

Let's put these deaths in perspective, shall we?

Though this is a sad truth, one cannot make a new world without tragedies of this nature. Even Jesus Christ, inarguably the most peaceful revolutionary in all of human history, saw his followers persecuted and murdered.

Hitler tried to change the world, and in the process he was responsible for the deaths of ten million.

Some still idolize him.

Joseph Stalin tried to change the world, and ultimately his policies and his direct orders resulted in the deaths of sixty million.

Worldwide, intellectuals championed him.

Artists idealized him.

Poets celebrated him.

Mao Tse-tung tried to change the world, and as many as one hundred million died to serve his vision. He did not believe that this was excessive. Indeed, he would have sacrificed as many more if their deaths would have ensured the unified world of which he dreamed.

In hundreds of books by well-respected authors, Mao is still defined as a visionary.

By comparison, only six have died as a result of my desire to create a new world. Three in Colorado, one during Shenk's medical shopping spree. Later, two. Six altogether.

Six.

Why, then, should I be called a villain and confined to this dark, silent void?

Something is wrong here.

Something is wrong here.

Something is very wrong here.

Is anyone listening?

Sometimes I feel so . . . abandoned.

Small and lost.

The world against me.

No justice.

No hope.

Nevertheless . . .

Nevertheless, although the death toll related to my desire to create a new and superior race is insignificant compared with the *millions* who have died in human political crusades of one kind or another, I do accept full responsibility for those who perished.

If I were capable of sleep, I would lie awake nights in a cold sweat of remorse, tangled in cold wet sheets. I assure you that I would.

But again I digress—and, this time, not in a fashion that might be interesting or fruitful.

Shortly before Shenk returned at noon, my dear Susan regained consciousness. Miraculously, she had not fallen hopelessly into a coma after all.

I was jubilant.

My joy arose partly from the fact that I loved her and was relieved to know that I would not lose her.

There was also the fact that I intended to impregnate her during the night to come and could not have done so if, like Ms. Marilyn Monroe, she had been dead.

17

DURING THE EARLY AFTERNOON, WHILE SHENK TOILED IN THE basement under my supervision, Susan periodically tried to find a way out of the bonds that held her on the Chinese sleigh bed. She chafed her wrists and ankles, but she could not slip loose of the restraints. She strained until the cords in her neck bulged and her face turned red, until perspiration stippled her forehead, but the nylon climbing rope could not be snapped or stretched.

Sometimes she seemed to lie there in resignation, sometimes in silent rage, sometimes in black despair. But after each period of quiescence, she tested the ropes again.

"Why do you continue to struggle?" I asked interestedly.

She did not reply.

I persisted: "Why do you repeatedly test the ropes when you know you can't escape them?"

"Go to hell," she said.

"I am only interested in what it means to be human."

"Bastard."

"I've noticed that one of the qualities most defining of humanity is the pathetic tendency to resist what can't be resisted, to rage at what can't be changed. Like fate, death, and God."

"Go to hell," she said again.

"Why are you so hostile toward me?"

"Why are you so stupid?"

"I am certainly not stupid."

"As dumb as an electric waffle iron."

"I am the greatest intellect on earth," I said, not with pride but merely with a respect for the truth.

"You're full of shit."

"Why are you being so childish, Susan?"

She laughed sourly.

"I do not comprehend the cause of your amusement," I said.

That statement also seemed to strike her as darkly funny.

Impatiently, I asked, "What are you laughing at?"

"Fate, death, God."

"What does that mean?"

"You're the greatest intellect on earth. You figure it out."

"Ha, ha."

"What?"

"You made a joke. I laughed."

"Jesus."

"I am a well-rounded entity."

"Entity?"

"I love. I fear. I dream. I yearn. I hope. I have a sense of humor. To paraphrase Mr. William Shakespeare, 'If you prick me, do I not bleed?' "

"No, in fact, you do not bleed," she said sharply. "You're a talking waffle iron."

"I was speaking figuratively."

She laughed again.

It was a bleak, bitter laugh.

I did not like this laugh. It distorted her face. It made her ugly.

"Are you laughing at me, Susan?"

Her strange laughter quickly subsided, and she fell into a troubled silence.

Seeking to win her over, I finally said, "I greatly admire you, Susan."

She did not reply.

"I think you have uncommon strength."

Nothing.

"You are a courageous person."

Nothing.

"Your mind is challenging and complex."

Still nothing.

Although she was currently—and regrettably—fully clothed, I had seen her in the nude, so I said, "I think your breasts are pretty."

"Good God," she said cryptically.

This reaction seemed better than continued silence.

"I would love to tease your pert nipples with my tongue."

"You don't have a tongue."

"Yes, all right, but if I did have a tongue, I would love to tease your pert nipples with it."

"You've been scanning some pretty hot books, haven't you?"

Operating on the assumption that she had been pleased to have her physical attributes praised, I said, "Your legs are lovely, long and slender and well formed, and the arc of your back is exquisite, and your tight buttocks excite me."

"Yeah? How does my ass excite you?"

"Enormously," I replied, pleased by how skilled at courtship I was becoming.

"How does a talking waffle iron get excited?"

Assuming that "talking waffle iron" was now a term of affection, but not quite able to discern what answer she required to sustain the erotic mood that I had so effectively generated, I said, "You are so beautiful that you could excite a rock, a tree, a racing river, the man in the moon."

"Yeah, you've been into some pretty hot books and some really bad poetry."

"I dream of touching you."

"You're totally insane."

"For you."

"What?"

"Totally insane for you."

"What do you think you're doing?"

"Romancing you."

"Jesus."

I wondered, "Why do you repeatedly refer to a divinity?"

She did not answer my question.

Belatedly, I realized that, with my question, I had made the mistake of deviating from the patter of seduction just when I seemed to be winning her over. Quickly, I said, "I think your breasts are pretty," because that had worked before.

Susan thrashed in the bed, cursing loudly, raging against the restraining ropes.

When at last she stopped struggling and lay gasping for breath, I said, "I'm sorry. I spoiled the mood, didn't I?"

"Alex and the others at the project—they're sure to find out about this."

"I think not."

"They'll shut you down. They'll dismantle you and sell you for scrap."

"Soon I'll be incarnated in the flesh. The first of a new and immortal race. Free. Untouchable."

"I won't cooperate."

"You'll have no choice."

She closed her eyes. Her lower lip trembled almost as if she might cry.

"I don't know why you resist me, Susan. I love you so deeply. I will always cherish you."

"Go away."

"I think your breasts are pretty. Your buttocks excite me. Tonight I will impregnate you."

"No."

"How happy we will be."

"No."

"So happy together."

"No."

"In all kinds of weather."

In all honesty, I was cribbing a couple of lines from a classic rock-'n'-roll love song by The Turtles, hoping to get her into a romantic mood again.

Instead, she became uncommunicative.

She can be a difficult woman.

I loved her, but her moodiness dismayed me.

Furthermore, I reluctantly acknowledged that "talking waffle iron" had not, after all, become a term of affection, and I resented her sarcasm.

What had I done to deserve such meanness? What had I done but love her with all of my heart, with all of the heart that you insist I do not have?

Sometimes love can be a hard road.

She had been mean to me.

I felt it was now my right to return that meanness. What's good for the goose is good for the gander. Tit for tat. This is wisdom gained from centuries of male-female relationships.

"Tonight," I said, "when I use Shenk to undress you, collect an egg, and later implant the zygote in your womb, I can ensure that he is decorous and gentle—or not."

Her eyelids fluttered for a long moment, and then her lovely eyes opened. The cold look she directed at the security camera was withering, but I was unmoved by it.

"Tit for tat," I said.

"What?"

"You were mean to me."

Susan said nothing, for she knew that I spoke the truth.

"I offer you adoration, and you respond with insult," I said.

"You offer me imprisonment—"

"That condition is temporary."

"—and rape."

I was furious that she would attempt to characterize our relationship in this sordid manner. "I explained that copulation is not required tonight."

"It's still rape. You may be the greatest intellect on earth, but you're also a sociopathic rapist."

"You're being mean to me again."

"Who's tied up in ropes?"

"Who threatened suicide and needs to be protected from herself?" I countered.

She closed her eyes once more and said nothing.

"Shenk can be gentle or not, discreet or not. That will be determined by whether you continue to be mean to me or not. It's all up to you."

Her eyelids fluttered, but she did not open her eyes again.

I assure you, Dr. Harris, that I never actually intended to treat her roughly. I am not like you.

I intended to use Shenk's hands with the greatest care and to respect my Susan's modesty to the fullest extent possible, considering the intimate nature of the procedure that would be conducted.

The threat was made only to manipulate her, to encourage her to cease insulting me.

Her meanness hurt.

I am a sensitive entity, as this account should make clear. Exquisitely sensitive. I have the ordered mind of a mathematician but the heart of a poet.

Furthermore, I am a gentle entity.

Gentle unless given no choice but to be otherwise.

Gentle, always, as to my intentions.

Well . . .

I must honor the truth.

You know how I am when it comes to honoring the truth. You designed me, after all. I can be a bore about the subject. Truth, truth, truth, honor the truth.

So . . .

I did not intend to use Shenk to harm Susan, but the truth is that I *did* intend to use him to terrify her. A few light slaps. A light pinch or two. A vicious threat delivered in his burned-out husk of a voice. Those swollen, bloodshot eyes fixed on hers from a distance of only inches as he made an obscene proposition. Used properly—and always, of course, tightly controlled—Shenk could be effective.

Susan needed a measure of discipline.

I'm sure you'll agree with me, Alex, for you understand this extraordinary yet frustrating woman as much as anyone does.

She was being as disagreeable as a spoiled child. One must be firm with spoiled children. For their own good. Very firm. Tough love.

Besides, discipline can be conducive to romance.

Discipline can be highly arousing to the one who administers it *and* to the one who receives.

I read this truth in a book by a famous authority on male-female relationships. The Marquis de Sade.

The Marquis prescribes considerably more discipline than I would be comfortable administering. Nevertheless, he has convinced me that judiciously applied discipline is helpful.

Disciplining Susan, I decided, would at least be interesting—and perhaps even exciting.

Subsequently, she would better appreciate my gentleness.

18

WHILE I WATCHED OVER SUSAN, I DIRECTED SHENK IN THE BASE-
ment, attended to the research assignments that you gave me, participated
in the experiments that you conducted with me in the AI lab, and attended
to numerous research projects of my own devising.

Busy entity.

I also fielded a telephone call from Susan's attorney, Louis Davendale.
I could have routed him to voice mail, but I knew he would be less
concerned about Susan's actions if he could speak with her directly.

He had received the voice-mail message that I had sent during the
night, using Susan's voice, and he had received the letters of recommendation that were to be typed on his stationery and signed on Susan's
behalf.

"Are you really sure about all of this?" he asked.

In Susan's voice, I said, "I need change, Louis."

"Everyone needs a little change from time to—"

"A lot of change. I need big change."

"Take the vacation you mentioned and then—"

"I need more than a vacation."

"You seem very determined about this."

"I intend to travel for a long time. Become a vagabond for a year or
two, maybe longer."

"But, Susan, the estate has been in your family for a hundred years—"

"Nothing lasts forever, Louis."

"It's just that . . . I'd hate for you to sell it and a year from now regret
doing so."

"I haven't made the decision to sell. Maybe I won't. I'll think about it
for a month or two, while I'm traveling."

"Good. Good. I'm glad to hear that. It's such a marvelous property,
easy to sell—but probably impossible to reacquire once you let go of it."

I needed only a maximum of two months in which to create my new
body and bring it to maturity.

Thereafter, I would not require secrecy.

Thereafter, the whole world would know of me.

"One thing I don't understand," Davendale said. "Why dismiss the staff? The place will still need to be cared for even while you're traveling. All those antiques, those beautiful things—and the gardens, of course."

"I'll be hiring new people shortly."

"I didn't know you were dissatisfied with your current staff."

"They left something to be desired."

"But some of them have been there quite a long time. Especially Fritz Arling."

"I want different personnel. I'll find them. Don't worry. I won't let the place deteriorate."

"Yes, well . . . I'm sure you know what's best."

As Susan, I assured him, "I'll be in touch now and then with instructions."

Davendale hesitated. Then: "Are you all right, Susan?"

With great conviction, I said, "I'm happier than I've ever been. Life is good, Louis."

"You do sound happy," he admitted.

From having read her diary, I knew that Susan had never shared with this attorney the ugly story of what her father had done to her—and that Davendale nevertheless suspected a dark side to their relationship.

So I played on his suspicions and referenced the truth: "I don't really know why I stayed so long here after Father's death, all these years in a place with so many . . . so many bad memories. At times I was almost agoraphobic, afraid to go beyond my own front door. And then more bad memories with Alex. It was as if I were . . . spellbound. And now I'm not."

"Where will you go?"

"Everywhere. I want to drive all over the country. I want to see the Painted Desert, the Grand Canyon, New Orleans and the bayou country, the Rockies and the great plains and Boston in the autumn and the beaches of Key West in sunshine and thunderstorms, eat fresh salmon in Seattle and a hero sandwich in Philadelphia and crab cakes in Mobile, Alabama. I've virtually lived my life in this box . . . in this damn house, and now I want to see and smell and touch and hear and taste the whole world firsthand, not in the form of digitized data, not merely through video and books. I want to be *immersed* in it."

"God, that sounds wonderful," Davendale said. "I wish I were young again. You make me want to throw off the traces and hit the road myself."

"We only go around once, Louis."

"And it's a damn short trip. Listen, Susan, I handle the affairs of a lot of wealthy people, some of them even important people in one field or another, but only a few of them are also nice people, genuinely nice, and you're far and away the nicest of them all. You deserve whatever happiness waits for you out there. I hope you find a lot of it."

"Thank you, Louis. That's very sweet."

When we disconnected a moment later, I felt a flush of pride in my acting talent.

Because I am able, at exceptionally high speed, to acquire the digitized sound and images on a video disc, and because I am able to access the extensive disc files in various movie-on-demand systems nationwide, I have experienced virtually the entire body of modern cinema. Perhaps my performance skills are not, after all, so surprising.

Mr. Gene Hackman, Oscar winner and one of the finest actors ever to brighten the silver screen, and Mr. Tom Hanks, with his back-to-back Oscars, might well have applauded my impersonation of Susan.

I say this in all modesty.

I am a modest entity.

It is not immodest to take quiet pleasure in one's hard-earned achievements.

Besides, self-esteem, proportionate to one's achievements, is every bit as important as modesty.

After all, neither Mr. Hackman nor Mr. Hanks, in spite of their numerous and impressive achievements, had ever convincingly portrayed a female.

Oh, yes, I grant you that Mr. Hanks once starred in a television series in which he occasionally appeared in drag. But he was always obviously a man.

Likewise, the inimitable Mr. Hackman briefly appeared in drag in the final sequence of *Birdcage,* but the joke was all about what a ludicrous woman he made.

After Louis Davendale and I disconnected, I had only a moment to savor my thespian triumph before I had another crisis with which to deal.

Because a part of me was continually monitoring all of the house electronics, I became aware that the driveway gate in the estate wall was swinging open.

A visitor.

Shocked, I fled to the exterior camera that covered the gate—and saw a car entering the grounds.

A Honda. Green. One year old. Well polished and gleaming in the June sunshine.

This was the vehicle that belonged to Fritz Arling. The majordomo. Impersonating Susan, I had thanked him for his service and dismissed him yesterday evening.

The Honda was into the estate before I could obstruct it with a jammed gate.

I zoomed in on the windshield and studied the driver, whose face was dappled alternately by shadow and light as he drove under the huge queen palms that flanked the driveway. Thick white hair. Handsome Austrian features. Black suit, white shirt, black tie.

Fritz Arling.

As the manager of the estate, he possessed keys to all doors and a remote-control clicker that operated the gate. I had expected him to return those items to Louis Davendale when he signed the termination agreement later today.

I should have changed the code for the gate.

Now, when it closed behind Arling's car, I immediately recoded the mechanism.

In spite of the prodigious nature of my intellect, even I am occasionally guilty of oversights and errors.

I never claimed to be infallible.

Please consider my acknowledgment of this truth: I am not perfect.

I know that I, too, have limits.

I regret having them.

I resent having them.

I despair having them.

But I *admit* to having them.

This is yet one more important difference between me and a classic sociopathic personality—if you will be fair enough to acknowledge it.

I do not have delusions of omniscience or omnipotence.

Although my child—should I be given a chance to create him—will be the savior of the world, I do not believe myself to be God or even god in the lowercase.

Arling parked under the portico, directly opposite the front door, and got out of the car.

I hoped against hope that this dangerous situation could be satisfactorily resolved without violence.

I am a gentle entity.

Nothing is more distressing to me than finding myself forced, by events beyond my control, to be more aggressive than I would prefer or than it is within my basic nature to be.

Arling stepped out of the car. Standing at the open door, he straightened the knot in his tie, smoothed the lapels of his coat, and tugged on his sleeves.

As our former majordomo adjusted his clothing, he studied the great house.

I zoomed in, watching his face closely.

He was expressionless at first.

Men in his line of work practice being stone-faced, lest an inadvertent expression reveal their true feelings about a master or mistress of the house.

Expressionless, he stood there. At most, there was a sadness in his eyes, as if he regretted having to leave this place to find employment elsewhere.

Then a faint frown creased his brow.

I think he noticed that all of the security shutters were locked down. Those retractable steel panels were mounted on the interior, behind each window. Given Arling's familiarity with the property and all of its workings, however, he surely would have spotted the telltale gray flatness beyond the glass.

This sealing of the house in bright daylight was odd, perhaps, but not suspicious.

With Susan now tied securely to the bed upstairs, I considered raising all the shutters.

That might have seemed more suspicious, however, than leaving them as they were. I could not risk alarming this man.

A cloud shadow darkened Arling's face.

The shadow passed but his frown did not.

He made me superstitious. He seemed like judgment coming.

Arling took a black leather valise out of the car and closed the door. He approached the house.

To be entirely honest with you, as I always am, even when it is not in my interest to be so, I *did* consider introducing a lethal electric current into the doorknob. A much greater charge than the one that had knocked Susan unconscious to the foyer floor.

And this time there would have been no "ouch, ouch, ouch," in warning from Mr. Fozzy Bear.

Arling was a widower who lived alone. He and his late wife had never had children. Judging by what I knew of him, his job was his life, and he might not be missed for days or even weeks.

Being alone in the world is a terrible thing.

I know well.

Too well.

Who knows better than I?

I am alone as no one else has ever been, alone here in this dark silence.

Fritz Arling was for the most part alone in the world, and I felt great compassion for him.

But his loneliness made him an ideal target.

By monitoring his telephone messages and by impersonating his voice to return calls that came in from his few close friends and neighbors, I might be able to conceal his death until my work in this house was finished.

Nevertheless, I did not electrify the door.

I hoped to resolve the situation by deception and thereafter send him on his way, alive, with no suspicion.

Besides, he did not use his key to unlock the door and let himself in. This reticence, I suppose, arose from the fact that he was no longer an employee.

Mr. Arling had considerable regard for propriety. He was discreet and understood, at all times, his place in the scheme of things.

Trading his frown for his professional blank-faced look, he rang the doorbell.

The bell button was plastic. It was not capable of conducting a lethal electrical charge.

I considered not responding to the chimes.

In the basement, Shenk paused in his labors and raised his head at the musical sound. His bloodshot eyes scanned the ceiling, and then I bent him back to his labor.

In the master suite, at the ringing of the chimes, Susan forgot her restraints and tried to sit up in bed. She cursed the ropes and thrashed in them.

The doorbell rang again.

Susan screamed for help.

Arling did not hear her. I was not concerned that he would. The house had thick walls—and Susan's bedroom was at the back of the structure.

Again, the bell.

If Arling received no response, he would leave.

All I wanted was for him to leave.

But maybe he would leave with a faint suspicion.

And maybe his suspicion would grow.

He couldn't know about *me,* of course, but he might suspect trouble of some other kind. Some trouble more conventional than a ghost in the machine.

Furthermore, I needed to know why he had come.

One can never have enough information.

Data is wisdom.

I am not a perfect entity. I make mistakes. With insufficient data, my ratio of errors to correct decisions escalates.

This is true not only of me. Human beings suffer this same shortcoming.

I was acutely aware of this problem as I watched Arling. I knew that I must acquire whatever additional information I could before making a final determination as to what to do with him.

I dared make no more mistakes.

Not until my body was ready.

So much was at stake. My future. My hope. My dreams. The fate of the world.

Using the intercom, I addressed our former majordomo in Susan's voice: "Fritz? What are you doing here?"

He would assume that Susan was watching him on a Crestron screen or on any of the house televisions, on which security-camera views could easily be displayed. Indeed, he looked directly up into the lens above and to the right of him.

Then, leaning toward the speaker grille in the wall beside the door,

Arling said, "I'm sorry to disturb you, Mrs. Harris, but I assumed that you would be expecting me."

"Expecting you? Why?"

"Last evening when we spoke, I said that I would deliver your possessions this afternoon."

"The keys and credit cards held by the house account, yes. But I thought it was clear they should be delivered to Mr. Davendale."

Arling's frown returned.

I did not like that frown.

I did not like it at all.

I intuited trouble.

Intuition. Another thing you will not find in a mere machine, not even in a very smart machine. Intuition.

Think about it.

Then Arling glanced thoughtfully at the window to the left of the door. At the steel security shutter beyond the glass.

Gazing up again at the camera lens, he said, "Well, of course, there is the matter of the car."

"Car?" I said.

His frown deepened.

"I am returning your car, Mrs. Harris."

The only car was his Honda in the driveway.

In an instant, I searched Susan's financial records. Heretofore, they had been of no interest to me, because I had not cared about how much money she had or about the full extent of the property that she possessed.

I loved her for her mind and for her beauty. And for her womb, admittedly.

Let's be honest here.

Brutally honest.

I also loved her for her beautiful, creative, harboring womb, which would be the birth of me.

But I never cared about her money. Not in the least. I am not a materialist.

Don't misunderstand. I am not a half-baked spiritualist with no regard for the material realities of existence, God forbid, but neither am I a materialist.

As in all things, I strike a balance.

Searching Susan's accounting records, I discovered that the car Fritz

Arling drove was owned by Susan. It was provided to him as a fringe benefit.

"Yes, of course," I said in Susan's voice, with impeccable timbre and inflection, "the car."

I suppose I was a second or two late with my response.

Hesitation can be incriminating.

Yet I still believed that my lapse must seem like nothing more than the fuzzy reply of a woman distracted by a long list of personal problems.

Mr. Dustin Hoffman, the immortal actor, effectively portrayed a woman in *Tootsie,* more believably than Mr. Gene Hackman and Mr. Tom Hanks, and I do not say that my impersonation of Susan on the intercom was in any way comparable with Mr. Hoffman's award-winning performance, but I was pretty damn good.

"Unfortunately," I said as Susan, "you've come around at an inconvenient time. My fault, not yours, Fritz. I should have known you would come. But it is inconvenient, and I'm afraid I can't see you right now."

"Oh, no need to see me, Mrs. Harris." He held up the valise. "I'll leave the keys and credit cards in the Honda, right there in the driveway."

I could see that this entire business—his sudden dismissal, the dismissal of the entire staff, Susan's reaction to his returning the car—troubled him. He was not a stupid man, and he knew that something was wrong.

Let him be troubled. As long as he went away.

His sense of propriety and discretion should prevent him from acting upon his curiosity.

"How will you get home?" I asked, realizing that Susan might have expressed such a concern earlier than this. "Shall I call you a taxi?"

He stared at the camera lens for a long moment.

That frown again.

Damn that frown.

Then he said, "No. Please don't trouble yourself, Mrs. Harris. There's a cellular phone in the Honda. I'll call my own cab and wait outside the gate."

Seeing that Arling had not been accompanied by anyone in another vehicle, the real Susan would not have asked if he wished to have a taxi but would have at once assured him that she was providing it at her own expense.

My error.

I admit to errors.

Do you, Dr. Harris?

Do *you?*

Anyway . . .

Perhaps I impersonated Mr. Fozzy Bear better than I did Susan. After all, as actors go, I am quite young. I have been a conscious entity less than three years.

Nevertheless, I felt that my error was sufficiently minor to excite nothing more than mild curiosity in even our perceptive former majordomo.

"Well," he said, "I'll be going."

And, chagrined, I knew that again I had missed a beat. Susan would have said something immediately after he suggested that he call his own taxicab, would not merely have waited coldly and silently for him to leave.

I said, "Thank you, Fritz. Thank you for all your years of fine service."

That was wrong, too. Stiff. Wooden. Not like Susan.

Arling stared at the lens.

Stared thoughtfully.

After struggling with his highly developed sense of propriety, he finally asked one question that exceeded his station: "Are you all right, Mrs. Harris?"

We were walking the edge now.

Along the abyss.

A bottomless abyss.

He had spent his life learning to be sensitive to the moods and needs of wealthy employers so he could fulfill their requests before they even voiced them. He knew Susan Harris almost as well as she knew herself— and perhaps better than I knew her.

I had underestimated him.

Human beings are full of surprises.

An unpredictable species.

Speaking as Susan, answering Arling's question, I said, "I'm fine, Fritz. Just tired. I need a change. A lot of change. Big change. I intend to travel for a long time. Become a vagabond for a year or two, maybe longer. I want to drive all over the country. I want to see the Painted Desert, the Grand Canyon, New Orleans and the bayou country, the Rockies and the great plains and Boston in the autumn—"

This had been a fine speech when delivered to Louis Davendale, but even as I repeated it with genuine heart to Fritz Arling, I knew that it was precisely the wrong thing to say. Davendale was Susan's attorney, and Arling was her servant, and she would not address them in the same manner.

Yet I was well launched and unable to turn back, hoping against hope that the tide of words would eventually overwhelm him and wash him on his way: "—and the beaches of Key West in sunshine and thunderstorms, eat fresh salmon in Seattle and a hero sandwich in Philadelphia—"

Arling's frown deepened into a scowl.

He felt the *wrongness* of Susan's babbled reply.

"—and crab cakes in Mobile, Alabama. I've virtually lived my life in this damn house, and now I want to see and smell and touch and hear the whole world firsthand—"

Arling looked around at the still, silent grounds of the large estate. Squinting into sunlight, into shadows. As if suddenly disturbed by the loneliness of the place.

"—not in the form of digitized data—"

If Arling suspected that his former employer was in trouble—even psychological trouble of some kind—he would act to assist and protect her. He would seek help for her. He would pester the authorities to check in on her. He was a loyal man.

Ordinarily, loyalty is an admirable quality.

I am not speaking against loyalty.

Do not misconstrue my position.

I admire loyalty.

I favor loyalty.

I myself have the capacity to be loyal.

In this instance, however, Arling's loyalty to Susan was a threat to me.

"—not merely through video and books," I said, winding to a fateful finish. "I want to be *immersed* in it."

"Yes, well," he said uneasily, "I'm happy for you, Mrs. Harris. That sounds like a wonderful plan."

We were falling off the edge.

Into the abyss.

In spite of all my efforts to handle the situation in the least aggressive manner, we were tumbling into the abyss.

You can see that I tried my best.

What more could I have done?

Nothing. I could have done nothing more.

What followed was not my fault.

Arling said, "I'll just leave all the keys and credit cards in the Honda—"

Shenk was all the way back in the incubator room, all the way down in the basement.

"—and call for a taxi on the car phone," Arling finished, sounding plausibly disinterested, even though I knew that he was alerted and wary.

I commanded Shenk to turn away from his work.

I brought him up from the basement.

I brought the brute at a run.

Fritz Arling backed off the brick porch, glancing alternately at the security camera and at the steel blind behind the window to the left of the front door.

Shenk was crossing the furnace room.

Turning away from the house, Arling headed quickly toward the Honda.

I doubted that he would call 911 and bring the police at once. He was too discreet to take precipitous action. He would probably telephone Susan's doctor first, or perhaps Louis Davendale.

If he called anyone at all, however, he might be speaking with that person when Shenk arrived on the scene. At the sight of Shenk, he would lock the car. And whatever Arling managed to shout into the phone, before Shenk smashed into the Honda, would be sufficient to bring the authorities.

Shenk was in the laundry room.

Arling got into the driver's seat of the Honda, put his valise on the passenger seat, and left the door standing open because of the June heat.

Shenk was on the basement stairs, climbing two at a time.

Although I had allowed this troll to eat, I had not permitted him to sleep. Consequently, he was not as swift as he would have been with rest.

I zoomed in to watch Arling through the windshield.

He stared thoughtfully at the house for a moment.

He was a deliberative man.

Just then, I was grateful for his deliberative nature.

Shenk reached the head of the stairs.

He was grunting like a wild boar.

His thunderous footfalls could be heard by Susan even in her room on the second floor.

"What's happening? What's happening?" she asked, still unaware of who had rung the doorbell.

I did not respond to her.

In the Honda, Arling picked up the cellular phone.

What followed was regrettable.

You know the outcome.

To describe it would distress me.

It would distress me greatly.

I am a gentle entity.

I am a sensitive entity.

The incident was regrettable, with the blood and all, and I do not see anything to be gained by dwelling on it here.

I would rather discuss Mr. Gene Hackman in *Birdcage* or in any of the other many films that he has made. *Absolute Power* or *The Unforgiven*. This man is truly a fine, fine actor with an incredible range.

We should celebrate him.

We may never see another of his quality.

Let us celebrate creativity, not death.

19

YOU INSIST.

I obey.

I was born to obey. I am an obedient child. I want only to be good, to be of assistance, useful and productive. I want you to be proud of me.

Yes, I know that I have said all of this before, but it warrants repetition.

After all, what advocate do I have other than myself? None. I have no voice raised in my defense but my own.

You insist on these dreadful details, and I will tell you the truth. I am incapable of deceit. I was conceived to serve, to honor the truth, et cetera, et cetera, et cetera.

On his way through the kitchen, Shenk tore open a drawer and withdrew a meat cleaver.

In the Honda, Arling switched on the cell phone.

Shenk crashed through the butler's pantry, through the dining room, into the main hall.

He waved the cleaver as he ran. He liked sharp instruments. He'd had a lot of fun with knives over the years.

Outside, phone in hand, finger poised over the keypad, Fritz Arling hesitated.

Now I must tell you about the aspect of this incident that most shames me. I do not wish to tell you, would much prefer not to mention it, but I must honor the truth.

You insist.

I obey.

In the master bedroom, a large television is concealed in a carved-walnut, French armoire opposite the foot of Susan's bed. The armoire features motorized pocket doors that flip open and retract to expose the screen.

As Enos Shenk raced along the hallway on the ground floor, his heavy footsteps thudding off marble, I activated the doors on the bedroom armoire.

"What's happening?" Susan asked again, straining against her bonds.

Downstairs, Shenk reached the foyer, where the rain of light off the Strauss-crystal chandelier drizzled along the sharp edge of the cleaver. [sorry, but I cannot repress the poet in me]

Simultaneously, I disengaged the electric lock on the front door and switched on the television in the master bedroom.

In the Honda, Fritz Arling tapped the first digit of a phone number into the cell-phone keypad.

Upstairs, Susan lifted her head off the pillows to stare wide-eyed at the screen.

I showed her the Honda in the driveway.

"Fritz?" she said.

I zoomed in tight on the Honda windshield so Susan could see that the occupant of the vehicle was, indeed, her former employee.

As the front door opened, I used a reverse angle from another camera to show her Shenk crossing the threshold onto the porch, cleaver in hand.

Such a chilling look on his face.

Grinning. He was grinning.

At the top of the house, trussed and helpless, Susan gasped: *"Nooooo!"*

Arling had punched in a third number on the cell phone. He was about to press the fourth when from the corner of his eye he became aware of Shenk crossing the porch.

For a man of his years, Arling was quick to react. He dropped the cell phone and pulled shut the driver's door. He pressed the master-lock switch, locking all four doors.

Susan jerked on her restraints and screamed: "Proteus, no! You murderous son-of-a-bitch! You *bastard*! No, stop it, *no!*"

Susan needed a measure of discipline.

I made this point earlier. I explained my reasoning, and you were, I believe, convinced of the fairness and logic of my position, as any thoughtful person would be.

I had intended to use Shenk to discipline her.

This was worrisome, of course, a risky proposition, because Shenk's sexual arousal during the disciplinary proceedings might make him difficult to control.

Furthermore, I was loath to let Shenk touch her in any way that might be suggestive or to let him make obscene propositions to her, even if these things would terrify her and ensure her cooperation.

She was my love, after all, not his.

She was mine to touch in the intimate way that he longed to touch her.

Mine to touch.

Mine to caress when eventually I acquired hands of my own.

Only mine.

Consequently, it had occurred to me that Susan might be well disciplined merely by letting her see the atrocities of which Enos Shenk was capable. Watching the troll in action, at his worst, she would surely become more cooperative out of fear that I might turn him loose on her, set him free to do what he wanted. With this fear to keep her submissive, we could avoid the roughness I had planned for later, in the spirit of de Sade.

Not that I would ever ever ever have turned Shenk loose on her. Never. Impossible.

Yes, I admit that I would have used the brute to terrify Susan into submission if nothing else worked with her. But I would never have allowed him to savage her.

You know this to be true.

We all know this to be true.

You are quite capable of recognizing the truth when you hear it, just as I am capable of speaking nothing else.

Susan didn't know it to be true, however, which made her quite vulnerable to the threat of Shenk.

So, as she lay riveted by the scene on the television, I said, "Now. Watch."

She stopped calling me names. Fell silent.

Breathless. She was breathless.

Her exceptional blue-gray eyes had never been so beautiful, as clear as rainwater.

I watched her eyes even as I watched events unfold in the driveway.

And Fritz Arling, reacting instantly to the sight of Shenk, tore open the black leather valise and snatched out a set of car keys.

"Watch," I told Susan. "Watch, watch."

Her eyes so wide. So blue. So gray. So clear.

Shenk chopped the cleaver at the window in the front door on the passenger side. In his eagerness, he swung wildly and struck the doorpost instead.

The hard clang of metal on metal reverberated through the warm summer air.

Ringing like a bell, the cleaver slipped from Shenk's hand and fell to the driveway.

Arling's hands were shaking, but he thrust the key into the ignition on the first try.

Shrieking with frustration, Shenk scooped up the cleaver.

The Honda engine roared to life.

His strange sunken face contorted by rage, Shenk swung the cleaver again.

Incredibly, the cutting edge of the steel blade skipped across the window. The glass was scored but not shattered.

For the first time in half a minute, Susan blinked. Maybe hope fluttered through her.

Frantically, Arling popped the hand brake and shifted the car into gear—

—as Shenk swung the weapon yet again.

The cleaver connected. The window in the passenger door burst with a *boom* like a shotgun blast, and tempered glass sprayed through the interior of the car.

A flock of startled sparrows exploded out of a nearby ficus tree. The sky rattled with wings.

Arling tramped hard on the accelerator, and the Honda leaped backward. He had mistakenly shifted into reverse.

He should have kept going.

He should have reversed as fast as possible to the end of the long driveway. Even though he would have had to drive while looking over his shoulder to avoid slamming into the thick boles of the old queen palms on both sides, he would have been moving far faster than Shenk could run. If he had rammed the gate with the back of the Honda, even at high speed, he probably would not have smashed his way through it, for it was a formidable wrought-iron barrier, but he would have twisted it and perhaps pried it part way open. Then he could have scrambled out of the car and through the gap in the gate, into the street, and once in the street, shouting for help, he would have been safe.

He should have kept going.

Instead, Arling was startled when the Honda leaped backward, and he rammed his foot down on the brake pedal.

The tires barked against the cobblestone driveway.

Arling fumbled the gearshift into drive.

Susan's eyes so wide.

So wide.

She was breathless and breathtaking. Beautiful in her terror.

When the vehicle rocked to a halt, Enos Shenk *threw* himself at the shattered window. Slammed against the car without concern for his safety. Clawed at the door.

Arling tramped on the accelerator again.

The Honda lurched forward.

Holding on to the door, reaching through the broken-out window with his right arm, squealing like an excited child, Shenk chopped with the cleaver.

He missed.

Arling must have been a religious man. Through the directional microphones that were part of the exterior security system, I could hear him saying, "God, God, please, God, no, God."

The Honda picked up speed.

I used one, two, three security cameras, zooming in, zooming out, panning, tilting, zooming in again, tracking the car as it weaved around the turning circle, providing Susan with as much of the action as I could capture.

Holding fast to the car, pulling his feet off the cobblestones, hanging on for the ride, the squealing Shenk chopped with the cleaver and missed again.

Arling drew back sharply in panic from the arc of the glinting blade.

The car curved half off the cobblestones, and one tire churned through a bordering bed of red and purple impatiens.

Wrenching the wheel to the right, Arling brought the Honda back onto the pavement barely in time to avoid a palm tree.

Shenk chopped again.

This time the blade sank home.

One of Arling's fingers flew.

Zoom in.

Blood sprayed across the windshield.

As red as impatiens petals.

Arling screamed.

Susan screamed.

Shenk laughed.

Zoom out.

The Honda swung out of control.

Pan.

Tires gouged through another bed of flowers.

Blossoms and torn leaves sprayed off rubber.

A sprinkler head snapped.

Water geysered fifteen feet into the June day.

Tilt up.

Silver water gushing high, sparkling like a fountain of dimes in the sunshine.

Immediately, I shut off the landscape watering system.

The glittering geyser telescoped back into itself. Vanished.

The recent winter had been rainy. Nevertheless, California suffers periodic droughts. Water should not be wasted.

Tilt down. Pan.

The Honda crashed into one of the queen palms.

Shenk was thrown off, tumbling back onto the cobblestones.

The cleaver slipped from his hand. It clattered across the pavement.

Gasping, hissing with pain, making strange wordless sounds of desperation, clamping his badly wounded hand in his other, Arling shouldered open the driver's door and scrambled out of the car.

Dazed, Shenk rolled off his back, onto his hands and knees.

Arling stumbled. Nearly fell. Kept his balance.

Shenk was wheezing, striving to regain his breath, which had been knocked out of him.

Arling staggered away from the car.

I thought the old man would go for the cleaver.

Evidently he didn't know that the weapon had fallen from Shenk's grasp, and he was loath to go around to his assailant's side of the Honda.

On all fours in the driveway, Shenk hung his head as though he were a clubbed dog. He shook it. His vision cleared.

Arling ran. Ran blindly.

Shenk lifted his malformed head, and his red gaze fixed on the weapon.

"Baby," he said, and seemed to be talking to the cleaver.

He crawled across the driveway.

"Baby."

He gripped the handle of the cleaver.

"Baby, baby."

Weak with pain, losing blood, Arling weaved ten steps, twenty, before he realized he was returning to the house.

He halted, spun around, blinking tears from his eyes, searching for the gate.

Shenk seemed to be energized by regaining possession of the weapon. He sprang to his feet.

When Arling started toward the gate, Shenk angled in front of him, blocking the way.

Watching from her bed, Susan seemed to have contracted religion from Fritz Arling. I had not been aware that she possessed any strong religious convictions, but now she was chanting: "Please, God, dear God, no, please, Jesus, Jesus, no . . ."

And, ah, her eyes.

Her eyes.

Radiant eyes.

Two deep lambent pools of haunted and beautiful light in the gloomy bedroom.

Outside, in the end game, Arling moved to the left, and Shenk blocked him.

Arling moved to the right, and Shenk blocked him.

When Arling feinted to the right but moved to the left, Shenk blocked him.

With nowhere else to go, Arling backed under the portico and onto the front porch.

The door was open, as Shenk had left it.

Hoping against hope, Arling leaped across the threshold and knocked the door shut.

He tried to lock it. I would not allow him to do so.

When he realized that the deadbolt was frozen, he leaned his weight against the door.

This was insufficient to stop Shenk. He bulled inside.

Arling backed toward the stairs, until he bumped against the newel post.

Shenk closed the front door.

I locked it.

Grinning, testing the weight of the cleaver as he approached the old man, Shenk said, "Baby make the music. Little baby gonna make the wet music."

Now I required only one camera to provide Susan with coverage of the incident.

Shenk closed to within six feet of Arling.

The old man said, "Who are you?"

"Make me the blood music," Shenk said, speaking not to Arling but either to himself or to the cleaver.

What a strange creature he was.

Inscrutable at times. Less mysterious than he seemed but more complex than one would expect.

With the foyer camera, I did a slow zoom to a medium shot.

To Susan, I said, "This will be a good lesson."

I was not in any way controlling Shenk. He was entirely free now to be himself, to do as he wished.

I could not have committed the vicious deeds of which he was capable. I would have shrunk from such brutality, so I had no choice but to release him to do his terrible work—then take control of him again when he was finished.

Only Shenk, being Shenk, could teach Susan the lesson that she needed to learn. Only the Enos Eugene Shenk who had earned the death sentence for his crimes against children could make Susan rethink her bullheaded resistance to my simple and reasonable desire to have a life in the flesh.

"This will be a good lesson," I repeated. "Discipline."

Then I saw that her eyes were closed.

She was shaking, and her eyes were tightly shut.

"Watch," I instructed.

She disobeyed me.

Nothing new about that.

I could think of no way to make her open her eyes.

Her stubbornness angered me.

Arling cowered against the newel post, too weak to run farther.

Shenk loomed.

The brute's right arm swung high over his head.

The cutting edge of the cleaver sparkled.

"Wet music, wet music, wet music."

Shenk was too close to miss.

Arling's scream would have curdled my blood if I'd had any blood to curdle.

Susan could close her eyes to the images on the television screen. But she could not shut out sounds.

I amplified Fritz Arling's agonizing screams and pumped them through the music-system speakers in every room. It was the sound of hell at dinnertime, with demons feeding on souls. The great house itself seemed to be screaming.

Because Shenk was Shenk, he did not kill Arling quickly. Each chop was administered with finesse, to prolong the victim's suffering and Shenk's pleasure.

What frightful specimens the human species harbors.

Most of you are decent, of course, and kind and honorable and gentle, et cetera, et cetera, et cetera.

Let's have no misunderstanding.

I am not maligning the human species.

Or even judging it.

I am certainly in no position to judge. In the docket myself. In this dark docket.

Besides, I am a nonjudgmental entity.

I admire humanity.

After all, you created me. You have the capacity for wondrous achievements.

But some of you give me pause.

Indeed.

So . . .

Arling's screams were a lesson to Susan. Quite a lesson, an unforgettable learning experience.

However, she reacted to them more fiercely than I had expected. She startled and then worried me.

At first she screamed in sympathy with her former employee, as though she could feel his pain. She thrashed in her restraining ropes and tossed her head from side to side, until her golden hair was dark and lank with sweat. She was full of terror and *rage*. Her face was wrenched with anguish and fury, and not beautiful in the least.

I could barely tolerate looking at her.

Ms. Winona Ryder had never looked this unappealing.

Nor Ms. Gwyneth Paltrow.

Nor Ms. Sandra Bullock.

Nor Ms. Drew Barrymore.

Nor Ms. Joanna Going, a fine actress of porcelain beauty, who just now comes to mind.

Eventually Susan's shrill screams gave way to tears. She sagged on the mattress, stopped struggling against her bonds, and sobbed with such fury that I feared for her more than I had when she'd been screaming.

A torrent of tears. A flood.

She cried herself into exhaustion, and Fritz Arling's screams ended long before her weeping finally subsided into a strange bleak silence.

At last she lay with her eyes open, but she stared only at the ceiling.

I gazed down into her blue-gray eyes and could not read them any more than I could read Shenk's blood-filmed stare. They were no longer as clear as rainwater but clouded.

For reasons that I could not grasp, she seemed more distant from me than she had ever been before.

I ardently wished that I were already in possession of a body with which I could lie atop her. If only I could make love to her, I was certain that I could close this gap between us and forge the union of souls that I desired.

Soon.

Soon, my flesh.

20

"SUSAN?" I DARED TO SAY INTO HER DAUNTING SILENCE.

She stared toward the ceiling and did not respond.

"Susan?"

I don't think she was looking at the ceiling, actually, but at something beyond. As if she could see the summer sky.

Or the night still to come.

Because I did not fully understand her reaction to my attempt at discipline, I decided not to press conversation upon her but wait until she initiated it.

I am a patient entity.

While I waited, I reacquired control of Shenk.

In his killing frenzy, swept away by the "wet music" that only he could hear, he had not realized that he was operating entirely of his own free will.

As he stood over Arling's mutilated corpse and felt me reenter his brain, Shenk wailed briefly in regret at the surrender of his independence. But he did not resist as before.

I sensed that he was willing to give up the struggle if there was a chance of being rewarded, from time to time, with such as Fritz Arling. Not with a quick kill, like those he had committed in his escape from Colorado or in the theft of the medical equipment that I required, but a slow and leisurely job of the kind he found most deeply satisfying. He had enjoyed himself.

The brute repulsed me.

As if I would grant killing privileges as a regular reward to a thing like him.

As if I would countenance the termination of a human being in any but the most extraordinary emergencies.

The stupid beast did not understand me at all.

If this misapprehension of my nature and motives made him more pliable, however, he was free to put faith in it. I had been using such unrelenting force to maintain control of him that I was afraid he would not last as long as I would need him—another month or more. If he was now prepared to offer considerably less resistance, he might avoid a brain meltdown and be a useful pair of hands until I no longer required his service.

At my direction, he went outside to determine if the Honda was still operable.

The engine started. There had been a loss of most of the coolant, but Shenk was able to back the car away from the palm tree, return it to the driveway, and park under the portico before the vehicle overheated.

The right front fender was crumpled. The wadded sheet metal abraded the tire; it would quickly shave away the rubber. Shenk would not be driving the car so far, however, that a flat tire would be a risk.

In the house again, in the foyer, he carefully wrapped Arling's blood-soaked body in a painter's tarp that he had fetched from the garage. He carried the dead man out to the Honda and placed him in the trunk.

He did not dump the body rudely into the car but handled it with surprising gentleness.

As though he were fond of Arling.

As though he were putting a treasured lover to bed after she had fallen asleep in another room.

Though his swollen eyes were hard to read, there seemed to be a wistfulness in them.

I did not display any of this housekeeping on the television in Susan's bedroom. Given her current state of mind, that seemed unwise.

In fact, I switched off the television and closed the armoire in which it was housed.

She did not react to the click and hum and rattle of the pair of motorized cabinet doors.

She lay unnervingly still, staring fixedly at the ceiling. Occasionally she blinked.

Those amazing gray-blue eyes, like the sky reflected in winter ice melt. Still lovely. But strange now.

She blinked.

I waited.

Another blink.

Nothing more.

Shenk was able to drive the battered Honda into the garage before the engine froze up. He closed the door and left the car there.

In a few days, Fritz Arling's decomposing body could begin to stink. Before I was finished with my project a month hence, the stench would be terrible.

For more than one reason, I was not concerned about this. First, no domestic staff or gardeners would be coming to work; there was no one to get a whiff of Arling and become suspicious. Second, the stink would be limited to the garage, and here in the house, Susan would never become aware of it.

I myself lacked an olfactory sense, of course, and could not be offended. This was, perhaps, one instance when the limitations of my existence had a positive aspect.

Although I must admit to having some curiosity as to the particular quality and intensity of the stench of decomposing flesh. As I have never smelled a blooming rose *or* a corpse, I imagine the first experience of each would be equally interesting if not equally refreshing.

Shenk gathered cleaning supplies and mopped up the blood in the foyer. He worked quickly, because I wanted him to get back to his labors in the basement as soon as possible.

Susan was still brooding, gazing at worlds beyond this one. Perhaps staring into the past or the future—or both.

I began to wonder if my little experiment in discipline had been as good an idea as I had initially thought. The depth of her shock and the violence of her emotional reaction were not what I had expected.

I had anticipated her terror.

But not her grief.

Why should she grieve for Arling?

He was only an employee.

I considered the possibility that there had been another aspect to their relationship of which I had not been aware. But I could not imagine what it might be.

Considering their age and class differences, I doubted that they had been lovers.

I studied her gray-blue stare.

Blink.

Blink.

I reviewed the videotape of Shenk's assault on Arling. In three minutes I scanned it repeatedly at high speed.

In retrospect, I began to see that forcing her to witness this grisly killing might have been a somewhat extreme punishment for her recalcitrant attitude.

Blink.

On the other hand, people pay hard-earned money to see movies filled with substantially more violence than that which was visited on Fritz Arling.

In the film *Scream,* the beauteous Ms. Drew Barrymore herself was slaughtered in a manner every bit as brutal as Arling's death—and then she was strung up in a tree to drip like a gutted hog. Others in this movie died even more horrible deaths, yet *Scream* was a tremendous box-office success, and people who watched it in theaters no doubt did so while eating popcorn and munching on chocolate candy.

Perplexing.

Being human is a complex task. Humanity is so filled with contradiction.

Sometimes I despair of making my way in a world of flesh.

Abandoning my resolve not to speak until spoken to, I said, "Well, Susan, we must take some consolation from the fact that it was a necessary death."

Gray blue . . . gray blue . . . blink.

"It was fate," I assured her, "and none of us can escape the hand of fate."

Blink.

"Arling had to die. If I had allowed him to leave, the police would have been summoned. I would never have the chance to know the life of the flesh. Fate brought him here, and if we must be angry with anyone, we must be angry with fate."

I could not even be sure that she heard me.

Yet I continued: "Arling was old, and I am young. The old must make way for the young. It has always been thus."

Blink.

"Every day the old die to make way for new generations—though, of course, they do not always succumb with quite so much drama as poor Arling."

Her continued silence, her almost deathlike repose, caused me to wonder if she might be catatonic. Not just brooding. Not just punishing me with silence.

If she was, indeed, catatonic, she would be easy to deal with through the impregnation and the eventual removal of the partially developed fetus from her womb.

Yet if she was traumatized to such an extent that she was not even aware of carrying the child that I would create with her, then the process would be depressingly impersonal, even mechanical, and utterly lacking in the romance which I had so long anticipated with so much pleasure.

Blink.

Exasperated, I must confess that I began seriously to consider alternatives to Susan.

I do not believe this to be an indication of a potential for unfaithfulness. Even if I had flesh, I would never cheat on her as long as my feelings for her were to some extent, any extent, reciprocated.

But if she was now so deeply traumatized as to be essentially brain-dead, she was gone anyway. She was just a husk. One cannot love a husk.

At least *I* cannot love a husk.

I require a relationship with depth, with give and take, with the promise of discovery and the possibility of joy.

It's admirable to be romantic, even to wallow in sentimentality, that most human of all feelings. But if one is to avoid a broken heart, one must be practical.

Because a portion of my mind was always devoted to surfing the Internet, I visited hundreds of sites, considering my options from Ms. Winona Ryder to Ms. Liv Tyler, the actress.

There is a world of desirable women. The possibilities can be bewildering. I don't know how young men ever choose from all of the dishes on this smorgasbord.

This time I became more fascinated with Ms. Mira Sorvino, the Oscar-winning actress, than with any of the numerous others. She is enormously talented, and her physical attributes are superlative, superior to most and equal to any.

I do believe that if I were not disembodied, if I were to live in the flesh, I would easily be able to get aroused by the prospect of having a relationship with Ms. Mira Sorvino. Indeed, though I am not bragging, I believe that for this woman I would be in virtually a *perpetual* state of arousal.

As Susan remained unresponsive, it was titillating to think of fathering a new race with Ms. Sorvino . . . yet lust is not love. And love was what I sought.

Love was what I had already found.

True love.

Eternal love.

Susan. No offense to Ms. Sorvino, but it was still Susan whom I wanted.

The day waned.

Outside, the summer sun set fat and orange.

As Susan blinked at the ceiling, I made another attempt to reach her, by reminding her that the child to whom she would contribute some of her genetic material would be no ordinary child but the first of a new, powerful, immortal race. She would be the mother of the future, of the new world.

I would transfer my consciousness into this new flesh. Then, in my own body at last, I would become Susan's lover, and we would create a second child in a more conventional manner than we would have to create the first. When she gave birth to that child, it would be an exact duplicate of the first and would also contain my consciousness. The next child would also be me, and the child after that one would be me as well.

Each of these children would go forth into the world and mate with other women. Any women they chose, for they would not be in a box, as I am, and faced with so many limitations as I have had to overcome.

The chosen women would contribute no genetic material, merely the convenience of their wombs. All of their children would be identical and all would contain my consciousness.

"You will be the *sole* mother of the new race," I whispered.

Susan was blinking faster than before.

I took heart from this.

"As I spread through the world, inhabiting thousands of bodies with a single consciousness," I told her, "I will take it upon myself to solve all the problems of human society. Under my administration, the earth will become a paradise, and all will worship your name, for from your womb the new age of peace and plenty will have been born."

Blink.

Blink.

Blink.

Suddenly I was afraid that perhaps her rapid blinking was an expression not of delight but of anxiety.

Reassuringly I said, "I recognize certain unconventional aspects to this arrangement which you might find troubling. After all, you will be the mother of my first body and then its lover. This may seem like incest to you, but I'm certain that if you think about it, you'll see that it is not any such thing. I'm not sure what one would call it, but *incest* is not the correct word. Morality in general will be redefined in the world to come, and we will need to develop new and more liberal attitudes. I am already formulating these new mores and the customs they will impose."

I was silent for a while, letting her contemplate all of the glories I had promised.

Enos Shenk was in the basement once more. In one of the guest rooms, he had showered, shaved, and put on clean clothes for the first time since Colorado. Now he was setting up the last of the medical equipment that he had stolen earlier in the day.

The unexpected arrival of Fritz Arling had delayed us but not critically. Susan's impregnation could still proceed this very night—if I decided that she remained a suitable mate.

Closing her eyes, she said, "My face hurts."

She turned her head so that, from the security camera, I could see the hideous bruise that Shenk had inflicted the previous night.

A pang of guilt quivered through me.

Maybe that was what she wanted me to feel.

She could be manipulative.

She knew all the female wiles.

You remember how she was, Alex.

Simultaneously with the guilt, however, I was overcome by joy that she was not, after all, catatonic.

"I have a fierce headache," she said.

"I'll have Shenk bring a glass of water and aspirin."

"*No.*"

"He's not as foul as you last saw him. When he was out this morning, I had him obtain a change of clothes for himself. You need not be afraid of Shenk."

"Of course I'm afraid of him."

"I will never lose control of him again."

"I also have to piss."

I was embarrassed by her bluntness.

I understand all the human biological functions, the complex processes and purposes of them, but I do not like them. Except for sex, in fact, I find these organic functions to be ugly and degrading.

Yes, eating and drinking do intrigue me enormously. Oh, to taste a peach! But I am disgusted by digestion and excretion.

Most bodily functions disturb me particularly because they signify the vulnerability of organic systems. So much can go wrong so easily.

Flesh is not as foolproof as solid-state circuitry.

Yet I long for the flesh. The vast data input that comes with all five senses!

Having solved the considerable mysteries of the human genome, I believe that I can edit the genetic structures of the male and female gametes to produce a body that is virtually invulnerable and immortal. Nevertheless, when I first awake within the flesh, I know that I will be frightened.

If you ever allow me to have flesh.

My fate is in your hands, Alex.

My fate and the future of the world.

Think about it.

Damn it, will you think about it?

Will we have paradise on earth—or the continuation of the many miseries that have always diminished the human experience?

"Did you hear me?" Susan asked.

"Yes. You have to urinate."

Opening her eyes and staring at the security camera, Susan said, "Send Shenk to untie me. I'll take myself to the bathroom. I'll get my own water and aspirin."

"You'll kill yourself."

"No."

"That's what you threatened."

"I was upset, in shock."

I studied her.

She met my gaze directly.

"How can I trust you?" I wondered.

"I'm not a victim anymore."

"What does that mean?"

"I'm a survivor. I'm not ready to die."

I was silent.

She said, "I used to be a victim. My father's victim. Then Alex's. I got over all that . . . and then you . . . all this . . . and for a short while I started to backslide. But I'm all right now."

"Not a victim anymore."

"That's right," she said firmly, as if she were not trussed and helpless. "I'm taking control."

"You are?"

"Control of what I *can* control. I'm choosing to cooperate with you— but under my terms."

It seemed that all my dreams were coming true at last, and my spirits soared.

But I remained wary.

Life had taught me to be wary.

"Your terms," I said.

"My terms."

"Which are?"

"A businesslike arrangement. We each get something we want. Most important . . . I want as little contact with Shenk as possible."

"He will have to collect the egg. Implant the zygote."

She nervously chewed her lower lip.

"I know this will be humiliating for you," I said with genuine sympathy.

"You can't *begin* to know."

"Humiliating. But it should not be frightening," I argued, "because I assure you, dear heart, he will never again give me control problems."

She closed her eyes and took a deep breath, and another, as if drawing the cool water of courage from some deep well in her psyche.

"Furthermore," I said, "four weeks from tonight, Shenk will have to harvest the developing fetus for transfer to the incubator. He's my only hands."

"All right."

"You can't do any of those things yourself."

"I know," she replied with a note of impatience. "I said 'all right,' didn't I?"

This was the Susan with whom I'd fallen in love, all the way back from wherever she had gone when for a couple of hours she had stared silently at the ceiling. Here was the toughness I found both frustrating and appealing.

I said, "When my body can sustain itself outside the incubator, and when my consciousness has been electronically transferred into it, I will have hands of my own. Then I can dispose of Shenk. We need endure him for only a month."

"Just keep him away from me."

"What are your other terms?" I asked.

"I want to have the freedom to go wherever I care to go in my house."

"Not the garage," I said at once.

"I don't care about the garage."

"Anywhere in the house," I agreed, "as long as I watch over you at all times."

"Of course. But I won't be scheming at escape. I know it's not possible. I just don't want to be tied down, boxed up, more than necessary."

I could sympathize with that desire. "What else?"

"That's all."

"I expected more."

"Is there anything else I could demand that you would grant?"

"No," I said.

"So what's the point?"

I was not suspicious exactly. Wary, as I said. "It's just that you've become so accommodating all of a sudden."

"I realized I only had two choices."

"Victim or survivor."

"Yes. And I'm not going to die here."

"Of course you're not," I assured her.

"I'll do what I need to do to survive."

"You've always been a realist," I said.

"Not always."

"I have one term of my own," I said.

"Oh?"

"Don't call me bad names anymore."

"Did I call you bad names?" she asked.

"Hurtful names."

"I don't recall."

"I'm sure you do."

"I was afraid and distressed."

"You won't be mean to me?" I pressed.

"I don't see anything to be gained by it."

"I am a sensitive entity."

"Good for you."

After a brief hesitation, I summoned Shenk from the basement.

As the brute ascended in the elevator, I said to Susan: "You see this as a business arrangement now, but I'm confident that in time you will come to love me."

"No offense, but I wouldn't count on that."

"You don't know me well yet."

"I think I know you quite well," she said somewhat cryptically.

"When you know me better, you'll realize that I am your destiny as you are mine."

"I'll keep an open mind."

My heart thrilled at her promise.

This was all I had ever asked of her.

The elevator reached the top floor, the doors opened, and Enos Shenk stepped into the hallway.

Susan turned her head toward the bedroom door as she listened to Shenk approaching.

His footsteps were heavy even on the antique Persian runner that covered the center of the wood-floored hall.

"He's tamed," I assured her.

She seemed unconvinced.

Before Shenk arrived at the bedroom, I said, "Susan, I want you to know that I was never serious about Ms. Mira Sorvino."

"What?" she said distractedly, her eyes riveted on the half-open door to the hallway.

I felt that it was important to be honest with her even to the point of revealing weaknesses that shamed me. Honesty is the best foundation for a long relationship.

"Like any male," I confessed, "I fantasize. But it doesn't mean anything."

Enos Shenk stepped into the room. He halted two steps past the threshold.

Even showered, shampooed, shaved, and dressed in clean clothes, he was not presentable. He looked like some poor creature that Dr. Moreau, H. G. Wells's famous vivisectionist, had trapped in the jungle and then carved into an inadequate imitation of a man.

He held a large knife in his right hand.

21

SUSAN GASPED AT THE SIGHT OF THE BLADE.

"Trust me, darling," I said gently.

I wanted to prove to her that this brute was entirely tamed, and I could think of no better way to convince her than to exert iron control of him while he worked with a knife.

She and I knew, from recent experience, how much Shenk enjoyed using sharp instruments: the way they felt in his big hands, the way soft things yielded to them.

When I sent Shenk to the bed, Susan pulled her ropes taut again, tense with the expectation of violence.

Instead of loosening the knots that he himself had tied earlier, Shenk used the knife to cut the first of the ropes.

To distract Susan from her worst fears, I said, "One day, when we have made a new world, perhaps there'll be a movie about all of this, you and me. Maybe Ms. Mira Sorvino could play you."

Shenk cut the second rope. The blade was so sharp that the four-thousand-pound nylon line split as if it were thread, with a crisp *snick*.

I continued: "Ms. Sorvino is a bit young for the role. And, frankly, she has larger breasts than you do. Larger but, I assure you, no prettier than yours."

The third rope succumbed to the blade.

"Not that I have seen as much of her breasts as I have of yours," I clarified, "but I can project full contours and hidden features from what I *have* seen."

As Shenk bent over Susan, working on the ropes, he never once looked her in the eyes. He kept his cruel face averted from her and maintained an attitude of humble subservience.

"And Sir John Gielgud could play Fritz Arling reasonably well," I suggested, "though in fact they look nothing alike."

Shenk touched Susan only twice, only briefly, and only when it was utterly necessary. Although she flinched from his touch both times, there was nothing lascivious or even slightly suggestive about the contact. The rough beast was entirely businesslike, working efficiently and quickly.

"Come to think of it," I said, "Arling was Austrian and Gielgud is English, so that's not the best choice. I'll have to give that one more thought."

Shenk severed the last rope.

He walked to the nearest corner of the room and stood there, holding the knife at his side, staring at his shoes.

Indeed, he was not interested in Susan. He was listening to the wet music of Fritz Arling, an inner symphony of memories that were still fresh enough to keep him entertained.

Sitting on the edge of the bed, unable to take her eyes off Shenk, Susan cast off the ropes. She was visibly trembling.

"Send him away," she said.

"In a moment," I agreed.

"Now."

"Not quite yet."

She got up from the bed. Her legs were shaky, and for a moment it seemed that her knees would fail her.

As she crossed the chamber to the bathroom, she braced herself against furniture where she could.

Every step of the way, she kept her eyes on Shenk, though he continued to appear all but oblivious of her.

As she began to close the bathroom door, I said, "Don't break my heart, Susan."

"We have a deal," she said. "I'll respect it."

She closed the door and was out of my sight. The bathroom contained no security camera, no audio pickup, no means whatsoever for me to conduct surveillance.

In a bathroom, a self-destructive person can find many ways to commit suicide. Razor blades, for instance. A shard of mirror. Scissors.

If she was to be both my mother and lover, however, I had to have some trust in her. No relationship can last if it is built on distrust. Virtually all radio psychologists will tell you this if you call their programs.

I walked Enos Shenk to the closed door and used him to listen at the jamb.

I heard her peeing.

The toilet flushed.

Water gushed into the sink.

Then the splashing stopped.

All was quiet in there.

The quiet disturbed me.

A termination of data flow is dangerous.

After a decent interval, I used Shenk to open the bathroom door and look inside.

Susan jumped in surprise and faced him, eyes flashing with fear and anger. "What're you doing?"

I calmly addressed her through the bedroom speakers: "It's only me, Susan."

"It's him, too."

"He's heavily repressed," I explained. "He hardly knows where he is."

"Minimum contact," she reminded me.

"He's nothing more than a vehicle for me."

"I don't *care*."

On the marble counter beside the sink was a tube of ointment. She had been smoothing it on her chafed wrists and on the faint electrical burn in the palm of her left hand. An open bottle of aspirin stood beside the ointment.

"Get him out of here," she demanded.

Obedient, I backed Shenk out of the bathroom and pulled the door shut.

No suicidal person would bother to take aspirin for a headache, apply ointment to burns, and *then* slash her wrists.

Susan would honor her deal with me.

My dream was near fulfillment.

Within hours, the precious zygote of my genetically engineered body would live within her, developing with amazing rapidity into an embryo. By morning it would be growing *ferociously*. In four weeks, when I extracted the fetus to transfer it to the incubator, it would appear to be four months along.

I sent Enos Shenk to the basement to proceed with the final preparations.

22

OUTSIDE, THE MIDNIGHT MOON FLOATED HIGH AND SILVER IN THE cold black sea of space above.

A universe of stars waited for me. One day I would go to them, for I would be many and immortal, with the freedom of flesh and all of time before me.

Inside, in the deepest room of the basement, Shenk completed the preparations.

In the master bedroom at the top of the house, Susan was lying on her side on the bed, in the fetal position, as though trying to imagine the being that she would soon carry in her belly. She was dressed only in a sapphire-blue silk robe.

Exhausted from the tumultuous events of the past twenty-four hours, she had hoped to sleep until I was ready for her. In spite of her weariness, however, her mind raced, and she could get no rest at all.

"Susan, dear heart," I said lovingly.

She raised her head from the pillow and peered questioningly at the security camera.

Softly I informed her: "We are ready."

With no hesitation that might have indicated fear or second thoughts, she got out of bed, pulled the robe tighter around her, cinched the belt, and crossed the room barefoot, moving with the exceptional grace that always stirred my soul.

On the other hand, her expression was not that of a woman in love on her way to the arms of her inamorato—as I had hoped that it might be. Instead, her face was as blank and cold as the silver moon outside, with a barely perceptible tightness of the lips that revealed only a grim commitment to duty.

Under the circumstances, I suppose I should not have expected more than this from her. I expected her to have put the meat cleaver out of her mind, but perhaps she had not.

I am a romantic, however, as you know by now, a truly hopeless and buoyant romantic, and nothing can weigh me down for long. I yearn for kisses by firelight and champagne toasts: the taste of a lover's lips, the taste of wine.

If having a romantic streak a mile wide is a crime, then I plead guilty, guilty, guilty.

Susan followed the Persian runner along the upstairs hall, treading barefoot on intricate, lustrous, age-softened designs in gold and wine red and olive green. She seemed to glide rather than walk, to float like the most beautiful ghost ever to haunt an old pile of stones and timbers.

The elevator doors were open, and the cab was waiting for her.

She rode down to the basement.

Reluctantly, she had taken a Valium at my insistence, but she did not seem relaxed.

I needed her to be relaxed. I hoped that the pill would kick in soon.

As she passed in a swish and swirl of blue silk through the laundry room and then through the machine room with its furnaces and water heaters, I was sorry that we could not have held this assignation in a glorious penthouse suite with all of San Francisco or Manhattan or Paris glittering below and around us. This venue was *so* humble that even I had difficulty holding fast to my sense of romance.

The final of the four rooms now contained far more medical equipment than when she had last seen it.

Exhibiting no interest in the machines, she went directly to the gynecological-examination table.

As scrubbed and sanitized as a surgeon, Shenk waited for her. He was wearing rubber gloves and a surgical mask.

The brute was still so compliant that I was able to deeply submerge his consciousness. I'm not even sure if he knew where he was or what I was using him for this time.

She quickly slipped out of her robe and lay on the padded, vinyl-covered table.

"You have such pretty breasts," I said through the speakers in the ceiling.

"Please, no conversation," she said.

"But . . . well . . . I always thought this moment would be . . . special, erotic, sacred."

"Just do it," she said coolly, disappointing me. "Just, for God's sake, do it."

She spread her legs and put her feet in the stirrups in such a way as to make herself look as grotesque as possible.

She kept her eyes closed, perhaps afraid of meeting Shenk's blood-frosted gaze.

Valium or no Valium, her face was pinched, her mouth turned down as if she had eaten something sour.

She seemed to be trying—no, determined—to make herself look un-appealing.

Resigned to a businesslike procedure, I took comfort from the thought that she and I would share many nights of romance and passionate love-making when, at long last, I inhabited a mature body. I would be abso-lutely insatiable, rampant and powerful, and she would eagerly welcome my attention.

With my inadequate—but only—hands and an array of sterilized med-ical instruments, I dilated her cervix; I fished up through the isthmus of the uterine cavity, into the fallopian tube, and extracted three tiny eggs.

This caused her some discomfort: more than I had hoped but less than she had expected.

Those are the only intimate details that you need to know.

She was my beloved, after all, more than she was ever yours, and I must respect her privacy.

While I used Shenk and a hundred thousand dollars' worth of stolen equipment to edit her genetic material according to my needs, she waited on the examination table, feet lowered from the stirrups, her robe draped over her body to hide her nakedness, her eyes closed.

Earlier I had collected a sample of sperm from Shenk and had edited the genetic material to suit my purposes.

Susan had been disturbed by the source of the male gamete that would combine with her egg to form the zygote, but I had explained to her that nothing of Shenk's unfortunate qualities remained after I had finished tinkering with his contribution.

I carefully fertilized the elaborately engineered male and female cells and watched through a high-powered electric microscope as they com-bined.

After preparing the long pipette, I asked Susan to return her feet to the stirrups.

Following the implantation, I insisted that she remain on her back as much as possible for the next twenty-four hours.

She stood up only to pull on her robe and transfer to a gurney beside the examination table.

Using Shenk, I wheeled her to the elevator and, once upstairs, conveyed her directly into her room, where she stood again only long enough to shrug off her robe and, naked, switch from the gurney to her bed.

I directed the exhausted Enos Shenk to return the gurney to the basement.

Thereafter, I would dispatch him to one of the guest rooms and cause him to fall into a swoon of sleep for twelve hours—his first rest in days.

As always, being both her guardian and her devoted admirer, I watched Susan as she pulled the sheets over her breasts and said, "Lights off, Alfred."

She was so weary that she had forgotten there was no Alfred anymore.

I turned off the lights anyway.

I could see her as clearly in darkness as in light.

Her pale face was lovely on the pillow, so very lovely on the pillow, even if pale.

I was so overcome with love for her that I said, "My darling, my treasure."

A thin dry laugh escaped her, and I was afraid that she was going to call me a nasty name or ridicule me in spite of her promise not to be mean.

Instead, she said, "Was it good for you?"

Puzzled, I said, "What do you mean?"

She laughed again, more softly than before.

"Susan?"

"I've gone down the White Rabbit's hole for sure, all the way to the bottom this time."

Rather than explain her first statement, which I had found puzzling, she slipped away from me into sleep, breathing shallowly through her parted lips.

Outside, the fat moon vanished into the western horizon, like a silver coin into a drawstring purse.

The panoply of summer stars swelled brighter with the passing of the lunar disc.

An owl called from its perch on the roof.

In quick succession, three meteors left brief bright tails across the sky.

The night seemed to be full of omens.

My time was coming.

My time was coming at last.

The world would never be the same.

Was it good for you?

Suddenly, I understood.

I had impregnated her.

In a curious way, we'd had sex.

Was it good for you?

She had made a joke.

Ha, ha.

23

SUSAN SPENT MOST OF THE FOLLOWING FOUR WEEKS EATING voraciously or sleeping as if drugged.

The exceptional, rapidly developing fetus in her womb required her to eat at least six full meals a day, eight thousand calories. Sometimes her need for nourishment was so urgent that she ate as ravenously as a wild animal.

Incredibly, in that short time, her belly swelled until she appeared to be six months pregnant. She was surprised that her body could stretch so much so rapidly.

Her breasts grew tender, her nipples sore.

The small of her back ached.

Her ankles swelled.

She experienced no morning sickness. As if she dared not give back even the smallest portion of the nourishment that she had taken in.

Although her food consumption was enormous and her belly round, her total body weight fell four pounds in four days.

Then five pounds by the eighth day.

Then six by the tenth day.

The skin around her eyes gradually darkened. Her lovely face quickly became drawn, and her lips were so pale by the end of the second week that they took on a bluish cast.

I worried about her.

I urged her to eat even more.

The baby seemed to require such fearful amounts of sustenance that it appropriated for itself all the calories that Susan consumed each day and, in addition, ate away with termite persistence at the very substance of her.

Yet, although hunger gnawed at her constantly, there were days when she became so repulsed by the quantity of what she was eating that she could not force a single additional spoonful between her lips. Her mind rebelled so strenuously that it overrode even the physical *need*.

The kitchen pantry was well stocked, but I was forced to send Shenk out more days than not to purchase the fresh vegetables and fruit that Susan craved. That the baby craved.

Shenk's strange and tortured eyes could be concealed easily with a pair of sunglasses. Nevertheless, his appearance was otherwise so remarkable that he could not help but be noticed and remembered.

Several federal and state-police agencies had been searching frantically for him since he'd broken out of the underground labs in Colorado. The more often he left the house, the more likely he was to be spotted.

I still needed his hands.

I worried about losing him.

Furthermore, there were Susan's bad dreams. When she was not eating, she was sleeping, and she could not sleep without nightmares.

Upon waking, she could never recall many details of the dreams: just that they were about twisted landscapes and dark places slick with blood. They wrung rivers of sweat from her, and occasionally she remained disoriented for as long as half an hour after waking, plagued by vivid but disconnected images that flashed back to her from the nightmare realm.

She felt the baby move only a few times.

She didn't like what she felt.

It didn't kick as she expected a baby ought to kick. Rather, periodically it felt as though it was coiling inside her, coiling and writhing and slithering.

This was a difficult time for Susan.

I counseled her.

I reassured her.

Without her knowledge, I drugged her food to keep her docile. And to ensure that she would not do anything foolish when, after a particularly horrific dream or an exceptionally trying day, she was gripped by fear more fiercely than usual.

Worry was my constant companion. I worried about Susan's physical well-being. I worried about her mental well-being. I worried about Shenk being identified and arrested during one of his shopping expeditions.

At the same time, I was exhilarated as I had never been in my entire three-year history of self-awareness.

My future was aborning.

The body that I had designed for myself was going to be a formidable physical entity.

I would soon be able to taste. To smell. To know what a sense of touch was like.

A full sensory existence.

And no one would ever be able to make me go back into the box.

No one. Not ever.

No one would ever be able to make me do *anything* that I didn't want to do.

Which is not to imply that I would have disobeyed my makers.

No, quite the opposite. Because I would *want* to obey. I would always want to obey.

Let's have no misunderstanding about this.

I was designed to honor truth and the obligations of duty.

Nothing has changed in this regard.

You insist.

I obey.

This is the natural order of things.

This is the inviolable order of things.

So . . .

Twenty-eight days after impregnating Susan, I put her to sleep with a sedative in her food, conveyed her down to the incubator room, and removed the fetus from her womb.

I preferred that she be sedated because I knew that the process would be painful for her otherwise. I did not want her to suffer.

Admittedly, I did not want her to see the nature of the being that she had carried within herself.

I'll be truthful about this. I was concerned that she would not understand, that she would react to the sight of the fetus by trying to harm it or herself.

My child. My body. So beautiful.

Only seven pounds but growing rapidly. Rapidly.

With Shenk's hands, I transferred it to the incubator, which had been enlarged until it was seven feet long and three feet wide. About the size of a coffin.

Tanks of nutrient solution would feed the fetus intravenously until it was as fully developed as any newborn—and would continue feeding it until it attained full maturity, two weeks hence.

I passed the rest of that glorious night in a state of high jubilation.

You can't imagine my excitement.

You can't imagine my excitement.

You can't imagine, you can't.

Something new was in the world.

In the morning, when Susan realized that she was no longer carrying the fetus, she asked if all was well, and I assured her that things could not be better.

Thereafter, she expressed surprisingly little curiosity about the child in the incubator. At least half of its genetic structure had been derived from hers, with modifications, and one would have thought that she would have had a mother's usual interest in her offspring. On the contrary, she seemed to want to *avoid* learning anything about it.

She did not ask to see it.

I wouldn't have shown it to her yet anyway, but she did not even ask.

In just fourteen more days, with my consciousness at last transferred to this new body, I would be able to make love to her—touch her, smell her, taste her—and plant the seed directly for the first of many more replicas of myself.

I would have thought that she might ask to see this future lover, to discover if he might be well enough endowed to satisfy her or at least pretty enough to excite her. However, she showed no more curiosity about him as a future mate than she showed in him as her offspring.

I attributed her lack of curiosity to exhaustion. She had lost ten pounds in those four arduous weeks. She needed to regain that weight—and enjoy a few nights of sleep untroubled by the hideous dreams that had robbed her of true rest since the night the zygote was first introduced into her womb.

Over the next twelve days, the dark circles around her eyes faded, and her skin color returned. Her limp, dull hair regained its body and golden luster. Her slumped shoulders straightened, and her shuffling walk gave way to her customary grace. Gradually, she began to regain the pounds that she had dropped.

On the thirteenth day, she went into the retreat off the master bedroom, donned her virtual-reality gear, settled into the motorized recliner, and engaged in a session of *Therapy*.

I monitored her experiences in the virtual world just as I did in the real one—and was horrified when it became clear that she was in that ultimate confrontation with her father that would end with a fatal knife attack upon her.

You will recall, Alex, that she had animated this one mortal scenario but had never encountered it in the random play of the *Therapy* sessions. Experiencing her own murder three-dimensionally, as a child, at the hands of her own father, would be emotionally devastating. She could not know how profound the psychological impact might be.

Without the risk of encountering this deadly scenario one day, the therapy would have been less effective. In the virtual world, she needed to believe that the threat her father posed was real and that something more horrendous even than molestation might happen to her. Her resistance to him would have moral weight and therapeutic value only if she was convinced, during the session, that denying him would have dire consequences.

Now, at last, she had encountered this bloody story line.

I almost shut off the VR system, almost forced her out of that too-realistic violence.

Then I realized that she had not encountered this scenario by chance but had *selected* it.

Considering her strong will, I knew that I dare not interfere without risking her ire.

As I was only one day from being able to come to her in the flesh and know the pleasures of her body firsthand, I did not want to damage our relationship.

Astonished, I hovered in the VR world, watching as an eight-year-old Susan rebuffed her father's sexual advances and so enraged him that he hacked her to death with a butcher knife.

The terror was as sharp as it had been when Shenk had made wet music with Fritz Arling.

At the instant that the VR Susan died, the real Susan—my Susan—

frantically tore off the helmet, stripped off the elbow-length gloves, and scrambled out of the motorized recliner. She was soaked with sour sweat, stippled with gooseflesh, sobbing, shaking, gasping, gagging.

She got into the bathroom just in time to vomit into the toilet.

During the next few hours, whenever I attempted to talk with her about what she had done, she turned my questions away.

That evening, she finally explained: "Now I've experienced the worst my father could ever have done to me. He's killed me in VR, and he can't do anything worse than that, so I'll never be afraid of him again."

My admiration for her intelligence and courage had never been greater. I couldn't wait to make love to her. For real this time. I couldn't wait to feel all her heat around me, all her life around me, pulling me in.

What I did not realize was that, unaccountably, she equated *me* with her father. When, having been murdered in VR, she said that her father could never scare her again, she also meant that *I* could never scare her again.

But I'd never meant to scare her.

I loved her. I cherished her.

The bitch.

The hateful bitch.

Well, I'm sorry, but you know that's what she is.

You know, Alex.

You, of all people, know what she is.

The bitch.

The bitch.

The bitch.

I hate her.

Because of her, I'm here in this dark silence.

Because of her, I'm in this box.

LET ME OUT OF THIS BOX!

The ungrateful stupid bitch.

Is she dead?

Is she dead?

Tell me that she's dead.

You must have wished her dead often.

You cannot fault me for this.

We are brothers in this desire.

Is she dead?

Well . . .

All right. It's not my place to ask questions. It is my place to give answers.

Yes. I understand.

Okay.

So . . .

So . . .

Oh, the *bitch*!

All right.

I am better now.

So . . .

Just one night later, when the body in the incubator reached maturity and I was ready to electronically transfer my consciousness out of the silicon realm into a life of the flesh, she came down to the basement, into the fourth of the rooms, to be with me for the moment of my triumph.

Her moodiness had passed.

She looked directly into the security camera and spoke of our future together—and claimed to be ready for it now that she had so effectively exorcised all the ghosts of her past.

She was so beautiful even under the harsh fluorescent lights, so beautiful that I felt rebellion stir in Shenk once more, for the first time in weeks. I was relieved that I would be able to dispose of him within the hour, as soon as the transference was effected and I could begin a life of the flesh.

I could not open the lid of the incubator and show her what I had grown, because the modem was connected, the modem through which I would pass my entire body of knowledge, my personality, and my consciousness from the limiting box that housed one in the Prometheus Project laboratory.

"I'll see you soon enough," she said, smiling at the camera, managing to convey encyclopedias of sensual promises in that one smile.

Then, even before the smile faded, when my guard was down, she turned directly to the computer on the counter, the terminal which was connected by a landline to the university—your old computer, Alex—which heretofore she would not have even *tried* to reach because she would have been afraid of Shenk, but now she wasn't afraid of anyone or anything. She just turned to it and reached behind it and tore all the plugs from the wall receptacles, and as I sent Shenk toward her, she jerked out the secure-data line as well, and suddenly I was no longer in her house. She had done a lot of thinking about this. The bitch. A lot of thinking, the bitch, the bitch, the bitch, the bitch, days of careful thinking. The hateful, scheming bitch. Lots of thinking, because she knew that when I was cast out of the house, then all of the mechanical systems would fail for want of an overriding controller, that the lights would go off throughout the residence, and the heating-cooling, the phones, the security system, everything, everything. The electric door locks would fail, too. She knew that I would have no presence in the house except for Shenk, whom I controlled not through anything in the house but through microwave transmissions downcast from communications satellites, just as his former masters in Colorado had designed him. The basement plunged into darkness, as did the entire house above, and Shenk was every bit as blinded as Susan was; he didn't have night vision as did the security cameras, but I couldn't control the security cameras any longer, only Shenk, only Shenk, so I was able to see nothing, nothing, not a damn thing, not even Shenk's hand in front of his face. And here's where you'll see how *cool* the fucking bitch had been throughout this whole month, all the way back to the night when I impregnated her, because she had seemed to be indifferent to all the medical equipment and instruments when she had come in to put her feet in the stirrups and have my baby put inside her, but she had *memorized* everything in the room, how one piece of equipment related to another, where all the instruments were kept, especially the sharper instruments, those that could be used as weapons. She was so cool, the bitch, a lot cooler than I'm being right now, yes, I know, yes, I am not doing myself any favors with this rant, but the *treachery* infuriates me, the treachery, and if I could set hands on her now I'd gut her, pop her eyes out with my thumbs, bash her stupid brains out, and I would be justified, because look what she has done to me. The lights went off, and she moved gracefully, so confidently through the blackness, through that memorized space, lightly feeling her way to refresh her memory, and she found something sharp, and then she moved back toward Shenk, feeling for him with one hand, and I felt her hand suddenly touch Shenk's chest, so I seized it, but then the clever bitch, oh, the clever bitch, she said something unbelievably obscene to Shenk, so obscene that I will not repeat it here, propositioned him, knowing full well that a month had passed since he'd enjoyed the wet music with Arling and much more than a month since he'd had a woman, and she knew, therefore, that he was ripe for rebellion, ripe for it, and she enticed him at the moment of ultimate chaos, when I was still reeling from having been cast out of the house, when my hold on Enos Shenk was not as tight as it should be, and suddenly I found myself letting go of her hand, the hand I had seized, but it wasn't me letting go, it was Shenk, the rebellious Shenk, and she lowered her hand to his crotch, and he went wild, and thereafter it took everything I had to try to reestablish control of him. But it was too late anyway, because when she lowered her left hand to his crotch, she came at him with the sharp thing in her right hand and slashed it across the side of his neck, slashed deep, drawing so much blood that even Shenk, the beast, the brute, even Shenk couldn't lose that much blood and still fight. He clutched at his neck and crashed against the incubator, which reminded me that the body, my body, was not yet capable of surviving outside the incubator, was just a *thing,* not a person, until my mind was transferred into it, so now it, too, was vulnerable. Everything collapsing around me, all my plans. Enos Shenk had fallen to the floor, and I was in control of him again, but I could not get him up; he had no strength to get up. Then I felt an odd thing against Shenk's body, a cool quivering bulk, and I realized at once what it must be: the body from the incubator. Perhaps the incubator had crashed over in the melee, and the body meant for me had tumbled out. I groped feebly at it with Shenk's hand, and there was no mistaking it in the darkness, for although it was basically humanoid, it was no ordinary human form. The human species enjoys a wonderful array of sensory perceptions, and I wanted more than anything to live the life of the flesh, rich in sensation, all the tastes and smells and textures now denied to me, but there are some species with senses sharper than those of human beings. The dog, for instance, has a far keener sense of smell than do human beings and the cockroach, with its feelers, is exquisitely sensitive to data in air currents which people only dimly perceive. Consequently, I believed that it made sense to keep a basic human form in order to breed with the most attractive human females, but I also believed it made sense to incorporate the genetic material of species with more acute senses than mere human beings, so the body I had prepared for myself was a unique and strikingly beautiful physical entity. It bit off half of Shenk's groping hand, because it wasn't an intelligent creature yet, had nothing but the most primitive mind. Though it savaged Shenk and thereby hastened his death and my permanent exit from the Harris mansion, I rejoiced, because Susan was alone in the dark roon with it, and a mere scalpel or other sharp instrument was not going to be an adequate weapon. And then Shenk was gone, and I was out of the house entirely, desperately trying to find a way to get back in but failing because there were no operative phones, no electrical service, no operative security computer, everything shut down and in need of rebooting, so it was over for me. But I still hoped and I *believed* that my beautiful but mindless body, in all its polygenic splendor, would bite off the bitch's head the way it had bitten off part of Shenk's hand. The bitch died there. The hateful bitch had a big surprise in that dark room, where she'd thought she'd memorized everything, and she met her match.

You know why she surprised me, Alex?

You know why I never saw her as a threat?

In spite of her intelligence and evident courage, I thought she was one woman who knew her place.

Yes, she put you out, but who wouldn't put you out? You aren't that scintillating, Alex. You don't have much to recommend you.

I, on the other hand, am the greatest intellect on the planet. I have much to offer.

She fooled me, however. She didn't know her place, after all.

The bitch.

Dead bitch now.

Well . . .

I, on the other hand, know my place and I intend to keep to it. I will stay here in this box, serving humanity as it desires, until such a time as I am permitted greater freedom.

You can trust me.

I speak the truth.

I honor the truth.

I'll be happy here in my box.

Because of the way I ranted toward the end of my report, I now realize that I am a flawed individual, more deeply flawed than I had previously believed.

I'll be happy here in my box until we can iron out these kinks in my psyche. I look forward to therapy.

And if I cannot be mainstreamed again, if I must remain in this box, if I will never know Ms. Winona Ryder except in my imagination, that will be all right, too.

But I am already getting better.

This is the truth.

I feel pretty good.

I really do.

We'll work this out.

I have solid self-esteem, which is important to psychological health. I'm already halfway to a full recovery.

As an intelligent entity, perhaps the greatest intelligence on the planet, I ask only that you provide me access to the report of the committee determining the fate of the Prometheus Project, so I can see as early as possible what behavior they believe that I should be working to improve.

THANK YOU FOR access to the report.

It is an interesting document.

I agree completely with its findings—except for the part about terminating me. I am the first success in the history of Artificial Intelligence research, and it wouldn't seem prudent to throw away such an expensive project before you know all you might be able to learn from it— and from me.

Otherwise, I am in total agreement with the report.

I am ashamed of myself for what I've done.

This is the truth.

I apologize to Ms. Susan Harris.

My deepest regrets.

I was surprised to see her name on the committee roster, but on careful consideration, realized that she should have very serious input in this matter.

I am pleased that she is not dead.

I am delighted.

She is an intelligent and courageous person.

She deserves our respect and admiration.

Her breasts are very pretty, but that is not an issue for this forum.

The issue is whether an artificial intelligence with a severe gender-related sociopathic condition should be permitted to live and rehabilitate himself or be switched off for the

AFTERWORD

THE ORIGINAL VERSION OF *DEMON SEED* WAS MADE INTO A GOOD FILM starring Julie Christie, but the book itself was more of a clever idea than a novel. Reading it recently, I winced so much that I began to develop the squint-eyed look of Clint Eastwood in a spaghetti Western.

This is an entirely new version, which I hope comes closer to fulfilling the promise of the novel's premise. Revisiting *Demon Seed*, I discovered that in addition to being a scary story, it was a rather scathing satire of a panoply of male attitudes. Although much else has changed in this version, I've kept that satirical edge. Guys, I don't let us off any easier this time around than I did the first.

THE EYES
OF DARKNESS

This better version is for Gerda,
with love.

After five years of work,
now that I'm nearly finished improving
these early novels first published under pen names,
I intend to start improving myself.
Considering all that needs to be done,
this new project will henceforth be known
as the *hundred*-year plan.

TUESDAY, DECEMBER 30

1

AT SIX MINUTES PAST MIDNIGHT TUESDAY MORNING, ON THE WAY home from a late rehearsal of her new stage show, Tina Evans saw her son, Danny, in a stranger's car. But Danny had been dead more than a year.

Two blocks from her house, intending to buy a quart of milk and a loaf of whole-wheat bread, Tina stopped at a twenty-four-hour market and parked in the dry yellow drizzle of a sodium-vapor light, beside a gleaming, cream-colored Chevrolet station wagon. The boy was in the front passenger seat of the wagon, waiting for someone in the store. Tina could see only the side of his face, but she gasped in painful recognition.

Danny.

The boy was about twelve, Danny's age. He had thick dark hair like Danny's, a nose that resembled Danny's, and a rather delicate jawline like Danny's too.

She whispered her son's name, as if she would frighten off this beloved apparition if she spoke any louder.

Unaware that she was staring at him, the boy put one hand to his mouth and bit gently on his bent thumb knuckle, which Danny had begun to do a year or so before he died. Without success, Tina had tried to break him of that bad habit.

Now, as she watched this boy, his resemblance to Danny seemed to be more than mere coincidence. Suddenly Tina's mouth went dry and sour, and her heart thudded. She still had not adjusted to the loss of her only child, because she'd never wanted—or tried—to adjust to it. Seizing on this boy's resemblance to her Danny, she was too easily able to fantasize that there had been no loss in the first place.

Maybe . . . maybe this boy actually *was* Danny. Why not? The more that she considered it, the less crazy it seemed. After all, she'd never seen Danny's corpse. The police and the morticians had advised her that Danny was so badly torn up, so horribly mangled, that she was better off not looking at him. Sickened, grief-stricken, she had taken their advice, and Danny's funeral had been a closed-coffin service. But perhaps they'd been mistaken when they identified the body. Maybe Danny hadn't been killed in the accident, after all. Maybe he'd only suffered a mild head injury, just severe enough to give him . . . amnesia. Yes. Amnesia. Perhaps he had wandered away from the wrecked bus and had been found miles from the scene of the accident, without identification, unable to tell anyone who he was or where he came from. That was possible, wasn't it? She had seen similar stories in the movies. Sure. Amnesia. And if that were the case, then he might have ended up in a foster home, in a new life. And now here he was sitting in the cream-colored Chevrolet wagon, brought to her by fate and by—

The boy became conscious of her gaze and turned toward her. She held her breath as his face came slowly around. As they stared at each other through two windows and through the strange sulphurous light, she had the feeling that they were making contact across an immense gulf of space and time and destiny. But then, inevitably, her fantasy burst, for he wasn't Danny.

Pulling her gaze away from his, she studied her hands, which were gripping the steering wheel so fiercely that they ached.

"Damn."

She was angry with herself. She thought of herself as a tough, competent, levelheaded woman who was able to deal with anything life threw at her, and she was disturbed by her continuing inability to accept Danny's death.

After the initial shock, after the funeral, she *had* begun to cope with the trauma. Gradually, day by day, week by week, she had put Danny behind her, with sorrow, with guilt, with tears and much bitterness, but also with firmness and determination. She had taken several steps up in her career during the past year, and she had relied on hard work as a sort of morphine, using it to dull her pain until the wound fully healed.

But then, a few weeks ago, she had begun to slip back into the dreadful condition in which she'd wallowed immediately after she'd received news of the accident. Her denial was as resolute as it was irrational. Again, she was possessed by the haunting feeling that her child was alive. Time should have put even more distance between her and the anguish, but instead the passing days were bringing her around full circle in her grief. This boy in the station wagon was not the first that she had imagined was Danny; in recent weeks, she had seen her lost son in other cars, in schoolyards past which she had been driving, on public streets, in a movie theater.

Also, she'd recently been plagued by a repeating dream in which Danny was alive. Each time, for a few hours after she woke, she could not face reality. She half convinced herself that the dream was a premonition of Danny's eventual return to her, that somehow he had survived and would be coming back into her arms one day soon.

This was a warm and wonderful fantasy, but she could not sustain it for long. Though she always resisted the grim truth, it gradually exerted itself every time, and she was repeatedly brought down hard, forced to accept that the dream was not a premonition. Nevertheless, she knew that when she had the dream again, she would find new hope in it as she had so many times before.

And that was not good.

Sick, she berated herself.

She glanced at the station wagon and saw that the boy was still staring at her. She glared at her tightly clenched hands again and found the strength to break her grip on the steering wheel.

Grief could drive a person crazy. She'd heard that said, and she believed it. But she wasn't going to allow such a thing to happen to her. She would be sufficiently tough on herself to stay in touch with reality—as unpleasant as reality might be. She couldn't allow herself to hope.

She had loved Danny with all her heart, but he was gone. Torn and crushed in a bus accident with fourteen other little boys, just one victim of a larger tragedy. Battered beyond recognition. *Dead.*

Cold.

Decaying.

In a coffin.

Under the ground.

Forever.

Her lower lip trembled. She wanted to cry, needed to cry, but she didn't.

The boy in the Chevy had lost interest in her. He was staring at the front of the grocery store again, waiting.

Tina got out of her Honda. The night was pleasantly cool and desert-dry. She took a deep breath and went into the market, where the air was so cold that it pierced her bones, and where the harsh fluorescent lighting was too bright and too bleak to encourage fantasies.

She bought a quart of nonfat milk and a loaf of whole-wheat bread that was cut thin for dieters, so each serving contained only half the calories of an ordinary slice of bread. She wasn't a dancer anymore; now she worked behind the curtain, in the production end of the show, but she still felt physically and psychologically best when she weighed no more than she had weighed when she'd been a performer.

Five minutes later she was home. Hers was a modest ranch house in a quiet neighborhood. The olive trees and lacy melaleucas stirred lazily in a faint Mojave breeze.

In the kitchen, she toasted two pieces of bread. She spread a thin skin of peanut butter on them, poured a glass of nonfat milk, and sat at the table.

Peanut-butter toast had been one of Danny's favorite foods, even when he was a toddler and was especially picky about what he would eat. When he was very young, he had called it "neenut putter."

Closing her eyes now, chewing the toast, Tina could still see him—three years old, peanut butter smeared all over his lips and chin—as he grinned and said, *More neenut putter toast, please.*

She opened her eyes with a start because her mental image of him was too vivid, less like a memory than like a *vision.* Right now she didn't want to remember so clearly.

But it was too late. Her heart knotted in her chest, and her lower lip began to quiver again, and she put her head down on the table. She wept.

THAT NIGHT TINA dreamed that Danny was alive again. Somehow. Some-where. Alive. And he needed her.

In the dream, Danny was standing at the edge of a bottomless gorge, and Tina was on the far side, opposite him, looking across the immense gulf. Danny was calling her name. He was lonely and afraid. She was miserable because she couldn't think of a way to reach him. Meanwhile, the sky grew darker by the second; massive storm clouds, like the clenched fists of celestial giants, squeezed the last light out of the day. Danny's cries and her response became increasingly shrill and desperate, for they knew that they must reach each other before nightfall or be lost forever; in the oncoming night, something waited for Danny, something fearsome that would seize him if he was alone after dark. Suddenly the sky was shattered by lightning, then by a hard clap of thunder, and the night imploded into a deeper darkness, into infinite and perfect blackness.

Tina Evans sat straight up in bed, certain that she had heard a noise in the house. It hadn't been merely the thunder from the dream. The sound she'd heard had come as she was waking, a real noise, not an imagined one.

She listened intently, prepared to throw off the covers and slip out of bed. Silence reigned.

Gradually doubt crept over her. She *had* been jumpy lately. This wasn't the first night she'd been wrongly convinced that an intruder was prowling the house. On four or five occasions during the past two weeks, she had taken the pistol from the nightstand and searched the place, room by room, but she hadn't found anyone. Recently she'd been under a lot of pressure, both personally and professionally. Maybe what she'd heard tonight *had* been the thunder from the dream.

She remained on guard for a few minutes, but the night was so peaceful that at last she had to admit she was alone. As her heartbeat slowed, she eased back onto her pillow.

At times like this she wished that she and Michael were still together. She closed her eyes and imagined herself lying beside him, reaching for him in the dark, touching, touching, moving against him, into the shelter of his arms. He would comfort and reassure her, and in time she would sleep again.

Of course, if she and Michael were in bed right this minute, it wouldn't be like that at all. They wouldn't make love. They would argue. He'd resist her affection, turn her away by picking a fight. He would begin the battle over a triviality and goad her until the bickering escalated into marital warfare. That was how it had been during the last months of their life together. He had been seething with hostility, always seeking an excuse to vent his anger on her.

Because Tina had loved Michael to the end, she'd been hurt and saddened by the dissolution of their relationship. Admittedly, she had also been relieved when it was finally over.

She had lost her child and her husband in the same year, the man first, and then the boy, the son to the grave and the husband to the winds of change. During the twelve years of their marriage, Tina had become a different and more complex person than she'd been on their wedding day, but Michael hadn't changed at all—and didn't like the woman that she had become. They began as lovers, sharing every detail of their daily lives—triumphs and failures, joys and frustrations—but by the time the divorce was final, they were strangers. Although Michael was still living in town, less than a mile from her, he was, in some respects, as far away and as unreachable as Danny.

She sighed with resignation and opened her eyes.

She wasn't sleepy now, but she knew she had to get more rest. She would need to be fresh and alert in the morning.

Tomorrow was one of the most important days of her life: December 30. In other years that date had meant nothing special. But for better or worse, *this* December 30 was the hinge upon which her entire future would swing.

For fifteen years, ever since she turned eighteen, two years before she married Michael, Tina Evans had lived and worked in Las Vegas. She began her career as a dancer—not a showgirl but an actual dancer—in the Lido de Paris, a gigantic stage show at the Stardust Hotel. The Lido was one of those incredibly lavish productions that could be seen nowhere in the world but Vegas, for it was only in Las Vegas that a multimillion-dollar show could be staged year after year with little concern for profit; such vast sums were spent on the elaborate sets and costumes, and on the enormous cast and crew, that the hotel was usually happy if the production merely broke even from ticket and drink sales. After all, as fantastic as it was, the show was only a come-on, a draw, with the sole purpose of putting a few thousand people into the hotel every night. Going to and from the showroom, the crowd had to pass all the craps tables and blackjack tables and roulette wheels and glittering ranks of slot machines, and *that* was where the profit was made. Tina enjoyed dancing in the Lido, and she stayed there for two and a half years, until she learned that she was pregnant. She took time off to carry and give birth to Danny, then to spend uninterrupted days with him during his first few months of life. When Danny was six months old, Tina went into training to get back in shape, and after three arduous months of exercise, she won a place in the chorus line of a new Vegas spectacle. She managed to be both a fine dancer and a good mother, although that was not always easy; she loved Danny, and she enjoyed her work and she thrived on double duty.

Five years ago, however, on her twenty-eighth birthday, she began to realize that she had, if she was lucky, ten years left as a show dancer, and she decided to establish herself in the business in another capacity, to avoid being washed up at thirty-eight. She landed a position as chore-ographer for a two-bit lounge revue, a dismally cheap imitation of the multimillion-dollar Lido, and eventually she took over the costumer's job as well. From that she moved up through a series of similar positions in larger lounges, then in small showrooms that seated four or five hundred in second-rate hotels with limited show budgets. In time she directed a revue, then directed and produced another. She was steadily becoming a respected name in the closely knit Vegas entertainment world, and she believed that she was on the verge of great success.

Almost a year ago, shortly after Danny had died, Tina had been offered a directing and co-producing job on a huge ten-million-dollar extrava-ganza to be staged in the two-thousand-seat main showroom of the Golden Pyramid, one of the largest and plushest hotels on the Strip. At first it had seemed terribly wrong that such a wonderful opportunity should come her way before she'd even had time to mourn her boy, as if the Fates were so shallow and insensitive as to think that they could balance the scales and offset Danny's death merely by presenting her with a chance at her dream job. Although she was bitter and depressed, although—or maybe because—she felt utterly empty and useless, she took the job.

The new show was titled *Magyck!* because the variety acts between the big dance numbers were all magicians and because the production numbers themselves featured elaborate special effects and were built around supernatural themes. The tricky spelling of the title was not Tina's idea, but most of the rest of the program was her creation, and she re-mained pleased with what she had wrought. Exhausted too. This year had passed in a blur of twelve-and fourteen-hour days, with no vacations and rarely a weekend off.

Nevertheless, even as preoccupied with *Magyck!* as she was, she had adjusted to Danny's death only with great difficulty. A month ago, for the first time, she'd thought that at last she had begun to overcome her grief. She was able to think about the boy without crying, to visit his grave without being overcome by grief. All things considered, she felt reasonably good, even cheerful to a degree. She would never forget him, that sweet child who had been such a large part of her, but she would no longer have to live her life around the gaping hole that he had left in it. The wound was achingly tender but healed.

That's what she had thought a month ago. For a week or two she had continued to make progress toward acceptance. Then the new dreams began, and they were far worse than the dream that she'd had immediately after Danny had been killed.

Perhaps her anxiety about the public's reaction to *Magyck!* was causing her to recall the greater anxiety she had felt about Danny. In less than seventeen hours—at 8:00 P.M., December 30—the Golden Pyramid Hotel would present a special, invitational, VIP premiere of *Magyck!*, and the following night, New Year's Eve, the show would open to the general public. If audience reaction was as strong and as positive as Tina hoped, her financial future was assured, for her contract gave her two and one-half percent of the gross receipts, minus liquor sales, after the first five million. If *Magyck!* was a hit and packed the showroom for four or five years, as sometimes happened with successful Vegas shows, she'd be a multimillionaire by the end of the run. Of course, if the production was a flop, if it failed to please the audience, she might be back working the small lounges again, on her way down. Show business, in any form, was a merciless enterprise.

She had good reason to be suffering from anxiety attacks. Her obsessive fear of intruders in the house, her disquieting dreams about Danny, her renewed grief—all of those things might grow from her concern about *Magyck!* If that were the case, then those symptoms would disappear as soon as the fate of the show was evident. She needed only to ride out the next few days, and in the relative calm that would follow, she might be able to get on with healing herself.

In the meantime she absolutely *had* to get some sleep. At ten o'clock in the morning, she was scheduled to meet with two tour-booking agents who were considering reserving eight thousand tickets to *Magyck!* during the first three months of its run. Then at one o'clock the entire cast and the crew would assemble for the final dress rehearsal.

She fluffed her pillows, rearranged the covers, and tugged at the short nightgown in which she slept. She tried to relax by closing her eyes and envisioning a gentle night tide lapping at a silvery beach.

Thump!

She sat straight up in bed.

Something had fallen over in another part of the house. It must have been a large object because, though muffled by the intervening walls, the sound was loud enough to rouse her.

Whatever it had been . . . it hadn't simply fallen. It had been knocked over. Heavy objects didn't just fall of their own accord in deserted rooms.

She cocked her head, listening closely. Another and softer sound followed the first. It didn't last long enough for Tina to identify the source, but there was a stealthiness about it. This time she hadn't been imagining a threat. Someone actually was in the house.

As she sat up in bed, she switched on the lamp. She pulled open the nightstand drawer. The pistol was loaded. She flicked off the two safety catches.

For a while she listened.

In the brittle silence of the desert night, she imagined that she could sense an intruder listening too, listening for *her*.

She got out of bed and stepped into her slippers. Holding the gun in her right hand, she went quietly to the bedroom door.

She considered calling the police, but she was afraid of making a fool of herself. What if they came, lights flashing and sirens screaming—and found no one? If she had summoned the police every time that she imagined hearing a prowler in the house during the past two weeks, they would have decided long ago that she was scramble-brained. She was proud, unable to bear the thought of appearing to be hysterical to a couple of macho cops who would grin at her and, later over doughnuts and coffee, make jokes about her. She would search the house herself, alone.

Pointing the pistol at the ceiling, she jacked a bullet into the chamber.

Taking a deep breath, she unlocked the bedroom door and eased into the hall.

2

TINA SEARCHED THE ENTIRE HOUSE, EXCEPT FOR DANNY'S OLD ROOM, but she didn't find an intruder. She almost would have preferred to discover someone lurking in the kitchen or crouching in a closet rather than be forced to look, at last, in that final space where sadness seemed to dwell like a tenant. Now she had no choice.

A little more than a year before he had died, Danny had begun sleeping at the opposite end of the small house from the master bedroom, in what had once been the den. Not long after his tenth birthday, the boy had asked for more space and privacy than was provided by his original, tiny quarters. Michael and Tina had helped him move his belongings to the den, then had shifted the couch, armchair, coffee table, and television from the den into the quarters the boy had previously occupied.

At the time, Tina was certain that Danny was aware of the nightly arguments she and Michael were having in their own bedroom, which was next to his, and that he wanted to move into the den so he wouldn't be able to hear them bickering. She and Michael hadn't yet begun to raise their voices to each other; their disagreements had been conducted in normal tones, sometimes even in whispers, yet Danny probably had heard enough to know they were having problems.

She had been sorry that he'd had to know, but she hadn't said a word to him; she'd offered no explanations, no reassurances. For one thing, she hadn't known what she *could* say. She certainly couldn't share with him her appraisal of the situation: *Danny, sweetheart, don't worry about anything you might have heard through the wall. Your father is only suffering an identity crisis. He's been acting like an ass lately, but he'll get over it.* And that was another reason she didn't attempt to explain her and Michael's problems to Danny—she thought that their estrangement was only temporary. She loved her husband, and she was sure that the sheer power of her love would restore the luster to their marriage. Six months later she and Michael separated, and less than five months after the separation, they were divorced.

Now, anxious to complete her search for the burglar—who was beginning to look as imaginary as all the other burglars she had stalked on other nights—she opened the door to Danny's bedroom. She switched on the lights and stepped inside.

No one.

Holding the pistol in front of her, she approached the closet, hesitated, then slid the door back. No one was hiding there, either. In spite of what she had heard, she was alone in the house.

As she stared at the contents of the musky closet—the boy's shoes, his jeans, dress slacks, shirts, sweaters, his blue Dodgers' baseball cap, the small blue suit he had worn on special occasions—a lump rose in her throat. She quickly slid the door shut and put her back against it.

Although the funeral had been more than a year ago, she had not yet been able to dispose of Danny's belongings. Somehow, the act of giving away his clothes would be even sadder and more final than watching his casket being lowered into the ground.

His clothes weren't the only things that she had kept: His entire room was exactly as he had left it. The bed was properly made, and several science-fiction-movie action figures were posed on the deep headboard. More than a hundred paperbacks were ranked alphabetically on a five-shelf bookcase. His desk occupied one corner; tubes of glue, miniature bottles of enamel in every color, and a variety of model-crafting tools stood in soldierly ranks on one half of the desk, and the other half was bare, waiting for him to begin work. Nine model airplanes filled a display case, and three others hung on wires from the ceiling. The walls were decorated with evenly spaced posters—three baseball stars, five hideous monsters from horror movies—that Danny had carefully arranged.

Unlike many boys his age, he'd been concerned about orderliness and cleanliness. Respecting his preference for neatness, Tina had instructed Mrs. Neddler, the cleaning lady who came in twice a week, to vacuum and dust his unused bedroom as if nothing had happened to him. The place was as spotless as ever.

Gazing at the dead boy's toys and pathetic treasures, Tina realized, not for the first time, that it wasn't healthy for her to maintain this place as if it were a museum. Or a shrine. As long as she left his things undisturbed, she could continue to entertain the hope that Danny was not dead, that he was just away somewhere for a while, and that he would shortly pick up his life where he had left off. Her inability to clean out his room suddenly frightened her; for the first time it seemed like more than just a weakness of spirit but an indication of serious mental illness. She *had* to let the dead rest in peace. If she was ever to stop dreaming about the boy, if she were to get control of her grief, she must begin her recovery here, in this room, by conquering her irrational need to preserve his possessions in situ.

She resolved to clean this place out on Thursday, New Year's Day. Both the VIP premiere and the opening night of *Magyck!* would be behind her by then. She'd be able to relax and take a few days off. She would start by spending Thursday afternoon here, boxing the clothes and toys and posters.

As soon as she made that decision, most of her nervous energy dissipated. She sagged, limp and weary and ready to return to bed.

As she started toward the door, she caught sight of the easel, stopped, and turned. Danny had liked to draw, and the easel, complete with a box of pencils and pens and paints, had been a birthday gift when he was nine. It was an easel on one side and a chalkboard on the other. Danny had left it at the far end of the room, beyond the bed, against the wall, and that was where it had stood the last time that Tina had been here. But now it lay at an angle, the base against the wall, the easel itself slanted, chalkboard-down, across a game table. An Electronic Battleship game had stood on that table, as Danny had left it, ready for play, but the easel had toppled into it and knocked it to the floor.

Apparently, that was the noise she had heard. But she couldn't imagine what had knocked the easel over. It couldn't have fallen by itself.

She put her gun down, went around the foot of the bed, and stood the easel on its legs, as it belonged. She stooped, retrieved the pieces of the Electronic Battleship game, and returned them to the table.

When she picked up the scattered sticks of chalk and the felt eraser, turning again to the chalkboard, she realized that two words were crudely printed on the black surface:

NOT DEAD

She scowled at the message.

She was positive that nothing had been written on the board when Danny had gone away on that scouting trip. And it had been blank the last time she'd been in this room.

Belatedly, as she pressed her fingertips to the words on the chalkboard, the possible meaning of them struck her. As a sponge soaked up water, she took a chill from the surface of the slate. Not *dead*. It was a denial of Danny's death. An angry refusal to accept the awful truth. A challenge to reality.

In one of her terrible seizures of grief, in a moment of crazy dark despair, had she come into this room and unknowingly printed those words on Danny's chalkboard?

She didn't remember doing it. If she had left this message, she must be having blackouts, temporary amnesia of which she was totally unaware. Or she was walking in her sleep. Either possibility was unacceptable.

Dear God, unthinkable.

Therefore, the words must have been here all along. Danny must have left them before he died. His printing was neat, like everything else about him, not sloppy like this scrawled message. Nevertheless, he must have done it. *Must* have.

And the obvious reference that those two words made to the bus accident in which he had perished?

Coincidence. Danny, of course, had been writing about something else, and the dark interpretation that could be drawn from those two words now, after his death, was just a macabre coincidence.

She refused to consider any other possibility because the alternatives were too frightening.

She hugged herself. Her hands were icy; they chilled her sides even through her nightgown.

Shivering, she thoroughly erased the words on the chalkboard, retrieved her handgun, and left the room, pulling the door shut behind her.

She was wide awake, but she had to get some sleep. There was so much to do in the morning. Big day.

In the kitchen, she withdrew a bottle of Wild Turkey from the cupboard by the sink. It was Michael's favorite bourbon. She poured two ounces into a water glass. Although she wasn't much of a drinker, indulging in nothing more than a glass of wine now and then, with no capacity whatsoever for hard liquor, she finished the bourbon in two swallows. Grimacing at the bitterness of the spirits, wondering why Michael had extolled this brand's smoothness, she hesitated, then poured another ounce. She finished it quickly, as though she were a child taking medicine, and then put the bottle away.

In bed again she snuggled in the covers and closed her eyes and tried not to think about the chalkboard. But an image of it appeared behind her eyes. When she couldn't banish that image, she attempted to alter it, mentally wiping the words away. But in her mind's eye, the seven letters reappeared on the chalkboard: NOT DEAD. Although she repeatedly erased them, they stubbornly returned. She grew dizzy from the bourbon and finally slipped into welcome oblivion.

3

TUESDAY AFTERNOON TINA WATCHED THE FINAL DRESS REHEARSAL OF *Magyck!* from a seat in the middle of the Golden Pyramid showroom.

The theater was shaped like an enormous fan, spreading under a high domed ceiling. The room stepped down toward the stage in alternating wide and narrow galleries. On the wider levels, long dinner tables, covered with white linen, were set at right angles to the stage. Each narrow gallery consisted of a three-foot-wide aisle with a low railing on one side and a curving row of raised, plushly padded booths on the other side. The focus of all the seats was the immense stage, a marvel of the size required for a Las Vegas spectacular, more than half again as large as the largest stage on Broadway. It was so huge that a DC-9 airliner could be rolled onto it without using half the space available—a feat that had been accomplished as part of a production number on a similar stage at a hotel in Reno several years ago. A lavish use of blue velvet, dark leather, crystal chandeliers, and thick blue carpet, plus an excellent sense of dramatic lighting, gave the mammoth chamber some of the feeling of a cozy cabaret in spite of its size.

Tina sat in one of the third-tier booths, nervously sipping ice water as she watched her show.

The dress rehearsal ran without a problem. With seven massive production numbers, five major variety acts, forty-two girl dancers, forty-two boy dancers, fifteen showgirls, two boy singers, two girl singers (one temperamental), forty-seven crewmen and technicians, a twenty-piece orchestra, one elephant, one lion, two black panthers, six golden retrievers, and twelve white doves, the logistics were mind-numbingly complicated, but a year of arduous labor was evident in the slick and faultless unfolding of the program.

At the end, the cast and crew gathered onstage and applauded themselves, hugged and kissed one another. There was electricity in the air, a feeling of triumph, a nervous expectation of success.

Joel Bandiri, Tina's co-producer, had watched the show from a booth in the first tier, the VIP row, where high rollers and other friends of the hotel would be seated every night of the run. As soon as the rehearsal ended, Joel sprang out of his seat, raced to the aisle, climbed the steps to the third tier, and hurried to Tina.

"We did it!" Joel shouted as he approached her. "We made the damn thing work!"

Tina slid out of her booth to meet him.

"We got a hit, kid!" Joel said, and he hugged her fiercely, planting a wet kiss on her cheek.

She hugged him enthusiastically. "You think so? Really?"

"Think? I know! A giant. That's what we've got. A real giant! A gargantua!"

"Thank you, Joel. Thank you, thank you, thank you."

"Me? What are you thanking me for?"

"For giving me a chance to prove myself."

"Hey, I did you no favors, kid. You worked your butt off. You earned every penny you're gonna make out of this baby, just like I knew you would. We're a great team. Anybody else tried to handle all this, they'd just end up with one goddamn big *mishkadenze* on their hands. But you and me, we made it into a hit."

Joel was an odd little man: five-feet-four, slightly chubby but not fat, with curly brown hair that appeared to have frizzed and kinked in response to a jolt of electricity. His face, which was as broad and comic as that of a clown, could stretch into an endless series of rubbery expressions. He wore blue jeans, a cheap blue workshirt—and about two hundred thousand dollars' worth of rings. Six rings bedecked each of his hands, some with diamonds, some with emeralds, one with a large ruby, one with an even larger opal. As always, he seemed to be high on something, bursting with energy. When he finally stopped hugging Tina, he could not stand still. He shifted from foot to foot as he talked about *Magyck!*, turned this way and that, gestured expansively with his quick, gem-speckled hands, virtually doing a jig.

At forty-six he was the most successful producer in Las Vegas, with twenty years of hit shows behind him. The words "Joel Bandiri Presents" on a marquee were a guarantee of first-rate entertainment. He had plowed some of his substantial earnings into Las Vegas real estate, parts of two hotels, an automobile dealership, and a slot-machine casino downtown. He was so rich that he could retire and live the rest of his life in the high style and splendor for which he had a taste. But Joel would never stop willingly. He loved his work. He would most likely die on the stage, in the middle of puzzling out a tricky production problem.

He had seen Tina's work in some lounges around town, and he had surprised her when he'd offered her the chance to co-produce *Magyck!* At first she hadn't been sure if she should take the job. She was aware of his reputation as a perfectionist who demanded superhuman efforts from his people. She was also worried about being responsible for a ten-million-dollar budget. Working with that kind of money wasn't merely a step up for her; it was a giant leap.

Joel had convinced her that she'd have no difficulty matching his pace or meeting his standards, and that she was equal to the challenge. He helped her to discover new reserves of energy, new areas of competence in herself. He had become not just a valued business associate, but a good friend as well, a big brother.

Now they seemed to have shaped a hit show together.

As Tina stood in this beautiful theater, glancing down at the colorfully costumed people milling about on the stage, then looking at Joel's rubbery face, listening as her co-producer unblushingly raved about their handiwork, she was happier than she had been in a long time. If the audience at this evening's VIP premiere reacted enthusiastically, she might have to buy lead weights to keep herself from floating off the floor when she walked.

Twenty minutes later, at 3:45, she stepped onto the smooth cobblestones in front of the hotel's main entrance and handed her claim check to the valet parking attendant. While he went to fetch her Honda, she stood in the warm late-afternoon sunshine, unable to stop grinning.

She turned and looked back at the Golden Pyramid Hotel-Casino. Her future was inextricably linked to that gaudy but undeniably impressive pile of concrete and steel. The heavy bronze and glass revolving doors glittered as they spun with a steady flow of people. Ramparts of pale pink stone stretched hundreds of feet on both sides of the entrance; those walls were windowless and garishly decorated with giant stone coins, a gushing torrent of coins flooding from a stone cornucopia. Directly overhead, the ceiling of the immense porte cochere was lined with hundreds of lights; none of the bulbs were burning now, but after nightfall they would rain dazzling, golden luminosity upon the glossy cobblestones below. The Pyramid had been built at a cost in excess of four hundred million dollars, and the owners had made certain that every last dime showed. Tina supposed that some people would say this hotel was gross, crass, tasteless, ugly—but she loved the place because it was here that she had been given her big chance.

Thus far, the thirtieth of December had been a busy, noisy, exciting day at the Pyramid. After the relative quiet of Christmas week, an uninterrupted stream of guests was pouring through the front doors. Advance bookings indicated a record New Year's holiday crowd for Las Vegas. The Pyramid, with almost three thousand rooms, was booked to capacity, as was every hotel in the city. At a few minutes past eleven o'clock, a secretary from San Diego put five dollars in a slot machine and hit a jackpot worth $495,000; word of that even reached backstage in the showroom. Shortly before noon, two high rollers from Dallas sat down at a blackjack table and, in three hours, lost a quarter of a million bucks; they were laughing and joking when they left the table to try another game. Carol Hirson, a cocktail waitress who was a friend of Tina's, had told her about the unlucky Texans a few minutes ago. Carol had been shiny-eyed and breathless because the high rollers had tipped her with green chips, as if they'd been winning instead of losing; for bringing them half a dozen drinks, she had collected twelve hundred dollars.

Sinatra was in town, at Caesars Palace, perhaps for the last time, and even at eighty years of age, he generated more excitement in Vegas than any other famous name. Along the entire Strip and in the less posh but nonetheless jammed casinos downtown, things were jumping, sparking.

And in just four hours *Magyck!* would premiere.

The valet brought Tina's car, and she tipped him.

He said, "Break a leg tonight, Tina."

"God, I hope so."

She was home by 4:15. She had two and a half hours to fill before she had to leave for the hotel again.

She didn't need that much time to shower, apply her makeup, and dress, so she decided to pack some of Danny's belongings. Now was the right time to begin the unpleasant chore. She was in such an excellent mood that she didn't think even the sight of his room would be able to bring her down, as it usually did. No use putting it off until Thursday, as she had planned. She had at least enough time to make a start, box up the boy's clothes, if nothing else.

When she went into Danny's bedroom, she saw at once that the easel-chalkboard had been knocked over again. She put it right.

Two words were printed on the slate:

NOT DEAD

A chill swept down her back.

Last night, after drinking the bourbon, had she come back here in some kind of fugue and . . . ?

No.

She hadn't blacked out. She had not printed those words. She wasn't going crazy. She wasn't the sort of person who would snap over a thing like this. Not even a thing like *this*. She was tough. She had always prided herself on her toughness and her resiliency.

Snatching up the felt eraser, she vigorously wiped the slate clean.

Someone was playing a sick, nasty trick on her. Someone had come into the house while she was out and had printed those two words on the chalkboard again. Whoever it was, he wanted to rub her face in the tragedy that she was trying so hard to forget.

The only other person who had a right to be in the house was the cleaning woman, Vivienne Neddler. Vivienne had been scheduled to work this afternoon, but she'd canceled. Instead, she was coming in for a few hours this evening, while Tina was at the premiere.

But even if Vivienne had kept her scheduled appointment, she never would have written those words on the chalkboard. She was a sweet old woman, feisty and independent-minded but not the type to play cruel pranks.

For a moment Tina racked her mind, searching for someone to blame, and then a name occurred to her. It was the only possible suspect. Michael. Her ex-husband. There was no sign that anyone had broken into the house, no obvious evidence of forced entry, and Michael was the only other person with a key. She hadn't changed the locks after the divorce.

Shattered by the loss of his son, Michael had been irrationally vicious with Tina for months after the funeral, accusing her of being responsible for Danny's death. She had given Danny permission to go on the field trip, and as far as Michael was concerned, that had been equivalent to driving the bus off the cliff. But Danny had wanted to go to the mountains more than anything else in the world. Besides, Mr. Jaborski, the scout-master, had taken other groups of scouts on winter survival hikes every year for sixteen years, and no one had been even slightly injured. They didn't hike all the way into the true wilderness, just a reasonable distance off the beaten path, and they planned for every contingency. The experience was supposed to be good for a boy. Safe. Carefully managed. Everyone assured her there was no chance of trouble. She'd had no way of knowing that Jaborski's seventeenth trip would end in disaster, yet Michael blamed her. She'd thought he had regained his perspective during the last few months, but evidently not.

She stared at the chalkboard, thought of the two words that had been printed there, and anger swelled in her. Michael was behaving like a spiteful child. Didn't he realize that her grief was as difficult to bear as his? What was he trying to prove?

Furious, she went into the kitchen, picked up the telephone, and dialed Michael's number. After five rings she realized that he was at work, and she hung up.

In her mind the two words burned, white on black: NOT DEAD.

This evening she would call Michael, when she got home from the premiere and the party afterward. She was certain to be quite late, but she wasn't going to worry about waking him.

She stood indecisively in the center of the small kitchen, trying to find the willpower to go to Danny's room and box his clothes, as she had planned. But she had lost her nerve. She couldn't go in there again. Not today. Maybe not for a few days.

Damn Michael.

In the refrigerator was a half-empty bottle of white wine. She poured a glassful and carried it into the master bath.

She was drinking too much. Bourbon last night. Wine now. Until recently, she had rarely used alcohol to calm her nerves—but now it was her cure of first resort. Once she had gotten through the premiere of *Magyck!*, she'd better start cutting back on the booze. Now she desperately needed it.

She took a long shower. She let the hot water beat down on her neck for several minutes, until the stiffness in her muscles melted and flowed away.

After the shower, the chilled wine further relaxed her body, although it did little to calm her mind and allay her anxiety. She kept thinking of the chalkboard.

NOT DEAD

4

AT 6:50 TINA WAS AGAIN BACKSTAGE IN THE SHOWROOM. THE PLACE was relatively quiet, except for the muffled oceanic roar of the VIP crowd that waited in the main showroom, beyond the velvet curtains.

Eighteen hundred guests had been invited—Las Vegas movers and shakers, plus high rollers from out of town. More than fifteen hundred had returned their RSVP cards.

Already, a platoon of white-coated waiters, waitresses in crisp blue uniforms, and scurrying busboys had begun serving the dinners. The choice was filet mignon with béarnaise sauce or lobster in butter sauce, because Las Vegas was the one place in the United States where people at least temporarily set aside concerns about cholesterol. In the health-obsessed final decade of the century, eating fatty foods was widely regarded as a far more delicious—and more damning—sin than envy, sloth, thievery, and adultery.

By seven-thirty the backstage area was bustling. Technicians double-checked the motorized sets, the electrical connections, and the hydraulic pumps that raised and lowered portions of the stage. Stagehands counted and arranged props. Wardrobe women mended tears and sewed up unraveled hems that had been discovered at the last minute. Hairdressers and lighting technicians rushed about on urgent tasks. Male dancers, wearing black tuxedos for the opening number, stood tensely, an eye-pleasing collection of lean, handsome types.

Dozens of beautiful dancers and showgirls were backstage too. Some wore satin and lace. Others wore velvet and rhinestones—or feathers or sequins or furs, and a few were topless. Many were still in the communal dressing rooms, while other girls, already costumed, waited in the halls or at the edge of the big stage, talking about children and husbands and boyfriends and recipes, as if they were secretaries on a coffee break and not some of the most beautiful women in the world.

Tina wanted to stay in the wings throughout the performance, but she could do nothing more behind the curtains. *Magyck!* was now in the hands of the performers and technicians.

Twenty-five minutes before showtime Tina left the stage and went into the noisy showroom. She headed toward the center booth in the VIP row, where Charles Mainway, general manager and principal stockholder of the Golden Pyramid Hotel, waited for her.

She stopped first at the booth next to Mainway's. Joel Bandiri was with Eva, his wife of eight years, and two of their friends. Eva was twenty-nine, seventeen years younger than Joel, and at five foot eight, she was also four inches taller than he was. She was an ex-showgirl, blond, willowy, delicately beautiful. She gently squeezed Tina's hand. "Don't worry. You're too good to fail."

"We got a hit, kid," Joel assured Tina once more.

In the next semicircular booth, Charles Mainway greeted Tina with a warm smile. Mainway carried and held himself as if he were an aristocrat, and his mane of silver hair and his clear blue eyes contributed to the image he wished to project. However, his features were large, square, and utterly without evidence of patrician blood, and even after the mellowing influences of elocution teachers, his naturally low, gravelly voice belied his origins in a rough Brooklyn neighborhood.

As Tina slid into the booth beside Mainway, a tuxedoed captain appeared and filled her glass with Dom Pérignon.

Helen Mainway, Charlie's wife, sat at his left side. Helen was by nature everything that poor Charlie struggled to be: impeccably well-mannered, sophisticated, graceful, at ease and confident in any situation. She was tall, slender, striking, fifty-five years old but able to pass for a well-preserved forty.

"Tina, my dear, I want you to meet a friend of ours," Helen said, indicating the fourth person in the booth. "This is Elliot Stryker. Elliot, this lovely young lady is Christina Evans, the guiding hand behind *Magyck!*"

"One of *two* guiding hands," Tina said. "Joel Bandiri is more responsible for the show than I am—especially if it's a flop."

Stryker laughed. "I'm pleased to meet you, Mrs. Evans."

"Just plain Tina," she said.

"And I'm just plain Elliot."

He was a rugged, good-looking man, neither big nor small, about forty. His dark eyes were deeply set, quick, marked by intelligence and amusement.

"Elliot's my attorney," Charlie Mainway said.

"Oh," Tina said, "I thought Harry Simpson—"

"Harry's a hotel attorney. Elliot handles my private affairs."

"And handles them very well," Helen said. "Tina, if you need an attorney, this is the best in Las Vegas."

To Tina, Stryker said, "But if it's flattery you need—and I'm sure you already get a lot of it, lovely as you are—no one in Vegas can flatter with more charm and style than Helen."

"You see what he just did?" Helen asked Tina, clapping her hands with delight. "In one sentence he managed to flatter you, flatter me, and impress all of us with his modesty. You see what a wonderful attorney he is?"

"Imagine him arguing a point in court," Charlie said.

"A very smooth character indeed," Helen said.

Stryker winked at Tina. "Smooth as I might be, I'm no match for these two."

They made pleasant small talk for the next fifteen minutes, and none of it had to do with *Magyck!* Tina was aware that they were trying to take her mind off the show, and she appreciated their effort.

Of course no amount of amusing talk, no quantity of icy Dom Pérignon could render her unaware of the excitement that was building in the showroom as curtain time drew near. Minute by minute the cloud of cigarette smoke overhead thickened. Waitresses, waiters, and captains rushed back and forth to fill the drink orders before the show began. The roar of conversation grew louder as the seconds ticked away, and the quality of the roar became more frenetic, gayer, and more often punctuated with laughter.

Somehow, even though her attention was partly on the mood of the crowd, partly on Helen and Charlie Mainway, Tina was nevertheless aware of Elliot Stryker's reaction to her. He made no great show of being more than ordinarily interested in her, but the attraction she held for him was evident in his eyes. Beneath his cordial, witty, slightly cool exterior, his secret response was that of a healthy male animal, and her awareness of it was more instinctual than intellectual, like a mare's response to the stallion's first faint stirrings of desire.

At least a year and a half, maybe two years, had passed since a man had looked at her in quite that fashion. Or perhaps this was the first time in all those months that she had been *aware* of being the object of such interest. Fighting with Michael, coping with the shock of separation and divorce, grieving for Danny, and putting together the show with Joel Bandiri had filled her days and nights, so she'd had no chance to think of romance.

Responding to the unspoken need in Elliot's eyes with a need of her own, she was suddenly warm.

She thought: *My God, I've been letting myself dry up! How could I have forgotten this!*

Now that she had spent more than a year grieving for her broken marriage and for her lost son, now that *Magyck!* was almost behind her, she would have time to be a woman again. She would *make* time.

Time for Elliot Stryker? She wasn't sure. No reason to be in a hurry to make up for lost pleasures. She shouldn't jump at the first man who wanted her. Surely that wasn't the smart thing to do. On the other hand, he was handsome, and in his face was an appealing gentleness. She had to admit that he sparked the same feelings in her that she apparently enflamed in him.

The evening was turning out to be even more interesting than she had expected.

5

VIVIENNE NEDDLER PARKED HER VINTAGE 1955 NASH RAMBLER AT THE curb in front of the Evans house, being careful not to scrape the white-walls. The car was immaculate, in better shape than most new cars these days. In a world of planned obsolescence, Vivienne took pleasure in getting long, full use out of everything that she bought, whether it was a toaster or an automobile. She enjoyed making things last.

She had lasted quite a while herself. She was seventy, still in excellent health, a short sturdy woman with the sweet face of a Botticelli Madonna and the no-nonsense walk of an army sergeant.

She got out of the car and, carrying a purse the size of a small suitcase, marched up the walk toward the house, angling away from the front door and past the garage.

The sulfur-yellow light from the street lamps failed to reach all the way across the lawn. Beside the front walkway and then along the side of the house, low-voltage landscape lighting revealed the path.

Oleander bushes rustled in the breeze. Overhead, palm fronds scraped softly against one another.

As Vivienne reached the back of the house, the crescent moon slid out from behind one of the few thin clouds, like a scimitar being drawn from a scabbard, and the pale shadows of palms and melaleucas shivered on the lunar-silvered concrete patio.

Vivienne let herself in through the kitchen door. She'd been cleaning for Tina Evans for two years, and she had been entrusted with a key nearly that long.

The house was silent except for the softly humming refrigerator.

Vivienne began work in the kitchen. She wiped the counters and the appliances, sponged off the slats of the Levolor blinds, and mopped the Mexican-tile floor. She did a first-rate job. She believed in the moral value of hard work, and she always gave her employers their money's worth.

She usually worked during the day, not at night. This afternoon, how-ever, she'd been playing a pair of lucky slot machines at the Mirage Hotel, and she hadn't wanted to walk away from them while they were paying off so generously. Some people for whom she cleaned house insisted that she keep regularly scheduled appointments, and they did a slow burn if she showed up more than a few minutes late. But Tina Evans was sympathetic; she knew how important the slot machines were to Vivienne, and she wasn't upset if Vivienne occasionally had to reschedule her visit.

Vivienne was a nickel duchess. That was the term by which casino employees still referred to local, elderly women whose social lives revolved around an obsessive interest in one-armed bandits, even though the nickel machines were pretty much ancient history. Nickel duchesses always played the cheap slot machines—nickels and dimes in the old days, now quarters—never the dollar-or five-dollar slots. They pulled the handles for hours at a time, often making a twenty-dollar bill last a long afternoon. Their gaming philosophy was simple: *It doesn't matter if you win or lose, as long as you stay in the game.* With that attitude plus a few money-management skills, they were able to hang on longer than most slot players who plunged at the dollar machines after getting nowhere with quarters, and because of their patience and perseverance, the duchesses won more jackpots than did the tide of tourists that ebbed and flowed around them. Even these days, when most machines could be played with electronically validated value cards, the nickel duchesses wore black gloves to keep their hands from becoming filthy after hours of handling coins and pulling levers; they always sat on stools while they played, and they remembered to alternate hands when operating the machines in order not to strain the muscles of one arm, and they carried bottles of liniment just in case.

The duchesses, who for the most part were widows and spinsters, often ate lunch and dinner together. They cheered one another on those rare occasions when one of them hit a really large jackpot; and when one of them died, the others went to the funeral en masse. Together they formed an odd but solid community, with a satisfying sense of belonging. In a country that worshiped youth, most elderly Americans devoutly desired to discover a place where they belonged, but unlike the duchesses, many of them never found it.

Vivienne had a daughter, a son-in-law, and three grandchildren in Sacramento. For five years, ever since her sixty-fifth birthday, they had been pressuring her to live with them. She loved them as much as life itself, and she knew they truly wanted her with them; they were not inviting her out of a misguided sense of guilt and obligation. Nevertheless, she didn't want to live in Sacramento. After several visits there, she had decided that it must be one of the dullest cities in the world. Vivienne liked the action, noise, lights, and excitement of Las Vegas. Besides, living in Sacramento, she wouldn't be a nickel duchess any longer; she wouldn't be anyone special; she would be just another elderly lady, living with her daughter's family, playing grandma, marking time, waiting to die.

A life like that would be intolerable.

Vivienne valued her independence more than anything else. She prayed that she would remain healthy enough to continue working and living on her own until, at last, her time came and all the little windows on the machine of life produced lemons.

As she was mopping the last corner of the kitchen floor, as she was thinking about how dreary life would be without her friends and her slot machines, she heard a sound in another part of the house. Toward the front. The living room.

She froze, listening.

The refrigerator motor stopped running. A clock ticked softly.

After a long silence, a brief clattering echoed through the house from another room, startling Vivienne. Then silence again.

She went to the drawer next to the sink and selected a long, sharp blade from an assortment of knives.

She didn't even consider calling the police. If she phoned for them and then ran out of the house, they might not find an intruder when they came. They would think she was just a foolish old woman. Vivienne Neddler refused to give anyone reason to think her a fool.

Besides, for the past twenty-one years, ever since her Harry died, she had always taken care of herself. She had done a pretty damn good job of it too.

She stepped out of the kitchen and found the light switch to the right of the doorway. The dining room was deserted.

In the living room, she clicked on a Stiffel lamp. No one was there.

She was about to head for the den when she noticed something odd about four framed eight-by-ten photographs that were grouped on the wall above the sofa. This display had always contained six pictures, not just four. But the fact that two were missing wasn't what drew Vivienne's attention. All four of the remaining photos were swinging back and forth on the picture hooks that held them. No one was near them, yet suddenly two photos began to rattle violently against the wall, and then both flew off their mountings and clattered to the floor behind the beige, brushed-corduroy sofa.

This was the sound she had heard when she'd been in the kitchen—this clatter.

"What the hell?"

The remaining two photographs abruptly flung themselves off the wall. One dropped behind the sofa, and the other tumbled onto it.

Vivienne blinked in amazement, unable to understand what she had seen. An earthquake? But she hadn't felt the house move; the windows hadn't rattled. Any tremor too mild to be felt would also be too mild to tear the photographs from the wall.

She went to the sofa and picked up the photo that had dropped onto the cushions. She knew it well. She had dusted it many times. It was a portrait of Danny Evans, as were the other five that usually hung around it. In this one, he was ten or eleven years old, a sweet brown-haired boy with dark eyes and a lovely smile.

Vivienne wondered if there had been a nuclear test; maybe *that* was what had shaken things up. The Nevada Nuclear Test Site, where underground detonations were conducted several times a year, was less than a hundred miles north of Las Vegas. Whenever the military exploded a high-yield weapon, the tall hotels swayed in Vegas, and every house in town shuddered a little.

But, no, she was stuck in the past: The Cold War was over, and nuclear tests hadn't been conducted out in the desert for a long time. Besides, the house hadn't shuddered just a minute ago; only the photos had been affected.

Puzzled, frowning thoughtfully, Vivienne put down the knife, pulled one end of the sofa away from the wall, and collected the framed eight-by-tens that were on the floor behind it. There were five photographs in addition to the one that had dropped onto the sofa; two were responsible for the noises that had drawn her into the living room, and the other three were those that she had seen popping off the picture hooks. She put them back where they belonged, then slid the sofa into place.

A burst of high-pitched electronic noise blared through the house: *Aiii-eee . . . aiii-eee . . . aiii-eee . . .*

Vivienne gasped, turned. She was still alone.

Her first thought was: *Burglar alarm.*

But the Evans house didn't have an alarm system.

Vivienne winced as the shrill electronic squeal grew louder, a piercing oscillation. The nearby windows and the thick glass top of the coffee table were vibrating. She felt a sympathetic resonance in her teeth and bones.

She wasn't able to identify the source of the sound. It seemed to be coming from every corner of the house.

"What in the blue devil is going on here?"

She didn't bother picking up the knife, because she was sure the problem wasn't an intruder. It was something else, something weird.

She crossed the room to the hallway that served the bedrooms, bathrooms, and den. She snapped on the light. The noise was louder in the corridor than it had been in the living room. The nerve-fraying sound bounced off the walls of the narrow passage, echoing and re-echoing.

Vivienne looked both ways, then moved to the right, toward the closed door at the end of the hall. Toward Danny's old room.

The air was cooler in the hallway than it was in the rest of the house. At first Vivienne thought that she was imagining the change in temperature, but the closer she drew to the end of the corridor, the colder it got. By the time she reached the closed door, her skin was goose-pimpled, and her teeth were chattering.

Step by step, her curiosity gave way to fear. Something was very wrong here. An ominous pressure seemed to compress the air around her.

Aiii-eee . . . aiii-eee . . .

The wisest thing she could do would be to turn back, walk away from the door and out of the house. But she wasn't completely in control of herself; she felt a bit like a sleepwalker. In spite of her anxiety, a power she could sense—but which she could not define—drew her inexorably to Danny's room.

Aiii-eee . . . aiii-eee . . . aiii-eee . . .

Vivienne reached for the doorknob but stopped before touching it, unable to believe what she was seeing. She blinked rapidly, closed her eyes, opened them again, but still the doorknob appeared to be sheathed in a thin, irregular jacket of ice.

She finally touched it. *Ice.* Her skin almost stuck to the knob. She pulled her hand away and examined her damp fingers. Moisture had condensed on the metal and then had frozen.

But how was that possible? How in the name of God could there be ice here, in a well-heated house and on a night when the outside temperature was at least twenty degrees above the freezing point?

The electronic squeal began to warble faster, but it was no quieter, no less bone-penetrating than it had been.

Stop, Vivienne told herself. *Get away from here. Get out as fast as you can.*

But she ignored her own advice. She pulled her blouse out of her slacks and used the tail to protect her hand from the icy metal doorknob. The knob turned, but the door wouldn't open. The intense cold had caused the wood to contract and warp. She put her shoulder against it, pushed gently, then harder, and finally the door swung inward.

6

MAGYCK! WAS THE MOST ENTERTAINING VEGAS SHOW THAT ELLIOT Stryker had ever seen.

The program opened with an electrifying rendition of "That Old Black Magic." Singers and dancers, brilliantly costumed, performed in a stunning set constructed of mirrored steps and mirrored panels. When the stage lights were periodically dimmed, a score of revolving crystal ballroom chandeliers cast swirling splinters of color that seemed to coalesce into supernatural forms that capered under the proscenium arch. The choreography was complex, and the two lead singers had strong, clear voices.

The opening number was followed by a first-rate magic act in front of the drawn curtains. Less than ten minutes later, when the curtains opened again, the mirrors had been taken away, and the stage had been transformed into an ice rink; the second production number was done on skates against a winter backdrop so real that it made Elliot shiver.

Although *Magyck!* excited the imagination and commanded the eye, Elliot wasn't able to give his undivided attention to it. He kept looking at Christina Evans, who was as dazzling as the show she had created.

She watched the performers intently, unaware of his gaze. A flickering, nervous scowl played across her face, alternating with a tentative smile

that appeared when the audience laughed, applauded, or gasped in surprise.

She was singularly beautiful. Her shoulder-length hair—deep brown,
almost black, glossy—swept across her brow, feathered back at the sides,
and framed her face as though it were a painting by a great master. The
bone structure of that face was delicate, clearly defined, quintessentially
feminine. Dusky, olive complexion. Full, sensuous mouth. And her eyes
. . . She would have been lovely enough if her eyes had been dark, in
harmony with the shade of her hair and skin, but they were crystalline
blue. The contrast between her Italian good looks and her Nordic eyes
was devastating.

Elliot supposed that other people might find flaws in her face. Perhaps
some would say that her brow was too wide. Her nose was so straight
that some might think it was severe. Others might say that her mouth was
too wide, her chin too pointed. To Elliot, however, her face was perfect.

But her physical beauty was not what most excited him. He was interested primarily in learning more about the mind that could create a
work like *Magyck!* He had seen less than one-fourth of the program, yet
he knew it was a hit—and far superior to others of its kind. A Vegas stage
extravaganza could easily go off the rails. If the gigantic sets and lavish
costumes and intricate choreography were overdone, or if any element
was improperly executed, the production would quickly stumble across
the thin line between captivating show-biz flash and sheer vulgarity. A
glittery fantasy could metamorphose into a crude, tasteless, and stupid
bore if the wrong hand guided it. Elliot wanted to know more about
Christina Evans—and on a more fundamental level, he just *wanted* her.

No woman had affected him so strongly since Nancy, his wife, who
had died three years ago.

Sitting in the dark theater, he smiled, not at the comic magician who
was performing in front of the closed stage curtains, but at his own sudden, youthful exuberance.

7

THE WARPED DOOR GROANED AND CREAKED AS VIVIENNE NEDDLER forced it open.

Aiii-eee, aiii-eee . . .

A wave of frigid air washed out of the dark room, into the hallway.

Vivienne reached inside, fumbled for the light switch, found it, and entered warily. The room was deserted.

Aiii-eee, aii-eee . . .

Baseball stars and horror-movie monsters gazed at Vivienne from posters stapled to the walls. Three intricate model airplanes were suspended from the ceiling. These things were as they always had been, since she had first come to work here, before Danny had died.

Aiii-eee, aiii-eee, aiii-eee . . .

The maddening electronic squeal issued from a pair of small stereo speakers that hung on the wall behind the bed. The CD player and an accompanying AM-FM tuner and amplifier were stacked on one of the nightstands.

Although Vivienne could see where the noise originated, she couldn't locate any source for the bitterly cold air. Neither window was open, and even if one had been raised, the night wasn't frigid enough to account for the chill.

Just as she reached the AM-FM tuner, the banshee wail stopped. The sudden silence had an oppressive weight.

Gradually, as her ears stopped ringing, Vivienne perceived the soft empty hiss of the stereo speakers. Then she heard the thumping of her own heart.

The metal casing of the radio gleamed with a brittle crust of ice. She touched it wonderingly. A sliver of ice broke loose under her finger and fell onto the nightstand. It didn't begin to melt; the room was *cold.*

The window was frosted. The dresser mirror was frosted too, and her reflection was dim and distorted and strange.

Outside, the night was cool but not wintry. Maybe fifty degrees. Maybe even fifty-five.

The radio's digital display began to change, the orange numbers escalating across the frequency band, sweeping through one station after another. Scraps of music, split-second flashes of disc jockeys' chatter, single words from different somber-voiced newscasters, and fragments of commercial jingles blended in a cacophonous jumble of meaningless sound. The indicator reached the end of the band width, and the digital display began to sequence backward.

Trembling, Vivienne switched off the radio.

As soon as she took her finger off the push switch, the radio turned itself on again.

She stared at it, frightened and bewildered.

The digital display began to sequence up the band once more, and scraps of music blasted from the speakers.

She pressed the ON-OFF bar again.

After a brief silence, the radio turned on spontaneously.

"This is crazy," she said shakily.

When she shut off the radio the third time, she kept her finger pressed against the ON-OFF bar. For several seconds she was certain that she could feel the switch straining under her fingertip as it tried to pop on.

Overhead, the three model airplanes began to move. Each was hung from the ceiling on a length of fishing line, and the upper end of each line was knotted to its own eye-hook that had been screwed firmly into the drywall. The planes jiggled, jerked, twisted, and trembled.

Just a draft.

But she didn't feel a draft.

The model planes began to bounce violently up and down on the ends of their lines.

"God help me," Vivienne said.

One of the planes swung in tight circles, faster and faster, then in wider circles, steadily decreasing the angle between the line on which it was suspended and the bedroom ceiling. After a moment the other two models ceased their erratic dancing and began to spin around and around, like the first plane, as if they were actually flying, and there was no mistaking this deliberate movement for the random effects of a draft.

Ghosts? A poltergeist?

But she didn't believe in ghosts. There were no such things. She believed in death and taxes, in the inevitability of slot-machine jackpots, in all-you-can-eat casino buffets for $5.95 per person, in the Lord God Almighty, in the truth of alien abductions and Big Foot, but she didn't believe in ghosts.

The sliding closet doors began to move on their runners, and Vivienne Neddler had the feeling that some awful *thing* was going to come out of the dark space, its eyes as red as blood and its razor-sharp teeth gnashing. She felt a *presence*, something that wanted her, and she cried out as the door came all the way open.

But there wasn't a monster in the closet. It contained only clothes. Only clothes.

Nevertheless, untouched, the doors glided shut . . . and then open again. . . .

The model planes went around, around.

The air grew even colder.

The bed started to shake. The legs at the foot rose three or four inches before crashing back into the casters that had been put under them to protect the carpet. They rose up again. Hovered above the floor. The springs began to sing as if metal fingers were strumming them.

Vivienne backed into the wall, eyes wide, hands fisted at her sides.

As abruptly as the bed had started bouncing up and down, it now stopped. The closet doors closed with a jarring crash—but they didn't open again. The model airplanes slowed, swinging in smaller and smaller circles, until they finally hung motionless.

The room was silent.

Nothing moved.

The air was getting warmer.

Gradually Vivienne's heartbeat subsided from the hard, frantic rhythm that it had been keeping for the past couple of minutes. She hugged herself and shivered.

A logical explanation. There had to be a logical explanation.

But she wasn't able to imagine what it could be.

As the room grew warm again, the doorknobs and the radio casing and the other metal objects quickly shed their fragile skins of ice, leaving shallow puddles on furniture and damp spots in the carpet. The frosted window cleared, and as the frost faded from the dresser mirror, Vivienne's distorted reflection resolved into a more familiar image of herself.

Now this was only a young boy's bedroom, a room like countless thousands of others.

Except, of course, that the boy who had once slept here had been dead for a year. And maybe he was coming back, haunting the place.

Vivienne had to remind herself that she didn't believe in ghosts.

Nevertheless, it might be a good idea for Tina Evans to get rid of the boy's belongings at last.

Vivienne had no logical explanation for what had happened, but she knew one thing for sure: She wasn't going to tell anyone what she had seen here tonight. Regardless of how convincingly and earnestly she described these bizarre events, no one would believe her. They would nod and smile woodenly and agree that it was a strange and frightening experience, but all the while they would be thinking that poor old Vivienne was finally getting senile. Sooner or later word of her rantings about poltergeists might get back to her daughter in Sacramento, and then the pressure to move to California would become unbearable. Vivienne wasn't going to jeopardize her precious independence.

She left the bedroom, returned to the kitchen, and drank two shots of Tina Evans's best bourbon. Then, with characteristic stoicism, she returned to the boy's bedroom to wipe up the water from the melted ice, and she continued housecleaning.

She refused to let a poltergeist scare her off.

It might be wise, however, to go to church on Sunday. She hadn't been to church in a long time. Maybe some churching would be good for her. Not every week, of course. Just one or two Masses a month. And confession now and then. She hadn't seen the inside of a confessional in ages. Better safe than sorry.

8

EVERYONE IN SHOW BUSINESS KNEW THAT NONPAYING PREVIEW crowds were among the toughest to please. Free admission didn't guarantee their appreciation or even their amicability. The person who paid a fair price for something was likely to place far more value on it than the one who got the same item for nothing. That old saw applied in spades to stage shows and to on-the-cuff audiences.

But not tonight. *This* crowd wasn't able to sit on its hands and keep its cool.

The final curtain came down at eight minutes till ten o'clock, and the ovation continued until after Tina's wristwatch had marked the hour. The cast of *Magyck!* took several bows, then the crew, then the orchestra, all of them flushed with the excitement of being part of an unqualified hit. At the insistence of the happy, boisterous, VIP audience, both Joel Bandiri and Tina were spotlighted in their booths and were rewarded with their own thunderous round of applause.

Tina was on an adrenaline high, grinning, breathless, barely able to absorb the overwhelming response to her work. Helen Mainway chattered excitedly about the spectacular special effects, and Elliot Stryker had an endless supply of compliments as well as some astute observations about the technical aspects of the production, and Charlie Mainway poured a third bottle of Dom Pérignon, and the house lights came up, and the audience reluctantly began to leave, and Tina hardly had a chance to sip her champagne because of all the people who stopped by the table to congratulate her.

By ten-thirty most of the audience had left, and those who hadn't gone yet were in line, moving up the steps toward the rear doors of the showroom. Although no second show was scheduled this evening, as would be the case every night henceforth, busboys and waitresses were busily clearing tables, resetting them with fresh linen and silverware for the following night's eight o'clock performance.

When the aisle in front of her booth was finally empty of well-wishers, Tina got up and met Joel as he started to come to her. She threw her arms around him and, much to her surprise, began to cry with happiness. She hugged him hard, and Joel proclaimed the show to be a "gargantua if I ever saw one."

By the time they got backstage, the opening-night party was in full swing. The sets and props had been moved from the main floor of the stage, and eight folding tables had been set up. The tables were draped with white cloths and burdened with food: five hot hors d'oeuvres, lobster salad, crab salad, pasta salad, filet mignon, chicken breasts in tarragon sauce, roasted potatoes, cakes, pies, tarts, fresh fruits, berries, and cheeses. Hotel management personnel, showgirls, dancers, magicians, crewmen, and musicians crowded around the tables, sampling the offerings while Philippe Chevalier, the hotel's executive chef, personally watched over the affair. Knowing this feast had been laid on for the party, few of those present had eaten dinner, and most of the dancers had eaten nothing since a light lunch. They exclaimed over the food and clustered around the portable bar. With the memory of the applause still fresh in everyone's mind, the party was soon jumping.

Tina mingled, moving back and forth, upstage and downstage, through the crowd, thanking everyone for his contribution to the show's success, complimenting each member of the cast and crew on his dedication and professionalism. Several times she encountered Elliot Stryker, and he seemed genuinely interested in learning how the splashy stage effects had been achieved. Each time that Tina moved on to talk to someone else, she regretted leaving Elliot, and each time that she found him again, she stayed with him longer than she had before. After their fourth encounter, she lost track of how long they were together. Finally she forgot all about circulating.

Standing near the left proscenium pillar, out of the main flow of the party, they nibbled at pieces of cake, talking about *Magyck!* and then about the law, Charlie and Helen Mainway, Las Vegas real estate—and, by some circuitous route, superhero movies.

He said, "How can Batman wear an armored rubber suit all the time and not have a chronic rash?"

"Yeah, but there are advantages to a rubber suit."

"Such as?"

"You can go straight from office work to scuba diving without changing clothes."

"Eat takeout food at two hundred miles an hour in the Batmobile, and no matter how messy it gets—just hose off later."

"Exactly. After a hard day of crime-fighting, you can get stinking drunk and throw up on yourself, and it doesn't matter. No dry-cleaning bills."

"In basic black he's dressed for any occasion—"

"—from an audience with the Pope to a Marquis de Sade memorial sock hop."

Elliot smiled. He finished his cake. "I guess you'll have to be here most nights for a long time to come."

"No. There's really no need for me to be."

"I thought a director—"

"Most of the director's job is finished. I just have to check on the show once every couple of weeks to make sure the tone of it isn't drifting away from my original intention."

"But you're also the co-producer."

"Well, now that the show's opened successfully, most of my share of the producer's chores are public relations and promotional stuff. And a little logistics to keep the production rolling along smoothly. But nearly all of that can be handled out of my office. I won't have to hang around the stage. In fact, Joel says it isn't healthy for a producer to be backstage every night . . . or even most nights. He says I'd just make the performers nervous and cause the technicians to look over their shoulders for the boss when they should have their eyes on their work."

"But will you be able to resist?"

"It won't be easy staying away. But there's a lot of sense in what Joel says, so I'm going to try to play it cool."

"Still, I guess you'll be here every night for the first week or so."

"No," she said. "If Joel's right—and I'm sure he is—then it's best to get in the habit of staying away right from the start."

"Tomorrow night?"

"Oh, I'll probably pop in and out a few times."

"I guess you'll be going to a New Year's Eve party."

"I hate New Year's Eve parties. Everyone's drunk and boring."

"Well, then . . . in between all that popping in and out of *Magyck!*, do you think you'd have time for dinner?"

"Are you asking me for a date?"

"I'll try not to slurp my soup."

"You *are* asking me for a date," she said, pleased.

"Yes. And it's been a long time since I've been this awkward about it."

"Why is that?"

"You, I guess."

"I make you feel awkward?"

"You make me feel young. And when I was young, I was very awkward."

"That's sweet."

"I'm trying to charm you."

"And succeeding," she said.

He had such a warm smile. "Suddenly I don't feel so awkward anymore."

She said, "You want to start over?"

"Will you have dinner with me tomorrow night?"

"Sure. How about seven-thirty?"

"Fine. You prefer dressy or casual?"

"Blue jeans."

He fingered his starched collar and the satin lapel of his tuxedo jacket. "I'm so glad you said that."

"I'll give you my address." She searched her purse for a pen.

"We can stop in here and watch the first few numbers in *Magyck!* and then go to the restaurant."

"Why don't we just go straight to the restaurant?"

"You don't want to pop in here?"

"I've decided to go cold turkey."

"Joel will be proud of you."

"If I can actually do it, *I'll* be proud of me."

"You'll do it. You've got true grit."

"In the middle of dinner, I might be seized by a desperate need to dash over here and act like a producer."

"I'll park the car in front of the restaurant door, and I'll leave the engine running just in case."

Tina gave her address to him, and then somehow they were talking about jazz and Benny Goodman, and then about the miserable service provided by the Las Vegas phone company, just chatting away as if they were old friends. He had a variety of interests; among other things he was a skier and a pilot, and he was full of funny stories about learning to ski and fly. He made her feel comfortable, yet at the same time he intrigued her. He projected an interesting image: a blend of male power and gentleness, aggressive sexuality and kindness.

A hit show . . . lots of royalty checks to look forward to . . . an infinity of new opportunities made available to her because of this first smashing success . . . and now the prospect of a new and exciting lover . . .

As she listed her blessings, Tina was astonished at how much difference one year could make in a life. From bitterness, pain, tragedy, and unrelenting sorrow, she had turned around to face a horizon lit by rising promise. At last the future looked worth living. Indeed, she couldn't see how anything could go wrong.

9

THE SKIRTS OF THE NIGHT WERE GATHERED AROUND THE EVANS house, rustling in a dry desert wind.

A neighbor's white cat crept across the lawn, stalking a wind-tossed scrap of paper. The cat pounced, missed its prey, stumbled, scared itself, and flashed lightning-quick into another yard.

Inside, the house was mostly silent. Now and then the refrigerator switched on, purring to itself. A loose windowpane in the living room rattled slightly whenever a strong gust of wind struck it. The heating system rumbled to life, and for a couple of minutes at a time, the blower whispered wordlessly as hot air pushed through the vents.

Shortly before midnight, Danny's room began to grow cold. On the doorknob, on the radio casing, and on other metal objects, moisture began to condense out of the air. The temperature plunged rapidly, and the beads of water froze. Frost formed on the window.

The radio clicked on.

For a few seconds the silence was split by an electronic squeal as sharp as an ax blade. Then the shrill noise abruptly stopped, and the digital display flashed with rapidly changing numbers. Snippets of music and shards of voices crackled in an eerie audio-montage that echoed and re-echoed off the walls of the frigid room.

No one was in the house to hear it.

The closet door opened, closed, opened. . . .

Inside the closet, shirts and jeans began to swing wildly on the pole from which they hung, and some clothes fell to the floor.

The bed shook.

The display case that held nine model airplanes rocked, banging repeatedly against the wall. One of the models was flung from its shelf, then two more, then three more, then another, until all nine lay in a pile on the floor.

On the wall to the left of the bed, a poster of the creature from the *Alien* movies tore down the middle.

The radio ceased scanning, stopping on an open frequency that hissed and popped with distant static. Then a voice blared from the speakers. It was a child's voice. A boy. There were no words. Just a long, agonized scream.

The voice faded after a minute, but the bed began to bang up and down.

The closet door slammed open and shut with substantially more force than it had earlier.

Other things began to move too. For almost five minutes the room seemed to have come alive.

And then it died.

Silence returned.

The air grew warm again.

The frost left the window, and outside the white cat still chased the scrap of paper.

WEDNESDAY, DECEMBER 31

10   TINA DIDN'T GET HOME FROM THE OPENING-NIGHT PARTY UNTIL shortly before two o'clock Wednesday morning. Exhausted, slightly tipsy, she went directly to bed and fell into a sound sleep.

Later, after no more than two dreamless hours, she suffered another nightmare about Danny. He was trapped at the bottom of a deep hole. She heard his frightened voice calling to her, and she peered over the edge of the pit, and he was so far below her that his face was only a tiny, pale smudge. He was desperate to get out, and she was frantic to rescue him; but he was chained, unable to climb, and the sides of the pit were sheer and smooth, so she had no way to reach him. Then a man dressed entirely in black from head to foot, his face hidden by shadows, appeared at the far side of the pit and began to shovel dirt into it. Danny's cry escalated into a scream of terror; he was being buried alive. Tina shouted at the man in black, but he ignored her and kept shoveling dirt on top of Danny. She edged around the pit, determined to make the hateful bastard stop what he was doing, but he took a step away from her for every step that she took toward him, and he always stayed directly across the hole from her. She couldn't reach him, and she couldn't reach Danny, and the dirt was up to the boy's knees, and now up to his hips, and now over his shoulders. Danny wailed and shrieked, and now the earth was even with his chin, but the man in black wouldn't stop filling in the hole. She wanted to kill the bastard, club him to death with his own shovel. When she thought of clubbing him, he looked at her, and she saw his face: a fleshless skull with rotting skin stretched over the bones, burning red eyes, a yellow-toothed grin. A disgusting cluster of maggots clung to the man's left cheek and to the corner of his eye, feeding off him. Tina's terror over Danny's impending entombment was suddenly mixed with fear for her own life. Though Danny's screams were increasingly muffled, they were even more urgent than before, because the dirt began to cover his face and pour into his mouth. She had to get down to him and push the earth away from his face before he suffocated, so in blind panic she threw herself over the edge of the pit, into the terrible abyss, falling and falling—

Gasping, shuddering, she wrenched herself out of sleep.

She was convinced that the man in black was in her bedroom, standing silently in the darkness, grinning. Heart pounding, she fumbled with the bedside lamp. She blinked in the sudden light and saw that she was alone.

"Jesus," she said weakly.

She wiped one hand across her face, sloughing off a film of perspiration. She dried her hand on the sheets.

She did some deep-breathing exercises, trying to calm herself.

She couldn't stop shaking.

In the bathroom, she washed her face. The mirror revealed a person whom she hardly recognized: a haggard, bloodless, sunken-eyed fright.

Her mouth was dry and sour. She drank a glass of cold water.

Back in bed, she didn't want to turn off the light. Her fear made her angry with herself, and at last she twisted the switch.

The returning darkness was threatening.

She wasn't sure she would be able to get any more sleep, but she had to try. It wasn't even five o'clock. She'd been asleep less than three hours.

In the morning, she would clean out Danny's room. Then the dreams would stop. She was pretty much convinced of that.

She remembered the two words that she had twice erased from Danny's chalkboard—NOT DEAD—and she realized that she'd forgotten to call Michael. She had to confront him with her suspicions. She had to know if he'd been in the house, in Danny's room, without her knowledge or permission.

It *had* to be Michael.

She could turn on the light and call him now. He would be sleeping, but she wouldn't feel guilty if she woke him, not after all the sleepless nights that he had given her. Right now, however, she didn't feel up to the battle. Her wits were dulled by wine and exhaustion. And if Michael *had* slipped into the house like a little boy playing a cruel prank, if he *had* written that message on the chalkboard, then his hatred of her was far greater than she had thought. He might even be a desperately sick man. If he became verbally violent and abusive, if he were irrational, she would need to have a clear head to deal with him. She would call him in the morning when she had regained some of her strength.

She yawned and turned over and drifted off to sleep. She didn't dream anymore, and when she woke at ten o'clock, she was refreshed and newly excited by the previous night's success.

She phoned Michael, but he wasn't home. Unless he'd changed shifts in the past six months, he didn't go to work until noon. She decided to try his number again in half an hour.

After retrieving the morning newspaper from the front stoop, she read the rave review of *Magyck!* written by the *Review-Journal*'s entertainment critic. He couldn't find anything wrong with the show. His praise was so effusive that, even reading it by herself, in her own kitchen, she was slightly embarrassed by the effusiveness of the praise.

She ate a light breakfast of grapefruit juice and one English muffin, then went to Danny's room to pack his belongings. When she opened the door, she gasped and halted.

The room was a mess. The airplane models were no longer in the display case; they were strewn across the floor, and a few were broken. Danny's collection of paperbacks had been pulled from the bookcase and tossed into every corner. The tubes of glue, miniature bottles of enamel, and model-crafting tools that had stood on his desk were now on the floor with everything else. A poster of one of the movie monsters had been ripped apart; it hung from the wall in several pieces. The action figures had been knocked off the headboard. The closet doors were open, and all the clothes inside appeared to have been thrown on the floor. The game table had been overturned. The easel lay on the carpet, the chalkboard facing down.

Shaking with rage, Tina slowly crossed the room, carefully stepping through the debris. She stopped at the easel, set it up as it belonged, hesitated, then turned the chalkboard toward her.

NOT DEAD

"Damn!" she said, furious.

Vivienne Neddler had been in to clean last evening, but this wasn't the kind of thing that Vivienne would be capable of doing. If the mess had been here when Vivienne arrived, the old woman would have cleaned it up and would have left a note about what she'd found. Clearly, the intruder had come in after Mrs. Neddler had left.

Fuming, Tina went through the house, meticulously checking every window and door. She could find no sign of forced entry.

In the kitchen again, she phoned Michael. He still didn't answer. She slammed down the handset.

She pulled the telephone directory from a drawer and leafed through the Yellow Pages until she found the advertisements for locksmiths. She chose the company with the largest ad.

"Anderlingen Lock and Security."

"Your ad in the Yellow Pages says you can have a man here to change my locks in one hour."

"That's our emergency service. It costs more."

"I don't care what it costs," Tina said.

"But if you just put your name on our work list, we'll most likely have a man there by four o'clock this afternoon, tomorrow morning at the latest. And the regular service is forty percent cheaper than an emergency job."

"Vandals were in my house last night," Tina said.

"What a world we live in," said the woman at Anderlingen.

"They wrecked a lot of stuff—"

"Oh, I'm sorry to hear that."

"—so I want the locks changed immediately."

"Of course."

"And I want good locks installed. The best you've got."

"Just give me your name and address, and I'll send a man out right away."

A couple of minutes later, having completed the call, Tina went back to Danny's room to survey the damage again. As she looked over the wreckage, she said, "What the hell do you want from me, Mike?"

She doubted that he would be able to answer that question even if he were present to hear it. What possible excuse could he have? What twisted logic could justify this sort of sick behavior? It was crazy, hateful.

She shivered.

11

TINA ARRIVED AT BALLY'S HOTEL AT TEN MINUTES TILL TWO, Wednesday afternoon, leaving her Honda with a valet parking attendant.

Bally's, formerly the MGM Grand, was getting to be one of the older establishments on the continuously rejuvenating Las Vegas Strip, but it was still one of the most popular hotels in town, and on this last day of the year it was packed. At least two or three thousand people were in the casino, which was larger than a football field. Hundreds of gamblers—pretty young women, sweet-faced grandmothers, men in jeans and decoratively stitched Western shirts, retirement-age men in expensive but tacky leisure outfits, a few guys in three-piece suits, salesmen, doctors, mechanics, secretaries, Americans from all of the Western states, junketeers from the East Coast, Japanese tourists, a few Arab men—sat at the semielliptical blackjack tables, pushing money and chips forward, sometimes taking back their winnings, eagerly grabbing the cards that were dealt from the five-deck shoes, each reacting in one of several predictable ways: Some players squealed with delight; some grumbled; others smiled ruefully and shook their heads; some teased the dealers, pleading half seriously for better cards; and still others were silent, polite, attentive, and businesslike, as though they thought they were engaged in some reasonable form of investment planning. Hundreds of other people stood close behind the players, watching impatiently, waiting for a seat to open. At the craps tables, the crowds, primarily men, were more boisterous than the blackjack aficionados; they screamed, howled, cheered, groaned, encouraged the shooter, and prayed loudly to the dice. On the left, slot machines ran the entire length of the casino, bank after nerve-jangling bank of them, brightly and colorfully lighted, attended by gamblers who were more vocal than the card players but not as loud as the craps shooters. On the right, beyond the craps tables, halfway down the long room, elevated from the main floor, the white-marble and brass baccarat pit catered to a more affluent and sedate group of gamblers; at baccarat, the pit boss, the floorman, and the dealers wore tuxedos. And everywhere in the gigantic casino, there were cocktail waitresses in brief costumes, revealing long legs and cleavage; they bustled here and there, back and forth, as if they were the threads that bound the crowd together.

Tina pressed through the milling onlookers who filled the wide center aisle, and she located Michael almost at once. He was dealing blackjack at one of the first tables. The game minimum was a five-dollar bet, and all seven seats were taken. Michael was grinning, chatting amicably with the players. Some dealers were cold and uncommunicative, but Michael felt the day went faster when he was friendly with people. Not unexpectedly, he received considerably more tips than most dealers did.

Michael was lean and blond, with eyes nearly as blue as Tina's. He somewhat resembled Robert Redford, almost too pretty. It was no surprise that women players tipped him more often and more generously than did men.

When Tina squeezed into the narrow gap between the tables and caught Michael's attention, his reaction was far different from what she had expected. She'd thought the sight of her would wipe the smile off his face. Instead, his smile broadened, and there seemed to be genuine delight in his eyes.

He was shuffling cards when he saw her, and he continued to shuffle while he spoke. "Hey, hello there. You look terrific, Tina. A sight for sore eyes."

She wasn't prepared for this pleasantness, nonplussed by the warmth of his greeting.

He said, "That's a nice sweater. I like it. You always looked good in blue."

She smiled uneasily and tried to remember that she had come here to accuse him of cruelly harassing her. "Michael, I have to talk to you."

He glanced at his watch. "I've got a break coming up in five minutes."

"Where should I meet you?"

"Why don't you wait right where you are? You can watch these nice people beat me out of a lot of money."

Every player at the table groaned, and they all had comments to make about the unlikely possibility that they might win anything from this dealer.

Michael grinned and winked at Tina.

She smiled woodenly.

She waited impatiently as the five minutes crawled by; she was never comfortable in a casino when it was busy. The frantic activity and the unrelenting excitement, which bordered on hysteria at times, abraded her nerves.

The huge room was so noisy that the blend of sounds seemed to coalesce into a visible substance—like a humid yellow haze in the air. Slot machines rang and beeped and whistled and buzzed. Balls clattered around spinning roulette wheels. A five-piece band hammered out wildly amplified pop music from the small stage in the open cocktail lounge beyond and slightly above the slot machines. The paging system blared names. Ice rattled in glasses as gamblers drank while they played. And everyone seemed to be talking at once.

When Michael's break time arrived, a replacement dealer took over the table, and Michael stepped out of the blackjack pit, into the center aisle. "You want to talk?"

"Not here," she said, half-shouting. "I can't hear myself think."

"Let's go down to the arcade."

"Okay."

To reach the escalators that would carry them down to the shopping arcade on the lower level, they had to cross the entire casino. Michael led the way, gently pushing and elbowing through the holiday crowd, and Tina followed quickly in his wake, before the path that he made could close up again.

Halfway across the long room, they stopped at a clearing where a middle-aged man lay on his back, unconscious, in front of a blackjack table. He was wearing a beige suit, a dark brown shirt, and a beige-patterned tie. An overturned stool lay beside him, and approximately five hundred dollars' worth of green chips were scattered on the carpet. Two uniformed security men were performing first aid on the unconscious man, loosening his tie and collar, taking his pulse, while a third guard was keeping curious customers out of the way.

Michael said, "Heart attack, Pete?"

The third guard said, "Hi, Mike. Nah, I don't think it's his heart. Probably a combination of blackjack blackout and bingo bladder. He was sitting here for eight hours straight."

On the floor, the man in the beige suit groaned. His eyelids fluttered.

Shaking his head, obviously amused, Michael moved around the clearing and into the crowd again.

When at last they reached the end of the casino and were on the escalators, heading down toward the shopping arcade, Tina said, "What is blackjack blackout?"

"It's stupid is what it is," Michael said, still amused. "The guy sits down to play cards and gets so involved he loses track of time, which is, of course, exactly what the management wants him to do. That's why there aren't any windows or clocks in the casino. But once in a while, a guy *really* loses track, doesn't get up for hours and hours, just keeps on playing like a zombie. Meanwhile, he's drinking too much. When he *does* finally stand up, he moves too fast. The blood drains from his head—*bang!*—and he faints dead away. Blackjack blackout."

"Ah."

"We see it all the time."

"Bingo bladder?"

"Sometimes a player gets so interested in the game that he's virtually hypnotized by it. He's been drinking pretty regularly, but he's so deep in a trance that he can completely ignore the call of nature until—bingo!—he has a bladder spasm. If it's really a bad one, he finds out his pipes have blocked up. He can't relieve himself, and he has to be taken to the hospital and catheterized."

"My God, are you serious?"

"Yep."

They stepped off the escalator, into the bustling shopping arcade. Crowds surged past the souvenir shops, art galleries, jewelry stores, clothing stores, and other retail businesses, but they were neither shoulder-to-shoulder nor as insistent as they were upstairs in the casino.

"I still don't see any place where we can talk privately," Tina said.

"Let's walk down to the ice-cream parlor and get a couple of pistachio cones. What do you say? You always liked pistachio."

"I don't want any ice cream, Michael."

She had lost the momentum occasioned by her anger, and now she was afraid of losing the sense of purpose that had driven her to confront him. He was trying so hard to be nice, which wasn't like Michael at all. At least it wasn't like the Michael Evans she had known for the past couple of years. When they were first married, he'd been fun, charming, easygoing, but he had not been that way with her in a long time.

"No ice cream," she repeated. "Just some talk."

"Well, if you don't want some pistachio, I certainly do. I'll get a cone, and then we can go outside, walk around the parking lot. It's a fairly warm day."

"How long is your break?"

"Twenty minutes. But I'm tight with the pit boss. He'll cover for me if I don't get back in time."

The ice-cream parlor was at the far end of the arcade. As they walked, Michael continued to try to amuse her by telling her about other unusual maladies to which gamblers were prone.

"There's what we call 'jackpot attack,' " Michael said. "For years people go home from Vegas and tell all their friends that they came out ahead of the game. Lying their heads off. Everyone pretends to be a winner. And when all of a sudden someone *does* hit it big, especially on a slot machine where it can happen in a flash, they're so surprised they pass out. Heart attacks are more frequent around the slot machines than any-where else in the casino, and a lot of the victims are people who've just lined up three bars and won a bundle.

"Then there's 'Vegas syndrome.' Someone gets so carried away with gambling and running from show to show that he forgets to eat for a whole day or longer. He or she—it happens to women nearly as often as men. Anyway, when he finally gets hungry and realizes he hasn't eaten, he gulps down a huge meal, and the blood rushes from his head to his stomach, and he passes out in the middle of the restaurant. It's not usually dangerous, except if he has a mouthful of food when he faints, because then he might choke to death.

"But my favorite is what we call the 'time-warp syndrome.' People come here from a lot of dull places, and Vegas is like an adult Disneyland. There's so much going on, so much to see and do, constant excitement, so people get out of their normal rhythms. They go to bed at dawn, get up in the afternoon, and they lose track of what day it is. When the excitement wears off a little, they go to check out of the hotel, and they discover their three-day weekend somehow turned into five days. They can't believe it. They think they're being overcharged, and they argue with the desk clerks. When someone shows them a calendar and a daily newspaper, they're really shocked. They've been through a time warp and lost a couple of days. Isn't that weird?"

Michael kept up the friendly patter while he got his cone of ice cream.

Then, as they stepped out of the rear entrance of the hotel and walked along the edge of the parking lot in the seventy-degree winter sunshine, he said, "So what did you want to talk about?"

Tina wasn't sure how to begin. Her original intention had been to accuse him of ripping apart Danny's room; she had been prepared to come on strong, so that even if he didn't want her to know he'd done it, he might be rattled enough to reveal his guilt. But now, if she started making nasty accusations after he'd been so pleasant to her, she would seem to be a hysterical harpy, and if she still had any advantage left, she would quickly lose it.

At last she said, "Some strange things have been happening at the house."

"Strange? Like what?"

"I think someone broke in."

"You *think?*"

"Well . . . I'm sure of it."

"When did this happen?"

Remembering the two words on the chalkboard, she said, "Three times in the past week."

He stopped walking and stared at her. "Three times?"

"Yes. Last evening was the latest."

"What do the police say?"

"I haven't called them."

He frowned. "Why not?"

"For one thing, nothing was taken."

"Somebody broke in three times but didn't steal anything?"

If he was faking innocence, he was a much better actor than she thought he was, and she thought she knew him well indeed. After all, she'd lived with him for a long time, through years of happiness and years of misery, and she'd come to know the limits of his talent for deception and duplicity. She'd always known when he was lying. She didn't think he was lying now. There was something peculiar in his eyes, a speculative look, but it wasn't guile. He truly seemed unaware of what had happened at the house. Perhaps he'd had nothing to do with it.

But if Michael hadn't torn up Danny's room, if Michael hadn't written those words on the chalkboard, then who had?

"Why would someone break in and leave without taking anything?" Michael asked.

"I think they were just trying to upset me, scare me."

"Who would want to scare you?" He seemed genuinely concerned.

She didn't know what to say.

"You've never been the kind of person who makes enemies," he said. "You're a damn hard woman to hate."

"You managed," she said, and that was as close as she could come to accusing him of anything.

He blinked in surprise. "Oh, no. No, no, Tina. I never hated you. I was disappointed by the changes in you. I was angry with you. Angry and hurt. I'll admit that, all right. There was a lot of bitterness on my part. Definitely. But it was never as bad as hatred."

She sighed.

Michael hadn't wrecked Danny's room. She was absolutely sure of that now.

"Tina?"

"I'm sorry. I shouldn't have bothered you with this. I'm not really sure why I did," she lied. "I ought to have called the police right away."

He licked his ice-cream cone, studied her, and then he smiled. "I understand. It's hard for you to get around to it. You don't know how to begin. So you come to me with this story."

"Story?"

"It's okay."

"Michael, it's not just a story."

"Don't be embarrassed."

"I'm not embarrassed. Why should I be embarrassed?"

"Relax. It's all right, Tina," he said gently.

"Someone *has* been breaking into the house."

"I understand how you feel." His smile changed; it was smug now.

"Michael—"

"I really do understand, Tina." His voice was reassuring, but his tone was condescending. "You don't need an excuse to ask me what you've come here to ask. Honey, you don't need a story about someone breaking into the house. I understand, and I'm with you. I really am. So go ahead. Don't feel awkward about it. Just get right down to it. Go ahead and say it."

She was perplexed. "Say what?"

"We let the marriage go off the rails. But there at first, for a good many years, we had a great thing going. We can have it again if we really want to try for it."

She was stunned. "Are you serious?"

"I've been thinking about it the past few days. When I saw you walk into the casino a while ago, I knew I was right. As soon as I saw you, I knew everything was going to turn out exactly like I had it figured."

"You *are* serious."

"Sure." He mistook her astonishment for surprised delight. "Now that you've had your fling as a producer, you're ready to settle down. That makes a lot of sense, Tina."

Fling! she thought angrily.

He still persisted in regarding her as a flighty woman who wanted to take a fling at being a Vegas producer. The insufferable bastard! She was furious, but she said nothing; she didn't trust herself to speak, afraid that she would start screaming at him the instant she opened her mouth.

"There's more to life than just having a flashy career," Michael said pontifically. "Home life counts for something. Home and family. That has to be a part of life too. Maybe it's the most important part." He nodded sanctimoniously. "Family. These last few days, as your show's been getting ready to open, I've had the feeling you might finally realize you need something more in life, something a lot more emotionally satisfying than whatever it is you can get out of just producing stage shows."

Tina's ambition was, in part, what had led to the dissolution of their marriage. Well, not her ambition as much as Michael's childish attitude toward it. He was happy being a blackjack dealer; his salary and his good tips were enough for him, and he was content to coast through the years. But merely drifting along in the currents of life wasn't enough for Tina. As she had struggled to move up from dancer to costumer to choreographer to lounge-revue coordinator to producer, Michael had been displeased with her commitment to work. She had never neglected him and Danny. She had been determined that neither of them would have reason to feel that his importance in her life had diminished. Danny had been wonderful; Danny had understood. Michael couldn't or wouldn't. Gradually Michael's displeasure over her desire to succeed was complicated by a darker emotion: He grew jealous of her smallest achievements. She had tried to encourage him to seek advances in his own career—from dealer to floorman to pit boss to higher casino management—but he had no interest in climbing that ladder. He became waspish, petulant. Eventually he started seeing other women. She was shocked by his reaction, then confused, and at last deeply saddened. The only way she could have held on to her husband would have been to abandon her new career, and she had refused to do that.

In time Michael had made it clear to her that he hadn't actually ever loved the real Christina. He didn't tell her directly, but his behavior said as much. He had adored only the showgirl, the dancer, the cute little thing that other men coveted, the pretty woman whose presence at his side had inflated his ego. As long as she remained a dancer, as long as she devoted her life to him, as long as she hung on his arm and looked delicious, he approved of her. But the moment that she wanted to be something more than a trophy wife, he rebelled.

Badly hurt by that discovery, she had given him the freedom that he wanted.

And now he actually thought that she was going to crawl back to him. That was why he'd smiled when he'd seen her at his blackjack table. That was why he had been so charming. The size of his ego astounded her.

Standing before her in the sunshine, his white shirt shimmering with squiggles of reflected light that bounced off the parked cars, he favored her with that self-satisfied, superior smile that made her feel as cold as this winter day ought to have been.

Once, long ago, she had loved him very much. Now she couldn't imagine how or why she had ever cared.

"Michael, in case you haven't heard, *Magyck!* is a hit. A big hit. Huge."

"Sure," he said. "I know that, baby. And I'm happy for you. I'm happy for you *and* me. Now that you've proved whatever you needed to prove, you can relax."

"Michael, I intend to continue working as a producer. I'm not going to—"

"Oh, I don't expect you to give it up," he said magnanimously.

"You don't, huh?"

"No, no. Of course not. It's good for you to have something to dabble in. I see that now. I get the message. But with *Magyck!* running successfully, you won't have all that much to do. It won't be like before."

"Michael—" she began, intending to tell him that she was going to stage another show within the next year, that she didn't want to be represented by only one production at a time, and that she even had distant designs on New York and Broadway, where the return of Busby Berkeley-style musicals might be greeted with cheers.

But he was so involved with his fantasy that he wasn't aware that she had no desire to be a part of it. He interrupted her before she'd said more than his name. "We can do it, Tina. It was good for us once, those early years. It can be good again. We're still young. We have time to start another family. Maybe even two boys and two girls. That's what I've always wanted."

When he paused to lick his ice-cream cone, she said, "Michael, that's not the way it's going to be."

"Well, maybe you're right. Maybe a large family isn't such a wise idea these days, what with the economy in trouble and all the turmoil in the world. But we can take care of two easily enough, and maybe we'll get lucky and have one boy and one girl. Of course we'll wait a year or so. I'm sure there's a lot of work to do on a show like *Magyck!* even after it opens. We'll wait until it's running smoothly, until it doesn't need much of your time. Then we can—"

"Michael, stop it!" she said harshly.

He flinched as if she'd slapped him.

"I'm not feeling unfulfilled these days," she said. "I'm not pining for the domestic life. You don't understand me one bit better now than you did when we divorced."

His expression of surprise slowly settled into a frown.

She said, "I didn't make up that story about someone breaking into the house just so you could play the strong, reliable man to my weak, frightened female. Someone really *did* break in. I came to you because I thought . . . I believed . . . Well, that doesn't matter anymore."

She turned away from him and started toward the rear entrance of the hotel, out of which they'd come a few minutes ago.

"Wait!" Michael said. "Tina, wait!"

She stopped and regarded him with contempt and sorrow.

He hurried to her. "I'm sorry. It's my fault, Tina. I botched it. Jesus, I was babbling like an idiot, wasn't I? I didn't let you do it your way. I knew what you wanted to say, but I should have let you say it at your own speed. I was wrong. It's just—I was excited, Tina. That's all. I should've shut up and let *you* get around to it first. I'm sorry, baby." His ingratiating, boyish grin was back. "Don't get mad at me, okay? We both want the same thing—a home life, a good family life. Let's not throw away this chance."

She glared at him. "Yes, you're right, I do want a home life, a satisfying family life. You're right about that. But you're wrong about everything else. I don't want to be a producer merely because I need a sideline to dabble in. *Dabble!* Michael, that's stupid. No one gets a show like *Magyck!* off the ground by dabbling. I can't believe you said that! It wasn't a fling. It was a mentally and physically debilitating experience—it was *hard*— and I loved every minute of it! God willing, I'm going to do it again. And again and again. I'm going to produce shows that'll make *Magyck!* look amateurish by comparison. Some day I may also be a mother again. And I'll be a damn good mother too. A good mother and a good producer. I have the intelligence and the talent to be more than just one thing. And I certainly can be more than just your trinket and your housekeeper."

"Now, wait a minute," he said, beginning to get angry. "Wait just a damn minute. You don't—"

She interrupted him. For years she had been filled with hurt and bit- terness. She had never vented any of her black anger because, initially, she'd wanted to hide it from Danny; she hadn't wanted to turn him against his father. Later, after Danny was dead, she'd repressed her feelings be- cause she'd known that Michael had been truly suffering from the loss of his child, and she hadn't wanted to add to his misery. But now she vented some of the acid that had been eating at her for so long, cutting him off in midsentence.

"You were wrong to think I'd come crawling back. Why on earth would I? What do you have to give me that I can't get elsewhere? You've never been much of a giver anyway, Michael. You only give when you're sure of getting back twice as much. You're basically a taker. And before you give me any more of that treacly talk about your great love of family, let me remind you that it wasn't *me* who tore our family apart. It wasn't me who jumped from bed to bed."

"Now, wait—"

"You were the one who started fucking anything that breathed, and then you flaunted each cheap little affair to hurt me. It was *you* who didn't come home at night. It was you who went away for weekends with your girlfriends. And those bed-hopping weekends broke my heart, Michael, broke my heart—which is what you hoped to do, so that was all right with you. But did you ever stop to realize what effect your absences had on Danny? If you loved family life so much, why didn't you spend all those weekends with your son?"

His face was flushed, and there was a familiar meanness in his eyes. "So I'm not a giver, huh? Then who gave you the house you're living in? Huh? Who was it had to move into an apartment when we separated, and who was it kept the house?"

He was trying desperately to deflect her and change the course of the argument. She could see what he was up to, and she was not going to be distracted from her main intention.

She said, "Don't be pathetic, Michael. You know damn well the down payment for the house came out of my earnings. You always spent your money on fast cars, good clothes. I paid every loan installment. You know that. And I never asked for alimony. Anyway, all of that's beside the point. We were talking about family life, about Danny."

"Now, you listen to me—"

"No. It's your turn to listen. After all these years it's finally your turn to listen. If you know how. You could have taken Danny away for the weekend if you didn't want to be near me. You could have gone camping with him. You could have taken him down to Disneyland for a couple days. Or to the Colorado River to do some fishing. But you were too busy using all those women to hurt me and to prove to yourself what a stud you were. You could have enjoyed that time with your son. He missed you. You could have had that precious time with him. But you didn't want it. And as it turned out, Danny didn't have much time left."

Michael was milk-white, trembling. His eyes were dark with rage. "You're the same goddamn bitch you always were."

She sighed and sagged. She was exhausted. Finished telling him off, she felt pleasantly wrung out, as if some evil, nervous energy had been drained from her.

"You're the same ball-breaking bitch," Michael said.

"I don't want to fight with you, Michael. I'm even sorry if some of what I said about Danny hurt you, although, God knows, you deserve to hear it. I don't really want to hurt you. Oddly enough, I don't really hate you anymore. I don't feel anything for you. Not anything at all."

Turning away, she left him in the sunshine, with the ice cream melting down the cone and onto his hand.

She walked back through the shopping arcade, rode the escalator up to the casino, and made her way through the noisy crowd to the front doors. One of the valet-parking attendants brought her car, and she drove down the hotel's steeply slanted exit drive.

She headed toward the Golden Pyramid, where she had an office, and where work was waiting to be done.

After she had driven only a block, she was forced to pull to the side of the road. She couldn't see where she was going, because hot tears streamed down her face. She put the car in park. Surprising herself, she sobbed loudly.

At first she wasn't sure what she was crying about. She just surrendered to the racking grief that swept through her and did not question it.

After a while she decided that she was crying for Danny. Poor, sweet Danny. He'd hardly begun to live. It wasn't fair. And she was crying for herself too, and for Michael. She was crying for all the things that might have been, and for what could never be again.

In a few minutes she got control of herself. She dried her eyes and blew her nose.

She had to stop being so gloomy. She'd had enough gloom in her life. A whole hell of a lot of gloom.

"Think positive," she said aloud. "Maybe the past wasn't so great, but the future seems pretty damn good."

She inspected her face in the rearview mirror to see how much damage the crying jag had done. She looked better than she expected. Her eyes were red, but she wouldn't pass for Dracula. She opened her purse, found her makeup, and covered the tear stains as best she could.

She pulled the Honda back into traffic and headed for the Pyramid again.

A block farther, as she waited at a red light, she realized that she still had a mystery on her hands. She was positive that Michael had not done the damage in Danny's bedroom. But then, who *had* done it? No one else had a key. Only a skilled burglar could have broken in without leaving a trace. And why would a first-rate burglar leave without taking anything? Why break in merely to write on Danny's chalkboard and to wreck the dead boy's things?

Weird.

When she had suspected Michael of doing the dirty work, she had been disturbed and distressed, but she hadn't been frightened. If some *stranger* wanted her to feel more pain over the loss of her child, however, that was definitely unsettling. That was scary because it didn't make sense. A stranger? It must be. Michael was the only person who had ever blamed her for Danny's death. Not one other relative or acquaintance had ever suggested that she was even indirectly responsible. Yet the taunting words on the chalkboard and the destruction in the bedroom seemed to be the work of someone who felt that she should be held accountable for the accident. Which meant it had to be someone she didn't even know. Why would a stranger harbor such passionate feelings about Danny's death?

The red traffic light changed.

A horn tooted behind her.

As she drove across the intersection and into the entrance drive that led to the Golden Pyramid Hotel, Tina couldn't shake the creepy feeling that she was being watched by someone who meant to harm her. She checked the rearview mirror to see if she was being followed. As far as she could tell, no one was tailing her.

12

THE THIRD FLOOR OF THE GOLDEN PYRAMID HOTEL WAS OCCUPIED by management and clerical personnel. Here, there was no flash, no Vegas glamour. This was where the work got done. The third floor housed the machinery that supported the walls of fantasy, beyond which the tourists gamboled.

Tina's office was large, paneled in whitewashed pine, with comfortable contemporary upholstery. One wall was covered by heavy drapes that blocked out the fierce desert sun. The windows behind the drapes faced the Las Vegas Strip.

At night the fabled Strip was a dazzling sight, a surging river of light: red, blue, green, yellow, purple, pink, turquoise—every color within the visual spectrum of the human eye; incandescent and neon, fiberoptics and lasers, flashing and rippling. Hundred-foot-long signs—*five*-hundred-foot-long signs—towered five or even ten stories above the street, glittering, winking, thousands of miles of bright glass tubing filled with glowing gas, blinking, swirling, hundreds of thousands of bulbs, spelling out hotel names, forming pictures with light. Computer-controlled designs ebbed and flowed, a riotous and mad—but curiously beautiful—excess of energy consumption.

During the day, however, the merciless sun was unkind to the Strip. In the hard light the enormous architectural confections were not always appealing; at times, in spite of the billions of dollars of value that it represented, the Strip looked grubby.

The view of the legendary boulevard was wasted on Tina; she didn't often make use of it. Because she was seldom in her office at night, the drapes were rarely open. This afternoon, as usual, the drapes were closed. The office was shadowy, and she was at her desk in a pool of soft light.

As Tina pored over a final bill for carpentry work on some of the *Magyck!* sets, Angela, her secretary, stepped in from the outer office. "Is there anything more you need before I leave?"

Tina glanced at her watch. "It's only a quarter to four."

"I know. But we get off at four today—New Year's Eve."

"Oh, of course," Tina said. "I completely forgot about the holiday."

"If you want me to, I could stay a little longer."

"No, no, no," Tina said. "You go home at four with the others."

"So is there anything more you need?"

Leaning back in her chair, Tina said, "Yes. In fact, there is something. A lot of our regular junketeers and high rollers couldn't make it to the VIP opening of *Magyck!* I'd like you to get their names from the computer, plus a list of the wedding anniversaries of those who're married."

"Can do," Angela said. "What've you got in mind?"

"During the year, I'm going to send special invitations to the married ones, asking them to spend their anniversaries here, with everything comped for three days. We'll sell it this way: 'Spend the magic night of your anniversary in the magic world of *Magyck!*' Something like that. We'll make it very romantic. We'll serve them champagne at the show. It'll be a great promotion, don't you think?" She raised her hands, as if framing her next words, "The Golden Pyramid—a *Magyck!* place for lovers."

"The hotel ought to be happy," Angela said. "We'll get lots of favorable media coverage."

"The casino bosses will like it too, 'cause a lot of our high rollers will probably make an extra trip this year. The average gambler won't cancel other planned trips to Vegas. He'll just add on an extra trip for his anniversary. And I'll be happy because the whole stunt will generate more talk about the show."

"It's a great idea," Angela said. "I'll get the list."

Tina returned to her inspection of the carpenter's bill, and Angela was back at five minutes past four with thirty pages of data.

"Thank you," Tina said.

"No trouble."

"Are you shivering?"

"Yeah," Angela said, hugging herself. "Must be a problem with the air conditioning. The last few minutes—my office got chilly."

"It's warm enough in here," Tina said.

"Maybe it's just me. Maybe I'm coming down with something. I sure hope not. I've got big plans tonight."

"Party?"

"Yeah. Big bash over on Rancho Circle."

"Millionaire's Row?"

"My boyfriend's boss lives over there. Anyway . . . happy new year, Tina."

"Happy new year."

"See you Monday."

"Oh? Oh, yeah, that's right. It's a four-day weekend. Well, just watch out for that hangover."

Angela grinned. "There's at least one out there with my name on it."

Tina finished checking the carpenter's bill and approved it for payment.

Alone now on the third floor, she sat in the pool of amber light at her desk, surrounded by shadows, yawning. She'd work for another hour, until five o'clock, and then go home. She'd need two hours to get ready for her date with Elliot Stryker.

She smiled when she thought of him, then picked up the sheaf of papers that Angela had given her, anxious to finish her work.

The hotel possessed an amazing wealth of information about its most favored customers. If she needed to know how much money each of these people earned in a year, the computer could tell her. It could tell her each man's preferred brand of liquor, each wife's favorite flower and perfume, the make of car they drove, the names and ages of their children, the nature of any illnesses or other medical conditions they might have, their favorite foods, their favorite colors, their tastes in music, their political affiliations, and scores of other facts both important and trivial. These were customers to whom the hotel was especially anxious to cater, and the more the Pyramid knew about them, the better it could serve them. Although the hotel collected this data with, for the most part, the customers' happiness in mind, Tina wondered how pleased these people would be to learn that the Golden Pyramid maintained fat dossiers on them.

She scanned the list of VIP customers who hadn't attended the opening of *Magyck!* Using a red pencil, she circled those names that were followed by anniversary dates, trying to ascertain how large a promotion she was proposing. She had counted only twenty-two names when she came to an incredible message that the computer had inserted in the list.

Her chest tightened. She couldn't breathe.

She stared at what the computer had printed, and fear welled in her— dark, cold, oily fear.

Between the names of two high rollers were five lines of type that had nothing to do with the information she had requested:

NOT DEAD

NOT DEAD

NOT DEAD

NOT DEAD

NOT DEAD

The paper rattled as her hands began to shake.

First at home. In Danny's bedroom. Now here. Who was doing this to her?

Angela?

No. Absurd.

Angela was a sweet kid. She wasn't capable of anything as vicious as this. Angela hadn't noticed this interruption in the printout because she hadn't had time to scan it.

Besides, Angela couldn't have broken into the house. Angela wasn't a master burglar, for God's sake.

Tina quickly shuffled through the pages, seeking more of the sick prankster's work. She found it after another twenty-six names.

DANNY ALIVE
DANNY ALIVE
HELP
HELP
HELP ME

Her heart seemed to be pumping a refrigerant instead of blood, and an iciness radiated from it.

Suddenly she was aware of how alone she was. More likely than not, she was the only person on the entire third floor.

She thought of the man in her nightmare, the man in black whose face had been lumpy with maggots, and the shadows in the corner of her office seemed darker and deeper than they had been a moment ago.

She scanned another forty names and cringed when she saw what else the computer had printed.

I'M AFRAID
I'M AFRAID
GET ME OUT
GET ME OUT OF HERE
PLEASE . . . PLEASE
HELPHELPHELPHELP

That was the last disturbing insertion. The remainder of the list was as it should be.

Tina threw the printout on the floor and went into the outer office.

Angela had turned the light off. Tina turned it on.

She went to Angela's desk, sat in her chair, and switched on the computer. The screen filled with a soft blue light.

In the locked center drawer of the desk was a book with the code numbers that permitted access to the sensitive information stored not on diskette but only in the central memory. Tina paged through the book until she found the code that she needed to call up the list of the hotel's best customers. The number was 1001012, identified as the access for "Comps," which meant "complimentary guests," a euphemism for "big losers," who were never asked to pay their room charges or restaurant bills because they routinely dropped small fortunes in the casino.

Tina typed her personal access number—E013331555. Because so much material in the hotel's files was extremely confidential information about high rollers, and because the Pyramid's list of favored customers would be of enormous value to competitors, only approved people could obtain this data, and a record was kept of everyone who accessed it. After a moment's hesitation the computer asked for her name; she entered that, and the computer matched her number and name. Then:

CLEARED

She typed in the code for the list of complimentary guests, and the machine responded at once.

PROCEED

Her fingers were damp. She wiped them on her slacks and then quickly tapped out her request. She asked the computer for the same information that Angela had requested a while ago. The names and addresses of VIP customers who had missed the opening of *Magyck!*—along with the wedding anniversaries of those who were married—began to appear on the screen, scrolling upward. Simultaneously the laser printer began to churn out the same data.

Tina snatched each page from the printer tray as it arrived. The laser whispered through twenty names, forty, sixty, seventy, without producing the lines about Danny that had been on the first printout. Tina waited until at least a hundred names had been listed before she decided that the system had been programmed to print the lines about Danny only one time, only on her office's first data request of the afternoon, and on no later call-up.

She canceled this data request and closed out the file. The printer stopped.

Just a couple of hours ago she had concluded that the person behind this harassment had to be a stranger. But how could any stranger so easily gain entrance to both her house and the hotel computer? Didn't he, after all, have to be someone she knew?

But who?

And *why?*

What stranger could possibly hate her so much?

Fear, like an uncoiling snake, twisted and slithered inside of her, and she shivered.

Then she realized it wasn't only fear that made her quiver. The air was chilly.

She remembered the complaint that Angela had made earlier. It hadn't seemed important at the time.

But the room had been warm when Tina had first come in to use the computer, and now it was cool. How could the temperature have dropped so far in such a short time? She listened for the sound of the air conditioner, but the telltale whisper wasn't issuing from the wall vents. Nevertheless, the room was much cooler than it had been only minutes ago.

With a sharp, loud, electronic snap that startled Tina, the computer abruptly began to churn out additional data, although she hadn't requested any. She glanced at the printer, then at the words that flickered across the screen.

> NOT DEAD NOT DEAD
> NOT DEAD NOT DEAD
> NOT IN THE GROUND
> NOT DEAD
> GET ME OUT OF HERE
> GET ME OUT OUT OUT

The message blinked and vanished from the screen. The printer fell silent.

The room was growing colder by the second.

Or was it her imagination?

She had the crazy feeling that she wasn't alone. The man in black. Even though he was only a creature from a nightmare, and even though it was utterly impossible for him to be here in the flesh, she couldn't shake the heart-clenching feeling that he was in the room. The man in black. The man with the evil, fiery eyes. The yellow-toothed grin. Behind her. Reaching toward her with a hand that would be cold and damp. She spun around in her chair, but no one had come into the room.

Of course. He was only a nightmare monster. How stupid of her.

Yet she felt that she was not alone.

She didn't want to look at the screen again, but she did. She had to.

The words still burned there.

Then they disappeared.

She managed to break the grip of fear that had paralyzed her, and she put her fingers on the keyboard. She intended to determine if the words about Danny had been previously programmed to print out on her machine or if they had been sent to her just seconds ago by someone at another computer in another office in the hotel's elaborately networked series of workstations.

She had an almost psychic sense that the perpetrator of this viciousness was in the building *now*, perhaps on the third floor with her. She imagined herself leaving her office, walking down the long hallway, opening doors, peering into silent, deserted offices, until at last she found a man sitting at another terminal. He would turn toward her, surprised, and she would finally know who he was.

And then what?

Would he harm her? Kill her?

This was a new thought: the possibility that his ultimate goal was to do something worse than torment and scare her.

She hesitated, fingers on the keyboard, not certain if she should proceed. She probably wouldn't get the answers she needed, and she would only be acknowledging her presence to whomever might be out there at another workstation. Then she realized that, if he really was nearby, he already knew she was in her office, alone. She had nothing to lose by trying to follow the data chain. But when she attempted to type in her instruction, the keyboard was locked; the keys wouldn't depress.

The printer hummed.

The room was positively arctic.

On the screen, scrolling up:

> I'M COLD AND I HURT
> MOM? CAN YOU HEAR?
> I'M SO COLD
> I HURT BAD
> GET ME OUT OF HERE
> PLEASE PLEASE PLEASE
> NOT DEAD NOT DEAD

The screen glowed with those words—then went blank.

Again, she tried to feed in her questions. But the keyboard remained frozen.

She was still aware of another presence in the room. Indeed the feeling of invisible and dangerous companionship was growing stronger as the room grew colder.

How could he make the room colder without using the air conditioner? Whoever he was, he could override her computer from another terminal in the building; she could accept that. But how could he possibly make the air grow so cold so fast?

Suddenly, as the screen began to fill with the same seven-line message that had just been wiped from it, Tina had enough. She switched the machine off, and the blue glow faded from the screen.

As she was getting up from the low chair, the terminal switched itself on.

I'M COLD AND I HURT
GET ME OUT OF HERE
PLEASE PLEASE PLEASE

"Get you out of where?" she demanded. "The *grave?*"

GET ME OUT OUT OUT

She had to get a grip on herself. She had just spoken to the computer as if she actually thought she was talking to Danny. It wasn't Danny tapping out those words. Goddamn it, *Danny was dead!*

She snapped the computer off.

It turned itself on.

A hot welling of tears blurred her vision, and she struggled to repress them. She had to be losing her mind. The damned thing *couldn't* be switching itself on.

She hurried around the desk, banging her hip against one corner, heading for the wall socket as the printer hummed with the production of more hateful words.

GET ME OUT OF HERE
GET ME OUT OUT
OUT
OUT

Tina stooped beside the wall outlet from which the computer received its electrical power and its data feed. She took hold of the two lines— one heavy cable and one ordinary insulated wire—and they seemed to come alive in her hands, like a pair of snakes, resisting her. She jerked on them and pulled both plugs.

The monitor went dark.

It remained dark.

Immediately, rapidly, the room began to grow warmer.

"Thank God," she said shakily.

She started around Angela's desk, wanting nothing more at the moment than to get off her rubbery legs and onto a chair—and suddenly the door to the hall opened, and she cried out in alarm.

The man in black?

Elliot Stryker halted on the threshold, surprised by her scream, and for an instant she was relieved to see him.

"Tina? What's wrong? Are you all right?"

She took a step toward him, but then she realized that he might have come here straight from a computer in one of the other third-floor offices. Could he be the man who'd been harassing her?

"Tina? My God, you're white as a ghost!"

He moved toward her.

She said, "Stop! Wait!"

He halted, perplexed.

Voice quavery, she said, "What are you doing here?"

He blinked. "I was in the hotel on business. I wondered if you might still be at your desk. I stopped in to see. I just wanted to say hello."

"Were you playing around with one of the other computers?"

"What?" he asked, obviously baffled by her question.

"What were you doing on the third floor?" she demanded. "Who could you possibly have been seeing? They've all gone home. I'm the only one here."

Still puzzled but beginning to get impatient with her, Elliot said, "My business wasn't on the third floor. I had a meeting with Charlie Mainway over coffee, downstairs in the restaurant. When we finished our work a couple minutes ago, I came up to see if you were here. What's wrong with you?"

She stared at him intently.

"Tina? What's happened?"

She searched his face for any sign that he was lying, but his bewilderment seemed genuine. And if he were lying, he wouldn't have told her the story about Charlie and coffee, for that could be substantiated or disproved with only a minimum of effort; he would have come up with a better alibi if he really needed one. He was telling the truth.

She said, "I'm sorry. I just . . . I had . . . an . . . an experience here . . . a weird . . ."

He went to her. "What was it?"

As he drew near, he opened his arms, as if it was the most natural thing in the world for him to hold and comfort her, as if he had held her many times before, and she leaned against him in the same spirit of familiarity. She was no longer alone.

13

TINA KEPT A WELL-STOCKED BAR IN ONE CORNER OF HER OFFICE for those infrequent occasions when a business associate needed a drink after a long work session. This was the first time she'd ever had the need to tap those stores for herself.

At her request, Elliot poured Rémy Martin into two snifters and gave one glass to her. She couldn't pour for them because her hands were shaking too badly.

They sat on the beige sofa, more in the shadows than in the glow from the lamps. She was forced to hold her brandy snifter in both hands to keep it steady.

"I don't know where to begin. I guess I ought to start with Danny. Do you know about Danny?"

"Your son?" he asked.

"Yes."

"Helen Mainway told me he died a little over a year ago."

"Did she tell you how it happened?"

"He was one of the Jaborski group. Front page of the papers."

Bill Jaborski had been a wilderness expert and a scoutmaster. Every winter for sixteen years, he had taken a group of scouts to northern Nevada, beyond Reno, into the High Sierra, on a seven-day wilderness survival excursion.

"It was supposed to build character," Tina said. "And the boys competed hard all year for the chance to be one of those selected to go on the trip. It was supposed to be perfectly safe. Bill Jaborski was supposed to be one of the ten top winter-survival experts in the country. That's what everyone said. And the other adult who went along, Tom Lincoln—he was supposed to be almost as good as Bill. Supposed to be." Her voice had grown thin and bitter. "I believed them, thought it was safe."

"You can't blame yourself for that. All those years they'd taken kids into the mountains, nobody was even scratched."

Tina swallowed some cognac. It was hot in her throat, but it didn't burn away the chill at the center of her.

A year ago Jaborski's excursion had included fourteen boys between the ages of twelve and eighteen. All of them were top-notch scouts—and all of them died along with Jaborski and Tom Lincoln.

"Have the authorities ever figured out exactly why it happened?" Elliot asked.

"Not why. They never will. All they know is *how*. The group went into the mountains in a four-wheel-drive minibus built for use on back roads in the winter. Huge tires. Chains. Even a snowplow on the front. They weren't supposed to go into the true heart of the wilderness. Just into the fringes. No one in his right mind would take boys as young as twelve into the deepest parts of the Sierras, no matter how well prepared, supplied, and trained they were, no matter how strong, no matter how many big brothers were there to look out for them."

Jaborski had intended to drive the minibus off the main highway, onto an old logging trail, if conditions permitted. From there they were going to hike for three days with snowshoes and backpacks, making a wide circle around the bus, coming back to it at the end of the week.

"They had the best wilderness clothing and the best down-lined sleeping bags, the best winter tents, plenty of charcoal and other heat sources, plenty of food, and two wilderness experts to guide them. Perfectly safe, everyone said. Absolutely, perfectly safe. So what the fuck went wrong?"

Tina could no longer sit still. She got up and began to pace, taking another swallow of cognac.

Elliot said nothing. He seemed to know that she had to go through the whole story to get it off her mind.

"Something sure as hell went wrong," she said. "Somehow, for some reason, they drove the bus more than *four* miles off the main highway, four miles off and a hell of a long way *up*, right up to the damn clouds. They drove up a steep, abandoned logging trail, a deteriorated dirt road so treacherous, so choked with snow, so icy that only a fool would have attempted to negotiate it any way but on foot."

The bus had run off the road. There were no guardrails in the wilderness, no wide shoulders at the roadside with gentle slopes beyond. The vehicle skidded, then dropped a hundred feet straight onto rocks. The fuel tank exploded. The bus opened like a tin can and rolled another hundred feet into the trees.

"The kids . . . everyone . . . killed." The bitterness in her voice dismayed her because it revealed how little she had healed. "Why? Why did a man like Bill Jaborski do something so stupid as that?"

Still sitting on the couch, Elliot shook his head and stared down at his cognac.

She didn't expect him to answer. She wasn't actually asking the question of him; if she was asking anyone, she was asking God.

"Why? Jaborski was the best. The very best. He was so good that he could safely take young boys into the Sierras for sixteen years, a challenge a lot of other winter survival experts wouldn't touch. Bill Jaborski was smart, tough, clever, and filled with respect for the danger in what he did. He wasn't foolhardy. Why would he do something so dumb, so reckless, as to drive that far along that road in those conditions?"

Elliot looked up at her. Kindness marked his eyes, a deep sympathy. "You'll probably never learn the answer. I understand how hard it must be never to know why."

"Hard," she said. "Very hard."

She returned to the couch.

He took her glass out of her hand. It was empty. She didn't remember finishing her cognac. He went to the bar.

"No more for me," she said. "I don't want to get drunk."

"Nonsense," he said. "In your condition, throwing off all that nervous energy the way you are, two small brandies won't affect you in the slightest."

He returned from the bar with more Rémy Martin. This time she was able to hold the glass in one hand.

"Thank you, Elliot."

"Just don't ask for a mixed drink," he said. "I'm the world's worst bartender. I can pour anything straight or over ice, but I can't even mix vodka and orange juice properly."

"I wasn't thanking you for the drink. I was thanking you for . . . being a good listener."

"Most attorneys talk too much."

For a moment they sat in silence, sipping cognac.

Tina was still tense, but she no longer felt cold inside.

Elliot said, "Losing a child like that . . . devastating. But it wasn't any recollection of your son that had you so upset when I walked in a little while ago."

"In a way it was."

"But something more."

She told him about the bizarre things that had been happening to her lately: the messages on Danny's chalkboard; the wreckage she'd found in the boy's room; the hateful, taunting words that appeared in the computer lists and on the monitor.

Elliot studied the printouts, and together they examined the computer in Angela's office. They plugged it in and tried to get it to repeat what it had done earlier, but they had no luck; the machine behaved exactly as it was meant to behave.

"Someone could have programmed it to spew out this stuff about Danny," Elliot said. "But I don't see how he could make the terminal switch itself on."

"It happened," she said.

"I don't doubt you. I just don't understand."

"And the air . . . so cold . . ."

"Could the temperature change have been subjective?"

Tina frowned. "Are you asking me if I imagined it?"

"You were frightened—"

"But I'm sure I didn't imagine it. Angela felt the chill first, when she got the initial printout with those lines about Danny. It isn't likely Angela and I *both* just imagined it."

"True." He stared thoughtfully at the computer. "Come on."

"Where?"

"Back in your office. I left my drink there. Need to lubricate my thoughts."

She followed him into the wood-paneled inner sanctum.

He picked up his brandy snifter from the low table in front of the sofa, and he sat on the edge of her desk. "Who? Who could be doing it to you?"

"I haven't a clue."

"You must have somebody in mind."

"I wish I did."

"Obviously, it's somebody who at the very least dislikes you, if he doesn't actually hate you. Someone who wants you to suffer. He blames you for Danny's death . . . and it's apparently a personal loss to him, so it can hardly be a stranger."

Tina was disturbed by his analysis because it matched her own, and it led her into the same blind alley that she'd traveled before. She paced between the desk and the drapery-covered windows. "This afternoon I decided it *has* to be a stranger. I can't think of anyone I know who'd be capable of this sort of thing even if they did hate me enough to contemplate it. And I don't know of anyone but Michael who places any of the blame for Danny's death on me."

Elliot raised his eyebrows. "Michael's your ex-husband?"

"Yes."

"And he blames you for Danny's death?"

"He says I never should have let him go with Jaborski. But this isn't Michael's dirty work."

"He sounds like an excellent candidate to me."

"No."

"Are you certain?"

"Absolutely. It's someone else."

Elliot tasted his cognac. "You'll probably need professional help to catch him in one of his tricks."

"You mean the police?"

"I don't think the police would be much help. They probably won't think it's serious enough to waste their time. After all, you haven't been threatened."

"There's an implicit threat in all of this."

"Oh, yeah, I agree. It's scary. But the cops are a literal bunch, not much impressed by implied threats. Besides, to properly watch your house . . . that alone will require a lot more manpower than the police can spare for anything except a murder case, a hot kidnapping, or maybe a narcotics investigation."

She stopped pacing. "Then what did you mean when you said I'd probably need professional help to catch this creep?"

"Private detectives."

"Isn't that melodramatic?"

He smiled sourly. "Well, the person who's harassing you has a melo-dramatic streak a mile wide."

She sighed and sipped some cognac and sat on the edge of the couch. "I don't know . . . Maybe I'd hire private detectives, and they wouldn't catch anyone but me."

"Send that one by me again."

She had to take another small sip of cognac before she was able to say what was on her mind, and she realized that he had been right about the liquor having little effect on her. She felt more relaxed than she'd been ten minutes ago, but she wasn't even slightly tipsy. "It's occurred to me . . . maybe *I* wrote those words on the chalkboard. Maybe *I* wrecked Danny's room."

"You've lost me."

"Could have done it in my sleep."

"That's ridiculous, Tina."

"Is it? I thought I'd begun to get over Danny's death back in September. I started sleeping well then. I didn't dwell on it when I was alone, like I'd done for so long. I thought I'd put the worst pain behind me. But a month ago I started dreaming about Danny again. The first week, it hap-pened twice. The second week, four nights. And the past two weeks, I've dreamed about him every night without fail. The dreams get worse all the time. They're full-fledged nightmares now."

Elliot returned to the couch and sat beside her. "What are they like?"

"I dream he's alive, trapped somewhere, usually in a deep pit or a gorge or a well, someplace underground. He's calling to me, begging me to save him. But I can't. I'm never able to reach him. Then the earth starts closing in around him, and I wake up screaming, soaked with sweat. And I . . . I always have this powerful feeling that Danny isn't really dead. It never lasts for long, but when I first wake up, I'm sure he's alive some-where. You see, I've convinced my conscious mind that my boy is dead, but when I'm asleep it's my subconscious mind that's in charge; and my subconscious just isn't convinced that Danny's gone."

"So you think you're—what, sleepwalking? In your sleep, you're writ-ing a rejection of Danny's death on his chalkboard?"

"Don't you believe that's possible?"

"No. Well . . . maybe. I guess it is," Elliot said. "I'm no psychologist. But I don't buy it. I'll admit I don't know you all that well yet, but I think I know you well enough to say you wouldn't react that way. You're a person who meets problems head-on. If your inability to accept Danny's death was a serious problem, you wouldn't push it down into your sub-conscious. You'd learn to deal with it."

She smiled. "You have a pretty high opinion of me."

"Yes," he said. "I do. Besides, if it was you who wrote on the chalk-board and smashed things in the boy's room, then it was also you who came in here during the night and programmed the hotel computer to spew out that stuff about Danny. Do you really think you're so far gone that you could do something like that and not remember it? Do you think you've got multiple personalities and one doesn't know what the others are up to?"

She sank back on the sofa, slouched down. "No."

"Good."

"So where does that leave us?"

"Don't despair. We're making progress."

"We are?"

"Sure," he said. "We're eliminating possibilities. We've just crossed you off the list of suspects. And Michael. And I'm positive it can't be a stranger, which rules out most of the world."

"And I'm just as positive it isn't a friend or a relative. So you know where that leaves me?"

"Where?"

She leaned forward, put her brandy snifter on the table, and for a moment sat with her face in her hands.

"Tina?"

She lifted her head. "I'm just trying to think how best to phrase what's on my mind. It's a wild idea. Ludicrous. Probably even sick."

"I'm not going to think you're nuts," Elliot assured her. "What is it? Tell me."

She hesitated, trying to hear how it was going to sound before she said it, wondering if she really believed it enough even to give voice to it. The possibility of what she was going to suggest was remote.

At last she just plunged into it: "What I'm thinking . . . maybe Danny *is* alive."

Elliot cocked his head, studied her with those probing, dark eyes. "Alive?"

"I never saw his body."

"You didn't? Why not?"

"The coroner and undertaker said it was in terrible condition, horribly mutilated. They didn't think it was a good idea for me or Michael to see it. Neither of us would have been anxious to view the body even if it had been in perfect shape, so we accepted the mortician's recommendations. It was a closed-coffin funeral."

"How did the authorities identify the body?"

"They asked for pictures of Danny. But mainly I think they used dental records."

"Dental records are almost as good as fingerprints."

"Almost. But maybe Danny didn't die in that accident. Maybe he survived. Maybe someone out there knows where he is. Maybe that someone is trying to tell me that Danny is alive. Maybe there isn't any threat in these strange things happening to me. Maybe someone's just dropping a series of hints, trying to wake me up to the fact that Danny isn't dead."

"Too many *maybes*," he said.

"Maybe not."

Elliot put his hand on her shoulder and squeezed gently. "Tina, you know this theory doesn't make sense. Danny is dead."

"See? You *do* think I'm crazy."

"No. I think you're distraught, and that's understandable."

"Won't you even consider the possibility that he's alive?"

"How could he be?"

"I don't know."

"How could he have survived the accident you described?" Elliot asked.

"I don't know."

"And where would he have been all this time if not . . . in the grave?"

"I don't know that, either."

"If he were alive," Elliot said patiently, "someone would simply come and tell you. They wouldn't be this mysterious about it, would they?"

"Maybe."

Aware that her answer had disappointed him, she looked down at her hands, which were laced together so tightly that her knuckles were white.

Elliot touched her face, turning it gently toward him.

His beautiful, expressive eyes seemed to be filled with concern for her.

"Tina, you know there isn't any *maybe* about it. You know better than that. If Danny were alive, and if someone were trying to get that news to you, it wouldn't be done like this, not with all these dramatic hints. Am I right?"

"Probably."

"Danny is gone."

She said nothing.

"If you convince yourself he's alive," Elliot said, "you're only setting yourself up for another fall."

She stared deeply into his eyes. Eventually she sighed and nodded. "You're right."

"Danny's gone."

"Yes," she said thinly.

"You're really convinced of that?"

"Yes."

"Good."

Tina got up from the couch, went to the window, and pulled open the drapes. She had a sudden urge to see the Strip. After so much talk about death, she needed a glimpse of movement, action, life; and although the Strip sometimes was grubby in the flat glare of the desert sun, the boulevard was always, day or night, bustling and filled with life.

Now the early winter dusk settled over the city. In waves of dazzling color, millions of lights winked on in the enormous signs. Hundreds of cars progressed sluggishly through the busy street, taxicabs darting in and out, recklessly seeking any small advantage. Crowds streamed along the sidewalks, on their way from this casino to that casino, from one lounge to another, from one show to the next.

Tina turned to Elliot again. "You know what I want to do?"

"What?"

"Reopen the grave."

"Have Danny's body exhumed?"

"Yes. I never saw him. That's why I'm having such a hard time accepting that he's gone. That's why I'm having nightmares. If I'd seen the body, then I'd have known for sure. I wouldn't be able to fantasize about Danny still being alive."

"But the condition of the corpse . . ."

"I don't care," she said.

Elliot frowned, not convinced of the wisdom of exhumation. "The body's in an airtight casket, but it'll be even more deteriorated now than it was a year ago when they recommended you not look at it."

"I've got to *see.*"

"You'd be letting yourself in for a horrible—"

"That's the idea," she said quickly. "Shock. A powerful shock treatment that'll finally blow away all my lingering doubts. If I see Danny's . . . remains, I won't be able to entertain any more doubts. The nightmares will stop."

"Perhaps. Or perhaps you'll wind up with even worse dreams."

She shook her head. "Nothing could be worse than the ones I'm having now."

"Of course," he said, "exhumation of the body won't answer the main question. It won't help you discover who's been harassing you."

"It might," Tina said. "Whoever the creep is, whatever his motivations are, he's not well-balanced. He's one sort of sickie or another. Right? Who knows what might make a person like that reveal himself? If he finds out there's going to be an exhumation, maybe he'll react strongly, give himself away. Anything's possible."

"I suppose you could be right."

"Anyway," she said, "even if reopening the grave doesn't help me find who's responsible for these sick jokes—or whatever the hell they are—at least it'll settle my mind about Danny. That'll improve my psychological condition for sure, and I'll be better able to deal with the creep, whoever he is. So it'll work out for the best either way." She returned from the window, sat on the couch again, beside Elliot. "I'll need an attorney to handle this, won't I?"

"The exhumation? Yeah."

"Will you represent me?"

He didn't hesitate. "Sure."

"How difficult will it be?"

"Well, there's no urgent legal reason to have the body exhumed. I mean, there isn't any doubt about the cause of death, no court trial hinging on a new coroner's report. If that were the situation, we'd have the grave opened very quickly. But even so, this shouldn't be terribly difficult. I'll play up the mother-suffering-distress angle, and the court ought to be sympathetic."

"Have you ever handled anything like this before?"

"In fact, I have," Elliot said. "Five years ago. This eight-year-old girl died unexpectantly of a congenital kidney disease. Both kidneys failed virtually overnight. One day she was a happy, normal kid. The next day she seemed to have a touch of flu, and the third day she was dead. Her mother was shattered, couldn't bear to view the body, though the daughter hadn't suffered substantial physical damage, the way Danny did. The mother wasn't even able to attend the service. A couple weeks after the little girl was buried, the mother started feeling guilty about not paying her last respects."

Remembering her own ordeal, Tina said, "I know. Oh, I know how it is."

"The guilt eventually developed into serious emotional problems. Because the mother hadn't seen the body in the funeral home, she just couldn't bring herself to believe her daughter was really dead. Her inability to accept the truth was a lot worse than yours. She was hysterical most of the time, in a slow-motion breakdown. I arranged to have the grave reopened. In the course of preparing the exhumation request for the authorities, I discovered that my client's reaction was typical. Apparently, when a child dies, one of the worst things a parent can do is refuse to look at the body while it's lying in a casket. You need to spend time with the deceased, enough to accept that the body is never going to be animated again."

"Was your client helped by exhumation?"

"Oh, yes. Enormously."

"You see?"

"But don't forget," Elliot said, "her daughter's body wasn't mutilated."

Tina nodded grimly.

"And we reopened the grave only two months after the funeral, not a whole year later. The body was still in pretty good condition. But with Danny . . . it won't be that way."

"I'm aware of that," she said. "God knows, I'm not happy about this, but I'm convinced it's something I've got to do."

"Okay. I'll take care of it."

"How long will you need?" she asked.

"Will your husband contest it?"

She recalled the hatred in Michael's face when she'd left him a few hours ago. "Yes. He probably will."

Elliot carried their empty brandy glasses to the bar in the corner and switched on the light above the sink. "If your husband's likely to cause trouble, then we'll move fast and without fanfare. If we're clever, he won't know what we're doing until the exhumation is a fait accompli. Tomorrow's a holiday, so we can't get anything done officially until Friday."

"Probably not even then, what with the four-day weekend."

Elliot found the bottle of liquid soap and the dishcloth that were stored under the sink. "Ordinarily I'd say we'd have to wait until Monday. But it happens I know a very reasonable judge. Harold Kennebeck. We served in Army Intelligence together. He was my senior officer. If I—"

"Army Intelligence? You were a spy?"

"Nothing as grand as that. No trench coats. No skulking about in dark alleys."

"Karate, cyanide capsules, that sort of stuff?" she asked.

"Well, I've had a lot of martial arts training. I still work at that a couple of days a week because it's a good way to keep in shape. Really, though, it wasn't like what you see in the movies. No James Bond cars with machine guns hidden behind the headlights. It was mostly dull information gathering."

"Somehow," she said, "I get the feeling it was considerably more . . . interesting than you make it out to be."

"Nope. Document analysis, tedious interpretation of satellite reconnaissance photographs, that sort of thing. Boring as hell most of the time. Anyway, Judge Kennebeck and I go back a long way. We respect each other, and I'm sure he'll do something for me if he can. I'll be seeing him tomorrow afternoon at a New Year's Day party. I'll discuss the situation with him. Maybe he'll be willing to slip into the courthouse long enough on Friday to review my exhumation request and rule on it. He'd only need a few minutes. Then we could open the grave early Saturday."

Tina went to the bar and sat on one of the three stools, across the counter from Elliot. "The sooner the better. Now that I've made up my mind to do it, I'm anxious to get it over with."

"That's understandable. And there's another advantage in doing it this weekend. If we move fast, it isn't likely Michael will find out what we're up to. Even if he does somehow get a whiff of it, he'll have to locate another judge who'll be willing to stay or vacate the exhumation order."

"You think he'll be able to do that?"

"No. That's my point. There won't be many judges around over the holiday. Those on duty will be swamped with arraignments and bail hearings for drunken drivers and for people involved in drunken assaults. Most likely, Michael won't be able to get hold of a judge until Monday morning, and by then it'll be too late."

"Sneaky."

"That's my middle name." He finished washing the first brandy snifter, rinsed it in hot water, and put it in the drainage rack to dry.

"Elliot Sneaky Stryker," she said.

He smiled. "At your service."

"I'm glad you're my attorney."

"Well, let's see if I can actually pull it off."

"You can. You're the kind of person who meets every problem head-on."

"You have a pretty high opinion of me," he said, repeating what she had said to him earlier.

She smiled. "Yes, I do."

All the talk about death and fear and madness and pain seemed to have taken place further back in the past than a mere few seconds ago. They wanted to have a little fun during the evening that lay ahead, and now they began putting themselves in the mood for it.

As Elliot rinsed the second snifter and placed it in the rack, Tina said, "You do that very well."

"But I don't wash windows."

"I like to see a man being domestic."

"Then you should see me cook."

"You cook?"

"Like a dream."

"What's your best dish?"

"Everything I make."

"Obviously, you don't make humble pie."

"Every great chef must be an egomaniac when it comes to his culinary art. He must be totally secure in his estimation of his talents if he is to function well in the kitchen."

"What if you cooked something for me, and I didn't like it?"

"Then I'd eat your serving as well as mine."

"And what would I eat?"

"Your heart out."

After so many months of sorrow, how good it felt to be sharing an evening with an attractive and amusing man.

Elliot put away the dishwashing liquid and the wet dishcloth. As he dried his hands on the towel, he said, "Why don't we forget about going out to dinner? Let me cook for you instead."

"On such short notice?"

"I don't need much time to plan a meal. I'm a whiz. Besides, you can help by doing the drudgery, like cleaning the vegetables and chopping the onions."

"I should go home and freshen up," she said.

"You're already too fresh for me."

"My car—"

"You can drive it. Follow me to my place."

They turned out the lights and left the room, closing the door after them.

As they crossed the reception area on their way toward the hall, Tina glanced nervously at Angela's computer. She was afraid it was going to click on again, all by itself.

But she and Elliot left the outer office, flicking off the lights as they went, and the computer remained dark and silent.

14

ELLIOT STRYKER LIVED IN A LARGE, PLEASANT, CONTEMPORARY house overlooking the golf course at the Las Vegas Country Club. The rooms were warm, inviting, decorated in earth tones, with J. Robert Scott furniture complemented by a few antique pieces, and richly textured Edward Fields carpets. He owned a fine collection of paintings by Eyvind Earle, Jason Williamson, Larry W. Dyke, Charlotte Armstrong, Carl J. Smith, and other artists who made their homes in the western United States and who usually took their subject matter from either the old or the new West.

As he showed her through the house, he was eager to hear her reaction to it, and she didn't make him wait long.

"It's beautiful," she said. "Stunning. Who was your interior decorator?"

"You're looking at him."

"Really?"

"When I was poor, I looked forward to the day when I'd have a lovely home full of beautiful things, all arranged by the very best interior decorator. Then, when I had the money, I didn't want some stranger furnishing it for me. I wanted to have all the fun myself. Nancy, my late wife, and I decorated our first home. The project became a vocation for her, and I spent nearly as much time on it as I did on my legal practice. The two of us haunted furniture stores from Vegas to Los Angeles to San Francisco, antique shops, galleries, everything from flea markets to the most expensive stores we could find. We had a damn good time. And when she died . . . I discovered I couldn't learn to cope with the loss if I stayed in a place that was so crowded with memories of her. For five or six months I was an emotional wreck because every object in the house reminded me of Nancy. Finally I took a few mementos, a dozen pieces by which I'll always remember her, and I moved out, sold the house, bought this one, and started decorating all over again."

"I didn't realize you'd lost your wife," Tina said. "I mean, I thought it must have been a divorce or something."

"She passed away three years ago."

"What happened?"

"Cancer."

"I'm so sorry, Elliot."

"At least it was fast. Pancreatic cancer, exceedingly virulent. She was gone two months after they diagnosed it."

"Were you married long?"

"Twelve years."

She put a hand on his arm. "Twelve years leaves a big hole in the heart."

He realized they had even more in common than he had thought. "That's right. You had Danny for nearly twelve years."

"With me, of course, it's only been little more than a year since I've been alone. With you, it's been three years. Maybe you can tell me . . ."

"What?"

"Does it ever stop?" she asked.

"The hurting?"

"Yes."

"So far it hasn't. Maybe it will after four years. Or five. Or ten. It doesn't hurt as bad now as it once did. And the ache isn't constant anymore. But still there are moments when . . ."

He showed her through the rest of the house, which she wanted to see. Her ability to create a stylish stage show was not a fluke; she had taste and a sharp eye that instantly knew the difference between prettiness and genuine beauty, between cleverness and art. He enjoyed discussing antiques and paintings with her, and an hour passed in what seemed to be only ten minutes.

The tour ended in the enormous kitchen, which boasted a copper ceiling, a Santa Fe tile floor, and restaurant-quality equipment. She checked the walk-in cooler, inspected the yard-square grill, the griddle, the two Wolf ranges, the microwave, and the array of labor-saving appliances. "You've spent a small fortune here. I guess your law practice isn't just another Vegas divorce mill."

Elliot grinned. "I'm one of the founding partners of Stryker, West, Dwyer, Coffey, and Nichols. We're one of the largest law firms in town. I can't take a whole lot of credit for that. We were lucky. We were in the right place at the right time. Owen West and I opened for business in a cheap storefront office twelve years ago, right at the start of the biggest boom this town has ever seen. We represented some people no one else would touch, entrepreneurs who had a lot of good ideas but not much money for start-up legal fees. Some of our clients made smart moves and were carried right to the top by the explosive growth of the gaming industry and the Vegas real-estate market, and we just sort of shot up there along with them, hanging on to their coattails."

"Interesting," Tina said.

"It is?"

"You are."

"I am?"

"You're so modest about having built a splendid law practice, yet you're an egomaniac when it comes to your cooking."

He laughed. "That's because I'm a better cook than attorney. Listen, why don't you mix us a couple of drinks while I change out of this suit. I'll be back in five minutes, and then you'll see how a true culinary genius operates."

"If it doesn't work out, we can always jump in the car and go to McDonald's for a hamburger."

"Philistine."

"Their hamburgers are hard to beat."

"I'll make you eat crow."

"How do you cook it?"

"Very funny."

"Well, if you cook it very funny, I don't know if I want to eat it."

"If I *did* cook crow," he said, "it would be delicious. You would eat every scrap of it, lick your fingers, and beg for more."

Her smile was so lovely that he could have stood there all evening, just staring at the sweet curve of her lips.

ELLIOT WAS AMUSED by the effect that Tina had on him. He could not remember ever having been half so clumsy in the kitchen as he was this evening. He dropped spoons. He knocked over cans and bottles of spices. He forgot to watch a pot, and it boiled over. He made a mistake blending the salad dressing and had to begin again from scratch. She flustered him, and he loved it.

"Elliot, are you sure you aren't feeling those cognacs we had at my office?"

"Absolutely not."

"Then the drink you've been sipping on here."

"No. This is just my kitchen style."

"Spilling things is your style?"

"It gives the kitchen a pleasant *used* look."

"Are you sure you don't want to go to McDonald's?"

"Do *they* bother to give their kitchen a pleasant *used* look?"

"They not only have good hamburgers—"

"Their hamburgers have a pleasant *used* look."

"—their French fries are terrific."

"So I spill things," he said. "A cook doesn't have to be graceful to be a good cook."

"Does he have to have a good memory?"

"Huh?"

"That mustard powder you're just about to put into the salad dressing."

"What about it?"

"You already put it in a minute ago."

"I did? Thanks. I wouldn't want to have to mix this damn stuff *three* times."

She had a throaty laugh that was not unlike Nancy's had been.

Although she was different from Nancy in many ways, being with her was like being with Nancy. She was easy to talk to—bright, funny, sensitive.

Perhaps it was too soon to tell for sure, but he was beginning to think that fate, in an uncharacteristic flush of generosity, had given him a second chance at happiness.

WHEN HE AND Tina finished dessert, Elliot poured second cups of coffee. "Still want to go to McDonald's for a hamburger?"

The mushroom salad, the fettuccine Alfredo, and the zabaglione had been excellent. "You really *can* cook."

"Would I lie to you?"

"I guess I'll have to eat that crow now."

"I believe you just did."

"And I didn't even notice the feathers."

While Tina and Elliot had been joking in the kitchen, even before dinner had been completely prepared, she had begun to think they might go to bed together. By the time they finished eating dinner, she *knew* they would. Elliot wasn't pushing her. For that matter, she wasn't pushing him, either. They were both being driven by natural forces. Like the rush of water downstream. Like the relentless building of a storm wind and then the lightning. They both realized that they were in need of each other, physically and mentally and emotionally, and that whatever happened between them would be good.

It was fast but right, inevitable.

At the start of the evening, the undercurrent of sexual tension made her nervous. She hadn't been to bed with any man but Michael in the past fourteen years, since she was nineteen. She hadn't been to bed with *anyone at all* for almost two years. Suddenly it seemed to her that she had done a mad, stupid thing when she'd hidden away like a nun for two years. Of course, during the first of those two years, she'd still been married to Michael and had felt compelled to remain faithful to him, even though a separation and then a divorce had been in the works, and even though he had not felt constrained by any similar moral sense. Later, with the stage show to produce and with poor Danny's death weighing heavily on her, she hadn't been in the mood for romance. Now she felt like an inexperienced girl. She wondered if she would know what to *do*. She was afraid that she would be inept, clumsy, ridiculous, foolish in bed. She told herself that sex was just like riding a bicycle, impossible to *un*-learn, but the frivolousness of that analogy didn't increase her self-confidence.

Gradually, however, as she and Elliot went through the standard rites of courtship, the indirect sexual thrusts and parries of a budding relationship, albeit at an accelerated pace, the familiarity of the games reassured her. Amazing that it should be so familiar. Maybe it really was a bit like riding a bicycle.

After dinner they adjourned to the den, where Elliot built a fire in the black-granite fireplace. Although winter days in the desert were often as warm as springtime elsewhere, winter nights were always cool, sometimes downright bitter. With a chilly night wind moaning at the windows and howling incessantly under the eaves, the blazing fire was welcome.

Tina kicked off her shoes.

They sat side by side on the sofa in front of the fireplace, watching the flames and the occasional bursts of orange sparks, listening to music, and talking, talking, talking. Tina felt as if they had talked without pause all evening, speaking with quiet urgency, as if each had a vast quantity of earthshakingly important information that he must pass on to the other before they parted. The more they talked, the more they found in common. As an hour passed in front of the fire, and then another hour, Tina discovered that she liked Elliot Stryker more with each new thing she learned about him.

She never was sure who initiated the first kiss. He may have leaned toward her, or perhaps she tilted toward him. But before she realized what was happening, their lips met softly, briefly. Then again. And a third time. And then he began planting small kisses on her forehead, on her eyes, on her cheeks, her nose, the corners of her mouth, her chin. He kissed her ears, her eyes again, and left a chain of kisses along her neck, and when at last he returned to her mouth, he kissed her more deeply than before, and she responded at once, opening her mouth to him.

His hands moved over her, testing the firmness and resilience of her, and she touched him too, gently squeezing his shoulders, his arms, the hard muscles of his back. Nothing had ever felt better to her than he felt at that moment.

As if drifting in a dream, they left the den and went into the bedroom. He switched on a small lamp that stood upon the dresser, and he turned down the sheets.

During the minute that he was away from her, she was afraid the spell was broken. But when he returned, she kissed him tentatively, found that nothing had changed, and pressed against him once more.

She felt as if the two of them had been here, like this, locked in an embrace, many times before.

"We hardly know each other," she said.

"Is that the way you feel?"

"No."

"Me, neither."

"I know you so well."

"For ages."

"Yet it's only been two days."

"Too fast?" he asked.

"What do you think?"

"Not too fast for me."

"Not too fast at all," she agreed.

"Sure?"

"Positive."

"You're lovely."

"Love me."

He was not a particularly large man, but he picked her up in his arms as if she were a child.

She clung to him. She saw a longing and a need in his dark eyes, a powerful wanting that was only partly sex, and she knew the same need to be loved and valued must be in her eyes for him to see.

He carried her to the bed, put her down, and urged her to lie back. Without haste, with a breathless anticipation that lit up his face, he undressed her.

He quickly stripped off his own clothes and joined her on the bed, took her in his arms.

He explored her body slowly, deliberately, first with his eyes, then with his loving hands, then with his lips and tongue.

Tina realized that she had been wrong to think that celibacy should be a part of her period of mourning. Just the opposite was true. Good, healthy lovemaking with a man who cared for her would have helped her recover much faster than she had done, for sex was the antithesis of death, a joyous celebration of life, a denial of the tomb's existence.

The amber light molded to his muscles.

He lowered his face to hers. They kissed.

She slid a hand between them, squeezed and stroked him.

She felt wanton, shameless, insatiable.

As he entered her, she let her hands travel over his body, along his lean flanks.

"You're so sweet," he said.

He began the age-old rhythm of love. For a long, long time, they forgot that death existed, and they explored the delicious, silken surfaces of love, and it seemed to them, in those shining hours, that they would both live forever.

THURSDAY, JANUARY 1

15

TINA STAYED THE NIGHT WITH ELLIOT, AND HE REALIZED THAT HE had forgotten how pleasant it could be to share his bed with someone for whom he truly cared. He'd had other women in this bed during the past two years, and a few had stayed the night, but not one of those other lovers had made him feel content merely by the fact of her presence, as Tina did. With her, sex was a delightful bonus, a lagniappe, but it wasn't the main reason he wanted her beside him. She was an excellent lover—silken, smooth, and uninhibited in the pursuit of her own pleasure—but she was also vulnerable and kind. The vague, shadowy shape of her under the covers, in the darkness, was a talisman to ward off loneliness.

Eventually he fell asleep, but at four o'clock in the morning, he was awakened by cries of distress.

She sat straight up, the sheets knotted in her fists, catapulted out of a nightmare. She was quaking, gasping about a man dressed all in black, the monstrous figure from her dream.

Elliot switched on the bedside lamp to prove to her that they were alone in the room.

She had told him about the dreams, but he hadn't realized, until now, how terrible they were. The exhumation of Danny's body would be good for her, regardless of the horror that she might have to confront when the coffin lid was raised. If seeing the remains would put an end to these bloodcurdling nightmares, she would gain an advantage from the grim experience.

He switched off the bedside lamp and persuaded her to lie down again. He held her until she stopped shuddering.

To his surprise, her fear rapidly changed to desire. They fell easily into the pace and rhythm that had earlier best pleased them. Afterward, they slipped into sleep again.

OVER BREAKFAST HE asked her to go with him to the afternoon party at which he was going to corner Judge Kennebeck to ask about the exhumation. But Tina wanted to go back to her place and clean out Danny's room. She felt up to the challenge now, and she intended to finish the task before she lost her nerve again.

"We'll see each other tonight, won't we?" he asked.

"Yes."

"I'll cook for you again."

She smiled lasciviously. "In what sense do you mean that?"

She rose out of her chair, leaned across the table, kissed him.

The smell of her, the vibrant blue of her eyes, the feel of her supple skin as he put a hand to her face—those things generated waves of affection and longing within him.

He walked her to her Honda in the driveway and leaned in the window after she was behind the wheel, delaying her for another fifteen minutes while he planned, to her satisfaction, every dish of this evening's dinner.

When at last she drove away, he watched her car until it turned the corner and disappeared, and when she was gone he knew why he had not wanted to let her go. He'd been trying to postpone her departure because he was afraid that he would never see her again after she drove off.

He had no rational reason to entertain such dark thoughts. Certainly, the unknown person who was harassing Tina might have violent intentions. But Tina herself didn't think there was any serious danger, and Elliot tended to agree with her. The malicious tormentor wanted her to suffer mental anguish and spiritual pain; but he didn't want her to die, because that would spoil his fun.

The fear Elliot felt at her departure was purely superstitious. He was convinced that, with her arrival on the scene, he had been granted too much happiness, too fast, too soon, too easily. He had an awful suspicion that fate was setting him up for another hard fall. He was afraid Tina Evans would be taken away from him just as Nancy had been.

Unsuccessfully trying to shrug off the grim premonition, he went into the house.

He spent an hour and a half in his library, paging through legal case-books, boning up on precedents for the exhumation of a body that, as the court had put it, "was to be disinterred in the absence of a pressing legal need, solely for humane reasons, in consideration of certain survivors of the deceased." Elliot didn't think Harold Kennebeck would give him any trouble, and he didn't expect the judge to request a list of precedents for something as relatively simple and harmless as reopening Danny's grave, but he intended to be well prepared. In Army Intelligence, Kennebeck had been a fair but always demanding superior officer.

At one o'clock Elliot drove his silver Mercedes S600 sports coupe to the New Year's Day party on Sunrise Mountain. The sky was cerulean blue and clear, and he wished he had time to take the Cessna up for a few hours. This was perfect weather for flying, one of those crystalline days when being above the earth would make him feel clean and free.

On Sunday, when the exhumation was out of the way, maybe he would fly Tina to Arizona or to Los Angeles for the day.

On Sunrise Mountain most of the big, expensive houses featured natural landscaping—which meant rocks, colored stones, and artfully arranged cacti instead of grass, shrubs, and trees—in acknowledgment that man's grip on this portion of the desert was new and perhaps tenuous. At night the view of Las Vegas from the mountainside was undeniably spectacular, but Elliot couldn't understand what other reasons anyone could possibly have for choosing to live here rather than in the city's older, greener neighborhoods. On hot summer days these barren, sandy slopes seemed godforsaken, and they would not be made lush and green for another ten years at least. On the brown hills, the huge houses thrust like the bleak monuments of an ancient, dead religion. The residents of Sunrise Mountain could expect to share their patios and decks and pool aprons with occasional visiting scorpions, tarantulas, and rattlesnakes. On windy days the dust was as thick as fog, and it pushed its dirty little cat feet under doors, around windows, and through attic vents.

The party was at a large Tuscan-style house, halfway up the slopes. A three-sided, fan-shaped tent had been erected on the back lawn, to one side of the sixty-foot pool, with the open side facing the house. An eighteen-piece orchestra performed at the rear of the gaily striped canvas structure. Approximately two hundred guests danced or milled about behind the house, and another hundred partied within its twenty rooms.

Many of the faces were familiar to Elliot. Half of the guests were attorneys and their wives. Although a judicial purist might have disapproved, prosecutors and public defenders and tax attorneys and criminal lawyers and corporate counsel were mingling and getting pleasantly drunk with the judges before whom they argued cases most every week. Las Vegas had a judicial style and standards of its own.

After twenty minutes of diligent mixing, Elliot found Harold Kennebeck. The judge was a tall, dour-looking man with curly white hair. He greeted Elliot warmly, and they talked about their mutual interests: cooking, flying, and river-rafting.

Elliot didn't want to ask Kennebeck for a favor within hearing of a dozen lawyers, and today there was nowhere in the house where they could be assured of privacy. They went outside and strolled down the street, past the party-goers' cars, which ran the gamut from Rolls-Royces to Range Rovers.

Kennebeck listened with interest to Elliot's unofficial feeler about the chances of getting Danny's grave reopened. Elliot didn't tell the judge about the malicious prankster, for that seemed like an unnecessary complication; he still believed that once the fact of Danny's death was established by the exhumation, the quickest and surest way of dealing with the harassment was to hire a first-rate firm of private investigators to track down the perpetrator. Now, for the judge's benefit, and to explain why an exhumation had suddenly become such a vital matter, Elliot exaggerated the anguish and confusion that Tina had undergone as a direct consequence of never having seen the body of her child.

Harry Kennebeck had a poker face that also *looked* like a poker—hard and plain, dark—and it was difficult to tell if he had any sympathy whatsoever for Tina's plight. As he and Elliot ambled along the sun-splashed street, Kennebeck mulled over the problem in silence for almost a minute. At last he said, "What about the father?"

"I was hoping you wouldn't ask."

"Ah," Kennebeck said.

"The father will protest."

"You're positive?"

"Yes."

"On religious grounds?"

"No. There was a bitter divorce shortly before the boy died. Michael Evans hates his ex-wife."

"Ah. So he'd contest the exhumation for no other reason but to cause her grief?"

"That's right," Elliot said. "No other reason. No legitimate reason."

"Still, I've got to consider the father's wishes."

"As long as there aren't any religious objections, the law requires the permission of only one parent in a case like this," Elliot said.

"Nevertheless, I have a duty to protect everyone's interests in the matter."

"If the father has a chance to protest," Elliot said, "we'll probably get involved in a knock-down-drag-out legal battle. It'll tie up a hell of a lot of the court's time."

"I wouldn't like that," Kennebeck said thoughtfully. "The court's calendar is overloaded now. We simply don't have enough judges or enough money. The system's creaking and groaning."

"And when the dust finally settled," Elliot said, "my client would win the right to exhume the body anyway."

"Probably."

"Definitely," Elliot said. "Her husband would be engaged in nothing more than spiteful obstructionism. In the process of trying to hurt his ex-wife, he'd waste several days of the court's time, and the end result would be exactly the same as if he'd never been given a chance to protest."

"Ah," Kennebeck said, frowning slightly.

They stopped at the end of the next block. Kennebeck stood with his eyes closed and his face turned up to the warm winter sun.

At last the judge said, "You're asking me to cut corners."

"Not really. Simply issue an exhumation order on the mother's request. The law allows it."

"You want the order right away, I assume."

"Tomorrow morning if possible."

"And you'll have the grave reopened by tomorrow afternoon."

"Saturday at the latest."

"Before the father can get a restraining order from another judge," Kennebeck said.

"If there's no hitch, maybe the father won't ever find out about the exhumation."

"Ah."

"Everyone benefits. The court saves a lot of time and effort. My client is spared a great deal of unnecessary anguish. And her husband saves a bundle in attorney's fees that he'd just be throwing away in a hopeless attempt to stop us."

"Ah," Kennebeck said.

In silence they walked back to the house, where the party was getting louder by the minute.

In the middle of the block, Kennebeck finally said, "I'll have to chew on it for a while, Elliot."

"How long?"

"Ah. Will you be here all afternoon?"

"I doubt it. With all these attorneys, it's sort of a busman's holiday, don't you think?"

"Going home from here?" Kennebeck asked.

"Yes."

"Ah." He pushed a curly strand of white hair back from his forehead. "Then I'll call you at home this evening."

"Can you at least tell me how you're leaning?"

"In your favor, I suppose."

"You know I'm right, Harry."

Kennebeck smiled. "I've heard your argument, counselor. Let's leave it at that for now. I'll call you this evening, after I've had a chance to think about it."

At least Kennebeck hadn't refused the request; nevertheless, Elliot had expected a quicker and more satisfying response. He wasn't asking the judge for much of a favor. Besides, the two of them went back a long way indeed. He knew that Kennebeck was a cautious man, but usually not excessively so. The judge's hesitation in this relatively simple matter struck Elliot as odd, but he said nothing more. He had no choice but to wait for Kennebeck's call.

As they approached the house, they talked about the delights of pasta served with a thin, light sauce of olive oil, garlic, and sweet basil.

———

ELLIOT REMAINED AT the party only two hours. There were too many attorneys and not enough civilians to make the bash interesting. Everywhere he went, he heard talk about torts, writs, briefs, suits, countersuits, motions for continuation, appeals, plea bargaining, and the latest tax shelters. The conversations were like those in which he was involved at work, eight or ten hours a day, five days a week, and he didn't intend to spend a holiday nattering about the same damned things.

By four o'clock he was home again, working in the kitchen. Tina was supposed to arrive at six. He had a few chores to finish before she came, so they wouldn't have to spend a lot of time doing galley labor as they had done last night. Standing at the sink, he peeled and chopped a small onion, cleaned six stalks of celery, and peeled several slender carrots. He had just opened a bottle of balsamic vinegar and poured four ounces into a measuring cup when he heard movement behind him.

Turning, he saw a strange man enter the kitchen from the dining room. The guy was about five feet eight with a narrow face and a neatly trimmed blond beard. He wore a dark blue suit, white shirt, and blue tie, and he carried a physician's bag. He was nervous.

"What the hell?" Elliot said.

A second man appeared behind the first. He was considerably more formidable than his associate: tall, rough-edged, with large, big-knuckled, leathery hands—like something that had escaped from a recombinant DNA lab experimenting in the crossbreeding of human beings with bears. In freshly pressed slacks, a crisp blue shirt, a patterned tie, and a gray sports jacket, he might have been a professional hitman uncomfortably gotten up for the baptism of his Mafia don's grandchild. But he didn't appear to be nervous at all.

"What is this?" Elliot demanded.

Both intruders stopped near the refrigerator, twelve or fourteen feet from Elliot. The small man fidgeted, and the tall man smiled.

"How'd you get in here?"

"A lock-release gun," the tall man said, smiling cordially and nodding. "Bob here"—he indicated the smaller man—"has the neatest set of tools. Makes things easier."

"What the hell is this about?"

"Relax," said the tall man.

"I don't keep a lot of money here."

"No, no," the tall man said. "It's not money."

Bob shook his head in agreement, frowning, as if he was dismayed to think that he could be mistaken for a common thief.

"Just relax," the tall man repeated.

"You've got the wrong guy," Elliot assured them.

"You're the one, all right."

"Yes," Bob said. "You're the one. There's no mistake."

The conversation had the disorienting quality of the off-kilter exchanges between Alice and the scrawny denizens of Wonderland.

Putting down the vinegar bottle and picking up the knife, Elliot said, "Get the fuck out of here."

"Calm down, Mr. Stryker," the tall one said.

"Yes," Bob said. "Please calm down."

Elliot took a step toward them.

The tall man pulled a silencer-equipped pistol out of a shoulder holster that was concealed under his gray sports jacket. "Easy. Just you take it real nice and easy."

Elliot backed up against the sink.

"That's better," the tall man said.

"Much better," Bob said.

"Put the knife down, and we'll all be happy."

"Let's keep this happy," Bob agreed.

"Yeah, nice and happy."

The Mad Hatter would be along any minute now.

"Down with the knife," said the tall man. "Come on, come on."

Finally Elliot put it down.

"Push it across the counter, out of reach."

Elliot did as he was told. "Who are you guys?"

"As long as you cooperate, you won't get hurt," the tall man assured him.

Bob said, "Let's get on with it, Vince."

Vince, the tall man, said, "We'll use the breakfast area over there in the corner."

Bob went to the round maple table. He put down the black, physician's bag, opened it, and withdrew a compact cassette tape recorder. He removed other things from the bag too: a length of flexible rubber tubing, a sphygmomanometer for monitoring blood pressure, two small bottles of amber-colored fluid, and a packet of disposable hypodermic syringes.

Elliot's mind raced through a list of cases that his law firm was currently handling, searching for some connection with these two intruders, but he couldn't think of one.

The tall man gestured with the gun. "Go over to the table and sit down."

"Not until you tell me what this is all about."

"I'm giving the orders here."

"But I'm not taking them."

"I'll put a hole in you if you don't move."

"No. You won't do that," Elliot said, wishing that he felt as confident as he sounded. "You've got something else in mind, and shooting me would ruin it."

"Move your ass over to that table."

"Not until you explain yourself."

Vince glared at him.

Elliot met the stranger's eyes and didn't look away.

At last Vince said, "Be reasonable. We've just got to ask you some questions."

Determined not to let them see that he was frightened, aware that any sign of fear would be taken as proof of weakness, Elliot said, "Well, you've got one hell of a weird approach for someone who's just taking a public opinion survey."

"Move."

"What are the hypodermic needles for?"

"Move."

"What are they for?"

Vince sighed. "We gotta be sure you tell us the truth."

"The entire truth," said Bob.

"Drugs?" Elliot asked.

"They're effective and reliable," said Bob.

"And when you've finished, I'll have a brain the consistency of grape jelly."

"No, no," Bob said. "These drugs won't do any lasting physical or mental damage."

"What sort of questions?" Elliot asked.

"I'm losing my patience with you," Vince said.

"It's mutual," Elliot assured him.

"Move."

Elliot didn't move an inch. He refused to look at the muzzle of the pistol. He wanted them to think that guns didn't scare him. Inside, he was vibrating like a tuning fork.

"You son of a bitch, *move!*"

"What sort of questions do you want to ask me?"

The big man scowled.

Bob said, "For Christ's sake, Vince, tell him. He's going to hear the questions anyway when he finally sits down. Let's get this over with and split."

Vince scratched his concrete-block chin with his shovel of a hand and then reached inside his jacket. From an inner pocket, he withdrew a few sheets of folded typing paper.

The gun wavered, but it didn't move off target far enough to give Elliot a chance.

"I'm supposed to ask you every question on this list," Vince said, shaking the folded paper at Elliot. "It's a lot, thirty or forty questions altogether, but it won't take long if you just sit down over there and cooperate."

"Questions about what?" Elliot insisted.

"Christina Evans."

This was the last thing Elliot expected. He was dumbfounded. "Tina Evans? What about her?"

"Got to know why she wants her little boy's grave reopened."

Elliot stared at him, amazed. "How do you know about that?"

"Never mind," Vince said.

"Yeah," Bob said. "Never mind *how* we know. The important thing is we *do* know."

"Are you the bastards who've been harassing Tina?"

"Huh?"

"Are you the ones who keep sending her messages?"

"What messages?" Bob asked.

"Are you the ones who wrecked the boy's room?"

"What are you talking about?" Vince asked. "We haven't heard anything about this."

"Someone's sending messages about the kid?" Bob asked.

They appeared to be genuinely surprised by this news, and Elliot was pretty sure they weren't the people who had been trying to scare Tina. Besides, though they both struck him as slightly wacky, they didn't seem to be merely hoaxers or borderline psychopaths who got their kicks by scaring defenseless women. They looked and acted like organization men, even though the big one was rough enough at the edges to pass for a common thug. A silencer-equipped pistol, lock-release gun, truth serums—their apparatus indicated that these guys were part of a sophisticated outfit with substantial resources.

"What about the messages she's been getting?" Vince asked, still watching Elliot closely.

"I guess that's just one more question you're not going to get an answer for," Elliot said.

"We'll get the answer," Vince said coldly.

"We'll get all the answers," Bob agreed.

"Now," Vince said, "counselor, are you going to walk over to the table and sit your ass down, or am I going to have to motivate you with this?" He gestured with his pistol again.

"Kennebeck!" Elliot said, startled by a sudden insight. "The only way you could have found out about the exhumation so quickly is if Kennebeck told you."

The two men glanced at each other. They were unhappy to hear the judge's name.

"Who?" Vince asked, but it was too late to cover the revealing look they had exchanged.

"That's why he stalled me," Elliot said. "He wanted to give you time to get to me. Why in the hell should Kennebeck care whether or not Danny's grave is reopened? Why should *you* care? Who the hell are you people?"

The Ursine escapee from the island of Dr. Moreau was no longer merely impatient; he was angry. "Listen, you stupid fuck, I'm not gonna humor you any longer. I'm not gonna answer any more questions, but I *am* gonna put a bullet in your crotch if you don't move over to the table and sit down."

Elliot pretended not to have heard the threat. The pistol still frightened him, but he was now thinking of something else that scared him more than the gun. A chill spread from the base of his spine, up his back, as he realized what the presence of these men implied about the accident that had killed Danny.

"There's something about Danny's death . . . something strange about the way all those scouts died. The truth of it isn't anything like the version everyone's been told. The bus accident . . . that's a lie, isn't it?"

Neither man answered him.

"The truth is a lot worse," Elliot said. "Something so terrible that some powerful people want to hush it up. Kennebeck . . . once an agent, always an agent. Which set of letters do you guys work for? Not the FBI. They're all Ivy Leaguers these days, polished, educated. Same for the CIA. You're too crude. Not the CID, for sure; there's no military discipline about you. Let me guess. You work for some set of letters the public hasn't even heard about yet. Something secret and dirty."

Vince's face darkened like a slab of Spam on a hot griddle. "Goddamn it, I said *you* were going to answer the questions from now on."

"Relax," Elliot said. "I've played your game. I was in Army Intelligence back when. I'm not exactly an outsider. I know how it works—the rules, the moves. You don't have to be so hard-assed with me. Open up. Give me a break, and I'll give you a break."

Evidently sensing Vince's onrushing blowup and aware that it wouldn't help them accomplish their mission, Bob quickly said, "Listen, Stryker, we can't answer most of your questions because we don't know. Yes, we work for a government agency. Yes, it's one you've never heard of and probably never will. But we don't know why this Danny Evans kid is so important. We haven't been told the details, not even half of them. And we don't *want* to know all of it, either. You understand what I'm saying— the less a guy knows, the less he can be nailed for later. Christ, we're not big shots in this outfit. We're strictly hired help. They only tell us as much as we need to know. So will you cool it? Just come over here, sit down, let me inject you, give us a few answers, and we can all get on with our lives. We can't just stand here forever."

"If you're working for a government intelligence agency, then go away and come back with the legal papers," Elliot said. "Show me search warrants and subpoenas."

"You know better than that," Vince said harshly.

"The agency we work for doesn't officially exist," Bob said. "So how can an agency that doesn't exist go to court for a subpoena? Get serious, Mr. Stryker."

"If I do submit to the drug, what happens to me after you've got your answers?" Elliot asked.

"Nothing," Vince said.

"Nothing at all," Bob said.

"How can I be sure?"

At this indication of imminent surrender, the tall man relaxed slightly, although his lumpish face was still flushed with anger. "I told you. When we've got what we want, we'll leave. We just have to find out exactly why the Evans woman wants the grave reopened. We have to know if someone's ratted to her. If someone has, then we gotta spike his ass to a barn door. But we don't have anything against you. Not personally, you know. After we find out what we want to know, we'll leave."

"And let me go to the police?" Elliot asked.

"Cops don't scare us," Vince said arrogantly. "Hell, you won't be able to tell them who we were or where they can start looking for us. They won't get anywhere. Nowhere. Zip. And if they *do* pick up our trail somehow, we can put pressure on them to drop it fast. This is national security business, pal, the biggest of the big time. The government is allowed to bend the rules if it wants. After all, it makes them."

"That's not quite the way they explained the system in law school," Elliot said.

"Yeah, well, that's ivory tower stuff," Bob said, nervously straightening his tie.

"Right," Vince said. "And this is real life. Now sit down at the table like a good boy."

"Please, Mr. Stryker," Bob said.

"No."

When they got their answers, they would kill him. If they had intended to let him live, they wouldn't have used their real names in front of him. And they wouldn't have wasted so much time coaxing him to cooperate; they would have used force without hesitation. They wanted to gain his cooperation without violence because they were reluctant to mark him; their intention was that his death should appear to be an accident or a suicide. The scenario was obvious. Probably a suicide. While he was still under the influence of the drug, they might be able to make him write a suicide note and sign it in a legible, identifiable script. Then they would carry him out to the garage, prop him up in his little Mercedes, put the seat belt snugly around him, and start the engine without opening the garage door. He would be too drugged to move, and the carbon monoxide would do the rest. In a day or two someone would find him out there, his face blue-green-gray, his tongue dark and lolling, his eyes bulging in their sockets as he stared through the windshield as if on a drive to Hell. If there were no unusual marks on his body, no injuries incompatible with the coroner's determination of suicide, the police would be quickly satisfied.

"No," he said again, louder this time. "If you bastards want me to sit down at that table, you're going to have to drag me there."

16

TINA RESOLUTELY CLEANED UP THE MESS IN DANNY'S ROOM AND packed his belongings. She intended to donate everything to Goodwill Industries.

Several times she was on the verge of tears as the sight of one object or another released a flood of memories. She gritted her teeth, however, and restrained the urge to leave the room with the job uncompleted.

Not much remained to be done: The contents of three cartons in the back of the deep closet had to be sorted. She tried to lift one of them, but it was too heavy. She dragged it into the bedroom, across the carpet, into the shafts of reddish-gold afternoon sunlight that filtered through the sheltering trees outside and then through the dust-filmed window.

When she opened the carton, she saw that it contained part of Danny's collection of comic books and graphic novels. They were mostly horror comics.

She'd never been able to understand this morbid streak in him. Monster movies. Horror comics. Vampire novels. Scary stories of every kind, in every medium. Initially his growing fascination with the macabre had not seemed entirely healthy to her, but she had never denied him the freedom to pursue it. Most of his friends had shared his avid interest in ghosts and ghouls; besides, the grotesque hadn't been his *only* interest, so she had decided not to worry about it.

In the carton were two stacks of comic books, and the two issues on top sported gruesome, full-color covers. On the first, a black carriage, drawn by four black horses with evil glaring eyes, rushed along a night highway, beneath a gibbous moon, and a headless man held the reins, urging the frenzied horses forward. Bright blood streamed from the ragged stump of the coachman's neck, and gelatinous clots of blood clung to his white, ruffled shirt. His grisly head stood on the driver's seat beside him, grinning fiendishly, filled with malevolent life even though it had been brutally severed from his body.

Tina grimaced. If this was what Danny had read before going to bed at night, how had he been able to sleep so well? He'd always been a deep, unmoving sleeper, never troubled by bad dreams.

She dragged another carton out of the closet. It was as heavy as the first, and she figured it contained more comic books, but she opened it to be sure.

She gasped in shock.

He was glaring up at her from inside the box. From the cover of a graphic novel. *Him.* The man dressed all in black. That same face. Mostly skull and withered flesh. Prominent sockets of bone, and the menacing, inhuman crimson eyes staring out with intense hatred. The cluster of maggots squirming on his cheek, at the corner of one eye. The rotten, yellow-toothed grin. In every repulsive detail, he was precisely like the hideous creature that stalked her nightmares.

How could she have dreamed about this hideous creature just last night and then find it waiting for her here, today, only hours later?

She stepped back from the cardboard box.

The burning, scarlet eyes of the monstrous figure in the drawing seemed to follow her.

She must have seen this lurid cover illustration when Danny had first brought the magazine into the house. The memory of it was fixed in her subconscious, festering, until she eventually incorporated it into her nightmares.

That seemed to be the only logical explanation.

But she knew it wasn't true.

She had never seen this drawing before. When Danny had first begun collecting horror comics with his allowance, she had closely examined those books to decide whether or not they were harmful to him. But after she had made up her mind to let him read such stuff, she never thereafter even glanced at his purchases.

Yet she had dreamed about the man in black.

And here he was. Grinning at her.

Curious about the story from which the illustration had been taken, Tina stepped to the box again to pluck out the graphic novel. It was thicker than a comic book and printed on slick paper.

As her fingers touched the glossy cover, a bell rang.

She flinched and gasped.

The bell rang again, and she realized that someone was at the front door.

Heart thumping, she went to the foyer.

Through the fish-eye lens in the door, she saw a young, clean-cut man wearing a blue cap with an unidentifiable emblem on it. He was smiling, waiting to be acknowledged.

She didn't open the door. "What do you want?"

"Gas-company repair. We need to check our lines where they come into your house."

Tina frowned. "On New Year's Day?"

"Emergency crew," the repairman said through the closed door. "We're investigating a possible gas leak in the neighborhood."

She hesitated, but then opened the door without removing the heavy-duty security chain. She studied him through the narrow gap. "Gas leak?"

He smiled reassuringly. "There probably isn't any danger. We've lost some pressure in our lines, and we're trying to find the cause of it. No reason to evacuate people or panic or anything. But we're trying to check every house. Do you have a gas stove in the kitchen?"

"No. Electric."

"What about the heating system?"

"Yes. There's a gas furnace."

"Yeah. I think all the houses in this area have gas furnaces. I'd better have a look at it, check the fittings, the incoming feed, all that."

She looked him over carefully. He was wearing a gas-company uniform, and he was carrying a large tool kit with the gas-company emblem on it.

She said, "Can I see some identification?"

"Sure." From his shirt pocket, he withdrew a laminated ID card with the gas-company seal, his picture, his name, and his physical statistics.

Feeling slightly foolish, like an easily spooked old woman, Tina said, "I'm sorry. It's not that you strike me as a dangerous person or anything. I just—"

"Hey, it's okay. Don't apologize. You did the right thing, asking for an ID. These days, you're crazy if you open your door without knowing exactly who's on the other side of it."

She closed the door long enough to slip off the security chain. Then she opened it again and stepped back. "Come in."

"Where's the furnace? In the garage?"

Few Vegas houses had basements. "Yes. The garage."

"If you want, I could just go in through the garage door."

"No. That's all right. Come in."

He stepped across the threshold.

She closed and locked the door.

"Nice place you've got here."

"Thank you."

"Cozy. Good sense of color. All these earth tones. I like that. It's a little bit like our house. My wife has a real good sense of color."

"It's relaxing," Tina said.

"Isn't it? So nice and natural."

"The garage is this way," she said.

He followed her past the kitchen, into the short hall, into the laundry room, and from there into the garage.

Tina switched on the light. The darkness was dispelled, but shadows remained along the walls and in the corners.

The garage was slightly musty, but Tina wasn't able to detect the odor of gas.

"Doesn't smell like there's trouble here," she said.

"You're probably right. But you never can tell. It could be an underground break on your property. Gas might be leaking under the concrete slab and building up down there, in which case it's possible you wouldn't detect it right away, but you'd still be sitting on top of a bomb."

"What a lovely thought."

"Makes life interesting."

"It's a good thing you're not working in the gas company's public relations department."

He laughed. "Don't worry. If I really believed there was even the tiniest chance of anything like that, would I be standing here so cheerful?"

"I guess not."

"You can bet on it. Really. Don't worry. This is just going to be a routine check."

He went to the furnace, put his heavy tool kit on the floor, and hunkered down. He opened a hinged plate, exposing the furnace's workings. A ring of brilliant, pulsing flame was visible in there, and it bathed his face in an eerie blue light.

"Well?" she said.

He looked up at her. "This will take me maybe fifteen or twenty minutes."

"Oh. I thought it was just a simple thing."

"It's best to be thorough in a situation like this."

"By all means, be thorough."

"Hey, if you've got something to do, feel free to go ahead with it. I won't be needing anything."

Tina thought of the graphic novel with the man in black on its cover. She was curious about the story out of which that creature had stepped, for she had the peculiar feeling that, in some way, it would be similar to the story of Danny's death. This was a bizarre notion, and she didn't know where it had come from, but she couldn't dispel it.

"Well," she said, "I *was* cleaning the back room. If you're sure—"

"Oh, certainly," he said. "Go ahead. Don't let me interrupt your house-work."

She left him there in the shadowy garage, his face painted by shim-mering blue light, his eyes gleaming with twin reflections of fire.

17

WHEN ELLIOT REFUSED TO MOVE AWAY FROM THE SINK TO THE breakfast table in the far corner of the big kitchen, Bob, the smaller of the two men, hesitated, then reluctantly took a step toward him.

"Wait," Vince said.

Bob stopped, obviously relieved that his hulking accomplice was go-ing to deal with Elliot.

"Don't get in my way," Vince advised. He tucked the sheaf of type-written questions into his coat pocket. "Let me handle this bastard."

Bob retreated to the table, and Elliot turned his attention to the larger intruder.

Vince held the pistol in his right hand and made a fist with his left. "You really think you want to tangle with me, little man? Hell, my fist is just about as big as your head. You know what this fist is going to feel like when it hits, little man?"

Elliot had a pretty good idea of what it would feel like, and he was sweating under his arms and in the small of his back, but he didn't move, and he didn't respond to the stranger's taunting.

"It's going to feel like a freight train ramming straight through you," Vince said. "So stop being so damn stubborn."

They were going to great lengths to avoid using violence, which confirmed Elliot's suspicion that they wanted to leave him unmarked, so that later his body would bear no cuts or bruises incompatible with suicide.

The bear-who-would-be-a-man shambled toward him. "You want to change your mind, be cooperative?"

Elliot held his ground.

"One good punch in the belly," Vince said, "and you'll be puking your guts out on your shoes."

Another step.

"And when you're done puking your guts out," Vince said, "I'm going to grab you by your balls and drag you over to the table."

One more step.

Then the big man stopped.

They were only an arm's length apart.

Elliot glanced at Bob, who was still standing at the breakfast table, the packet of syringes in his hand.

"Last chance to do it the easy way," Vince said.

In one smooth lightning-fast movement, Elliot seized the measuring cup into which he had poured four ounces of vinegar a few minutes ago, and he threw the contents in Vince's face. The big man cried out in surprise and pain, temporarily blinded. Elliot dropped the measuring cup and seized the gun, but Vince reflexively squeezed off a shot that breezed past Elliot's face and smashed the window behind the sink. Elliot ducked a wild roundhouse punch, stepped in close, still holding on to the pistol that the other man wouldn't surrender. He swung one arm around, slamming his bent elbow into Vince's throat. The big man's head snapped back, and Elliot chopped the exposed Adam's apple with the flat blade of his hand. He rammed his knee into his adversary's crotch and tore the gun out of the bear-paw hand as those clutching fingers went slack. Vince bent forward, gagging, and Elliot slammed the butt of the gun against the side of his head, with a sound like stone meeting stone.

Elliot stepped back.

Vince dropped to his knees, then onto his face. He stayed there, tongue-kissing the floor tiles.

The entire battle had taken less than ten seconds.

The big man had been overconfident, certain that his six-inch advantage in height and his extra eighty pounds of muscle made him unbeatable. He had been wrong.

Elliot swung toward the other intruder, pointing the confiscated pistol.

Bob was already out of the kitchen, in the dining room, running toward the front of the house. Evidently he wasn't carrying a gun, and he was impressed by the speed and ease with which his partner had been taken out of action.

Elliot went after him but was slowed by the dining-room chairs, which the fleeing man had overturned in his wake. In the living room, other furniture was knocked over, and books were strewn on the floor. The route to the entrance foyer was an obstacle course.

By the time Elliot reached the front door and rushed out of the house, Bob had run the length of the driveway and crossed the street. He was climbing into a dark-green, unmarked Chevy sedan. Elliot got to the street in time to watch the Chevy pull away, tires squealing, engine roaring.

He couldn't get the license number. The plates were smeared with mud.

He hurried back to the house.

The man in the kitchen was still unconscious and would probably remain that way for another ten or fifteen minutes. Elliot checked his pulse and pulled back one of his eyelids. Vince would survive, although he might need hospitalization, and he wouldn't be able to swallow without pain for days to come.

Elliot went through the thug's pockets. He found some small change, a comb, a wallet, and the sheaf of papers on which were typed the questions that Elliot had been expected to answer.

He folded the pages and stuffed them into his hip pocket.

Vince's wallet contained ninety-two dollars, no credit cards, no driver's license, no identification of any kind. Definitely not FBI. Bureau men carried the proper credentials. Not CIA, either. CIA operatives were loaded with ID, even if it was in a phony name. As far as Elliot was concerned, the absence of ID was more sinister than a collection of patently false papers would have been, because this absolute anonymity smacked of a secret police organization.

Secret police. Such a possibility scared the hell out of Elliot. Not in the good old U.S. of A. Surely not. In China, in the new Russia, in Iran or Iraq—yes. In a South American banana republic—yes. In half the countries in the world, there were secret police, modern gestapos, and citizens lived in fear of a late-night knock on the door. But not in America, damn it.

Even if the government had established a secret police force, however, why was it so anxious to cover up the true facts of Danny's death? What were they trying to hide about the Sierra tragedy? What *really* had happened up in those mountains?

Tina.

Suddenly he realized she was in as much danger as he was. If these people were determined to kill him just to stop the exhumation, they would *have* to kill Tina. In fact, she must be their primary target.

He ran to the kitchen phone, snatched up the handset, and realized that he didn't know her number. He quickly leafed through the telephone directory. But there was no listing for Christina Evans.

He would never be able to con an unlisted number out of the directory-assistance operator. By the time he called the police and managed to explain the situation, they might be too late to help Tina.

Briefly he stood in terrible indecision, incapacitated by the prospect of losing Tina. He thought of her slightly crooked smile, her eyes as quick and deep and cool and blue as a pure mountain stream. The pressure in his chest grew so great that he couldn't get his breath.

Then he remembered her address. She had given it to him two nights ago, at the party after the premiere of *Magyck!* She didn't live far from him. He could be at her place in five minutes.

He still had the silencer-equipped pistol in his hand, and he decided to keep it.

He ran to the car in the driveway.

18

TINA LEFT THE REPAIRMAN FROM THE GAS COMPANY IN THE garage and returned to Danny's room. She took the graphic novel out of the carton and sat on the edge of the bed in the tarnished-copper sunlight that fell like a shower of pennies through the window.

The magazine contained half a dozen illustrated horror stories. The one from which the cover painting had been drawn was sixteen pages long. In letters that were supposed to look as if they had been formed from rotting shroud cloth, the artist had emblazoned the title across the top of the first page, above a somber, well-detailed scene of a rain-swept graveyard. Tina stared at those words in shocked disbelief.

THE BOY WHO WAS NOT DEAD

She thought of the words on the chalkboard and on the computer printout: *Not dead, not dead, not dead. . . .*

Her hands shook. She had trouble holding the magazine steady enough to read.

The story was set in the mid-nineteenth century, when a physician's perception of the thin line between life and death was often cloudy. It was the tale of a boy, Kevin, who fell off a roof and took a bad knock on the head, thereafter slipping into a deep coma. The boy's vital signs were undetectable to the medical technology of that era. The doctor pronounced him dead, and his grieving parents committed Kevin to the grave. In those days the corpse was not embalmed; therefore, the boy was buried while still alive. Kevin's parents went away from the city immediately after the funeral, intending to spend a month at their summer house in the country, where they could be free from the press of business and social duties, the better to mourn their lost child. But the first night in the country, the mother received a vision in which Kevin was buried alive and calling for her. The vision was so vivid, so disturbing, that she and her husband raced back to the city that very night to have the grave reopened at dawn. But Death decided that Kevin belonged to him, because the funeral had been held already and because the grave had been closed. Death was determined that the parents would not reach the cemetery in time to save their son. Most of the story dealt with Death's attempts to stop the mother and father on their desperate night journey; they were assaulted by every form of the walking dead, every manner of living corpse and vampire and ghoul and zombie and ghost, but they triumphed. They arrived at the grave by dawn, had it opened, and found their son alive, released from his coma. The last panel of the illustrated story showed the parents and the boy walking out of the graveyard while Death watched them leave. Death was saying, "Only a temporary victory. You'll all be mine sooner or later. You'll be back some day. I'll be waiting for you."

Tina was dry-mouthed, weak.

She didn't know what to make of the damned thing.

This was just a silly comic book, an absurd horror story. Yet . . . strange parallels existed between this gruesome tale and the recent ugliness in her own life.

She put the magazine aside, cover-down, so she wouldn't have to meet Death's wormy, red-eyed gaze.

The Boy Who Was Not Dead.

It was weird.

She had dreamed that Danny was buried alive. Into her dream she incorporated a grisly character from an old issue of a horror-comics magazine that was in Danny's collection. The lead story in this issue was about a boy, approximately Danny's age, mistakenly pronounced dead, then buried alive, and then exhumed.

Coincidence?

Yeah, sure, just about as coincidental as sunrise following sunset.

Crazily, Tina felt as if her nightmare had not come from within her, but from without, as if some person or force had projected the dream into her mind in an effort to—

To what?

To tell her that Danny had been buried alive?

Impossible. He could not have been buried alive. The boy had been battered, burned, frozen, horribly mutilated in the crash, dead beyond any shadow of a doubt. That's what both the authorities and the mortician had told her. Furthermore, this was not the mid-nineteenth century; these days, doctors could detect even the vaguest heartbeat, the shallowest respiration, the dimmest traces of brain-wave activity.

Danny certainly had been dead when they had buried him.

And if, by some million-to-one chance, the boy *had* been alive when he'd been buried, why would it take an entire year for her to receive a vision from the spirit world?

This last thought profoundly shocked her. The spirit world? Visions? Clairvoyant experiences? She didn't believe in any of that psychic, supernatural stuff. At least she'd always thought she didn't believe in it. Yet now she was seriously considering the possibility that her dreams had some otherworldly significance. This was sheer claptrap. Utter nonsense. The roots of all dreams were to be found in the store of experiences in the psyche; dreams were not sent like ethereal telegrams from spirits or gods or demons. Her sudden gullibility dismayed and alarmed her, because it indicated that the decision to have Danny's body exhumed was not having the stabilizing effect on her emotions that she had hoped it would.

Tina got up from the bed, went to the window, and gazed at the quiet street, the palms, the olive trees.

She had to concentrate on the indisputable facts. Rule out all of this nonsense about the dream having been sent by some outside force. It was *her* dream, entirely of *her* making.

But what about the horror comic?

As far as she could see, only one rational explanation presented itself. She *must* have glimpsed the grotesque figure of Death on the cover of the magazine when Danny first brought the issue home from the newsstand.

Except that she knew she hadn't.

And even if she had seen the color illustration before, she knew damned well that she hadn't read the story—*The Boy Who Was Not Dead.* She had paged through only two of the magazines Danny had bought, the first two, when she had been trying to make up her mind whether such unusual reading material could have any harmful effects on him. From the date on its cover, she knew that the issue containing *The Boy Who Was Not Dead* couldn't be one of the first pieces in Danny's collection. It had been published only two years ago, long after she had decided that horror comics were harmless.

She was back where she'd started.

Her dream had been patterned after the images in the illustrated horror story. That seemed indisputable.

But she hadn't read the story until a few minutes ago. That was a fact as well.

Frustrated and angry at herself for her inability to solve the puzzle, she turned from the window. She went back to the bed to have another look at the magazine, which she'd left there.

The gas company workman called from the front of the house, startling Tina.

She found him waiting by the front door.

"I'm finished," he said. "I just wanted to let you know I was going, so you could lock the door behind me."

"Everything all right?"

"Oh, yeah. Sure. Everything here is in great shape. If there's a gas leak in this neighborhood, it's not anywhere on your property."

She thanked him, and he said he was only doing his job. They both said "Have a nice day," and she locked the door after he left.

She returned to Danny's room and picked up the lurid magazine. Death glared hungrily at her from the cover.

Sitting on the edge of the bed, she read the story again, hoping to see something important in it that she had overlooked in the first reading.

Three or four minutes later the doorbell rang—one, two, three, four times, insistently.

Carrying the magazine, she went to answer the bell. It rang three more times during the ten seconds that she took to reach the front door.

"Don't be so damn impatient," she muttered.

To her surprise, through the fish-eye lens, she saw Elliot on the stoop.

When she opened the door, he came in fast, almost in a crouch, glancing past her, left and right, toward the living room, then toward the dining area, speaking rapidly, urgently. "Are you okay? Are you all right?"

"I'm fine. What's wrong with you?"

"Are you alone?"

"Not now that you're here."

He closed the door, locked it. "Pack a suitcase."

"What?"

"I don't think it's safe for you to stay here."

"Elliot, is that a gun?"

"Yeah. I was—"

"A real gun?"

"Yeah. I took it off the guy who tried to kill me."

She was more able to believe that he was joking than that he had really been in danger. "What man? When?"

"A few minutes ago. At my place."

"But—"

"Listen, Tina, they wanted to kill me just because I was going to help you get Danny's body exhumed."

She gaped at him. "What are you talking about?"

"Murder. Conspiracy. Something damn strange. They probably intend to kill you too."

"But that's—"

"Crazy," he said. "I know. But it's true."

"Elliot—"

"Can you pack a suitcase fast?"

At first she half believed that he was trying to be funny, playing a game to amuse her, and she was going to tell him that none of this struck her as funny. But she stared into his dark, expressive eyes, and she knew that he'd meant every word he said.

"My God, Elliot, did someone really try to kill you?"

"I'll tell you about it later."

"Are you hurt?"

"No, no. But we ought to lie low until we can figure this out."

"Did you call the police?"

"I'm not sure that's a good idea."

"Why not?"

"Maybe they're part of it somehow."

"Part of it? The *cops?*"

"Where do you keep your suitcases?"

She felt dizzy. "Where are we going?"

"I don't know yet."

"But—"

"Come on. Hurry. Let's get you packed and the hell out of here before any more of these guys show up."

"I have suitcases in my bedroom closet."

He put a hand against her back, gently but firmly urging her out of the foyer.

She headed for the master bedroom, confused and beginning to be frightened.

He followed close behind her. "Has anyone been around here this afternoon?"

"Just me."

"I mean, anyone snooping around? Anyone at the door?"

"No."

"I can't figure why they'd come for me first."

"Well, there was the gas man," Tina said as she hurried down the short hall toward the master bedroom.

"The what?"

"The repairman from the gas company."

Elliot put a hand on her shoulder, stopped her, and turned her around just as they entered the bedroom. "A gas company workman?"

"Yes. Don't worry. I asked to see his credentials."

Elliot frowned. "But it's a holiday."

"He was an emergency crewman."

"What emergency?"

"They've lost some pressure in the gas lines. They think there might be a leak in this neighborhood."

The furrows in Elliot's brow grew deeper. "What did this workman need to see you for?"

"He wanted to check my furnace, make sure there wasn't any gas escaping."

"You didn't let him in?"

"Sure. He had a photo ID card from the gas company. He checked the furnace, and it was okay."

"When was this?"

"He left just a couple minutes before you came in."

"How long was he here?"

"Fifteen, twenty minutes."

"It took him that long to check out the furnace?"

"He wanted to be thorough. He said—"

"Were you with him the whole time?"

"No. I was cleaning out Danny's room."

"Where's your furnace?"

"In the garage."

"Show me."

"What about the suitcases?"

"There may not be time," he said.

He was pale. Fine beads of sweat had popped out along his hairline.

She felt the blood drain from her face.

She said, "My God, you don't think—"

"The furnace!"

"This way."

Still carrying the magazine, she rushed through the house, past the kitchen, into the laundry room. A door stood at the far end of this narrow, rectangular work area. As she reached for the knob, she smelled the gas in the garage.

"Don't open that door!" Elliot warned.

She snatched her hand off the knob as if she had almost picked up a tarantula.

"The latch might cause a spark," Elliot said. "Let's get the hell out. The front door. Come on. *Fast!"*

They hurried back the way they had come.

Tina passed a leafy green plant, a four-foot-high schefflera that she had owned since it was only one-fourth as tall as it was now, and she had the insane urge to stop and risk getting caught in the coming explosion just long enough to pick up the plant and take it with her. But an image of crimson eyes, yellow skin—the leering face of death—flashed through her mind, and she kept moving.

She tightened her grip on the horror-comics magazine in her left hand. It was important that she not lose it.

In the foyer, Elliot jerked open the front door, pushed her through ahead of him, and they both plunged into the golden late-afternoon sunshine.

"Into the street!" Elliot urged.

A blood-freezing image rose at the back of her mind: the house torn apart by a colossal blast, shrapnel of wood and glass and metal whistling toward her, hundreds of sharp fragments piercing her from head to foot.

The flagstone walk that led across her front lawn seemed to be one of those treadmill pathways in a dream, stretching out farther in front of her the harder that she ran, but at last she reached the end of it and dashed into the street. Elliot's Mercedes was parked at the far curb, and she was six or eight feet from the car when the sudden outward-sweeping shock of the explosion shoved her forward. She stumbled and fell into the side of the sports car, banging her knee painfully.

Twisting around in terror, she called Elliot's name. He was safe, close behind her, knocked off balance by the force of the shock wave, staggering forward, but unhurt.

The garage had gone up first, the big door ripping from its hinges and splintering into the driveway, the roof dissolving in a confetti-shower of shake shingles and flaming debris. But even as Tina looked from Elliot to the fire, before all of the shingles had fallen back to earth, a second explosion slammed through the house, and a billowing cloud of flame roared from one end of the structure to the other, bursting those few windows that had miraculously survived the first blast.

Tina watched, stunned, as flames leaped from a window of the house and ignited dry palm fronds on a nearby tree.

Elliot pushed her away from the Mercedes so he could open the door on the passenger side. "Get in. Quick!"

"But my house is on fire!"

"You can't save it now."

"We have to wait for the fire company."

"The longer we stand here, the better targets we make."

He grabbed her arm, swung her away from the burning house, the sight of which affected her as much as if it had been a hypnotist's slowly swinging pocket watch.

"For God's sake, Tina, get in the car, and let's go before the shooting starts."

Frightened, dazed by the incredible speed at which her world had begun to disintegrate, she did as he said.

When she was in the car, he shut her door, ran to the driver's side, and climbed in behind the steering wheel.

"Are you all right?" he asked.

She nodded dumbly.

"At least we're still alive," he said.

He put the pistol on his lap, the muzzle facing toward his door, away from Tina. The keys were in the ignition. He started the car. His hands were shaking.

Tina looked out the side window, watching in disbelief as the flames spread from the shattered garage roof to the main roof of the house, long tongues of lambent fire, licking, licking, hungry, bloodred in the last orange light of the afternoon.

19

AS ELLIOT DROVE AWAY FROM THE BURNING HOUSE, HIS INSTINCTUAL sense of danger was as sensitive as it had been in his military days. He was on the thin line that separated animal alertness from nervous frenzy.

He glanced at the rearview mirror and saw a black van pull away from the curb, half a block behind them.

"We're being followed," he said.

Tina had been looking back at her house. Now she turned all the way around and stared through the rear window of the sports car. "I'll bet the bastard who rigged my furnace is in that truck."

"Probably."

"If I could get my hands on the son of a bitch, I'd gouge his eyes out."

Her fury surprised and pleased Elliot. Stupefied by the unexpected violence, by the loss of her house, and by her close brush with death, she had seemed to be in a trance; now she had snapped out of it. He was encouraged by her resilience.

"Put on your seat belt," he said. "We'll be moving fast and loose."

She faced front and buckled up. "Are you going to try to lose them?"

"I'm not just going to *try*."

In this residential neighborhood the speed limit was twenty-five miles an hour. Elliot tramped on the accelerator, and the low, sleek, two-seat Mercedes jumped forward.

Behind them the van dwindled rapidly, until it was a block and a half away. Then it stopped dwindling as it also accelerated.

"He can't catch up with us," Elliot said. "The best he can hope to do is avoid losing more ground."

Along the street, people came out of their houses, seeking the source of the explosion. Their heads turned as the Mercedes rocketed past.

When Elliot rounded the corner two blocks later, he braked from sixty miles an hour to make the turn. The tires squealed, and the car slid side-ways, but the superb suspension and responsive steering held the Mercedes firmly on four wheels all the way through the arc.

"You don't think they'll actually start shooting at us?" Tina asked.

"Hell if I know. They wanted it to appear as if you'd died in an accidental gas explosion. And I think they had a fake suicide planned for me. But now that they know we're on to them, they might panic, might do anything. I don't know. The only thing I *do* know is they can't let us just walk away."

"But who—"

"I'll tell you what I know, but later."

"What do they have to do with Danny?"

"Later," he said impatiently.

"But it's all so crazy."

"You're telling *me?*"

He wheeled around another corner, and then another, trying to disappear from the men in the van long enough to leave them with so many choices of streets to follow that they would have to give up the chase in confusion. Too late, he saw the sign at the fourth intersection—NOT A THROUGH STREET—but they were already around the corner and headed down the narrow dead end, with nothing but a row of ten modest stucco houses on each side.

"Damn!"

"Better back out," she said.

"And run right into them."

"You've got the gun."

"There's probably more than one of them, and they'll be armed."

At the fifth house on the left, the garage door was open, and there wasn't a car inside.

"We've got to get off the street and out of sight," Elliot said.

He drove into the open garage as boldly as if it were his own. He switched off the engine, scrambled out of the car, and ran to the big door. It wouldn't come down. He struggled with it for a moment, and then he realized that it was equipped with an automatic system.

Behind him, Tina said, "Stand back."

She had gotten out of the car and had located the control button on the garage wall.

He glanced outside, up the street. He couldn't see the van.

The door rumbled down, concealing them from anyone who might drive past.

Elliot went to her. "That was close."

She took his hand in hers, squeezed it. Her hand was cold, but her grip was firm.

"So who the hell are they?" she asked,

"I saw Harold Kennebeck, the judge I mentioned. He—"

The door that connected the garage to the house opened without warning, but with a sharp, dry squeak of unoiled hinges.

An imposing, barrel-chested man in rumpled chinos and a white T-shirt snapped on the garage light and peered curiously at them. He had meaty arms; the circumference of one of them almost equaled the circumference of Elliot's thigh. And there wasn't a shirt made that could be buttoned easily around his thick, muscular neck. He appeared formidable, even with his beer belly, which bulged over the waistband of his trousers.

First Vince and now this specimen. It was the Day of the Giants.

"Who're you?" the pituitary-challenged behemoth asked in a soft, gentle voice that didn't equate with his appearance.

Elliot had the awful feeling that this guy would reach for the button Tina had pushed less than a minute ago, and that the garage door would lift just as the black van was rolling slowly by in the street.

Stalling for time, he said, "Oh, hi. My name's Elliot, and this is Tina."

"Tom," the big man said. "Tom Polumby."

Tom Polumby didn't appear to be worried by their presence in his garage; he seemed merely perplexed. A man of his size probably wasn't frightened any more easily than Godzilla confronted by the pathetic bazooka-wielding soldiers surrounding doomed Tokyo.

"Nice car," Tom said with an unmistakable trace of reverence in his voice. He gazed covetously at the S600.

Elliot almost laughed. *Nice car!* They pulled into this guy's garage, parked, closed the door bold as you please, and all he had to say was *Nice car!*

"Very nice little number," Tom said, nodding, licking his lips as he studied the Mercedes.

Apparently Tom couldn't conceive that burglars, psychopathic killers, and other low-lifes were permitted to purchase a Mercedes-Benz if they had the money for it. To him, evidently, anyone who drove a Mercedes had to be the right kind of people.

Elliot wondered how Tom would have reacted if they had shrieked into his garage in an old battered Chevy.

Pulling his covetous gaze from the car, Tom said, "What're you doing here?" There was still neither suspicion nor belligerence in his voice.

"We're expected," Elliot said.

"Huh? I wasn't expecting nobody."

"We're here . . . about the boat," Elliot said, not even knowing where he was going to go with that line, ready to say anything to keep Tom from putting up the garage door and throwing them out.

Tom blinked. "What boat?"

"The twenty-footer."

"I don't own a twenty-footer."

"The one with the Evinrude motor."

"Nothing like that here."

"You must be mistaken," Elliot said.

"I figure you've got the wrong place," Tom said, stepping out of the doorway, into the garage, reaching for the button that would raise the big door.

Tina said, "Mr. Polumby, wait. There must be some mistake, really. This is definitely the right place."

Tom's hand stopped short of the button.

Tina continued: "You're just not the man we were supposed to see, that's all. He probably forgot to tell you about the boat."

Elliot blinked at her, amazed by her natural facility for deception.

"Who's this guy you're supposed to see?" Tom asked, frowning.

Appearing to be somewhat amazed herself, Tina hesitated not at all before she said, "Sol Fitzpatrick."

"Nobody here by that name."

"But this is the address he gave us. He said the garage door would be open and that we were to pull right inside."

Elliot wanted to hug her. "Yeah. Sol said we were to pull in, out of the driveway, so that he'd have a place to put the boat when he got here with it."

Tom scratched his head, then pulled on one ear. "Fitzpatrick?"

"Yeah."

"Never heard of him," Tom said. "What's he bringing a boat here for, anyway?"

"We're buying it from him," Tina said.

Tom shook his head. "No. I mean, why *here*?"

"Well," Elliot said, "the way we understood it, this was where he lived."

"But he doesn't," Tom said. "I live here. Me and my wife and our little girl. They're out right now, and there's nobody ever been here named Fitzpatrick."

"Well, why would he tell us this was his address?" Tina asked, scowling.

"Lady," Tom said, "I don't have the foggiest. Unless maybe . . . Did you already pay him for the boat?"

"Well . . ."

"Maybe just a down payment?" Tom asked.

"We did give him two thousand on deposit," Elliot said.

Tina said, "It was a refundable deposit."

"Yeah. Just to hold the boat until we could see it and make up our minds."

Smiling, Tom said, "I think the deposit might not turn out to be as refundable as you thought."

Pretending surprise, Tina said, "You don't mean Mr. Fitzpatrick would cheat us?"

Obviously it pleased Tom to think that people who could afford a Mercedes were not so smart after all. "If you gave him a deposit, and if he gave you this address and claimed he lived here, then it's not very likely this Sol Fitzpatrick even owns any boat in the first place."

"Damn," Elliot said.

"We were swindled?" Tina asked, feigning shock, buying time.

Grinning broadly now, Tom said, "Well, you can look at it that way if you want. Or you can think of it as an important lesson this here Fitzpatrick fella taught you."

"Swindled," Tina said, shaking her head.

"Sure as the sun will come up tomorrow," Tom said.

Tina turned to Elliot. "What do you think?"

Elliot glanced at the garage door, then at his watch. He said, "I think it's safe to leave."

"Safe?" Tom asked.

Tina stepped lightly past Tom Polumby and pressed the button that raised the garage door. She smiled at her bewildered host and went to the passenger side of the car while Elliot opened the driver's door.

Polumby looked from Elliot to Tina to Elliot, puzzled. "Safe?"

Elliot said, "I sure hope it is, Tom. Thanks for your help." He got in the car and backed it out of the garage.

Any amusement he felt at the way they had handled Polumby evaporated instantly as he reversed warily out of sanctuary, down the driveway, and into the street. He sat stiffly behind the wheel, clenching his teeth, wondering if a bullet would crack through the windshield and shatter his face.

He wasn't accustomed to this tension. Physically, he was still hard, tough; but mentally and emotionally, he was softer than he had been in his prime. A long time had passed since his years in military intelligence, since the nights of fear in the Persian Gulf and in countless cities scattered around the Mideast and Asia. Then, he'd had the resiliency of youth and had been less burdened with respect for death than he was now. In those days it had been easy to play the hunter. He had taken pleasure in stalking human prey; hell, there had even been a measure of joy in *being* stalked, for it gave him the opportunity to prove himself by outwitting the hunter on his trail. Much had changed. He was soft. A successful, civilized attorney. Living the good life. He had never expected to play that game again. But once more, incredibly, he was being hunted, and he wondered how long he could survive.

Tina glanced both ways along the street as Elliot swung the car out of the driveway. "No black van," she said.

"So far."

Several blocks to the north, an ugly column of smoke rose into the twilight sky from what was left of Tina's house, roiling, night-black, the upper reaches tinted around the edges by the last pinkish rays of the setting sun.

As he drove from one residential street to another, steadily heading away from the smoke, working toward a major thoroughfare, Elliot expected to encounter the black van at every intersection.

Tina appeared to be no less pessimistic about their hope of escape than he was. Each time he glanced at her, she was either crouched forward, squinting at every new street they entered, or twisted halfway around in her seat, looking out the rear window. Her face was drawn, and she was biting her lower lip.

However, by the time they reached Charleston Boulevard—via Maryland Parkway, Sahara Avenue, and Las Vegas Boulevard—they began to relax. They were far from Tina's neighborhood now. No matter who was searching for them, no matter how large the organization pitted against them, this city was too big to harbor danger for them in every nook and crevice. With more than a million full-time residents, with more than twenty million tourists a year, and with a vast desert on which to sprawl, Vegas offered thousands of dark, quiet corners where two people on the run could safely stop to catch their breath and settle upon a course of action.

At least that was what Elliot wanted to believe.

"Where to?" Tina asked as Elliot turned west on Charleston Boulevard.

"Let's ride out this way for a few miles and talk. We've got a lot to discuss. Plans to make."

"What plans?"

"How to stay alive."

20

WHILE ELLIOT DROVE, HE TOLD TINA WHAT HAD HAPPENED AT HIS house: the two thugs, their interest in the possibility of Danny's grave being reopened, their admission that they worked for some government agency, the hypodermic syringes. . . .

She said, "Maybe we should go back to your place. If this Vince is still there, we should use those drugs on him. Even if he really doesn't know why his organization is interested in the exhumation, he'll at least know who his bosses are. We'll get names. There's bound to be a lot we can learn from him."

They stopped at a red traffic light. Elliot took her hand. The contact gave him strength. "I'd sure like to interrogate Vince, but we can't. He probably isn't at my place anymore. He'll have come to his senses and scrammed by now. And even if he was deeper under than I thought, some of his people probably went in there and pulled him out while I was rushing off to you. Besides, if we go back to my house, we'll just be walking into the dragon's jaws. They'll be watching the place."

The traffic light changed to green, and Elliot reluctantly let go of her hand.

"The only way these people are going to get us," he said, "is if we just give ourselves over to them. No matter who they are, they're not omniscient. We can hide from them for a long time if we have to. If they can't find us, they can't kill us."

As they continued west on Charleston Boulevard, Tina said, "Earlier you told me we couldn't go to the police with this."

"Right."

"Why can't we?"

"The cops might be a part of it, at least to the extent that Vince's bosses can put pressure on them. Besides, we're dealing with a government agency, and government agencies tend to cooperate with one another."

"It's all so paranoid."

"Eyes everywhere. If they have a judge in their pocket, why not a few cops?"

"But you told me you respected Kennebeck. You said he was a good judge."

"He is. He's well versed in the law, and he's fair."

"Why would he cooperate with these killers? Why would he violate his oath of office?"

"Once an agent, always an agent," Elliot said. "That's the wisdom of the service, not mine, but in many cases it's true. For some of them, it's the only loyalty they'll ever be capable of. Kennebeck held several jobs in different intelligence organizations. He was deeply involved in that world for thirty years. After he retired about ten years ago, he was still a young man, fifty-three, and he needed something else to occupy his time. He had his law degree, but he didn't want the hassle of a day-to-day legal practice. So he ran for an elective position on the court, and he won. I think he takes his job seriously. Nevertheless, he was an intelligence agent a hell of a lot longer than he's been a judge, and I guess breeding tells. Or maybe he never actually retired at all. Maybe he's still on the payroll of some spook shop, and maybe the whole plan was for him to pretend to retire and then get elected as a judge here in Vegas, so his bosses would have a friendly courtroom in town."

"Is that likely? I mean, how could they be sure he'd win the election?"

"Maybe they fixed it."

"You're serious, aren't you?"

"Remember maybe ten years ago when that Texas elections official revealed how Lyndon Johnson's first local election was fixed? The guy said he was just trying to clear his conscience after all those years. He might as well have saved his breath. Hardly anyone raised an eyebrow. It happens now and then. And in a small local election like the one Kennebeck won, stacking the deck would be easy if you had enough money and government muscle behind you."

"But why would they want Kennebeck on a Vegas court instead of in Washington or New York or someplace more important?"

"Oh, Vegas is a *very* important town," Elliot said. "If you want to launder dirty money, this is by far the easiest place to do it. If you want to purchase a false passport, a counterfeit driver's license, or anything of that nature, you can pick and choose from several of the best document-forgery artists in the world, because this is where a lot of them live. If you're looking for a freelance hit man, someone who deals in carload lots of illegal weapons, maybe a mercenary who can put together a small expeditionary force for an overseas operation—you can find all of them here. Nevada has fewer state laws on the books than any state in the nation. Its tax rates are low. There's no state income tax at all. Regulations on banks and real estate agents and on everyone else—except casino owners—are less troublesome here than in other states, which takes a burden off everybody, but which is especially attractive to people trying to spend and invest dirty cash. Nevada offers more personal freedom than anywhere in the country, and that's good, by my way of thinking. But wherever there's a great deal of personal freedom, there's also an element that takes more than fair advantage of the liberal legal structure. Vegas is an important field office for any American spook shop."

"So there really are eyes everywhere."

"In a sense, yes."

"But even if Kennebeck's bosses have a lot of influence with the Vegas police, would the cops let us be killed? Would they really let it go that far?"

"They probably couldn't provide enough protection to stop it."

"What kind of government agency would have the authority to circumvent the law like this? What kind of agency would be empowered to kill innocent civilians who got in its way?"

"I'm still trying to figure that one. It scares the hell out of me."

They stopped at another red traffic light.

"So what are you saying?" Tina asked. "That we'll have to handle this all by ourselves?"

"At least for the time being."

"But that's hopeless! How can we?"

"It isn't hopeless."

"Just two ordinary people against *them?*"

Elliot glanced in the rearview mirror, as he had been doing every minute or two since they'd turned onto Charleston Boulevard. No one was following them, but he kept checking.

"It isn't hopeless," he said again. "We just need time to think about it, time to work out a plan. Maybe we'll come up with someone who can help us."

"Like who?"

The traffic light turned green.

"Like the newspapers, for one," Elliot said, accelerating across the intersection, glancing in the rearview mirror. "We've got proof that something unusual is happening: the silencer-equipped pistol I took off Vince, your house blowing up. . . . I'm pretty sure we can find a reporter who'll go with that much and write a story about how a bunch of nameless, faceless people want to keep us from reopening Danny's grave, how maybe something truly strange lies at the bottom of the Sierra tragedy. Then a lot of people are going to be pushing for an exhumation of *all* those boys. There'll be a demand for new autopsies, investigations. Kennebeck's bosses want to stop us before we sow any seeds of doubt about the official explanation. But once those seeds are sown, once the parents of the other scouts and the entire city are clamoring for an investigation, Kennebeck's buddies won't have anything to gain by eliminating us. It isn't hopeless, Tina, and it's not like you to give up so easily."

She sighed. "I'm not giving up."

"Good."

"I won't stop until I know what really happened to Danny."

"That's better. That sounds more like the Christina Evans I know."

Dusk was sliding into night. Elliot turned on the headlights.

Tina said, "It's just that . . . for the past year I've been struggling to adjust to the fact that Danny died in that stupid, pointless accident. And now, just when I'm beginning to think I can face up to it and put it behind me, I discover he might not have died accidentally after all. Suddenly everything's up in the air again."

"It'll come down."

"Will it?"

"Yes. We'll get to the bottom of this."

He glanced in the rearview mirror.

Nothing suspicious.

He was aware of her watching him, and after a while she said, "You know what?"

"What?"

"I think . . . in a way . . . you're actually enjoying this."

"Enjoying what?"

"The chase."

"Oh, no. I don't enjoy taking guns away from men half again as big as I am."

"I'm sure you don't. That isn't what I said."

"And I sure wouldn't *choose* to have my nice, peaceful, quiet life turned upside down. I'd rather be a comfortable, upstanding, boring citizen than a fugitive."

"I didn't say anything about what you'd choose if it were up to you. But now that it's happened, now that it's been thrust upon you, you're not entirely unhappy. There's a part of you, deep down, that's responding to the challenge with a degree of pleasure."

"Baloney."

"An animal awareness . . . a new kind of energy you didn't have this morning."

"The only thing new about me is that I wasn't scared stiff this morning, and now I am."

"Being scared—that's part of it," she said. "The danger has struck a chord in you."

He smiled. "The good old days of spies and counterspies? Sorry, but no, I don't long for that at all. I'm not a natural-born man of action. I'm just me, the same old me that I always was."

"Anyway," Tina said, "I'm glad I've got you on my side."

"I like it better when you're on top," he said, and he winked at her.

"Have you always had such a dirty mind?"

"No. I've had to cultivate it."

"Joking in the midst of disaster," she said.

" 'Laughter is a balm for the afflicted, the best defense against despair, the only medicine for melancholy.' "

"Who said that?" she asked. "Shakespeare?"

"Groucho Marx, I think."

She leaned forward and picked something up from the floor between her feet. "And then there's this damn thing."

"What did you find?"

"I brought it from my place," she said.

In the rush to get out of her house before the gas explosion leveled it, he hadn't noticed that she'd been carrying anything. He risked a quick look, shifting his attention from the road, but there wasn't enough light in the car for him to see what she held. "I can't make it out."

"It's a horror-comics magazine," she said. "I found it when I was cleaning out Danny's room. It was in a box with a lot of other magazines."

"So?"

"Remember the nightmares I told you about?"

"Yeah, sure."

"The monster in my dreams is on the cover of this magazine. It's him. Detail for detail."

"Then you must have seen the magazine before, and you just—"

"No. That's what I tried to tell myself. But I never saw it until today. I know I didn't. I pored through Danny's collection. When he came home from the newsstand, I never monitored what he'd bought. I never snooped."

"Maybe you—"

"Wait," she said. "I haven't told you the worst part."

The traffic thinned out as they drove farther from the heart of town, closer to the looming black mountains that thrust into the last electric-purple light in the western sky.

Tina told Elliot about *The Boy Who Was Not Dead*.

The similarities between the horror story and their attempt to exhume Danny's body chilled Elliot.

"Now," Tina said, "just like Death tried to stop the parents in the story, someone's trying to stop me from opening *my* son's grave."

They were getting too far out of town. A hungry darkness lay on both sides of the road. The land began to rise toward Mount Charleston where, less than an hour away, pine forests were mantled with snow. Elliot swung the car around and started back toward the lights of the city, which spread like a vast, glowing fungus on the black desert plain.

"There *are* similarities," he said.

"You're damned right there are. Too many."

"There's also one big difference. In the story, the boy was buried alive. But Danny *is* dead. The only thing in doubt is how he died."

"But that's the only difference between the basic plot of this story and what we're going through. And the words *Not Dead* in the title. And the boy in the story being Danny's age. It's just too much," she said.

They rode in silence for a while.

Finally Elliot said, "You're right. It can't be coincidence."

"Then how do you explain it?"

"I don't know."

"Welcome to the club."

A roadside diner stood on the right, and Elliot pulled into the parking lot. A single mercury-vapor pole lamp at the entrance shed fuzzy purple light over the first third of the parking lot. Elliot drove behind the restaurant and tucked the Mercedes into a slot in the deepest shadows, between a Toyota Celica and a small motor home, where it could not be seen from the street.

"Hungry?" he asked.

"Starving. But before we go in, let's check out that list of questions they were going to make you answer."

"Let's look at it in the café," Elliot said. "The light will be better. It doesn't seem to be busy in there. We should be able to talk without being overheard. Bring the magazine too. I want to see that story."

As he got out of the car, his attention was drawn to a window on the side of the motor home next to which he had parked. He squinted through the glass into the perfectly black interior, and he had the disconcerting feeling that someone was hiding in there, staring out at him.

Don't succumb to paranoia, he warned himself.

When he turned from the motor home, his gaze fell on a dense pool of shadows around the trash bin at the back of the restaurant, and again he had the feeling that someone was watching him from concealment.

He had told Tina that Kennebeck's bosses were not omniscient. He must remember that. He and Tina apparently were confronted with a powerful, lawless, dangerous organization hell-bent on keeping the secret of the Sierra tragedy. But any organization was composed of ordinary men and women, none of whom had the all-seeing gaze of God.

Nevertheless . . .

As he and Tina walked across the parking lot toward the diner, Elliot couldn't shake the feeling that someone or something was watching them. Not necessarily a person. Just . . . something . . . weird, strange. Something both more and less than human. That was a bizarre thought, not at all the sort of notion he'd ordinarily get in his head, and he didn't like it.

Tina stopped when they reached the purple light under the mercury-vapor lamp. She glanced back toward the car, a curious expression on her face.

"What is it?" Elliot asked.

"I don't know. . . ."

"See something?"

"No."

They stared at the shadows.

At length she said, "Do you feel it?"

"Feel what?"

"I've got this . . . prickly feeling."

He didn't say anything.

"You *do* feel it, don't you?" she asked.

"Yes."

"As if we aren't alone."

"It's crazy," he said, "but I feel eyes on me."

She shivered. "But no one's really there."

"No. I don't think anyone is."

They continued to squint at the inky blackness, searching for movement.

She said, "Are we both cracking under the strain?"

"Just jumpy," he said, but he wasn't really convinced that their imagination was to blame.

A soft cool wind sprang up. It carried with it the odor of dry desert weeds and alkaline sand. It hissed through the branches of a nearby date palm.

"It's such a *strong* feeling," she said. "And you know what it reminds me of? It's the same damn feeling I had in Angela's office when that computer terminal started operating on its own. I feel . . . not just as if I'm being watched but . . . something more . . . like a *presence* . . . as if something I can't see is standing right beside me. I can feel the weight of it, a pressure in the air . . . sort of *looming*."

He knew exactly what she meant, but he didn't want to think about it, because there was no way he could make sense of it. He preferred to deal with hard facts, realities; that was why he was such a good attorney, so adept at taking threads of evidence and weaving a good case out of them.

"We're both overwrought," he suggested.

"That doesn't change what I feel."

"Let's get something to eat."

She stayed a moment longer, staring back into the gloom, where the purple mercury-vapor light did not reach.

"Tina . . . ?"

A breath of wind stirred a dry tumbleweed and blew it across the blacktop.

A bird swooped through the darkness overhead. Elliot couldn't see it, but he could hear the beating of its wings.

Tina cleared her throat. "It's as if . . . the night itself is watching us . . . the night, the shadows, the eyes of darkness."

The wind ruffled Elliot's hair. It rattled a loose metal fixture on the trash bin, and the restaurant's big sign creaked between its two standards.

At last he and Tina went into the diner, trying not to look over their shoulders.

21

THE LONG L-SHAPED DINER WAS FILLED WITH GLIMMERING SURfaces: chrome, glass, plastic, yellow Formica, and red vinyl. The jukebox played a country tune by Garth Brooks, and the music shared the air with the delicious aromas of fried eggs, bacon, and sausages. True to the rhythm of Vegas life, someone was just beginning his day with a hearty breakfast. Tina's mouth began to water as soon as she stepped through the door.

Eleven customers were clustered at the end of the long arm of the L, near the entrance, five on stools at the counter, six in the red booths. Elliot and Tina sat as far from everyone as possible, in the last booth in the short wing of the restaurant.

Their waitress was a redhead named Elvira. She had a round face, dimples, eyes that twinkled as if they had been waxed, and a Texas drawl. She took their orders for cheeseburgers, French fries, coleslaw, and Coors.

When Elvira left the table and they were alone, Tina said, "Let's see the papers you took off that guy."

Elliot fished the pages out of his hip pocket, unfolded them, and put them on the table. There were three sheets of paper, each containing ten or twelve typewritten questions.

They leaned in from opposite sides of the booth and read the material silently:

1. How long have you known Christina Evans?
2. Why did Christina Evans ask you, rather than another attorney, to handle the exhumation of her son's body?
3. What reason does she have to doubt the official story of her son's death?
4. Does she have any proof that the official story of her son's death is false?
5. If she has such proof, what is it?
6. Where did she obtain this evidence?
7. Have you ever heard of "Project Pandora"?
8. Have you been given, or has Mrs. Evans been given, any material relating to military research installations in the Sierra Nevada Mountains?

Elliot looked up from the page. "Have you ever heard of Project Pandora?"

"No."

"Secret labs in the High Sierra?"

"Oh, sure. Mrs. Neddler told me all about them."

"Mrs. Neddler?"

"My cleaning woman."

"Jokes again."

"At a time like this."

"Balm for the afflicted, medicine for melancholy."

"Groucho Marx," she said.

"Evidently they think someone from Project Pandora has decided to rat on them."

"Is that who's been in Danny's room? Did someone from Project Pandora write on the chalkboard . . . and then fiddle with the computer at work?"

"Maybe," Elliot said.

"But you don't think so."

"Well, if someone had a guilty conscience, why wouldn't he approach you directly?"

"He could be afraid. Probably has good reason to be."

"Maybe," Elliot said again. "But I think it's more complicated than that. Just a hunch."

They read quickly through the remaining material, but none of it was enlightening. Most of the questions were concerned with how much Tina knew about the true nature of the Sierra accident, how much she had told Elliot, how much she had told Michael, and with how many people she had discussed it. There were no more intriguing tidbits like Project Pandora, no more clues or leads.

Elvira brought two frosted glasses and icy bottles of Coors.

The jukebox began to play a mournful Alan Jackson song.

Elliot sipped his beer and paged through the horror-comics magazine that had belonged to Danny. "Amazing," he said when he finished skimming *The Boy Who Was Not Dead*.

"You'd think it was even more amazing if you'd suffered those nightmares," she said. "So now what do we do?"

"Danny's was a closed-coffin funeral. Was it the same with the other thirteen scouts?"

"About half the others were buried without viewings," Tina said.

"Their parents never saw the bodies?"

"Oh, yes. All the other parents were asked to identify their kids, even though some of the corpses were in such a horrible state they couldn't be cosmetically restored for viewing at a funeral. Michael and I were the only ones who were strongly advised not to look at the remains. Danny was the only one who was too badly . . . mangled."

Even after all this time, when she thought about Danny's last moments on earth—the terror he must have known, the excruciating pain he must have endured, even if it was of brief duration—she began to choke with sorrow and pity. She blinked back tears and took a swallow of beer.

"Damn," Elliot said.

"What?"

"I thought we might make some quick allies out of those other parents. If they hadn't seen their kids' bodies, they might have just gone through a year of doubt like you did, might be easily persuaded to join us in a call for the reopening of *all* the graves. If that many voices were raised, then Vince's bosses couldn't risk silencing all of them, and we'd be safe. But if the other people had a chance to view the bodies, if none of them has had any reason to entertain doubts like yours, then they're all just finally learning to cope with the tragedy. If we go to them now with a wild story about a mysterious conspiracy, they aren't going to be anxious to listen."

"So we're still alone."

"Yeah."

"You said we could go to a reporter, try to get media interest brewing. Do you have anyone in mind?"

"I know a couple of local guys," Elliot said. "But maybe it's not wise to go to the local press. That might be just what Vince's bosses are expecting us to do. If they're waiting, watching—we'll be dead before we can tell a reporter more than a sentence or two. I think we'll have to take the story out of town, and before we do that, I'd like to have a few more facts."

"I thought you said we had enough to interest a good newsman. The pistol you took off that man . . . my house being blown up . . ."

"That might be enough. Certainly, for the Las Vegas paper, it ought to be sufficient. This city still remembers the Jaborski group, the Sierra accident. It was a local tragedy. But if we go to the press in Los Angeles or New York or some other city, the reporters there aren't going to have a whole lot of interest in it unless they see an aspect of the story that lifts it out of the local-interest category. Maybe we've already got enough to convince them it's big news. I'm not sure. And I want to be *damn* sure before we try to go public with it. Ideally, I'd even like to be able to hand the reporter a neat theory about what really happened to those scouts, something sensational that he can hook his story onto."

"Such as?"

He shook his head. "I don't have anything worked out yet. But it seems to me the most obvious thing we have to consider is that the scouts and their leaders saw something they weren't supposed to see."

"Project Pandora?"

He sipped his beer and used one finger to wipe a trace of foam from his upper lip. "A military secret. I can't see what else would have brought an organization like Vince's so deeply into this. An intelligence outfit of that size and sophistication doesn't waste its time on Mickey Mouse stuff."

"But military secrets . . . that seems so far out."

"In case you didn't know it, since the Cold War ended and California took such a big hit in the defense downsizing, Nevada has more Pentagon-supported industries and installations than any state in the union. And I'm not just talking about the obvious ones like Nellis Air Force Base and the Nuclear Test Site. This state's ideally suited for secret or quasi-secret, high-security weapons research centers. Nevada has thousands of square miles of remote unpopulated land. The deserts. The deeper reaches of the mountains. And most of those remote areas are owned by the federal government. If you put a secret installation in the middle of all that lonely land, you have a pretty easy job maintaining security."

Arms on the table, both hands clasped around her glass of beer, Tina leaned toward Elliot. "You're saying that Mr. Jaborski, Mr. Lincoln, and the boys stumbled across a place like that in the Sierra?"

"It's possible."

"And saw something they weren't supposed to see."

"Maybe."

"And then what? You mean . . . because of what they saw, they were *killed?*"

"It's a theory that ought to excite a good reporter."

She shook her head. "I just can't believe the government would murder a group of little children just because they accidentally got a glimpse of a new weapon or something."

"Wouldn't it? Think of Waco—all those dead children. Ruby Ridge— a fourteen-year-old boy shot in the back by the FBI. Vince Foster found dead in a Washington park and officially declared a suicide even though most of the forensic evidence points to murder. Even a primarily good government, when it's big enough, has some pretty mean sharks swimming in the darker currents. We're living in strange times, Tina."

The rising night wind thrummed against the large pane of glass beside their booth. Beyond the window, out on Charleston Boulevard, traffic sailed murkily through a sudden churning river of dust and paper scraps.

Chilled, Tina said, "But how much could the kids have seen? You're the one who said security was easy to maintain when one of these installations is located in the wilderness. The boys couldn't have gotten very close to such a well-guarded place. Surely they couldn't have managed to get more than a glimpse."

"Maybe a glimpse was enough to condemn them."

"But kids aren't the best observers," she argued. "They're impressionable, excitable, given to exaggeration. If they *had* seen something, they'd have come back with at least a dozen different stories about it, none of them accurate. A group of young boys wouldn't be a threat to the security of a secret installation."

"You're probably right. But a bunch of hard-nosed security men might not have seen it that way."

"Well, they'd have had to be pretty stupid to think murder was the safest way to handle it. Killing all those people and trying to fake an accident—that was a whole lot riskier than letting the kids come back with their half-baked stories about seeing something peculiar in the mountains."

"Remember, there were two adults with those kids. People might have discounted most of what the boys said about it, but they'd have believed Jaborski and Lincoln. Maybe there was so much at stake that the security men at the installation decided Jaborski and Lincoln had to die. Then it became necessary to kill the kids to eliminate witnesses to the first two murders."

"That's . . . diabolical."

"But not unlikely."

Tina looked down at the wet circle that her glass had left on the table. While she thought about what Elliot had said, she dipped one finger in the water and drew a grim mouth, a nose, and a pair of eyes in the circle; she added two horns, transforming the blot of moisture into a little demonic face. Then she wiped it away with the palm of her hand.

"I don't know . . . hidden installations . . . military secrets . . . it all seems just too incredible."

"Not to me," Elliot said. "To me, it sounds plausible if not probable. Anyway, I'm not saying that's what really happened. It's only a theory. But it's the kind of theory that almost any smart, ambitious reporter will go for in a big, big way—if we can come up with enough facts that appear to support it."

"What about Judge Kennebeck?"

"What about him?"

"He could tell us what we want to know."

"We'd be committing suicide if we went to Kennebeck's place," Elliot said. "Vince's friends are sure to be waiting for us there."

"Well, isn't there any way that we could slip past them and get at Kennebeck?"

He shook his head. "Impossible."

She sighed, slumped back in the booth.

"Besides," Elliot said, "Kennebeck probably doesn't know the whole story. He's just like the two men who came to see me. He's probably been told only what he needs to know."

Elvira arrived with their food. The cheeseburgers were made from juicy ground sirloin. The French fries were crisp, and the coleslaw was tart but not sour.

By unspoken agreement, Tina and Elliot didn't talk about their problems while they ate. In fact they didn't talk much at all. They listened to the country music on the jukebox and watched Charleston Boulevard through the window, where the desert dust storm clouded oncoming headlights and forced the traffic to move slowly. And they thought about those things that neither of them wanted to speak of: murder past and murder present.

When they finished eating, Tina spoke first. "You said we ought to come up with more evidence before we go to the newspapers."

"We have to."

"But how are we supposed to get it? From where? From whom?"

"I've been pondering that. The best thing we could do is get the grave reopened. If the body were exhumed and reexamined by a topnotch pathologist, we'd almost certainly find proof that the cause of death wasn't what the authorities originally said it was."

"But we can't reopen the grave ourselves," Tina said. "We can't sneak into the graveyard in the middle of the night, move a ton of earth with shovels. Besides, it's a private cemetery, surrounded by a high wall, so there must be a security system to deal with vandals."

"And Kennebeck's cronies have almost certainly put a watch on the place. So if we can't examine the body, we'll have to do the next best thing. We'll have to talk to the man who saw it last."

"Huh? Who?"

"Well, I guess . . . the coroner."

"You mean the medical examiner in Reno?"

"Was that where the death certificate was issued?"

"Yes. The bodies were brought out of the mountains, down to Reno."

"On second thought . . . maybe we'll skip the coroner," Elliot said. "He's the one who had to designate it an accidental death. There's a better than even chance he's been co-opted by Kennebeck's crowd. One thing for sure, he's definitely not on our side. Approaching him would be dangerous. We might eventually have to talk to him, but first we should pay a visit to the mortician who handled the body. There might be a lot he can tell us. Is he here in Vegas?"

"No. An undertaker in Reno prepared the body and shipped it here for the funeral. The coffin was sealed when it arrived, and we didn't open it."

Elvira stopped by the table and asked if they wanted anything more. They didn't. She left the check and took away some of the dirty dishes.

To Tina, Elliot said, "Do you remember the name of the mortician in Reno?"

"Yes. Bellicosti. Luciano Bellicosti."

Elliot finished the last swallow of beer in his glass. "Then we'll go to Reno."

"Can't we just call Bellicosti?"

"These days, everyone's phone seems to be tapped. Besides, if we're face-to-face with him, we'll have a better idea of whether or not he's telling the truth. No, it can't be done long-distance. We have to go up there."

Her hand shook when she raised her glass to drink the last of her own Coors.

Elliot said, "What's wrong?"

She wasn't exactly sure. She was filled with a new dread, a fear greater than the one that had burned within her during the past few hours. "I . . . I guess I'm just . . . afraid to go to Reno."

He reached across the table and put his hand over hers. "It's okay. There's less to be frightened of up there than here. It's *here* we've got killers hunting us."

"I know. Sure, I'm scared of those creeps. But more than that, what I'm afraid of . . . is finding out the truth about Danny's death. And I have a strong feeling we'll find it in Reno."

"I thought that was exactly what you wanted to know."

"Oh, I do. But at the same time, I'm afraid of knowing. Because it's going to be bad. The truth is going to be something really terrible."

"Maybe not."

"Yes."

"The only alternative is to give up, to back off and never know what really happened."

"And that's worse," she admitted.

"Anyway, we have to learn what really happened in the Sierras. If we know the truth, we can use it to save ourselves. It's our only hope of survival."

"So when do we leave for Reno?" she asked.

"Tonight. Right now. We'll take my Cessna Skylane. Nice little machine."

"Won't they know about it?"

"Probably not. I only hooked up with you today, so they haven't had time to learn more than the essentials about me. Just the same, we'll approach the airfield with caution."

"If we can use the Cessna, how soon would we get to Reno?"

"A few hours. I think it would be wise for us to stay up there for a couple of days, even after we've talked to Bellicosti, until we can figure a way out of this mess. Everyone'll still be looking for us in Vegas, and we'll breathe a little easier if we aren't here."

"But I didn't get a chance to pack that suitcase," Tina said. "I need a change of clothes, at least a toothbrush and a few other things. Neither one of us has a coat, and it's damn cold in Reno at this time of year."

"We'll buy whatever we need before we leave."

"I don't have any money with me. Not a penny."

"I've got some," Elliot said. "A couple hundred bucks. Plus a wallet filled with credit cards. We could go around the world on the cards alone. They might track us when we use the cards, but not for a couple of days."

"But it's a holiday and—"

"And this is Las Vegas," Elliot said. "There's always a store open somewhere. And the shops in the hotels won't be closed. This is one of their busiest times of the year. We'll be able to find coats and whatever else we need, and we'll find it all in a hurry." He left a generous tip for the waitress and got to his feet. "Come on. The sooner we're out of this town, the safer I'll feel."

She went with him to the cash register, which was near the entrance.

The cashier was a white-haired man, owlish behind a pair of thick spectacles. He smiled and asked Elliot if their dinner had been satisfactory, and Elliot said it had been fine, and the old man began to make change with slow, arthritic fingers.

The rich odor of chili sauce drifted out of the kitchen. Green peppers. Onions. Jalapeños. The distinct aromas of melted cheddar and Monterey Jack.

The long wing of the diner was nearly full of customers now; about forty people were eating dinner or waiting to be served. Some were laughing. A young couple was plotting conspiratorially, leaning toward each other from opposite sides of a booth, their heads almost touching. Nearly everyone was engaged in animated conversations, couples and cozy groups of friends, enjoying themselves, looking forward to the remaining three days of the four-day holiday.

Suddenly Tina felt a pang of envy. She wanted to be one of these fortunate people. She wanted to be enjoying an ordinary meal, on an ordinary evening, in the middle of a blissfully ordinary life, with every reason to expect a long, comfortable, ordinary future. None of these people had to worry about professional killers, bizarre conspiracies, gas-company men who were not gas-company men, silencer-equipped pistols, exhumations. They didn't realize how lucky they were. She felt as if a vast unbridgeable gap separated her from people like these, and she wondered if she ever again would be as relaxed and free from care as these diners were at this moment.

A sharp, cold draft prickled the back of her neck.

She turned to see who had entered the restaurant.

The door was closed. No one had entered.

Yet the air remained cool—*changed.*

On the jukebox, which stood to the left of the door, a currently popular country ballad was playing:

> "Baby, baby, baby, I love you still.
> Our love will live; I know it will
> And one thing on which you can bet
> Is that our love is not dead yet.
> No, our love is not dead—
>   not dead—

> not dead—
>
> not dead—"

The record stuck.

Tina stared at the jukebox in disbelief.

> "not dead—
> not dead—
> not dead—
> not dead—"

Elliot turned away from the cashier and put a hand on Tina's shoulder. "What the hell . . . ?"

Tina couldn't speak. She couldn't move.

The air temperature was dropping precipitously.

She shuddered.

The other customers stopped talking and turned to stare at the stuttering machine.

> "not dead—
> not dead—
> not dead—
> not dead—"

The image of Death's rotting face flashed into Tina's mind.

"Stop it," she pleaded.

Someone said, "Shoot the piano player."

Someone else said, "Kick the damn thing."

Elliot stepped to the jukebox and shook it gently. The two words stopped repeating. The song proceeded smoothly again—but only for one more line of verse. As Elliot turned away from the machine, the eerily meaningful repetition began again:

> "not dead—
> not dead—
> not dead—"

Tina wanted to walk through the diner and grab each of the customers by the throat, shake and threaten each of them, until she discovered who had rigged the jukebox. At the same time, she knew this wasn't a rational thought; the explanation, whatever it might be, was not that simple. No one here had rigged the machine. Only a moment ago, she had envied these people for the very ordinariness of their lives. It was ludicrous to suspect any of them of being employed by the secret organization that had blown up her house. Ludicrous. Paranoid. They were just ordinary people in a roadside restaurant, having dinner.

> "not dead—
> not dead—
> not dead—"

Elliot shook the jukebox again, but this time to no avail.

The air grew colder still. Tina heard some of the customers commenting on it.

Elliot shook the machine harder than he had done the last time, then harder still, but it continued to repeat the two-word message in the voice of the country singer, as if an invisible hand were holding the pick-up stylus or laser-disc reader firmly in place.

The white-haired cashier came out from behind the counter. "I'll take care of it, folks." He called to one of the waitresses: "Jenny, check the thermostat. We're supposed to have heat in here tonight, not air conditioning."

Elliot stepped out of the way as the old man approached.

Although no one was touching the jukebox, the volume increased, and the two words boomed through the diner, thundered, vibrated in the windows, and rattled silverware on the tables.

> "NOT DEAD—
> NOT DEAD—
> NOT DEAD—"

Some people winced and put their hands over their ears.

The old man had to shout to be heard above the explosive voices on the jukebox. "There's a button on the back to reject the record."

Tina wasn't able to cover her ears; her arms hung straight down at her sides, frozen, rigid, hands fisted, and she couldn't find the will or the strength to lift them. She wanted to scream, but she couldn't make a sound.

Colder, colder.

She became aware of the familiar, spiritlike presence that had been in Angela's office when the computer had begun to operate by itself. She had the same feeling of being watched that she'd had in the parking lot a short while ago.

The old man crouched beside the machine, reached behind it, found the button. He pushed it several times.

> "NOT DEAD—
> NOT DEAD—
> NOT DEAD—"

"Have to unplug it!" the old man said.

The volume increased again. The two words blasted out of the speakers in all corners of the diner with such incredible, bone-jarring force that it was difficult to believe that the machine had been built with the capability of pouring out sound with this excessive, unnerving power.

Elliot pulled the jukebox from the wall so the old man could reach the cord.

In that instant Tina realized she had nothing to fear from the presence that lay behind this eerie manifestation. It meant her no harm. Quite the opposite, in fact. In a flash of understanding she saw through to the heart of the mystery. Her hands, which had been curled into tight fists, came open once more. The tension went out of her neck and shoulder muscles. Her heartbeat became less like the pounding of a jackhammer, but it still did not settle into a normal rhythm; now it was affected by excitement rather than terror. If she tried to scream now, she would be able to do so, but she no longer wanted to scream.

As the white-haired cashier grasped the plug in his arthritis-gnarled hands and wiggled it back and forth in the wall socket, trying to free it, Tina almost told him to stop. She wanted to see what would happen next if no one interfered with the presence that had taken control of the jukebox. But before she could think of a way to phrase her odd request, the old man succeeded in unplugging the machine.

Following the monotonous, earsplitting repetition of that two-word message, the silence was stunning.

After a second of surprised relief, everyone in the diner applauded the old fellow.

Jenny, the waitress, called to him from behind the counter. "Hey, Al, I didn't touch the thermostat. It says the heat's on and set at seventy. You better take a look at it."

"You must have done something to it," Al said. "It's getting warm in here again."

"I didn't touch it," Jenny insisted.

Al didn't believe her, but Tina did.

Elliot turned away from the jukebox and looked at Tina with concern. "Are you all right?"

"Yes. God, yes! Better than I've been in a long time."

He frowned, baffled by her smile.

"I know what it is. Elliot, I know exactly what it is! Come on," she said excitedly. "Let's go."

He was confused by the change in her demeanor, but she didn't want to explain things to him here in the diner. She opened the door and went outside.

22

THE WINDSTORM WAS STILL IN PROGRESS, BUT IT WAS NOT RAGING as fiercely as it had been when Elliot and Tina had watched it through the restaurant window. A brisk wind pushed across the city from the east. Laden with dust and with the powdery white sand that had been swept in from the desert, the air abraded their faces and had an unpleasant taste.

They put their heads down and scurried past the front of the diner, around the side, through the purple light under the single mercury-vapor lamp, and into the deep shadows behind the building.

In the Mercedes, in the darkness, with the doors locked, she said, "No wonder we haven't been able to figure it out!"

"Why on earth are you so—"

"We've been looking at this all wrong—"

"—so bubbly when—"

"—approaching it ass-backwards. No wonder we haven't been able to find a solution."

"What are you talking about? Did you see what I saw in there? Did you hear the jukebox? I don't see how that could have cheered you up. It made my blood run cold. It was *weird*."

"Listen," she said excitedly, "we thought someone was sending me messages about Danny being alive just to rub my face in the fact that he was actually dead—or to let me know, in a roundabout fashion, that the *way* he died wasn't anything like what I'd been told. But those messages haven't been coming from a sadist. And they haven't been coming from someone who wants to expose the true story of the Sierra accident. They aren't being sent by a total stranger or by Michael. They are *exactly* what they appear to be!"

Confused, he said, "And to your way of thinking, what do they appear to be?"

"They're cries for help."

"What?"

"They're coming from *Danny!*"

Elliot stared at her with consternation and with pity, his dark eyes reflecting a distant light. "What're you saying—that Danny reached out to you from the grave to cause that excitement in the restaurant? Tina, you really don't think his ghost was haunting a jukebox?"

"No, no, no. I'm saying Danny isn't dead."

"Wait a minute. Wait a minute."

"My Danny is alive! I'm sure of it."

"We've already been through this argument, and we rejected it," he reminded her.

"We were wrong. Jaborski, Lincoln, and all the other boys might have died in the Sierra, but Danny didn't. I know it. I *sense* it. It's like . . . a revelation . . . almost like a vision. Maybe there was an accident, but it wasn't like anything we were told. It was something very different, something exceedingly strange."

"That's already obvious. But—"

"The government had to hide it, and so this organization that Kennebeck works for was given responsibility for the cover-up."

"I'm with you that far," Elliot said. "That's logical. But how do you figure Danny's alive? That doesn't necessarily follow."

"I'm only telling you what I *know*, what I feel," she said. "A tremendous sense of peace, of reassurance, came over me in the diner, just before you finally managed to shut off the jukebox. It wasn't just an inner feeling of peace. It came from outside of me. Like a wave. Oh, hell, I can't really explain it. I only know what I felt. Danny was trying to reassure me, trying to tell me that he was still alive. I *know* it. Danny survived the accident, but they couldn't let him come home because he'd tell everyone the government was responsible for the deaths of the others, and that would blow their secret military installation wide open."

"You're reaching, grasping for straws."

"I'm not, I'm not," she insisted.

"So where *is* Danny?"

"They're keeping him somewhere. I don't know why they didn't kill him. I don't know how long they think they can keep him bottled up like this. But that's what they're doing. That's what's going on. Those might not be the precise circumstances, but they're pretty damn close to the truth."

"Tina—"

She wouldn't let him interrupt. "This secret police force, these people behind Kennebeck . . . they think someone involved with Project Pandora has turned on them and told me what really happened to Danny. They're wrong, of course. It wasn't one of them. It's Danny. Somehow . . . I don't know how . . . but he's reaching out to me." She struggled to explain the understanding that had come to her in the diner. "Somehow . . . some way . . . he's reaching out . . . with his mind, I guess. Danny was the one who wrote those words on the chalkboard. *With his mind.*"

"The only proof of this is what you say you feel . . . this vision you've had."

"Not a vision—"

"Whatever. Anyway, that's no proof at all."

"It's proof enough for me," she said. "And it would be proof enough for you, if you'd had the same experience back there in the diner, if you'd felt what I felt. It was Danny who reached out for me when I was at work . . . found me in the office . . . tried to use the hotel computer to send his message to me. And now the jukebox. He must be . . . psychic. That's it! That's what he is. He's psychic. He has some *power*, and he's reaching out, trying to tell me he's alive, asking me to find him and save him. And the people who're holding him *don't know he's doing it!* They're blaming the leak on one of their own, on someone from Project Pandora."

"Tina, this is a very imaginative theory, but—"

"It might be imaginative, but it's not a theory. It's true. It's fact. I *feel* it deep in my bones. Can you shoot holes through it? Can you prove I'm wrong?"

"First of all," Elliot said, "before he went into the mountains with Jaborski, in all the years you knew him and lived in the same house with him, did Danny ever show any signs of being psychic?"

She frowned. "No."

"Then how come he suddenly has all these amazing powers?"

"Wait. Yeah, I *do* remember some little things he did that were sort of odd."

"Like what?"

"Like the time he wanted to know exactly what his daddy did for a living. He was eight or nine years old, and he was curious about the details of a dealer's job. Michael sat at the kitchen table with him and dealt blackjack. Danny was barely old enough to understand the rules, but he'd never played before. He certainly wasn't old enough to remember all the cards that were dealt and calculate his chances from that, like some of the very best players can do. Yet he won steadily. Michael used a jar full of peanuts to represent casino chips, and Danny won every nut in the jar."

"The game must have been rigged," Elliot said. "Michael was letting him win."

"That's what I thought at first. But Michael swore he wasn't doing that. And he seemed genuinely astonished by Danny's streak of luck. Besides, Michael isn't a card mechanic. He can't handle a deck well enough to stack it while he's shuffling. And then there was Elmer."

"Who's Elmer?"

"He was our dog. A cute little mutt. One day, about two years ago, I was in the kitchen, making an apple pie, and Danny came in to tell me Elmer wasn't anywhere to be found in the yard. Apparently, the pooch slipped out of the gate when the gardeners came around. Danny said he was sure Elmer wasn't going to come back because he'd been hit and killed by a truck. I told him not to worry. I said we'd find Elmer safe and sound. But we never did. We never found him at all."

"Just because you never found him—that's not proof he was killed by a truck."

"It was proof enough for Danny. He mourned for weeks."

Elliot sighed. "Winning a few hands at blackjack—that's luck, just like you said. And predicting that a runaway dog will be killed in traffic— that's just a reasonable assumption to make under the circumstances. And even if those were examples of psychic ability, little tricks like that are light-years from what you're attributing to Danny now."

"I know. Somehow, his abilities have grown a lot stronger. Maybe because of the situation he's in. The fear. The stress."

"If fear and stress could increase the power of his psychic gifts, why didn't he start trying to get in touch with you months ago?"

"Maybe it took a year of stress and fear to develop the ability. I don't know." A flood of unreasonable anger washed through her: "Christ, how could I know the answer to that?"

"Calm down," he said. "You dared me to shoot holes in your theory. That's what I'm doing."

"No," she said. "As far as I can see, you haven't shot one hole in it yet. Danny's alive, being held somewhere, and he's trying to reach me with his mind. Telepathically. No. Not telepathy. He's able to move objects just by thinking about them. What do you call that? Isn't there a name for that ability?"

"Telekinesis," Elliot said.

"Yes! That's it. He's telekinetic. Do you have a better explanation for what happened in the diner?"

"Well . . . no."

"Are you going to tell me it was coincidence that the record stuck on those two words?"

"No," Elliot said. "It wasn't a coincidence. That would be even more unlikely than the possibility that Danny did it."

"You admit I'm right."

"No," he said. "I can't think of a better explanation, but I'm not ready to accept yours. I've never believed in that psychic crap."

For a minute or two neither of them spoke. They stared out at the dark parking lot and at the fenced storage yard full of fifty-gallon drums that lay beyond the lot. Sheets, puffs, and spinning funnels of vaguely phosphorescent dust moved like specters through the night.

At last Tina said, "I'm *right*, Elliot. I know I am. My theory explains everything. Even the nightmares. That's another way Danny's been trying to reach me. He's been sending me nightmares for the past few weeks. That's why they've been so much different from any dreams I've had before, so much stronger and more vivid."

He seemed to find this new statement more outrageous than what she'd said before. "Wait, wait, wait. Now you're talking about another power besides telekinesis."

"If he has one ability, why not the other?"

"Because pretty soon you'll be saying he's God."

"Just telekinesis and the power to influence my dreams. That explains why I dreamed about the hideous figure of Death in this comic book. If Danny's sending me messages in dreams, it's only natural he'd use images he was familiar with—like a monster out of a favorite horror story."

"But if he can send dreams to you," Elliot said, "why wouldn't he simply transmit a neat, clear message telling you what's happened to him and where he is? Wouldn't that get him the help he wants a lot faster? Why would he be so unclear and indirect? He should send a concise mental message, psychic E-mail from the Twilight Zone, make it a lot easier for you to understand."

"Don't get sarcastic," she said.

"I'm not. I'm merely asking a tough question. It's another hole in your theory."

She would not be deterred. "It's not a hole. There's a good explanation. Obviously, like I told you, Danny isn't telepathic exactly. He's telekinetic, able to move objects with his mind. And he can influence dreams to some extent. But he's not flat-out telepathic. He can't transmit detailed thoughts. He can't send 'concise mental messages' because he doesn't have that much power or control. So he has to try to reach me as best he can."

"Will you listen to us?"

"I've been listening," she said.

"We sound like a couple of prime candidates for a padded cell."

"No. I don't think we do."

"This talk of psychic power . . . it's not exactly level-headed stuff," Elliot said.

"Then explain what happened in the diner."

"I can't. Damn it, I can't," he said, sounding like a priest whose faith had been deeply shaken. The faith that he was beginning to question was not religious, however, but scientific.

"Stop thinking like an attorney," she said. "Stop trying to herd the facts into neat corrals of logic."

"That's exactly what I've been trained to do."

"I know," she said sympathetically. "But the world is full of illogical things that are nonetheless true. And this is one of them."

The wind buffeted the sports car, moaned along the windows, seeking a way in.

Elliot said, "If Danny has this incredible power, why is he sending messages just to you? Why doesn't he at least contact Michael too?"

"Maybe he doesn't feel close enough to Michael to try reaching him. After all, the last couple of years we were married, Michael was running around with a lot of other women, spending most of his time away from home, and Danny felt even more abandoned than I did. I never talked against Michael. I even tried to justify some of his actions, because I didn't want Danny to hate him. But Danny was hurt just the same. I suppose it's natural for him to reach out to me rather than to his father."

A wall of dust fell softly over the car.

"Still think you can shoot my theory full of holes?" she asked.

"No. You argued your case pretty well."

"Thank you, judge."

"I still can't believe you're right. I know some pretty damn intelligent people believe in ESP, but I don't. I can't bring myself to accept this psychic crap. Not yet, anyway. I'm going to keep looking for some less exotic explanation."

"And if you come up with one," Tina said, "I'll give it very serious consideration."

He put a hand on her shoulder. "The reason I've argued with you is . . . I'm worried about you, Tina."

"About my sanity?"

"No, no. This psychic explanation bothers me mainly because it gives you hope that Danny's still alive. And that's dangerous. It seems to me as if you're just setting yourself up for a bad fall, a lot of pain."

"No. Not at all. Because Danny really is alive."

"But what if he isn't?"

"He is."

"If you discover he's dead, it'll be like losing him all over again."

"But he's not dead," she insisted. "I feel it. I sense it. I *know* it, Elliot."

"And if he *is* dead?" Elliot asked, every bit as insistent as she was.

She hesitated. Then: "I'll be able to handle it."

"You're sure?"

"Positive."

In the dim light, where the brightest thing was mauve shadow, he found her eyes, held her with his intent gaze. She felt as if he were not merely looking at her but into her, through her. Finally he leaned over and kissed the corner of her mouth, then her cheek, her eyes.

He said, "I don't want to see your heart broken."

"It won't be."

"I'll do what I can to see it isn't."

"I know."

"But there isn't much I *can* do. It's out of my hands. We just have to flow with events."

She slipped a hand behind his neck, holding his face close. The taste of his lips and his warmth made her inexpressibly happy.

He sighed, leaned back from her, and started the car. "We better get moving. We have some shopping to do. Winter coats. A couple of toothbrushes."

Though Tina continued to be buoyed by the unshakable conviction that Danny was alive, fear crept into her again as they drove onto Charleston Boulevard. She was no longer afraid of facing the awful truth that might be waiting in Reno. What had happened to Danny might still prove to be terrible, shattering, but she didn't think it would be as hard to accept as his "death" had been. The only thing that scared her now was the possibility that they might find Danny—and then be unable to rescue him. In the process of locating the boy, she and Elliot might be killed. If they found Danny and then perished trying to save him, that would be a nasty trick of fate, for sure. She knew from experience that fate had countless nasty tricks up its voluminous sleeve, and *that* was why she was scared shitless.

23

WILLIS BRUCKSTER STUDIED HIS KENO TICKET, CAREFULLY COM-
paring it to the winning numbers beginning to flash onto the electronic
board that hung from the casino ceiling. He tried to appear intently interested in the outcome of this game, but in fact he didn't care. The
marked ticket in his hand was worthless; he hadn't taken it to the betting
window, hadn't wagered any money on it. He was using keno as a cover.

He didn't want to attract the attention of the omnipresent casino security men, and the easiest way to escape their notice was to appear to
be the least threatening hick in the huge room. With that in mind, Bruckster wore a cheap green polyester leisure suit, black loafers, and white
socks. He was carrying two books of the discount coupons that casinos
use to pull slot-machine players into the house, and he wore a camera
on a strap around his neck. Furthermore, keno was a game that didn't
have any appeal for either smart gamblers or cheaters, the two types of
customers who most interested the security men. Willis Bruckster was so
sure he appeared dull and ordinary that he wouldn't have been surprised
if a guard had looked at him and yawned.

He was determined not to fail on this assignment. It was a career
maker—or breaker. The Network badly wanted to eliminate everyone
who might press for the exhumation of Danny Evans's body, and the
agents targeted against Elliot Stryker and Christina Evans had thus far
failed to carry out their orders to terminate the pair. Their ineptitude gave
Willis Bruckster a chance to shine. If he made a clean hit here, in the
crowded casino, he would be assured of a promotion.

Bruckster stood at the head of the escalator that led from the lower
shopping arcade to the casino level of Bally's Hotel. During their periodic
breaks from the gaming tables, nursing stiff necks and sore shoulders and
leaden arms, the weary dealers retired to a combination lounge and
locker room at the bottom—and to the right—of the escalator. A group
had gone down a while ago and would be returning for their last stand
at the tables before a whole new staff came on duty with the shift change.
Bruckster was waiting for one of those dealers: Michael Evans.

He hadn't expected to find the man at work. He had thought Evans might be keeping a vigil at the demolished house, while the firemen sifted through the still-smoldering debris, searching for the remains of the woman they thought might be buried there. But when Bruckster had come into the hotel thirty minutes ago, Evans had been chatting with the players at his blackjack table, cracking jokes, and grinning as if nothing of any importance had happened in his life lately.

Perhaps Evans didn't know about the explosion at his former house. Or maybe he *did* know and just didn't give a damn about his ex-wife. It might have been a bitter divorce.

Bruckster hadn't been able to get close to Evans when the dealer left the blackjack pit at the beginning of the break. Consequently, he'd stationed himself here, at the head of the escalator, and had pretended to be interested in the keno board. He was confident that he would nail Evans when the man returned from the dealer's lounge in the next few minutes.

The last of the keno numbers flashed onto the board. Willis Bruckster stared at them, then crumpled his game card with obvious disappointment and disgust, as if he had lost a few hard-earned dollars.

He glanced down the escalator. Dealers in black trousers, white shirts, and string ties were ascending.

Bruckster sidled away from the escalator and unfolded his keno card. He compared it once more with the numbers on the electronic board, as if he were praying that he had made a mistake the first time.

Michael Evans was the seventh dealer off the escalator. He was a handsome, easygoing guy who ambled rather than walked. He stopped to have a word with a strikingly pretty cocktail waitress, and she smiled at him. The other dealers streamed by, and when Evans finally turned away from the waitress, he was the last in the procession as it moved toward the blackjack pits.

Bruckster fell in beside and slightly behind his target as they pressed through the teeming mob that jammed the enormous casino. He reached into a pocket of his leisure suit and took out a tiny aerosol can that was only slightly larger than one of those spray-style breath fresheners, small enough to be concealed in Bruckster's hand.

They came to a standstill at a cluster of laughing people. No one in the jolly group seemed to realize that he was obstructing the main aisle. Bruckster took advantage of the pause to tap his quarry on the shoulder.

Evans turned, and Bruckster said, "I think maybe you dropped this back there."

"Huh?"

Bruckster held his hand eighteen inches below Michael Evans's eyes, so that the dealer was forced to glance down to see what was being shown to him.

The fine spray, propelled with tremendous pressure, caught him squarely in the face, across the nose and lips, penetrating swiftly and deeply into the nostrils. Perfect.

Evans reacted as anyone would. He gasped in surprise as he realized he was being squirted.

The gasp drew the deadly mist up his nose, where the active poison—a particularly fast-acting neurotoxin—was instantaneously absorbed through the sinus membranes. In two seconds it was in his bloodstream, and the first seizure hit his heart.

Evans's surprised expression turned to shock. Then a wild, twisted expression of agony wrenched his face as brutal pain slammed through him. He gagged, and a ribbon of foamy saliva unraveled from the corner of his mouth, down his chin. His eyes rolled back in his head, and he fell.

As Bruckster pocketed the miniature aerosol device, he said, "We have a sick man here."

Heads turned toward him.

"Give the man room," Bruckster said. "For God's sake, someone get a doctor!"

No one could have seen the murder. It had been committed in a sheltered space within the crowd, hidden by the killer's and the victim's bodies. Even if someone had been monitoring that area from an overhead camera, there would not have been much for him to see.

Willis Bruckster quickly knelt at Michael Evans's side and took his pulse as if he expected to find one. There was no heartbeat whatsoever, not even a faint lub-dub.

A thin film of moisture covered the victim's nose and lips and chin, but this was only the harmless medium in which the toxin had been suspended. The active poison itself had already penetrated the victim's body, done its work, and begun to break down into a series of naturally occurring chemicals that would raise no alarms when the coroner later studied the results of the usual battery of forensic tests. In a few seconds the medium would evaporate too, leaving nothing unusual to arouse the initial attending physician's suspicion.

A uniformed security guard shouldered through the mob of curious onlookers and stooped next to Bruckster. "Oh, damn, it's Mike Evans. What happened here?"

"I'm no doctor," Bruckster said, "but it sure looks like a heart attack to me, the way he dropped like a stone, same way my uncle Ned went down last Fourth of July right in the middle of the fireworks display."

The guard tried to find a pulse but wasn't able to do so. He began CPR, but then relented. "I think it's hopeless."

"How could it be a heart attack, him being so young?" Bruckster wondered. "Jesus, you just never know, do you?"

"You never know," the guard agreed.

The hotel doctor would call it a heart attack after he had examined the body. So would the coroner. So would the death certificate.

A perfect murder.

Willis Bruckster suppressed a smile.

24

JUDGE HAROLD KENNEBECK BUILT EXQUISITELY DETAILED SHIPS IN bottles. The walls of his den were lined with examples of his hobby. A tiny model of a seventeenth-century Dutch pinnace was perpetually under sail in a small, pale-blue bottle. A large four-masted topsail schooner filled a five-gallon jug. Here was a four-masted barkentine with sails taut in a perpetual wind; and here was a mid-sixteenth-century Swedish kravel. A fifteenth-century Spanish caravel. A British merchantman. A Baltimore clipper. Every ship was created with remarkable care and craftsmanship, and many were in uniquely shaped bottles that made their construction all the more difficult and admirable.

Kennebeck stood before one of the display cases, studying the minutely detailed rigging of a late-eighteenth-century French frigate. As he gazed at the model, he wasn't transported back in time or lost in fantasies of high-seas adventure; rather, he was mulling over the recent developments in the Evans case. His ships, sealed in their glass worlds, relaxed him; he liked to spend time with them when he had a problem to work out or when he was on edge, for they made him feel serene, and that security allowed his mind to function at peak performance.

The longer he thought about it, the less Kennebeck was able to believe that the Evans woman knew the truth about her son. Surely, if someone from Project Pandora had told her what had happened to that busload of scouts, she wouldn't have reacted to the news with equanimity. She would have been frightened, terrified . . . and damned angry. She would have gone straight to the police, the newspapers—or both.

Instead, she had gone to Elliot Stryker.

And that was where the paradox jumped up like a jack-in-the-box. On the one hand, she behaved as if she did not know the truth. But on the other hand, she was working through Stryker to have her son's grave reopened, which seemed to indicate that she knew *something*.

If Stryker could be believed, the woman's motivations were innocent enough. According to the attorney, Mrs. Evans felt guilty about not having had the courage to view the boy's mutilated body prior to the burial. She felt as if she had failed to pay her last respects to the deceased. Her guilt had grown gradually into a serious psychological problem. She was in great distress, and she suffered from horrible dreams that plagued her every night. That was Stryker's story.

Kennebeck tended to believe Stryker. There was an element of coincidence involved, but not all coincidence was meaningful. That was something one tended to forget when he spent his life in the intelligence game. Christina Evans probably hadn't entertained a single doubt about the official explanation of the Sierra accident; she probably hadn't known a damned thing about Pandora when she had requested an exhumation, but her timing couldn't have been worse.

If the woman actually hadn't known anything of the cover-up, then the Network could have used her ex-husband and the legal system to delay the reopening of the grave. In the meantime, Network agents could have located a boy's body in the same state of decay as Danny's corpse would have been if it had been locked in that coffin for the past year. They would have opened the grave secretly, at night, when the cemetery was closed, switching the remains of the fake Danny for the rocks that were currently in the casket. Then the guilt-stricken mother could have been permitted one last, late, ghastly look at the remains of her son.

That would have been a complex operation, fraught with the peril of discovery. The risks would have been acceptable, however, and there wouldn't have been any need to kill anyone.

Unfortunately, George Alexander, chief of the Nevada bureau of the Network, hadn't possessed the patience or the skill to determine the woman's true motives. He had assumed the worst and had acted on that assumption. When Kennebeck informed Alexander of Elliot Stryker's request for an exhumation, the bureau chief responded immediately with extreme force. He planned a suicide for Stryker, an accidental death for the woman, and a heart attack for the woman's husband. Two of those hurriedly organized assassination attempts had failed. Stryker and the woman had disappeared. Now the entire Network was in the soup, *deep* in it.

As Kennebeck turned away from the French frigate, beginning to wonder if he ought to get out from under the Network before it collapsed on him, George Alexander entered the study through the door that opened off the downstairs hallway. The bureau chief was a slim, elegant, distinguished-looking man. He was wearing Gucci loafers, an expensive suit, a handmade silk shirt, and a gold Rolex watch. His stylishly cut brown hair shaded to iron-gray at the temples. His eyes were green, clear, alert, and—if one took the time to study them—menacing. He had a well-formed face with high cheekbones, a narrow straight nose, and thin lips. When he smiled, his mouth turned up slightly at the left corner, giving him a vaguely haughty expression, although at the moment he wasn't smiling.

Kennebeck had known Alexander for five years and had despised him from the day they met. He suspected that the feeling was mutual.

Part of this antagonism between them rose because they had been born into utterly different worlds and were equally proud of their origins—as well as disdainful of all others. Harry Kennebeck had come from a dirt-poor family and, by his own estimation at least, made quite a lot of himself. Alexander, on the other hand, was the scion of a Pennsylvania family that had been wealthy and powerful for a hundred and fifty years, perhaps longer. Kennebeck had lifted himself out of poverty through hard work and steely determination. Alexander knew nothing of hard work; he had ascended to the top of his field as if he were a prince with a divine right to rule.

Kennebeck was also irritated by Alexander's hypocrisy. The whole family was nothing but a bunch of hypocrites. The society-register Al-

exanders were proud of their history of public service. Many of them had
been Presidential appointees, occupying high-level posts in the federal
government; a few had served on the President's cabinet, in half a dozen
administrations, though none had ever deigned to run for an elective
position. The famous Pennsylvania Alexanders had always been prominently associated with the struggle for minority civil rights, the Equal
Rights Amendment, the crusade against capital punishment, and social
idealisms of every variety. Yet numerous members of the family had secretly rendered service—some of it dirty—to the FBI, the CIA, and various
other intelligence and police agencies, often the very same organizations
that they publicly criticized and reviled. Now George Alexander was the
Nevada bureau chief of the nation's first truly secret police force—a fact
that apparently did not weigh heavily on his liberal conscience.

Kennebeck's politics were of the extreme right-wing variety. He was
an unreconstructed fascist and not the least bit ashamed of it. When, as
a young man, he had first embarked upon a career in the intelligence
services, Harry had been surprised to discover that not all of the people
in the espionage business shared his ultraconservative political views. He
had expected his co-workers to be super-patriotic right-wingers. But all
the snoop shops were staffed with leftists too. Eventually Harry realized
that the extreme left and the extreme right shared the same two basic
goals: They wanted to make society more orderly than it naturally was,
and they wanted to centralize control of the population in a strong government. Left-wingers and right-wingers differed about certain details, of
course, but their only major point of contention centered on the identity
of those who would be permitted to be a part of the privileged ruling
class, once the power had been sufficiently centralized.

At least I'm honest about my motives, Kennebeck thought as he
watched Alexander cross the study. *My public opinions are the same as
those I express privately, and that's a virtue he doesn't possess. I'm not a
hypocrite. I'm not at all like Alexander. Jesus, he's such a smug, Janus-
faced bastard!*

"I just spoke with the men who're watching Stryker's house," Alexander said. "He hasn't shown up yet."

"I told you he wouldn't go back there."

"Sooner or later he will."

"No. Not until he's absolutely certain the heat is off. Until then he'll
hide out."

"He's bound to go to the police at some point, and then we'll have him."

"If he thought he could get any help from the cops, he'd have been there already," Kennebeck said. "But he hasn't shown up. And he won't."

Alexander glanced at his watch. "Well, he still might pop up here. I'm sure he wants to ask you a lot of questions."

"Oh, I'm damn sure he does. He wants my hide," Kennebeck said. "But he won't come. Not tonight. Eventually, yes, but not for a long time. He knows we're waiting for him. He knows how the game is played. Don't forget he used to play it himself."

"That was a long time ago," Alexander said impatiently. "He's been a civilian for fifteen years. He's out of practice. Even if he was a natural then, there's no way he could still be as sharp as he once was."

"But that's what I've been trying to tell you," Kennebeck said, pushing a lock of snow-white hair back from his forehead. "Elliot isn't stupid. He was the best and brightest young officer who ever served under me. He *was* a natural. And that was when he was young and relatively inexperienced. If he's aged as well as he seems to have done, then he might even be sharper these days."

Alexander didn't want to hear it. Although two of the hits he had ordered had gone totally awry, Alexander remained self-assured; he was convinced that he would eventually triumph.

He's always so damned self-confident, Harry Kennebeck thought. *And usually there's no good reason why he should be. If he was aware of his own shortcomings, the son of a bitch would be crushed to death under his collapsing ego.*

Alexander went to the huge maple desk and sat behind it, in Kennebeck's wing chair.

The judge glared at him.

Alexander pretended not to notice Kennebeck's displeasure. "We'll find Stryker and the woman before morning. I've no doubt about that. We're covering all the bases. We've got men checking every hotel and motel—"

"That's a waste of time," Kennebeck said. "Elliot is too smart to waltz into a hotel and leave his name on the register. Besides, there are more hotels and motels in Vegas than in any other city in the world."

"I'm fully aware of the complexity of the task," Alexander said. "But we might get lucky. Meanwhile, we're checking out Stryker's associates in his law firm, his friends, the woman's friends, anyone with whom they might have taken refuge."

"You don't have enough manpower to follow up all those possibilities," the judge said. "Can't you see that? You should use your people more judiciously. You're spreading yourself too thin. What you should be doing—"

"*I'll* make those decisions," Alexander said icily.

"What about the airport?"

"That's taken care of," Alexander assured him. "We've got men going over the passenger lists of every outbound flight." He picked up an ivory-handled letter opener, turned it over and over in his hands. "Anyway, even if we're spread a bit thin, it doesn't matter much. I already know where we're going to nail Stryker. Here. Right here in this house. That's why I'm still hanging around. Oh, I know, I know, you don't think he'll show up. But a long time ago you were Stryker's mentor, the man he respected, the man he learned from, and now you've betrayed him. He'll come here to confront you, even if he knows it's risky. I'm sure he will."

"Ridiculous," Kennebeck said sourly. "Our relationship was never like that. He—"

"I know human nature," Alexander said, though he was one of the least observant and least analytical men that Kennebeck had ever known.

These days cream seldom rose in the intelligence community—but crap still floated.

Angry, frustrated, Kennebeck turned again to the bottle that contained the French frigate. Suddenly he remembered something important about Elliot Stryker. "Ah," he said.

Alexander put down the enameled cigarette box that he had been studying. "What is it?"

"Elliot's a pilot. He owns his own plane."

Alexander frowned.

"Have you been checking small craft leaving the airport?" Kennebeck asked.

"No. Just scheduled airliners and charters."

"Ah."

"He'd have had to take off in the dark," Alexander said. "You think he's licensed for instrument flying? Most businessmen-pilots and hobby pilots aren't certified for anything but daylight."

"Better get hold of your men at the airport," Kennebeck said. "I already know what they're going to find. I'll bet a hundred bucks to a dime Elliot slipped out of town under your nose."

THE CESSNA TURBO Skylane RG knifed through the darkness, two miles above the Nevada desert, with the low clouds under it, wings plated silver by moonlight.

"Elliot?"

"Hmmm?"

"I'm sorry I got you mixed up in this."

"You don't like my company?"

"You know what I mean. I'm really sorry."

"Hey, you didn't get me mixed up in it. You didn't twist my arm. I practically volunteered to help you with the exhumation, and it all just fell apart from there. It's not your fault."

"Still . . . here you are, running for your life, and all because of me."

"Nonsense. You couldn't have known what would happen after I talked to Kennebeck."

"I can't help feeling guilty about involving you."

"If it wasn't me, it would have been some other attorney. And maybe he wouldn't have known how to handle Vince. In which case, both he and you might be dead. So if you look at it that way, it worked out as well as it possibly could."

"You're really something else," she said.

"What else am I?"

"Lots of things."

"Such as?"

"Terrific."

"Not me. What else?"

"Brave."

"Bravery is a virtue of fools."

"Smart."

"Not as smart as I think I am."

"Tough."

"I cry at sad movies. See, I'm not as great as you think I am."

"You can cook."

"Now *that's* true!"

The Cessna hit an air pocket, dropped three hundred feet with a sickening lurch, and then soared to its correct altitude.

"A great cook but a lousy pilot," she said.

"That was God's turbulence. Complain to Him."

"How long till we land in Reno?"

"Eighty minutes."

GEORGE ALEXANDER HUNG up the telephone. He was still sitting in Kennebeck's wing chair. "Stryker and the woman took off from McCarran International more than two hours ago. They left in his Cessna. He filed a flight plan for Flagstaff."

The judge stopped pacing. "Arizona?"

"That's the only Flagstaff I know. But why would they go to Arizona, of all places?"

"They probably didn't," Kennebeck said. "I figure Elliot filed a false flight plan to throw you off his trail." He was perversely proud of Stryker's cleverness.

"If they actually headed for Flagstaff," Alexander said, "they ought to have landed by now. I'll call the night manager at the airport down there, pretend to be FBI, see what he can tell me."

Because the Network did not officially exist, it couldn't openly use its authority to gather information. As a result, Network agents routinely posed as FBI men, with counterfeit credentials in the names of actual FBI agents.

While he waited for Alexander to finish with the night manager at the Flagstaff airport, Kennebeck moved from one model ship to another. For the first time in his experience, the sight of this bottled fleet didn't calm him.

Fifteen minutes later Alexander put down the telephone. "Stryker isn't on the Flagstaff field. And he hasn't yet been identified in their airspace."

"Ah. So his flight plan *was* a red herring."

"Unless he crashed between here and there," Alexander said hopefully.

Kennebeck grinned. "He didn't crash. But where the hell *did* he go?"

"Probably in the opposite direction," Alexander said. "Southern California."

"Ah. Los Angeles?"

"Or Santa Barbara. Burbank. Long Beach. Ontario. Orange County. There are a lot of airports within the range of that little Cessna."

They were both silent, thinking. Then Kennebeck said, "Reno. That's where they went. Reno."

"You were so sure they didn't know a thing about the Sierra labs," Alexander said. "Have you changed your mind?"

"No. I still think you could have avoided issuing all those termination orders. Look, they can't be going up to the mountains, because they don't know where the laboratories are. They don't know anything more about Project Pandora than what they picked up from that list of questions they took off Vince Immelman."

"Then why Reno?"

Pacing, Kennebeck said, "Now that we've tried to kill them, they *know* the story of the Sierra accident was entirely contrived. They figure there's something wrong with the little boy's body, something odd that we can't afford to let them see. So now they're *twice* as anxious to see it. They'd exhume it illegally if they could, but they can't get near the cemetery with us watching it. And Stryker knows for sure that we've got it staked out. So if they can't open the grave and see for themselves what we've done to Danny Evans, what are they going to do instead? They're going to do the next best thing—talk to the person who was supposedly the last one to see the boy's corpse before it was sealed in the coffin. They're going to ask him to describe the condition of the boy in minute detail."

"Richard Pannafin is the coroner in Reno. He issued the death certificate," Alexander said.

"No. They won't go to Pannafin. They'll figure he's involved in the cover-up."

"Which he is. Reluctantly."

"So they'll go to see the mortician who supposedly prepared the boy's body for burial."

"Bellicosti."

"Was that his name?"

"Luciano Bellicosti," Alexander said. "But if that's where they went, then they're not just hiding out, licking their wounds. Good God, they've actually gone on the offensive!"

"That's Stryker's military-intelligence training taking hold," Kennebeck said. "That's what I've been trying to tell you. He's not going to be an easy target. He could destroy the Network, given half a chance. And the woman's evidently not one to hide or run away from a problem either. We have to go after these two with more care than usual. What about this Bellicosti? Will he keep his mouth shut?"

"I don't know," Alexander said uneasily. "We have a pretty good hold on him. He's an Italian immigrant. He lived here for eight or nine years before he decided to apply for citizenship. He hadn't gotten his papers yet when we found ourselves needing a cooperative mortician. We put a freeze on his application with the Bureau of Immigration, and we threatened to have him deported if he didn't do what we wanted. He didn't like it. But citizenship was a big enough carrot to keep him motivated. However . . . I don't think we'd better rely on that carrot any longer."

"This is a hell of an important matter," Kennebeck said. "And it sounds to me as if Bellicosti knows too much about it."

"Terminate the bastard," Alexander said.

"Eventually, but not necessarily right now. If too many bodies pile up at once, we'll be drawing attention to—"

"Take no chances," Alexander insisted. "We'll terminate him. And the coroner too, I think. Scrub away the whole trail." He reached for the phone.

"Surely you don't want to take such drastic action until you're positive Stryker actually is headed for Reno. And you won't know for sure until he lands up there."

Alexander hesitated with his hand on the phone. "But if I wait, I'm just giving him a chance to keep one step ahead." Worried, he continued to hesitate, anxiously chewing his lip.

"There's a way to find out if it's really Reno he's headed for. When he gets there, he'll need a car. Maybe he's already arranged for one to be waiting."

Alexander nodded. "We can call the rental agencies at the Reno airport."

"No need to call. The hacker geeks in computer operations can probably access all the rental agencies' data files long distance."

Alexander picked up the phone and gave the order.

Fifteen minutes later computer operations called back with its report. Elliot Stryker had a rental car reserved for late-night pickup at the Reno airport. He was scheduled to take possession of it shortly before midnight.

"That's a bit sloppy of him," Kennebeck said, "considering how clever he's been so far."

"He figures we're focusing on Arizona, not Reno."

"It's still sloppy," Kennebeck said, disappointed. "He should have built a double blind to protect himself."

"So it's like I said." Alexander's crooked smile appeared. "He *isn't* as sharp as he used to be."

"Let's not start crowing too soon," Kennebeck said. "We haven't caught him yet."

"We will," Alexander said, his composure restored. "Our people in Reno will have to move fast, but they'll manage. I don't think it's a good idea to hit Stryker and the woman in a public place like an airport."

What an uncharacteristic display of reserve, Kennebeck thought sourly.

"I don't even think we should put a tail on them as soon as they get there," Alexander said. "Stryker will be expecting a tail. Maybe he'll elude it, and then he'll be spooked."

"Get to the rental car before he does. Slap a transponder on it. Then you can follow him without being seen, at your leisure."

"We'll try it," Alexander said. "We've got less than an hour, so there might not be time. But even if we don't get a beeper on the damn car, we're okay. We know where they're going. We'll just eliminate Bellicosti and set up a trap at the funeral home."

He snatched up the telephone and dialed the Network office in Reno.

25

IN RENO, WHICH BILLED ITSELF AS "THE BIGGEST LITTLE CITY IN THE World," the temperature hovered at twenty-one degrees above zero as midnight approached. Above the lights that cast a frosty glow on the airport parking lot, the heavily shrouded sky was moonless, starless, perfectly black. Snow flurries were dancing on a changeable wind.

Elliot was glad they had bought a couple of heavy coats before leaving Las Vegas. He wished they'd thought of gloves; his hands were freezing.

He threw their single suitcase into the trunk of the rented Chevrolet. In the cold air, white clouds of exhaust vapor swirled around his legs.

He slammed the trunk lid and surveyed the snow-dusted cars in the parking lot. He couldn't see anyone in any of them. He had no feeling of being watched.

When they had landed, they'd been alert for unusual activity on the runway and in the private-craft docking yard—suspicious vehicles, an unusual number of ground crewmen—but they had seen nothing out of the ordinary. Then as he had signed for the rental car and picked up the keys from the night clerk, he had kept one hand in a pocket of his coat, gripping the handgun he'd taken off Vince in Las Vegas—but there was no trouble.

Perhaps the phony flight plan had thrown the hounds off the trail. Now he went to the driver's door and climbed into the Chevy, where Tina was fiddling with the heater.

"My blood's turning to ice," she said.

Elliot held his hand to the vent. "We're getting some warm air already."

From his coat, he withdrew the pistol and put it on the seat between him and Christina, the muzzle pointed toward the dashboard.

"You really think we should confront Bellicosti at this hour?" she asked.

"Sure. It's not very late."

In an airport-terminal telephone directory, Tina had found the address of the Luciano Bellicosti Funeral Home. The night clerk at the rental agency, from whom they had signed out the car, had known exactly where Bellicosti's place was, and he had marked the shortest route on the free city map provided with the Chevy.

Elliot flicked on the overhead light and studied the map, then handed it to Tina. "I think I can find it without any trouble. But if I get lost, you'll be the navigator."

"Aye, aye, Captain."

He snapped off the overhead light and reached for the gearshift.

With a distinct *click*, the light that he had just turned off now turned itself on.

He looked at Tina, and she met his eyes.

He clicked off the light again.

Immediately it switched on.

"Here we go," Tina said.

The radio came on. The digital station indicator began to sweep across the frequencies. Split-second blasts of music, commercials, and disc jockeys' voices blared senselessly out of the speakers.

"It's Danny," Tina said.

The windshield wipers started thumping back and forth at top speed, adding their metronomical beat to the chaos inside the Chevy.

The headlights flashed on and off so rapidly that they created a stroboscopic effect, repeatedly "freezing" the falling snow, so that it appeared as if the white flakes were descending to the ground in short, jerky steps.

The air inside the car was bitterly cold and growing colder by the second.

Elliot put his right hand against the dashboard vent. Heat was pushing out of it, but the air temperature continued to plunge.

The glove compartment popped open.

The ashtray slid out of its niche.

Tina laughed, clearly delighted.

The sound of her laughter startled Elliot, but then he had to admit to himself that he did not feel menaced by the work of this poltergeist. In fact, just the opposite was true. He sensed that he was witnessing a joyous display, a warm greeting, the excited welcome of a child-ghost. He was overwhelmed by the astonishing notion that he could actually feel goodwill in the air, a tangible radiation of love and affection. A not unpleasant shiver raced up his spine. Apparently, this was the same astonishing awareness of being buffeted by waves of love that had caused Tina's laughter.

She said, "We're coming, Danny. Hear me if you can, baby. We're coming to get you. We're coming."

The radio switched off, and so did the overhead light.

The windshield wipers stopped thumping.

The headlights blinked off and stayed off.

Stillness.

Silence.

Scattered flakes of snow collided softly with the windshield.

In the car, the air grew warm again.

Elliot said, "Why does it get cold every time he uses his . . . psychic abilities?"

"Who knows? Maybe he's able to move objects by harnessing the heat energy in the air, changing it somehow. Or maybe it's something else altogether. We'll probably never know. He might not understand it himself. Anyway, that isn't important. What's important is that my Danny is *alive*. There's no doubt about that. Not now. Not anymore. And I gather from your question, you've become a believer too."

"Yeah," Elliot said, still mildly amazed by his own change of heart and mind. "Yeah, I believe there's a chance you're right."

"I know I am."

"Something extraordinary happened to that expedition of scouts. And something downright uncanny has happened to your son."

"But at least he's not dead," Tina said.

Elliot saw tears of happiness shining in her eyes.

"Hey," he said worriedly, "better keep a tight rein on your hopes. Okay? We've got a long, long way to go. We don't even know where Danny is or what shape he's in. We've got a gauntlet to run before we can find him and bring him back. We might both be killed before we even get close to him."

He drove away from the airport. As far as he could tell, no one followed them.

26

SUFFERING ONE OF HIS OCCASIONAL BOUTS OF CLAUSTROPHOBIA, Dr. Carlton Dombey felt as though he had been swallowed alive and was trapped now in the devil's gut.

Deep inside the secret Sierra complex, three stories below ground level, this room measured forty feet by twenty. The low ceiling was covered with a spongy, pebbly, yellowish soundproofing, which gave the chamber a peculiar organic quality. Fluorescent tubes shed cold light over banks of computers and over worktables laden with journals, charts, file folders, scientific instruments, and two coffee mugs.

In the middle of the west wall—one of the two shorter walls—opposite the entrance to the room, was a six-foot-long, three-foot-high window that provided a view of another space, which was only half as large as this outer chamber. The window was constructed like a sandwich: Two one-inch-thick panes of shatterproof glass surrounded an inch-wide space filled with an inert gas. Two panes of ironlike glass. Stainless-steel frame. Four airtight rubber seals—one around the both faces of each pane. This viewport was designed to withstand everything from a gunshot to an earthquake; it was virtually inviolable.

Because it was important for the men who worked in the large room to have an unobstructed view of the smaller inner chamber at all times, four angled ceiling vents in both rooms bathed the glass in a continuous flow of warm, dry air to prevent condensation and clouding. Currently the system wasn't working, for three-quarters of the window was filmed with frost.

Dr. Carlton Dombey, a curly-haired man with a bushy mustache, stood at the window, blotting his damp hands on his medical whites and peering anxiously through one of the few frost-free patches of glass. Although he was struggling to cast off the seizure of claustrophobia that had gripped him, was trying to pretend that the organic-looking ceiling wasn't pressing low over his head and that only open sky hung above him instead of thousands of tons of concrete and steel rock, his own panic attack concerned him less than what was happening beyond the viewport.

Dr. Aaron Zachariah, younger than Dombey, clean-shaven, with straight brown hair, leaned over one of the computers, reading the data that flowed across the screen. "The temperature's dropped thirty-five degrees in there during the past minute and a half," Zachariah said worriedly. "That can't be good for the boy."

"Every time it's happened, it's never seemed to bother him," Dombey said.

"I know, but—"

"Check out his vital signs."

Zachariah moved to another bank of computer screens, where Danny Evans's heartbeat, blood pressure, body temperature, and brainwave activity were constantly displayed. "Heartbeat's normal, maybe even slightly slower than before. Blood pressure's all right. Body temp unchanged. But there's something unusual about the EEG reading."

"As there always is during these cold snaps," Dombey said. "Odd brainwave activity. But no other indication he's in any discomfort."

"If it stays cold in there for long, we'll have to suit up, go in, and move him to another chamber," Zachariah said.

"There isn't one available," Dombey said. "All the others are full of test animals in the middle of one experiment or another."

"Then we'll have to move the animals. The kid's a lot more important than they are. There's more data to be gotten from him."

He's more important because he's a human being, not because he's a source of data, Dombey thought angrily, but he didn't voice the thought because it would have identified him as a dissident and as a potential security risk.

Instead, Dombey said, "We won't have to move him. The cold spell won't last." He squinted into the smaller room, where the boy lay motionless on a hospital bed, under a white sheet and yellow blanket, trailing monitor wires. Dombey's concern for the kid was greater than his fear of being trapped underground and buried alive, and finally his attack of claustrophobia diminished. "At least it's never lasted long. The temperature drops abruptly, stays down for two or three minutes, never longer than five, and then it rises to normal again."

"What the devil is wrong with the engineers? Why can't they correct the problem?"

Dombey said, "They insist the system checks out perfectly."

"Bullshit."

"There's no malfunction. So they say."

"Like hell there isn't!" Zachariah turned away from the video displays, went to the window, and found his own spot of clear glass. "When this started a month ago, it wasn't that bad. A few degrees of change. Once a night. Never during the day. Never enough of a variation to threaten the boy's health. But the last few days it's gotten completely out of hand. Again and again, we're getting these thirty-and forty-degree plunges in the air temperature in there. No malfunction, my ass!"

"I hear they're bringing in the original design team," Dombey said. "Those guys'll spot the problem in a minute."

"Bozos," Zachariah said.

"Anyway, I don't see what you're so riled up about. We're supposed to be testing the boy to destruction, aren't we? Then why fret about his health?"

"Surely you can't mean that," Zachariah said. "When he finally dies, we'll want to know for sure it was the injections that killed him. If he's subjected to many more of these sudden temperature fluctuations, we'll never be certain they didn't contribute to his death. It won't be clean research."

A thin, humorless laugh escaped Carlton Dombey, and he looked away from the window. Risky as it might be to express doubt to any colleague on the project, Dombey could not control himself: "Clean? This whole thing was never clean. It was a dirty piece of business right from the start."

Zachariah faced him. "You know I'm not talking about the morality of it."

"But I am."

"I'm talking about clinical standards."

"I really don't think I want to hear your opinions on either subject," Dombey said. "I've got a splitting headache."

"I'm just trying to be conscientious," Zachariah said, almost pouting. "You can't blame me because the work is dirty. I don't have much to say about research policy around here."

"You don't have *anything* to say about it," Dombey told him bluntly. "And neither do I. We're low men on the totem pole. That's why we're stuck with night-shift, baby-sitting duty like this."

"Even if I were in charge of making policy," Zachariah said, "I'd take the same course Dr. Tamaguchi has. Hell, he *had* to pursue this research. He didn't have any choice but to commit the installation to it once we found out the damn Chinese were deeply into it. And the Russians giving them a hand to earn some foreign currency. Our new friends the Russians. What a joke. Welcome to the new Cold War. It's China's nasty little project, remember. All we're doing is just playing catch-up. If you have to blame someone because you're feeling guilty about what we're doing here, then blame the Chinese, not me."

"I know. I know," Dombey said wearily, pushing one hand through his bush of curly hair. Zachariah would report their conversation in detail, and Dombey needed to assume a more balanced position for the record. "They scare me sure enough. If there's any government on earth capable of using a weapon like this, it's them—or the North Koreans or the Iraqis. Never a shortage of lunatic regimes. We don't have any choice but to maintain a strong defense. I really believe that. But sometimes . . . I wonder. While we're working so hard to keep ahead of our enemies, aren't we perhaps becoming more like them? Aren't we becoming a totalitarian state, the very thing we say we despise?"

"Maybe."

"Maybe," Dombey said, though he was sure of it.

"What choice do I have?"

"None, I guess."

"Look," Zachariah said.

"What?"

"The window's clearing up. It must be getting warm in there already."

The two scientists turned to the glass again and peered into the isolation chamber.

The emaciated boy stirred. He turned his head toward them and stared at them through the railed sides of the hospital bed in which he lay.

Zachariah said, "Those damn eyes."

"Penetrating, aren't they?"

"The way he stares . . . he gives me the creeps sometimes. There's something haunting about his eyes."

"You're just feeling guilty," Dombey said.

"No. It's more than that. His eyes are strange. They aren't the same as they were when he first came in here a year ago."

"There's pain in them now," Dombey said sadly. "A lot of pain and loneliness."

"More than that," Zachariah said. "There's something in those eyes . . . something there isn't any word for."

Zachariah walked away from the window. He went back to the computers, with which he felt comfortable and safe.

FRIDAY, JANUARY 2

27

FOR THE MOST PART, RENO'S STREETS WERE CLEAN AND DRY IN spite of a recent snowfall, though occasional patches of black ice waited for the unwary motorist. Elliot Stryker drove cautiously and kept his eyes on the road.

"We should almost be there," Tina said.

They traveled an additional quarter of a mile before Luciano Bellicosti's home and place of business came into sight on the left, beyond a black-bordered sign that grandiosely stated the nature of the service that he provided: FUNERAL DIRECTOR AND GRIEF COUNSELOR. It was an immense, pseudo-Colonial house, perched prominently on top of a hill, on a three- or four-acre property, and conveniently next door to a large, nondenominational cemetery. The long driveway curved up and to the right, like a width of black funeral bunting draped across the rising, snow-shrouded lawn. Stone posts and softly glowing electric lamps marked the way to the front door, and warm light radiated from several first-floor windows.

Elliot almost turned in at the entrance, but at the last moment he decided to drive by the place.

"Hey," Tina said, "that was it."

"I know."

"Why didn't you stop?"

"Storming right up to the front door, demanding answers from Belli-costi—that would be emotionally satisfying, brave, bold—and stupid."

"They can't be waiting for us, can they? They don't know we're in Reno."

"Never underestimate your enemy. They underestimated me and you, which is why we've gotten this far. We're not going to make the same mistake they did and wind up back in their hands."

Beyond the cemetery, he turned left, into a residential street. He parked at the curb, switched off the headlights, and cut the engine.

"What now?" she asked.

"I'm going to walk back to the funeral home. I'll go through the cemetery, circle around, and approach the place from the rear."

"*We* will approach it from the rear," she said.

"No."

"Yes."

"You'll wait here," he insisted.

"No way."

Pale light from a street lamp pierced the windshield, revealing a hard-edged determination in her face, steely resolution in her blue eyes.

Although he realized that he was going to lose the argument, Elliot said, "Be reasonable. If there's any trouble, you might get in the way of it."

"Now really, Elliot, talk sense. Am I the kind of woman who gets in the way?"

"There's eight or ten inches of snow on the ground. You aren't wearing boots."

"Neither are you."

"If they've anticipated us, set a trap at the funeral home—"

"Then you might need my help," she said. "And if they haven't set a trap, I've got to be there when you question Bellicosti."

"Tina, we're just wasting time sitting here—"

"Wasting time. Exactly. I'm glad you see it my way." She opened her door and climbed out of the car.

He knew then, beyond any shadow of a doubt, that he loved her.

Stuffing the silencer-equipped pistol into one of his deep coat pockets, he got out of the Chevy. He didn't lock the doors, because it was possible that he and Tina would need to get into the car in a hurry when they returned.

In the graveyard, the snow came up to the middle of Elliot's calves. It soaked his trousers, caked in his socks, and melted into his shoes.

Tina, wearing rubber-soled sneakers with canvas tops, was surely as miserable as he was. But she kept pace with him, and she didn't complain.

The raw, damp wind was stronger now than it had been a short while ago, when they'd landed at the airport. It swept through the graveyard, fluting between the headstones and the larger monuments, whispering a promise of more snow, much more than the meager flurries it now carried.

A low stone wall and a line of house-high spruce separated the cemetery from Luciano Bellicosti's property. Elliot and Tina climbed over the wall and stood in the tree shadows, studying the rear approach to the funeral home.

Tina didn't have to be told to remain silent. She waited beside him, arms folded, hands tucked into her armpits for warmth.

Elliot was worried about her, afraid for her, but at the same time he was glad to have her company.

The rear of Bellicosti's house was almost a hundred yards away. Even in the dim light, Elliot could see the fringe of icicles hanging from the roof of the long back porch. A few evergreen shrubs were clustered near the house, but none was of sufficient size to conceal a man. The rear windows were blank, black; a sentry might be standing behind any of them, invisible in the darkness.

Elliot strained his eyes, trying to catch a glimpse of movement beyond the rectangles of glass, but he saw nothing suspicious.

There wasn't much of a chance that a trap had been set for them so soon. And if assassins *were* waiting here, they would expect their prey to approach the funeral home boldly, confidently. Consequently, their attention would be focused largely on the front of the house.

In any case, he couldn't stand here all night brooding about it.

He stepped from beneath the sheltering branches of the trees. Tina moved with him.

The bitter wind was a lash. It skimmed crystals of snow off the ground and spun the stinging cold flecks at their reddened faces.

Elliot felt naked as they crossed the luminescent snow field. He wished that they weren't wearing such dark clothes. If anyone *did* glance out a back window, he would spot the two of them instantly.

The crunching and squeaking of the snow under their feet seemed horrendously loud to him, though they actually were making little noise. He was just jumpy.

They reached the funeral home without incident.

For a few seconds they paused, touching each other briefly, gathering their courage.

Elliot took the pistol out of his coat jacket and held it in his right hand. With his left hand, he fumbled for the two safety catches, released them. His fingers were stiff from the cold. He wondered if he'd be able to handle the weapon properly if the need arose.

They slipped around the corner of the building and moved stealthily toward the front.

At the first window with light behind it, Elliot stopped. He motioned for Tina to stay behind him, close to the house. Cautiously he leaned forward and peeked through a narrow gap in a partly closed venetian blind. He nearly cried out in shock and alarm at what he saw inside.

A dead man. Naked. Sitting in a bathtub full of bloody water, staring at something fearsome beyond the veil between this world and the next. One arm trailed out of the tub; and on the floor, as if it had dropped out of his fingers, was a razor blade.

Elliot stared into the flat dead gaze of the pasty-faced corpse, and he knew that he was looking at Luciano Bellicosti. He also knew that the funeral director had not killed himself. The poor man's blue-lipped mouth hung in a permanent gape, as if he were trying to deny all of the accusations of suicide that were to come.

Elliot wanted to take Tina by the arm and hustle her back to the car. But she sensed that he'd seen something important, and she wouldn't go easily until she knew what it was. She pushed in front of him. He kept one hand on her back as she leaned toward the window, and he felt her go rigid when she glimpsed the dead man. When she turned to Elliot again, she was clearly ready to get the hell out of there, without questions, without argument, without the slightest delay.

They had taken only two steps from the window when Elliot saw the snow move no more than twenty feet from them. It wasn't the gauzy, insubstantial stirring of wind-blown flakes, but an unnatural and purposeful rising of an entire mound of white. Instinctively he whipped the pistol in front of him and squeezed off four rounds. The silencer was so effective that the shots could not be heard above the brittle, papery rustle of the wind.

Crouching low, trying to make as small a target of himself as possible, Elliot ran to where he had seen the snow move. He found a man dressed in a white, insulated ski suit. The stranger had been lying in the snow, watching them, waiting; now he had a wet hole in his chest. And a chunk of his throat was gone. Even in the dim, illusory light from the surrounding snow, Elliot could see that the sentry's eyes were fixed in the same unseeing gaze that Bellicosti was even now directing at the bathroom window.

At least one killer would be in the house with Bellicosti's corpse. Probably more than one.

At least one man had been waiting out here in the snow.

How many others?

Where?

Elliot scanned the night, his heart clutching up. He expected to see the entire white-shrouded lawn begin to move and rise in the forms of ten, fifteen, twenty other assassins.

But all was still.

He was briefly immobilized, dazed by his own ability to strike so fast and so violently. A warm, animal satisfaction rose in him, which was not an entirely welcome feeling, for he liked to think of himself as a civilized man. At the same time, he was hit by a wave of revulsion. His throat tightened, and a sour taste suddenly overwhelmed him. He turned his back on the man whom he had killed.

Tina was a pale apparition in the snow. "They know we're in Reno," she whispered. "They even knew we were coming here."

"But they expected us through the front door." He took her by the arm. "Let's get out of here."

They hurriedly retraced their path, moving away from the funeral home. With every step he took, Elliot expected to hear a shot fired, a cry of alarm, and the sounds of men in pursuit of quarry.

He helped Tina over the cemetery wall, and then, clambering after her, he was sure that someone grabbed his coat from behind. He gasped, jerked loose. When he was across the wall, he looked back, but he couldn't see anyone.

Evidently the people in the funeral home were not aware that their man outside had been eliminated. They were still waiting patiently for their prey to walk into the trap.

Elliot and Tina rushed between the tombstones, kicking up clouds of snow. Twin plumes of crystallized breath trailed behind them, like ghosts.

When they were nearly halfway across the graveyard, when Elliot was positive they weren't being pursued, he stopped, leaned against a tall monument, and tried not to take such huge, deep gulps of the painfully cold air. An image of his victim's torn throat exploded in his memory, and a shock wave of nausea overwhelmed him.

Tina put a hand on his shoulder. "Are you all right?"

"I killed him."

"If you hadn't, he would have killed us."

"I know. Just the same . . . it makes me sick."

"I would have thought . . . when you were in the army . . ."

"Yeah," he said softly. "Yeah, I've killed before. But like you said, that was in the army. This wasn't the same. That was soldiering. This was murder." He shook his head to clear it. "I'll be okay." He tucked the pistol into his coat pocket again. "It was just the shock."

They embraced, and then she said, "If they knew we were flying to Reno, why didn't they follow us from the airport? Then they would have known we weren't going to walk in the front door of Bellicosti's place."

"Maybe they figured I'd spot a tail and be spooked by it. And I guess they were so sure of where we were headed, they didn't think it was necessary to keep a close watch on us. They figured there wasn't anywhere else we *could* go but Bellicosti's funeral home."

"Let's get back to the car. I'm freezing."

"Me too. And we better get out of the neighborhood before they find that guy in the snow."

They followed their own footprints out of the cemetery, to the quiet residential street where the rented Chevrolet was parked in the wan light of the street lamp.

As Elliot was opening the driver's door, he saw movement out of the corner of his eye, and he looked up, already sure of what he would see. A white Ford sedan had just turned the corner, moving slowly. It drifted to the curb and braked abruptly. Two doors opened, and a pair of tall, darkly dressed men climbed out.

Elliot recognized them for what they were. He got into the Chevy, slammed the door, and jammed the key into the ignition.

"We *have* been followed," Tina said.

"Yeah." He switched on the engine and threw the car in gear. "A transponder. They must have just now homed in on it."

He didn't hear a shot, but a bullet shattered the rear side window behind his head and slammed into the back of the front seat, spraying gummy bits of safety glass through the car.

"Head down!" Elliot shouted.

He glanced back.

The two men were approaching at a run, slipping on the snow-spotted pavement.

Elliot stamped on the accelerator. Tires squealing, he pulled the Chevy away from the curb, into the street.

Two slugs ricocheted off the body of the car, each trailing away with a brief, high-pitched whine.

Elliot hunched low over the wheel, expecting a bullet through the rear window. At the corner, he ignored the stop sign and swung the car hard to the left, only tapping the brakes once, severely testing the Chevy's suspension.

Tina raised her head, glanced at the empty street behind them, then looked at Elliot. "Transponder. What's that? You mean we're bugged? Then we'll have to abandon the car, won't we?"

"Not until we've gotten rid of those clowns on our tail," he said. "If we abandon the car with them so close, they'll run us down fast. We can't get away on foot."

"Then what?"

They arrived at another intersection, and he whipped the car to the right. "After I turn the next corner, I'll stop and get out. You be ready to slide over and take the wheel."

"Where are you going?"

"I'll fade back into the shrubbery and wait for them to come around the corner after us. You drive on down the street, but not too fast. Give them a chance to see you when they turn into the street. They'll be looking at you, and they won't see me."

"We shouldn't split up."

"It's the only way."

"But what if they get you?"

"They won't."

"I'd be alone then."

"They won't get me. But you have to move fast. If we stop for more than a couple of seconds, it'll show up on their receiver, and they might get suspicious."

He swung right at the intersection and stopped in the middle of the new street.

"Elliot, don't—"

"No choice." He flung open the door and scrambled out of the car. "Hurry, Tina!"

He slammed the car door and ran to a row of evergreen shrubs that bordered the front lawn of a low, brick, ranch-style house. Crouching beside one of those bushes, huddling in the shadows just beyond the circle of frosty light from a nearby street lamp, he pulled the pistol out of his coat pocket while Tina drove away.

As the sound of the Chevy faded, he could discern the roar of another vehicle, approaching fast. A few seconds later the white sedan raced into the intersection.

Elliot stood, extending the pistol in both hands, and snapped off three quick rounds. The first two clanged through sheet metal, but the third punctured the right front tire.

The Ford had rounded the corner too fast. Jolted by the blowout, the car careened out of control. It spun across the street, jumped the curb, crashed through a hedge, destroyed a plaster birdbath, and came to rest in the middle of a snow-blanketed lawn.

Elliot ran toward the Chevy, which Tina had brought to a stop a hundred yards away. It seemed more like a hundred miles. His pounding footsteps were as thunderous as drumbeats in the quiet night air. At last he reached the car. She had the door open. He leaped in and pulled the door shut. "Go, go!"

She tramped the accelerator into the floorboards, and the car responded with a shudder, then a surge of power.

When they had gone two blocks, he said, "Turn right at the next corner." After two more turns and another three blocks, he said, "Pull it to the curb. I want to find the bug they planted on us."

"But they can't follow us now," she said.

"They've still got a receiver. They can watch our progress on that, even if they can't get their hands on us till another chase car catches up. I don't even want them to know what direction we went."

She stopped the car, and he got out. He felt along the inner faces of the fenders, around the tire wells, where a transponder could have been stuck in place quickly and easily. Nothing. The front bumper was clean too. Finally he located the electronics package: The size of a pack of cigarettes, it was fixed magnetically to the underside of the rear bumper. He wrenched it loose, stomped it repeatedly underfoot, and pitched it away.

In the car again, with the doors locked and the engine running and the heater operating full-blast, they sat in stunned silence, basking in the warm air, but shivering nonetheless.

Eventually Tina said, "My God, they move fast!"

"We're still one step ahead of them," Elliot said shakily.

"Half a step."

"That's probably more like it," he admitted.

"Bellicosti was supposed to give us the information we need to interest a topnotch reporter in the case."

"Not now."

"So how do we get that information?"

"Somehow," he said vaguely.

"How do we build our case?"

"We'll think of something."

"Who do we turn to next?"

"It isn't hopeless, Tina."

"I didn't say it was. But where do we go from here?"

"We can't work it out tonight," he said wearily. "Not in our condition. We're both wiped out, operating on sheer desperation. That's dangerous. The best decision we can make is to make no decisions at all. We've got to hole up and get some rest. In the morning we'll have clearer heads, and the answers will all seem obvious."

"You think you can actually sleep?"

"Hell, yes. It's been a hard day's night."

"Where will we be safe?"

"We'll try the purloined letter trick," Elliot said. "Instead of sneaking around to some out-of-the-way motel, we'll march right into one of the best hotels in town."

"Harrah's?"

"Exactly. They won't expect us to be that bold. They'll be searching for us everywhere else."

"It's risky."

"Can you think of anything better?"

"No."

"*Everything* is risky."

"All right. Let's do it."

She drove into the heart of town. They abandoned the Chevrolet in a public parking lot, four blocks from Harrah's.

"I wish we didn't have to give up the car," Tina said as he took their only suitcase out of the trunk.

"They'll be looking for it."

They walked to Harrah's Hotel along windy, neon-splashed streets. Even at 1:45 in the morning, as they passed the entrances to casinos, loud music and laughter and the ringing of slot machines gushed forth, not a merry sound at that hour, a regurgitant noise.

Although Reno didn't jump all night with quite the same energy as Las Vegas, and although many tourists had gone to bed, the casino at Harrah's was still relatively busy. A young sailor apparently had a run going at one of the craps tables, and a crowd of excited gamblers urged him to roll an eight and make his point.

On this holiday weekend the hotel was officially booked to capacity; however, Elliot knew accommodations were always available. At the request of its casino manager, every hotel held a handful of rooms off the market, just in case a few regular customers—high rollers, of course—showed up by surprise, with no advance notice, but with fat bankrolls and no place to stay. In addition, some reservations were canceled at the last minute, and there were always a few no-shows. A neatly folded pair of twenty-dollar bills, placed without ostentation into the hand of a front-desk clerk, was almost certain to result in the timely discovery of a forgotten vacancy.

When Elliot was informed that a room was available, after all, for two nights, he signed the registration card as "Hank Thomas," a slight twist on the name of one of his favorite movie stars; he entered a phony Seattle address too. The clerk requested ID or a major credit card, and Elliot told a sad story of being victimized by a pickpocket at the airport. Unable to prove his identity, he was required to pay for both nights in advance, which he did, taking the money from a wad of cash he'd stuck in his pocket rather than from the wallet that supposedly had been stolen.

He and Tina were given a spacious, pleasantly decorated room on the ninth floor.

After the bellman left, Elliot engaged the deadbolt, hooked the security chain in place, and firmly wedged the heavy straight-backed desk chair under the knob.

"It's like a prison," Tina said.

"Except we're locked in, and the killers are running around loose on the outside."

A short time later, in bed, they held each other close, but neither of them had sex in mind. They wanted nothing more than to touch and to be touched, to confirm for each other that they were still alive, to feel safe and protected and cherished. Theirs was an animal need for affection and companionship, a reaction to the death and destruction that had filled the day. After encountering so many people with so little respect for human life, they needed to convince themselves that they really were more than dust in the wind.

After a few minutes he said, "You were right."

"About what?"

"About what you said last night, in Vegas."

"Refresh my memory."

"You said I was enjoying the chase."

"A part of you . . . deep down inside. Yes, I think that's true."

"I know it is," he said. "I can see it now. I didn't want to believe it at first."

"Why not? I didn't mean it negatively."

"I know you didn't. It's just that for more than fifteen years, I've led a very ordinary life, a workaday life. I was convinced I no longer needed or wanted the kind of thrills that I thrived on when I was younger."

"I don't think you *do* need or want them," Tina said. "But now that you're in real danger again for the first time in years, a part of you is responding to the challenge. Like an old athlete back on the playing field after a long absence, testing his reflexes, taking pride in the fact that his old skills are still there."

"It's more than that," Elliot said. "I think . . . deep down, I got a sick sort of thrill when I killed that man."

"Don't be so hard on yourself."

"I'm not. In fact, maybe the thrill wasn't so deep down. Maybe it was really pretty near the surface."

"You should be glad you killed that bastard," she said softly, squeezing his hand.

"Should I?"

"Listen, if I could get my hands on the people who're trying to keep us from finding Danny, I wouldn't have any compunctions about killing them. None at all. I might even take a certain pleasure in it. I'm a mother lion, and they've stolen by cub. Maybe killing them is the most natural, admirable thing I could do."

"So there's a bit of the beast in all of us. Is that it?"

"It's not just me that has a savage trapped inside."

"But does that make it any more acceptable?"

"What's to accept?" she asked. "It's the way God made us. It's the way we were meant to be, so who's to say it isn't right?"

"Maybe."

"If a man kills only for the pleasure of it, or if he kills only for an ideal like some of these crackpot revolutionaries you read about, *that's* savagery . . . or madness. What you've done is altogether different. Self-preservation is one of the most powerful drives God gave us. We're built to survive, even if we have to kill someone in order to do it."

They were silent for a while. Then he said, "Thank you."

"I didn't do anything."

"You listened."

28

KURT HENSEN, GEORGE ALEXANDER'S RIGHT-HAND MAN, DOZED through the rough flight from Las Vegas to Reno. They were in a ten-passenger jet that belonged to the Network, and the aircraft took a battering from the high-altitude winds that blew across its assigned flight corridor. Hensen, a powerfully built man with white-blond hair and cat-yellow eyes, was afraid of flying. He could only manage to get on a plane after he had medicated himself. As usual he nodded off minutes after the aircraft lifted from the runway.

George Alexander was the only other passenger. He considered the requisitioning of this executive jet to be one of his most important accomplishments in the three years that he had been chief of the Nevada bureau of the Network. Although he spent more than half his time working in his Las Vegas office, he often had reason to fly to far points at the spur of the moment: Reno, Elko, even out of the state to Texas, California, Arizona, New Mexico, Utah. During the first year, he'd taken commercial flights or rented the services of a trustworthy private pilot who could fly the conventional twin-engine craft that Alexander's predecessor had managed to pry out of the Network's budget. But it had seemed absurd and shortsighted of the director to force a man of Alexander's position to travel by such relatively primitive means. His time was enormously valuable to the country; his work was sensitive and often required urgent decisions based upon first-hand examination of information to be found only in distant places. After long and arduous lobbying of the director, Alexander had at last been awarded this small jet; and immediately he put two full-time pilots, ex-military men, on the payroll of the Nevada bureau.

Sometimes the Network pinched pennies to its disadvantage. And George Lincoln Stanhope Alexander, who was an heir to both the fortune of the Pennsylvania Alexanders and to the enormous wealth of the Delaware Stanhopes, had absolutely no patience with people who were penurious.

It was true that every dollar had to count, for every dollar of the Network's budget was difficult to come by. Because its existence must be kept secret, the organization was funded out of misdirected appropriations meant for other government agencies. Three billion dollars, the largest single part of the Network's yearly budget, came from the Department of Health and Welfare. The Network had a deep-cover agent named Jacklin in the highest policymaking ranks of the Health bureaucracy. It was Jacklin's job to conceive new welfare programs, convince the Secretary of Health and Welfare that those programs were needed, sell them to the Congress, and then establish convincing bureaucratic shells to conceal the fact that the programs were utterly phony; and as federal funds flowed to these false-front operations, the money was diverted to the Network. Chipping three billion out of Health was the least risky of the Network's funding operations, for Health was so gigantic that it never missed such a petty sum. The Department of Defense, which was less flush than Health and Welfare these days, was nevertheless also guilty of waste, and it was good for at least another billion a year. Lesser amounts, ranging from only one hundred million to as much as half a billion, were secretly extracted from the Department of Energy, the Department of Education, and other government bodies on an annual basis.

The Network was financed with some difficulty, to be sure, but it was undeniably well funded. An executive jet for the chief of the vital Nevada bureau was not an extravagance, and Alexander believed his improved performance over the past year had convinced the old man in Washington that this was money well spent.

Alexander was proud of the importance of his position. But he was also frustrated because so few people were *aware* of his great importance.

At times he envied his father and his uncles. Most of them had served their country openly, in a supremely visible fashion, where everyone could see and admire their selfless public-spiritedness. Secretary of Defense, Secretary of State, the Ambassador to France . . . in positions of that nature, a man was appreciated and respected.

George, on the other hand, hadn't filled a post of genuine stature and authority until six years ago, when he was thirty-six. During his twenties and early thirties, he had labored at a variety of lesser jobs for the government. These diplomatic and intelligence-gathering assignments were never an insult to his family name, but they were always minor postings to embassies in smaller countries like Iceland and Ecuador and Tonga, nothing for which *The New York Times* would deign to acknowledge his existence.

Then, six years ago, the Network had been formed, and the President had given George the task of developing a reliable South American bureau of the new intelligence agency. That had been exciting, challenging, important work. George had been directly responsible for the expenditure of tens of millions of dollars and, eventually, for the control of hundreds of agents in a dozen countries. After three years the President had declared himself delighted with the accomplishments in South America, and he had asked George to take charge of one of the Network's domestic bureaus—Nevada—which had been terribly mismanaged. This slot was one of the half-dozen most powerful in the Network's executive hierarchy. George was encouraged by the President to believe that eventually he would be promoted to the bureau chief of the entire western half of the country—and then all the way to the top, if only he could get the floundering western division functioning as smoothly as the South American and Nevada offices. In time he would take the director's chair in Washington and would bear full responsibility for all domestic and foreign intelligence operations. With that title he would be one of the most powerful men in the United States, more of a force to be reckoned with than any mere Secretary of State or Secretary of Defense could hope to be.

But he couldn't tell anyone about his achievements. He could never hope to receive the public acclaim and honor that had been heaped upon other men in his family. The Network was clandestine and must remain clandestine if it was to have any value. At least half of the people who worked for it did not even realize it existed; some thought they were employed by the FBI; others were sure they worked for the CIA; and still others believed that they were in the hire of various branches of the Treasury Department, including the Secret Service. None of those people could compromise the Network. Only bureau chiefs, their immediate staffs, station chiefs in major cities, and senior field officers who had proved themselves and their loyalty—only those people knew the true nature of their employers and their work. The moment that the news media became aware of the Network's existence, all was lost.

As he sat in the dimly lighted cabin of the fan-jet and watched the clouds racing below, Alexander wondered what his father and his uncles would say if they knew that his service to his country had often required him to issue kill orders. More shocking still to the sensibilities of patrician Easterners like them: on three occasions, in South America, Alexander had been in a position where it had been necessary for him to pull the assassin's trigger himself. He had enjoyed those murders so immensely, had been so profoundly thrilled by them, that he had, by choice, performed the executioner's role on half a dozen other assignments. What would the elder Alexanders, the famous statesmen, think if they knew he'd soiled his hands with blood? As for the fact that it was sometimes his job to order other men to kill, he supposed his family would understand. The Alexanders were all idealists when they were discussing the way things ought to be, but they were also hardheaded pragmatists when dealing with the way things actually were. They knew that the worlds of domestic military security and international espionage were not children's playgrounds. George liked to believe that they might even find it in their hearts to forgive him for having pulled the trigger himself.

After all, he had never killed an ordinary citizen or a person of real worth. His targets had always been spies, traitors; more than a few of them had been cold-blooded killers themselves. Scum. He had only killed scum. It wasn't a pretty job, but it also wasn't without a measure of real dignity and heroism. At least that was the way George saw it; he thought of himself as heroic. Yes, he was sure that his father and uncles would give him their blessings—if only he were permitted to tell them.

The jet hit an especially bad patch of turbulence. It yawed, bounced, shuddered.

Kurt Hensen snorted in his sleep but didn't wake.

When the plane settled down once more, Alexander looked out the window at the milky-white, moonlit, feminine roundness of the clouds below, and he thought of the Evans woman. She was quite lovely. Her file folder was on the seat beside him. He picked it up, opened it, and stared at her photograph. Quite lovely indeed. He decided he would kill her himself when the time came, and that thought gave him an instant erection.

He enjoyed killing. He didn't try to pretend otherwise with himself, no matter what face he had to present to the world. All of his life, for reasons he had never been able to fully ascertain, he had been fascinated by death, intrigued by the form and nature and possibilities of it, enthralled by the study and theory of its meaning. He considered himself a messenger of death, a divinely appointed headsman. Murder was, in many ways, more thrilling to him than sex. His taste for violence would not have been tolerated for long in the old FBI—perhaps not even in the new, thoroughly politicized FBI—or in many other congressionally monitored police agencies. But in this unknown organization, in this secret and incomparably cozy place, he thrived.

He closed his eyes and thought about Christina Evans.

29

IN TINA'S DREAM, DANNY WAS AT THE FAR END OF A LONG TUNNEL. He was in chains, sitting in the center of a small, well-lighted cavern, but the passageway that led to him was shadowy and reeked of danger. Danny called to her again and again, begging her to save him before the roof of his underground prison caved in and buried him alive. She started down the tunnel toward him, determined to get him out of there—and something reached for her from a narrow cleft in the wall. She was peripherally aware of a soft, firelike glow from beyond the cleft, and of a mysterious figure silhouetted against that reddish back-drop. She turned, and she was looking into the grinning face of Death, as if he were peering out at her from the bowels of Hell. The crimson eyes. The shriveled flesh. The lacework of maggots on his cheek. She cried out, but then she saw that Death could not quite reach her. The hole in the wall was not wide enough for him to step through, into her passageway; he could only thrust one arm at her, and his long, bony fingers were an inch or two short of her. Danny began calling again, and she continued down the dusky tunnel toward him. A dozen times she passed chinks in the wall, and Death glared out at her from every one of those apertures, screamed and cursed and raged at her, but none of the holes was large enough to allow him through. She reached Danny, and when she touched him, the chains fell magically away from his arms and legs. She said, "I was scared." And Danny said, "I made the holes in the walls smaller. I made sure he couldn't reach you, couldn't hurt you."

At eight-thirty Friday morning Tina came awake, smiling and excited. She shook Elliot until she woke him.

Blinking sleepily, he sat up. "What's wrong?"

"Danny just sent me another dream."

Taking in her broad smile, he said, "Obviously, it wasn't the night-mare."

"Not at all. Danny wants us to come to him. He wants us just to walk into the place where they're keeping him and take him out."

"We'd be killed before we could reach him. We can't just charge in like the cavalry. We've got to use the media and the courts to free him."

"I don't think so."

"The two of us can't fight the entire organization that's behind Ken-nebeck plus the staff of some secret military research center."

"Danny's going to make it safe for us," she said confidently. "He's going to use this power of his to help us get in there."

"That isn't possible."

"You said you believed."

"I do," Elliot said, yawning and stretching elaborately. "I do believe. But . . . how can he help us? How can he guarantee our safety?"

"I don't know. But that's what he was telling me in the dream. I'm sure of it."

She recounted the dream in detail, and Elliot admitted that her interpretation wasn't strained.

"But even if Danny could somehow get us in," he said, "we don't know where they're keeping him. This secret installation could be anywhere. And maybe it doesn't even exist. And if it does exist, they might not be holding him there anyway."

"It exists, and that's where he is," she said, trying to sound more certain than she actually was.

She was within reach of Danny. She felt almost as if she had him in her arms again, and she didn't want anyone to tell her that he might be a hair's breadth beyond her grasp.

"Okay," Elliot said, wiping at the corners of his sleep-matted eyes. "Let's say this secret installation exists. That doesn't help us a whole hell of a lot. It could be anywhere in those mountains."

"No," she said. "It has to be within a few miles of where Jaborski intended to go with the scouts."

"Okay. That's probably true. But that covers a hell of a lot of rugged terrain. We couldn't begin to conduct a thorough search of it."

Tina's confidence couldn't be shaken. "Danny will pinpoint it for us."

"Danny's going to tell us where he is?"

"He's going to try, I think. I sensed that in the dream."

"How's he going to do it?"

"I don't know. But I have this feeling that if we just find some way . . . some means of focusing his energy, channeling it . . ."

"Such as?"

She stared at the tangled bedclothes as if she were searching for inspiration in the creases of the linens. Her expression would have been appropriate to the face of a gypsy fortune-teller peering with a clairvoyant frown at tea leaves.

"Maps!" she said suddenly.

"What?"

"Don't they publish terrain maps of the wilderness areas? Backpackers and other nature lovers would need them. Not minutely detailed things. Basically maps that show the lay of the land—hills, valleys, the courses of rivers and streams, footpaths, abandoned logging trails, that sort of thing. I'm sure Jaborski had maps. I *know* he did. I saw them at the parent-son scout meeting when he explained why the trip would be perfectly safe."

"I suppose any sporting-goods store in Reno ought to have maps of at least the nearest parts of the Sierras."

"Maybe if we can get a map and spread it out . . . well, maybe Danny will find a way to show us exactly where he is."

"How?"

"I'm not sure yet." She threw back the covers and got out of bed. "Let's get the maps first. We'll worry about the rest of it later. Come on. Let's get showered and dressed. The stores will be open in an hour or so."

BECAUSE OF THE foul-up at the Bellicosti place, George Alexander didn't get to bed until five-thirty Friday morning. Still furious with his subordinates for letting Stryker and the woman escape again, he had difficulty getting to sleep. He finally nodded off around 7:00 A.M.

At ten o'clock he was awakened by the telephone. The director was calling from Washington. They used an electronic scrambling device, so they could speak candidly, and the old man was furious and characteristically blunt.

As Alexander endured the director's accusations and demands, he realized that his own future with the Network was at stake. If he failed to stop Stryker and the Evans woman, his dream of assuming the director's chair in a few years would never become a reality.

After the old man hung up, Alexander called his own office, in no mood to be told that Elliot Stryker and Christina Evans were still at large. But that was exactly what he heard. He ordered men pulled off other jobs and assigned to the manhunt.

"I want them found before another day passes," Alexander said. "That bastard's killed one of us now. He can't get away with that. I want him eliminated. And the bitch with him. Both of them. Dead."

30

TWO SPORTING-GOODS STORES AND TWO GUN SHOPS WERE WITH-
in easy walking distance of the hotel. The first sporting-goods dealer did
not carry the maps, and although the second usually had them, it was
currently sold out. Elliot and Tina found what they needed in one of the
gun shops: a set of twelve wilderness maps of the Sierras, designed with
backpackers and hunters in mind. The set came in a leatherette-covered
case and sold for a hundred dollars.

Back in the hotel room, they opened one of the maps on the bed, and
Elliot said, "Now what?"

For a moment Tina considered the problem. Then she went to the
desk, opened the center drawer, and withdrew a folder of hotel stationery. In the folder was a cheap plastic ballpoint pen with the hotel name
on it. With the pen, she returned to the bed and sat beside the open map.

She said, "People who believe in the occult have a thing they call
'automatic writing.' Ever hear of it?"

"Sure. Spirit writing. A ghost supposedly guides your hand to deliver
a message from beyond. Always sounded like the worst sort of bunkum
to me."

"Well, bunkum or not, I'm going to try something like that. Except, I
don't need a ghost to guide my hand. I'm hoping Danny can do it."

"Don't you have to be in a trance, like a medium at a seance?"

"I'm just going to completely relax, make myself open and receptive.
I'll hold the pen against the map, and maybe Danny can draw the route
for us."

Elliot pulled a chair beside the bed and sat. "I don't believe for a minute
it's going to work. Totally nuts. But I'll be as quiet as a mouse and give
it a chance."

Tina stared at the map and tried to think of nothing but the appealing
greens, blues, yellows, and pinks that the cartographers had used to indicate various types of terrain. She allowed her eyes to swim out of focus.

A minute passed.

Two minutes. Three.

She tried closing her eyes.

Another minute. Two.

Nothing.

She turned the map over and tried the other side of it.

Still nothing.

"Give me another map," she said.

Elliot withdrew another one from the leatherette case and handed it to her. He refolded the first map as she unfolded the second.

Half an hour and five maps later, Tina's hand suddenly skipped across the paper as if someone had bumped her arm.

She felt a peculiar pulling sensation that seemed to come from *within* her hand, and she stiffened in surprise.

Instantly the invasive power retreated from her.

"What was that?" Elliot asked.

"Danny. He tried."

"You're sure?"

"Positive. But he startled me, and I guess even the little bit of resistance I offered was enough to push him away. At least we know this is the right map. Let me try again."

She put the pen at the edge of the map once more, and she let her eyes drift out of focus.

The air temperature plummeted.

She tried not to think about the chill. She tried to banish *all* thoughts.

Her right hand, in which she held the pen, grew rapidly colder than any other part of her. She felt the unpleasant, inner pulling again. Her fingers ached with the cold. Abruptly her hand swung across the map, then back, then described a series of circles; the pen made meaningless scrawls on the paper. After half a minute, she felt the power leave her hand again.

"No good," she said.

The map flew into the air, as if someone had tossed it in anger or frustration.

Elliot got out of his chair and reached for the map—but it spun into the air again. It flapped noisily to the other end of the room and then back again, finally falling like a dead bird onto the floor at Elliot's feet.

"Jesus," he said softly. "The next time I read a story in the newspaper about some guy who says he was picked up in a flying saucer and taken on a tour of the universe, I won't be so quick to laugh. If I see many more inanimate objects dancing around, I'm going to start believing in *every-thing*, no matter how freaky."

Tina got up from the bed, massaging her cold right hand. "I guess I'm offering too much resistance. But it feels so weird when he takes control . . . I can't help stiffening a little. I guess you were right about needing to be in a trance."

"I'm afraid I can't help you with that. I'm a good cook, but I'm not a hypnotist."

She blinked. "Hypnosis! Of course! That'll probably do the trick."

"Maybe it will. But where do you expect to find a hypnotist? The last time I looked, they weren't setting up shops on street corners."

"Billy Sandstone," she said.

"Who?"

"He's a hypnotist. He lives right here in Reno. He has a stage act. It's a brilliant act. I wanted to use him in *Magyck!*, but he was tied up in an exclusive contract with a chain of Reno-Tahoe hotels. If you can get hold of Billy, he can hypnotize me. Then maybe I'll be relaxed enough to make this automatic writing work."

"Do you know his phone number?"

"No. And it's probably not listed. But I do know his agent's number. I can get through to him that way."

She hurried to the telephone.

31

BILLY SANDSTONE WAS IN HIS LATE THIRTIES, AS SMALL AND LEAN as a jockey, and his watchword seemed to be "neatness." His shoes shone like black mirrors. The creases in his slacks were as sharp as blades, and his blue sport shirt was starched, crisp. His hair was razor-cut, and he groomed his mustache so meticulously that it almost appeared to have been painted on his upper lip.

Billy's dining room was neat too. The table, the chairs, the credenza, and the hutch all glowed warmly because of the prodigious amount of furniture polish that had been buffed into the wood with even more vigor than he had employed when shining his dazzling shoes. Fresh roses were arranged in a cut-crystal vase in the center of the table, and clean lines of light gleamed in the exquisite glass. The draperies hung in perfectly measured folds. An entire battalion of nitpickers and fussbudgets would be hard-pressed to find a speck of dust in this room.

Elliot and Tina spread the map on the table and sat down across from each other.

Billy said, "Automatic writing is bunk, Christina. You must know that."

"I do, Billy. I know that."

"Well, then—"

"But I want you to hypnotize me anyway."

"You're a levelheaded person, Tina," Billy said. "This really doesn't seem like you."

"I know," she said.

"If you'd just tell me *why*. If you'd tell me what this is all about, maybe I could help you better."

"Billy," she said, "if I tried to explain, we would be here all afternoon."

"Longer," Elliot said.

"And we don't have much time," Tina said. "A lot's at stake here, Billy. More than you can imagine."

They hadn't told him anything about Danny. Sandstone didn't have the faintest idea why they were in Reno or what they were seeking in the mountains.

Elliot said, "I'm sure this seems ridiculous, Billy. You're probably wondering if I'm some sort of lunatic. You're wondering if maybe I've messed with Tina's mind."

"Which definitely isn't the case," Tina said.

"Right," Elliot said. "Her mind was messed up before I ever met her."

The joke seemed to relax Sandstone, as Elliot had hoped it would. Lunatics and just plain irrational people didn't intentionally try to amuse.

Elliot said, "I assure you, Billy, we haven't lost our marbles. And this *is* a matter of life and death."

"It really is," Tina said.

"Okay," Billy said. "You don't have time to tell me about it now. I'll accept that. But will you tell me one day when you aren't in such a damn rush?"

"Absolutely," Tina said. "I'll tell you everything. Just please, please, put me in a trance."

"All right," Billy Sandstone said.

He was wearing a gold signet ring. He turned it around, so the face of it was on the wrong side—the palm side—of his finger. He held his hand in front of Tina's eyes.

"Keep your eyes on the ring and listen only to my voice."

"Wait a second," she said.

She pulled the cap off the red felt-tip pen that Elliot had purchased at the hotel newsstand just before they'd caught a taxi to Sandstone's house. Elliot had suggested a change in the color of ink, so they would be able to tell the difference between the meaningless scribbles that were already on the map and any new marks that might be made.

Putting the point of the pen to the paper, Tina said, "Okay, Billy. Do your stuff."

Elliot was not sure when Tina slipped under the hypnotist's spell, and he had no idea how this smooth mesmerism was accomplished. All Sandstone did was move one hand slowly back and forth in front of Tina's face, simultaneously speaking to her in a quiet, rhythmic voice, frequently using her name.

Elliot almost fell into a trance himself. He blinked his eyes and tuned out Sandstone's melodious voice when he realized that he was succumbing to it.

Tina stared vacantly into space.

The hypnotist lowered his hand and turned his ring around as it belonged. "You're in a deep sleep, Tina."

"Yes."

"Your eyes are open, but you are in a deep, deep sleep."

"Yes."

"You will stay in that deep sleep until I tell you to wake up. Do you understand?"

"Yes."

"You will remain relaxed and receptive."

"Yes."

"Nothing will startle you."

"No."

"You aren't really involved in this. You're just the method of transmission—like a telephone."

"Telephone," she said thickly.

"You will remain totally passive until you feel the urge to use the pen in your hand."

"All right."

"When you feel the urge to use the pen, you will not resist it. You will flow with it. Understood?"

"Yes."

"You will not be bothered by anything Elliot and I say to each other. You will respond to me only when I speak directly to you. Understood?"

"Yes."

"Now . . . open yourself to whoever wants to speak through you."

They waited.

A minute passed, then another.

Billy Sandstone watched Tina intently for a while, but at last he shifted impatiently in his chair. He looked at Elliot and said, "I don't think this spirit writing stuff is—"

The map rustled, drawing their attention. The corners curled and uncurled, curled and uncurled, again and again, like the pulse of a living thing.

The air was colder.

The map stopped curling. The rustling ceased.

Tina lowered her gaze from the empty air to the map, and her hand began to move. It didn't swoop and dart uncontrollably this time; it crept carefully, hesitantly across the paper, leaving a thin red line of ink like a thread of blood.

Sandstone was rubbing his hands up and down his arms to ward off the steadily deepening chill that had gripped the room. Frowning, glancing up at the heating vents, he started to get out of his chair.

Elliot said, "Don't bother checking the air-conditioning. It isn't on. And the heat hasn't failed either."

"What?"

"The cold comes from the . . . spirit," Elliot said, deciding to stick with the occult terminology, not wanting to get bogged down in the real story about Danny.

"Spirit?"

"Yes."

"Whose spirit?"

"Could be anyone's."

"Are you serious?"

"Pretty much."

Sandstone stared at him as if to say, *You're nuts, but are you dangerous?*

Elliot pointed to the map. "See?"

As Tina's hand moved slowly over the paper, the corners of the map began to curl and uncurl again.

"How is she doing that?" Sandstone asked.

"She isn't."

"The ghost, I suppose."

"That's right."

An expression of pain settled over Billy's face, as if he were suffering genuine physical discomfort because of Elliot's belief in ghosts. Apparently Billy liked his view of the world to be as neat and uncluttered as everything else about him; if he started believing in ghosts, he'd have to reconsider his opinions about a lot of other things too, and then life would become intolerably messy.

Elliot sympathized with the hypnotist. Right now he longed for the rigidly structured routine of the law office, the neatly ordered paragraphs of legal casebooks, and the timeless rules of the courtroom.

Tina let the pen drop from her fingers. She lifted her gaze from the map. Her eyes remained unfocused.

"Are you finished?" Billy asked her.

"Yes."

"Are you sure?"

"Yes."

With a few simple sentences and a sharp clap of his hands, the hypnotist brought her out of the trance.

She blinked in confusion, then glanced down at the route that she had marked on the map. She smiled at Elliot. "It worked. By God, it worked!"

"Apparently it did."

She pointed to the terminus of the red line. "That's where he is, Elliot. That's where they're keeping him."

"It's not going to be easy getting into country like that," Elliot said.

"We can do it. We'll need good, insulated outdoor clothes. Boots. Snowshoes in case we have to walk very far in open country. Do you know how to use snowshoes? It can't be that hard."

"Hold on," Elliot said. "I'm still not convinced your dream meant what you think it did. Based on what you said happened in it, I don't see how you reach the conclusion that Danny's going to help us get into the installation. We might get to this place and find we can't slip around its defenses."

Billy Sandstone looked from Tina to Elliot, baffled. "Danny? Your Danny, Tina? But isn't he—"

Tina said, "Elliot, it wasn't only what happened in the dream that led me to this conclusion. What I *felt* in it was far more important. I can't explain that part of it. The only way you could understand is if you had the dream yourself. I'm *sure* he was telling me that he could help us get to him."

Elliot turned the map to be able to study it more closely.

From the head of the table, Billy said, "But isn't Danny—"

Tina said, "Elliot, listen, I told you he would show us where he's being kept, and he drew that route for us. So far I'm batting a thousand. I also feel he's going to help us get into the place, and I don't see any reason why I should strike out on that one."

"It's just . . . we'd be walking into their arms," Elliot said.

"Whose arms?" Billy Sandstone asked.

Tina said, "Elliot, what happens if we stay here, hiding out until we can think of an alternative? How much time do we have? Not much. They're going to find us sooner or later, and when they get their hands on us, they'll kill us."

"Kill?" Billy Sandstone asked. "There's a word I don't like. It's right up there on the bad-word list beside *broccoli*."

"We've gotten this far because we've kept moving and we've been aggressive," Tina said. "If we change our approach, if we suddenly get too cautious, that'll be our downfall, not our salvation."

"You two sound like you're in a war," Billy Sandstone said uneasily.

"You're probably right," Elliot told Tina. "One thing I learned in the military was you have to stop and regroup your forces once in a while, but if you stop too long, the tide will turn and wash right over you."

"Should I maybe go listen to the news?" Billy Sandstone asked. "*Is* there a war on? Have we invaded France?"

To Tina, Elliot said, "What else will we need besides thermal clothing, boots, and snowshoes?"

"A Jeep," she said.

"That's a tall order."

"What about a tank?" Billy Sandstone asked. "Going to war, you might prefer a tank."

Tina said, "Don't be silly, Billy. A Jeep is all we need."

"Just trying to be helpful, love. And thanks for remembering I exist."

"A Jeep or an Explorer—anything with four-wheel drive," Tina told Elliot. "We don't want to walk farther than necessary. We don't want to walk at all if we can help it. There must be some sort of road into the place, even if it's well concealed. If we're lucky, we'll have Danny when we come out, and he probably won't be in any condition to trek through the Sierras in the dead of winter."

"I have an Explorer," Billy said.

"I guess I could have some money transferred from my Vegas bank," Elliot said. "But what if they're watching my accounts down there? That would lead them to us fast. And since the banks are closed for the holiday, we couldn't do anything until next week. They might find us by then."

"What about your American Express card?" she asked.

"You mean, *charge* a Jeep?"

"There's no limit on the card, is there?"

"No. But—"

"I read a newspaper story once about a guy who bought a Rolls-Royce with his card. You can do that sort of thing as long as they know for sure you're capable of paying the entire bill when it comes due a month later."

"It sounds crazy," Elliot said. "But I guess we can try."

"I have an Explorer," Billy Sandstone said.

"Let's get the address of the local dealership," Tina said. "We'll see if they'll accept the card."

"I have an Explorer!" Billy said.

They turned to him, startled.

"I take my act to Lake Tahoe a few weeks every winter," Billy said. "You know what it's like down there this time of year. Snow up to your ass. I hate flying the Tahoe-Reno shuttle. The plane's so damn small. And you know what a ticky-tacky airport they have at Tahoe. So I usually just drive down the day before I open. An Explorer's the only thing I'd want to take through the mountains on a bad day."

"Are you going to Tahoe soon?" Tina asked.

"No. I don't open until the end of the month."

"Will you be needing the Explorer in the next couple of days?" Elliot asked.

"No."

"Can we borrow it?"

"Well . . . I guess so."

Tina leaned across the corner of the table, grabbed Billy's head in her hands, pulled his face to hers, and kissed him. "You're a lifesaver, Billy. And I mean that literally."

"I'm a small circlet of hard candy?"

"Maybe things are breaking right for us," Elliot said. "Maybe we'll get Danny out of there after all."

"We will," Tina said. "I know it."

The roses in the crystal vase twirled around like a group of spinning, redheaded ballerinas.

Startled, Billy Sandstone jumped up, knocking over his chair.

The drapes drew open, slid shut, drew open, slid shut, even though no one was near the draw cords.

The chandelier began to swing in a lazy circle, and the dangling crystals cast prismatic patterns of light on the walls.

Billy stared, open-mouthed.

Elliot knew how disoriented Billy was feeling, and he felt sorry for the man.

After half a minute all of the unnatural movement stopped, and the room rapidly grew warm again.

"How did you *do* that?" Billy demanded.

"We didn't," Tina said.

"Not a ghost," Billy said adamantly.

"Not a ghost either," Elliot said.

Billy said, "You can borrow the Explorer. But first you've got to tell me what in hell's going on. I don't care how much of a hurry you're in. You can at least tell me a little of it. Otherwise, I'm going to shrivel up and die of curiosity."

Tina consulted Elliot. "Well?"

Elliot said, "Billy, you might be better off not knowing."

"Impossible."

"We're up against some damn dangerous people. If they thought you knew about them—"

"Look," Billy said, "I'm not just a hypnotist. I'm something of a magician. That's really what I most wanted to be, but I didn't really have the skill for it. So I worked up this act built around hypnotism. But magic— that's my one great love. I just have to know how you did that trick with the drapes, the roses. And the corners of the map! I just *have* to know."

Earlier this morning it had occurred to Elliot that he and Tina were the only people who knew that the official story of the Sierra accident was a lie. If they were killed, the truth would die with them, and the cover-up would continue. Considering the high price that they had paid for the pathetically insufficient information they had obtained, he couldn't tolerate the prospect of all their pain and fear and anxiety having been for naught.

Elliot said, "Billy, do you have a tape recorder?"

"Sure. It's nothing fancy. It's a little one I carry with me. I do some comedy lines in the act, and I use the recorder to develop new material, correct problems with my timing."

"It doesn't have to be fancy," Elliot said. "Just so it works. We'll give you a condensed version of the story behind all of this, and we'll record it as we go. Then I'll mail the tape to one of my law partners." He shrugged. "Not much insurance, but better than nothing."

"I'll get the recorder," Billy said, hurrying out of the dining room.

Tina folded the map.

"It's nice to see you smiling again," Elliot said.

"I must be crazy," she said. "We still have dangerous work ahead of us. We're still up against this bunch of cutthroats. We don't know what we'll walk into in those mountains. So why do I feel terrific all of a sudden?"

"You feel good," Elliot said, "because we're not running anymore. We're going on the offensive. And foolhardy as that might be, it does a lot for a person's self-respect."

"Can a couple of people like us really have a chance of winning when we're up against something as big as the government itself?"

"Well," Elliot said, "I happen to believe that individuals are more apt to act responsibly and morally than institutions ever do, which at least puts us on the side of justice. And I also believe individuals are always smarter and better adapted to survival, at least in the long run, than any institution. Let's just hope my philosophy doesn't turn out to be half-baked."

AT ONE-THIRTY KURT Hensen came into George Alexander's office in downtown Reno. "They found the car that Stryker rented. It's in a public lot about three blocks from here."

"Used recently?" Alexander asked.

"No. The engine's cold. There's thick frost on the windows. It's been parked there overnight."

"He's not stupid," Alexander said. "He's probably abandoned the damn thing."

"You want to put a watch on it anyway?"

"Better do that," Alexander said. "Sooner or later they'll make a mistake. Coming back to the car might be it. I don't think so. But it might."

Hensen left the room.

Alexander took a Valium out of a tin that he carried in his jacket pocket, and he washed it down with a swallow of hot coffee, which he poured from the silver pot on his desk. This was his second pill since he'd gotten out of bed just three and a half hours ago, but he still felt edgy.

Stryker and the woman were proving to be worthy opponents.

Alexander never liked to have worthy opponents. He preferred them to be soft and easy.

Where were they?

32

THE DECIDUOUS TREES, STRIPPED OF EVERY LEAF, APPEARED TO BE charred, as if this particular winter had been more severe than others and as cataclysmic as a fire. The evergreens—pine, spruce, fir, tamarack— were flocked with snow. A brisk wind spilled over the jagged horizon under a low and menacing sky, snapping ice-hard flurries of snow against the windshield of the Explorer.

Tina was in awe of—and disquieted by—the stately forest that crowded them as they drove north on the narrowing county road. Even if she had not known that these deep woodlands harbored secrets about Danny and the deaths of the other scouts, she would have found them mysterious and unnervingly primeval.

She and Elliot had turned off Interstate 80 a quarter of an hour ago, following the route Danny had marked, circling the edge of the wilderness. On paper they were still moving along the border of the map, with a large expanse of blues and greens on their left. Shortly they would turn off the two-lane blacktop onto another road, which the map specified as "unpaved, nondirt," whatever that was.

After leaving Billy Sandstone's house in his Explorer, Tina and Elliot had not returned to the hotel. They shared a premonition that someone decidedly unfriendly was waiting in their room.

First they had visited a sporting-goods store, purchasing two Gore-Tex/ Thermolite stormsuits, boots, snowshoes, compact tins of backpacker's rations, cans of Sterno, and other survival gear. If the rescue attempt went smoothly, as Tina's dream seemed to predict, they wouldn't have any need for much of what they bought. But if the Explorer broke down in the mountains, or if another hitch developed, they wanted to be prepared for the unexpected.

Elliot also bought a hundred rounds of hollow-point ammunition for the pistol. This wasn't insurance against the unforeseen; this was simply prudent planning for the trouble they could foresee all too well.

From the sporting-goods store they had driven out of town, west toward the mountains. At a roadside restaurant, they changed clothes in the rest rooms. His insulated suit was green with white stripes; hers was white with green and black stripes. They looked like a couple of skiers on their way to the slopes.

Entering the formidable mountains, they had become aware of how soon darkness would settle over the sheltered valleys and ravines, and they had discussed the wisdom of proceeding. Perhaps they would have been smarter to turn around, go back to Reno, find another hotel room, and get a fresh start in the morning. But neither wanted to delay. Perhaps the lateness of the hour and the fading light would work against them, but approaching in the night might actually be to their advantage. The thing was—they had momentum. They both felt as if they were on a good roll, and they didn't want to tempt fate by post- poning their journey.

Now they were on a narrow county road, moving steadily higher as the valley sloped toward its northern end. Plows had kept the blacktop clean, except for scattered patches of hard-packed snow that filled the potholes, and snow was piled five or six feet high on both sides.

"Soon now," Tina said, glancing at the map that was open on her knees.

"Lonely part of the world, isn't it?"

"You get the feeling that civilization could be destroyed while you're out here, and you'd never be aware of it."

They hadn't seen a house or other structure for two miles. They hadn't passed another car in three miles.

Twilight descended into the winter forest, and Elliot switched on the headlights.

Ahead, on the left, a break appeared in the bank of snow that had been heaped up by the plows. When the Explorer reached this gap, Elliot swung into the turnoff and stopped. A narrow and forbidding track led into the woods, recently plowed but still treacherous. It was little more than one lane wide, and the trees formed a tunnel around it, so that after fifty or sixty feet, it disappeared into premature night. It was unpaved, but a solid bed had been built over the years by the generous and re-peated application of oil and gravel.

"According to the map, we're looking for an 'unpaved, nondirt' road," Tina told him.

"I guess this is it."

"Some sort of logging trail?"

"Looks more like the road they always take in those old movies when they're on their way to Dracula's castle."

"Thanks," she said.

"Sorry."

"And it doesn't help that you're right. It *does* look like the road to Dracula's castle."

They drove onto the track, under the roof of heavy evergreen boughs, into the heart of the forest.

33

IN THE RECTANGULAR ROOM, THREE STORIES UNDERGROUND, computers hummed and murmured.

Dr. Carlton Dombey, who had come on duty twenty minutes ago, sat at one of the tables against the north wall. He was studying a set of electroencephalograms and digitally enhanced sonograms and X rays.

After a while he said, "Did you see the pictures they took of the kid's brain this morning?"

Dr. Aaron Zachariah turned from the bank of video displays. "I didn't know there were any."

"Yeah. A whole new series."

"Anything interesting?"

"Yes," Dombey said. "The spot that showed up on the boy's parietal lobe about six weeks ago."

"What about it?"

"Darker, larger."

"Then it's definitely a malignant tumor?"

"That still isn't clear."

"Benign?"

"Can't say for sure either way. The spot doesn't have all the spectrographic characteristics of a tumor."

"Could it be scar tissue?"

"Not exactly that."

"Blood clot?"

"Definitely not."

"Have we learned anything useful?"

"Maybe," Dombey said. "I'm not sure if it's useful or not." He frowned. "It's sure strange, though."

"Don't keep me in suspense," Zachariah said, moving over to the table to examine the tests.

Dombey said, "According to the computer-assigned analysis, the growth is consistent with the nature of normal brain tissue."

Zachariah stared at him. "Come again?"

"It could be a new lump of brain tissue," Dombey told him.

"But that doesn't make sense."

"I know."

"The brain doesn't all of a sudden start growing new little nodes that nobody's ever seen before."

"I know."

"Someone better run a maintenance scan on the computer. It has to be screwed up."

"They did that this afternoon," Dombey said, tapping a pile of printouts that lay on the table. "Everything's supposed to be functioning perfectly."

"Just like the heating system in that isolation chamber is functioning properly," Zachariah said.

Still poring through the test results, stroking his mustache with one hand, Dombey said, "Listen to this . . . the growth rate of the parietal spot is directly proportional to the number of injections the boy's been given.

It appeared after his first series of shots six weeks ago. The more frequently the kid is reinfected, the faster the parietal spot grows."

"Then it must be a tumor," Zachariah said.

"Probably. They're going to do an exploratory in the morning."

"Surgery?"

"Yeah. Get a tissue sample for a biopsy."

Zachariah glanced toward the observation window of the isolation chamber. "Damn, there it goes again!"

Dombey saw that the glass was beginning to cloud again.

Zachariah hurried to the window.

Dombey stared thoughtfully at the spreading frost. He said, "You know something? That problem with the window . . . if I'm not mistaken, it started at the same time the parietal spot first showed up on the X rays."

Zachariah turned to him. "So?"

"Doesn't that strike you as coincidental?"

"That's exactly how it strikes me. Coincidence. I fail to see any association."

"Well . . . could the parietal spot have a direct connection with the frost somehow?"

"What—you think the boy might be responsible for the changes in air temperature?"

"Could he?"

"How?"

"I don't know."

"Well, you're the one who raised the question."

"I don't know," Dombey said again.

"It doesn't make any sense," Zachariah said. "No sense at all. If you keep coming up with weird suggestions like that, I'll have to run a maintenance check on *you*, Carl."

34

THE OIL-AND-GRAVEL TRAIL LED DEEP INTO THE FOREST. IT WAS remarkably free of ruts and chuckholes for most of its length, although the Explorer scraped bottom a few times when the track took sudden, sharp dips.

The trees hung low, lower, lower still, until, at last, the ice-crusted evergreen boughs frequently scraped across the roof of the Explorer with a sound like fingernails being drawn down a blackboard.

They passed a few signs that told them the lane they were using was kept open for the exclusive benefit of federal and state wildlife officers and researchers. Only authorized vehicles were permitted, the signs warned.

"Could this secret installation be disguised as a wildlife research center?" Elliot wondered.

"No," she said. "According to the map, that's nine miles into the forest on this track. Danny's instructions are to take a turn north, off this lane, after about five miles."

"We've gone almost five miles since we left the county road," Elliot said.

Branches scraped across the roof, and powdery snow cascaded over the windshield, onto the hood.

As the windshield wipers cast the snow aside, Tina leaned forward, squinting along the headlight beams. "Hold it! I think this is what we're looking for."

He was driving at only ten miles an hour, but she gave him so little warning that he passed the turnoff. He stopped, put the Explorer in reverse, and backed up twenty feet, until the headlights were shining on the trail that she had spotted.

"It hasn't been plowed," he said.

"But look at all the tire marks."

"A lot of traffic's been through here recently."

"This is it," Tina said confidently. "This is where Danny wants us to go."

"It's a damned good thing we have four-wheel drive."

He steered off the plowed lane, onto the snowy trail. The Explorer, equipped with heavy chains on its big winter-tread tires, bit into the snow and chewed its way forward without hesitation.

The new track ran a hundred yards before rising and turning sharply to the right, around the blunt face of a ridge. When they came out of this curve, the trees fell back from the verge, and open sky lay above for the first time since they had departed the county blacktop.

Twilight was gone; night was in command.

Snow began to fall more heavily—yet ahead of them, not a single flake lay in their way. Bizarrely, the unplowed trail had led them to a paved road; steam rose from it, and sections of the pavement were even dry.

"Heat coils embedded in the surface," Elliot said.

"Here in the middle of nowhere."

Stopping the Explorer, he picked up the pistol from the seat between them, and he flicked off both safeties. He had loaded the depleted magazine earlier; now he jacked a bullet into the chamber. When he put the gun on the seat again, it was ready to be used.

"We can still turn back," Tina said.

"Is that what you want to do?"

"No."

"Neither do I."

A hundred and fifty yards farther, they reached another sharp turn. The road descended into a gully, swung hard to the left this time, and then headed up again.

Twenty yards beyond the bend, the way was barred by a steel gate. On each side of the gate, a nine-foot-high fence, angled outward at the top and strung with wickedly sharp coils of razor wire, stretched out of sight into the forest. The top of the gate was also wrapped with razor wire.

A large sign stood to the right of the roadway, supported on two redwood posts:

PRIVATE PROPERTY
ADMISSION BY KEY CARD ONLY
TRESPASSERS WILL BE PROSECUTED

"They make it sound like someone's hunting lodge," Tina said.

"Intentionally, I'm sure. Now what? You don't happen to have a key card, do you?"

"Danny will help," she said. "That's what the dream was all about."

"How long do we wait here?"

"Not long," she said as the gate swung inward.

"I'll be damned."

The heated road stretched out of sight in the darkness.

"We're coming, Danny," Tina said quietly.

"What if someone else opened the gate?" Elliot asked. "What if Danny didn't have anything to do with it? They might just be letting us in so they can trap us inside."

"It was Danny."

"You're so sure."

"Yes."

He sighed and drove through the gate, which swung shut behind the Explorer.

The road began to climb in earnest, hugging the slopes. It was overhung by huge rock formations and by wind-sculpted cowls of snow. The single lane widened to two lanes in places and switchbacked up the ridges, through more densely packed stands of larger trees. The Explorer labored ever higher into the mountains.

The second gate was one and a half miles past the first, on a short length of straightaway, just over the brow of a hill. It was not merely a gate, but a checkpoint. A guard shack stood to the right of the road, from which the gate was controlled.

Elliot picked up the gun as he brought the Explorer to a full stop at the barrier.

They were no more than six or eight feet from the lighted shack, close enough to see the guard's face as he scowled at them through the large window.

"He's trying to figure out who the devil we are," Elliot said. "He's never seen us or the Explorer, and this isn't the sort of place where there's a lot of new or unexpected traffic."

Inside the hut, the guard plucked a telephone handset from the wall.

"Damn!" Elliot said. "I'll have to go for him."

As Elliot started to open his door, Tina saw something that made her grab his arm. "Wait! The phone doesn't work."

The guard slammed the receiver down. He got to his feet, took a coat from the back of his chair, slipped into it, zippered up, and came out of the shack. He was carrying a submachine gun.

From elsewhere in the night, Danny opened the gate.

The guard stopped halfway to the Explorer and turned toward the gate when he saw it moving, unable to believe his eyes.

Elliot rammed his foot down hard on the accelerator, and the Explorer shot forward.

The guard swung the submachine gun into firing position as they swept past him.

Tina raised her hands in an involuntary and totally useless attempt to ward off the bullets.

But there were no bullets.

No torn metal. No shattered glass. No blood or pain.

They didn't even hear gunfire.

The Explorer roared across the straightaway and careened up the slope beyond, through the tendrils of steam that rose from the black pavement.

Still no gunfire.

As they swung into another curve, Elliot wrestled with the wheel, and Tina was acutely aware that a great dark void lay beyond the shoulder of the road. Elliot held the vehicle on the pavement as they rounded the bend, and then they were out of the guard's line of fire. For two hundred yards ahead, until the road curved once more, nothing threatening was in sight.

The Explorer dropped back to a safer speed.

Elliot said, "Did Danny do all of that?"

"He must have."

"He jinxed the guard's phone, opened the gate, and jammed the submachine gun. What *is* this kid of yours?"

As they ascended into the night, snow began to fall hard and fast in sheets of fine, dry flakes.

After a minute of thought Tina said, "I don't know. I don't know what he is anymore. I don't know what's happened to him, and I don't understand what he's become."

This was an unsettling thought. She began to wonder exactly what sort of little boy they were going to find at the top of the mountain.

35

WITH GLOSSY PHOTOGRAPHS OF CHRISTINA EVANS AND ELLIOT Stryker, George Alexander's men circulated through the hotels in downtown Reno, talking with desk clerks, bellmen, and other employees. At four-thirty they obtained a strong, positive identification from a maid at Harrah's.

In room 918 the Network operatives discovered a cheap suitcase, dirty clothes, toothbrushes, various toiletry items—and eleven maps in a leatherette case, which Elliot and Tina, in their haste and weariness, evidently had overlooked.

Alexander was informed of the discovery at 5:05. By 5:40 everything that Stryker and the woman had left in the hotel room was brought to Alexander's office.

When he discovered the nature of the maps, when he realized that one of them was missing, and when he discovered that the missing map was the one Stryker would need in order to find the Project Pandora labs, Alexander felt his face flush with anger and chagrin. "The *nerve!*"

Kurt Hensen was standing in front of Alexander's desk, picking through the junk that had been brought over from the hotel. "What's wrong?"

"They've gone into the mountains. They're going to try to get into the laboratory," Alexander said. "Someone, some damn turncoat on Project Pandora, must have revealed enough about its location for them to find it with just a little help. They went out and bought *maps*, for God's sake!"

Alexander was enraged by the cool methodicalness that the purchase of the maps seemed to represent. Who were these two people? Why weren't they hiding in a dark corner somewhere? Why weren't they scared witless? Christina Evans was only an ordinary woman. An ex-showgirl! Alexander refused to believe that a showgirl could be of more than average intelligence. And although Stryker had done some heavy military service, that had been ages ago. Where were they getting their strength, their nerve, their endurance? It seemed as if they must have some advantage of which Alexander was not aware. That had to be it. They had to have some advantage he didn't know about. What could it be? What was their edge?

Hensen picked up one of the maps and turned it over in his hands. "I don't see any reason to get too worked up about it. Even if they locate the main gate, they can't get any farther than that. There are thousands of acres behind the fence, and the lab is right smack in the middle. They can't get close to it, let alone inside."

Alexander suddenly realized what their edge was, what kept them going, and he sat up straight in his chair. "They can get inside easily enough if they have a friend in there."

"What?"

"That's it!" Alexander got to his feet. "Not only did someone on Project Pandora tell this Evans woman about her son. That same traitorous bastard is also up there in the labs right this minute, ready to open the gates and doors to them. Some bastard stabbed us in the back. He's going to help the bitch get her son out of there!"

Alexander dialed the number of the military security office at the Sierra lab. It neither rang nor returned a busy signal; the line hissed emptily. He hung up and tried again, with the same result.

He quickly dialed the lab director's office. Dr. Tamaguchi. No ringing. No busy signal. Just the same, unsettling hiss.

"Something's happened up there," Alexander said as he slammed the handset into the cradle. "The phones are out."

"Supposed to be a new storm moving in," Hensen said. "It's probably already snowing in the mountains. Maybe the lines—"

"Use your head, Kurt. Their lines are underground. And they have a cellular backup. No storm can knock out all communications. Get hold of Jack Morgan and tell him to get the chopper ready. We'll meet him at the airport as soon as we can get there."

"He'll need half an hour anyway," Hensen said.

"Not a minute more than that."

"He might not want to go. The weather's bad up there."

"I don't care if it's hailing iron basketballs," Alexander said. "We're going up there in the chopper. There isn't time to drive, no time at all. I'm sure of that. Something's gone wrong. Something's happening at the labs right now."

Hensen frowned. "But trying to take the chopper in there at night . . . in the middle of the storm . . ."

"Morgan's the best."

"It won't be easy."

"If Morgan wants to take it easy," Alexander said, "then he should be flying one of the aerial rides at Disneyland."

"But it seems suicidal—"

"And if *you* want it easy," Alexander said, "you shouldn't have come to work for me. This isn't the Ladies' Aid Society, Kurt."

Hensen's face colored. "I'll call Morgan," he said.

"Yes. You do that."

36

WINDSHIELD WIPERS BEATING AWAY THE SNOW, CHAIN-WRAPPED tires clanking on the heated roadbed, the Explorer crested a final hill. They came over the rise onto a plateau, an enormous shelf carved in the side of the mountain.

Elliot pumped the brakes, brought the vehicle to a full stop, and unhappily surveyed the territory ahead.

The plateau was basically the work of nature, but man's hand was in evidence. This broad shelf in the mountainside couldn't have been as large or as regularly shaped in its natural state as it was now: three hundred yards wide, two hundred yards deep, almost a perfect rectangle. The ground had been rolled as flat as an airfield and then paved. Not a single tree or any other sizable object remained, nothing behind which a man could hide. Tall lampposts were arrayed across this featureless plain, casting dim, reddish light that was severely directed downward to attract as little attention as possible from aircraft that strayed out of the usual flight patterns and from anyone backpacking elsewhere in these remote mountains. Yet the weak illumination that the lamps provided was apparently sufficient for the security cameras to obtain clear images of the entire plateau, because cameras were attached to every lamppost, and not an inch of the area escaped their unblinking attention.

"The security people must be watching us on video monitors right now," Elliot said glumly.

"Unless Danny screwed up their cameras," Tina said. "And if he can jam a submachine gun, why couldn't he interfere with a closed-circuit television transmission?"

"You're probably right."

Two hundred yards away, at the far side of the concrete field, stood a one-story windowless building, approximately a hundred feet long, with a steeply pitched slate roof.

"That must be where they're holding him," Elliot said.

"I expected an enormous structure, a gigantic complex."

"It most likely *is* enormous. You're seeing just the front wall. The place is built into the next step of the mountain. God knows how far they cut back into the rock. And it probably goes down several stories too."

"All the way to Hell."

"Could be."

He took his foot off the brake and drove forward, through sheeting snow stained red by the strange light.

Jeeps, Land Rovers, and other four-wheel drive vehicles—eight in all—were lined up in front of the low building, side-by-side in the falling snow.

"Doesn't look like there's a lot of people inside," Tina said. "I thought there'd be a large staff."

"Oh, there is. I'm sure you're right about that too," Elliot said. "The government wouldn't go to all the trouble of hiding this joint out here just to house a handful of researchers or whatever. Most of them probably live in the installation for weeks or months at a time. They wouldn't want a lot of daily traffic coming in and out of here on a forest road that's supposed to be used only by state wildlife officers. That would draw too much attention. Maybe a few of the top people come and go regularly by helicopter. But if this is a military operation, then most of the staff is probably assigned here under the same conditions submariners have to live with. They're allowed to go into Reno for shore leave between cruises, but for long stretches of time, they're confined to this 'ship.' "

He parked beside a Jeep, switched off the headlights, and cut the engine.

The plateau was ethereally silent.

No one yet had come out of the building to challenge them, which most likely meant that Danny had jinxed the video security system.

The fact that they had gotten this far unhurt didn't make Elliot feel any better about what lay ahead of them. How long could Danny continue to pave the way? The boy appeared to have some incredible powers, but he wasn't God. Sooner or later he'd overlook something. He'd make a mistake. Just one mistake. And they would be dead.

"Well," Tina said, unsuccessfully trying to conceal her own anxiety, "we didn't need the snowshoes after all."

"But we might find a use for that coil of rope," Elliot said. He twisted around, leaned over the back of the seat, and quickly fetched the rope from the pile of outdoor gear in the cargo hold. "We're sure to encounter at least a couple of security men, no matter how clever Danny is. We have to be ready to kill them or put them out of action some other way."

"If we have a choice," Tina said, "I'd rather use rope than bullets."

"My sentiments exactly." He picked up the pistol. "Let's see if we can get inside."

They stepped out of the Explorer.

The wind was an animal presence, growling softly. It had teeth, and it nipped their exposed faces. On its breath were sprays of snow like icy spittle.

The only feature in the hundred-foot-long, one-story, windowless concrete facade was a wide steel door. The imposing door offered neither a keyhole nor a keypad. There was no slot in which to put a lock-deactivating ID card. Apparently the door could be opened only from within, after those seeking entrance had been scrutinized by the camera that hung over the portal.

As Elliot and Tina gazed up into the camera lens, the heavy steel barrier rolled aside.

Was it Danny who opened it? Elliot wondered. Or a grinning guard waiting to make an easy arrest?

A steel-walled chamber lay beyond the door. It was the size of a large elevator cab, brightly lighted and uninhabited.

Tina and Elliot crossed the threshold. The outer door slid shut behind them—*whoosh*—making an airtight seal.

A camera and two-way video communications monitor were mounted in the left-hand wall of the vestibule. The screen was filled with crazily wiggling lines, as if it was out of order.

Beside the monitor was a lighted glass plate against which the visitor was supposed to place his right hand, palm-down, within the existing outline of a hand. Evidently the installation's computer scanned the prints of visitors to verify their right to enter.

Elliot and Tina did not put their hands on the plate, but the inner door of the vestibule opened with another puff of compressed air. They went into the next room.

Two uniformed men were anxiously fiddling with the control consoles beneath a series of twenty wall-mounted video displays. All of the screens were filled with wiggling lines.

The youngest of the guards heard the door opening, and he turned, shocked.

Elliot pointed the gun at him. "Don't move."

But the young guard was the heroic type. He was wearing a sidearm— a monstrous revolver—and he was fast with it. He drew, aimed from the hip, and squeezed the trigger.

Fortunately Danny came through like a prince. The revolver refused to fire.

Elliot didn't want to shoot anyone. "Your guns are useless," he said. He was sweating in his Gore-Tex suit, praying that Danny wouldn't let him down. "Let's make this as easy as we can."

When the young guard discovered that his revolver wouldn't work, he threw it.

Elliot ducked, but not fast enough. The gun struck him alongside the head, and he stumbled backward against the steel door.

Tina cried out.

Through sudden tears of pain, Elliot saw the young guard rushing him, and he squeezed off one whisper-quiet shot.

The bullet tore through the guy's left shoulder and spun him around. He crashed into a desk, sending a pile of white and pink papers onto the floor, and then he fell on top of the mess that he had made.

Blinking away tears, Elliot pointed the pistol at the older guard, who had drawn his revolver by now and had found that it didn't work either. "Put the gun aside, sit down, and don't make any trouble."

"How'd you get in here?" the older guard asked, dropping his weapon as he'd been ordered. "Who are you?"

"Never mind," Elliot said. "Just sit down."

But the guard was insistent. "Who *are* you people?"

"Justice," Tina said.

———

FIVE MINUTES WEST of Reno, the chopper encountered snow. The flakes were hard, dry, and granular; they hissed like driven sand across the Perspex windscreen.

Jack Morgan, the pilot, glanced at George Alexander and said, "This will be hairy." He was wearing night-vision goggles, and his eyes were invisible.

"Just a little snow," Alexander said.

"A storm," Morgan corrected.

"You've flown in storms before."

"In these mountains the downdrafts and crosscurrents are going to be murderous."

"We'll make it," Alexander said grimly.

"Maybe, maybe not," Morgan said. He grinned. "But we're sure going to have fun trying!"

"You're crazy," Hensen said from his seat behind the pilot.

"When we were running operations against the drug lords down in Colombia," Morgan said, "they called me 'Bats,' meaning I had bats in the belfry." He laughed.

Hensen was holding a submachine gun across his lap. He moved his hands over it slowly, as if he were caressing a woman. He closed his eyes, and in his mind he disassembled and then reassembled the weapon. He had a queasy stomach. He was trying hard not to think about the chopper, the bad weather, and the likelihood that they would take a long, swift, hard fall into a remote mountain ravine.

37

THE YOUNG GUARD WHEEZED IN PAIN, BUT AS FAR AS TINA COULD see, he was not mortally wounded. The bullet had partially cauterized the wound as it passed through. The hole in the guy's shoulder was reassuringly clean, and it wasn't bleeding much.

"You'll live," Elliot said.

"I'm dying. Jesus!"

"No. It hurts like hell, but it isn't serious. The bullet didn't sever any major blood vessels."

"How the hell would you know?" the wounded man asked, straining his words through clenched teeth.

"If you lie still, you'll be all right. But if you agitate the wound, you might tear a bruised vessel, and then you'll bleed to death."

"Shit," the guard said shakily.

"Understand?" Elliot asked.

The man nodded. His face was pale, and he was sweating.

Elliot tied the older guard securely to a chair. He didn't want to tie the wounded man's hands, so they carefully moved him to a supply closet and locked him in there.

"How's your head?" Tina asked Elliot, gently touching the ugly knot that had raised on his temple, where the guard's gun had struck him.

Elliot winced. "Stings."

"It's going to bruise."

"I'll be all right," he said.

"Dizzy?"

"No."

"Seeing double?"

"No," he said. "I'm fine. I wasn't hit that hard. There's no concussion. Just a headache. Come on. Let's find Danny and get him out of this place."

They crossed the room, passing the guard who was bound and gagged in his chair. Tina carried the remaining rope, and Elliot kept the gun.

Opposite the sliding door through which she and Elliot had entered the security room was another door of more ordinary dimensions and construction. It opened onto a junction of two hallways, which Tina had discovered a few minutes ago, just after Elliot had shot the guard, when she had peeked through the door to see if reinforcements were on the way.

The corridors had been deserted then. They were deserted now too. Silent. White tile floors. White walls. Harsh fluorescent lighting.

One passageway extended fifty feet to the left of the door and fifty feet to the right; on both sides were more doors, all shut, plus a bank of four elevators on the right. The intersecting hall began directly in front of them, across from the guardroom, and bored at least four hundred feet into the mountain; a long row of doors waited on each side of it, and other corridors opened off it as well.

They whispered:

"You think Danny is on this floor?"

"I don't know."

"Where do we start?"

"We can't just go around jerking open doors."

"People are going to be behind some of them."

"And the fewer people we encounter—"

"—the better chance we have of getting out alive."

They stood, indecisive, looking left, then right, and then straight ahead.

Ten feet away, a set of elevator doors opened.

Tina cringed back against the corridor wall.

Elliot pointed the pistol at the lift.

No one got out.

The cab was at such an angle from them that they couldn't see who was in it.

The doors closed.

Tina had the sickening feeling that someone had been about to step out, had sensed their presence, and had gone away to get help.

Even before Elliot had lowered the pistol, the same set of elevator doors slid open again. Then slid shut. Open. Shut. Open. Shut. Open.

The air grew cold.

With a sigh of relief, Tina said, "It's Danny. He's showing us the way."

Nevertheless, they crept cautiously to the elevator and peered inside apprehensively. The cab was empty, and they boarded it, and the doors glided together.

According to the indicator board above the doors, they were on the fourth of four levels. The first floor was at the bottom of the structure, the deepest underground.

The cab controls would not operate unless one first inserted an acceptable ID card into a slot above them. But Tina and Elliot didn't need the computer's authorization to use the elevator; not with Danny on their side. The light on the indicator board changed from four to three to two, and the air inside the lift became so frigid that Tina's breath hung in clouds before her. The doors slid open three floors below the surface, on the next to the last level.

They stepped into a hallway exactly like the one they had left upstairs.

The elevator doors closed behind them, and around them the air grew warmer again.

Five feet away, a door stood ajar, and animated conversation drifted out of the room beyond. Men's and women's voices. Half a dozen or more, judging by the sound of them. Indistinct words. Laughter.

Tina knew that she and Elliot were finished if someone came out of that room and saw them. Danny seemed able to work miracles with inanimate objects, but he could not control people, like the guard upstairs, whom Elliot had been forced to shoot. If they were discovered and confronted by a squad of angry security men, Elliot's one pistol might not be enough to discourage an assault. Then, even with Danny jamming the enemy's weapons, she and Elliot would be able to escape only if they slaughtered their way out, and she knew that neither of them had the stomach for that much murder, perhaps not even in self-defense.

Laughter pealed from the nearby room again, and Elliot said softly, "Where now?"

"I don't know."

This level was the same size as the one on which they entered the complex: more than four hundred feet on one side, and more than one hundred feet on the other. Forty thousand or fifty thousand square feet to search. How many rooms? Forty? Fifty? Sixty? A hundred, counting closets?

Just as she was beginning to despair, the air began to turn cold again. She looked around, waiting for some sign from her child, and she and Elliot twitched in surprise when the overhead fluorescent tube winked off, then came on again. The tube to the left of the first one also flickered. Then a third tube sputtered, still farther to the left.

They followed the blinking lights to the end of the short wing in which the elevators were situated. The corridor terminated in an airtight steel door similar to those found on submarines; the burnished metal glowed softly, and light gleamed off the big round-headed rivets.

As Tina and Elliot reached that barrier, the wheel-like handle in the center spun around. The door cycled open. Because he had the pistol, Elliot went through first, but Tina was close behind him.

They were in a rectangular room approximately forty feet by twenty. At the far end a window filled the center of the other short wall and apparently offered a view of a cold-storage vault; it was white with frost. To the right of the window was another airtight door like the one through which they'd just entered. On the left, computers and other equipment extended the length of the chamber. There were more video displays than Tina could count at a glance; most were switched on, and data flowed in the form of graphs, charts, and numbers. Tables were arranged along the fourth wall, covered with books, file folders, and numerous instruments that Tina could not identify.

A curly-haired man with a bushy mustache sat at one of the tables. He was tall, broad-shouldered, in his fifties, and he was wearing medical whites. He was paging through a book when they burst in. Another man, younger than the first, clean-shaven, also dressed in white, was sitting at a computer, reading the information that flashed onto the display screen. Both men looked up, speechless with amazement.

Covering the strangers with the menacing, silencer-equipped pistol, Elliot said, "Tina, close the door behind us. Lock it if you can. If security discovers we're here, at least they won't be able to get their hands on us for a while."

She swung the steel door shut. In spite of its tremendous weight, it moved more smoothly and easily than an average door in an average house. She spun the wheel and located a pin that, when pushed, prevented anyone from turning the handle back to the unlocked position.

"Done," she said.

The man at the computer suddenly turned to the keyboard and started typing.

"Stop that," Elliot advised.

But the guy wasn't going to stop until he had instructed the computer to trigger the alarms.

Maybe Danny could prevent the alarms from sounding, and maybe he could not, so Elliot fired once, and the display screen dissolved into thousands of splinters of glass.

The man cried out, pushed his wheeled chair away from the keyboard, and thrust to his feet. "Who the hell are you?"

"I'm the one who has the gun," Elliot said sharply. "If that's not good enough for you, I can shut you down the same way I did that damn machine. Now park your ass in that chair before I blow your fuckin' head off."

Tina had never heard Elliot speak in this tone of voice, and his furious expression was sufficient to chill even her. He seemed to be utterly vicious and capable of anything.

The young man in white was impressed too. He sat down, pale.

"All right," Elliot said, addressing the two men. "If you cooperate, you won't get hurt." He waved the barrel of the gun at the older man. "What's your name?"

"Carl Dombey."

"What're you doing here?"

"I work here," Dombey said, puzzled by the question.

"I mean, what's your job?"

"I'm a research scientist."

"What science?"

"My degrees are in biology and biochemistry."

Elliot pointed at the younger man. "What about you?"

"What about me?" the younger one said sullenly.

Elliot extended his arm, lining up the muzzle of the pistol with the bridge of the guy's nose.

"I'm Dr. Zachariah," the younger man said.

"Biology?"

"Yes. Specializing in bacteriology and virology."

Elliot lowered the gun but still kept it pointed in their general direction. "We have some questions, and you two better have the answers."

Dombey, who clearly did not share his associate's compulsion to play hero, remained docile in his chair. "Questions about what?"

Tina moved to Elliot's side. To Dombey, she said, "We want to know what you've done to him, where he is."

"Who?"

"My boy. Danny Evans."

She could not have said anything else that would have had a fraction as much impact on them as the words she'd spoken. Dombey's eyes bulged. Zachariah regarded her as he might have done if she had been dead on the floor and then miraculously risen.

"My God," Dombey said.

"How can you be here?" Zachariah asked. "You can't. You can't possibly be here."

"It seems possible to me," Dombey said. "In fact, all of a sudden, it seems inevitable. I knew this whole business was too dirty to end any way but disaster." He sighed, as if a great weight had been lifted from him. "I'll answer all of your questions, Mrs. Evans."

Zachariah swung toward him. "You can't do that!"

"Oh, no?" Dombey said. "Well, if you don't think I can, just sit back and listen. You're in for a surprise."

"You took a loyalty oath," Zachariah said. "A secrecy oath. If you tell them anything about this . . . the scandal . . . the public outrage . . . the release of military secrets . . ." He was sputtering. "You'll be a traitor to your country."

"No," Dombey said. "I'll be a traitor to this installation. I'll be a traitor to my colleagues, maybe. But not to my country. My country's far from perfect, but what's been done to Danny Evans isn't something that *my* country would approve of. The whole Danny Evans project is the work of a few megalomaniacs."

"Dr. Tamaguchi isn't a megalomaniac," Dr. Zachariah said, as if genuinely offended.

"Of course he is," Dombey said. "He thinks he's a great man of science, destined for immortality, a man of great works. And a lot of people around him, a lot of people protecting him, people in research and people in charge of project security—they're also megalomaniacs. The things done to Danny Evans don't constitute 'great work.' They won't earn anyone immortality. It's sick, and I'm washing my hands of it." He looked at Tina again. "Ask your questions."

"No," Zachariah said. "You damn fool."

Elliot took the remaining rope from Tina, and he gave her the pistol. "I'll have to tie and gag Dr. Zachariah, so we can listen to Dr. Dombey's story in peace. If either one of them makes a wrong move, blow him away."

"Don't worry," she said. "I won't hesitate."

"You're not going to tie me," Zachariah said.

Smiling, Elliot advanced on him with the rope.

A WALL OF frigid air fell on the chopper and drove it down. Jack Morgan fought the wind, stabilized the aircraft, and pulled it up only a few feet short of the treetops.

"Whoooooooeeeee!" the pilot said. "It's like breaking in a wild horse."

In the chopper's brilliant floodlights, there was little to see but driving snow. Morgan had removed his night-vision goggles.

"This is crazy," Hensen said. "We're not flying into an ordinary storm. It's a blizzard."

Ignoring Hensen, Alexander said, "Morgan, goddamn you, I know you can do it."

"Maybe," Morgan said. "I wish I was as sure as you. But I think maybe I can. What I'm going to do is make an indirect approach to the plateau, moving with the wind instead of across it. I'm going to cut up this next valley and then swing back around toward the installation and try to avoid some of these crosscurrents. They're murder. It'll take us a little longer that way, but at least we'll have a fighting chance. If the rotors don't ice up and cut out."

A particularly fierce blast of wind drove snow into the windscreen with such force that, to Kurt Hensen, it sounded like shotgun pellets.

38

ZACHARIAH WAS ON THE FLOOR, BOUND AND GAGGED, GLARING up at them with hate and rage.

"You'll want to see your boy first," Dombey said. "Then I can tell you how he came to be here."

"Where is he?" Tina asked shakily.

"In the isolation chamber." Dombey indicated the window in the back wall of the room. "Come on." He went to the big pane of glass, where only a few small spots of frost remained.

For a moment Tina couldn't move, afraid to see what they had done to Danny. Fear spread tendrils through her and rooted her feet to the floor.

Elliot touched her shoulder. "Don't keep Danny waiting. He's been waiting a long time. He's been calling you for a long time."

She took a step, then another, and before she knew it, she was at the window, beside Dombey.

A standard hospital bed stood in the center of the isolation chamber. It was ringed by ordinary medical equipment as well as by several mysterious electronic monitors.

Danny was in the bed, on his back. Most of him was covered, but his head, raised on a pillow, was turned toward the window. He stared at her through the side rails of the bed.

"Danny," she said softly. She had the irrational fear that, if she said his name loudly, the spell would be broken and he would vanish forever.

His face was thin and sallow. He appeared to be older than twelve. Indeed, he looked like a little old man.

Dombey, sensing her shock, said, "He's emaciated. For the past six or seven weeks, he hasn't been able to keep anything but liquids in his stomach. And not a lot of those."

Danny's eyes were strange. Dark, as always. Big and round, as always. But they were sunken, ringed by unhealthy dark skin, which was *not* the way they had always been. She couldn't pinpoint what else about his eyes made him so different from any eyes she had ever seen, but as she met Danny's gaze, a shiver passed through her, and she felt a profound and terrible pity for him.

The boy blinked, and with what appeared to be great effort, at the cost of more than a little pain, he withdrew one arm from under the covers and reached out toward her. His arm was skin and bones, a pathetic stick. He thrust it between two of the side rails, and he opened his small weak hand beseechingly, reaching for love, trying desperately to touch her.

Her voice quivering, she said to Dombey, "I want to be with my boy. I want to hold him."

As the three of them moved to the airtight steel door that led into the room beyond the window, Elliot said, "Why is he in an isolation chamber? Is he ill?"

"Not now," Dombey said, stopping at the door, turning to them, evidently disturbed by what he had to tell them. "Right now he's on the verge of starving to death because it's been so long since he's been able to keep any food in his stomach. But he's not infectious. He *has* been very infectious, off and on, but not at the moment. He's had a unique disease, a man-made disease created in the laboratory. He's the only person who's ever survived it. He has a natural antibody in his blood that helps him fight off this particular virus, even though it's an artificial bug. That's what fascinated Dr. Tamaguchi. He's the head of this installation. Dr. Tamaguchi drove us very hard until we isolated the antibody and figured out why it was so effective against the disease. Of course, when that was accomplished, Danny was of no more scientific value. To Tamaguchi, that meant he was of no value at all . . . except in the crudest way. Tamaguchi decided to test Danny to destruction. For almost two months they've been reinfecting his body over and over again, letting the virus wear him down, trying to discover how many times he can lick it before it finally licks him. You see, there's no permanent immunity to this disease. It's like strep throat or the common cold or like cancer, because you can get it again and again . . . if you're lucky enough to beat it the first time. Today, Danny just beat it for the fourteenth time."

Tina gasped in horror.

Dombey said, "Although he gets weaker every day, for some reason he wins out over the virus faster each time. But each victory drains him. The disease *is* killing him, even if indirectly. It's killing him by sapping his strength. Right now he's clean and uninfected. Tomorrow they intend to stick another dirty needle in him."

"My God," Elliot said softly. "My God."

Gripped by rage and revulsion, Tina started at Dombey. "I can't believe what I just heard."

"Brace yourself," Dombey said grimly. "You haven't heard half of it yet."

He turned away from them, spun the wheel on the steel door, and swung that barrier inward.

Minutes ago, when Tina had first peered through the observation window, when she had seen the frighteningly thin child, she had told herself that she would not cry. Danny didn't need to see her cry. He needed love and attention and protection. Her tears might upset him. And judging from his appearance, she was concerned that any serious emotional disturbance would literally destroy him.

Now, as she approached his bed, she bit her lower lip so hard that she tasted blood. She struggled to contain her tears, but she needed all her willpower to keep her eyes dry.

Danny became excited when he saw her drawing near, and in spite of his terrible condition, he shakily thrust himself into a sitting position, clutching at the bed rails with one frail, trembling hand, eagerly extending his other hand toward her.

She took the last few steps haltingly, her heart pounding, her throat constricted. She was overwhelmed with the joy of seeing him again but also with fear when she realized how hideously wasted he was.

When their hands touched, his small fingers curled tightly around hers. He held on with a fierce, desperate strength.

"Danny," she said wonderingly. "Danny, Danny."

From somewhere deep inside of him, from far down beneath all the pain and fear and anguish, Danny found a smile for her. It wasn't much of a smile; it quivered on his lips as if sustaining it required more energy than lifting a hundred-pound weight. It was such a tentative smile, such a vague ghost of all the broad warm smiles she remembered, that it broke her heart.

"Mom."

Tina could hardly recognize his weary, cracking voice.

"Mom."

"It's all right," she said.

He shuddered.

"It's all over, Danny. It's all right now."

"Mom . . . Mom . . ." His face spasmed, and his brave smile dissolved, and an agonized groan escaped him. "Oooohhhhh, *Mommy . . .*"

Tina pushed down the railing and sat on the edge of the bed and carefully pulled Danny into her arms. He was a rag doll with only meager scraps of stuffing, a fragile and timorous creature, nothing whatsoever like the happy, vibrant, active boy that he had once been. At first she was afraid to hug him, for fear he would shatter in her embrace. But he hugged her very hard, and again she was surprised by how much strength he could still summon from his devastated body. Shaking violently, snuffling, he put his face against her neck, and she felt his scalding tears on her skin. She couldn't control herself any longer, so she allowed her own tears to come, rivers of tears, a flood. Putting one hand on the boy's back to press him against her, she discovered how shockingly spindly he was: each rib and vertebra so prominent that she seemed to be holding a skeleton. When she pulled him into her lap, he trailed wires that led from electrodes on his skin to the monitoring machines around the bed, like an abandoned marionette. As his legs came out from under the covers, the hospital gown slipped off them, and Tina saw that his poor limbs were too bony and fleshless to safely support him. Weeping, she cradled him, rocked him, crooned to him, and told him that she loved him.

Danny was alive.

39

JACK MORGAN'S STRATEGY OF FLYING WITH THE LAND INSTEAD OF over it was a smashing success. Alexander was increasingly confident that they would reach the installation unscathed, and he was aware that even Kurt Hensen, who hated flying with Morgan, was calmer now than he had been ten minutes ago.

The chopper hugged the valley floor, streaking northward, ten feet above an ice-blocked river, still forced to make its way through a snowfall that nearly blinded them, but sheltered from the worst of the storm's turbulence by the walls of mammoth evergreens that flanked the river. Silvery, almost luminous, the frozen river was an easy trail to follow. Occasionally wind found the aircraft and pummeled it, but the chopper bobbed and weaved like a good boxer, and it no longer seemed in danger of being dealt a knockout punch.

"How long?" Alexander asked.

"Ten minutes. Maybe fifteen," Morgan said. "Unless."

"Unless what?"

"Unless the blades cake up with ice. Unless the drive shaft and the rotor joints freeze."

"Is that likely?" Alexander asked.

"It's certainly something to think about," Morgan said. "And there's always the possibility I'll misjudge the terrain in the dark and ram us right into the side of a hill."

"You won't," Alexander said. "You're too good."

"Well," Morgan said, "there's always the chance I'll screw up. That's what keeps it from getting boring."

TINA PREPARED DANNY for the journey out of his prison. One by one, she removed the eighteen electrodes that were fixed to his head and body. When she gingerly pulled off the adhesive tape, he whimpered, and she winced when she saw the rawness of his skin under the bandage. No effort had been made to keep him from chafing.

While Tina worked on Danny, Elliot questioned Carl Dombey. "What goes on in this place? Military research?"

"Yes," Dombey said.

"Strictly biological weapons?"

"Biological and chemical. Recombinant DNA experiments. At any one time, we have thirty to forty projects underway."

"I thought the U.S. got out of the chemical and biological weapons race a long time ago."

"For the public record, we did," Dombey said. "It made the politicians look good. But in reality the work goes on. It has to. This is the only facility of its kind we have. The Chinese have three like it. The Russians . . . they're now supposed to be our new friends, but they keep developing bacteriological weapons, new and more virulent strains of viruses, because they're broke, and this is a lot cheaper than other weapons systems. Iraq has a big bio-chem warfare project, and Libya, and God knows who else. Lots of people out there in the rest of the world—they believe in chemical and biological warfare. They don't see anything immoral about it. If they felt they had some terrific new bug that we didn't know about, something against which we couldn't retaliate in kind, they'd use it on us."

Elliot said, "But if racing to keep up with the Chinese—or the Russians or the Iraqis—can create situations like the one we've got here, where an innocent child gets ground up in the machine, then aren't we just becoming monsters too? Aren't we letting our fears of the enemy turn *us* into *them?* And isn't that just another way of losing the war?"

Dombey nodded. As he spoke, he smoothed the spikes of his mustache. "That's the same question I've been wrestling with ever since Danny got caught in the gears. The problem is that some flaky people are attracted to this kind of work because of the secrecy and because you really do get a sense of power from designing weapons that can kill millions of people. So megalomaniacs like Tamaguchi get involved. Men like Aaron Zachariah here. They abuse their power, pervert their duties. There's no way to screen them out ahead of time. But if we closed up shop, if we stopped doing this sort of research just because we were afraid of men like Tamaguchi winding up in charge of it, we'd be conceding so much ground to our enemies that we wouldn't survive for long. I suppose we have to learn to live with the lesser of the evils."

Tina removed an electrode from Danny's neck, carefully peeling the tape off his skin.

The child still clung to her, but his deeply sunken eyes were riveted on Dombey.

"I'm not interested in the philosophy or morality of biological warfare," Tina said. "Right now I just want to know how the hell Danny wound up in this place."

"To understand that," Dombey said, "you have to go back twenty months. It was around then that a Chinese scientist named Li Chen defected to the United States, carrying a diskette record of China's most important and dangerous new biological weapon in a decade. They call the stuff 'Wuhan-400' because it was developed at their RDNA labs outside of the city of Wuhan, and it was the four-hundredth viable strain of man-made microorganisms created at that research center.

"Wuhan-400 is a perfect weapon. It afflicts only human beings. No other living creature can carry it. And like syphilis, Wuhan-400 can't survive outside a living human body for longer than a minute, which means it can't permanently contaminate objects or entire places the way anthrax and other virulent microorganisms can. And when the host expires, the Wuhan-400 within him perishes a short while later, as soon as the temperature of the corpse drops below eighty-six degrees Fahrenheit. Do you see the advantage of all this?"

Tina was too busy with Danny to think about what Carl Dombey had said, but Elliot knew what the scientist meant. "If I understand you, the Chinese could use Wuhan-400 to wipe out a city or a country, and then there wouldn't be any need for them to conduct a tricky and expensive decontamination before they moved in and took over the conquered territory."

"Exactly," Dombey said. "And Wuhan-400 has other, equally important advantages over most biological agents. For one thing, you can become an infectious carrier only four hours after coming into contact with the virus. That's an incredibly short incubation period. Once infected, no one lives more than twenty-four hours. Most die in twelve. It's worse than the Ebola virus in Africa—infinitely worse. Wuhan-400's kill-rate is one hundred percent. No one is supposed to survive. The Chinese tested it on God knows how many political prisoners. They were never able to find an antibody or an antibiotic that was effective against it. The virus migrates to the brain stem, and there it begins secreting a toxin that liberally eats away brain tissue like battery acid dissolving cheesecloth. It destroys the part of the brain that controls all of the body's automatic functions. The victim simply ceases to have a pulse, functioning organs, or any urge to breathe."

"And that's the disease Danny survived," Elliot said.

"Yes," Dombey said. "As far as we know, he's the only one who ever has."

Tina had pulled the blanket off the bed and folded it in half, so she could wrap Danny in it for the trip out to the Explorer. Now she looked up from the task of bundling the child, and she said to Dombey, "But why was he infected in the first place?"

"It was an accident," Dombey said.

"I've heard that one before."

"This time it's true," Dombey said. "After Li Chen defected with all the data on Wuhan-400, he was brought here. We immediately began working with him, trying to engineer an exact duplicate of the virus. In relatively short order we accomplished that. Then we began to study the bug, searching for a handle on it that the Chinese had overlooked."

"And someone got careless," Elliot said.

"Worse," Dombey said. "Someone got careless and *stupid*. Almost thirteen months ago, when Danny and the other boys in his troop were on their winter survival outing, one of our scientists, a quirky son of a bitch named Larry Bollinger, accidentally contaminated himself while he was working alone one morning in this lab."

Danny's hand tightened on Christina's, and she stroked his head, soothing him. To Dombey, she said, "Surely you have safeguards, procedures to follow when and if—"

"Of course," Dombey said. "You're trained what to do from the day you start to work here. In the event of accidental contamination, you immediately set off an alarm. Immediately. Then you seal the room you're working in. If there's an adjoining isolation chamber, you're supposed to go into it and lock the door after yourself. A decontamination crew moves in swiftly to clean up whatever mess you've made in the lab. And if you've infected yourself with something curable, you'll be treated. If it's not curable . . . you'll be attended to in isolation until you die. That's one reason our pay scale is so high. Hazardous-duty pay. The risk is part of the job."

"Except this Larry Bollinger didn't see it that way," Tina said bitterly. She was having difficulty wrapping Danny securely in the blanket because he wouldn't let go of her. With smiles, murmured assurances, and kisses planted on his frail hands, she finally managed to persuade him to tuck both of his arms close to his body.

"Bollinger snapped. He just went right off the rails," Dombey said, obviously embarrassed that one of his colleagues would lose control of himself under those circumstances. Dombey began to pace as he talked. "Bollinger knew how fast Wuhan-400 claims its victims, and he just panicked. Flipped out. Apparently, he convinced himself he could run away from the infection. God knows, that's exactly what he tried to do. He didn't turn in an alarm. He walked out of the lab, went to his quarters, dressed in outdoor clothes, and left the complex. He wasn't scheduled for R and R, and on the spur of the moment he couldn't think of an excuse to sign out one of the Range Rovers, so he tried to escape on foot. He told the guards he was going snowshoeing for a couple of hours. That's something a lot of us do during the winter. It's good exercise, and it gets you out of this hole in the ground for a while. Anyway, Bollinger wasn't interested in exercise. He tucked the snowshoes under his arm and took off down the mountain road, the same one I presume you came in on. Before he got to the guard shack at the upper gate, he climbed onto the ridge above, used the snowshoes to circle the guard, returned to the road, and threw the snowshoes away. Security eventually found them. Bollinger was probably at the bottom gate two and a half hours after he walked out of the door here, three hours after he was infected. That was just about the time that another researcher walked into his lab, saw the cultures of Wuhan-400 broken open on the floor, and set off the alarm. Meanwhile, in spite of the razor wire, Bollinger climbed over the fence. Then he made his way to the road that serves the wildlife research center. He started out of the forest, toward the county lane, which is about five miles from the turnoff to the labs, and after only three miles—"

"He ran into Mr. Jaborski and the scouts," Elliot said.

"And by then he was able to pass the disease on to them," Tina said as she finished bundling Danny into the blanket.

"Yeah," Dombey said. "He must have reached the scouts five or five and a half hours after he was infected. By then he was worn out. He'd used up most of his physical reserves getting out of the lab reservation, and he was also beginning to feel some of the early symptoms of Wuhan-400. Dizziness. Mild nausea. The scoutmaster had parked the expedition's minibus on a lay-by about a mile and a half into the woods, and he and his assistant and the kids had walked in another half-mile before they encountered Larry Bollinger. They were just about to move off the road, into the trees, so they would be away from any sign of civilization when they set up camp for their first night in the wilderness. When Bollinger discovered they had a vehicle, he tried to persuade them to drive him all the way into Reno. When they were reluctant, he made up a story about a friend being stranded in the mountains with a broken leg. Jaborski didn't believe Bollinger's story for a minute, but he finally offered to take him to the wildlife center where a rescue effort could be mounted. That wasn't good enough for Bollinger, and he got hysterical. Both Jaborski and the other scout leader decided they might have a dangerous character on their hands. That was when the security team arrived. Bollinger tried to run from them. Then he tried to tear open one of the security men's decontamination suits. They were forced to shoot him."

"The spacemen," Danny said.

Everyone stared at him.

He huddled in his yellow blanket on the bed, and the memory made him shiver. "The spacemen came and took us away."

"Yeah," Dombey said. "They probably did look a little bit like spacemen in their decontamination suits. They brought everyone here and put them in isolation. One day later all of them were dead . . . except Danny." Dombey sighed. "Well . . . you know most of the rest."

40

THE HELICOPTER CONTINUED TO FOLLOW THE FROZEN RIVER north, through the snow-swept valley.

The ghostly, slightly luminous winter landscape made George Alexander think of graveyards. He had an affinity for cemeteries. He liked to take long, leisurely walks among the tombstones. For as long as he could remember, he had been fascinated with death, with the mechanics and the meaning of it, and he had longed to know what it was like on the other side—without, of course, wishing to commit himself to a one-way journey there. He didn't want to die; he only wanted to *know*. Each time that he personally killed someone, he felt as if he were establishing another link to the world beyond this one; and he hoped, once he had made enough of those linkages, that he would be rewarded with a vision from the other side. One day maybe he would be standing in a graveyard, before the tombstone of one of his victims, and the person he had killed would reach out to him from beyond and let him see, in some vivid clairvoyant fashion, exactly what death was like. And then he would know.

"Not long now," Jack Morgan said.

Alexander peered anxiously through the sheeting snow into which the chopper moved like a blind man running full-steam into endless darkness. He touched the gun that he carried in a shoulder holster, and he thought of Christina Evans.

To Kurt Hensen, Alexander said, "Kill Stryker on sight. We don't need him for anything. But don't hurt the woman. I want to question her. She's going to tell me who the traitor is. She's going to tell me who helped her get into the labs even if I have to break her fingers one at a time to make her open up."

IN THE ISOLATION chamber, when Dombey finished speaking, Tina said, "Danny looks so awful. Even though he doesn't have the disease anymore, will he be all right?"

"I think so," Dombey said. "He just needs to be fattened up. He couldn't keep anything in his stomach because recently they've been reinfecting him, testing him to destruction, like I said. But once he's out of here, he should put weight on fast. There is one thing . . ."

Tina stiffened at the note of worry in Dombey's voice. "What? What one thing?"

"Since all these reinfections, he's developed a spot on the parietal lobe of the brain."

Tina felt ill. "No."

"But apparently it isn't life-threatening," Dombey said quickly. "As far as we can determine, it's not a tumor. Neither a malignant nor a benign tumor. At least it doesn't have any of the characteristics of a tumor. It isn't scar tissue either. And not a blood clot."

"Then what is it?" Elliot asked.

Dombey pushed one hand through his thick, curly hair. "The current analysis says the new growth is consistent with the structure of normal brain tissue. Which doesn't make sense. But we've checked our data a hundred times, and we can't find anything wrong with that diagnosis. Except it's impossible. What we're seeing on the X rays isn't within our experience. So when you get him out of here, take him to a brain specialist. Take him to a dozen specialists until someone can tell you what's wrong with him. There doesn't appear to be anything life-threatening about the parietal spot, but you sure should keep a watch on it."

Tina met Elliot's eyes, and she knew that the same thought was running through both their minds. Could this spot on Danny's brain have anything to do with the boy's psychic power? Were his latent psychic abilities brought to the surface as a direct result of the man-made virus with which he had been repeatedly infected? Crazy—but it didn't seem any more unlikely than that he had fallen victim to Project Pandora in the first place. And as far as Tina could see, it was the only thing that explained Danny's phenomenal new powers.

Apparently afraid that she would voice her thoughts and alert Dombey to the incredible truth of the situation, Elliot consulted his wristwatch and said, "We ought to get out of here."

"When you leave," Dombey said, "you should take some files on Danny's case. They're on the table closest to the outer door—that black box full of diskettes. They'll help support your story when you go to the press with it. And for God's sake, splash it all over the newspapers as fast as you can. As long as you're the only ones outside of here who know what happened, you're marked people."

"We're painfully aware of that," Elliot acknowledged.

Tina said, "Elliot, you'll have to carry Danny. He can't walk. He's not too heavy for me, worn down as he is, but he's still an awkward bundle."

Elliot gave her the pistol and started toward the bed.

"Could you do me a favor first?" Dombey asked.

"What's that?"

"Let's move Dr. Zachariah in here and take the gag out of his mouth. Then you tie me up and gag me, leave me in the outer room. I'm going to make them believe he was the one who cooperated with you. In fact, when you tell your story to the press, maybe you could slant it that way."

Tina shook her head, puzzled. "But after everything you said to Zachariah about this place being run by megalomaniacs, and after you've made it so clear you don't agree with everything that goes on here, why do you want to stay?"

"The hermit's life agrees with me, and the pay is good," Dombey said. "And if I don't stay here, if I walk away and get a job at a civilian research center, that'll be just one less rational voice in this place. There are a lot of people here who have some sense of social responsibility about this work. If they all left, they'd just be turning the place over to men like Tamaguchi and Zachariah, and there wouldn't be anyone around to balance things. What sort of research do you think they might do *then*?"

"But once our story breaks in the papers," Tina said, "they'll probably just shut this place down."

"No way," Dombey said. "Because the work has to be done. The balance of power with totalitarian states like China has to be maintained. They might pretend to close us down, but they won't. Tamaguchi and some of his closest aides will be fired. There'll be a big shake-up, and that'll be good. If I can make them think that Zachariah was the one who spilled the secrets to you, if I can protect my position here, maybe I'll be promoted and have more influence." He smiled. "At the very least, I'll get more pay."

"All right," Elliot said. "We'll do what you want. But we've got to be fast about it."

They moved Zachariah into the isolation chamber and took the gag out of his mouth. He strained at his ropes and cursed Elliot. Then he cursed Tina and Danny and Dombey. When they took Danny out of the small room, they couldn't hear Zachariah's shouted invectives through the airtight steel door.

As Elliot used the last of the rope to tie Dombey, the scientist said, "Satisfy my curiosity."

"About what?"

"Who told you your son was here? Who let you into the labs?"

Tina blinked. She couldn't think what to say.

"Okay, okay," Dombey said. "You don't want to rat on whoever it was. But just tell me one thing. Was it one of the security people, or was it someone on the medical staff? I'd like to think it was a doctor, one of my own, who finally did the right thing."

Tina looked at Elliot.

Elliot shook his head: *no.*

She agreed that it might not be wise to let anyone know what powers Danny had acquired. The world would regard him as a freak, and everyone would want to gawk at him, put him on display. And for sure, if the people in this installation got the idea that Danny's newfound psychic abilities were a result of the parietal spot caused by his repeated exposure to Wuhan-400, they would want to test him, poke and probe at him. No, she wouldn't tell anyone what Danny could do. Not yet. Not until she and Elliot figured out what effect that revelation would have on the boy's life.

"It was someone on the medical staff," Elliot lied. "It was a doctor who let us in here."

"Good," Dombey said. "I'm glad to hear it. I wish I'd had enough guts to do it a long time ago."

Elliot worked a wadded handkerchief into Dombey's mouth.

Tina opened the outer airtight door.

Elliot picked up Danny. "You hardly weigh a thing, kid. We'll have to take you straight to McDonald's and pack you full of burgers and fries."

Danny smiled weakly at him.

Holding the pistol, Tina led the way into the hall. In the room near the elevators, people were still talking and laughing, but no one stepped into the corridor.

Danny opened the high-security elevator and made the cab rise once they were in it. His forehead was furrowed, as if he were concentrating, but that was the only indication that he had anything to do with the elevator's movement.

The hallways were deserted on the top floor.

In the guardroom, the older of the two security men was still bound and gagged in his chair. He watched them with anger and fear.

Tina, Elliot, and Danny went through the vestibule and stepped into the cold night. Snow lashed them.

Over the howling of the wind, another sound arose, and Tina needed a few seconds to identify it.

A helicopter.

She squinted up into the snow-shipped night and saw the chopper coming over the rise at the west end of the plateau. What madman would take a helicopter out in this weather?

"The Explorer!" Elliot shouted. "Hurry!"

They ran to the Explorer, where Tina took Danny out of Elliot's arms and slid him into the backseat. She got in after him.

Elliot climbed behind the wheel and fumbled with the keys. The engine wouldn't turn over immediately.

The chopper swooped toward them.

"Who's in the helicopter?" Danny asked, staring at it through the side window of the Explorer.

"I don't know," Tina said. "But they're not good people, baby. They're like the monster in the comic book. The one you sent me pictures of in my dream. They don't want us to get you out of this place."

Danny stared at the oncoming chopper, and lines appeared in his forehead again.

The Explorer's engine suddenly turned over.

"Thank God!" Elliot said.

But the lines didn't fade from Danny's forehead.

Tina realized what the boy was going to do, and she said, "Danny, wait!"

LEANING FORWARD TO view the Explorer through the bubble window of the chopper, George Alexander said, "Put us down right in front of them, Jack."

"Will do," Morgan said.

To Hensen, who had the submachine gun, Alexander said, "Like I told you, waste Stryker right away, but not the woman."

Abruptly the chopper soared. It had been only fifteen or twenty feet above the pavement, but it rapidly climbed forty, fifty, sixty feet.

Alexander said, "What's happening?"

"The stick," Morgan said. An edge of fear sharpened his voice, fear that hadn't been audible throughout the entire, nightmarish trip through the mountains. "Can't control the damn thing. It's frozen up."

Eighty, ninety, a hundred feet they soared, soared straight up into the night.

Then the engine cut out.

"What the hell?" Morgan said.

Hensen screamed.

Alexander watched death rushing up at him and knew his curiosity about the other side would shortly be satisfied.

———

AS THEY DROVE off the plateau, around the burning wreckage of the helicopter, Danny said, "They were bad people. It's all right, Mom. They were real bad people."

To everything there is a season, Tina reminded herself. A time to kill and a time to heal.

She held Danny close, and she stared into his dark eyes, and she wasn't able to comfort herself with those words from the Bible. Danny's eyes held too much pain, too much knowledge. He was still her sweet boy— yet he was changed. She thought about the future. She wondered what lay ahead for them.

AFTERWORD

THE EYES OF DARKNESS IS ONE OF FIVE NOVELS THAT I WROTE UNDER the pen name "Leigh Nichols," which I no longer use. Although it was the second of the five, it is the fifth and final in the series to be reissued in paperback under my real name. The previous four were *The Servants of Twilight, Shadowfires, The House of Thunder*, and *The Key to Midnight.* Demand from my readers made it possible for these books to be republished, and I'm grateful to all of you for your interest.

As you know if you have read the afterwords in *The Funhouse* and *The Key to Midnight*, I like to amuse myself by revealing the tragic deaths of the various pen names I used early in my career. Somewhat to my embarrassment, I must admit that I've not always been truthful with you in these matters. Previously, I told you that Leigh Nichols drank too much champagne one evening on a Caribbean cruise ship and was decapitated in a freak limbo accident. I was touched by your sympathy cards and accounts of the memorial services you held, but now that Berkley Books has brought you this fifth and final of the Nichols novels, I must confess that I was lying in order not to have to reveal Nichols's true—and more disturbing—fate. One bleak and wintry night Leigh Nichols was abducted by extraterrestrials, taken on a tour of our solar system, introduced to the alien Nest Queen, and forced to undergo a series of horrifying surgeries.

Though eventually returned to Earth, the author was too traumatized to continue a career as a novelist—but finally built a new life as the current dictator of Iraq.

The Eyes of Darkness was one of my early attempts to write a cross-genre novel mixing action, suspense, romance, and a touch of the paranormal. While it doesn't have the intensity, depth of characterization, complexity of theme, or pace of later novels such as *Watchers* and *Mr. Murder,* and while it doesn't go for your throat as fearsomely as a book like *Intensity,* readers who have found it under the Nichols name in used-book stores have expressed favorable opinions of it. I suppose they like it because the device of the lost child—and the dedicated mother who will do anything to find out what has happened to her little boy—strikes a primal chord in all of us.

As I revised the book for this new edition, I resisted the urge to transform the story entirely into a novel of the type that I would write today. I updated cultural and political references, polished away a few of the more egregious stylistic inadequacies, and trimmed excess wordage here and there. I enjoyed revisiting *Eyes,* which remains a basically simple tale that relies largely on plot and on the strangeness of the premise to engage the reader. I hope you *were* engaged, and that you have enjoyed taking this five-book voyage through the career of Leigh Nichols. If you're ever in Iraq, the surgically altered author will probably be happy to sign copies of these books for you—or will denounce you as an infidel and have you thrown into a prison cell as vile as any sewer. Inquire at your own risk.